FIRST BLOOD

The noise was deafening. But more spectacular was the fireball, followed by another, bigger fireball as over a thousand pounds of fuel in the aircraft ignited. The first explosion killed the half-dozen men close to the Super Stallion instantly. The second mowed down another ten who had managed to move away from the bird. What the flame and heat didn't do, the flying shrapnel did.

As the sun set in the Arabian Gulf, emergency messages went up and across the U.S. military chain of command. At Fifth Fleet Headquarters, in Manama, Bahrain; at the National Military Command Center in the Pentagon; at the National Security Council in the Old Executive Office Building; in the White House Situation Room; and in a score of other headquarters and locations they all knew what had happened. But they could not answer the question:

Who had done this?

Other Titles by
George Galdorisi
from Avon Books

THE CORONADO CONSPIRACY

FOR DUTY

AND

HONOR

GEORGE GALDORISI

AVON BOOKS ◆ NEW YORK

AVON BOOKS, INC.
An Imprint of HarperCollins*Publishers*
10 East 53rd Street
New York, New York 10022-5299

Copyright © 2000 by George Galdorisi
Inside cover author photo by Becky Galdorisi
Published by arrangement with the author
Library of Congress Catalog Card Number: 99-96440
ISBN: 0-380-80892-7
www.harpercollins.com

First Avon Books Printing: April 2000

AVON TRADEMARK REG. U.S. PAT. OFF. AND IN OTHER COUNTRIES, MARCA REGISTRADA, HECHO EN U.S.A.

Printed in the U.S.A.

WCD   10   9   8   7   6   5   4   3   2   1

For Becky

ACKNOWLEDGMENTS

THE CORONADO CONSPIRACY WAS A RELATIVELY EASY book to write. Call it beginner's luck, call it what you will, but it came through into its final form without too many changes. *For Duty and Honor* was much more difficult and required a great deal of help and support before it reached its final, publishable form. I owe a tremendous debt of gratitude to those who helped make this second book a reality.

First and foremost, my family—my wife Becky, my son Brian, and my daughter Laura provided the support and encouragement necessary for me to continue cobbling together this story through draft after not-good-enough draft. They never wavered in their support or even hinted that I was not on a fruitful quest. Without their sincere "you can do it" attitude, I might have passed on this story and moved on to another one.

My agent, John Boswell, cheerfully endured reviewing several earlier efforts to put together an interesting yarn and patiently provided just the right mixture of enthusiasm and criticism to lift this story out of the doldrums. John went the extra mile early on when he just as easily might have moved on to other authors with other stories. His patience was near-infinite.

If my editor, Stephen Power, is not the world's best, then he certainly must be among the chosen few. His insightful commentary and on-the-mark suggestions led to a near-total re-crafting of this tale. Each round of comments made the story better and Stephen's unique ability to find the heart of a good story was the engine that drove this novel forward.

Several friends and colleagues reviewed the final draft of this novel and unselfishly provided invaluable suggestions. My eternal gratitude to Dr. Kay Krohne, Rear Admiral Ham Tallent, and Alice Jacobson for giving so freely of their time and priceless insights to make this work a better one.

I might not have attempted a second novel if I had not received tremendous encouragement from family, friends and other special people who had read *The Coronado Conspiracy*. My father, Victor Galdorisi, Captain Jim Stavridis, Mr. Fred Rainbow, Vice Admiral Doug Katz, Captain Dick Couch and Captain P.T. Deutermann, provided a tremendous boost as did many, many classmates from the Naval Academy Class of 1970 who read and commented favorably on *The Coronado Conspiracy*. I know that *For Duty and Honor* was borne up and reached fruition based in no small part on their contagious enthusiasm for my first novel.

Finally, but by no means last, my thanks to the Officers, Chief Petty Officers, and men and women of the United States Navy. This is the last book I will write while on active duty in the Navy. The daily inspiration of watching these professionals at work and play in peace and in war has inspired—and will continue to inspire—my writing. Without their unselfish sacrifice of going down to the sea in ships, there would be no stories.

CAST OF MAJOR CHARACTERS

U.S. Characters

Lieutenant General Robert Allen	Joint Staff Director of Operations
Patrick Browne	President of the United States
Captain Jake Busch	Commanding Officer, USS *Shiloh*
Victor Creazzo	Attorney General
Michael Curtis	National Security Adviser
General Alfred Cutler	Vice-Chairman of the Joint Chiefs of Staff
Commander "Boomer" Davison	*Carl Vinson*'s Air Boss
Captain "Bolter" Dennis	Fifth Fleet Chief of Staff
Captain Bill Durham	CARGRU SEVEN Operations Officer
Commander Alex Fitzgerald	Flight Surgeon aboard *Carl Vinson*
Vice Admiral Harry Flowers	Commander of the U.S. Fifth Fleet
Captain "Wizard" Foster	Commander Carrier Air Group in *Carl Vinson*

Lieutenant Anne O'Connor	VS-35 pilot aboard USS *Carl Vinson*
Captain Terry O'Donnell	Staff officer on the Joint Staff
Petty Officer Donald Parker	Flight deck crewmember aboard *Carl Vinson*
Captain Tom Perry	Naval officer assigned to the NSC; Harry Flowers protégé
Becky Philips	*Carl Vinson* Battle Group Flag Secretary
Philip Quinn	Secretary of State
Commander "Bingo" Reynolds	VS-35 Executive Officer
Rear Admiral "Heater" Robinson	CARGRU SEVEN Commander
Captain George Sampson	CARGRU SEVEN Chief of Staff
Commander "Benny" Tallent	VF-11 Executive Officer
Captain Craig Vandegrift	Commanding Officer, USS *Carl Vinson*
Commander Joe Willard	Commanding Officer, USS *Jefferson City*

Iranian Characters

Ahmad Mohammad Besharati	Iran's Minister of the Interior
Achmed Boleshari	Iranian terrorist
Hasan Ebrahhim Habibi	President of the Islamic Republic of Iran
Mejid Homani	Iranian terrorist

Commander Farhad Kani	Commanding officer of Iranian frigate
Hala Karomi	Iranian terrorist
Commander Mohtaj	Commanding officer of Iranian frigate
Major General Najafi	Chief of Iran's Armed Forces
Ayatollah Ali Akbar Nateq-Nuri	Iranian spiritual leader and commander in chief
Hojjatolislam Rouhani	Secretary of the Iranian Supreme Council
Hossein Shiekholeslam	Iranian Foreign Ministry official and terrorist
Ali Akbar Velayati	Iran's Minister of Foreign Affairs

Iraqi Characters

Raid Abd Bakr	Iraqi MIG pilot
Saddam Hussein	President of Iraq
Sergeant Majid Khadduri	Iraqi air controller at Habbaniyah
Raid Faud Muhammad	Air control chief at Habbaniyah

1

FROM A MILE AND A HALF AWAY, ACROSS THE HOT tarmac shimmering in the 110 degree heat, the CH-53E Sikorsky Super Stallion looked like a huge praying mantis to the men in the van. Its massive blades hung so low that they seemed to touch the ground, and its wide, squat body gave the impression of the big bug—angry, foreboding. All around and on top of the bug, men working on her looked like tiny ants trying vainly to overwhelm her. Framed by the hangar at the U.S. military's Aviation Support Unit in a corner of Bahrain International Airport, the bug was going through its final maintenance checks before its evening flight.

Inside the hangar, its huge doors wide open to take advantage of what little breeze there was, two sweating Navy pilots waited in their flight gear for the maintenance chief to finish directing his exhausted crew. Wearing blue coveralls dropped halfway down and tied around their waists, their once-white T-shirts stained with a rainbow of colors—grease, hydraulic fluid, engine, and transmission oil the maintenance men bent to their tasks of ensuring that their bird was ready for flight.

"Hong, get that damned hydraulic bowser off the deck and get it moved inside."

"Bohem, I told you to clean those damn windshields, how the hell are the lieutenants gonna see where they're flying with that grease you've smeared all over them?"

"Van Wagner, go get the tow tractor and let's get ready to pull this beast out to the fight line."

"Roger," replied the maintenance man. Neither he nor his companions moved with enthusiasm or alacrity. The searing

Bahrain heat sucked the life out of them, and the interior of the hangar provided the only cover from the intensity of the desert sun. They were about to lose even that as they towed the helo outside to ready it for launch.

Lieutenant Jake Watson and Lieutenant Harold Johnson stood ready, nodding sagely as the chief barked orders to the men. They recognized that this was tough, thankless duty for their maintenance crew. The two pilots were hot, sweaty, and dirty too, but at least they'd be flying soon, maybe even bag some night time after their hop taking supplies out to the Navy aircraft carrier in the northern Arabian Gulf was complete. The chief upset their quiet musings.

"One of you lieutenants mind riding the brakes so we can tow this beast out of the hangar?"

"Sure, I'll get it," replied Johnson.

"Ready, Ahmad."

"May you be with him today, Mohammad. Do your duty."

Ahmad and their other companion got out of the van and walked quickly away into the lengthening shadows of the airport building. They never looked back at Mohammad, whose foot had already come off the brake and pressed smoothly down on the accelerator, sending the van across the tarmac. It instantly caught the attention of the Bahraini airport security police, and a police truck started towards it, but Mohammad, unconcerned, just sped up and turned slightly to head directly for the Super Stallion looming ahead of him less than half a mile away.

As the van accelerated, its carriage started rattling from the bounce of the load in back, the load which Mohammad, Ahmad, and their companion had so carefully packed there. He prayed not for his own life—he knew where he would be in the next minute—but that what they had set up would work properly. The Bahraini police truck was another quarter mile back, but gaining.

The maintenance crew walked backwards, keeping their eyes on the blades of the helicopter as they cleared the sides of the hangar. Emerging into the intense heat, the men trudged on, just hoping to get another hot, dirty, evolution over with so they could find some shade and catch some rest.

Harold Johnson saw the van first as he lifted his eye momentarily from the taxi director. He blinked in disbelief for only an instant. Then, instinctively, he started to climb out of the aircraft and shout to his men.

"LOOK OUT, LOOK OUT, GET AWAY FROM THE BIRD, GET AWAY FROM THE BIRD!"

The men were momentarily perplexed. They just stared at Johnson. What the hell was the lieutenant talking about? Maybe the damned heat had gotten to him. Then one of them turned around and saw what the lieutenant saw.

"Goddamnit, stop, stop!" he shouted at the van.

Only a hundred yards away now, Mohammad had the accelerator on the deck. The van was shaking violently, protesting both the weight of the C-4 explosive it was carrying and the speed being demanded of it. Mohammad suppressed an urge to yell, but he wouldn't give the infidels the pleasure of hearing him scream. They would die like the dogs they were.

As the van's objective became clear, the maintenance men started to move away from the bird, looking to their officers and their chief, for some rationale for what was happening. There was none.

Yards away now, Mohammad gripped the steering wheel so hard that surely he would bend it. The men were scattering, and he could see it now, fear in their faces, their not knowing which way to run. Perhaps they prayed to their god. What futility in that, he thought.

The van contacted the helicopter right on its nose, impacting the chin bubble. The wire connected to the bumper of the van and threaded back through its interior was connected to the detonator and set it off, causing the van's cargo to explode spectacularly. Investigators would eventually be able to pinpoint the exact spot where the van struck the helo, correctly estimate that the van was traveling at 110 miles per hour, and calculate the van was carrying approximately 400 pounds of C-4 explosive.

The noise was deafening, but more spectacular was the fireball from the explosives in the van, followed by another, bigger fireball as 10,000 pounds of fuel in the aircraft ignited.

The first explosion instantly killed the half-dozen men close to the Super Stallion, while the second mowed down another ten who had managed to scurry a little farther away from the bird, as well as the police security van, even as it tried to veer away. What the flame and the heat didn't do, the flying shrapnel of what was once a helicopter did.

Those killed instantly in the blast were perhaps the most fortunate, as the men who were a bit farther away died more slowly, their bodies ripped apart by countless metal fragments that seared their torsos and limbs and started bleeding that could not be stopped. The hot metal shrapnel found its way to the far corners of the hangar, starting fires in various places and adding to the carnage and the confusion. Sirens soon came on all around the airport as emergency vehicles converged on the scene—too late to help any of the men of the Super Stallion crew.

As the sun set in the Arabian Gulf, emergency messages went up and across the U.S. military chain of command. CNN had a crew on scene in less than four hours. At Fifth Fleet Headquarters in Manama, Bahrain, at the National Military Command Center in the Pentagon, at the National Security Council in the Old Executive Office Building, in the White House Situation Room, and in a score of other headquarters and locations they all knew what had happened but they could not answer the question, Who had done this?

2

Two weeks later

THE SUICIDE CAR ATTACK ON THE NAVY CH-53E detachment in Bahrain had shocked not just America but also the world. Fourteen Americans had died, pilots and maintenance people alike. The president had been sufficiently moved—or his imagemakers had told him it was the right thing to do—to invite the families of the victims from that squadron, HC-4 in Sigonella, Sicily, to the White House to present posthumous awards to the men and women who had died in the blast, as well as other awards to some of the survivors.

He had barely noticed her in the corner, but as other family members queued up to talk with the president or be comforted by the First Lady, a smallish black woman walked up to National Security Adviser Michael Curtis.

"Are you Mr. Curtis, the national security adviser?" she asked.

"Yes ma'am, I am," he replied warily, not knowing what was coming.

"I'm Margaret Johnson. Harold Johnson was my son."

"Yes ma'am," continued Curtis. "We are all saddened by his death—and the death of his fellow men. . . ."

The woman wouldn't let him finish his sentence. "Mr. Curtis, tell me my Harold died for a reason. Tell me he didn't die just to keep the price of gasoline down."

Curtis was thrown off guard. He tried to empathize with the woman, but why was she asking him this? "Ma'am, your son was a fine patriot, and he—"

Again she cut him off. "Don't patronize me, Mr. Curtis. You didn't know my Harold, so you can't know that. His daddy did three tours in Vietnam—Army infantry—made it home in one piece, but the war took too much out of him, he died when Harold was little. I raised him and his two sisters alone. Harold was a good boy—and a smart one. Got a scholarship to North Carolina State. The Navy recruited him to be a pilot—recruited him hard—don't have too many black pilots, you know. He liked helicopters and he liked his squadron. He was a helicopter commander. He called the Super Stallion—that's the nickname for his helicopter, you know—his baby. Took me inside of one, Mr. Curtis, when I made my first trip out there to Sigonella, then had one of his buddies take this picture of me and him in front of it."

As she finished her sentence she fished a well-worn picture from her large straw purse and handed it to Curtis. The national security adviser handled it, almost tenderly: Harold Johnson, in his flight suit, standing in front of his CH-53E Super Stallion, with his arm around his diminutive mother, proud, unafraid, invincible. It contrasted sharply with the more recent scene at Dover Air Force Base, when fourteen flag-draped coffins had arrived on the C5-A Galaxy. She let him look at the picture for a while, then spoke.

"Tell me that this fine boy didn't die for nothing, Mr. Curtis."

Holding that picture and seeing the tears well up in her eyes had a sobering effect on the national security adviser. He knew what he had to do. He couldn't open his mouth unless he made that commitment. Curtis swallowed hard.

"Mrs. Johnson, Harold did not die in vain. I promise you we will punish the people who did this, we will punish them severely."

"Harold loved his country . . . don't let his country let him down, Mr. Curtis." She was sobbing softly now, and Curtis was about to lose control. He had to do something.

"Mrs. Johnson, please let me introduce you to the president. I know that he would be disappointed if he did not get to meet you," he said, while gently taking her elbow in one hand. Then he tried to give her the picture back.

She walked the way he steered her, but she looked at him with resolution in her eyes—those eyes that he would never forget.

"No, you keep this picture, Mr. Curtis. I remember what Harold looked like—I want you to remember too."

"Yes ma'am," was his only possible reply.

"I want you to keep this on your desk until justice is done."

Again, all he could muster was "Yes ma'am."

As Harold Johnson's mother talked with the president, the great man comforting her with soothing words and the first lady hugging her tightly, Michael Curtis turned away. He wanted to run away, but he couldn't. Damn the president! He knew what the problem was. He knew how to get to the enemy. They *were* the enemy too, every bit as much as if they had landed on our own shores and killed these Americans. Michael Curtis knew that soon he would have to energize the National Security Council.

3

Six weeks later

THE NIMITZ CLASS NUCLEAR AIRCRAFT CARRIER, USS *Carl Vinson*, sliced through the hot, 90 degree waters of the Arabian Gulf, her two nuclear reactors propelling her in excess of 30 knots. Displacing almost 100,000 tons, *Carl Vinson* moved all-but noiselessly, parting the waves with her powerful bow, her four 20-foot propellers biting into the Gulf waters with incredible torque. Yet, for all her power, the massive ship seemed to glide through the water almost effortlessly, not as an intruder on the sea but as one with it.

Built in Newport News Shipyard over the span of seven years at the cost of well in excess of four billion dollars, *Carl Vinson*, like her sister Nimitz Class aircraft carriers, is one of the eight wonders of the modern world. Almost 1,100 feet in length, her flight deck encompasses four and one half acres. Over 240 feet from her keel to the top of her main mast, she literally dwarfs other warships. On her flight deck and in her cavernous hangar bay, over seventy of the most sophisticated warplanes on the planet comprise her striking arm.

Over five thousand officers, chief petty officers, and sailors live and work in this floating city. The ship is perhaps the greatest engineering and social achievement that the United States has ever constructed—a weapon of war deployed to the seven seas to keep the peace. *Carl Vinson* was in the Arabian Gulf doing exactly that, the greater good motivating the crew as, about her decks and in her workspaces, they began their everyday chores, conducting the thousands of necessary and important duties that kept this behemoth functioning. Their routine was just that—routine—until . . .

"GENERAL QUARTERS, GENERAL QUARTERS, all hands man your battle stations, go down and aft on the port side, up and forward on the starboard side, Zebra must be set in twelve minutes, now General Quarters."

Lieutenant Anne O'Connor shot up in her rack in the small stateroom she shared with Lieutenant Chrissie Linder. Anne was in the Alert 15 crew and was supposed to be able to get her S-3B Viking off *Carl Vinson*'s deck within the next fifteen minutes, ready to refuel the thirsty, fuel-guzzling, F-14D Tomcats and F/A-18C Hornets that were being scrambled to defend the carrier. She had been dozing, well, it had started off as reading, when the 1 MC general announcing system had brought her to. Within two minutes, she was in her flight suit and torso harness and groping around on the deck furiously trying to put on her flight boots. Anne knew that if the ship was going to general quarters, she would be launching soon.

"Now launch the Alert 7 fighters," intoned the disembodied voice on the 1 MC. "GQ time, one minute," the voice continued, noting how long the ship had been at general quarters.

Launch the alert. This could be trouble. Or could it be a drill? She didn't know which, but you always had to assume the worst. Anne knew the entire defensive package lineup by heart. The SH-60 planeguard helo was sitting on spot four on the carrier's angled deck, its pilots sitting in their aircraft watching the temperature gauge creep slowly past 40 degrees Celsius. They would launch first. Two Hornets were in Alert 7, their pilots already in their aircraft so they could get off *Carl Vinson*'s deck in seven minutes or less. They would be the first DLIs—deck-launched interceptors. Then Anne's Viking in Alert 15 would be the next to go, taking her station in the "tanker track" at 7,000 feet, ready to refuel the thirsty fighters after they had roared out to their stations to do battle with whatever enemy aircraft were closing the carrier. Two Tomcats were also in Alert 15; they would be next off the catapults—"the cats." After that, the Alert 30 launch; another planeguard helo, the E-2C Hawkeye radar control aircraft, the EA-6B Prowler jammer aircraft, and two more Hornets rounded out the complete package. If all those aircraft had to launch, Anne knew the carrier was in serious trouble.

"Chrissie, what the hell time is it?" yelled Anne as she wrapped the long laces of her left boot around her ankle and back again. *Damn, what sadist makes these things this friggin' long*, she thought as she mentally shifted to trying to get the second boot on in a hurry.

"Only 0830," responded her roommate, who was still undressed and lounging in her upper bunk, cramped as it and the stateroom were. Anne was a first-tour "nugget" pilot on her first deployment and Chrissie was only a few years senior, so they only rated one of the smallest staterooms on the ship. Theirs was typical of those that junior officers inhabited on *Carl Vinson*—a set of bunk beds, several lockers, two pull-out desks built into the lockers, a small sink and mirror. That was about it. The room was austere—almost stark— although they had dressed it up as best they could.

"What? 0830?" Anne shouted. "Goddamnit, we're not supposed to be flying until noon today. I can't believe this!" she said as she slid the second boot onto her right foot and struggled with the too-long laces.

"GQ time, two minutes," said the voice.

"Better get moving roomie, sounds serious," said Chrissie with just a hint of sarcasm as she rolled out of her top bunk and began to put on her flight suit. She needed to show up in the Blue Wolf Ready Room too, but she wasn't part of the ready alert crew, having flown a hop the night before. There was no need for her to panic, plus she was almost sure that this was a drill. She hoped.

Anne, though, was perplexed. GQs were usually carefully orchestrated events aboard the Gold Eagle—*Carl Vinson*'s nickname—even in the potentially hostile Arabian Gulf. An unannounced GQ was a rarity, and one where the ship actually launched fighters in response to a "hostile threat" was even rarer. Even lowly JOs knew that something was up. They just weren't sure what.

Anne was also a bit scared. Not of what would happen in the air—she was a naval aviator and every bit as courageous as her male counterparts, of that she was sure. Nothing that could happen in the air worried her, she had trained and trained hard for her mission. Once airborne she knew she would succeed.

No, she was scared of Bingo. Craig "Bingo" Reynolds was the Blue Wolf XO—executive officer—and he was not the kinder, gentler type. Anne, Chrissie, and the other JOs thought that he was a throwback to some pre-human species who existed for one reason and one reason only, to make their lives as junior officers as miserable as possible. As a brand-new lieutenant, Anne had absorbed more than a fair share of Bingo's wrath, and she didn't know whether he was trying to make it harder or easier on her because she was one of only four women officers in the squadron. The jury was still out on that, but perhaps it was about to come in. Because he would be in the Blue Wolf Ready Room for certain and would see her come in late.

She was dealing with an operational matter now, a matter of warfighting, not some XO's pettiness. The Alert 15 crew was supposed to already be in the Blue Wolf Ready Room, Ready Room Four on *Carl Vinson*, not in the rack. Since entering the Gulf, though, the admiral had them in Alert Alpha with a spread of birds in states from Alert 7 to Alert 30 almost continuously. The problem was that being in Alert 15 broke their crew rest cycle and meant missing out on flying later in the day or that night if they were stuck with Alert 15 duty during the day.

So they had cut a deal with the squadron operations officer that if they could get back to the ready room in less than five minutes after GQ sounded, he would let them slide back to their staterooms during Alert 15. This was more than altruism on the operations officer's part. Having a bunch of pilots waste their crew day standing Alert 15 meant that he could come perilously close to not being able to fill the flight schedule, and this might cause the Blue Wolves to miss sorties. In the intensely competitive world of naval aviation, missing these carrier flights was akin to being a mass-murderer. Do that as an ops officer and it wouldn't be the squadron exec but the squadron commander himself who would have his head.

"GQ time, three minutes," intoned the voice on the 1 MC as Anne sprang to her feet and bolted toward the door, determined not to get burned on this one, not as a pilot, not as a female. Damnit, damnit, damnit, why hadn't she just left her flight boots on? She could make it to the ready room in under two minutes, couldn't she?

Anne's mind was racing as she flung the door to her stateroom open, leaving Chrissie behind, casually zipping on her flight suit. Room 03-95-L (the Navy way of numbering everything on a ship, 03 standing for the third deck above the main deck, 95 standing for the "frame," or numbered divisions that started at the bow and ran aft—each frame marking off approximately four feet on these Nimitz Class nuclear aircraft carriers—and L standing for living space) was a long way from the ready room, but at least it was on the same deck, and that would speed her progress. Her room was just starboard of the ship's centerline, as was the back entrance to Ready Four, almost ninety frames aft, but traveling on the starboard side passageway meant traveling through the Blue Tile Area, the Flag Spaces that were home to Admiral "Heater" Robinson and his staff. The ever-present sentry frequently stopped anyone who was not on the admiral's staff who was trying to pass through there. She changed her route to the port side, a few dozen steps longer, but more of a sure thing. Besides that, that was the direction of the "flow" during GQ—moving up ladders and running forward on the starboard, or right, side of the ship—and opposite that on the port, or left, side. A "ship thing" that most pilots didn't pay much attention to, but now it was working to Anne's advantage.

Anne turned right out of her stateroom and headed athwartships—Navy slang for anything running perpendicular to the ship's centerline—at a full run, then turned left, picked up the fore and aft passageway, and started at full sprint toward the after end of the ship and Ready Four. Every three strides she would lift her feet just a little higher and pull her arms and legs in just a little closer to avoid the "knee knockers" that punctuated the ship's two main length-wise passageways every five frames. There weren't many sailors in this passageway, and those that were there moved aside instinctively as Anne barreled aft with a look of semi-desperation in her eyes. This couldn't be the real thing—but if it were, she'd be ready.

Anne Claire O'Connor came by her bent for naval avia-tion naturally. The only child of now-retired Captain Jeff "Boxman" O'Connor, who had flown F-4 Phantoms in Viet-nam and gone on to command his own carrier air wing, Anne had grown up in the midst of the lore of naval avia-tion. An honor student and varsity athlete at Coronado High School in southern California, she had won an appointment to the United States Naval Academy and had excelled there as a swimmer. Tall, slim, and strikingly attractive, at five foot nine and a lithe 130 pounds, Anne O'Connor turned heads. She knew that her stunning good looks did not help her "blend" as a naval aviator—there were fewer than a dozen women among *Carl Vinson*'s over two hundred pilots and naval flight officers. Unlike everything else she did in her life, Anne O'Connor failed in her mission to not stand out. She was, simply put, a knockout. As the sailors in the pas-sageway stepped aside to let her pass by, they tried not to stare, but most couldn't help themselves.

Anne was oblivious to them, though, as she gauged her progress aft along the port side passageway by familiar land-marks; back door to the Flag Mess, getting closer, Flag Intel, Flag Comms, TFCC—the Tactical Flag Coordination Cen-ter, closer still, ship's CDC—Combat Direction Center, even closer, up and over a half-foot high rise in the deck at CATCC—Carrier Air Traffic Control Center room—frame 170, almost there, athwartship passageway, yes! She hung a hard left and headed back to the starboard side passageway, well aft of the Blue Tile Area. She began to slow down as she passed the Fist and Stinger Ready Rooms, then hung a quick right and was at the back door to Ready Four.

"GQ time, four minutes," intoned the voice.

Anne heaved a sigh of relief. OK, so far, so good, now the hard part. This has got to look casual, she told herself.

She was about to enter the Blue Wolf Ready Room. Head call, that would be the cover story, she just had to go to the head. Anne didn't like playing this kind of ruse, it went against her basic sense of honesty, but they were doing it for the greater good, weren't they? After all, it was the ops o's plan, wasn't it? She'd just as soon be sitting in Ready Four than lying in her rack. *BS, Anne*, she told herself, *quit rationalizing*. Just get into the ready room, get the brief from the squadron duty officer—the SDO—and get out there and get in your Viking.

Anne took a deep breath as she pushed the back door to Ready Four open and looked around furtively. No Bingo. Yes, there was a god! No ops officer either. Yes! She knew that they'd be there soon, though. What she saw was just the usual assemblage of pilots filing into their chairs—if he or she wasn't flying, a pilot's GQ station was supposed to be in the Ready Room. She grabbed her survival vest from her chair and walked up to the particularly harried SDO, Lieutenant Mike "Shooter" Patterson.

"Damnit Anne, where were you—" He caught himself. No sense yelling at her. "The rest of your crew is already up in the aircraft—they walked a minute ago. Mike Hart's gonna get the systems started, the rest of your crew's up there with him."

"GQ time, five minutes."

Her fellow JOs who had now filled about half of the chairs in Ready Four looked at her with a mixture of bemusement and concern—bemusement that they weren't the ones who'd been caught napping, literally, and concern that the Blue Wolves would look bad if she didn't launch on time.

Anne didn't waste any time, but wheeled to sprint out of the ready room, almost colliding with the squadron ops officer as she did. Just as she exited the door she heard the sound of the shuttle traveling down the catapult track as the first Hornet launched from cat 4. That shuttling sound was followed by the reassuring *pop* as the cat stroke was absorbed and the energy was directed throughout the ship. The first Alert 7 Hornet had launched. This was looking less and less like a drill. She had to get into the air and gas those fighters, or they would be on fumes in no time.

"GQ time, six minutes."

Anne didn't wait for the shudder of the cat to stop—geez, sometimes it felt like the entire ship would shake apart. She turned left out of the ready room, ran forward just a few feet, then turned right, heading outboard toward the skin of the ship. She continued outward, toting her bulky gear past several maintenance shops, then finally to the hatch, which led out to the starboard side catwalk.

Anne pulled the long handle securing the hatch up and to the right and opened the huge door, taking her outside of the skin of the ship. Turn left, up the seven steps to the catwalk.

"GQ time, seven minutes."

The searing heat outside hit her like a bat between the brows. Summer in the Arabian Gulf, not a cloud in the sky, and even at this hour of the morning, the temperature was over 100. The radiated heat off the flight deck made it feel at least 15 degrees hotter than that, and the combined thickness of her flight suit, torso harness, and survival vest made her start sweating instantly.

Clack, clack, clack—the sound of the shuttle as the second Alert 7 Hornet roared down cat 3. Anne could hear the roar and caught the Hornet out of her peripheral vision as she bounded up the additional few steps from the catwalk to the flight deck. Then the ship shuddered again with the force of the cat stroke. However, the shock of the cat never felt as bad out on the flight deck as it did inside the ship.

"GQ time, eight minutes."

The Hornets got airborne in time, thought Anne. Good for them. Now the pressure was on her and her Viking and on the two Tomcats in Alert 15. If this wasn't a drill, the Hornets would need relief on station by the "Toms" soon, and she would need to be in position to refuel the Hornets.

Sweating more profusely now, Anne dashed past the "bomb farm"—the staging area for all manner of bombs and missiles jammed between *Carl Vinson*'s island structure and the edge of the flight deck. She passed the island and the "crash and smash" crew as she headed for her aircraft. The Viking was just aft of the island, in good position to taxi to the cat now that the Hornets had launched.

"GQ time, nine minutes."

No time to preflight her aircraft again; she had done that when they had set the alert last night. She ducked down and entered the small hatch that led inside the Viking. She looked quickly left toward the back of the plane and nodded to Lieutenant Todd Kuntz, her other NFO, and to Antisubmarine Warfare Operator—AW2—Marty Walker. Twisting her body right she stepped up into the cockpit and sat down in the left seat. All the time, her COTAC's hands moved around the cockpit as he flicked switches and completed the taxi and takeoff checklists. Mike Hart looked at Anne as she sat down and managed a thin smile.

"Anne, nice of you to join us," kidded Mike. He didn't kid her too hard, though. Mike had been in the same position once before, and she had bailed him out.

"Yeah, well, I wasn't doing anything else this morning, thought I'd provide the adult supervision you boys needed," Anne replied as she strapped in as rapidly as she could.

"GQ time, ten minutes. Zebra set, main deck and below."

"They're ready to taxi us as soon as you're strapped in," said Mike. Though a naval flight officer trained to operate weapons systems and sensors and not a pilot like Anne, Mike Hart's position as COTAC made him essentially a co pilot, and he had a full set of flight controls on the right side of the aircraft. Anne had been paired with Mike for most of the deployment, and they made a good team.

Finally strapped in, her helmet on and talking with her crew over the ICS—internal communications system—Anne grabbed the NATOPS pocket checklist on the center console and helped Mike complete the remainder of the pre-taxi checklist.

"GQ time, eleven minutes."

Not much time left. Checklist complete, Anne turned to Mike.

"Ready to go?"

"Let's rock and roll," he replied.

"You guys ready in back?"

"Let's do it," Todd Kuntz said.

Anne looked up and saw the yellow-shirted plane captain standing just a few feet in front of her, ready to taxi the aircraft. A thumbs-up from Anne let him know that he could start moving the Viking. Anne taxied the aircraft to cat 4. A Tomcat was already on cat 3, completing its final hookups. As she taxied into position, the flight deck crew hooked up the holdback bar and the launch bar to the nose gear of the Viking. The huge, rectangular JBD—jet blast deflector— moved up into position behind the aircraft to protect planes and people further aft on the flight deck from the Viking's two powerful turbofan engines. To her right, the Tomcat was just starting to run up its powerful engines, the incredible heat running up the JBD and making the air shimmer all around it.

"GQ time, twelve minutes."

The final checkers gave Anne's aircraft the last lookover prior to granting it the final go-ahead for flight. No room for error. A bad hookup, a missed procedure, and four people and a multi-million-dollar aircraft could be lost. Anne and Mike completed the last items of their checklist.

One deck below the flight deck in *Carl Vinson*'s Blue Tile Area, in the ship's TFCC, Admiral "Heater" Robinson had seen enough. His Alert 7 fighters had gotten off the deck in time and were already up for control with "strike"—the controllers who directed the aircraft toward the engagement area—and his Alert 15 crews would be off the cats early. He was satisfied that he could defend *Carl Vinson* and her support ships. Robinson put his hand on his flag tactical action officer's shoulder.

"Call it off Steve," he said as he turned and left TFCC, walking the few short steps through the War Room back to his cabin.

Lieutenant Commander Steve Rawls picked up the Bogen phone—*Carl Vinson*'s internal communications system— and punched button 22, which linked him directly to *Carl Vinson*'s commanding officer, Captain Craig Vandegrift.

"Captain, this is the Flag TAO. Stand down from the alert launch."

"Admiral's orders?" asked the captain. Vandegrift had been burned before by junior staff officers who had misinterpreted the task group commander's orders, and he didn't want that to happen here.

"Admiral's orders," responded Rawls.

"Roger," replied Vandegrift. Then, with a fluid motion, he picked up the phone connecting him directly to *Carl Vinson*'s air boss in the Primary Flight Control Tower, one deck above.

"Stand 'em down, Boss."

"Aye, Captain," responded the air boss.

Anne did the "cockpit wipeout," ensuring that all of her controls were free. The Tomcat was running its engines at full power as the "Shooter" in the launch bubble in the portside catwalk prepared to launch the fighter. Anne prepared to run her throttles up to full power. A dozen other details ran through her mind.

"Secure from General Quarters. Secure from General Quarters. Stand down the Alert 15 package. I say again. Stand down the Alert 15 package."

DAMNIT, thought Anne. *All of this and we don't go flying. What is wrong with this boat?*

But there was nothing wrong with *Carl Vinson* nor with what had just happened. Tensions in the Arabian Gulf were rising, and Admiral "Hunter" Robinson wanted to make sure his task group—and especially his pilots—were ready for anything. An unannounced GQ got everyone on their toes and kept them there.

As Anne looked out on the calm waters of the Arabian Gulf and into the perpetual haze that hung in the skies around *Carl Vinson* and got ready to taxi her Viking back to its original position on deck, she wondered what part she would play in any conflict. She knew, however, she would be ready.

4

THE MEETING OF THE NATIONAL SECURITY COUNCIL was not going well.

National Security Adviser Michael Curtis had tried his level best to form a consensus among the many players—each with a seemingly different agenda—who were present: Secretary of Defense Bryce Jacobs, Secretary of State Philip Quinn, Attorney General Victor Creazzo, the DCI—Director of Central Intelligence—Peter Hernandez, the chairman of the Joint Chiefs of Staff, Admiral Jake Monroe, as well as some of their key deputies; but consensus was not to be had. The president wanted answers, and all Curtis could get from them was more questions. In the many years that he had known the president, he had shown him failure just wasn't in his vocabulary. He didn't want it to be there now. He would go to the mat one more time.

"Look," Curtis began, not speaking to anyone in particular, but looking toward Secretary of State Philip Quinn. "We have to get to the bottom of this. Don't our people in the field overseas have any leads?"

"Sure, we have some," said Quinn, "but none convincing enough to take action."

"I agree," added JCS Chairman Monroe, somewhat spontaneously. Admiral Jake Monroe was an oftentimes vocal critic of the use of U.S. military forces for anything but the most compelling reasons. "We can't be certain exactly where the threats are being directed from. Barring that, we can't begin to plan for any contingencies."

"Well, Admiral, we're pressing hard to try to obtain that information," said the DCI, Pete Hernandez. "We just don't have that many in-country sources."

"We don't have the right information and until we do, I say we shouldn't move," added Monroe.

"Gentlemen, I believe that we are more in agreement than we may think," said Bryce Jacobs, looking directly at the chairman and arching his eyebrows as a signal for him to restrain his arguments a bit. "The Chairman is merely suggesting that we be certain before taking any overt action."

Admiral Monroe looked back at the defense secretary and signaled that he understood.

Michael Curtis pressed again. "All right, Mr. Secretary," he said. "I understand the desirability of moving deliberately, but as the evidence mounts that this terrorism might be Iranian sponsored, we should at least have contingency plans, don't you think?"

"We have those plans," replied the secretary of defense, "but it takes presidential direction to implement them."

"Yes, I know that," replied Curtis, "but we need to know more than we know right now, we need a comprehensive intelligence estimate," he said, now looking directly at the director of central intelligence.

"Gentlemen, we *are* striving to know more. We have operatives who we are attempting to obtain information from. I think that it won't be too long before we will have what we need," said the DCI, now sounding a bit defensive.

"We may not have all the time you think you need," said the national security adviser. "You all must understand that the president is very firm that he wants to take action to stop these attacks." He spoke forcefully, as if with the voice of the president himself.

"We need to take the right actions though, Michael, not just lash out," said the secretary of state.

"WE'RE NOT JUST LASHING OUT," shouted Curtis, smashing his fist on the desk, startling everyone in the room.

And so it went. The president's key advisors could not agree on what action to take, or whether to take any action at all. The national security adviser was barely able to keep order. They were at an impasse.

"Let's break for lunch now and reconvene at one-thirty," offered Curtis, hoping that a midday respite would help break the ice.

After the others filed out of the room, Curtis paused a moment and reflected back on the events of the past several months. Several terrorist acts against America had been committed and at what some would say was an accelerated pace. Although there was not yet a definite "smoking gun," very strong circumstantial evidence pointed to Iran. The Iranians vehemently denied any responsibility for any of the attacks, but they were becoming increasingly disingenuous when asked for assistance in trying to track down the source of these attacks.

He, along with his fellow NSC members, was both staggered by the attacks' ferocity and confused by their seeming randomness: the suicide van attack on the U.S. Navy CH-53E detachment at the Aviation Support Unit in Bahrain, the explosion in the marketplace frequented by Americans in Kuwait City, the small truck that exploded on a sunny Sunday afternoon in the quiet neighborhood populated by primarily American expatriates in Dhahran, Saudi Arabia. They suspected the Iranian regime, suspected it strongly, and most investigations sought not so much to get at the truth as to find a way to somehow tie the attacks to the clerical regime that had been vocal in its disdain for America. But no direct link had been found—yet.

But his president demanded action. Patrick Browne was acutely aware of the opinion polls, and those polls, fed by constant commentary from the diplomatic and military officials of the administration Browne had supplanted, as well as by a consistent stream of editorials bashing his "do nothing" policy on terrorism, had him sinking rapidly. Similar polls indicated that most Americans—an overwhelming majority, in fact—believed that Iran supported state-sponsored terrorism. The fact that there were active terrorist training camps within Iran made a compelling case to launch something against the camps at the very least. The president did not want to seem to jump to conclusions—that would not be presidential—so he turned it over to the ecumenical NSC, not directing, but strongly hinting, what an acceptable finding would be.

The NSC, and especially National Security Adviser Michael

Curtis, had been continually frustrated however, by their inability to deliver that finding. All they had were consistent themes for the attacks. They had usually targeted Americans and, by their very nature, were destabilizing to an area that the United States very much wanted to keep stable. With over two-thirds of the world's proven oil reserves and close to forty percent of the world's daily oil production, the Arabian Gulf littoral was an area of enormous—and increasing—importance to the United States and to its principal allies in Europe, as well as to its Asian anchor in Japan. Any disruption of this flow would be enough to send the western economies in general, and the United States economy in particular, into a tailspin. It was a situation that demanded action.

Sitting alone in that room, Curtis determined that there would be action, too, well-hidden smoking gun be damned. Even though Patrick Browne wanted to be as justified as possible before striking back at anyone; even though he wanted the situation painted in black and white, not the muted grays Curtis had to deal with; even though this was an almost impossible position for the national security adviser; Curtis knew that the only way to get closure was to make the president agree to focus the energies of the nation against the Islamic Republic. He would have to force his president to make that decision

Then he would go back to his office and hope he was able to face again that picture of Harold Johnson and his still-grieving mama.

5

ANNE O'CONNOR AND MIKE HART ENTERED THE SEA combat commander's module within *Carl Vinson*'s Combat Direction Center to get their briefing from the destroyer squadron commander, Commodore Jim Hughes, prior to launching on their ASR—armed surface reconnaissance—mission. Though many of her fellow pilots just wanted to be in the air flying, Anne enjoyed taking the time to see the "big picture" as the commodore briefed her on the surface picture in the Gulf.

"OK, Lieutenant," the commodore began, "you can see it here on our fusion plot. Up north we've got two of our ships doing maritime interception operations. Want you to go up there and have a look first, check in with USS *Jarrett*, she's the on-scene commander. They'll have some contacts that they want you to identify."

"Wilco, sir," replied Anne. She enjoyed going on these missions—they were more tactical than flying endless circles in the tanker track refueling other aircraft. Captain Hughes liked to use the Vikings assigned—"fragged"—to him on the flight schedule aggressively, flying ASR missions throughout the Gulf, ready to respond to any contingency while building a coherent surface picture of this incredibly jammed body of water.

"After that, would appreciate it if you and your crew would head south. I want you to check out our Maritime Prepositioning ships at anchor just north of Jebel Ali. We've had reports of small high-speed boats approaching close to them from time to time but no one has been able to identify a country of origin."

"Do you think that they might be Iranian Revolutionary Guard Corps Navy boats?" asked Anne.

"We don't know for sure, anything that you can give us on that, well, we'd sure appreciate it."

"Roger sir," replied Anne. She let her eyes wander to the three-foot-square, large-screen display in front of them that displayed a complete picture of surface ships in the Gulf. As the embarked destroyer squadron commander, Commodore Hughes was responsible for maintaining the complete surface and subsurface picture throughout the Arabian Gulf, as well as running all maritime interception operations there.

Although she was just a junior lieutenant and he was a senior captain, Anne was struck by the fact that the commodore always brought the aircrews working with him into his module and took pains to give them the "big picture." It was a professional association Anne valued almost as much as those with her own squadronmates. If her damned exec, Bingo, were half as gracious as the commodore, her life as a JO might be more bearable.

"OK, Lieutenant O'Connor. I appreciate your taking the time to come on down for this brief. We really have a lot for you to do on this mission. We'll talk with you when you get airborne."

"Wilco, Commodore, we'll come up on the net ASAP," she replied as she turned to leave.

"Oh, Lieutenant," he replied when she had one foot out the door. She turned to hear the rest of his sentence. "Fly 'em safe."

The fact that Anne had developed this association with Commodore Hughes said a lot about Anne as a professional naval officer. Anne loved to fly, but flying was just part of what she was about. Women still made up only a small percentage—barely double digits—of the Navy's officer corps, less when you culled out specialties like legal and medical, and far less when you looked at the percentages of pilots who were women. Above all else, she wanted to be treated like a professional, respected for what she could do in the air and for what she contributed to the mission on the ground.

* * *

"ADMIRAL'S IN TFCC," shouted the petty officer as Rear Admiral Mike "Heater" Robinson returned to his Tactical Flag Coordination Center aboard USS *Carl Vinson* just a few frames forward of where Anne O'Connor and Commodore Jim Hughes had just finished their briefing. Announcing the admiral's presence in TFCC was more than protocol—it alerted the Carrier Group SEVEN watchstanders to be just a little more alert and let them get a jump on thinking through the answers to what were certain to be a series of penetrating questions from the task group commander. The admiral was one of the most well liked "one stars" in the Navy, but he brooked no inattentiveness among his watchstanders in TFCC. He expected them to use their considerable resources to have a complete tactical picture at all times. Pity the Flag Tactical Action Officer—or TAO— who didn't know where every task force ship and aircraft was, where every potential hostile platform was, and who hadn't thought through what actions the task force needed to take to both protect itself and take offensive action if necessary.

The admiral did not need to say anything upon entering TFCC to inspire this sort of activity. A combination of his physical presence and the intense training he had put the entire task group—and especially his staff—through during *Carl Vinson*'s workups were sufficient to inspire this kind of activity. Heater Robinson was a big man, six foot four inches tall and a hefty 240 pounds. Powerfully built, with close-cropped blonde hair and penetrating blue eyes, the admiral had a commanding presence and still looked like he could strap on a jet anytime and duel with any one of the fighter pilots in Carrier Air Wing Fourteen, *Carl Vinson*'s embarked wing.

After graduating from the Naval Academy in 1970 and earning his wings at Meridian, Mississippi, less than a year later, Heater Robinson had flown Phantoms in Vietnam and Tomcats from the mid-1970s. He had come up through the system before Washington duty and duty with multi-service joint staffs made staff tours a necessity, and he still boasted more flight hours and traps—carrier arrested landings—than any pilot on board *Carl Vinson*. He flew often during his tour, commanding the carrier USS *John F. Kennedy*, a fact that he constantly laid on *Carl Vinson*'s commanding officer, Captain Craig Vandegrift. The captain was an "A-6 puke," and the admiral never lost an opportunity to give him some of the good-natured ribbing that was always passed between pilots in different carrier jet communities.

Lieutenant Commander Steve Rawls was still Flag TAO and rose as the admiral returned to TFCC. The TAOs recognized that the best way to head off a thousand penetrating questions from the task group commander was to start briefing him immediately upon his arrival in TFCC. There was much to tell. Dominated by two Large Screen Displays—LSDs—on the port bulkhead of the small space, this nerve center of the task group's activities was only 15 feet by 30 feet and looked much smaller; TFCC packed a great deal of equipment and presented a great deal of information in a small space. On the left-hand LSD was the ACDS—Advanced Combat Direction System—display, a radar depiction of contacts within several hundred miles of *Carl Vinson*. On the right was the NTCS-A—Naval Tactical Command System Afloat—with a depiction of the position of every ship and aircraft worldwide based on multi-sensor inputs.

Flanking the two LSDs were a series of smaller displays showing a variety of information; the commercial air routes crisscrossing the Arabian Gulf, the PUs—participating units—in the data link connecting all of the ships in the task force electronically, other information that fed the LSDs, the latest weather briefing, the status of aircraft in the air and on alert, a TV monitor tuned continuously to CNN, and a wealth of additional information. To the uninitiated, it overwhelmed the senses and threatened to put the viewer into information overload, but to the experienced watchstander, it all served to increase his or her SA—situational awareness—that most vital ingredient of effective decision making.

Closer to him than the LSDs, at the far end of his T-Table, the TAO had two other officers working for him. Lieutenant John Clarke manned the surface display, and Lieutenant Paul Barton manned the air display. Both officers constantly manipulated their displays, hooking any one of the scores of tracks displayed on the NTCS-A on the right-hand LSD that were displaying additional information about the track; its course, speed, altitude in the case of an aircraft, type of contact, and other pertinent details. They had learned the admiral's rules well: if it appeared on their screen, they'd better know everything about it.

To his left, several OSs—Operations Specialists—manned a variety of consoles, all of which drew information from a variety of sources, ship's radars, aircraft radars, IFF—Identification Friend or Foe interrogations—link inputs, and visual sightings. They, in turn, inputted this information into the system, which, in turn, fed the LSDs. To the right were various status boards, displaying all matter of information, from ship call signs, to warfare commander assignments, to positioning data on key contacts. Interspersed throughout TFCC were over a dozen radio speakers and handsets, all monitored by one or another TFCC watchstanders, who somehow managed to hear the transmission that they keyed in on above the din of all the other radio noise.

Rawls began to brief the admiral on the tactical situation. Using his laser pointer, he walked it around the right-hand LSD.

"Admiral, lot of activity for this early in the morning," he began. "We're gonna let the two Hornets we launched burn up their bag of gas and do a little tracking for the boys in CDC before we bring 'em back aboard 'bout thirty minutes from now." Rawls was a "black shoe," a surface warfare officer, who was still trying to figure out what he was doing on an aircraft carrier briefing an "Airedale" admiral. His detailer, or assignment officer, had told him this was a "great career opportunity" when he cut him this set of orders.

"That accounts for the good guys," responded the admiral. "What do you make of what the other side's doing so far?"

"Activity in Iran today is really consistent with their activity over the last few days," said Rawls as he focused his laser pointer on that country. "Couple of jets out of Bushehr, some others out of Shiraz and Dezful—and of course their P-3 patrol plane making its standard maritime patrol."

"OK, seems pretty normal," said the admiral, looking primarily at the screen, but letting his eyes meet Rawls's occasionally to let him know that he valued his analysis. "What's the situation on the other side of the Gulf?"

"Kind of a slow start with Iraq this morning," Rawls began again. "Some MIGs out of Al Asad. Also have a single MIG out of Al Taq. It was up for about an hour. Balad and Q West have only had a few tactical flights each all morning. They don't seem to be the focused fields today."

"I think that makes sense. Anything else?"

"No sir, Admiral, not really. . . ."

The admiral could tell something about the air activity bothered his TAO, but that he would have to draw him out. "Go ahead Steve. What's on your mind?" he said.

"Well, Admiral, you know, I'm not an Airedale or anything, but I've been standing TAO for a while, and, this is just a theory, I guess, but Iran is flying a little higher rate than they have a week or so ago."

"Yes, I know, but do you make anything of it?"

"Well, sort of. I haven't even mentioned this to the intel guys, but it seems that their flights are, well, more organized . . ."

"More organized?"

"Yes sir, Admiral. I know that this sounds weird, but weeks ago, they were flying from all of these different fields at different times and going in different directions. Sometimes they'd come out over the water. Remember the time a little over two weeks ago when we were in the northern Gulf and their two Phantoms were flying out over the Gulf? We went to GQ and got all spun up. Turned out that they were just doing practice runs against their patrol boats for training."

"Sure, I remember that. Things were tense for a while, weren't they?"

"Yes sir, and that sort of thing happened quite a bit. They just didn't pay much attention. Wasn't a big sweat item for them."

"And now?"

"Now sir, well, Admiral, they don't do that anymore. Haven't seen an Iranian aircraft gets its feet wet in three or four days. Seems like they're very focused on not doing that.

And there's something else. They don't just launch at random times and go in different directions. A large number of their strike and attack aircraft launch around the same time and go off in the same general direction over the desert—it even looks like some of them refuel enroute. Then they all form up and come back to the southwest at the same time. Admiral, it sure looks a little funny."

"Perhaps so. Certainly worthy of us putting some analysis into, don't you think so?"

"Yes sir, I sure do," said Rawls.

"Carry on then. I'm going back to the cabin. You know how to get hold of me if you need to."

The admiral again walked the short distance through the War Room and back into his spacious cabin. He sat down in his large black leather chair and slumped a bit as he looked at the foot-high pile of paper in his burgeoning in-basket. He considered his conversation with Steve Rawls. Every professional instinct he had made him pause. What Rawls had described to him ominously sounded like the Iranians were practicing mirror-image strikes against his battle group. If the aircraft formations that Rawls described flew northwest instead of southwest they would be on top of CVOA4 and on top of his battle group.

He had a feeling that his potential adversaries—not just Iran, but Iraq, too—were poised and ready to inflict devastation on his battle group. It was a thought that filled him with dread. How had he missed what Rawls had just told him? He didn't have time to analyze this. He needed to act—protecting his battle group was his most important job.

He reached for the KY-68 secure phone on his desk. A push of the internal staff intercom button and his administrative people were working on connecting him with Fifth Fleet Headquarters and his immediate operational boss, Vice Admiral Harry Flowers. His flag lieutenant, Lieutenant Mike Lumme, did as the admiral asked him and stood by and listened to Heater Robinson's end of the conversation. It was shorter than either of them expected.

"Good afternoon, Admiral Flowers," Admiral Robinson began.

"Yes sir, we're training hard out here . . ." he continued.

"Yes sir, Admiral. Sir. I had something that I thought I needed to bring to your attention . . ."

"Yes sir. It is a rather large concern, sir . . ."

"Admiral, if I may . . ."

"No sir, Admiral. We have been observing Iranian air activity . . ."

"No sir, I am sure that your intelligence people have been observing it too . . ."

"Admiral . . . the level of activity has picked up and the patterns of activity . . ."

"No sir, Admiral, if I may continue. I have concerns that we may need to take more of a defensive posture . . ."

"Yes sir. I said defensive posture. It's only prudent that . . ."

"Admiral . . . yes sir . . . no, I don't think that I am raising any alarm bells unnecessarily . . ."

"No sir, you are certainly in charge of the overall naval matters in the Arabian Gulf, but I am . . ."

Lumme watched as the admiral suddenly pulled the receiver away from his ear. He looked visibly pained.

"Did you lose the connection, Admiral? Shall we try to reestablish it?"

"No Mike, we're done. I just need a little time alone."

"Yes sir," said Lumme as he beat a hasty retreat from the admiral's cabin.

One hundred and fifty miles away, at Fifth Fleet Headquarters in Manama, Bahrain, the man who had been at the other end of the clipped dialogue with Heater Robinson stood at his desk and completed that conversation. "WE'LL SEE WHO THE HELL IS IN CHARGE!" shouted Vice Admiral Harry Flowers as he slammed the receiver down in its cradle. Small, pale, and gaunt, Vice Admiral Flowers was the complete physical—and in many ways—psychological opposite of Rear Admiral Robinson. Admiral Flowers had only recently taken command of Fifth Fleet as the Navy commander in the Arabian Gulf, and he intended to set the tone for his expected two-year command tour early. Word would spread to follow-on carrier task group commanders that the admiral was not someone to be dealt with lightly. Task group commanders indeed! He viewed them as mere custodians of a group of ships. He wielded the real power. He controlled the United States Navy in the Arabian Gulf. He would decide how its forces would be used!

Vice Admiral Flowers's career in the Navy differed as much from that of Heater Robinson as their respective physical appearances did. A nuclear trained officer who grew up on surface ships, Admiral Flowers had a natural disdain for Airedales. He had succeeded in a series of junior officer jobs on now-obsolescent nuclear-powered cruisers by his diligence, attention to detail, scrupulous adherence to the strict regulations and procedures of the Navy's nuclear-power program, and by his willingness to professionally assassinate any peer or subordinate who broke those rules.

Harry Flowers had never commanded a Navy carrier task group and had little empathy for the predicament Heater Robinson found himself in. After command of a frigate and subsequent command of a nuclear cruiser, USS *Truxton*, Flowers had gained notice for his performance in a series of Washington assignments, many with the Navy's nuclear power bureaucracy within the Naval Reactors Division and the Naval Sea Systems Command. Most recently, and most notably, he served as the Navy inspector general, where his job was to inspect other Navy commands and find fault or uncover wrongdoing. It was an assignment that suited his temperament and his training, and he earned enough recognition uncovering genuine scandals that—partly to assuage a Congress that continually chided the Navy for not policing itself—he was given his third star and his current command.

The only tour that Vice Admiral Flowers had ever had on an aircraft carrier was his two-year stint as RO—Reactor Officer—aboard the aircraft carrier USS *Nimitz*. While this was typically a tour where nuclear surface officers learn to live with and appreciate aviation officers, Flowers's disdain for aviators only grew during his tour as he constantly bickered with *Nimitz*'s commanding officer, whom he considered his intellectual inferior. During this tour as RO, Flowers usually took his meals in his stateroom to avoid eating with his fellow department heads—a luxury that *Nimitz*'s executive officer allowed him—only because Flowers outranked him by several years and because the exec did not wish to inflict Flowers's acerbic personality on the rest of his wardroom.

Vice Admiral Flowers pulled his spare five-foot, six-inch frame out of his leather chair and pushed himself up on his desk. He called his chief of staff, Captain Roger "Bolter" Dennis, an aviator, into his office. He wanted to get to the bottom of just what it was Admiral Robinson was telling him.

"Chief of Staff, does our intel have anything changing dramatically recently regarding threats in the Gulf?"

"No sir," responded Captain Dennis.

"Any change in THREATCONs passed down from higher authority?"

"No sir." Bolter Dennis was baffled by the admiral's line of questioning. He tried to do the mental gymnastics to bring himself up to speed.

"Any reason that you can think of why the battle group commander might be worried?"

"No sir," responded the chief of staff, still unclear as to where the admiral was going with this.

"Any reason why the battle group shouldn't posture aggressively and carry out the exercise the way we have told them to?"

"No, sir, no reason at all. . . ." Dennis was beginning to see why the admiral was quizzing him on this. As the chief of staff—as well as the senior aviator on the staff—the chief of staff was becoming accustomed to receiving the majority of the admiral's general wrath against aviators.

"Is it clear, then, who is in charge of naval forces in the Gulf?"

"Crystal, sir."

"Good, Chief of Staff, I'm glad that we agree on that."

As the chief of staff departed, the Fifth Fleet commander had a few more moments to reflect. Admiral Flowers knew why the Navy had sent him here. They wanted him to die professionally. Traditionally, few Fifth Fleet commanders had ever risen to four-star rank, and the Navy was a service long on tradition. It seemed counterintuitive, given the importance of the Gulf region—one would think that the naval forces commander in the region would be an important player in the great scheme of things. But CENTCOM—the United States Central Command—was always commanded by an Army, Air Force, or Marine Corps officer, and the entire focus of the AOR—Area of Responsibility—was on land warfare and air warfare, and on checkmating the two premier land powers there, Iran and Iraq.

Although naval forces, represented by his Fifth Fleet, were the only ones always in theater, it always worked out that Army and Air Force units were the focus of effort when it came time to develop campaign plans, take major military action, or make any significant move, and Navy forces were relegated to a supporting role. Flowers vividly recalled operation Desert Strike against Saddam Hussein in 1996. Precluded by political considerations from striking Iraq from bases in the Middle East in early September of that year, the Air Force blocked attempts to use Navy carrier-based tactical aircraft already in theater. Instead, those same Navy jets had been used to escort B-52s that were flown all the way from Barksdale Air Force Base in Louisiana to launch CALCM cruise missiles against Iraqi surface to air missile sites. The bottom line remained—there was a strong prejudice among his Army and Air Force seniors against the effective use of naval forces in this AOR.

Admiral Flowers was not going to spend two years commanding Fifth Fleet merely to have it be a sideshow for the Army and the Air Force in the region. That would gain him no visibility and would guarantee that he would labor in obscurity for two years only to be shuffled off to some nondescript job and then into retirement long before he was ready. If Robinson was too timid to use his precious task group aggressively, he would direct the efforts of the task group himself. Robinson was coming perilously close to having no other purpose than to carry out his direct orders.

One thing that Flowers had done during his career was to develop a network of officers who were in some way beholden to him—officers whose careers he had pushed, others whom he had spared when he could have ended their careers abruptly, still others hoping to garner favors when he gained his fourth star. While some other senior officers moved on from one assignment to another and barely remembered most of the officers they served with, Flowers kept meticulous files and had already, on a number of occasions, called in some markers. More would be called in soon.

He summoned one of his yeoman. The admiral didn't bother to use the man's name. He would most likely be of little long-term use to him.

"Yeoman, I want you to place a call to the NSC—that's National Security Council," he said gratuitously. "I want you to reach a Captain Perry. Tell him I want to talk with him immediately. Have his office find him if he's not immediately available."

"Yes sir," replied the yeoman and wheeled out of the office to do the admiral's bidding. He had learned during Flowers's first few days on the staff never to question the admiral's orders, even if he knew that the time zone difference meant it was very early in the morning Washington, D.C. time. He'd let the duty people at the other end worry about contacting this captain at home.

"And another thing, Yeoman," shouted Flowers after him. "Get the operations officer in here right now."

Captain Carl Mullen appeared within three minutes, extracting himself immediately from an important meeting. However, it was not fast enough for the admiral.

"About time, Ops O," snarled Flowers, not even looking up at the harried officer.

"Yes sir," was all that Mullen could offer.

"Are we monitoring the flight schedule for *Carl Vinson* every day?"

"Yes sir," offered Mullen, not sure where the admiral was going with this.

"Well, I want to be briefed more thoroughly on their operations every day, not just three times a week. How many sorties did they have yesterday?"

"Admiral, I'll have to consult my message traffic, but I believe that it was just over one hundred—"

The admiral cut him off. "Just over a hundred. We've got

the biggest damn exercise going that we've had here in years and that's all they can muster? How many of those are strike sorties?"

"I think about forty-five," offered Mullen, now clearly on the defensive and baffled as to why the admiral wanted such specific information.

"FORTY-FIVE?" Flowers shot out of his chair. He had barely calmed down from railing at Heater Robinson, and now he was boiling again. Mullen was to be the new object of his wrath. Didn't these drones understand? The damn Air Force was getting too big a piece of the action in the Gulf, and this timid admiral on *Carl Vinson* was just laying back generating the minimal number of sorties for the Navy. Flowers would be damned before he would let Robinson torpedo his ambitions.

Flowers pointed his thin index finger at Mullen and began to shout. "You talk to those people now, I mean right now. I want sorties, all they can generate. I want them playing this exercise to the hilt. I don't want to hear about defensive counter-air, I want simulated strikes. You tell them. I want strikes! I want us to fill the sky in the Gulf, not the damned Air Force. What do they think we send a carrier to the Gulf for, just to defend itself? I want that message sent and I want it sent loud and clear!"

"Yes sir, Admiral. I'm sure that we can fix this. I'll get right on it," Mullen replied as he beat a hasty retreat.

As Mullen left, the admiral collapsed back down into his chair. Why was this so damn hard, motivating these drudges? Once he talked to Captain Tom Perry, things would begin to change in the Gulf—and his star would rise one way or the other.

6

PRESIDENT HASAN EBRAHHIM HABIBI SAT AT HIS DESK in his office in the heart of Tehran. He had been president of the Islamic Republic of Iran for four years, following the assassination of President Ali Akhbar Hashemi Rafsanjani. He recalled the tumultuous days following that event and even now reflected on his good fortune at being able to hold together the country's diverse radical, pragmatic, and conservative factions. Although western observers were sanguine about the survival of the regime, he was not. He had been there. He had witnessed the turmoil and the carnage. He did not think that the nation would survive another such upheaval.

President Habibi had just finished chairing a particularly factious meeting of the Supreme National Security Council and had been unsuccessful in forging a consensus among the clerics, diplomats, and top-ranking officers from the Army and Revolutionary Guard as to how to deal with the Islamic Republic's deteriorating economic condition and concomitant spiraling internal unrest. The fragile coalition of conservatives and pragmatists that he had cobbled together was under intense attack by the recalcitrant radical faction, which seemed blind to the economic malaise and internal strife and seemed singularly focused on the charismatic Ayatollah Khomeini's doctrine of permanent revolution. The exchanges still rang in his ears.

"We must continue to expand our exports of oil," began Minister of the Interior, Ahmad Mohammad Besharati. "We can dramatically increase oil revenues. The U.S. dollar has risen fifteen percent in the last two years and we can increase our revenues in Europe, and especially in Asia—"

"But not in the United States," interrupted Hojjatolislam Rouhani, the Supreme Council's secretary and a representative of spiritual leader Ayatollah Ali Akbar Nateq-Nuri. "The American pigs still refuse to buy our oil and they have poisoned the Paris Club of Bankers. We had to negotiate more than a dozen different debt agreements to refinance our loans—at exorbitant rates."

The nodding of heads around the table by the eleven council members signaled that they agreed with Hojjatolislam Rouhani's assessment.

"You are correct, we cannot yet trade with the U.S.," continued Besharati. "But it is not for us to let that deter us from generating the revenues we can. Our production of crude oil last year averaged over four million barrels per day, second only to the Saudis'. They now realize we are a powerful partner in keeping oil prices stable. They recognize, too, the influence we have with the Emirates and with Oman. Our commerce with those two states gives us tremendous leverage with them."

"Agreed," President Habibi replied. "We must increase oil revenues. The opportunity for increased revenues has never been better."

"So you think that we can buy off our people with more money, with more exposure to western values?" asked Ayatollah Ali Ghoreishi. "Do you think that is the way to solve the problems facing the country?"

"I do!" Habibi said forcefully. "You forget that our unemployment rate is almost twenty percent—among our young men it is almost twice that. Our cities swell with squatters setting up shantytowns even as we speak. You recall, I am sure, the riots just a few miles from this building last year, as well as the recent riots in Mashhad, Araq, Ghazvin, and Shiraz. Major General Najafi, how many were killed and wounded in the rioting in Araq in June?" he asked the chief of the Armed Forces of the Islamic Republic.

"Over forty killed, several hundred wounded, Mr. President. But it was all handled very quickly."

"Indeed it was," continued Habibi, knowing the next answer, but wanting the general to say it himself. "But did you handle it all with your forces?"

"My forces?" said General Najafi.

"Yes. Was it your forces alone that you used, or did you have to rely on the Basij Militia?"

"Yes, the militia was of some help."

"And the anti-riot force sent all the way from Tehran? Were they of 'some help' too?" pressed Habibi, not wanting to let the general dictate the terms of the debate. He knew that his nation was in trouble. He had to press the point.

"Yes," answered General Najafi, now clearly angered by Habibi.

And so the debate went. President Habibi continued to drive for a consensus, for a moderate, pragmatic approach. Above all else he wanted to ensure that European nations and Japan continued their policy of constructive engagement with the Islamic Republic rather than follow the more doctrinaire position of the United States, which seemed to never have recovered from the overthrow of the shah. His long-term goal included some sort of rapprochement with the United States, but that would have to wait until the immediate crisis passed.

But not all those present at that meeting of the Supreme National Security Council participated in the debate. Listening, but sullen and noncommunicative, had been the minister of foreign affairs, Ali Akbar Velayati. Velayati, Habibi knew, was strongly influenced by another official within the Foreign Ministry, Hossein Shiekholeslam. Educated in the United States, Shiekholeslam was strongly anti-American, and Habibi knew that he had diverted government funds and that he was now the chief financier of the numerous terrorist training camps within the Islamic Republic, as well as the chief architect of the recent terrorist attacks in the region.

Although most of those advocating Khomeini's doctrine of "permanent revolution," like Shiekholeslam, had been purged from formal government entities, many had built a strong power base in the Revolutionary Guard and in the Basij Militia. This was evidenced by such situations as the continued existence of the revolutionary magazine *Bayan*, published by a radical former minister of the interior, which attacked Habibi personally for being an "American lackey."

Abiding the terrorist camps while denying their existence was a compromise that Habibi felt he had to make to avoid the questioning of his revolutionary credentials and to fend off accusations of his diverging from the path of the Imam Khomeini.

These were the internal conflicts that Habibi pondered as he sat in his large office. Perhaps if he were a bigger man, he thought, maybe he could control these meetings better. But at a mere five feet, five inches in height, with unremarkable features, the slight, thin, bespectacled Habibi looked more like a harried accountant than the president of the Islamic Republic. He would just work harder, he thought, to make all of his countrymen work together.

But above all else, Hasan Ebrahhim Habibi wanted to do the right thing for his beloved Islamic Republic. Sometimes he felt that he was single-handedly holding together the fractious groups within the Republic. He had placated the radicals by allowing them to pursue their "permanent revolution." Thus far, those tacitly approving the attacks— he knew that Shiekholeslam was the mastermind—had made them oblique enough to avoid having the United States find a smoking gun and take reprisals. How long he would be able to maintain this precarious balance was a question he was afraid to ask.

7

"LAUNCH COMPLETE, LAUNCH COMPLETE," SAID *CARL Vinson's* boss, Commander Jack "Boomer" Davison, over the ship's 5 MC announcing system as the last Hornet climbed out ahead of the carrier. Davison would have much rather been in one of those Hornets than in *Carl Vinson's* Primary Flight Control high above the flight deck on the ship's O-10 level, but he had had his share of flying tours, including command of VFA-192 flying with Carrier Air Wing Five off USS *Independence*.

Carrier Air Wing Fourteen's package was inbound to the box to conduct one of their Operation Southern Watch missions for the day. Their job was to patrol the no-fly zone in southern Iraq established in 1991 and expanded in 1996 as a result of Iraq's suppression of its Kurdish minority and the subsequent Operation Desert Strike. These operations had become routine, and patrolling the no-fly zone no longer held the suspense that it did years earlier when the Iraqis used to send an occasional surface to air missile—SAM— hurtling at a Navy or Air Force jet.

Brian McDonald was part of "package Charlie" that day, the third group of aircraft the Navy had sent toward the box. As the group of four Hornets, two Tomcats, and one Prowler all finished taking their drinks from the KC-10 tanker over Saudi Arabia and got ready to "push"—move toward the box—it occurred to him that this wasn't a bad way to spend the day. Sitting comfortably in Stinger 304, he twisted his neck to the right and looked over at his wingman, Tiny Baker, in Stinger 308, who gave him a nod. Tiny must be thinking the same thing. Back to his left, a section of Hornets from the "Fistles" of VFA-25—Fist 402 and Fist 405—flew along with them. All the Hornets were armed with two AIM-7 Sparrows and two AIM-9 Sidewinders and a full gun load. To his right, two Tomcats from the Red Rippers of VF-11—Ripper 100 and Ripper 106—flew in tight formation armed with their single Sparrow, two Sidewinders, and single AIM-54 Phoenix missile. The EA-6B Prowler from the Cougars of VAQ-139, with its sophisticated jamming pods, rounded out the package.

Brian loved what the Hornet could do as a flying machine, but he was even more enamored by what it could do as a weapons platform. A fly-by-wire aircraft with a fully digital glass cockpit, the Hornet defined state-of-the-art flying, systems performance, sensor capability, and weapons delivery. In the air-to-air mode the aircraft utilized the APG-65 radar to track multiple targets simultaneously, and then engage the target using the full range of air-to-air missiles in the inventory, including the AIM-120 AMRAAM, as well as the older Sparrows and Sidewinders. In the air-to-ground mode, Brian's Hornet could use all Navy precision guided munitions, including laser-guided bombs, SLAM, Maverick, and Harpoon. Even though he was aloft on another routine, boring, mission, the Hornet was a joy to fly and operate.

At Al Taqaddum airfield in southern Iraq, Raid Abd Bakr climbed into his MIG-25 Foxbat and went through his preflight checks prior to taxiing out for his mission. He had a single AS-6 anti-surface missile—a training missile—slung under his aircraft. It was scheduled to be a good training hop, a GCI—ground control intercept—flight that would take him close to the thirty-third parallel, the top of the southern no-fly zone that the United States and its allies enforced on a daily basis. He considered his good fortune. Assignment to Al Taqaddum—Al Taq as the Americans called it—and to a MIG-25 Foxbat squadron was a career plum. Importantly, this posting would ensure that he experienced more flying than his compatriots at nearby airfields at Balad and Al Asad, and much more than those at the northern airfields of Qayyarah West and Kirkuk. Being posted at a base less than forty miles from the capital, Baghdad, had its advantages. President Saddam Hussein demanded the highest vigilance in and around Iraq's capital city.

The GCI flight was excellent training. A major, or raid, in the Iraqi Air Force could receive no better opportunity. It would be a challenging flight. The ground controller would first fly him northwest towards Al Asad, following the Euphrates River at low level, then south over Iraq's portion of the vast Syrian Desert, a continuum of wide stony plains interspersed with occasional sandy stretches and long wandering wadis—the watercourses that are dry most of the year—then east across still more wadis as far as Iraq's second largest lake, Bamr Al Milh, than east-south-east toward Al Kut, then northwest for his longest leg back to Al Taq. Raid Bakr's job was to follow the instructions of the controller precisely. It had been over two weeks since he had last flown—too long—and he knew that he was rusty, but this was an excellent way to regain his proficiency.

His checks completed, Raid Bakr taxied his MIG out onto the southeast end of the closest northwest-southeast runway at Al Taq. Once there, he checked in with his GCI controller at the nearby base of Habbaniyah. All the controller was to him was a disembodied voice that would keep him safe. That was all he needed to know as he pushed the throttles forward, powering his aircraft northwest along the runway, speeding past the few buildings on the base on his right-hand side, pushing his MIG up into the early afternoon sky.

Shortly after *Carl Vinson*'s package Charlie took off, Air Force Captain Brad Weiss was airborne in his U-2. Launching from Prince Sultan Air Base in the vast Saudi Arabian desert, Weiss figured that this would be another routine mission. The U-2s patrolled the sky along the southern edge of the Iraqi no-fly zone, and Weiss was one of the most experienced pilots in his highly secret squadron. He would utilize his aircraft's cameras to take extensive pictures of Iraqi positions on the other side of the no-fly zone, seeking bits and pieces of intelligence regarding Iraqi movements or build-ups, flights or missile positions.

Captain Brad Weiss did not lack for courage, but he felt incredibly vulnerable as he flew this mission. "Alone and unafraid" he and his squadronmates called it with their pilot's gallows humor. There were no "routine" missions as far as he was concerned. Even a half-witted Iraqi pilot could shoot him down. He took some comfort in the fact that both the Air Force and the Navy put fighter jet packages into the box whenever the U-2 flew to protect his highly valuable aircraft by engaging any Iraqi jet that threatened him. Due to the position of the U-2s along the edge of the no-fly zone, and the close proximity of many Iraqi airfields just north of the no-fly zone, there was very little time for the U.S. jets to react to protect the U-2s. Brad Weiss felt more vulnerable than he liked to feel.

*　　*　　*

As the package Charlie approached CAP station Colorado, they anchored over a convenient geographic checkpoint, the small town of Ar Rumaythah. Two Hornets and two Tomcats set up "mixed sections"—a Hornet and a Tomcat flying together to take advantage of their respective sensor capabilities—while the Prowler set up a good jamming station south of them and the two additional Hornets flew slightly west of the north-south racetrack the mixed section jets set up. Flying their north-south racetrack enabled the jets to have at least one mixed section of fighters pointing toward Iraqi airspace at all times, ready to engage any Iraqi jet attempting to threaten the U-2. Further to the south, the ever-present Air Force AWACS radar plane kept a wary eye on everything in the air, ready to give an instant alert should an Iraqi jet make any threatening move.

Brian was flying one of the mixed sections, his Stinger 304 married up with Ripper 100, piloted by the Red Ripper's executive officer, Commander Tim "Benny" Tallent. Benny had been at this a long time, so Brian was content with flying Benny's wing and learning anything the Red Ripper's skipper could teach him. Once package Charlie was set in its station, Benny radioed the AWACS that the U-2 was cleared to begin its flight.

Raid Bakr began the first leg of his GCI hop along the Euphrates River with a mixture of exhilaration and frustration. Exhilaration to be in the air once again, but frustration that his jet was not operating to his liking. His gyrocompass was acting balky again—he knew that he had flown this very aircraft almost a month ago and had told the maintenance crew to fix it. His standby compass was completely out of the aircraft, no doubt removed to place in another aircraft with even more severe material problems. Worse still, his radios produced a great deal of static and background noise. He had to ask the GCI controller to repeat his instructions frequently. The damned Americans and their embargo—spare parts were dwindling to critical proportions. The condition of his aircraft was annoying and bordering on the unsatisfactory, but he was not about to return to base and wait—who knew how long—to fly again. He would just try to make the best of it. Flying south now, across the Syrian desert, he was thankful that there was a GCI controller at all: there were no navigational landmarks in this vast wasteland.

"Roger, Joker," said Captain Brad Weiss as the AWACS controller cleared him to begin his flight along the northern edge of the no-fly zone. He switched his camera equipment on and banked right, heading for his first way point. No freelancing here, he thought. He had a definite flight path that he needed to follow. The AWACS had cleared him along his route, and that meant that his defensive CAP station was set—didn't it? Wasn't it Navy pilots flying protection today? What if they had some emergency on the aircraft carrier and they had to recall them? He felt the hair on the back of his neck stand up just a little bit more than usual.

Raid Bakr found himself speaking more and more loudly just to make himself understood to his GCI controller. He knew that the enlisted man at the other end was just trying to do his job, but senior officers were monitoring his flight, and if he did not perform well it would not be the controller who would be censured, but him.

"Turn now—"

"Say again, control, you are very garbled," Bakr shouted.

"102, I say . . . turn . . . one . . . zero . . ."

"You are broken, say again."

"I say . . . turn . . . zero."

He thought he understood the command, and the turn didn't seem exactly right—south-south-east—but the radios were now getting worse, and picking up every second or third word was about the best he could do. He stared at his fuel gauge for a while and tried to concentrate on managing his fuel supply. How embarrassing it would be to run low on fuel and have to land at another field short of his home base. Let's see, at a speed of 450 knots, consuming . . .

Brian and Benny's mixed section continued to fly lazy race track patterns over their anchor point, surveying the Iraqi landscape below. While Benny kept up a constant chatter with his RIO, or radar intercept officer, in the back of his Tomcat, Brian was alone with his thoughts in the single-seat Hornet. They were broken out of their respective musings by an unexpected call from the AWACS.

"Ripper 100 and flight, Joker, over." The controller sounded excited.

"Go ahead, Joker."

"100, I've got a bogey headed south-southeast, type unknown, about ninety miles from your posit."

"Roger, Joker. Say intentions," said Benny. He'd been doing this long enough that he realized that the AWACS was good—but not perfect. They had radar "ghosts"—false images—just like any other radar. Benny wanted a little more info before getting his pucker factor too high.

"Ripper 100, on its current course, contact will pass within thirty miles of the U-2 in about ten minutes. We may have a problem here." The Air Force controller was identifying the problem, but he wasn't coming up with any specifics.

"Joker, this is Ripper 100. Rules of engagement are pretty clear on this one. It's your call if we engage."

"Roger, 100, checking . . . wait."

"Joker, 100, say range to bogey."

"Ripper 100, Joker, bogey still closing our man, now inside of thirty miles, request you begin to close. Vector 320, seventy-five miles."

"Joker, Ripper. Vectoring."

Almost instinctively, Benny banked his Tomcat hard, and Brian followed as if on cue. They had practiced this dozens of times. Was this really the genuine article?

In his MIG-25, Raid Bakr continued on his path. His fuel calculations complete, he looked out of his cockpit at the formless desert below, trying to pick up some landmark, something that would tell him where he was. The GCI controller wasn't helping, though Bakr did note the pitch of his voice in his almost inaudible communications pickup.

Captain Brad Weiss continued on course, but listening to the conversations coming from the AWACS made a tight knot form in the pit of his stomach. He was as brave as the next man, but the AWACS needed to tell him to reverse course and steer out of danger away from the Iraqi intruder. When were they going to call him? He'd give it a few seconds before calling them.

Aboard the AWACS the mission commander had less than a minute to make two decisions. The first was relatively easy. He called Brad Weiss on the secure net.

"Dragon, this is Joker. You are steering into danger, turn right now, reverse course and come to a heading of 250. Acknowledge."

"Joker, Dragon, wilco," said Weiss as he banked his U-2 as hard as he dared and retreated toward safety. Satisfied that his charge was turning away from danger, the AWACS mission commander, knowing it was his only recourse based on the intelligence at hand, made his second decision.

"Ripper flight, this is Joker. Dragon is clearing the area, target at your one o'clock, sixty-five miles. Stand by to engage. I say again, stand by to engage. Out."

Benny and Brian quickly rehearsed their procedures as they simultaneously shed their disbelief that this was actually happening. They determined that the best tactic was for Benny to engage the MIG-25 at long range with his Phoenix missile. Brian would be prepped with his shorter-range missiles if Benny missed.

Raid Bakr was shouting now, trying to make the GCI controller hear him. Damn these radios. His instincts told him that he was on this leg for too long a time, but the Iraqi military booked no freelancing by its pilots. Following the rules was his only recourse. He just needed the controller to talk to him. His shouting seemed to have some impact. Now the controller was talking very loudly and very excitedly. What was he saying, though? The high pitch of his voice started to make Bakr anxious.

"Ripper flight, target now at your twelve-thirty, fifty-five miles. You are cleared to engage. I say again. You are cleared to engage. Light 'em up, Ripper." Satisfied that he was lined up for a good shot, and now cleared to fire, Benny's RIO turned on his fire control radar. Immediately, he had contact.

"Engaging."

The display was unmistakable to Raid Bakr in his MIG-25. His ES—electronic surveillance—gear picked up the Tomcat's fire control radar as soon as it came on. But how could it be? He was targeted? Raid Bakr began to call his GCI controller, but then his survival instincts took over.

"Fox three," shouted Benny's RIO, stating the obvious but following procedures nonetheless. The Phoenix missile coming off a fast-moving Tomcat moves at over 1,500 miles an hour. It headed straight for the MIG-25. It would take less than two minutes to get there.

Raid Bakr did not know what was coming, and he did not know what was to soon hit him. He mustered all of the flying skills he had learned in all his years of flying and yanked and banked his plane wildly to try to defeat the unseen foe.

Aboard the AWACS, the mission commander and his crew tracked the Phoenix missile as it sped toward the MIG. "Seconds to go now . . ."

Brian spotted it first. "Ripper 100, flash, twelve o'clock, a little low. No chute that I can see from here."

"Roger 304, we're breaking off." Break. "Joker, Ripper flight, scratch one bogey, returning to station."

"Roger, Ripper," replied the AWACS mission commander, but he had moved on. Over his secure net he was preparing a short, pre-formatted message to the Joint Task Force-Southwest Asia—JTF-SWA. Simultaneously, the E-2 loitering off the coast had picked up all of the transmissions and was preparing a similar message to send to *Carl Vinson*'s Combat Direction Center—CDC.

As the operators in the field followed their well-rehearsed procedures for pushing this information up the chain of command, it was only a matter of minutes before the word of this shootdown reached the National Military Command Center in the Pentagon. Minutes later it reached military headquarters in Baghdad.

8

GENERAL DANIEL XAVIER LAWRENCE SAT AT HIS DESK at United States Central Command Headquarters in MacDill Air Force Base in Tampa, Florida. Sensitive to Arabian Gulf nations' concerns that the United States' "footprint" in the Gulf was too large, the Americans had set up the command responsible for military activities in that region at this sprawling Florida base. CENTCOM directed activities in the Arabian Gulf from this distant headquarters, and that unique situation led to challenges that the general was dealing with now. Tensions were heating up in the Arabian Gulf, and he was not there. The only senior officers in the Gulf AOR were Air Force Major General Anthony Gaylord, the Commander of JTF-SWA, running Operation Southern Watch, and Vice Admiral Harry Flowers, "dual hatted" as U.S. Naval Forces Central command and Fifth Fleet commander. Lawrence could barely tolerate the Air Force and couldn't abide the Navy at all. He was getting his information secondhand, and from officers in whom he had no personal confidence.

CENTCOM was the most unique of the nine Unified Combatant Commands that were assigned operational control of United States combat forces. While other Unified Combatant commanders—like those of the United States Pacific Command headquartered in Honolulu, Hawaii, or the United States European Command headquartered in Stuttgart-Vaihingen, Germany—had vast forces continually under their command (and were also located permanently in the area of their operations), the CENTCOM commander had a grand total of fewer than seven hundred full-time military personnel permanently assigned to his headquarters located seven thousand miles from where the action would be in case of a conflict.

The theory had it that, in time of crisis, CENTCOM would forward deploy to the Arabian Gulf and would draw forces from its component commanders; the U.S. Army Forces Central Command (ARCENT) at Fort McPherson, Georgia; U.S. Central Command Air Forces (CENTAF) at Shaw Air Force Base, South Carolina; U.S. Naval Forces Central Command (NAVCENT) in Manama, Bahrain; U.S. Marine Corps Forces Central Command (MARCENT) at Camp Lejeune, North Carolina; and U.S. Special Operations Command Central (SOCCENT), also at MacDill. That was the theory, but Lawrence had seen that theory come apart during Operation Desert Strike in 1996 when his predecessor's staff had never moved forward and when forces were drawn from wherever the National Command Authorities had deemed necessary. He wasn't in control of the situation, and it bothered him deeply.

Control is what had propelled General Daniel Xavier Lawrence to four stars in the United States Army and what had made him one of the most powerful men in the United States military. His looks accentuated that power. Lawrence had been a boxer at the U. S. Military Academy at West Point and still practiced in the ring frequently. At just over six feet tall and a lean 190 pounds, he looked like a professional athlete and looked a decade younger than his fifty years. Lawrence had made a near religion out of physical fitness, and part of Army lore was that he often held sway at contentious meetings with peers because other officers feared that he might invite them into a boxing ring. He was not afraid to flaunt his physical power.

He was just finishing his first cup of coffee and going through his message queue when his executive assistant (EA) Colonel Carter Samuels knocked and walked briskly into his office.

"Yes, Carter?" The general looked up and immediately sensed alarm in his assistant's eyes.

"General, call from General Gaylord. He says there's been a shootdown over Iraq."

"Shootdown!" exclaimed General Lawrence as he leapt out of his chair. "Put him through. One of our planes?"

"No sir, an Iraqi Foxbat."

Colonel Samuels left and put the call through within seconds. "Lawrence here!" said the general, picking up the phone on the first ring.

"General, good morning. I have not confirmed this report, but initial indications from our AWACS are that one of our jets just shot down a MIG-25 Foxbat crossing the thirty-third parallel. It was heading right for our U-2 when it was shot down."

"Heading for our U-2? Why? When?"

"Just ten minutes ago, General. I called you as soon as I could. We have already made our voice report to the National Military Command Center—and to your command center, of course. But I wanted to call you personally."

"Well, who the hell shot at him?"

"It was one of our Navy Tomcats off *Carl Vinson*, General."

"NAVY! Goddamnit! I told you we had to keep the fucking Navy out of the fucking box. Goddamnit! Who gave the shoot order?" Lawrence was working himself into a full rage now.

"Our AWACS gave the final order, General—in accordance with the Rules of Engagement," continued Gaylord, now trying to somehow mollify his enraged senior.

"Fuck the ROE!" shouted Lawrence. "I'm the Goddamned unified commander. Did you ever think of consulting me?"

"General," protested Gaylord, "there just wasn't time . . ."

"Wasn't time?! You let that Navy cowboy Flowers screw the pooch on this one. When the hell is he going to call me? I want that Tomcat crew debriefed right away and a full transcript sent to me."

"Yes sir," was all that Gaylord could offer. Lawrence

wasn't thinking clearly—he was barely thinking at all. But Gaylord could not make him understand that now. Lawrence was in the "full blaster" mode he was famous for. There was never time to check such things through. U.S. aircraft had been playing this cat and mouse game with Saddam Hussein's Air Force for a long time. Now something had happened.

"Send me a full report, General, and send it in a hurry. I want to see anything else that comes out of JTF-SWA before it goes out to any other commands."

"Yes sir," responded Gaylord, eager to get off the phone as quickly as possible, before Lawrence exploded again.

Lawrence's EA was the next to receive a blast.

"Carter, get in here," Lawrence shouted into the intercom. Samuels was there before the general's finger was off the intercom button. "You get Admiral Flowers on the line and get him on it now! Then I want his deputy, Rear Admiral Bowling, in here immediately." Samuels was gone as quickly as he had appeared.

General Lawrence was too agitated to sit down, so he paced back and forth across the length and breadth of his large office. Finally, his deputy director for intelligence brought in the charts that he had asked for, then beat a hasty retreat as the general told him to do just that.

General Lawrence spread the large map of the CENTCOM AOR on his desk. The general had a fascination with geography, and somehow, spreading this chart out and staring at it while he waited for various phone calls to be placed helped focus his mind. Looking at the sprawling AOR, which stretched over 3,000 miles from east to west and almost 3,500 miles north to south, he reminded himself of the complexity of the twenty countries that comprised the area he was responsible for. In addition to the Arabian Gulf littoral states of Bahrain, Iran, Iraq, Kuwait, Oman, Qatar, Saudi Arabia, and the United Arab Emirates, his AOR stretched to the borders of Kenya and Tanzania in the south; to the borders of Egypt and Libya in the west; to the borders of Iran and Azerbaijan in the north; to the borders that Pakistan shared with China and India in the east.

While looking at the map did help focus his mind, it increased his frustration. How the hell did they expect him to be able to manage from his headquarters in Florida the complex interactions in this area that spanned three continents and was the birthplace of three of the world's major religions—Christianity, Judaism, and Islam—and where contentions among those religions still gave rise to continuous strife? How was he supposed to safeguard from seven thousand miles away a region that contained more than seventy percent of the world's oil reserves, and that was the juncture of the major maritime trade routes linking the Middle East, Europe, South and East Asia and the Western Hemisphere, including maritime choke points like the Strait of Hormuz and the Suez Canal? He would find a way to get himself and his headquarters staff into the AOR or bust!

The intercom rang again. "General, I have Admiral Flowers on the line," said his secretary.

"Put him on," said General Lawrence, pushing the maps aside, "and tell Samuels to get on his line, I may want to replay this one."

Having their executive assistants listen in on all of their important calls was a time-honored tradition of very senior military officers. They dealt with many issues and felt that their time was too valuable to take notes on their conversations, so the EA was assigned to listen in to those calls to keep a near-verbatim transcription of what was discussed. Little wonder that rumors and leaks abounded throughout the military establishment.

Lawrence let the phone ring several times as he settled back into his large brown leather chair. Finally, he picked it up. "Lawrence here."

"General, this is Vice Admiral Harry Flowers. How are you this morning, sir?" began the admiral, knowing what General Lawrence was calling about but not being certain of what his reaction would be. He found out immediately.

"Not worth a damn, Admiral. How in the hell did you let one of your planes shoot down a goddamned Iraqi aircraft?"

"The MIG was making a beeline for one of our U2s, General. Under the circumstances, I'd say that we probably saved our pilot's life." Flowers was taking a hard line. He was new in his job, but he had already drawn his own conclusions about General Daniel Xavier Lawrence. "Dumb jock" was the phrase that he used in his most private conversations with intimates. He would show him who had the real clout in the CENTCOM AOR.

The general was silent for a moment as he considered Admiral Flowers's comments. The admiral took that silence as assent and was mentally congratulating himself on his persuasiveness. He thought that he now had General Lawrence where he wanted him. He was wrong.

"You'd say we probably saved the pilot's life, eh, Admiral. What do you base that on, your extensive experience in the AOR, or your actual combat experience?" said Lawrence loudly and with a heavy dose of sarcasm in his voice. He had no respect for Flowers. None. But now, this . . . this dilettante was defying him. General Lawrence was working himself up into a full rage.

Admiral Flowers was undaunted and brushed off the personal and professional slight as he attempted to continue. "General Lawrence, I think that if you—"

The general cut him off. "No, Admiral, now you just go into the listen mode. You didn't think, that's the Goddamn problem—you and whoever is in charge of your battle group launching these guys over Iraq without really having control over them. You just started blasting away. Who in the hell do you think you are? You call yourself the fleet commander out there? You responsible for those Navy jets?" Lawrence hesitated for a second to allow Flowers to get in just a word.

"Yes, I am responsible . . ."

"You are, huh? So you've spent time on *Carl Vinson*—in your capacity as fleet commander, that is?" General Lawrence clearly baited Admiral Flowers.

"Yes, General, I've been out to *Carl Vinson*."

"Yes. I'm sure that you have. And you've visited the ready rooms and talked with the pilots, correct?"

"Well, General—" Lawrence knew the answer and poured it on.

"And since what we do during Operation Southern Watch is so important, you've impressed on them *personally* the delicacy of the situation over Iraq. You've explained to them the overarching guidance regarding the various combinations and permutations of what they should or should not do in the box, how they should think through the situation and use force only as a last resort. You have done that, haven't you, Admiral?"

"No, General, not exactly."

"Not exactly?"

"No, General, well, I mean, I have not personally done that. I didn't feel that that was my role. The task group commander—"

General Lawrence went for the jugular now. "So, Admiral Flowers. Let me understand this. You're there in the AOR full time. You have one carrier task group working for you. You have a whole host of assets that can take you out to the carrier anytime you want—hell, you can embark in the carrier full time for all I care. And given all that, you haven't made the time to take a personal interest in something so important, and brief the pilots on what they are supposed to do, but have left it up to some cowboy out there on the carrier. Do I understand this right? My, Admiral, you must be awfully busy doing other things. It's just not clear to me what those things are."

Admiral Flowers hadn't expected his conversation with General Lawrence to be a love-in, but he hadn't expected the attacks to be so vehement or so personal. He attempted to recover some shred of dignity. "General, I will fix the problem. You have my assurance on that."

"YOU ARE THE GODDAMNED PROBLEM, FLOWERS. YOU AND THAT IDIOT IN CHARGE OF YOUR BATTLE GROUP, ROBINSON, ISN'T THAT HIS NAME? HE'S SUPPOSED TO BE A HOT SHOT WITH THE OTHER FLYBOYS IN THE NAVY. THEY HAVEN'T HEARD FROM ME YET, SO STAND BY!" shouted General Lawrence as he slammed the phone down in its cradle. Colonel Samuels winced as he pulled the phone away from his ear.

"Mandy," the General yelled, loud enough for his secretary to hear, "you got that call placed to the chairman yet?"

"We'll get a call back as soon as he comes out of the NMCC, General."

General Lawrence was frustrated beyond words. He needed to be where the action was. He couldn't do his job from this desk in a building half a world away. He was going to be in charge, and he was going to be in control. He would make that happen above all else.

9

CARL VINSON HAD BEEN AT GENERAL QUARTERS FOR over three hours. Immediately after the E-2C Hawkeye had reported the Foxbat shootdown, Captain Craig Vandegrift had sent his ship to GQ to prepare for the worst. The ready alert fighters had been launched, a tanker package had been sent up, and some of the aircraft in the just returned package Charlie had been refueled on deck and immediately sent up again. Rear Admiral "Heater" Robinson, Captain Vandegrift, and the CAG (Commander Air Group), Captain Ryan "Wizard" Foster, had caucused regarding how to get the largest number of fighters in the air in the least amount of time.

The "handler," the officer responsible for positioning all the carrier's aircraft in the hangar bay and on Carl Vinson's huge flight deck, was not as well prepared for this contingency as he might have been, and as aircraft were respotted—moved to different positions on the flight deck—to enable the carrier to get more fighters into the air, a heavier burden fell to the airborne tankers, the S-3B Vikings, to keep gas in the air and support the growing number of airborne fighters.

Lieutenant Anne O'Connor was piloting one of those Vikings. Immediately after the Foxbat shootdown she had been pulled off her ASR mission, brought back to the carrier, hot-refueled, and sent aloft as one of the primary tankers. This was the real thing. Aircraft were being shot down. Anne knew it was critical to do the best job she could.

She was running racetracks at 7,000 feet and 250 knots high above *Carl Vinson* in Blue Wolf 702, and she and her crew had just refueled their third fighter. There were more coming off *Carl Vinson*'s flight deck. Navy fighters were notorious fuel hogs, and these jets used a lot of fuel during start-up, taxi, and especially during their launch and initial climb out, so much so that it was necessary to top them off with fuel before sending them off to continue their mission. Anne and her crew had been airborne as the mission tanker for a while, and, coming on the heels of their long ASR mission, they were getting a little ragged. The urgency of the mission, however, made them hang in there. For Anne O'Connor this was what being in the Navy and being a naval aviator was all about.

As she piloted Blue Wolf 702 around the tanker track, making endless left-hand turns and fueling more and more fighters, none of those thoughts worried her. She was completely focused on her mission. A major part of that focus was concentrating on her aircraft, the S-3B Viking. Anne loved the Viking. Built by Lockheed primarily as an anti-submarine warfare, or ASW, aircraft, designed to protect the aircraft carrier from Soviet submarines, the Viking still performed the ASW mission but had evolved a host of other missions, including electronic surveillance, over-the-horizon targeting, anti-surface warfare, mining, and the mission Anne was on now—tanking other Airwing aircraft.

The Viking was ideal for the tanking mission. Its two General Electric TF34-GE-400B turbofan engines were extremely fuel efficient and allowed it to remain on station for almost seven hours. With a maximum gross weight for carrier operations of over 40,000 pounds, it could carry thousands of pounds of fuel to provide to its tanked aircraft. With a crew of four, a pilot and naval flight officer in the front and another naval flight officer and an enlisted sensor operator in the back, there were enough people on board to conduct the tanking mission and still monitor the plane's sophisticated Inverse Synthetic Aperture Radar—ISAR—

and provide task group surveillance at the same time. With a top speed of 450 knots it could dash to station and refuel aircraft anywhere in the carrier's sphere of operations.

Right now, that mission involved anchoring overhead the carrier and providing fuel to aircraft as they came off *Carl Vinson*'s busy flight deck, and then sending them on to their TCP—timing control point—en route to their box missions. Anne was totally focused on this mission, that is, until she spotted the next fighter on her list of planes to refuel— Stinger 304. Brian McDonald's jet. It reminded her of how being a naval aviator—or even being a naval officer—was such a near thing for her.

Like all of the 1,200 or so new plebes, Anne O'Connor entered the United States Naval Academy on that sultry day in June determined to do her best to graduate and become a commissioned naval officer, and then to enter flight training and earn her wings. Based on all she had accomplished in high school, it seemed like a very achievable goal. Anne had an intense but successful plebe summer and was ready to begin her academic year when the brigade returned in the fall.

Anne hit the ground running, becoming a peer leader among her classmates, making the varsity swimming team— a real accomplishment for a plebe or freshman—and keeping up with her studies, though that part was harder than she had anticipated. Anne had been an honor student in high school, but the level of academics at the Academy was extremely high and a big leap from Coronado High. She kept up by burning the midnight oil and just toughing it out. She made no secret of the fact that she was almost totally focused on naval aviation and started collecting naval aviation squadron stickers to post in her room—unlike most of the other women at the academy, who had pictures of their boyfriends adorning their walls.

A month after Christmas, during a period known at the Naval Academy as the dark ages, when the Annapolis sky is perpetually gray, when the joys of Christmas are a distant memory, and when spring seems just too far out there to even think about, Anne O'Connor hit a tough spot. Her grades were slipping badly. She was starting on the swimming team, which was taking up a great deal of her time, and she did not want to back off on that. Swimming was more than just something she did; it helped define who she was. She had been dating—they weren't allowed to call it dating at the academy—but she was involved with a former mid on the academy men's swimming team who had quit the academy a month earlier and transferred to USC, where he accepted a full swimming scholarship. Anne had been offered a swimming scholarship at USC out of Coronado High and, when she turned it down to attend the academy, she had received a great letter from that coach reminding her that if she ever changed her mind, a scholarship at Southern Cal was waiting for her.

Her company officer, the mentor for the hundred-plus midshipmen typically assigned to a company, was a crusty, non-athletic, surface warfare officer who was not enamored with athletes, prospective aviators, or women for that matter. He had chewed her out several times about her grades and further told her how stupid she was to be playing a varsity sport. The low ebb hit when she flunked her second math exam in a row and came down with the flu, missing several swim meets. Her friend at USC was calling her every other night to try to persuade her to drop out of the academy and come join him there—back in southern California, where her heart was.

Brian McDonald was a first class midshipman in her company and had already been selected for naval aviation. Although Anne was not in his individual squad, there were informal networks within the company, so when he learned that a fellow midshipman interested in naval aviation was thinking of quitting, he summoned her to his room in Bancroft Hall, the academy's cavernous dormitory.

"Midshipman O'Connor, reporting as ordered," said Anne as she knocked on Midshipman First Class McDonald's door at 2100 on a Tuesday night. Brian had picked the time because he knew his roommate would be in the library cramming for an exam.

"Come in, O'Connor. Stand at ease."

"Yes sir," Anne replied. She did not know why she had been summoned here, but if a plebe was summoned to a first class room, it was never a good thing. Probably just one more person who was going to rag on her about her failing math grades. This might be the final nail in the coffin that was going to make her decision to quit the academy that much easier. She still felt like hell from this flu, and she hoped that she wouldn't lose her cool and snap back if he chewed her out.

"OK, I guess you're wondering why I called you down here," said Brian. He was looking up from his small desk chair as she continued to stand at ease.

"Yes sir, I was," she replied as formally and officially as she knew how. *The less you say, the better, Anne*, she kept telling herself.

"Well, this may take a while, why don't you grab my roomie's chair there and sit down. I'm getting a crick in my neck looking up at you."

"Yes sir," she replied and hoped that he didn't see the puzzled look on her face. Upperclassmen never invited plebes to sit down in their rooms. Anne sat at attention in the chair.

"I understand that you've been having some trouble with math?"

"Yes, sir, a little, but I'm studying hard and going to math help sessions twice a week," she replied. She knew she was sounding defensive, but she couldn't help herself.

"Well, calc is pretty tough stuff. I figure you must be studying because you're not around the company area much, you must be at the library."

"Yes sir, I'm there a lot, that's for sure," she replied. She was still fencing.

"One thing that I noticed when we do company-wide inspections is that you've turned your room into an aviation shrine. You have an awful lot of stuff, memorabilia and all that."

"Yes sir, I think that it's all within regs, what I have posted, that is."

"O'Connor, look, relax will you? You look like Artoo-

Detoo without his can!" he said. That finally drew a smile, and Anne slumped a little bit.

"Look, a company here is a very small place. I think I know that you are really very interested in naval aviation. Am I safe in saying that?"

"Yes sir, more than interested, I've wanted to fly since I was five years old and I saw my first airshow. I saw myself in a Blue Angels uniform some day."

"OK, so have I, so we have something in common. You know that if you graduate from this place you're virtually a shoe-in to go to naval aviation training."

"That was my goal when I came here."

"It's also no secret that you're thinking of dropping out, transferring to USC."

"Yes sir, that's right. If I can't get good enough grades to stay here, I want to go somewhere where I can finish my education—"

"And what happens to flying?" he said, interrupting her.

"After I graduate from USC I can look into that—"

Brian interrupted her again. "O'Connor, look, you haven't been to all the briefings I have. The Navy is downsizing. They don't need that many pilots. If you're going to USC on a swimming scholarship they aren't going to let you join NROTC. And if you don't graduate from here or an NROTC school, the chances of getting into naval aviation are almost zero."

Anne hadn't considered that.

"Here, I want to show you something." Brian produced a thick photo album. It was filled with pictures of his summer training, all of it focused on naval aviation; pictures of him on USS *Enterprise* working and flying with their Tomcat squadron; pictures of him in Pensacola, home of the Navy's Blue Angels, including a picture with one of the Blues in front of their classy Hornets; pictures of him in various kinds of flight gear; even a picture of him going "down the chute" in the Dilbert Dunker, the device used to train pilots on how to get out of a ditched aircraft. As Brian went through the book, Anne was caught up in his contagious enthusiasm for flying—the same kind of enthusiasm she had had eight months ago when she'd entered the academy.

Finally, after regaling her for over twenty minutes, he closed the book. "Well, what do you think?"

"It looks like you are really looking forward to flying. I think that you will make a great pilot."

"So will you, O'Connor."

"I don't think that I will be one—or a graduate of this place," she replied. Brian could sense her opening up a bit.

"Look, O'Connor, I didn't call you down here to hit on you, okay. I just didn't want to see you give up your dream. I know because I was exactly where you are two years ago— I was in my sophomore slump when someone did for me what I'm trying to do for you."

He let that sink in. Anne finally looked up and made the first real eye contact that she had with him.

"Don't you see? If you think this company is tight, naval aviation is tighter. I could tell just looking at your room, but also from talking to your firsties, that you love naval aviation. Who do you think I want in my squadron flying wing on me; you, or someone who just picks naval aviation out of a hat on service selection night? If you want to say that those of us in this company who are going naval air have a little clique, you can say that. But we just try to support each other."

"Yes sir, but I can't hack the math," Anne replied, feeling a lump in her throat. Everything Brian was saying was so true—she desperately wanted to fly—but she wouldn't if she didn't get through academically.

"Bullshit, O'Connor," he said loudly, startling her. "Everyone says that at first. The math sucks and it's as boring as flying is fun." He pushed a sheet of paper across the desk toward her. "Here, recognize any of these names?"

"Yes sir, these are all midshipmen in our company."

"More than that, Anne, they are all going into naval aviation. Each one, each and every one of the six, has volunteered to tutor you day or night to get you through this. Now my personal recommendation is either Frank Noonan, he's a real math whiz, or Mary Williams, she took the same course you have now last year, but you go ahead and pick who you want. They all got help from somebody going into aviation at one time or another and now each one of them is eager to return the favor. You just have to say yes."

Anne looked at the piece of paper. More than just a list of names, Brian had carefully typed in what courses each one of them had taken, what math courses they were currently taking, and their room numbers. This wasn't some off-the-cuff thing, he had put a lot of time and effort into this.

"Sir, I'll think about this, I'll think about this a lot. I really will."

"O'Connor, I'm counting on you to do more than that. We're gonna get you over this math problem, we're gonna get you over this stupid flu you've got and back in the pool and winning swim meets for us, and we're gonna get you out of here and into the fleet and flying, you got it?"

With that Brian rose, and Anne did too. He extended his hand. "Yes sir," she said.

"I'm looking forward to you flying on my wing, O'Connor, don't screw it up!"

"No sir," she said.

That encounter with Brian McDonald had been just the tonic for Anne. She received an extraordinary amount of help, and while her math grades were not pretty, she got through it. She was soon back in the pool winning her events and shortly lost interest in USC and even in the former midshipman who was there.

Anne had never found a way to formally thank Brian for doing what he did, because there never seemed to be an end to his helping her. After he graduated he kept in touch, writing her letters occasionally when he was going through flight training, also sending her a little something to keep her psyched up for naval aviation—a squadron patch, a picture of a fighter aircraft, some other sort of aviation memorabilia, or the like. Subtly, Brian let her know that he had invested in her as a future naval aviator and that he didn't expect her to let him down—she had better make it through the academy and select for naval aviation.

Anne had done just that, and went directly to Pensacola after graduation. The constant moving from base to base as she began primary flight training, coupled with Brian's embarking on his first carrier deployment, caused them to lose touch. Now, several years later, they suddenly found themselves in the same Airwing. Anne tried to thank Brian formally, but he downplayed his role, insisting that she had done it all herself and pointing out that one of her classmates from their same company, Jake McLaughlin, who was flying with HS-4, had availed himself of the same type of help. Anne and Jake were fast friends, and, as they compared notes, they realized just how influential Brian had been in getting them to where they were now.

That was it. Brian was busy with his squadron and Anne with hers, but he always checked in on her and Jake from time to time—just to see how they were doing. A hint or a tip from a pilot three years senior to her was always a huge help, and Anne truly felt the mentoring on a frequent basis. Brian McDonald continued to play an important part in her life.

Anne O'Connor put those thoughts out of her mind as Stinger 304 moved in to refuel. It took only a few minutes to give the Hornet the 2,000 pounds of gas it needed. As 304 broke away to the left she allowed herself a look at his jet and saw his head turn toward her. No eye contact was possible behind those darkened visors, but she was sure that she saw a head nod. *Still checking on me*, she thought. Brian McDonald, tough Hornet pilot, making sure I'm doing all right. She knew that she wouldn't be there without him. Those thoughts were broken as Stinger 304 pushed up the throttles and headed back to the box.

Stinger 307 was next up for gas and was about halfway through refueling when the E-2C called. Anne could tell instantly that there was a problem. "Ninety-nine [the collective call sign for all the aircraft in the air], this is Black Eagle 601. Got a Tomcat with a combined hydraulic failure. Need to bring him aboard immediately. Break. Ripper 105, you'll be number one for landing, contact departure, expect a straight-in approach. Break. Blue Wolf, I'm sending you some more pups that need fuel prior to their push into the box."

"Blue Wolf 702, Roger. Send 'em on, Black Eagle."

"CAG LSO to the platform."

The announcement over *Carl Vinson*'s 1 MC told every-one onboard that an emergency of some kind was in prog-ress. An aircraft carrier's launch and recovery cycles are very stable, fixed events, and the LSOs, or Landing Signal Officers—the pilots who guide the planes to touchdown over the flight deck—are always on station before a scheduled recovery begins. When an LSO has to be called to the plat-form unexpectedly, it invariably means that an aircraft had to land early, often with one kind of emergency or another.

The emergency in this case was a combined hydraulic fail-ure on Ripper 105, one of the Tomcats returning from its flight in the box. The Tomcat's flight control system is crit-ically dependent on hydraulic fluid as a motive force for the jet's flight controls. Without hydraulic power the Tomcat would be totally out of control and would crash disastrously. Therefore, redundant hydraulic systems give the fighter backup hydraulic power in most scenarios, but if any one system fails, it is crucial to get the jet on deck as quickly as possible. The failure of the combined system means that the aircraft is still flyable but flying qualities are degraded and the controls feel "mushy" to the pilot.

On an aircraft carrier carrying over 5,000 people, it is usu-ally impossible to be singularly focused on any one thing for very long. Scores—if not hundreds—of very important things go on every hour of every day. When an Airwing aircraft has an emergency, however, the ship's focus is riv-eted on that aircraft, and everyone, from the captain to the most junior man or woman on the flight deck, does every-thing in his or her power to bring the aircraft back on deck safely.

Sitting at their scopes in CATCC, *Carl Vinson*'s OSs picked up Ripper 105 on their scopes as soon as he was handed off by the E-2C. Clearing all other aircraft out of the way, they set him up for an extended straight-in ap-proach, rather than a carrier "break," where the aircraft flies over the carrier and then breaks left abruptly to enter a downwind leg for landing. A straight-in would minimize the strain on the aircraft's hydraulic control systems. On the bridge, the captain called for more speed so *Carl Vinson* could have more wind over the flight deck to make it easier for the Tomcat to land. On the flight deck, on the LSO platform, and in Primary—the flight control tower—the first team was at the ready to get Ripper 105 back on deck safely.

The air boss got things moving in a hurry, booming into the 5 MC: "On the flight deck. Let's look sharp. We've got a Tomcat with a combined hydraulic failure coming in for a final approach thirty miles out. Let's get cranials on, sleeves rolled down, excess personnel clear the flight deck. Let's get all aircraft parked right now. Set the deck."

On the bridge, Captain Vandegrift instructed his officer of the deck to bring *Carl Vinson* to a course ten degrees to the right of where they were steaming to get the winds just a bit better for the Tomcat.

Ripper 105 rolled onto a twenty-mile final approach following the course of the ship. The pilot, Lieutenant Paul "Weasel" Weisbrook, and his naval flight officer, Lieutenant Charlie "Cyrus" Vance, nursed their jet along, making the minimum control inputs required to keep it heading toward *Carl Vinson*. The dialogue in the cockpit was as minimal as Weasel's control inputs.

"Looking good, Weasel," said Cyrus in as calm a tone as possible.

"Roger, feels OK, Cyrus, she's handling pretty good," replied Weasel.

"It's all you buddy, no problems back here. Feels like a magic carpet ride."

CCA—Carrier Control Approach—handed the jet off to the LSO, and the next voice that Weasel and Cyrus heard was that of the CAG LSO, Lieutenant Commander Mike "Dobie" Gillis.

"Ripper 105, paddles, looking good, call the ball." "Paddles" was the common name for the landing signal officer and was a throwback to the days before the "meatball" glide slope indicator that gave the pilots a more precise way of guiding their jet safely to the deck. In the days before the meatball, the LSO, armed with two landing paddles, visually directed the jet to the deck and used his paddles to wave the jet off if its approach was out of parameters. Now, the LSO worked in sync with the meatball and gave the pilot advisory commands, although he still had the authority to wave off any approach. He wanted to make this approach a good one. No one knew how long the Tomcat could go without having all its hydraulics fail, causing a disaster and the loss of the two aviators.

"Roger, Tomcat ball, 4.8," said Weasel, letting the LSO know how much fuel he had on board. 4,800 pounds.

"Roger, ball, looking good, bring it on in, Weasel."

"Roger."

That was the last transmission that Weasel was expected to provide; all he was supposed to do now was fly the ball and listen to the LSO and follow his directions. His controls were feeling mushy. He would be glad to get his jet down on *Carl Vinson*'s flight deck. Dobie worked him in.

"Looking good in the groove, 105. Looking good."

"Easy with the power."

Dobie was the best LSO in the Airwing—that's why he was out there bringing Weasel in. Dobie's modus operandi was to talk in a calm, soft voice, almost a whisper, working his pilot down. As Ripper 105 got closer, Dobie's voice got even softer.

"Looking good, 105, *easy* with the power, *easy*, really, really smooth buddy."

"Left for lineup."

Dobie was coaxing, cajoling, putting body language into his voice, into his every inflection. He wanted to make Weasel feel like he was in the cockpit with him, that he felt the mushy controls too, that he was working with him as closely as he possibly could to get the wounded jet on deck.

"You're a little low, power, *easy* with the power. Bring it on in."

"You're a little left, bring it back, *easy* . . . *easy*, work with it, *easy*."

Ripper 105 was closing rapidly, inside one-half mile, only seconds away from the deck. Dobie could see the Tomcat wallowing. He could feel Weasel's tightness as he tried to fight through the degraded hydraulics. He had to get him on deck. Still whispering, but talking much more rapidly now, he coaxed the Tomcat in.

"Steady, looking good."

"Little power."

"Right for lineup."

"Little more power."

"Easy with it."

"Right for lineup."

"Power, POWER!"

SLAM! 54,000 pounds of Tomcat smashed onto *Carl Vinson*'s deck at 135 knots—just over 150 miles per hour. Weasel had been low, and Ripper 105's tail hook caught the number one wire, the first wire on the deck. As soon as he hit, Weasel pushed his throttle full forward—standard procedure as a precaution in the event that the tail hook didn't engage the wire—so the Tomcat would have enough power to leap back off the deck. Anything less than full power, and the aircraft would almost certainly settle and crash into the water.

The opposing forces of the number one arresting wire catching the Tomcat and the full force of his throttles trying to thrust the plane forward whipped Weasel and Cyrus back in their seats as they absorbed the punishing Gs that accompany every carrier landing. But Weasel and Cyrus were bothered by the Gs perhaps less than on any other landing they had ever made. They were safe on deck. That was all that mattered. In the world of naval aviation professionals, there was no hoopla that went along with an event like this. Just business. The air boss broke the ice.

"On the flight deck, let's move the Tomcat onto elevator two. Prepare for the next recovery in twenty minutes."

One deck below, Heater Robinson walked out of TFCC and back toward his cabin. The pressure on his battle group was increasing, and he could do little about it. If only the leadership would decide how they wanted to use his battle group. Then the dangers his pilots were dealing with would be worth something.

10

MUCH OF THE BUSINESS OF THE NATION AND THE military forces that carry out the nation's mandates is routine. Hundreds of thousands of military people are deployed each day across the globe, but their actions and activities usually receive so little notice that even those in the executive branch, working directly for the commander in chief, pay scant attention to what goes on with the forward deployed Navy task groups, Marine Corps air-ground task organizations, Air Force wings, and Army brigades on a day-to-day basis.

When a crisis occurs, however, the president is almost instantly surrounded by a large coterie of civilian and military advisors, policy experts, interested staffers, and a large number of straphangers eager to be at the nexus of whatever action is occurring and is about to occur. The shootdown of the Iraqi Foxbat was no different, and the White House Situation Room was rapidly filling beyond capacity as more and more people filed down to the basement.

Word of the shootdown was flashed to the National Military Command Center—NMCC—by the JTF-SWA watch team in accordance with normal procedures immediately after they learned of it. The military was well-schooled in the absolute requirement to keep the chain of command informed at almost any cost. The NMCC immediately went through their notification checklist and, after dealing with one military assistant, got the word directly to the national security adviser. Michael Curtis interrupted the president in the family living quarters while he was having breakfast.

Now, the president entered the Situation Room and he

would, no doubt, want answers and quickly. Most of his key advisors—Michael Curtis, Defense Secretary Bryce Jacobs, Chairman of the Joint Chiefs of Staff Admiral Jake Monroe, CIA Director Pete Hernandez, and a few others were already gathered, the recipients of various "heads up" by their staff that something was brewing and that they ought to get in their cars, get on their car phones, and head for the White House. The secretary of state was still en route.

Michael Curtis stepped forward to brief the president. How ironic, he thought: just a day ago, he and many of the principals present had met to try to evolve a plan to deal with Iran, and today, the other powerful Gulf state, Iraq, had apparently tried to shoot down a U.S. military spy plane. Mideast politics was quickly becoming an all-consuming task for the administration and especially for him.

"Good morning, gentlemen," said the president, clearly a bit agitated. "OK, let me have it, what do we know?"

Curtis spoke forthrightly and forcefully. "We actually don't have the complete picture right now, Mr. President," he began. "We are just getting fragmentary reports thus far."

"Well, what *do* we know?" said the president. Patrick Browne was barely able to hide his annoyance. This was the White House Situation Room. It wasn't supposed to be a bunch of people standing around not knowing what was going on.

"We do know several things, Mr. President," Curtis began again cautiously. "We know that at 0722 Eastern Standard time, an F-14D Tomcat fighter off USS *Carl Vinson* shot down an Iraqi fighter jet. We believe that it was a MIG-25 Foxbat. We know that we had a U-2 flying along the northern edge of the southern no-fly zone at that time. We know that the AWACS reported that the MIG appeared to be heading directly for the U-2. We know that we have not yet heard anything from the Iraqi government. We do know that they have gone to a higher state of alert and that there is increased air activity on their part. We know that the *Carl Vinson* task force commander has sent the entire task group to General Quarters."

"That's fine, Michael," said the president. "But we don't

know why. Do your boys know anything, Pete?" he said, turning toward CIA Director Pete Hernandez.

"Not as much as we'd like to, Mr. President. We don't think that this is part of an overall offensive plan. There have been absolutely no indications or warnings that would lead us to that assumption. There have been no troop movements and no substantial and meaningful increase in air activity. It has been relatively quiet for the past several months and there were no precursors to today's events."

"Other theories?" replied the president.

"Well, Mr. President," continued Pete Hernandez, "there are always theories that we come up with. One, of course, is that this may have been a defector. That's a pretty low probability, because the pilots flying out of Al Taq, where this flight originated, are usually screened more thoroughly than any of their other pilots."

"Go on," said Patrick Browne, getting more agitated by the minute by the lack of definitive answers.

"Another theory," continued the DCI, "is that this guy might have been a rogue pilot who just wanted to start a conflict on his own. Maybe he or his family were hammered in Desert Storm or Desert Strike. But we discount that one the same way we do the defector theory; screening's probably too good in those southern bases."

The president let his stare tell the DCI he should come to the point quickly.

"Based on what little we do know, the most convincing theory that we can come up with right now is that this pilot just got lost."

"Got lost?!" said the president.

"Yes sir, got lost."

The president held up his hands as if waiting to catch something that wasn't going to be thrown. Admiral Jake Monroe decided to come to his colleague's rescue.

"Yes, Mr. President, it's a plausible scenario. Their pilots are not nearly as well trained as ours. They are almost totally dependent on their ground control interceptors to drive them from place to place and particularly to position them for an attack on another aircraft. It seems almost beyond belief that a controller would tell a pilot to do this, and just as unbelievable that a pilot would try to do it—attack one of our planes, that is."

"So you're saying that this poor bastard may have just strayed across the border by mistake?"

"Yes, Mr. President," said Admiral Jake Monroe.

"And we shot his ass out of the sky?"

"Yes, Mr. President."

"Goddamnit, Jake!" shouted the president. "Are your guys out there *trying* to start World War III?"

"No, they're not," said Secretary of Defense Bryce Jacobs. "The reaction times are so brief that the pilots must act quickly. You can imagine the disaster if one of our U-2s were shot down. It's unfortunate that this happened, Mr. President, but I think that everyone acted properly."

"Disaster if our U-2 was shot down . . . 'unfortunate' that this happened? Do you all not see what you've just done?!" Patrick Browne was in full rage now.

"Mr. President," continued Bryce Jacobs, "we had no intention of starting anything. From what we know thus far, our forces exercised prudent precautions. I promise you that we are already conducting a full investigation and that if culpability is found we will be swift in handing out punishment."

The president calmed down a bit, but only a bit. "Jake, who the hell is in charge out there?" he said, turning toward the chairman of the Joint Chiefs of Staff.

"Well, General Lawrence is the commander of the Central Command, and Admiral Flowers—"

"I know the Goddamned chain of command!" the president interrupted, his anger still boiling, "but who is in charge of the carrier sending these trigger-happy pilots up where they can start a war?"

"Sir, Admiral Mike Robinson is the battle group commander. Mr. President, I've served with Mike—"

"Yeah, yeah," the president interrupted again, "and you're gonna tell me what a fine fellow he is and how he's a fine battle group commander and how he's doing a great job."

"Yes sir," said the chairman, now realizing that Admiral Robinson was taking the heat for something that clearly was not his fault and now knowing that he needed to defuse the situation. "He is doing a fine job, Mr. President. We served together years ago. But I will personally contact him and ensure that he knows the rules of engagement and keeps things from escalating out of control."

"Personally, Jake, and don't wait too damned long."

"I will do that today, Mr. President," replied Jake Monroe, realizing that he had better make good on his promise.

"All right. Fine," replied the president. Turning to Michael Curtis he said, "Someone get Secretary Quinn and put him through to me here immediately. I want to know what the situation in Iraq is. I need to know what their reaction has been and what it will be." Then, turning to the secretary of defense, he said, "And I want to know what our options are—our full range of options."

Michael Curtis had welcomed the order to contact Secretary of State Philip Quinn. It got him out of the blast radius of the president's wrath. But more importantly, it got him away from the immediate conversation about Iraq. He was certain that this was just some tragic accident, a mistake, an error by a second-rate pilot flying for a third-rate air force. But instantaneously, it had distracted the president and his key advisors from the genuine, long-term menace in the Gulf. How long would it take to get their focus back in the right direction?

The national security adviser did not come by his opinion on Iran cavalierly or because of any ingrained prejudice or proclivities, and certainly not just because of recent events. He had studied the issue earnestly and saw in Iran a building power that had the potential to threaten the United States and its interests much more directly than Iraq had in 1990 when it invaded Kuwait. There was a wide array of facts that supported his reasoning.

Iran possessed a dozen Chinese made Hegu fast attack craft and had fitted them with powerful C-802 surface-to-surface missiles. These Hegu class craft gave Iran a mobile, anti-ship missile capability that could be used against merchant or naval shipping.

More ominously, Iran was equipping its aircraft with air-to-surface missiles. The C-801 air-to-surface missile had been fielded on Iranian aircraft operating out of the Bushehr naval base. Located on the Iranian coast perilously close to the carrier operating areas in the northern Gulf, F-4s taking off from Bushehr could be launching deadly missiles at the *Carl Vinson* only minutes after takeoff.

The national security adviser also knew that Iran possessed hundreds of Chinese-made Silkworm and Seersucker anti-ship missiles and that Iran had positioned these missiles along its coast flanking all normal shipping lanes in the Gulf.

Added to this offensive sea-based and land-based anti-shipping capability, the Iranians had also developed a significant coastal air defense capability. They had a total of almost two dozen Soviet-made mobile surface-to-air missile sites and were negotiating to purchase more and better surface-to-air missile systems.

One of the more troubling aspects of the Iranian arms buildup was its growing submarine force. Iran had obtained a total of three Kilo class diesel-electric submarines from Russia. Significantly, in addition to torpedos, these submarines carried twenty-four mines each and could place them anywhere while submerged. The potential for these submarines alone to choke the Strait of Hormuz was very real.

Tying together all of these military capabilities was the long and deep animosity that the ruling Iranian mullahs had against the United States. The Iranian clerics had convinced themselves that the United States would not rest until their clerical regime no longer ran the Islamic Republic. Nothing the United States did ever disabused the mullahs of this notion, and collectively, they viewed the United States as a long-term, implacable foe.

Of course, one of their planes hadn't just been shot down by one of ours, and Curtis had no doubt Iran would try to somehow use to their advantage their sudden position as "innocent bystander."

11

THE INTERCOM RANG INSISTENTLY ON THE DESK OF President Hasan Ebrahhim Habibi. He felt the hair on the back of his neck rise. He thought that he knew what this visit was going to be about, and he didn't want to be engaged in this way. But he had no choice.

"Minister Ali Akbar Velayati to see you, Mr. President," said the secretary.

"Send him in, please," replied Habibi, trying not to sound annoyed, or even resigned.

"Good afternoon, Mr. President," said Velayati as he entered. The minister of foreign affairs was a tall, spare man who was a decade younger than Habibi. The president always thought Velayati didn't show the proper reserve or respect he should in his presence.

"Good afternoon, Mr. Foreign Minister. My staff wasn't able to discern an agenda for this meeting. How may I help you today?" said Habibi.

"I think that you know why I am here, Mr. President. You have heard, I am sure, about the downing of the Iraqi plane by the Americans."

"I have. What concern is that of ours?" Habibi was being extremely cautious, measuring his words carefully. Velayati was clever and never initiated a meeting unless he wanted something.

"I think that it concerns us very much, my friend." There was a hint of sarcasm in his voice as Velayati paused on the word "friend." They were anything but friends.

"And how is that?" said Habibi, working hard to keep control and not lash out at Velayati.

"The Americans have shown us before that they can only

focus on one thing at a time. They will be conjuring up all kinds of theories to justify punishing the Iraqis. They will ignore us completely while this is going on."

"What does this mean to us, Mr. Foreign Minister?"

"It means we have an opportunity to rid our Gulf of the Americans."

"I don't share your compelling need to drive them out. They want to keep oil flowing through Hormuz, as do we. You seem to forget what supports our economy."

"I know very well!" said Velayati loudly. "But all commerce is on their terms."

"Be that as it may, Mr. Foreign Minister," continued Habibi, "we gain no advantage by going against the Americans, none whatsoever."

"And you see no advantage that would accrue to us if the Americans focus their wrath on Iraq, and if such a conflict weakens them both to the extent that we are once again supreme in the region?"

"You can't think that this incident will spark that. Surely this shootdown was an accident. There will be saber rattling, angry words, and then it will all be papered over," replied Habibi.

"Perhaps so, but I am not talking about this incident. I am talking about all that we are doing, and must continue to do, to keep the pressure on America, to make their presence in the Gulf ultimately too costly."

"So what is it you are asking me to do, Mr. Foreign Minister?" replied Habibi, now becoming annoyed with Velayati.

"Nothing, Mr. President."

"Nothing?" replied Habibi, not hiding his surprise.

"Nothing. Nothing at all."

"Then why have you come here to see me?"

"Because I know that you know that actions are underway already, actions that will deter the Americans from honoring their commitments here. They are being undertaken by our brave martyrs, many of whom have gone on to paradise already."

"If I know of these actions as you say I do, why are you telling me this now?"

"Because these actions must be stepped up. We have been doing this at a low level of intensity for a long time. We are getting results, but those results are minor—a pipe bomb here, an explosion in a marketplace there—they have not had the desired impact. We need no specific action on your part, Mr. President, just your assurance that you will look the other way as we intensify these preparations."

"Why, Mr. Foreign Minister, would I want to provide these assurances?"

"President Habibi, it is not for me to make rash statements about the way in which you are discharging your duties as president of the Islamic Republic of Iran."

"But you want me to follow your lead on this. Tell me why I should do that!"

"Mr. President, I will tell you, only because you insist. I need not remind you that we are an Islamic Republic and that we are responsible for providing leadership to the Islamic world. I should not need to remind you either that the Imam, Ayatollah Khomeini, preached a doctrine of permanent revolution and, as the leaders of the Islamic world, we are responsible for carrying this out. Those who are not behind the revolution are impeding it."

"So you question my revolutionary credentials, Velayati?" replied Habibi, rising to his feet.

"You have said it, Mr. President."

"And you propose to carry on these actions against the Americans, with my acquiescence, and for that, you will validate my credentials as a revolutionary in the cause of Islam."

This is exactly where Velayati wanted the conversation to go, because it enabled him to draw and play his trump card.

"I will, as will Ayatollah Ali Akbar Nateq-Nuri!" replied Velayati with a flourish. The mention of Ayatollah Nateq-Nuri, the country's religious leader and, by law, its commander in chief, set Habibi back. Velayati was too cautious to play this card cavalierly; he must have already consulted with Nateq-Nuri. Habibi was all too aware of the power of the Islamic Republic's religious leader. Not many years ago, the Ayatollah Ali Hoseini Khamenei had promoted Dr.

Hassan Firouzabadi, a veterinarian with no known army rank, to major general with nine years' seniority. Not long after that, the religious leader had Firouzabadi, whose strongest credential was his long record of service with the Basij Militia, installed as chief of staff for the Iranian armed forces. Therefore, Habibi proceeded very carefully.

"So, Mr. Minister. If you have already consulted with Ayatollah Nateq-Nuri, and you have, as you say, agreement on this, why are we having this conversation? As commander in chief, he has the authority to do all of the things you wish. How do my actions or inactions play into your plans?"

"As you know, Mr. President, there is strong precedent among our clerics to disassociate their temporal and spiritual activities. You recall in 1994 when the Ayatollah Mohammad Rezea Hahdavi-Kani, the secretary general of our Combatant Clerical Association, declared in public that our next president should not be a cleric. You also recall, I am sure, the admonition of our renowned revolutionary philosopher Abdulkarim Soroush that clerics should serve solely as religious leaders. The ayatollah has many duties of a religious nature that preclude his active, day-to-day involvement in affairs of state. He must remain aloof on many of the more mundane issues affecting the day-to-day things we do to run our government—"

Habibi cut him off. He wanted to say, "So, Mr. Minister. You want to insulate Ayatollah Nateq-Nuri and let me take the fall for having knowledge of such activities should they backfire," but he held his tongue. He knew Velayati's power, and he dared not confront him directly. Instead he said, "Mr. Minister, I see your point."

"You do?"

"Yes. If there is consensus that this must be done, then I will not stand in the way of it. I insist, though, that you keep me informed of what you are doing. I cannot conduct the affairs of state without full knowledge of these actions. You know all too well how my predecessor was embarrassed many times when he was not kept informed of various activities going on inside of our borders only to be called on it by others in the international arena."

"Of course, Mr. President. We would never do anything to complicate your handling of the affairs of the Islamic Republic." Velayati had not anticipated this response from Habibi and was himself proceeding carefully now. He was unsure where the president was going with this.

"That is appreciated, Mr. Minister. Now. Are you prepared today to tell me of the activities you have planned and initiated?"

Velayati backpedaled now, wanting to strike a deal with Habibi, but not wanting to reveal too much. "Well, not completely, Mr. President. I do not keep all of the details in my head, but I can tell you what I know."

"That will be sufficient. Please proceed," replied Habibi, now gaining the upper hand in his game of wits with Velayati.

"Very well, Mr. President. First, you know that we currently have just a dozen camps where those who support the permanent revolution preached by the Ayatollah Khomeini train. It is not our nation that has invented a need for these camps. The entire Islamic world has demanded them, we are merely a geographic convenience."

Habibi found Velayati patronizing. He didn't know how much more of this revolutionary sop he could endure, but he kept listening.

"Are all of these camps active now, Mr. Minister?"

"No, not all, Mr. President. The Imam Ali camp east of Tehran is our largest camp and is very active. It is there we are training members of the Saudi dissident groups, especially the Hezbollah of Hejaz and the Organization of Islamic Revolution. We also use it as a central point to plan many of our other activities."

"Yes, and the other camps?"

"The Nahaveand camp in Hamaden southwest of Tehran is a principal training ground for the Hezbollah, and we dispatch those who are trained back to many countries. The Fatah Ghani Husseini camp is just south of our capital outside of Qom, and is very active training Turkish militants, primarily in assassination techniques. The Alyeck camp to the northwest near Qazin is for more generalized training. These camps are operating at near maximum capacity already, and we need to bring some of the others back up to a more robust capability."

"And you say that funding is not an issue."

"Our brothers in the Islamic world have been more than generous. The many Shia movements have poured out their generosity on our fighters. We want for very little."

"Very good, Mr. Minister. You have told me enough about the camps, now tell me what else you are doing that I must know about."

Velayati thought for a moment. He wanted to be selective in what he told Habibi, but he wanted to tell him a sufficient amount to convince him that he had been candid with him so he would let him run with his plan. He also had no desire to embarrass the president of the Islamic Republic in the international forum, but that was a secondary consideration. He knew the power that Shiekholeslam had and how he had used that power already. It pained him to think that in many ways he was every bit as much of a functionary as Habibi. He would be sure that Shiekholeslam knew that he had secured the cooperation of the president of the Islamic Republic and that he alone could sustain that cooperation.

Then he laid out the basic outlines of his plan.

12

THE ADMIRAL'S CHIEF OF STAFF, CAPTAIN GEORGE Sampson, knocked on the door to the admiral's cabin.

"You asked to see me, Admiral?"

"Yes, COS, come in, please." Admiral Robinson rose, walked over to the large sofa in his office, and invited his chief of staff to sit down.

George Sampson had worked with the admiral long enough to see that he was in one of his reflective moods. He knew that one of his primary jobs as chief of staff was to be a sounding board for the admiral at moments like this.

"COS, you know that you or I could have called this, but our role is becoming more and more complex. Remember when our mission was defined only as naval presence?"

"I remember, Admiral. It wasn't that long ago, either, and duty here wasn't very exciting," said the chief of staff.

"Desert Storm changed that, didn't it? Now we've inherited all these new responsibilities in the Arabian Gulf. Operation Southern Watch and an expaned no-fly zone over Iraq demand constant patrolling by our aircraft."

It was a rhetorical question, and George Sampson didn't bother to answer; he just let the admiral continue.

"There's not much margin for error, George. Our aircraft have to be in an 'up' flight status every day, sorties have to be briefed, flown, and debriefed; more aircraft maintenance has to be performed, and the routine continues with us working literally around the clock. I know that I'm not telling you anything that you don't know."

"No sir, Admiral," continued Sampson. "Wouldn't be so bad if Operation Southern Watch was our only mission."

"You're right," continued the admiral. "OSW alone would be enough to keep us fully engaged. Do they have any clue how many assets it takes to enforce United Nations sanctions and run our maritime interdiction operation against Iraq? Shit, we're dedicating two to three ships to constantly patrol the northern Gulf, stopping ships attempting to make their way in and out of Iraq."

"It's tough, dirty work, Admiral."

"Hell, George, you've seen our ships patrolling these waters aggressively twenty-four hours a day, stopping sanctions violators and then, when necessary, escorting them to a neutral country that agrees to take their cargo and crews. It takes a huge effort to do that job."

"I know that we're constantly juggling our ships to fulfill the mission, Admiral. It's getting tougher every day."

"That's the bottom line, George. Ultimately, it falls to us—to our lone battle group—to provide the striking arm to enforce United States wishes here. That's exactly what Carl Vinson Task Group is being asked to do now. That's what Exercise "Swift Sword"—planning contingency operations against any state that threatens our interests in the Gulf littoral—is all about. I've just got to be damned sure that we're ready."

"I think that we'll be more than ready, Admiral," offered George Sampson, trying to put a positive spin on things.

"Good. Thanks for listening, George," said the admiral as he rose, signaling the chief of staff that it was time for him to leave. "I think we're on the same page on this. Let's get the other players together."

As he opened the door to the admiral's cabin and motioned for his key advisers to enter, George Sampson recognized that while this was a familiar overall scheme that presented itself to the senior officers of the Carl Vinson Task Group, there were aspects of it that seemed different from their previous trips to the Arabian Gulf. They all knew that something was different, not quite right.

The admiral was gathering his closest advisors in his cabin because he wanted to try to determine just what had changed. The cabin was large by any standards, and particularly for a seagoing office, with a working area of twenty feet by fifteen feet, and a separate living quarters further to starboard. Two large sofas dominated the after and starboard bulkheads of the working area, a large credenza with a thirty-one-inch television set filled the forward portion. Attractive prints of the Pacific Northwest—*Carl Vinson*'s home port area—covered the light wood-grain laminate on the bulkheads. A small conference table with cushioned captain's chairs filled the center of the room.

The admiral worked at a large wraparound curved desk, which had a group of phones on the far right-hand side and a small banker's lamp in the center. On the bulkhead in front of him he had the Bogen phone, which connected him to TFCC, SUPPLOT—Supplementary Plot—adjacent to TFCC, the captain on the bridge, and other key places throughout the ship, as well as a control box that allowed him to select one of twenty preset channels on either of the two TV monitors on a shelf high above his head. A "red phone" used for talking on any of a number of secure frequencies and a "bitch box" used for internal communications with a number of other locations—anywhere from his chief of staff's office to the flag intelligence office—completed the dizzying array of capabilities that the admiral had within easy reach of his large, high-backed chair.

Admiral Robinson took his place at the head of the table, the door to the Flag War Room—with its cipher lock and combination lock—on his right, a smaller door leading to the Flag Mess on his left. Seated at the table in the center of the room were his chief of staff, Captain George Sampson, *Carl Vinson*'s commanding officer, Captain Craig Vandegrift, CAG, Captain Wizard Foster, Captain Jim Hughes, his destroyer squadron commander, and his operations officer, Captain Bill Durham. CAG Foster was the first one to break the ice.

"Admiral," he began, leaning closer to Robinson from his chair just to the admiral's left. Foster was a big man, though not as robust as Admiral Robinson. An F-14 NFO and a former TOPGUN instructor, Wizard had earned his handle through his early mastery of airborne tactics and his encyclopedic knowledge of enemy and friendly systems, sensors, and weapons. At six foot five, with broad shoulders from years of lifting weights, Wizard exuded confidence. His deep blue eyes and rugged looks belied an agile mind, and he spoke in near whispers as he remained less than a foot away from the admiral. "Admiral, we've been working with CVIC and the intel folks at Fifth Fleet to come up with target sets for Exercise Swift Sword and I've got some problems with them."

"What kind of problems, Wizard?" probed Robinson.

"Well, Admiral. They give us target sets—actually, we have to extract them from them—and they seem to be really focused on hitting the Iranian Navy hard inport. Don't have any trouble doing that, but it seems like we're doin' overkill on the Navy boats—ah, ships, and ignoring everything else."

"Like what?" Wizard was not an alarmist, and if he was concerned about something, it was because his good instincts told him that he should be.

"Well, Admiral, the size of the strikes that we're sending

into Bandar Abbas and Bushehr is kind of awesome, I mean, big, big, packages."

"How big?"

"Well, sir, 'bout twenty to twenty-four plane raids."

"At each one?" said the admiral.

"Yes sir."

"And what's the timing on these raids?"

"They say that the fleet commander wants 'em pulled off simultaneously. Don't get me wrong, Admiral, we want to train the way we're gonna fight—if that's the way we're gonna fight."

Turning to Craig Vandegrift, the admiral said, "Skipper, can you get that big a package off the deck given the limited sea room you have?"

"Long as the wind keeps coming from the northwest, I've got plenty of sea room to run along the length of my assigned area. No problem getting them off. Recovery gets a little tougher, with the way visibility drops so rapidly at night."

"So some of these strikes are at night?" said Robinson, looking back toward Wizard.

"Yes, Admiral, well, they're day and night." Leaning closer to the admiral, the CAG spread out a small flow sheet in front of him, which showed the multiple strikes on each of Iran's two major naval bases. "The way their staff is directing it, we're doing three major attacks on each base, simultaneously for the first two, and then the third into Bandar Abbas, followed four hours later by the third into Bushehr. Course, this is only training, but the way they're coming at this, being so directive, makes me just a little curious."

"Me too," said the admiral.

"Then there's the weaponeering," added Craig Vandegrift.

"What about it?" asked the admiral, becoming more and more perplexed.

"Well sir, as I'm sure you remember all too well from your tour in command of *Kennedy*, building up the bombs is often the long pole in the tent. When CAG and I initially worked with your staff on this, we all felt that cluster bombs would be the best weapon for what we were trying to accomplish.

The blast and frag pattern that we'd get with them would put the Iranian boats out of commission for a long time, so that they'd be no threat to us. Then we could move on to strikes against terrorist camps, which was the purpose of this 'exercise.' "

"That makes a lot of sense to me," replied Heater Robinson.

"Us too, Admiral," said Wizard, jumping in. "But the Fifth Fleet staff guys said no, don't use cluster bombs, use laser-guided bombs. Said we wanted a probability of kill to, well, they said to send the Iranian Navy to the bottom."

"Why do they want to do that?"

"We can't get 'em to say, Admiral," continued CAG. "You know what it's gonna take to do that. More bombs, a lot more accuracy, riskier packages and all that. We're certainly willing to do that, but we kind of feel like mushrooms as we try to plan for all this . . ."

"Kept in the dark all the time and fed shit?" offered the admiral, trying to get a feel for just how much this bothered everyone else. It was starting to bother him a lot. The staff, ship, and Airwing had proposed blasting the Iranian Navy with cluster bombs that could be dropped from high altitude, that exploded at a predetermined height above the Iranian boats, raining down small bomblets onto their ships and craft, certainly rendering them out of commission for a lengthy period of time. The use of laser-guided bombs, which allowed aircrews to laser-designate targets and guide a 500, 1,000, or 2,000 pound bomb directly onto the target in question, would certainly increase the probability of sinking the vessel it hit, but it required the attacking aircraft to hold a laser designator on the target for the entire time of the bomb's flight, causing the aircrew to have to fly a much riskier flight profile. The admiral knew that flying high-performance jets off aircraft carriers and into combat was not risk free, but he was dead set against his pilots taking unnecessary risks for no apparent reason. "It's strange," continued the admiral, "damn strange."

"Exactly sir, and it gets even stranger. The commodore can fill you in."

Jim Hughes weighed in. "Admiral, I've been getting a lot

of 'guidance' from the Fifth Fleet ops folks regarding ship positioning for Swift Sword. They're telling me to basically forget about maritime interception ops and bring all my ships into position to simulate threatening Iran. First off, they want me to bring all the TLAM shooters into launch basket positions so we can use Tomahawk. That isn't a problem. We've been planning these sorts of things for years, and the going in has always been to use Tomahawk primarily to neutralize their integrated air defense system. . . ."

"Well isn't that what we've been doing?" asked Robinson.

"We are, Admiral," replied the commodore. "But we're doing a lot more. In addition to the TLAM we have programmed against IADS, they are telling us that we need to pour a lot of Tomahawks into their naval bases at Bandar Abbas and Bushehr . . ."

"In addition to the TACAIR strikes?" The admiral was becoming more and more perplexed.

"Yes sir. They want incredible probability of kills at both those bases. Additionally, they want Tomahawk shots—quite a few of them, actually—against the airfields at Shiraz, Bushehr, and Omideyeh. They've given us a long list of targets."

"What kind of Tomahawk inventory we talking about using?"

"That's just it, Admiral. The way they have us shooting them on the first two days of this 'exercise' we all but run out of TLAMs at the end of day two. I mean, no reserves, and certainly no backup missiles for the later salvos."

"Anything else?"

"Yes sir, Admiral. They are wanting us to move our cruisers in close to Bushehr and simulate pounding it with naval surface fire support. Doesn't seem like a prudent thing to do, but they want us to plan it that way."

"Who do they envision providing air defense for the carrier?"

"Well, no one sir. They said that we can cover that with our deck-launched interceptors."

"CAG. You got that covered?" asked the admiral, knowing the answer.

"No sir. Not even close. With strike packages this big, and

with the short turnaround time between strikes, I'm pressed to just make the flight schedule for the strikes—and that's if our availability is super."

Admiral Robinson paused and looked around the table. His senior commanders and staff assistants, with an incredible amount of collective experience, were staring at him almost blankly. What they were being told to do by Fifth Fleet just didn't track. It was common knowledge that "exercises" like Swift Sword mirrored reality, and if they practiced that intently for something, then at least at some level it was being considered as a real scenario. If that was the case, than it tracked even less well. The admiral was well aware of the growing consternation with the Iranian terrorist camps and had wargamed taking them out as part of the Carl Vinson Task Group's workup cycle. But this new level of escalation—sending their navy to the bottom, destroying their air force, using surface ship guns to pound their naval bases—this all signaled something more ominous. He knew that his seasoned commanders didn't feel at all comfortable with the plan, and he shared their discomfort. For now, Heater Robinson decided that he needed to take some action to help focus his staff and his principal warfare commanders.

"All right, gents. Here's what I want you to focus on for now. We're the only game in town. Lose this carrier or, hell, lose any of our combatant ships and we're out of business. Plan for the exercise, cooperate with the Fifth Fleet staff as best you can, but do not degrade the defense of this task group, is that understood?" The nodding of heads around the table signaled that they did. "Plan robust simulated strikes for Swift Sword, but give 'em a reality check. Until someone explains to my satisfaction why we're doing what we're doing, it's business as usual. We are *not* going to run strikes we can't reasonably put together and support. We are *not* going to run our supply of Tomahawks to zero. We are *not* going for overkill when we have a discrete mission that we can execute with far less cost. Is everyone clear on that?"

As Admiral Robinson pushed away from his end of the table and rose, he seemed to his commanders to be a decade older than the man who had led them from their West Coast home ports less than three months ago. The awesome responsibility of using his battle group as an instrument of national power, while not unduly hazarding the over 8,000 sailors assigned to the group, fell to him and him alone. It was a duty he would not shirk. Thus far, he had not been able to convince his seniors of the potential dangers to his battle group. As the last officer left his cabin, he picked his secure phone out of its cradle and determined to try to explain the situation to Admiral Flowers again. As he lifted the receiver, there was a knock on his cabin door.

"Come in," he said, trying to hide his annoyance that his train of thought had been broken by the knock.

"Hello, Admiral, sorry to bother you," began his communications officer, Lieutenant Commander Heather Wilson. "Just received this SPECAT message for you, I wanted Petty Officer Harris to bring it right down."

His communications officer now had his full attention, SPECAT messages were Special Category messages, those of such importance, needing such a degree of privacy, that only one trusted radioman on the staff was allowed to handle them. Was this the signal finally for action against the terrorists?

Just forty frames aft of where the admiral and his senior commanders were planning their strategy at the highest level, junior officers were also planning—planning to deal with the potential that some of the aircraft in any actual strike against Iran might be shot down.

In Ready Room Five, home of the Black Knights of HS-4, several officers bent over a topographical chart of the Iranian landmass and planned their mission.

"OK Jake," began Lieutenant Junior Grade Mary McGwire, the squadron's air intelligence officer, who had gathered a series of charts from CVIC. "We've put the route of flight for your birds over the beach on the charts as you see here. For these missions you'd ingress the coast right here—"

"For all our missions?" asked Lieutenant Jake McLaughlin, one of the Black Knights' senior aircraft commanders. Jake didn't like interrupting the AI, but these were important missions, the life and death stuff that they were responsible for.

"Yes, for all of them going to the four SAR pickup points that you see depicted here. I've got the other routes on these other charts, but they're the less likely scenarios."

"OK, I see it. Do these circles represent all of the Iranian surface-to-air missile batteries?" asked Bart Ellzey, Jake's copilot.

"All of the fixed ones, the mobile guys are just too hard to pin down," Mary continued. "Now, these small black circles represent all of the AAA sites we've charted. I think that it should be pretty accurate. This is high-priority stuff for our collection people."

"I think I've got it," replied Jake. He turned to the representative of Team Three. "Your guys are riding in the back of our birds for all of these missions, you got any questions?"

"No," he replied. "You boys just get us to the SAR dot where your guy needs to be rescued, we'll do the rest once we get on the ground."

"We can do it. You snake-eaters just live for this stuff, don't you?"

"That we do, Jake. That we do."

The SEAL had to think a bit about what he had just said. He really didn't like telling half-truths to Jake or to any of the other HS-4 bubbas. Hell, they had "adopted" his entire SEAL platoon. As a small group assigned to a 5,000-person aircraft carrier, the SEALs often got lost in the shuffle. Since the majority of their missions, including Combat Search and Rescue, would be flown with HS-4, the Black Knights had established a close working—and social—relationship with the SEAL and his team. He was especially close to Jake and his roommate, Warren Hardesty, both Naval Academy guys, but other than that pretty normal, he thought.

That's why it pained him to have to tell them what at best were half-truths. Sure he was with SEAL Team Three, and, sure, they would do all of these missions that they traditionally did. But while all of his men were SEALs through and through, he wasn't. Oh, his service record said that he had moved up through the ranks, had made chief petty officer, and then had been commissioned as a result of especially heroic action, but he was not entirely what he seemed.

Rick Holden was CIA. That was his parent organization, and that was where he began his career after graduating from the University of Virginia. He had been involved in many operations with the clandestine services section of the agency and had done especially valuable work for them in Eastern Europe and the then-Soviet Union. After becoming involved in an operation that went extremely bad—one that required the United States to expend considerable effort to extricate him from the Ukraine prison he was being held in—the agency needed to make a decision regarding Rick; either keep him working in clandestine services, assign him a headquarters position, or cut him loose from the agency altogether. The first choice was just too dangerous, Rick balked at the second, and all agreed that he was too valuable an asset to lose completely.

Therefore, a cover was set up. The service record of Chief Petty Officer Rick Holden, ostensibly just brought on active duty from the Reserves, happened to appear in the Navy Personnel Bureau. Rick was provided with comprehensive information regarding the SEALs so he could "walk the talk" and appear to be what they wanted him portrayed as—a Navy SEAL chief who had been in the service for approximately ten years or so. He was then assigned to SEAL Team Three and went out on deployment as an assistant platoon leader—the normal career progression point for someone of his age and with his experience. He was just supposed to keep his head down and blend in as a SEAL and be on-call to the agency if and when they needed him.

However, while assigned to USS *Coronado*, Rick became caught up in a scheme by senior military officers who caused a major operation to fail in an attempt to have the president impeached. Rick and a Navy intelligence officer discovered this plot and went through incredible efforts to expose the conspirators and thwart their plot. Although not able to stop them from carrying out their treason, Rick did reveal the truth to a very surprised Congress and kept the president from being impeached. This heroic action earned him a commission as a Navy ensign—a commission conferred by the president himself. The agency let his cover continue to play by just letting him make this enlisted-to-officer transition in the SEAL community and continue serving as a Navy SEAL while being "on call" to the agency. Rick enjoyed his role as a SEAL and, now that he had been commissioned for a while, was enjoying life as a naval officer too. He wanted this to continue for as long as possible, but he just didn't know how long that would be.

Or what role he might have in the hornet's nest that was the Arabian Gulf.

13

IN SPITE OF THE DAMAGE INFLICTED BY THE COALITION against Iraq during Desert Storm in 1991, Saddam Hussein used the time after the war to rebuild a great deal of his military infrastructure. One of the areas that he lavished a great deal of attention on was his vast air control and air defense network. Designed by the French aerospace firm Thomson-CSF and called Kari, which was Iraq spelled backwards in French, it represented the best technology that Iraq's oil profits could buy in the late 1980s. Although the network had been partially destroyed during Desert Storm, Iraq's president had painstakingly rebuilt the system and attempted to shield it with an even more robust air defense network of air-to-surface missiles.

Kari had a pyramidal structure. Observers at hundreds of posts fed tracking data into the system. This information was, in turn, fed into seventeen Intercept Operations Centers—IOCs—spread throughout the country. Like spokes in a wheel, the IOCs led to regional Sector Operations Centers—SOCs. There were four of these SOCs, which collectively controlled the entire land mass of Iraq. The Taji SOC was responsible for the area around Baghdad, including most of the area along the central portion of the northern edge of the southern no-fly zone. Taji, along with the three other SOCs, fed its information to Air Defense Headquarters in Baghdad, thereby providing the Iraqi high command with a nationwide air picture.

It was this system that instantly alerted all key political, military, and other leaders in Iraq that Raid Bakr had been shot down. Quick replay of tapes showed the path of his aircraft, the path of the American U-2 spy plane, and the attack profiles of the American fighters who had sent the doomed Iraqi major to his greater reward. It looked like what it was—an unfortunate accident. Still, those in the Iraqi command structure needed to report this officially to Iraqi president Saddam Hussein.

Once he had sorted out the details, chief of staff of the Air Force, Lieutenant General Sa'b Hassan Muzakim Al Tikriti, prepared to call the chief of the Armed Forces General Staff, General Ayad Fatih Khalifa Habib At Rawi. First, he checked with his political officer, who represented his link in the Ba'ath party chain of command, to ensure that he was doing what he was expected to do. Assured by Faud Baram that he was, indeed, doing the right thing, the general picked up his command center phone and was linked to Iraqi headquarters.

"General Ayad, this is General Sa'b. You have heard, no doubt, about the unfortunate shootdown of our MIG-25."

"Yes, General Sa'b, I am to report to Field Marshall Saddam Hussein Al Majid Al Tikriti about the situation immediately."

"General Ayad, I am gathering details still. It is very confusing, as you might imagine. All of our forces are on alert. Radars at Al Taq, at Balad, at Alasad, and at other sites have detected no movement of American planes outside of their normal patrol patterns."

"So you do not think that this is a prelude to some attack."

"No, I don't, General. I think that it was as it appears, a tragic, tragic blunder."

"We are reserving judgment. You had better come up with answers quickly, General. Field Marshall Saddam Hussein is not a man of infinite patience."

"Yes, General." That last statement need not be said, nor did Sa'b miss the use of the word "we" by Ayad. He could feel the full wrath of Saddam Hussein falling on him as chief of staff of the Air Force, and it was not readily apparent that any of his higher ranking military colleagues would step up to protect him. He picked up the phone and called Habbaniyah.

Raid Faud Muhammad was the chief of air controllers at the Habbaniyah air control facility. The GCI controller directing Raid Bakr's aircraft worked at this facility. By now, the raid and other officers had reconstructed events and had determined that the controller, Sergeant Majid Khadduri, had simply blundered. There was a series of reasons for this— he was inexperienced on the piece of gear that he was operating, he was in a brutal watch rotation due to failure of the headquarters command to provide enough controllers to man all the necessary watch stations, the communications with Raid Bakr's aircraft had been extremely poor, and he had not allowed enough safety margin to avoid the thirty-third parallel. All of these were excuses, Raid Faud Muhammad realized, and excuses were not what Field Marshall Saddam Hussein wanted to hear. The raid would question Sergeant Khadduri himself. He knew what he wanted to hear, and he knew what the sergeant must say.

A small group was gathered in the Spartan office in the basement of the Habbaniyah control site. Most of the supervisors and more experienced controllers stood around the periphery of the small, bare room with concrete walls and a flickering neon light on the ceiling. In the center of the room was a small table with two chairs. Raid Faud Muhammad sat in one chair, and Sergeant Majid Khadduri sat in the other. Sergeant Khadduri was extremely nervous, and the raid offered him a cigarette to calm his nerves—which he gratefully accepted.

Raid Faud Muhammad looked around the room for reassurance. As his eyes scanned the room, every set of eyes met his and signaled understanding. Their eyes and their body language signaled that they had done what needed to be done. The sergeant had been well coached. Raid Muhammad drew deeply on his cigarette and smiled at Sergeant Khadduri.

"Sergeant, do you know why I am here?" began Raid Muhammad.

"I think so sir," began the sergeant tentatively.

"Clearly it is about the tragic loss of Raid Bakr. You understand that no one is here to blame you for anything. Your loyalty is undisputed." That statement was designed for the ears of the Ba'ath party, lest anyone in the room be questioned later.

"Yes, thank you sir. I have been a loyal soldier all these years. I have performed my job diligently. No one has worked harder learning all of their systems—"

Faud Muhammad stopped him. "Sergeant, no one is questioning that at all. We want you to tell us about the American trickery."

Armed with that code word, Sergeant Khadduri began to relate the tale as he had been coached. He was controlling Raid Bakr's aircraft precisely, as he had been instructed. He knew exactly where he was sending him and had calculated sufficient margin of error to keep the aircraft safe. But then, in the later stages of the flight, as the MIG-25 came to its closest point of approach to the thirty-third parallel, an American Prowler aircraft flying only a few miles south of the parallel began jamming his station. He switched frequencies and did everything else that he had been instructed to do to break through the jamming, but to no avail.

At this point in his story, Faud Muhammad interrupted him. "Sergeant, you know the capabilities of all American aircraft. If the Prowler was close enough to jam your station, they could have shot a HARM missile at you—destroying you and your entire station."

"Yes sir, I considered that, and I alerted my supervisors. But I knew that I must continue to try to communicate with my aircraft. It was my responsibility and I had to ensure his flight safety."

Raid Faud Muhammad looked around the room. He arched his eyebrows and nodded slowly, signaling assent that this young sergeant had tried to do his job to the best of his ability and that he was willing to risk his life to protect his pilot. All heads around the room nodded assurance.

"What happened then, Sergeant?"

"It became very confusing. Many of my circuits were jammed, but I was able to pick up bits and pieces of various communications. Not entire conversations, just bits and pieces. I was trying so hard to do my job—"

"Yes we all know that you were," he said. "Just tell us, though, what you do recall."

Relieved by the raid's soothing tone, Sergeant Khadduri continued. "I heard a voice I did not recognize—but speaking our language—giving instructions to Raid Bakr. The communications were very scratchy, but it sounded like he used the same instructions that I give, that he even used the same phrases. I heard, I think, Raid Bakr question him about his instructions, but the controller said that he was to follow them and do what he was told."

"This, from a controller to a pilot in our Air Force?" said Faud Muhammad.

"Not only the controller, sir, but another voice. Again, the conversations were very broken, but when Raid Bakr questioned the instructions that he was receiving from the controller, another voice came on the same circuit and was very firm with him that he was to follow instructions. The voice was very angry and cursed at Raid Bakr, and he followed instructions. Seconds later, I thought I heard him yelling about American aircraft. Then I heard nothing."

The room was silent. Faud Muhammad looked sympathetically at the sergeant, who was now starting to shake. His hand was barely able to hold his cigarette. Finally he began to sob.

"There was nothing I could do, nothing. They were jamming my station. I tried to break through to my aircraft. I knew the risk to me and to my station but I kept trying to transmit. They were too powerful for me. It is not my fault, it is not."

Sergeant Majid Khadduri started to sob. But he had told

his story well and Faud Muhammad reached over and patted his shoulder.

Lieutenant General Sa'b Hassan Muzakim Al Tikriti answered the insistent intercom that jangled his already frayed nerves. "Yes, what is it?"

"Raid Faud Muhammad is on the line and wishes to speak with you," said his secretary.

"Send his call in—and close that door."

As he picked up his telephone, settled back into his overstuffed chair, and gazed up at the ceiling fan turning endless circles above him, the general listened to what the major told him. It had gone exactly as planned. The chief of staff of the Iraqi Air Force would report this to his president. He knew that he was safe for now.

14

"GENTLEMEN, THE ADMIRAL," ANNOUNCED HEATER Robinson's flag lieutenant, Mike Lumme as the admiral, stone-faced, walked into Carrier Group SEVEN's War Room aboard USS *Carl Vinson*. Adjacent to the admiral's large cabin and very close to both TFCC and SUPPLOT, where much of the most sensitive intelligence and I&W that *Carl Vinson* collected was displayed, analyzed, and then disseminated to other parts of the ship, the War Room was the location for most of the important meetings where Heater Robinson gathered his key warfare commanders and principal staff members.

Compared to the admiral's cabin, which was comfortable to the point of resembling an office ashore, the War Room was austere, even severe—befitting its name. Dominated by a massive table in the center and twelve high-backed chairs surrounding it, this large room emphasized function over aesthetics. An oversized chart table filled the port bulkhead, and small desks festooned with computers filled the forward and after bulkheads. Sound-absorptive padding covered the walls from floor to ceiling, and a large projector loomed over the table and pointed at a screen on the starboard end of the room. Massive wire bundles covered the overhead and the upper walls, and bright neon lights cast a harsh glow throughout the room.

"Seats, gentlemen," said Robinson as he took his chair at the head of the table. He pondered the array of talent he had at the War Room's main table, as well as sitting on desktops and standing in every nook and cranny of the room. Sitting at the table were Captain Craig Vandegrift, CAG Foster, Captain Jim Hughes, Captain George Sampson, Captain Bill Durham, and Captain Rocky Jacobson. The admiral had called this staff meeting to review their preparations for Exercise Swift Sword.

The meteorology officer, Lieutenant Commander Bart McCallum, began the briefing. After putting up an array of charts, the admiral asked McCallum just one question.

"Bart, what's the prognosis for weather over Iran for the next several weeks?"

"Pretty much the same trend we're seeing now, Admiral. Gradual cooling. Think that we'll continue to be affected by the low over the Gulf. Westerlies will be stronger in northern Iran than in the south this time of year. The shamal will kick up some dust storms and increase the haze over most of the western half of the country. If you have no questions, Admiral, I'll be followed by Lieutenant Commander Garrow."

"Morning, Admiral," began Lieutenant Commander Mary Garrow, the staff assistant intelligence officer. "This morning I've been asked to focus on the Iranian Navy. We assess their Navy as posing a significant threat to our task force."

"Let's focus on where they are now, in their bases, that is," said Admiral Robinson. Clearly he was searching for some specific information.

Garrow called up another slide on her power point display. "Admiral, this map shows the three Iranian naval districts; the first district at Bandar Abbas in the south, directly across from the Omani Peninsula; the second district at Bushehr in the northern Gulf, almost exactly on the twenty-ninth parallel, and the third district at Bandar Khomeini, in the extreme northern Gulf . . ."

Garrow was a good briefer, but she wasn't getting to the point quickly enough. "This is great, Lieutenant Commander Garrow—and what you're telling me is fine—but let's get to the point, the positions of the Iranian ships in the ports that do count."

"Yes, Admiral," she replied, and then to one of the staff lieutenants who was handling the briefing graphics, she said, "click ahead a few slides, I'll tell you where to stop."

As he did, all eyes in the room were on Admiral Robinson. They knew that he had recently had secure phone conversations with the Fifth Fleet commander. Swift Sword was an exercise—a major exercise but an exercise nonetheless. Military forces, and particularly naval forces at sea, always exercised and given the politics in the Arabian Gulf, they had been doing so for years to simulate strikes on either Iraq or Iran. These exercises were thinly disguised with generic names and enough papering over that the target nations were not supposed to feel threatened, but their pose had hardened in the past year or so.

Now Exercise Swift Sword would be much more aggressive than any exercises in recent memory. The conduct of the exercise, the movement of additional forces into the area, simulated strikes into Iran, simulated blockade of Iranian ports, and other actions all seemed very real and led to the strong suspicion that offensive action might actually take place. The staff knew only what they carried in their secret and top secret folders, but the admiral was privy to additional information. Some tried to read that information, but none could get beyond his tightly set jaw.

Garrow finally found the slide she wanted. "Admiral, we've confirmed by imagery the disposition of Iranian naval forces that you see on this slide. The major concentration of Iranian naval forces are, of course, at Bandar Abbas and Bushehr. At Bandar Abbas they have their three Kilo Class submarines, as well as a pretty robust surface combatant capability; a couple of Sumner Class DDGs, some SAAM Class FFGs, a large number of patrol craft, some Hengham Class LSTs and a number of service and support group ships, as well as about a dozen Revolutionary Guard Boghammars and many small boats."

"Good. Continue," said Robinson.

"Yes sir. At Bushehr they have a similar lineup. No submarines, of course, but that's where they have their large concentration of missile boats, mainly the French-made Kaman, but also some smaller patrol craft and less capable patrol boats. The Revolutionary Guard keeps almost twenty Boghammars here, as well as the usual collection of smaller stuff."

The previously blank TV screen situated on a large filing cabinet over her left shoulder came on, and a photo of the Bandar Abbas Naval Base was presented. As Admiral Robinson listened intently, Garrow went through a number of these photos, patiently showing the position of every Iranian naval vessel at their docks. The same scenario continued with photos of Bushehr Naval Base.

"Subject to any additional questions, that concludes my brief, Admiral."

"Thanks, Commander Garrow, outstanding. Now the question is, what do we do with it and where do we go with all of it?"

The entire assemblage wondered how the admiral would answer that question for them as he got up and strode to the front of the War Room.

"All right, folks, now I'm gonna tell you where I think we stand and what we're gonna do. We're going to press ahead with Exercise Swift Sword. First of all, we're not going to be distracted by this little incident over the box. CAG, you boys did a fine job up there and we're not gonna worry about the court of world opinion or anything else. If anyone wants to second-guess anyone, they're going to have to second-guess me. While we're doing Exercise Swift Sword, the Air Force is picking up all of the OSW missions. Wizard, you feel like your folks have given them a good enough pass down."

"Yes sir, Admiral," responded CAG.

"Good. Now our focus is on Swift Sword. I don't need to tell most of you, especially many of you who have served in the Gulf before, that sometimes these 'exercises' turn into 'opsercises,' which move into full-fledged operations. Now nobody's saying that we're getting ready to thump up on Iran—at least nobody who's willing to be quoted—but you know what they've been up to and you know what could happen. That's why we want to do this 'exercise' with as much realism and give it the best possible effort we can. I want real bombs on airplanes, your first teams in the aircraft, ships really at GQ—not some halfway compromise—and people practicing like the real McCoy could happen tomorrow, because it could."

Robinson looked around the room and watched what he was saying sink in, even with his more junior staffers. There were more concerned looks, more desire in their eyes.

"But remember, there is life after any exercise, there's life after any 'opsercise' and there's life after any strikes that we might do. We will complete whatever mission we are given and complete it well—but we will defend this task group at all costs. So I want you to plan your exercises and plan your contingency strikes, give it a robust effort, but, by God, don't you stretch it so thin that we can't take care of ourselves if something happens."

The heads around the table nodded.

"OK. I think that I've taken up enough of everyone's time. I appreciate all of the hard work that has gone into your planning."

Heater Robinson walked back into his flag cabin. He sat down heavily in his padded, high-backed, blue chair. He let out a heavy sigh. He hoped that he had not let his anger and confusion spill over and impact his people. He opened up his message folder and re-read the SPECAT message that he had read with disbelief a half-dozen times before the meeting.

FROM: JOINT CHIEFS OF STAFF
TO: CCG7
BT
SECRET SPECAT FOR ADMIRAL ROBINSON FROM MON-
ROE//N00000//
MSGID/GENADMIN/JOINT STAFF//
SUBJ/CRISIS OF CONFIDENCE (S)//
RMKS/1.(S) HEATER. WE GO BACK A LONG WAY AND I
TELL YOU THIS IN STRICTEST CONFIDENCE. DESTROY
THIS MESSAGE AFTER YOU READ IT.
2.(S) I'VE JUST HAD MY ASS ROUNDLY CHEWED BY THE
PRESIDENT OVER THIS FOXBAT SHOOTDOWN. HEATER, I
AM SKIPPING ECHELON AND NOT TELLING THE THEA-
TER COMMANDER OR YOUR IMMEDIATE BOSS, HARRY
FLOWERS. ONLY YOU. THE PRESIDENT WAS A HEART-
BEAT AWAY FROM PERSONALLY FIRING YOU OVER THIS.
I HAD TO PROSTRATE MYSELF TO KEEP HIM FROM DO-
ING IT. WHATEVER YOU DO, YOU'VE GOT TO GET IT TO-
GETHER OUT THERE AND KEEP YOUR GUYS FROM
STARTING A WAR. I'VE SHOT MY SILVER BULLET,
HEATER, ANOTHER SCREW-UP AND I CAN'T BAIL YOU
OUT AGAIN. WARM REGARDS, JAKE.
DECL/X4//
BT

Reading it again didn't help Heater Robinson understand
it any better. Had his longtime friend forgotten what it was
like out here? He'd helped him once, but now it was clear
that he was stepping away from him. What could he do? He
stared at the STU-III secure phone for a few moments and
then picked it up.

15

THE PRESIDENT SAT AT HIS DESK IN THE OVAL OFFICE and fiddled with some paperwork, but he was not really doing anything useful. He loved this office and all that went with it, and usually took the time to savor it and enjoy it. He put the papers down and rubbed the bridge of his nose. Patrick Browne was not a particularly big man, but he was a man of presence. At just under six feet tall and a well-built 200 pounds, he still looked younger than his fifty-eight years. His head was large, and he had what many described as "comforting" features, large brown eyes, bushy blonde eyebrows, a somewhat large nose, full lips, and a chin that jutted forward and gave a strength to his other features. Remarkably free of wrinkles and with a full head of light brown hair, he had that perpetual hail-fellow-well-met look about him that was so helpful to anyone in public office.

As he swung around in his Kevlar-backed chair and stared out the pale blue bulletproof windows, he was too preoccupied to enjoy the trappings of his office. The tall, narrow windows were framed by gold-colored damask draperies and should have formed a perfect setting to similarly frame his thoughts. He brought his gaze inside the room and looked for a moment at the American flag to his left and the presidential flag to his right, hoping to find some inspiration.

He was waiting for his national security adviser to update him on the shootdown of the Iraqi Foxbat aircraft. He was dodging the press, and he had specifically directed his press secretary, Pete Lockhart, to fend off the press with some of the standard sop that he served up in such situations: "The president was conferring with international leaders." "He will be available before too long." Anything to buy some time.

As he spun around in his chair again, now facing the small conference area just in front of his desk, and beyond that to the fireplace at the other end of the office, he tried to think how other presidents had handled crises in the Arabian Gulf—President George Bush's handling of Operations Desert Shield and Desert Storm, President Bill Clinton's handling of Operation Desert Strike. He hoped that it would not escalate to either of those levels, but President Patrick Browne was a cautious man who wanted to have all of his options laid out for him. He did not like to be surprised.

His secretary ushered in National Security Adviser Michael Curtis, along with vice-chairman of the Joint Chiefs of Staff, Air Force General Alfred Cutler. The chairman had stayed behind in the NMCC to monitor events as they were happening. Curtis also brought along his military assistant, Navy Captain Tom Perry. Perry was a rising star in Navy circles, and he had been recommended to Curtis by a Navy admiral in whom Curtis had a great deal of confidence. Perry had access and influence far beyond his pay grade, and this wasn't the first time he had accompanied the national security adviser to the Oval Office.

"Come in gentlemen, Michael, General, Captain, sit down," said the president, motioning for them to sit as he walked from behind his desk, past the two straight-backed chairs flanking it, to the sofas in the center of the Oval Office. "I appreciate your coming over here so quickly to brief me. What are the facts as we know them now?"

There was momentary silence, but then Michael Curtis nodded, indicating that General Cutler should begin speaking.

"Mr. President, good afternoon. The chairman sends his regrets, but due to the tense situation, he thought it best to remain in the NMCC. . . ."

"Of course," said the president with a friendly, dismissive wave. "I think it's important that he stay right there and monitor the situation."

"Yes sir, well, Mr. President, it appears that the shoot-down of the Iraqi MIG was just a very unfortunate accident.

The consensus is that the Iraqi plane was the victim of very sloppy GCI procedures and crossed the thirty-third parallel."

"How far did he cross before he was shot down?" asked the president.

"Less than five miles," continued General Cutler. "However, Mr. President, he was heading directly for one of our U-2 aircraft. The on-scene commander had to make a decision, and in this case I think they made the right one."

"Well, it appears that they may have done just that, General," replied the president, who was able to reflect more rationally on events now that some time had elapsed since his initial shock over the shootdown. Thinking about the man he replaced helped validate his change in attitude. He thought that the vice chairman was sounding defensive, but he understood why.

Damn his predecessor in the Oval Office. He and his administration had second-guessed the military to pieces—no wonder the senior military leadership was always waiting for the other shoe to drop whenever anything even hinted of a mistake. He was investing a lot of intellectual energy in mollifying them.

"I think that, under the circumstances, the Navy pilots did exactly the right thing," said the president. Then, looking at Captain Perry to try to put the conversation on a less tense basis, he added, "Don't you think so, Captain?"

"Yes sir I do!" said Perry emphatically. Drawn in by the president's encouraging eyes, he continued. "If I may say so, Mr. President, all this shootdown can do to us is to distract us from our primary focus in the Gulf. It—"

Michael Curtis cut him off. He didn't mind showcasing his bright young Navy captain with the president—hell, Perry worked eighty-hour weeks for him and was as loyal an underling as had ever served him, but he wasn't going to let Perry dominate the agenda. "Mr. President, if it's all right, may we close this matter out before moving on to the next one?"

"Certainly, Michael," responded the president, a bit perplexed.

"As I was saying, Mr. President," continued Curtis, "we

will have a more comprehensive picture over time, but all the initial indications are that our forces did exactly the right thing and that we have the high ground on this one."

"I understand that the Iraqi pilot was killed."

"Our aircraft reported the Iraqi plane exploding and did not see a parachute, Mr. President, so it's extremely unlikely that he survived."

"I see, and what has the Iraqi reaction been?"

"That's been a little mixed, Mr. President. On the one hand there has been no indication at all of stepped-up Iraqi military activity, validating that this was undoubtedly an accident, and indicating that they are not using it as an excuse to take aggressive action—it would be foolhardy to do so, of course. So right now on the military front, things are very calm."

"And on other fronts?" replied the president.

"It's a bit confusing thus far, Mr. President, but we have some initial indications that the Iraqis are claiming that we lured their aircraft across the border with electronic deception of some kind so that we could have an excuse to shoot it down."

"Did we?" said the president.

General Cutler subtly signaled Curtis that he wanted to take that one, and Curtis nodded his assent.

"Mr. President, I can tell you absolutely that we did not. We don't have the equipment to do that sort of thing, and even if we did, our people know that that is a serious action which is not condoned under any circumstances. But if I may, Mr. President, our intelligence people think that it's a plausible ruse by the Iraqis, maybe internally within their military. At some level— probably at several levels—heads would roll for a blunder of that type, therefore, it's always easy for someone in their military to blame us for acting in a hostile manner so they can save their own skin with Saddam."

"So what are you all recommending?" asked the president, now unsure of just what kind of advice he was getting.

Curtis took over the conversation. "I think that we should just wait it out, Mr. President. We should tell the truth, in as much detail as possible, and I think that we will have the high ground in the court of world opinion. In a few days we can go back to our normal OSW patrols."

"I agree," said the president. "Now, this wasn't all you wanted to talk about, was it?"

"No sir," said the national security adviser. "As Captain Perry alluded to earlier, this little incident shouldn't cause us to lose focus on the other side of the Gulf. The situation in Iran continues to worsen. As you know, Iran has supported terrorist camps for a long time. For the past few years the level of activity there has been fairly steady. Of late, the level of activity has picked up dramatically."

President Patrick Browne leaned forward on his sofa and looked directly at Michael Curtis. "This increase in activity, it hasn't translated into any additional terrorist activity, has it?"

"No, Mr. President. That's the problem. We see this significant step-up, but it hasn't resulted in a spike in terrorism in the region or in other forms of international terrorism."

"Well, what do you make of it, then?" The president was pressing, for now he was beginning to recognize the potential gravity of the situation.

"There are a number of different scenarios, Mr. President, but perhaps the worst is that the Islamic Republic is biding its time, continuing to train more and more agents. Then, at some time, they will strike simultaneously throughout the Gulf, primarily at our military forces, our embassies and consulates, and at concentrations of American citizens."

"When would they do this, and why?"

"The when is a totally open question, Mr. President," continued Curtis. "The why really lingers from the days of our support for the Shah. It's almost the chicken and the egg scenario, the same convoluted logic we used to go through with the Soviets—do we threaten them because they threaten us or do they threaten us because we threaten them? But be that as it may, there is the feeling in some intelligence circles that the mullahs believe—and believe sincerely—that the United States will not be satisfied until the clerical regime is overthrown and a populist, secular regime is placed into power. They further think that acts of terrorism will cause us to back off on some of our commitments in the Gulf and eventually try to exert less influence here."

"Do they feel that threatened?" asked the president. Patrick Browne had been briefed on the political and military situation in the Arabian Gulf before, but now he was beginning to put into context all the disparate bits of information that he had acquired from countless briefing folders, endless presentations, and other anecdotal information.

"I'm afraid that they often do, Mr. President, and our rhetoric in the past hasn't helped any."

"Our rhetoric in the past."

"Yes sir," continued Curtis. "We have tended to blame Iran for a large percentage of terrorist acts over the years, many of which could not reasonably have been attributed to them."

"Where do you assess that we stand now?"

"If this scenario plays itself out in a negative way, we will likely have very little notice that a series of terrorist attacks is about to occur. We need to be prepared to strike fast and strike hard the instant an attack occurs that we attribute to Iran. Only by coming at them with disproportionate force can we possibly dissuade them from follow-on terrorist attacks."

"We seem to have a lot of forces in the area. I would think that that's something we could do—attack them, I mean."

"Yes sir, Mr. President. But those forces can't respond with a strike on short notice. They have to assess the viability of various targets, analyze target folders, apportion strikes to various platforms, and then train specifically, ideally multiple times, to hit those targets in order to ensure a high probability of destroying those targets."

The president was frustrated. What should have been so simple sounded so complex. "Look, I know that I'm not a military man, but is it really that complex to hit a bunch of terrorist camps out in the middle of the Iranian desert?"

Curtis knew that the vice chairman could now respond with a military point of view, and he deflected the question to him. "General?" he said, looking directly at General Cutler.

"Yes sir, Mr. President. Our main goal is to strike the camps, but in addition we need to ensure that we are putting our forces at as little risk as possible."

"Well certainly, General. That sounds prudent."

"Yes sir, well, Mr. President, in order to do that we must neutralize their IADS—their Integrated Air Defense—their Air Force, and their Navy."

"Yes, well, all right, how do we do that?"

"Actually, Mr. President, the good news is that we practice such scenarios frequently when our forces are in the Gulf."

"Well, that sounds like the right thing to do. I assume that we are conducting these drills now."

"Yes, we are, Mr. President," continued General Cutler, "and with a higher level of intensity. We are directing particular attention at their Navy."

"Their Navy?" said the president.

Captain Perry shifted forward on the sofa and looked directly at the national security adviser. He wanted the go-ahead to speak. Curtis gave it to him with a nod.

"If I may, Mr. President," Perry began. "The Iranian Navy poses the greatest long-term threat to our interests in the Arabian Gulf. While more than fifty percent of their total military equipment was destroyed in their war with Iraq in the eighties, their Navy was relatively unscathed. What's more, they have added substantially to that Navy where it poses a viable threat to our carrier task groups. They have really put their emphasis on confining our access to the Gulf, especially in their deployment of anti-ship missiles such as the Hai Ying-2 Silkworm and the Ying Jai C-802 at various points along the Strait of Hormuz and have now added the C-802 missile to their patrol boats. They have also put Hawk anti-air missiles in several strategic locations, including Siri Island right in the Strait of Hormuz. Additionally, they could potentially, given their minelaying capability, close off the Strait of Hormuz—perhaps for an extended time."

"Would they do that?" asked the president.

"We assess that they would do that if provoked, Mr. President. Attacks on their terrorist camps would surely be thought of as provocative. Therefore, we could reasonably expect them to unleash their Navy to try to deal with us."

"What damage could they do to our Navy?"

"Virtually none, Mr. President, if we strike them first. That is why we think that an attack on their Navy is crucial to the success of any operation and to the ultimate safety of our forces."

"That sounds reasonable."

General Cutler jumped in. "Yes it does, Mr. President. It is just a question of degree, not kind. There are several ways to go at their Navy, each with different trade offs. One scenario would have us put their Navy out of action long enough to ensure the success of our strikes and ensure the safety of our carrier task group. Taking another approach, we could make a more robust attack on their Navy and sink it, ensuring that it was not a threat to us for years. That's the approach that Captain Perry here advocates, but it will take a lot more horsepower to achieve that level of destruction."

"Yes, I can see that it would," said the president, now more engaged in the analysis.

"We don't need to make a decision today, Mr. President, but ultimately, should we wind up in some sort of strike scenario, we will have to make a decision on which route to go," replied the national security adviser.

The president looked at Captain Perry. "You're concerned about the safety of your Navy, aren't you, Captain?"

"Yes, Mr. President, I am."

"Well I am too. General Cutler, I know that it will take some level of effort, but I'm not comfortable with leaving them with much of their key military forces intact. Hell, I thought we realized that from all these years of dealing with Saddam Hussein. Anything we don't obliterate, he just rebuilds and puts back into service. Yes, I think that we should be looking at sinking their Navy. Captain," he said, looking directly at Perry, "you have provided a compelling case for this, you know."

"Thank you, Mr. President," replied Captain Tom Perry. He was flattered that he was being complimented by the president of the United States—by his commander in chief—but he was more satisfied that he had pushed forward the agenda of his mentor who was on-scene, seven thousand miles away.

16

PACKAGE FOXTROT HAD COMPLETED THEIR OSW MISsion and was returning to the carrier. It had been an uneventful mission, but Brian McDonald was happy with the way events had turned out. The weather had been marginal at best and the thirteen-aircraft package had been almost double the size of normal packages, yet he had briefed and flown a near perfect mission and all of his pilots had performed well—even the first tour "nugget" pilots. Now all that remained was getting back aboard the boat.

To someone standing anywhere on a modern U.S. Nimitz Class aircraft carrier, the ship looks huge, monstrous, awe inspiring. It dwarfs any other ship in the United States Navy and makes the few aircraft carriers possessed by other navies seem puny. It is impossible to come away from one without being almost overwhelmed by the acres that comprise the flight deck. That is a perspective shared by all but about two hundred and fifty of the five-thousand-plus people aboard *Carl Vinson*.

To the pilot in the aircraft making an approach to land on a carrier, the "boat"—as the pilots irreverently insist on calling the vessel that is officially classified as a ship—looks about as big as a postage stamp. Throw in a bit of a sea state, and that postage stamp begins to bob and weave, pitch and roll, and do any number of gyrations that have no rhyme or reason. Add to that, darkness and the degree of difficulty goes up geometrically. Add marginal weather to that—exactly the kind of weather Brian was experiencing—and the difficulties involved in getting a twenty- to thirty-ton aircraft that was flying up to 150 miles per hour to hit the spot on the deck between the one and four wires, a distance of only 120 feet, tested the mettle of even the most experienced pilots. When aviators referred to flying as "hours of boredom punctuated by moments of terror," this was the terror they were talking about.

Brian was experienced enough to know that this would be a tough night back at the boat. As the aircraft left the box and went "feet wet," they would first check in with Red Crown, the Aegis Cruiser, USS *Shiloh*, who would ensure that the aircraft were all "friendlies" and that an Iraqi aircraft had not joined the large gaggle of U.S. planes in an attempt to sneak in close to the carrier. Then the aircraft would all head for the marshall stack—that section of airspace between fifteen and thirty or so miles behind the carrier—and await their turn to be brought in for landing.

On *Carl Vinson*'s flight deck, the flight deck crew listened to the 5 MC as the air boss encouraged his troops to hang in there for the night's last recovery. It was just past 2330—11:30 P.M. to civilians—and this recovery would last till past midnight. *Carl Vinson* had been flying fixed wing aircraft since 11.00 A.M. and helos before that, and the flight deck crew had been on duty continuously since then, save for quick breaks to grab some food and a brief respite in the very short time between launch and recovery cycles. It was a brutal pace that was taking its toll on the Air Department. Fatigue had reached acute proportions by this time of night.

Around the flight deck, the Air Department team went through their normal routine of handling the last recovery. Thirteen aircraft, not too bad. Airwing Fourteen's box mission, plus tankers, plus the E-2C, as well as armed surface reconnaissance aircraft. Petty Officer Donald Parker was one of those men. It was his job to push the rake, a device that shoved the arresting gear off any obstacles as it was pulled back into position after it had been stretched by a landing aircraft. It was one of the most basic jobs for the flight deck crew, but something that Parker's chief had told him that he would be moving out of next month when he was going to move up to phone talker in Primary.

Parker had been up since before sunrise, but he never complained. He was one of those hundreds of dedicated young sailors who put in incredible hours under appalling conditions just to do their job. Donald Parker, or "Parks" as his buddies called him, was completing his first Navy deployment, and was looking forward to seeing his wife and two-year-old son when *Carl Vinson* returned to her home port in Bremerton, Washington.

The Hornets were the first aircraft out of the marshall stack. Brian was number three and listened intently as he heard the lineup for all of the aircraft in his package. Sounded like everyone would be in good shape for fuel, no problems there, just had to ensure that everyone got back aboard safely.

Brian heard the first Hornet make its approach. "Fist 405, paddles, call the ball."

"Roger, Hornet ball, 4.2."

"Roger ball. Deck's lively, keep it coming."

"Roger."

So the conversations went, the LSOs bringing in the first two Hornets, working hard but each had good passes, Fist 405 caught the three wire, Fist 402 caught the four wire. Brian was next in the groove.

"Stinger 304, paddles, radio check, over."

"Roger paddles, 304 has you loud and clear."

"Keep it coming 304, setting the deck."

"Roger."

The LSOs knew each pilot well; better than their spouses was the familiar saying within the Airwing. Knew their habits, how they handled their aircraft, how each pilot would react to his calls. Knew just how much each one would advance the throttle at the call for power. Subtle differences. Almost imperceptible to the casual observer. But in the high-stakes game of putting a twenty-plus-ton aircraft on a moving flight deck, those were the finesse factors that spelled the difference between disaster and a successful landing.

As one of the more senior pilots in the squadron, Brian was a good "ball flyer," and his LSO tended to give him less direction than he did to more junior pilots. He would keep him within safe parameters, but he would let him work the problem.

"Stinger 304, call the ball."

"Roger, Hornet ball, 4.4."

"Roger, ball, keep it coming."

"Little power. Easy with it."

"Left for lineup."

"Power."

THUD! Brian put his Hornet precisely in the right spot. Three wire, yes! This one would bump his landing grades just a small decimal point higher. It was turning out to be a perfect night.

A Tomcat from the VF-11 Red Rippers was next for landing. The air boss set the deck for the heavier aircraft, changing the tension on the arresting wires to accommodate the additional weight. Ten more aircraft to go. He'd be glad when this one was in the bag.

On the flight deck, Petty Officer Parker pushed back toward the center line the three wire Brian had caught to ensure that it didn't snag. He was going to be glad when this recovery was over. He had long since sweated through his clothes, and he hadn't had the energy to refill his camelback after the last launch. The water fountain just inside the island was secured because of a leak, and he was too tired to go down the two decks necessary to find one that he could use. He was debating whether to try to grab some mid-rats—the meal that was served on the mess decks around midnight—or to just grab a shower and hit his rack. Reveille was coming at 0600, no matter what.

Parker had been trained to go back behind the "stubby" tow tractor or the N-16 crash cart after he pushed the wire each time. That would protect him somewhat if anything untoward happened on the flight deck—an aircraft crash, something flying off the aircraft, a wire snapping. But it was at least a dozen extra steps to do that, and Parker was exhausted. He just leaned on the tail pylon of Black Knight

613, one of the helos parked next to the island, just outside of the foul line. There, in the shadow of the helo, he escaped everyone's notice as he waited for the next recovery.

"Ripper 106, call the ball."

"Tomcat Ball, 4.7."

"Roger, ball."

"Left for lineup."

"Power."

"*Easy* with it. *EASY*!"

It wasn't the best approach he had ever seen, but the LSO knew the pilot, knew he was a good ball flyer, and knew also that the weather wasn't getting any better and he needed to get everyone back aboard. He was beat, too.

SLAM. The Tomcat landed a little long, caught the four wire, which started its runout. Then disaster struck. The cross deck pendant, the center part of the arresting wire, snapped. Broke right there. With a sickening sound much like a gunshot, the wire whipped through the air, moving with incredible speed. From his position in the de-arm area, hundreds of feet away, Brian heard the sound and snapped his head in that direction. Men everywhere instinctively hit the deck. Even up in the tower, the air boss and his crew ducked. Ripper 106 was already well off the deck and climbing at military power.

But it happened too fast for Petty Officer Parker. Holding on to the side of the helicopter, he watched the Tomcat hit as he had done thousands of times before, and he watched the cable start its runout. He heard a noise, but he was too startled to comprehend what it was. The cable moved so fast that he never knew what hit him—at least that's what they were going to tell his grieving widow and young son. The thick cable hit him just above the waist and literally cut his body in half. It might have kept going and thrown him over the side, except for Black Knight 613. It slammed his broken body into the helo, then lopped off 613's tail pylon, leaving it a mangle of metal, cables, control tubes, and wires as it slowed down its inertia and came to rest in the "junkyard" area aft of the island.

The mini-boss saw it first and reflexively buzzed the captain on the bridge. "Captain, mini-here. Yes sir, I saw it. Cable snapped. We've got a man-down. Need a 1 MC call, Captain."

The air boss was already booming over the 5 MC, the flight deck general announcing system. "On the flight deck, there's a man down, man down near the after portion of the island."

The mini-boss grabbed the UHF radio transmitter and called to the aircraft still in the air, "Ninety-nine, we have a snapped cable and an injury on the flight deck. Delta easy. I say again, delta easy." Delta easy—the signal for all aircraft to loiter around the carrier at their best fuel conservation altitude and airspeed—let all of them know that they might be airborne for a while before the deck was open again.

As the mini-boss made the call, the Bosn' mate on the bridge had taken his direction and now made his 1 MC call, which was heard throughout *Carl Vinson*. "Man down, man down. Man down on the flight deck, vicinity of the island. Away the medical alert team, away. MAN DOWN."

Five decks below the flight deck, Petty Officer First Class Adam Pierre grabbed his gear and joined two other petty officers as they raced out of medical, through the mess decks, and bounded up the starboard side ladder up toward the flight deck. They burst out of the interior of the island and headed for Petty Officer Parker. Pierre was the first to reach him. He instantly recognized it was too late.

The air boss and the mini-boss knew too. The air boss heard it from his flight deck director communicating via his "Mickey Mouse ears." Someone had to tell the captain. The air boss knew that he had to be the one.

"Captain, the man down on the flight deck is Petty Officer Parker. He . . . he didn't make it, Captain."

Craig Vandegrift listened impassively, then refocused his attention on what needed to be done. "OK Boss, let's get the flight deck cleared and get those aircraft on deck."

As his shipmates gingerly carried the broken body of Petty Officer Parker below decks, Captain Vandegrift, Boomer Davison, and many others aboard *Carl Vinson* knew that they had to complete the task at hand, but they also wanted to know why this had happened. Collectively, they hoped that it was a freak event and not a portent of things to come.

Six decks below the bridge, Heater Robinson hung up the Bogen phone after listening to Craig Vandegrift tell him of Petty Officer Parker's death. The chairman of the Joint Chiefs of Staff had chastised him for accidentally shooting down a damned Iraqi pilot. He wondered if Jake Monroe, or any of them sitting in their air conditioned offices in the Pentagon, in the Old Executive Office Building, or in the White House, cared one whit about men like Parker, who were dying so that the United States could do nothing in the Arabian Gulf.

17

FIELD MARSHALL SADDAM HUSSEIN AL MAJID AL TIK-riti summoned his key leaders to Baghdad in the wake of the Foxbat shootdown. He had been receiving disparate reports, and he wanted to gather all those leaders in one place so he could determine conclusively what had happened and decide what they should do next. He had already made up his own mind, but he wanted the validation from his top military commanders that he was embarking on the right course. It was surprising that he still thought he was getting sound advice. These men were not fools. They knew what Saddam Hussein wanted to hear and understood fully the penalty for not telling him exactly that.

He looked around the table and surveyed the sea of faces around it. All of his generals were attired in their battle uniforms. Saddam was wearing his also. The men who were gathered around the conference table thought, but dared not say, how incongruous it was Saddam would wear military garb at all.

Lieutenant General Muzakim, Air Force chief of staff, spoke first. "Field Marshall, we have investigated the loss of our Foxbat thoroughly and have determined conclusively that it was the work of American warplanes who lured it across the border and then shot it down, undoubtedly to provoke an incident with us."

"Why would they do such a thing?" asked Saddam.

"Their motives are not entirely clear to us," interjected Deputy Prime Minister Aziz. "We know that the U.S. has been chafing at the United Nations resolutions that allow us to trade oil once again. Perhaps they hope to have that ability restricted one more time."

"Perhaps?" said Saddam, raising his eyebrows to indicate that he was not happy with conjecture at this point.

"That is only a theory, of course. We have our agents trying to better determine where they are going with this," Aziz continued.

"General Muzakim, how is it that one of our aircraft, flown by one of our best pilots, could be lured across the border by such a simple ruse and then shot down?" asked Saddam, his tone of voice taking a harder edge.

"Excellency, as you know, the Americans spend an incredible amount of money on jamming and deception aircraft and other systems. We have watched as their aircraft carriers have displaced other aircraft in favor of the Prowler jamming airplanes. This is the aircraft that we learned has jammed the Habbaniyah control center. We have seen this many times before, Field Marshall. Unfortunately, the best technology that we are able to purchase from Europe is not as advanced as that in their aircraft."

"So when this jamming occurs, do our pilots and controllers not take prudent precautions?"

"Indeed they do, Excellency. However, it appears that the Americans evolved an elaborate plot. We think that they have been planning this for a long time. Looking back now, we have been jammed and deceived before, but it never had this disastrous result in the end."

"General Ali Hasan, is there no way that we can defeat this? Must we be doomed to suffer at the hands of the Americans indefinitely?" said Saddam, now raising his voice and gesturing almost wildly with his hand.

"No, Field Marshall. We will continue to explore ways of getting better equipment. I have a delegation in China now looking at some of their most modern equipment."

"I understand. And will the Chinese sell the equipment to us?" His eyes were riveted on the general.

"They have shown in the past that they will sell their arms to whoever will pay them," continued General Ali Hasan. "You know how much they sell to the Iranians. The Chinese are merchants above all else. They want to increase their sales throughout our region. They would like nothing better than an arms race," said the general.

The dialogue continued with the assembled underlings telling Saddam Hussein exactly what he wanted to hear; that the Americans had lured Raid Bakr across the border, that Iraq did not have the sophisticated equipment to defeat this tactic—but that they were going to get it. They were merely sycophants attempting to escape with their skins. Saddam Hussein seemed satisfied by the explanation of what had happened to Raid Bakr's aircraft, much to the relief of all.

Finally, the minister of defense, Staff General Ali Hasan Al Majid Al Tikriti, spoke. "Excellency, we are not merely waiting for new equipment to keep the American warplanes at bay. There has been almost no unrest among the Kurds and therefore we have moved many of our most capable aircraft from our northern airfields to our more southern ones. Additionally, we are moving our mobile surface-to-air missile sites every day, and moving them in very irregular patterns. We will impossibly complicate the Americans' efforts."

"So, Mr. Defense Minister, you guarantee that we will not have an incident again?"

"Yes, Field Marshall," he said, hoping that the use of his military title would further placate Saddam. "We have moved decisively to achieve this."

"Perhaps you have, Mr. Defense Minister," began Saddam Hussein. "Perhaps you have. But we are going to do more. The Americans have given us a golden opportunity. We cannot let it pass by. Here is what you are going to do next. . . ."

18

"COME IN," SAID ADMIRAL ROBINSON IN RESPONSE TO the knock on his cabin door. He had asked for this meeting and got up from his large desk chair, moving over to the small table just adjacent to his desk as his key senior aviators filed in; *Carl Vinson*'s CO, Captain Craig Vandegrift, the air boss, Commander Boomer Davison, CAG, Captain Wizard Foster, Deputy CAG, Captain Bob Keithly, and his staff operations officer, Captain Bill Durham. The men were all still in a somber mood. Parker's death the night before was sobering to all of them.

Robinson signaled for them all to be seated as he looked around his spacious cabin. He was almost embarrassed to have this huge space. In addition to his large, wraparound desk console, he had the conference table where they were now seated, a large reception area with sofa and easy chairs, and a huge wall-filling entertainment complex with television, VCR, stereo system—the works. Beyond that, a hallway led to his private bathroom and sleeping quarters. Heater Robinson thought that this space could have accommodated all the JOs from his first ready room—easily.

Heater Robinson looked around at the sea of morose faces at the table and decided that he needed to break the ice. "Gents, we all mourn the loss of Petty Officer Parker. He was a fine young man who wanted nothing but to serve his country. I know that many—perhaps all of you—are troubled by his loss, especially by a loss that was so avoidable. Do not misunderstand the reason for this meeting. I am not here to assess blame. I am not here to tell you that you must do better or try harder."

"Admiral, all of us strongly feel the loss of Petty Officer Parker," said Craig Vandegrift. "It was a tragic, tragic accident and clearly one that could have been prevented."

"What have we learned so far regarding what happened?" asked the Admiral.

"We've of course appointed an investigating officer," responded the air boss, Boomer Davison. "We are still in the beginning stages of the investigation, but one thing that we know is that Petty Officer Parker had been up since 0430 that morning."

"Since 0430?" said the admiral.

"Yes sir," responded Davison. "We had flight quarters at 0530 to launch the COD to the beach to pick up the media people that Fifth Fleet wanted to send us, then we moved right into helo flight ops to send our two HH-60s around the task group to push parts at the small boys, then we took the CH-53E hits from CTF-53 with cargo and mail—takes an awfully long time to unload those beasts, Admiral—then we had to take the LAMPS helo from *Shiloh* to bring some of their gear over for calibration. By that time, we were setting up for our first launch and it didn't let up after that."

"I read you, Boss," responded the admiral. He knew that these activities went on every day aboard *Carl Vinson*, he just hadn't focused on them in this context.

"I think it's safe to say, Admiral, that Parker was totally exhausted by that point. He just let down his guard. He should have been standing behind the tow tractor or in some other protected place, but he wasn't. No one saw him there, otherwise one of my flight deck supervisors would have made him move," continued the air boss.

"Has the pace picked up all of a sudden?" asked the admiral, intuitively knowing the answer to his question.

"Air Boss painted a really accurate picture of yesterday," interjected CAG, "and no sir, yesterday wasn't an atypical day. The pace hasn't picked up all of a sudden, it's been building gradually ever since we entered the Gulf. I think that it's fair to say it's never been higher."

"It certainly is higher than when I had *Kennedy* over here," said the admiral, understanding where they were coming from and wanting them to speak freely. "But what's changed specifically?"

"Well, Admiral, there's also the various P-3 type flights. Commodore needs 'em to do surveillance, we know that, but the Fifth Fleet staff now wants us to put up CAP in case they get threatened by any hostiles. Those guys patrol the Gulf just about all day long and that's a lot of CAP sorties we're putting up."

"I can see that it is, CAG. Anything else?" said the admiral, who was getting a very clear picture of what Wizard was telling him.

"Nothing major, Admiral. Seems like Fifth Fleet used to let us use CTF-53s, CH-53Es, and H-3s a lot more to bring parts, pax, and mail out to us. They're really holding them back now, say it's for 'higher priority missions.' That makes us launch a few extra COD flights every day, and has us shuttling our helos, especially our HH-60Hs, back and forth almost continuously."

"So we're getting nibbled to death on the margins, is that it?" said the admiral. "Ops Boss, what does your counterpart say when you talk to him about this?"

The operations officer—the N-3—thought a moment before responding. This trend had been evident to him, and he had tried to stem it at his level but had failed. He knew how Admiral Flowers had been treating his boss, and he had tried to shield him from any confrontations with the Fifth Fleet commander, but there was only so much that he could do. He had to tell him the truth.

"Admiral, I'm on the phone with their ops officer, Captain Gary Hoffman, several times a day. Gary's been there for almost two years. I challenge him on each one of these new requirements and he's hard pressed to explain why they're laying all these things on now. He can't really say it, but he hints pretty strongly that Vice Admiral Flowers is coming up with these ideas on his own."

"So, we're saying that we have pushed it to the limits, but that it's a Navy problem of our own making. Nothing that can't be fixed."

"Yes sir, we really are," chimed in *Carl Vinson*'s commanding officer. "This isn't an excuse, Admiral. We've got to find a way to make sure that what happened to Petty Officer Parker doesn't happen to another sailor."

"There's only one of us here who can take point on this one, fellas. I've got the ball, let me run with it a while? Thanks for coming in."

As Heater Robinson rose, the others rose also. They knew that the admiral was going to have to call Fifth Fleet and ask Admiral Flowers for some respite in their intense OP-TEMPO. They were all savvy enough to share a collective dread of what the response was going to be.

19

At Fifth Fleet headquarters in Manama, Bahrain, Admiral Flowers sat at his desk reading the day's intelligence summary. The news wasn't particularly encouraging. The Iraqis were still posturing in the wake of the Foxbat shootdown, and it appeared that the Iranians were both stepping up their terrorist training and starting to filter some of these terrorists to locations throughout the Gulf. He had marshaled sufficient U.S. forces in the Gulf to do something about it—now he just needed to be able to go forward.

He had the *Carl Vinson* Task Group commander on the phone several times a day, but had not been satisfied by his response regarding his preparations for Exercise Swift Sword. He wanted to see the strike briefs in person, not just whatever brief the admiral's staff concocted for him—no doubt some vanilla, watered down, bereft-of-details "executive summary"—no, he wanted to see the actual briefs by the strike leaders themselves. Robinson had protested— God, he had some nerve, didn't want to fly that many people in, didn't think it was necessary, tied up a lot of helo assets, all manner of excuses—but he had simply told him that he could either fly them in from the carrier's position over a hundred miles away or he could bring his carrier in toward Bahrain and anchor at "Bahrain Bell" and enjoy a shorter flight.

As Admiral Flowers sat in his well-appointed office at his headquarters, his thoughts were interrupted by the buzz on his intercom.

"Yes," he said impatiently.

"Admiral, Captain Perry is calling for you." The yeoman's voice was crisp and polite; he knew that Admiral Flowers wanted military precision in everything that went on in his office.

"Put him through," replied Flowers.

"Good day, Admiral," began Perry.

"Good day, Tom. What's the good word from Washington?"

"Admiral, the news is good, really good. We had a very positive session with the president. I laid out all of the advantages that would accrue if we struck the Iranian Navy particularly hard, and I think that I was convincing."

"That's great news, exactly what did he say, Tom?"

"He said, Admiral"—Perry paused for dramatic effect— "he said that we should sink their Navy."

"Not just take it out of action?"

"No sir. He definitely said sink it."

"That's great work, Tom. I'll take it from here." The admiral was standing now, and as his aide looked from his cubbyhole of an office through the small Plexiglas window into the admiral's large office, he could see the admiral now standing and becoming very animated. Evidently he was very excited about what he was hearing and he paced a few feet back and forth, almost dragging the secure STU-III phone off his desk. "You just keep in the loop there, you hear. I don't want anyone getting cold feet and changing their mind at this point."

"I won't let that happen, Admiral. You can count on that."

"I know that I can count on you, Tom."

The admiral was interrupted by another buzz on the intercom. Unlike his aide, the yeoman could not see into Admiral Flowers's office from his desk on the other side of the reception area. He had told them to find a way to fix that, but they hadn't yet, the dullards—he'd have to make them do it his way.

"Yes!" he said sharply, holding the STU-III phone with Captain Perry on the line away from his head for a moment.

"Admiral," began the somewhat shaken yeoman, "Admiral Robinson and his staff people are here."

"Well, I'm on a very important call to Washington, have the chief of staff take them down to the conference room. I'll get down there when I can."

As the yeoman relayed the message to Admiral Robinson, Captain Dennis, who could hear the yeoman's conversations from his office, quickly appeared to greet Admiral Robinson. "Admiral, welcome. Sorry that the boss is momentarily tied up. Won't you join me in our conference room, I'm sure that the admiral will be finished with his call soon."

Admiral Heater Robinson was not quick to anger, but he was doing a slow burn now. Admiral Flowers had summoned him here, insisted that he bring his senior staff members and strike leaders to the Fifth Fleet Headquarters with him. It had taken two of the carrier's HH-60H helicopters to haul this crowd from their position over 150 miles away, and Robinson had complied, not because it made any sense but because Flowers was his superior commander. And now Flowers was too busy talking with someone on the phone to personally greet the only other Navy Flag officer in the entire theater of operations?

"All right, Chief of Staff," began the admiral, not wanting to take his anger out on Dennis, "lead the way, my folks are down there already and I guess that we might as well get started."

Flowers's chief of staff led them down the narrow corridor that connected the newer portion of Fifth Fleet Headquarters with the older portion containing the large conference and briefing room. The Fifth Fleet staffers, as well as his own people, stood as Admiral Robinson entered the large room. Robinson seated himself at the center of the large table, facing the screen that dominated the center of one wall.

The Fifth Fleet operations officer, Captain Carl Mullen, stood at the briefer's podium to Heater Robinson's right and addressed the admiral and the other officers seated at the table. "Admiral, gentlemen, thank you all for coming," he began. "Admiral Flowers thought that it would be beneficial if we all gathered to review the preparations we are making for Exercise Swift Sword."

"We've got our plan pretty well laid out," offered Admiral Robinson's ops officer, Captain Bill Durham. "We've transmitted those to you via message and I think that we've met your requirements."

"Oh, you have and you've done an outstanding job," continued Mullen. "We just wanted to look at your plans in a little more depth so we can support you as best we can as we prepare for this important exercise."

"I know, Carl," continued Durham, "but you know as well as I do that this level of detail, having our strike leaders brief the actual conduct of their simulated strikes for this 'exercise' to your boss is a little bit unusual, to say the least. You know as well as I do that by bringing them here, we're taking them away from doing a lot of other important things that they need to be doing with their squadrons."

"I know Bill, but you've got to understand the importance of this 'exercise' and what might happen downstream. I'm sure that when Admiral Flowers comes in he will share some of his insights with us."

"That's right," the chief of staff offered. "We just wanted to get all the major players assembled in one . . ."

"Stop!" shouted Admiral Robinson as he shot up out of his chair. Professional courtesy—not going at the captains on the Fifth Fleet staff was all that had kept him in his chair this long—but he had now heard enough. "Maybe we need to wait for your boss to show up, Chief of Staff. I've brought a dozen and a half of the most senior people from *Carl Vinson* here today because your boss summoned us. We're working sixteen hours a day to put this damned exercise together to your specifications, and we're working as hard as we can to do that, but when you interrupt us in the middle of all that to come down here and present the plan to you all so you can . . . can nit-pick it to death, we just don't have time for that . . ." Admiral Robinson was looking right toward Dennis and Mullen and noticed that their eyes were slowly moving to the right, toward the door at his left. He turned slowly and saw the small, spare frame of Admiral Flowers standing in the doorway. He had evidently heard at least some of Robinson's monologue.

"Good, Admiral Robinson, you've had your moment in the sun. Now please be seated."

Shocked, Heater Robinson mustered all of the control that he possessed and sat down.

Flowers went to his chair without stopping to shake Robinson's hand. "Well. We welcome all of you from *Carl Vinson*." Admiral Flowers moved his eyes from person to person at the table, everyone but Admiral Robinson, an omission lost on no one. "I know that you might be a bit busy," he continued, "but we wanted to bring you here to better explain our position, which evidently gets lost somewhat in translation in the few hundred miles from my headquarters to your flagship," he said, looking directly at Heater Robinson.

"Now Admiral Robinson here was beginning to make his little speech," Flowers continued, his voice taking on an even nastier tone, "but I don't need to hear it, because those of you afloat just don't have the big picture. I'm gonna tell you what the big picture is."

All eyes were riveted on the Fifth Fleet commander, including Admiral Robinson's, whose eyes betrayed his seething hatred.

"The big picture is that I'm not gonna let you people on *Carl Vinson* waste everyone's time husbanding your precious task group. I'm not sure if you're saving it for the junior prom or what. Well, you didn't come all the way here to worry about a thousand 'what ifs' and about just defending yourselves.

"The job you're here to do is to do the national will. Right now, that includes threatening the Islamic Republic of Iran. Threatening them to stop their damned terrorist activities. Exercise Swift Sword could turn into an operation at any moment. I thought that I had made that perfectly clear. Therefore, we're going to train the way we are going to fight. I don't want any halfhearted, watered-down strike packages, I want everything you can throw into this."

"Yes sir," began Captain Bill Durham. "We are trying to balance . . ."

Flowers cut him off. "Balance? I don't want to hear about balance, Captain. I want you to build strike packages that put the fear of God into those damn people. Don't think for a moment that they aren't watching what you are doing in the Central Gulf during your practice strikes. And should we take this further . . ." He paused for dramatic effect. Almost shouting now, he continued, "Should we take this further, we are going after their Navy. We're not going to damage it. We're not going to put it out of action. We're going to sink it. Sink it where it lays. Iran won't have a Navy when we're through with them!"

The contingent from *Carl Vinson* had never heard anything like this, and even his own staff members had never seen Admiral Flowers this animated. He just stood, defiant, his small jaw jutting forward, almost panting from his outburst. No one dared speak.

"Well, now that we understand each other a little better, Admiral Robinson, why don't you have your people tell us how they're going to do all this."

"Certainly, Admiral," said Heater Robinson. He rose, barely controlling his rage. "My Ops O will lead off with the overall campaign plan, followed by CAG, followed by the various strike leads for different strikes during the first phase of the *exercise*."

Heater Robinson was determined to shield his people the best he could and absorb Admiral Flowers's wrath himself— and he did just that. Each briefer presented his portion of the plan and each time, predictably, it was not enough. As the Fifth Fleet commander expressed his dissatisfaction at each step along the way, Admiral Robinson chimed in for the briefer and assured Flowers that things would be changed to meet his needs. Demeaning as it was to him personally, the honorable officer in Heater Robinson demanded that he shield his officers from this, this *madman's* wrath.

Finally, the briefings were complete. Admiral Flowers absently thanked everyone for coming, although there was not the thinnest shred of sincerity in his voice. He left the conference room as abruptly as he had entered.

Back in his office, Admiral Flowers settled down into his chair—buoyed from making his point but drained by the effort. He would not be just another forgotten Fifth Fleet commander. He would be remembered as the man who sent the Iranian Navy to the bottom of the ocean. That would be his legacy.

20

SITTING IN THE CRAMPED SEAT OF AN S-3B VIKING for many hours a day wasn't doing a thing to help her stay in shape, mused Anne O'Connor as she bent over her right leg, which was propped up on an NC-8 cart on *Carl Vinson's* flight deck. During the limited time that the ship wasn't conducting air operations, Boomer Davison opened up the flight deck for jogging. Anne and many others planned their schedules around this time as the flight deck was the only place to run on this impossibly cramped ship.

It wasn't taking Anne long to warm up, for the oppressive noonday sun caused her to break a sweat instantly. As she stretched, she looked around the flight deck for some familiar faces, someone to jog with. It was boring enough running in circles on the hot, slick, steel deck, dodging airplanes as you did. At least running along with someone and making small talk would take her mind off what was always a tough run. She saw Jake McLaughlin and Rick Holden running toward her. Jake and Anne had been classmates in the same company at the Naval Academy, had many mutual interests, and had been fast friends since then. Both served in squadrons at the North Island Naval Air Station and lived an almost idyllic life, renting small apartments in the resort town of Coronado, just outside the gates of the air station. Anne waved at him as he came toward her.

"Hey, Anne," said Jake, raspy and a bit out of breath.

"Hey Jake, hey Rick." Anne had seen Rick around the ship, especially with Jake and the other HS-4 bubbas, but only knew him well enough to recognize who he was.

Jake had been running with Rick Holden—it seemed the natural thing to do, given how closely HS-4 worked with Rick's SEAL platoon and especially how tight Jake and Rick had become. Call it the experience of shared danger. Call it mutual professional respect. Whatever it was, they were a team.

"Anne, you just getting ready to go? It's hot as Hades out there," said Jake.

"Yeah, think that I'm pretty loose, I'm gonna give it a good couple of miles anyway. You hot, sweaty boys want to join me?"

"Not me," replied Jake. "This SEAL has run me into the ground. I may need help dragging my body into the shower."

Anne really did want to have someone run with her, so she pressed. "How about it, you guys, just a lap or two with me to get me warmed up."

Jake was silent, his hands on his knees, still trying to catch his breath.

"Sure, I'll give it a few turns around the deck," chimed in Rick. "Ol Jake here needs to limp on down to his stateroom and get a little nap before his flight later this afternoon. The lad isn't as young as he once was, you know."

"Sure. Great," said Anne, wanting to remain game. She didn't know Rick at all and was a bit flustered that he'd agreed to run with her. What were they going to talk about? Well, he seemed like he had a decent sense of humor.

As Jake walked around the island and toward the catwalk, Anne and Rick headed for the "stream," the group of runners going in clockwise circles around the deck. They both were silent for a short while. Finally, Anne spoke up.

"Rick, you're the OIC of the SEAL platoon, right?"

"Sure am. How about you? Jake says you're a Viking pilot. How is that bird to fly?"

Anne had to think a moment. Jake had been telling Rick about her. Why? Had Rick asked about her? Anne wasn't so much on guard or flattered as curious.

"It's a great aircraft. Flies like a dream. I was real lucky to get selected to fly it," she replied. "I see you and the HS-4 guys together a lot. I guess you do a lot of flying with them."

"Yeah, that's the only reason I knew what you flew. Jake and the other ringknockers spend ninety percent of their time talking about their days at the academy, and they have tales to tell about everyone there. I think that's where your name came up."

Anne looked toward him to see him flash a broad smile. He was baiting her and she knew it. She decided to play along.

"Oh, yes, and I'm certain that they told you some wild stories. I take it you weren't afflicted with going to the academy. Where'd you go to school, Rick?"

"Oh, I went to UVA. But that was a long time ago," he replied. Rick was understandably a bit on guard whenever any questions about his past came up.

"Oh, so you're one of those really smart guys!" she kidded. "Did you go ROTC or just decide to come in after you graduated?" Anne wasn't trying to pry into his life, she was just looking for a basis to keep the conversation going as they pounded their way around the flight deck.

Rick decided to switch the venue of the conversation. "No, I bummed around after college at a few different jobs before coming into the Navy," he said. Then, nimbly changing the subject, he continued. "So I see that your squadron has a bunch of aircraft on the ship. Do you mainly . . . do what, work as tankers for the other aircraft?"

"Yeah, that's our main mission, really. I think that we've got it down pat. Wouldn't mind doing something a little bit different. Think that I vaguely remember ASW—at least how to spell it," replied Anne, not breathless at all, and having no trouble keeping up with Rick's pace.

"Maybe the Iranians will get one of their mighty Kilo submarines underway," chided Rick, knowing enough about the Navy that he understood that these boats that Iran had bought from Russia rarely ventured out to sea.

"Maybe it will snow in August in the Gulf too," replied Anne, feigning disbelief that Rick could be so naive, but causing them both to laugh.

It felt good to laugh, and Anne was enjoying the light banter with Rick. She wasn't looking for anything remotely resembling a relationship—not with anyone onboard this ship—she had promised herself that. But there was such a small number of women on the ship that she couldn't restrict her relationships to women alone, and she would much rather talk and kid with a man who wasn't in the Airwing—too many problems and too much talk if that went anywhere or even seemed to be going anywhere.

No, Rick was "safe," and Anne was mildly curious about the SEAL mission. A number of her close friends from the academy had gone into the SEALs, but beyond seeing them in Coronado during their training, she pretty much lost track of them once they went to their first duty stations.

Talking with Rick was definitely safer than talking with any of her fellow pilots. Anne enjoyed the professionalism and keen competitiveness of naval aviation—but only up to a point. As a naval aviator, where everyone is supposed to have the "right stuff" and project an aura of infallibility, Anne could never feel comfortable confiding in her fellow aviators. She didn't have that problem with Rick.

"You try to work out every day, Anne?" asked Rick as they completed their second lap around the flight deck.

"Well, to tell you the truth, it just doesn't happen every day. Sometimes I'm so drained after flying all day—especially those long tanker hop days—that I just about look like

Jake did and bag it. I don't imagine that you SEALs have that problem. Don't we pay you guys to work out every day?" she kidded.

"Yep, and I'm trying to give the Navy their money's worth," he kidded back, glad that he was able to deflect questions about his past.

Rick found Anne easy to talk to also, but he felt very guarded about his professional past. Beyond that, he was not sure how involved he should become with any woman. During his last assignment, before he was Ensign Rick Holden, Rick had been incredibly close to someone—someone whom he had shared life or death experiences with. He knew that she loved him and he her—but they wanted to give a relationship that had burned in the crucible of shared danger time to mature, to make sure that it was the real thing.

They were both Navy and they were assigned to commands a world away from each other. They e-mailed each other frequently, and, although there were no promises or definite plans, they both saw the world the same way and felt that they could have a future together. They both needed time. With this relationship with Laura Peters in his mind, Rick Holden was not looking for a deep relationship with anyone else right now.

One deck below where Anne and Rick were now making their fourth circuit of the flight deck, Heater Robinson sat in his cabin alone. First the angry SPECAT message from his friend, Admiral Jake Monroe, then the needless death of Petty Officer Parker, and now this absolutely humiliating experience at the hands of Admiral Flowers. The admiral felt like a punch-drunk fighter.

Heater Robinson was not so much staggered by the personal attacks or even by whatever impact this would have on his professional reputation—hell, he had been promoted several pay grades higher than he ever thought he would be and had reached what he considered to be the pinnacle of his career. He was Teflon as far as that was concerned. What angered him was his country's vacillation, its unwillingness to act, its holding back and running only self-destructive busywork exercises that sapped both equipment and morale when it should be striking the enemies of the U.S. He had faith that the system would eventually do the right thing. But that faith was being sorely tested.

21

PATRICK BROWNE WAS PACING UP AND DOWN IN front of his desk. He had planned from the outset to make his economic stimulus package the crown jewel of his first term as president. He fervently believed in what he was doing, and he was primarily focused on making a good package part of the law of the land. The fact that this major package of tax cuts, incentives, and other attractive perks was going to reach fruition right before his reelection campaign kicked off was just a serendipitous bonus, he told himself. In fact, he had told himself this so many times that he actually believed it. He needed time and attention to bring this to closure, but his foreign policy wonks wouldn't give him enough time to rivet his attention the way he needed to.

The president was still pacing when the door to the Oval Office opened. Michael Curtis led a large group into the office. It included Bryce Jacobs, Philip Quinn, Admiral Jake Monroe, Lieutenant General Robert Allen, the JCS operations director, Joseph Nye, the assistant secretary of defense for international security affairs, Pete Hernandez, and Major General Thomas Prescott, the DIA deputy director for intelligence. Patrick Browne knew that this was not going to be a short or an easy meeting.

Once the president gestured for them to sit, Michael Curtis began the meeting. "Mr. President. We have come to update you on the situation in the Arabian Gulf. First of all, we believe that the situation with Iraq is stable. Saddam and his people will saber-rattle for a while, move aircraft from one field to another, move surface-to-air missiles from place to place in the no-fly zone and the like, but we don't expect any additional threats to our forces. Admiral Monroe has confirmed this with CENTCOM and they're on the same page."

"Admiral?" said the president.

"Yes, Mr. President. I have been in constant contact with General Lawrence. We both think that the Iraqis will posture for a while, but there's no point in taking a more aggressive stance for much longer. They've been really grinding away at this story that we lured their aircraft across the border—Saddam's got a whole team of our reporters over there, unwittingly beating the drum for him—but we feel that the real story will come out sooner or later and they'll realize that their guy just screwed up and drop the entire issue."

"No chance that they'll try to use it as a pretext to step up operations in the region counter to our interests?" asked Joseph Nye. Nye had been a fixture in the Defense Department for a long time and had more corporate knowledge than anyone in the room. He wanted to look at all the angles.

"We really don't think so," continued Admiral Monroe. "He's too weak now. The UN sanctions have really made it tight for him. We don't see any overt moves based on this."

"State agrees with that assessment, Mr. President," added Philip Quinn. "We always keep a weather eye on Iraq, but we are sharpening our focus on Iran based on the actions of the last several weeks."

"That's good," said the president.

"Yes sir," said Michael Curtis. "On the other hand, Mr. President, the extent of Iranian activity is sobering. It appears that they may be planning something major in the very near future. General Prescott has some additional details that he brought to share with us. General."

"Mr. President, as you have been briefed before, the Iranians have put a number of terrorist camps back on line and have intensified the activity at some others. Overall, we've seen the highest-ever level of activity at these camps based on both imagery and HUMINT."

The statement startled the president, since HUMINT, or human intelligence, indicated that the United States had agents in Iran reporting on the activities in the terrorist camps. This alone indicated that the nation's intelligence agencies were very concerned about the situation.

"Go ahead, General."

"Yes sir, Mr. President. We've seen an increase in activity in the camps, but we've also seen a substantial flow of people out of the camps. We strongly suspect that these people have completed their training and are now being sent out to perform various missions. It's not just the fact this is happening, Mr. President, but that it is happening in such numbers. We simply don't have the capability of tracking every person who leaves one of these camps."

The president recognized the general's concerns by nodding.

"Mr. President, we've shifted our focus a bit and have tried to zero in on any Gulf nations where known terrorists are entering. We have also increased the threat condition in some of the Gulf littoral states, and have warned American citizens about the increased threat. Barring that, our next step could be to have U.S. citizens leave some of those countries—voluntarily, of course."

"No, no!" said the president. "I don't want to start some wholesale panic. We will continue business as usual with regard to our consular people and ordinary citizens. Raising the threat levels is an overt enough act. I don't want us overreacting."

"Mr. President," chimed in Philip Quinn, "no one is overreacting. We want to move deliberately on this, but I'm afraid that the intelligence community has presented a very real threat. We just want to be prepared, Mr. President, and we want to take other, more definitive, action."

"What kind of action are you talking about?" asked the president.

"We have considered a wide range of options, Mr. President. The one that would have the most salutary effect at this point would be a demarche to the Islamic Republic of

Iran, warning them that any terrorist activities would be met by disproportionate force by the United States against their country."

"Isn't that a little strong?" asked the president. "I mean, do we have to issue a demarche to every nation that might threaten us in that way? What if we fail to demarche some nation? Do they then assume that attacks against us can be made with impunity? I have to tell you that I'll have to think about that one, Mr. Secretary. I'll have to think hard on that one."

"Of course," said Philip Quinn. He was not about to debate the president here in the Oval Office.

Sitting across from him on the other sofa, Michael Curtis merely looked down at the carpet. He had not been in favor of the secretary of state's demarche idea. Curtis had not preloaded the president and prejudiced him against the idea, but he was glad the president had vetoed it.

What Curtis had put into effect was much more comprehensive than any diplomatic demarche could be. Working with the chairman of the Joint Chiefs of Staff, as well as with General Lawrence at CENTCOM, they had put together Exercise Swift Sword. They hadn't kept the exercise a secret from Secretary of Defense Bryce Jacobs or from the president, but they had billed it as just another routine exercise. What the president did not know was that the exercise was designed to simulate strikes into Iran—deep and massive strikes, not pinpricks—with the objective of setting back their military infrastructure at least a decade, perhaps two. A terrorist act could secure for them the license to put that plan into action and turn the "exercise" into actual strikes. They didn't want any diplomatic posturing to derail their plan.

"Mr. President," said the national security adviser, "I believe that the secretary of state has presented a viable option that is available for your use should you so desire. Another view might be, however, that a demarche to Iran might tip our hand too much. There is some evidence, as you know, Mr. President, that would suggest that the Iranian clerics, the people who really run that country, would not be fazed by a demarche and that it even might have the opposite effect and cause them to take overt action sooner with respect to a terrorist action."

Philip Quinn just glared at the national security adviser. This was a test of wills between the secretary of state and Curtis, and right now, it appeared that the national security adviser had the upper hand. Philip Quinn was astute enough to know when he was being outmaneuvered and backed off as gracefully as he could.

"Of course, Mr. President, a demarche is only one of the host of options you have at your disposal. We can proceed in any of several different directions," said the secretary of state. "Perhaps as we gather more intelligence on exactly what the Iranians are doing we can chart a more precise course."

"Yes, perhaps we can," responded the president. "Pete, I'd like you and General Prescott to take another hard look at just what is going on with respect to Iranian-sponsored terrorist activity in the Gulf. Bryce, I want you and Admiral Monroe to continue this exercise that you are conducting and be ready to respond massively to an overt attack, but don't let our people get trigger-happy and start something that we don't mean to start, and don't tip our hand by disrupting any normal operating patterns."

Patrick Browne pushed his chair back from his desk and surveyed the room. His principals were all scribbling notes to record his instructions. He felt very . . . well . . . presidential. He had given instructions—the press would no doubt report that he had "taken charge"; his orders were being carried out; and now he could put this untidy business aside and return to working on his domestic agenda.

Michael Curtis smiled to himself. He had his victory. The instructions that the president had given to the others would take so long to carry out that a signal terrorist act was bound to happen. Exercise Swift Sword would soon be turned into an attack on the Islamic Republic of Iran. He would make sure that the military was prepared to do their part.

Michael Curtis left the Oval Office quickly. He had work to do. His first phone call would be to Captain Tom Perry.

The Fifth Fleet commander would be called moments after that. He wanted to be sure that Flowers was going to be absolutely ready. This was the opportunity that they had waited for.

22

ONE OF THE THINGS THAT THE UNITED STATES GOVernment does least well is keep secrets. Although they had no well-placed spies in the sense that most people understand the word, the Islamic Republic of Iran recognized early that it was in their best interest to stay tapped into the decision making apparatus of the nation that seemed all too prone to threaten their interests. A secretary here, a summer intern there, a media person with the appropriate contacts, and without an extraordinary degree of effort they had the capability to discern the moves that the American government was taking and, more importantly, intending to take. There was a well-established funnel to channel this information back to the Iranian capital in Tehran, and there it was analyzed and disseminated to the highest reaches of government.

Foreign Minister Ali Akbar Velayati and Chief of the Iranian Armed Forces Major General Abdollah Najafi had asked for an audience with the president of the Islamic Republic. Habibi thought it odd that these two men, who did not often agree on the form the Islamic Republic's policies should take, and who did not seem to get along personally, should ask for an audience together. He ushered them into his office and had them sit in two high-backed chairs in front of his desk. Minister Velayati spoke first.

"Mr. President, thank you for seeing us on such short notice."

Always cautious with anything that Velayati said, Habibi replied, "No affairs that I deal with are so important that I cannot make time to see you and General Najafi, Mr. Minister. How can I help you this morning?"

"Mr. President," Velayati continued, "when we met last I told you of actions that we were taking to make the infidels think twice about becoming a permanent presence in the Arabian Gulf—"

"And I told you that I don't share your urgent need to expel the Americans from the Gulf, Mr. Minister," Habibi interrupted.

"You did, Mr. President, and I know that we disagree on this. But in spite of your concerns, we felt that we must step up our actions and make them more organized. You asked to be kept informed. We are doing that right now. I have men in place ready to strike, and what General Najafi is about to tell you will convince you, I hope, that this is the right course."

Habibi was puzzled. If these two men were now in agreement on a course of action, he recognized that he might be powerless to interfere.

"General?" he said.

Major General Najafi cut an imposing figure even in his fatigue uniform, worn, no doubt, thought Habibi, to impress his warrior credentials on the decidedly non-warriorlike president. At six foot three and a robust 230 pounds, with rough-hewn features and a particularly large head, Najafi made no pretense of culture or subtlety. He was all business.

"I appreciate your seeing us, Mr. President. I will come right to the point. We—that is, Minister Velayati and I—have received some very, very disturbing information from our contacts in the United States. It is possible that the Americans may be planning an attack against the Islamic Republic."

"General, are you certain? What makes you think such a thing is possible?"

"There are several indicators, Mr. President, each one significant in its own right, and together, absolutely compelling, almost certain, that an attack by the Americans is imminent."

Habibi was concerned now. Whatever his other faults, Najafi was a cautious man and not one to overreact to events. He looked at Velayati, who just sat silently. If the general was this concerned, perhaps there was merit to his fears.

"General, what are those indications?"

"First, Mr. President, the foreign minister has learned that some circles within the United States Department of State are crafting a demarche that accuses us of fostering terrorism and threatens to attack our nation if there is a significant terrorist attack anywhere in the Arabian Gulf."

"Anywhere in the Gulf?"

"Yes, anywhere in the Gulf, Mr. President," replied Minister Velayati. "The tenor of what is being considered states that there will not even be a search for the culprits, but that our country will be immediately attacked."

"That is outrageous. Have the Americans gone mad?"

"I cannot answer that, Mr. President," Velayati continued. "Our diplomats assure us that this demarche has not been issued, but that it is being debated at the highest level of their government. We can't be certain that it will be issued, but the fact that it is being considered at all is indeed troubling."

"I should say it is! General Najafi, you said that there are indications of an impending American attack."

"Mr. President, the actions of the American military, and particularly the United States Navy, in the Arabian Gulf cause us a great deal of worry. While I cannot speak with certainty of some of the things we just discussed, I can tell you precisely what the Americans are doing with their military forces."

"I think that we have seen an increase in activity, especially after the shootdown of the Iraqi Foxbat fighter, but none of that seemed directed at us, General," said Habibi.

"The Americans are devious indeed to conceal that from the upper levels of the Islamic Republic, Mr. President. But they are menacing us in a direct and specific way."

"How so?" said Habibi, leaning forward; very much disturbed.

"Mr. President, the Americans are conducting an exercise called 'Swift Sword.' It is supposedly a general exercise to test their naval and air forces in the Gulf. But the object of this exercise is clear. It is our Islamic Republic. Our Orion aircraft have been monitoring this exercise most carefully. They note that the practice strikes that the Americans conduct are aimed at us, and they are thinly disguised. They conduct them in the middle of the Arabian Gulf, but it is clear where they are aiming their strikes. We are absolutely certain they intend to strike our naval bases at Bandar Abbas and also at Bushehr. There is also strong evidence that they will attack into the heartland of the Republic."

"Are you certain?"

"More certain than I have ever been, Mr. President. But these attacks will not only be conducted by the carrier *Carl Vinson*, but also by the dozens of aircraft of the so-called AEF that the traitors to the Islamic cause in Qatar have allowed to move into their nation. The American admiral on *Carl Vinson* has made many trips to Qatar to confer with his Air Force colleague. From watching their exercises we know that they will attack us together, overwhelming our brave defenders."

"Are we so poorly—if bravely—defended?" asked Habibi. He knew the answer to this, knew that the American forces could totally devastate the Islamic Republic. But he had to hear it from his most senior military man.

"Yes, Mr. President. It shames me to tell you this, but our forces are just too weak to withstand the American onslaught."

Minister Velayati chimed in. "Mr. President, that is why I am moving forward with the actions of the brave men that have been trained in our camps. Since the Americans plan to strike us anyway, we will not make our situation any worse by striking first. In just a few days the American aircraft carrier will make a port call in Muscat. We will strike against them there—"

"Strike the carrier?" interrupted Habibi.

"No, that is too hardened a target. We will strike at their people. That is what the Americans fear most."

"Then what do you think the Americans will do? Aren't you making it certain that they will strike us?"

"They intend to strike us anyway!" offered General Najafi.

"Yes, I understand, General. But Mr. Minister, will this not just enrage them and have them make even more devastating attacks against us?" Habibi was genuinely concerned now. This was spinning out of control.

"Mr. President, the Americans have a long history of running away from crises when they lose large numbers of their people. Look what they did in Lebanon when the Marine barracks there were bombed. And you recall that they got out of Somalia when video of their dead soldiers being dragged through the streets was shown on their newscasts. They have no stomach for these kinds of personal losses."

"What if they don't react as you predict, Mr. Minister?" asked Habibi.

"We—General Najafi and I—have considered this possibility and have set a plan in motion to raise the stakes so quickly that the Americans will surely leave the Gulf for good."

"Raise the stakes—higher than killing a large number of their sailors?"

"Yes, Mr. President," continued Velayati, who was becoming more and more animated. "The Americans will not rest until our regime is destroyed, or until they recognize that it is too painful for them to do it. We are increasing that threshold of pain."

"How?" was all that Habibi could say.

"By the time the attack in Muscat is complete, our agents in America will be in place ready to take these attacks to the American homeland. . . ."

Habibi looked toward General Najafi for affirmation, but he just nodded agreement with what Velayati was saying.

"Yes, Mr. President. And in a spectacular way. That is all I am prepared to say at this time, but I assure you that if we are struck, we will strike back harder."

"But if they do not choose to run as you assume they will, Minister Velayati, the American carrier will strike us again and again. General Najafi, you just told me that our defenses are too weak and will be overwhelmed."

"Mr. President, the carrier *Carl Vinson* poses the biggest threat to us. Eliminate that carrier and we stand a chance of surviving whatever blow the Americans can deliver and then striking back. I am not a political person, Mr. President, but I think that the court of world opinion would be with us if we lashed back after the Americans strike us."

"So, how do you propose to strike the Americans?"

"Mr. President, we do not have many weapons that can successfully attack a carrier. Our missiles both on shore and on our Navy ships have a good capability, but the Americans are very adept at thwarting them with their AEGIS cruisers and with other defensive means. Even armed with the newer C-802 cruise missiles, our Hegu fast attack craft have little chance of penetrating the ring of steel the Americans deploy around their carriers."

"But if our surface combatants cannot reach them, then surely our aircraft can. You don't doubt the bravery of our pilots, do you?"

"Not in the least, Mr. President. But our pilots fly obsolete and obsolescent aircraft like the F-4—a plane the Americans used during the Vietnam War—the F-6, and the F-7. Even the F-14 Tomcat, one of the best planes in our inventory, is one that the Americans have all but phased out of their inventory, and we are constantly in need of spare parts that we can only get at exorbitant prices on the black market."

"I have never been briefed on this," countered Habibi.

"This is normally not something that we would raise to your level, Mr. President, but something that we just learn to live with in the military. The bottom line, however, is that an attempt to attack the American carrier with our tactical aircraft would be a suicide mission for our brave pilots and one that would have no chance of even wounding the carrier." Habibi could tell that General Najafi was genuinely frustrated with the condition and especially the readiness of Iran's armed forces.

"What do you propose then, General?"

"Mr. President, our scientists have worked diligently to revive our nuclear program. Progress has been slow, sometimes agonizingly slow, as again we are impeded by western embargoes. But I am told that we have come up with enough enriched uranium to build a low-grade nuclear device. This device is awaiting testing in a remote desert site. We—that is, with your concurrence, Mr. President—propose to put this device on an aircraft and destroy the American carrier with it."

"But General, you have just finished telling me that the Americans can shoot down our jets with impunity. How do you propose to deliver such a nuclear device?"

"Mr. President, that will take some finesse. What we will do is put it on one of our transport aircraft. That aircraft can then take off from Shiraz International and fly toward Kuwait City."

"Why will this fool the Americans, General?"

"Mr. President, our government, in cooperation with the International Civilian Aviation Organization, has recently established a commercial airline route between Shiraz and Kuwait City. This is a normal path for commercial airline traffic and, because of the relatively short distance between the two cities, these airliners rarely climb above twenty thousand feet. Additionally, this path goes right by the area that the American carrier most commonly operates in. Our plane will join the airliner route, spacing itself appropriately in sequence with the normal flow of aircraft traffic. Then, when it is close to the carrier, it will make a beeline to it and drop its weapon."

"That is a bold plan, General. But what will happen to the crew? Surely the Americans will shoot them down."

"The crew has been selected well," chimed in Velayati. "They know the importance of their mission and they are prepared to die for the cause."

President Habibi could tell that this plan had been well coordinated between his foreign minister and the head of his armed forces. He dared not try to derail it—or even question it.

"I understand your plan, gentlemen. We must discuss it within the Supreme National Security Council. Such an action is something that must be decided only after much prayer and debate."

"Yes, Mr. President. But we must not pray too hard or debate too long. The Americans must be taught a lesson and taught one soon."

As the two men left his office, President Habibi slumped down in his chair. Events were spinning out of control. He no longer felt that he could effectively direct the efforts of his country.

23

COMMANDER, CARRIER AIRWING FOURTEEN—CAPTAIN Wizard Foster was displayed on a highly polished piece of brass on the upper part of the door. Below it was the rainbow on the inverted triangle that symbolized the Airwing's logo. Above the door was a small brass enunciator light with green illuminated, indicating that CAG Foster was in his cabin and did not currently have a visitor.

Commander Alex Fitzgerald could have walked right in, but he paced nervously outside of the door to CAG's stateroom in *Carl Vinson*'s Blue Tile Area. As he paced, CARGRU SEVEN staff officers coming and going in and out of their wardroom right across the passageway gave him a curious glance but thought nothing more about it as they went about their everyday tasks.

Fitzgerald was the Airwing Fourteen flight surgeon, and he was wrestling with a dilemma of doctor-patient privilege that he'd hoped he would never have to face. CAG was his immediate boss and had made it clear to his flight surgeon that he wanted to know everything about the health of every aviator aboard *Carl Vinson*. Alex Fitzgerald was torn, but ultimately his loyalty to his boss won out.

"Enter!" said Wizard Foster in response to the loud knock on his door.

"Hello, CAG," began Alex. "I apologize for just barging in. If this isn't a good time . . ."

"Naw, anytime's a good time for you, Doc," replied Wizard. "Glad to see you. What's on your mind?" he said as he guided Fitzgerald to the green sofa against his forward bulkhead and sat down next to him.

"CAG," Alex began, clearly a bit nervous, "I have a matter that I want to discuss with you that I could have tabled under the rubric of doctor-client privilege. However, you have made it clear in the past that you wanted to know about the health of our aviators on board."

"Yes I did, Doc." Wizard Foster couldn't help but speculate. He knew what kinds of corners aviators sometimes cut to try to keep flying when they shouldn't be—hell, he had pulled some of those tricks when he was a lieutenant—taking Motrin to kill the pain of athletic injuries, flying with the flu or with a cold, taking medication for a variety of ailments when he shouldn't have been flying at all. Sometimes he thought Fitzgerald was just a little bit too anal about this. Pilots knew their limits. What minor faux pas had the doc discovered now? "And I appreciate your dilemma— and your decision. Just tell me what you know about every Airwing aviator."

"CAG, well, this isn't exactly about an Airwing aviator— though it is about someone who flies with the Airwing— occasionally, that is."

"OK, Doc, well, who would that be?" replied Foster, now sounding mildly annoyed with Fitzgerald.

"Sir, this is very hard for me to discuss, you see, sir, well, it involves a very senior officer aboard *Carl Vinson*. . . ."

"Doc, for chrissake! Who the hell are you talking about?" shouted Wizard Foster. He was getting tired of his flight surgeon's elliptical beating around the bush.

"Sir. CAG. It's about Admiral Robinson."

"Admiral Robinson! Doc, are you serious?"

"Yes sir, CAG, very serious, and since the admiral sometimes flies with the Airwing, I felt it was my duty to inform you sir." Alex Fitzgerald felt that he was on shaky ground now. The CAG's exclamation had startled him and made him less sure of himself. He proceeded cautiously. "Sir, I think that his condition may be rather serious."

"Doc, what the heck is going on?"

"Well, CAG, it all started a few days ago. The admiral asked me to come up to his cabin. Said he wanted me to give him something to calm his nerves—"

"Calm his nerves?" CAG interrupted. "Did he look nervous or upset to you?"

"CAG, you let me come to the daily flag briefs once a week or so and I have to say that the admiral doesn't look the same as he did when we began the deployment—"

Wizard Foster interrupted again. "Hell, Doc, none of us probably do. We are in the Arabian Gulf. This is hard, stressful work. We lost a man on the flight deck a few days ago. The admiral's name is at the top of the page. Sure, he's probably a little bit stressed. What did you give him?" CAG had determined in his own mind that Fitzgerald was wasting his time. Damn, every time you thought you had one of these docs trained up right, they slipped back into this fantasy world where people worked nine to five and had no stress on them.

"Sir, on his direct orders, I finally prescribed a mild sleeping sedative. But that's not the point, CAG." Fitzgerald was sounding defensive, and for good reason.

"Well, what is the damn point, Doc? So far nothing you've told me sounds like any of our business!" Wizard Foster was raising his voice now, and Fitzgerald was looking alarmed.

"CAG, so I could prescribe the right medication, I persuaded the admiral to let me take his blood pressure and listen to his heart and feel his pulse—again, just so I could prescribe the right thing. CAG, his blood pressure is sky high—160 over 110. His heart is racing and his pulse is too. And sir, he just . . . just . . . looks bad."

"What did you do then?" asked Foster, moderating his tone a bit. The numbers were sinking in, and he was starting to see the flight surgeon's point.

"I suggested to him that we do a more robust battery of tests. Blood tests, that sort of thing, CAG, but he just threw me out of his office. Said that he 'wasn't going to take any damned tests' and that I had better have his prescription up to him right away or else. I did what he asked and now I'm here."

"When did this happen?"

"CAG, well . . ." Fitzgerald was stammering now. "It happened two days ago. I know now that I should have told you right away, but sir, he is a flag officer and a patient. Ultimately, though, I thought that you should know."

"No, Doc, you did the right thing. It was a tough call but I admire you coming forward. For the moment, though, why don't we just let this sit? The admiral hasn't flown much at all since we've been in the Gulf, just that one S-3 flight to Bahrain in the COTAC seat and twice with HS-4 on day VFR flights. I'm not worried from the standpoint of an aircrew being on medication."

"Yes sir, but from the standpoint of his overall health?"

"Right, Doc. I know that is something we have to look at. But the admiral is a professional. I'll find a way to bring it up with him. Hell, you know how we all are, Doc, we think that we're immortal and all that. I've got this one for action."

"Thanks CAG. I'm glad . . . well . . . I'm glad that I came up to see you."

"I am too, Doc."

As the door shut behind his flight surgeon, CAG sat down heavily in his desk chair. He now understood just how much stress Heater Robinson was under and how it was affecting him. He wanted to help him. He was just not sure how to do it.

Fifty frames forward, Anne O'Connor was pulling on her flight suit for yet another hop. She was one of the high-time pilots in VS-35 for this month, and she was rubbing it with her roommate.

"So Chrissie, are you in *double-digits* for flight time this month? If you're not, I *may* bag out of one of my hops and let you take it."

Chrissie sat at her desk reading a letter from "the beau," as Anne referred to her fiancé. She knew that Chrissie was pouring through that letter and that she could run her almost recklessly, knowing that Chrissie wouldn't be focused enough to slash back with any kind of good comeback.

"No, I'm getting plenty, roomie, you may be getting too much . . . by the way, *Brian* stopped me in the p-way the other day asking how you were doing," she said, her voice lingering on Brian's name.

"McDonald?" said Anne, feigning surprise.

"Oh, cut it out, Anne, you know who, it's always *Brian*," said Chrissie.

That hit a nerve with Anne. "Chrissie, you know that there's nothing going on with me and McDonald, don't you?"

"Sure I do, roomie. I know that he's just this big mentor guy from the academy. He's kinda gender neutral on this mentoring stuff, aren't there a bunch of you in the Airwing that he's looking out for?"

"Just a few of us, just kind of a sounding board about stuff like career patterns, good flying jobs, that sort of thing."

"Yeah, hey, I think it's great. Maybe I run you about it because I'm a little jealous. After all, even though we had a pretty big NROTC unit at Notre Dame, we sure don't have this worldwide network like you ring-knockers do," replied Chrissie, her tone of voice convincing Anne that she was really OK with all of this.

"Well, I think that McDonald keeps checking up on me because I need the most help. Maybe that's why I'm hogging this much flight time, you know, practice, practice, practice," said Anne.

"I guess," Chrissie said. "But, what's up with this guy you've been jogging with? Anything there?"

"Chrissie, now that you're engaged I know what you're up to. You can't stand for me to be single," Anne chided back. "No, there's nothing there. You know how it is in the Airwing, Chrissie. Gosh, I confide in you, but that's it. I don't dare talk to any guys in the Airwing, there's just too much scuttlebutt. Rick is, well, safe. He's a lot older and he's just easy to talk to."

"I think that's great, Anne. Go for it. You're not gonna stop talking to me now, are you?"

Anne knew that Chrissie was really running her now. It

wasn't just that Chrissie was her roommate, or that they were squadronmates, or that Anne constantly depended on her experience, or that they did a lot of things together; no, it went beyond that—Chrissie was her confidante. She told her everything. Every victory. Every defeat. Every worry. Every crisis. Everything. The thought that she would ever stop doing that and that Chrissie wouldn't be there for her was so bizarre that she pushed it out of her brain.

24

IT WAS DARK AS THE CARS PULLED UP TO THE OLD Executive Office Building and discharged their very important passengers. The joke among the security guards was that the National Security Council only met at night now—better to make their deliberations seem more clandestine. There was no joking among the participants. They were about serious business.

The national security adviser sat at his desk going over his notes for the meeting, waiting for the other participants to assemble in the Cabinet Room. Michael Curtis was edgy, but comfortable with driving the problem, becoming the pivotal person in determining the fate of nations. This is what had attracted him to public service and what had motivated and driven him for the last thirty years. Power. Nowhere but in government service—and government service at this level—could a person rise to a position that wielded this much. Certainly, the elected officials had to be allowed to believe that their positions let them wield the power, but ultimately it came to men like Curtis who had bent their backs to the yoke of service. They were the real decision makers.

It had not been an easy or a direct path to this pinnacle

for the national security adviser. Certainly his family connections and educational credentials gave him a favored starting position, but that starting position was crowded with hundreds—perhaps thousands—of young hopefuls like himself who were just as eager to succeed, just as desirous of rising to the top. Michael Curtis had simply outworked, outfought, and outmaneuvered all of the competition to achieve the status as principal adviser to the highest elected official of the most powerful nation in the world.

Michael Curtis was determined to best his historical competition, too. As he thought about some of the national security advisers to recent presidents—Zbigniew Brzezinski, Henry Kissinger, Brent Scowcroft, Colin Powell, Tony Lake, Sandy Berger, and others—it occurred to Curtis that only a few had wielded the full range of power that he could employ. Others had either been unwilling or unable to use the office as a personal tool for crafting a foreign policy agenda that met what he perceived to be the nation's vital interests. Failure to use power in this manner was anathema to Curtis.

Michael Curtis's view of the world was not necessarily out of consonance with his colleagues'. He just wanted to achieve his goals—the nation's goals really, he was merely an interpreter of them—more quickly and more directly than some of his more cautious colleagues. He did not fancy himself a Spanish bullfighter who slowly bleeds the bull to death. Rather, he thought of himself as the lone marksman, delivering the single shot to the threat, which would bring it down permanently. Iran was that threat, in his mind, the one nation on earth that posed the most compelling danger to the United States. He was not unhappy that the Iranians were unleashing terrorists throughout the Gulf region and maybe further than that.

He knew that the United States was prepared to respond to a terrorist attack of any kind with disproportionate force and that he had the ability to steer that response in a way that would not just persuade the Islamic Republic to cease its terrorist acts for the moment but would render it incapable of continuing terrorist training or even of posing a viable military threat in the ensuing decades. He wanted that to be his legacy—not that he successfully solved the "crisis du jour" but that he was successful in safeguarding America's interests for the long term.

His key military advisor, Captain Tom Perry, had worked hellish hours under near sweatshop conditions to provide him with background information to evolve an effective plan for doing this. The captain had evidently called in some markers to gather all of the information, but it was an impressive performance. He had presented the national security adviser with the information that they had subsequently given the president, emphasizing the need to destroy the Iranian Navy in its ports of Bushehr and Bandar Abbas before they had any chance of putting out to sea. It was a well thought through plan. The only way that the plan could go awry, thought Curtis, was if the Iranians did not give the United States reason enough to attack. He would ensure that that did not happen.

Michael Curtis strode into the Cabinet Room, where the small group had gathered—Admiral Monroe, Major General Prescott, Joseph Nye, Lieutenant General Allen, and Captain Perry. Curtis got right to the point.

"Gentlemen, you know why we are here. The president has given specific direction regarding our actions in the Arabian Gulf. I think that our most important role right now is communicating with the unified commander and ensuring that he is prepared to carry out the president's desires, should a terrorist act occur which requires a response on our part. Admiral Monroe, I will leave that to you and to General Allen to ensure that CENTCOM is thoroughly prepared to do this, but I would like a report back soon with some level of detail explaining this."

"Yes, Mr. Curtis. We can provide that for you."

"Splendid. General Prescott, I want you to continue to work closely with Mr. Hernandez to share vital intelligence. If Iran is responsible for a terrorist act and if we start shooting, he will need to have detailed information regarding the position of Iranian forces, especially Iranian naval forces."

"Yes sir, we can do that."

There was momentary silence in the room as each principal considered what his next series of actions would be. Each man now knew where Michael Curtis was driving. Although some, particularly the military officers who were not as adept at bureaucratic infighting and maneuvering, may have questioned his methods, none questioned his objective.

Michael Curtis cleared his throat. "Gentlemen," he said, "I have spoken with the president extensively about the situation in the Islamic Republic. The threat they pose to us and to our interests is very real indeed. In the event that any of our forces are struck, we must be prepared to move quickly with overwhelming force to deal a crippling blow to the Iranians. Nothing short of this will dissuade them from striking out at us again."

"Mr. Curtis," offered Admiral Monroe. He was the senior military man there and felt that he needed to be the one to speak up. "We are certainly making all preparations for any contingency, but you are speaking as if the Iranians have attacked our forces or our interests already. We may just want to wait a bit to be sure that we are not being preemptive about this."

Michael Curtis genuinely liked Admiral Monroe, but he could not let this pass. "Admiral, I appreciate what you are saying. However, we have to be ready for any contingency. General Lawrence and Admiral Flowers are on-scene, and they feel sufficiently alarmed to have asked for more forces and to have put the forces they have in a much higher state of alert. I'm just asking us to make commonsense preparations, that's all."

The men assembled knew that there was more to it than that, but they dared not confront the national security adviser directly. They would go along with the plan—at least for now. How long they would have to do this they could only speculate. Perhaps they would never know.

For his part, Michael Curtis was bothered that precautions that might have been taken and actions that might have been put in place could insulate U.S. forces from the threat of terrorism—but Curtis needed a spark to ignite his plan. He was determined that he would get that spark and soon.

25

TUESDAY WAS A "NO-FLY" DAY ABOARD *CARL VINSON* as the nuclear carrier steamed at twenty-five knots through the Central Arabian Gulf en route to its port call in Muscat, Oman. It was a long way to travel from their operating area in the northeastern portion of the Gulf—over 350 nautical miles to the beginning of the traffic separation scheme leading into the narrow Strait of Hormuz, and then another 150 nautical miles or so through the Strait and on to Muscat.

It seemed a long way to go for a liberty port, but to everyone aboard *Carl Vinson* it was an important trip. The pace of operations for their past several weeks in the Gulf had been unrelenting, and everyone, from Admiral Robinson to the newest seaman or airman aboard the ship, needed a break to recharge their batteries. There were limited opportunities inside the Gulf for shore liberty for American sailors and fewer still for sailors aboard a ninety-five-thousand-ton aircraft carrier, which had more restrictive anchoring and docking constraints than smaller ships. Muscat, with its close-in anchorage and adequate infrastructure of liberty barges, ship services, and the like needed to support an aircraft carrier like *Carl Vinson*, was one of the few good port calls in the entire region.

Heater Robinson sat in his large chair on the port side of the Flag Bridge watching the scores of sailors on the flight deck work on their aircraft. His chief of staff and his Airwing commander stood by him. Robinson was actually letting himself relax for a moment and enjoy some light banter with his two senior advisors.

"Admiral, looks like we've got everything on track for our port call in Muscat," said George Sampson.

"I think so, Chief of Staff. Boy, these kids are ready for a port call. Looking at them working out there is really an inspiration. Looks like they're getting pretty caught up on maintenance, CAG."

"They are," replied Wizard Foster. Then he continued.

"Admiral, so, how is everything else going? I know that we're keeping you super busy. Are you getting enough time to work out, sir?"

"Never enough, CAG, but I'm doing OK. How about you?" replied Heater Robinson. Nice of CAG to inquire about his health. Seemed like it was a little more than just a casual query, though.

"Oh, I'm just fine, Admiral. Just fine. Senior flight surgeon keeps me on the straight and narrow. He's my hero," he replied. Maybe he was being too elliptical, but Wizard Foster was just trying to gently nudge the admiral into taking better care of himself.

The ringing of the Bogen phone next to the admiral's chair preempted the admiral from responding to Wizard.

"Flag Bridge, Chief of Staff," said George Sampson as he picked up the phone. "Roger, we're on our way down," he said as he put the phone back in its cradle.

Heater Robinson looked quizzically at his chief of staff.

"Admiral, that was the Staff TAO. He's got the Fifth Fleet flag lieutenant on the line and he says that Admiral Flowers wants to speak with you. He says that it's urgent, sir."

"It usually is, COS," replied Heater Robinson as he lifted himself out of his chair, jumped down on the deck, and headed aft on the Flag Bridge. Moving quickly, with the CAG and chief of staff in tow, he pushed open the massive blast door marking the entry to the Flag Bridge and headed for the ladder. *What does Flowers want now?* he asked himself as he moved quickly down the five decks and reached the Blue Tile Area. As he got to the War Room, Lieutenant Mike Lumme was holding open the door.

"Admiral, Fifth Fleet is on the phone in TFCC. We can't seem to transfer it to your cabin, some glitch with the phones. Would you mind taking the call in TFCC sir?"

"No, I'll get it there, Mike. Just ask the folks working here to keep the noise down. Can't ever get a really good connection with these KY-68s."

"Admiral Robinson here," he said as he picked up the handset of the secure phone.

The Fifth Fleet flag lieutenant on the other end told him that he would put Admiral Flowers on momentarily. Heater Robinson's mind raced, trying to anticipate what Admiral Flowers would want to talk about.

"Hello, Admiral Flowers."

"Robinson, what's your location now?" replied Flowers. Admiral Robinson noted immediately that his tone was icy.

"Admiral, we're entering the Western Traffic Separation Scheme in the southern Gulf. We're right on track and should pass through the Strait of Hormuz on time."

"Of course. Never want to be late for a port call," snarled Admiral Flowers.

So that was it, thought Heater Robinson. The Fifth Fleet commander had been dead set against this port call from the start. Now he was going to grind him about it.

"No sir, we don't want to be late now that we have laid on our logistic requirements for Muscat."

"No, of course you don't. But do you expect to be ready for the next phase of Exercise Swift Sword when you come out of that visit?"

"Yes sir, we do, Admiral. We got our Airwing up to speed with night landing currency last night, and we've already identified the pilots we have to qualify the first night out of port. I think we'll be ready, sir."

There was a pregnant pause before Admiral Flowers continued.

"Well, you sure as hell better be ready—ready in all respects when you sortie. And another thing. I saw the message that your flagship put out regarding its force protection plans. They looked a little sketchy to me. Don't they believe that there is a threat out there?"

"They do indeed, Admiral," replied Heater Robinson. He had scanned the force protection plans—he couldn't say that he had read them thoroughly—but they had looked adequate to him. He didn't want to go to the wall with his superior officer on this one though, not yet. "I will review them again though, sir, and if there are extra measures that we need to add I'll be certain to add them and beef up our security as appropriate."

"See that you do, Admiral Robinson. You're the one who pushed for this port call—over my objections, I might add—and we finally let you have your way to throw a bone to the political wonks who want my ships to visit every damn port in this theater. But know this, Admiral. If you fail to protect your people against any attacks, I'll have your job. Is that clear?"

"Crystal, sir," replied Heater Robinson.

26

HARD BY THE GEORGE WASHINGTON PARKWAY, THE turnoff for the Central Intelligence Agency Headquarters is relatively obscure. All signs along this scenic drive, which is also a major commuter route in and out of Washington, DC, are relatively subdued, helping to retain the parkway's ambiance. However, the CIA sign is perhaps more subdued than the rest, creating the distinct impression that those who don't have business there should just pass by this exit quickly. No sightseeing.

CIA Headquarters—"Langley" for short, after the small berg closest to it—to those who do frequent it, is hidden away on the Virginia side of the Potomac River, sandwiched between the George Washington Parkway and Columbia Pike. To most of the residents of adjacent upscale McLean, Langley is a quiet, unobtrusive neighbor. The scandals and negative press that earlier made the agency the object of attention and dissension were now a thing of the past.

The DCI had left the nighttime meeting of the National Security Council determined to ensure that the contribution of the agency to solving the Iranian conundrum was both comprehensive and timely. He had gone directly home to his residence after the late-night meeting adjourned, but he was at the agency at 6:00 A.M., long before the busy commuter traffic on the parkway slowed things down.

As he entered the Crystal Palace and the main entry hall of the headquarters, Hernandez was met by a bevy of aides and assistants who had come in hours before their boss in order to begin to draw together the information that he had indicated he wanted. Pausing briefly to thank them for coming in so early, he strode off toward his office as they fell into step with him. He passed through his outer office, tossed his raincoat on one of the chairs in the reception area, and stopped long enough to greet his secretary.

"Good morning, Mr. Hernandez."

"Morning, Erin. Closed door meeting. Just me and the gaggle that followed me in here. We'll grab a pot of coffee and some cups and fend for ourselves."

With that, he and the group in tow were off to the small but well-appointed meeting room near the director's office.

"Ladies and gents, you all know why we are here," the DCI began. "Events in the Arabian Gulf are heating up and heating up fast. We want to be able to give the NSC our best estimate regarding threats to Americans there and we don't have a lot of time to do it. I know that we are working across a lot of time zones and that you all have had to put some people out—including yourselves—to do this quickly. Let's go around the table and see what we have."

Marty Adams spoke first. "Sir, we do not have a complete picture of the extent of terrorist infiltration into the countries around the Gulf littoral. We do feel very confident that due to the extent of the training that went on in the Iranian camps, there is an extremely high probability that any terrorist activity in the next several days or weeks would be logically attributable to Iran."

"Logically attributable to Iran might not be quite enough to rain destruction down on their country if some group somewhere gets pissed off and blows something up one day, Marty." The DCI didn't want to make Marty Adams look bad, but he needed to focus the group on pulling together hard evidence that would stand up to scrutiny at the NSC. "OK, what else?"

Sam Lipman spoke up next. "We have come into some specific information which may help us point the finger a little more specifically. Airport security at Bahrain International found two bags with explosives in the luggage that was unloaded from a flight from Tehran. Dogs lit on the stuff. No names on the bags of course. Security was very tight at the time and they speculate that the passengers who transported them into the country fled. The Bahrainis are working incredibly hard to comb for anyone who recently entered the country."

"What else?" said Hernandez, now happier because he was getting some definitive information.

"There are some reports, but we don't give them much credence, that an Iranian flagged merchant is headed for UAE, either Abu Dhabi or Dubai, perhaps via the port at Jabel Ali. We are watching the port facility really carefully and are pretty confident we won't miss anything that tries to slip in."

"Good, anything else?" Hernandez was impressed that his staff had been able to pull this much together in so short a time.

"There's one more, sir. It's based on pretty sketchy information, and we were inclined to discount it, but it's building a strong circumstantial case. We have been told at least four Hezbollah agents entered Muscat, Oman on a flight from Tehran almost a week ago. Usually we don't focus too much on them, because Muscat is just a convenient jumping-off point to travel to other locations such as Qatar, Bahrain, Saudi Arabia, and other countries. But no one can confirm that they have left Oman, and their arrival came very soon after the port call for *Carl Vinson* was announced. It may just be a coincidence, but we assess that they may pose a threat to the carrier or its crew."

"We announce our carrier visits?" said Hernandez.

"Not exactly announce, sir," said Admiral George Baldwin, the CIA deputy director, and the next most senior person to the DCI in the room. "There are some long lead time items incident to a carrier's visit to any port—arrangements with husbandry agents to procure supplies, advance permission to fly in that country's airspace, clearances for military personnel transferring to come in and out of the country, rerouting of the airborne logistics train that brings supplies from the States to support the carrier; that sort of thing. By the time the carrier arrives, it's a well-known happening."

Hernandez didn't particularly like having this news dropped on him in this forum. "Well, Admiral, that certainly doesn't make our job any easier, does it?"

Vice Admiral Baldwin realized that he had been giving his boss a tutorial and backed off immediately. "No sir, normally it's not a problem, but I suppose that when the terrorist threat is high we might want to modify our procedures."

"Good, Admiral. Thank you." Turning back to Lipman, Hernandez said, "Now Sam, what else do we know about this situation in Oman?"

"There's not a lot else we are certain of, sir. We have gotten an agreement from Ambassador Young and the US-DAO to brief *Carl Vinson* extensively on the potential threat. The carrier will be anchored out, and they should have no trouble maintaining adequate security for the ship itself. We also feel confident that they can make the crew aware of how to protect themselves while ashore; not being alone in bars or alleys in the wee hours of the morning, not being too conspicuous, that sort of thing."

"It's kind of hard to make, what, three thousand sailors inconspicuous."

"Five thousand," offered Vice Admiral Baldwin. He hesitated to speak up, but he wanted to be sure that the DCI understood the magnitude of the problem. Hernandez decided to tap into the admiral's expertise.

"Admiral, didn't you have command of a carrier task group assigned to the Arabian Gulf a while ago?"

"Yes sir, I did. Kitty Hawk Task Group. Not too many years ago."

"If you were the task group commander, and you knew what we know now, what would your concerns be?"

Vice Admiral Baldwin was glad that his expertise was being tapped for this. He had thought about just this sort of scenario and had some strong opinions.

"Well sir, whoever is supporting these terrorists—Iran, we have to assume from what we know—is probably not really pleased with the government of Oman for letting the carrier come here in the first place. They're probably especially angry because they like to think that they have some degree of influence with the sultanate. So they probably want to lash out, not only at the carrier but at the government too. I don't see any attack on government buildings in the offing, they're pretty well protected and that wouldn't make the connection with the United States. No, what my greatest fear would be is their attacking a large group of my sailors in a way that would also destroy some major building in the country."

"How would they accomplish such a thing?" asked the DCI, now genuinely concerned by the admiral's comments.

"My guess is that if there really are terrorists in-country bent on doing what we think they will do—and if they can pull it off—they'll probably look to target some hotel where we have a large group of sailors staying. Maybe one that contains a large collection of our officers, too. The Omanis don't have the type of security that we have seen the Bahrainis put up in places like the Manai Plaza in Manama. It would be an easy hit."

"So how do we protect against that? What recommendations can we push up to the NSC?" Hernandez was truly perplexed. A career bureaucrat, he had risen through the ranks via that great burcaucratic game, Playing It Safe. Of all the bureaucracies in government, the intelligence apparatus was perhaps the most conservative. The bureaucratic ethic of the CIA depended on never being wrong. To predict something with certainty, and then have it not happen, was professional suicide. The DCI had served for decades and had continued to succeed because he had avoided getting burned by a wrong guess. Now he was on the spot in a time-sensitive situation where he had to make a call. It was a situation that made him extremely uncomfortable.

"Well sir," Admiral Baldwin continued, "Mr. Lipman has given us what sounds like pretty reliable data that these Hezbollah agents are in Muscat. They just left the camps in Lebanon. Iran's rhetoric has been getting more and more strident lately. We don't know for certain that they intend to strike at our people, but it might be wise to deny them the opportunity to do that."

"What are you recommending?" asked the DCI.

"We can cancel the Muscat port visit for *Carl Vinson*, for openers," responded the admiral.

"How would the Navy feel about that?"

"If their people were in harm's way, I think they'd be glad that they weren't going there."

"Well, that would seem to make sense, from my perspective."

The discussions continued for a protracted time. The DCI was unsure of what to do and felt that the more they discussed it, the more readily a solution would present itself. It was not to be. The more they talked, the tougher the conundrum became. Finally, their meeting broke up just before 10:00 A.M. The DCI thanked all of his people for what they had contributed. As everyone departed, Admiral Baldwin stayed behind.

"Mr. Director, I don't want to press, but if we want to do something we need to move quickly. *Carl Vinson* passed through the Strait of Hormuz hours ago."

Pete Hernandez finally decided he had to do something. He would call Michael Curtis as soon as he could return to his office. "Thank you Admiral, I'll take it from here."

27

"ANCHORED, SHIFT COLORS!" THE CALL BY THE BOSN' mate over *Carl Vinson*'s 1 MC was followed by the long blast of a whistle. Simultaneously, the National Ensign that was flying from the mainmast was hauled down smartly, while the Union Jack was raised on the bow and another National Ensign was raised on the stern. It was a smart military maneuver that had occurred on *Carl Vinson* hundreds of times before, but this sunny morning off the coast of Muscat, Oman, her sailors had a little extra zip in their actions as the prospect of liberty in this old port city beckoned them.

As *Carl Vinson* turned and pointed up into the wind at her anchor, her crew busied themselves with a hundred different tasks. Her engineers shut down portions of the engineering plant not needed now that the ship was anchored, her deck crew worked at making fast the camel—the huge bargelike device used as a platform to launch and receive her liberty boats—to the stern of the ship, shore patrol groups got outfitted in their uniforms, and the like. Deep inside the berthing compartments throughout the ship, the mood was festive as the crew prepared for the first liberty that they had seen in over a month. Civilian clothing came out of lockers, sailors lined up at the ship's ATMs to fill their wallets with spending money, and there was a race to get up to the hangar bay to join the already swelling liberty lines of sailors waiting to go ashore.

Carl Vinson's advance party had been ashore for two days, making all the necessary arrangements incident to an aircraft carrier's pulling into a foreign port and all that seemed to remain was for *Carl Vinson* to put her extensive liberty party ashore.

Several miles down the coast, at the Intercontinental Hotel, were officers from various squadrons and departments aboard *Carl Vinson* who had flown in on the COD a day prior to make arrangements for admin rooms where groups of officers would gather to rest, relax, and unwind. The Intercontinental, which boasted great amenities and fronted a beautiful beach, appeared to be the hotel of choice for *Carl Vinson* while it was in Muscat. Her young, aggressive manager, Patrick Cox, was determined to make whatever concessions and arrangements he had to in order to make his hotel *the* place to be.

The Intercontinental's spacious lawns were already being roped off and a small bandstand was being constructed to accommodate a battle of the bands that would, Cox hoped, draw even more of *Carl Vinson*'s crew to the hotel. Cox cast a wide net throughout Muscat among local vendors to bring in sufficient quantities of beverages, food, and other items to accommodate the expected influx of crewmembers there. Throughout the capital, everyone, from cab drivers to merchants, knew that the Intercontinental was where sailors would want to go.

At the Intercontinental's imposing entrance, two shabbily dressed men, both in their early twenties, busied themselves washing the large all-glass inner and outer doorways to the hotel. The windows were washed frequently, not by hotel employees but by contracted maintenance personnel. As the two young men completed the outer windows and moved through the entry area, they didn't even stop to look at the spectacular stone murals on either wall of the entryway but began working on the inner glass doors. The Intercontinental's well-heeled clientele were too busy to notice, and if they did, they thought nothing of the fact that one of the two men had a collapsible tape measure and was taking measurements of the height and width of the center sliding doors. Their washing complete, the two young men melted away as quietly as they had come.

Back aboard *Carl Vinson*, the lines of sailors in the hangar bay swelled as the Deck Department made their final preparations to secure the large camel to the stern of the ship. The liberty boats that *Carl Vinson* had contracted for stood off a short way away, waiting for the opportunity to come alongside the camel and begin taking her sailors ashore. The lines had to move from time to time as a score of Bosn' mates maneuvered first the Admiral's Barge, and then the Captain's Gig, to elevator number four, where they were then lowered into the water.

In *Carl Vinson*'s War Room, Admiral Robinson gathered his key commanders for the final meeting they would have for the next few days. He was satisfied that they were well-prepared for Phase II of Exercise Swift Sword and was convinced that they would come out of this port visit refreshed and ready to perform well in the exercise.

"CAG, I know that we've got concerns about aircraft availability, how is it looking for resupply of spare parts while we're here?"

"Not too bad, Admiral. There are a lot of spare parts waiting for us in Muscat, and the supply channel's working pretty well too, I think."

"Good," said Heater Robinson. "Commodore, how are we covering things in the Gulf while we're in port?"

"Admiral, we've got things pretty well covered," said Jim Hughes. "Due to the distances and communications limitations, we're a little bit constrained down here in Oman. I've turned over Maritime Interception duties to DESRON 50, and they're embarking in *Laboon* in the Northern Gulf. *Doyle* will be up there with her and will help patrol with her LAMPS helos. We're not real deep, but we can cover it for the four days we're here."

"Great," responded the admiral. Heater Robinson had trained his senior officers well, and they knew how to get out ahead of the problem. "Ops O, how's the SOE looking for Phase II?" The SOE, or Schedule of Events, was just what its name implied—the master schedule for everything that the task group intended to do during the upcoming Exercise Swift Sword Phase II. The SOE for Swift Sword Phase II was absolutely jam-packed.

"Admiral. We've been round and round with Fifth Fleet staff on this," replied Bill Durham. "We've tried to narrow the scope of this exercise, but they keep insisting that we add more and more events. There is nothing that is planned that isn't doable, but it's very success-oriented, and if we have even a bit of a breakdown here or there, the whole SOE is in jeopardy. At this point, we just have to run with it and see what happens."

"I agree. If we get in a bind, I can work with Admiral Flowers to alter things as necessary." Heater Robinson was putting on the best professional face that he could in front of his senior commanders, but he was continuously frustrated by Admiral Flowers's micro-managing this exercise, possibly to the detriment of his crew.

"OK gents, from an operational and maintenance standpoint, I'm pretty happy with where we stand. Before we put too many sailors ashore we need to be sure that our force protection measures are airtight. Captain, have we done everything that we can?" the admiral asked, turning to Craig Vandegrift.

"I think that we have, Admiral," replied *Carl Vinson*'s CO, a little bit curious as to why Admiral Robinson was revisiting an issue that was typically handled by Vandegrift and his subordinates and not brought to the admiral's level. "We have taken all the specific measures that Fifth Fleet requires us to take."

"And we think that we'll be all right with what we have set up now?" inquired the admiral. He didn't himself want to micro-manage, but Admiral Flowers's cautions forced him to, to some extent.

"I think that we have taken all reasonable precautions that we can, Admiral. We have set a curfew for our people and have briefed them thoroughly on being cautious while they are here. The junior folks have to be off the streets by midnight. I think that we are OK, sir."

"Good. These people deserve liberty badly, but we've got to keep them safe."

Just a few yards from the War Room, CARGRU SEVEN's chief of staff, Captain George Sampson, dealt with the plethora of details incident to a carrier's making a port call. He talked with his command duty officer, spoke with the ship's executive officer several times, took custody of phones and beepers for him and the admiral, went over the admiral's busy social schedule with the flag lieutenant, reviewed the press guidance for the port visit that the public affairs officer had obtained from Fifth Fleet, and attended to a dozen other small, but significant, details. He did not have time to go through the early morning ritual of reading his message traffic. Had he done so, he might have noticed that the threat assessment for Oman had just been increased to the highest assignable level.

*   *   *

In a tiny garage a few miles from the Intercontinental, men were packing a van quickly, but with care. It really wasn't a complex task—the van was large, and their explosives were powerful. Bringing them into the sultanate had been laughably easy; they could have readily brought in much more. However, the size of the van had been selected specifically to do the job and just fit into the orifice that it needed to.

Back aboard *Carl Vinson*, in the Blue Tile Area, Lieutenant Mike Lumme helped Admiral Robinson with his uniforms as the admiral and other senior officers prepared for the obligatory round of calls on Omani dignitaries, as well as on the American ambassador. The admiral was not in a good mood—he still had a junior officer's love of liberty and he viewed these calls as a waste of his time and energy. Worse, he couldn't even start the calls until he welcomed the Naval Attaché aboard—and he wouldn't be there for another hour. He'd just as soon wave off all of the diplomatic niceties, but then that would give Admiral Flowers just one more thing to be on his case about. He'd be back at sea, on the line in the Gulf, and under Flowers's thumb soon enough.

28

VICE ADMIRAL HARRY FLOWERS SAT AT HIS DESK READING the morning's message traffic. His duty officer had reported that *Carl Vinson* was anchored off Muscat, and it just served to remind him how angry he was that he had been overruled regarding the carrier's port visit their need for some relief be damned. The admiral didn't like being overruled, hell, in his last job as inspector general no one dared overrule him. He was smart enough to know that this fight was already over. He would move on to the next one. He would turn up the gain on Exercise Swift Sword and run it at a level of intensity never before seen in the Arabian Gulf. He would make his mark early here. No slow ramp-up for him.

Admiral Flowers was happy enough with that thought to actually take a moment and survey his well-appointed office. Compared to the large office he had had at the Washington Navy Yard when he was inspector general, his Fifth Fleet Headquarters office was rather smallish, but it was magnificently appointed. From his imposing, modern desk he looked out on a well-manicured courtyard. He never went out there, actually—didn't much like the sun—but it presented an inviting appearance. Between his desk and the courtyard was a tastefully decorated reception area, with a large black leather sofa against the left-hand wall and two large matching chairs flanking a low table. Immediately to the left of his desk was the obligatory map of the region, better for his guests to understand that the admiral was always focused on his job. To the right was an impressive entertainment center with a thirty-one-inch television constantly tuned to CNN, as well as all the other accouterments. In the far right-hand corner, on either side of his flag display, were the entrance to his private rest room, a significant perk, and the private hallway to his chief of staff's office. Completing the ambiance were a number of beautiful Persian rugs and several ferns tastefully presented in large copper urns on low, four-legged stands. It was an office designed to impress, and Admiral Flowers used it wisely to do that with visiting ambassadors, military leaders, businessmen, and other dignitaries.

He was interrupted from his musings as his chief of staff knocked first, then entered from the private hallway. Flowers was finding Captain Dennis a little easier to work with once he had given him a few tongue lashings and the aviator had bent to his will.

"Admiral, Intel and Ops wanted to get on your calendar this morning as soon as they could," said Bolter Dennis.

"What's the issue, can't it wait for the normal staff meeting at 10:00?"

"They don't think so, Admiral. It has to do with some

sensitive reports that have come in during the early hours of the morning about threat conditions in Oman. I don't have all the details, but they're ready to present them as soon as you are available, sir."

Flowers would have more respect for Dennis if he had his shit together. He should have grilled the other officers and extracted all the info from them, not come in here unarmed. Damn, he'd just have to put up with it.

"OK, five minutes, my conference room."

"Seats, gents," said Admiral Flowers as he entered his small executive meeting room, just across the reception area from his office. With its beautiful polished wood table and chairs, its recessed lighting, and its multi-panel sliding glass doors, this small conference room was appointed as well as many corporate boardrooms. Harry Flowers felt very at home here.

He surveyed the faces around the table looking back at him. In addition to Bolter Dennis, the group included his operations officer, Captain Carl Mullen, his intelligence officer, Captain Don Fraser, and his legal officer, Commander Mike Oakes. It was a small, select group, but that was all that was necessary for this meeting.

"OK, let's have it," said the admiral, looking at his chief of staff. "You all asked for this meeting."

"Admiral, we have just come across some disturbing intelligence," began Captain Don Fraser. "The report that we have indicates there are at least four Hezbollah agents in Muscat, and we assess that there is a probability that they will try to make an attack on our sailors while they are in Oman. I got this report via flash precedence message at 0200 this morning. I elected not to awaken you, Admiral. However, I sent a message to Admiral Robinson's staff on *Carl Vinson* to alert them."

Admiral Flowers was actually glad to see that his staff was taking some kind of initiative. Manama, Bahrain, was not at the top of anyone's preference card as a place to be assigned, and too often, Fifth Fleet wound up saddled with officers who were unassignable elsewhere. Maybe if he continued to work on them they would come around.

"Good, have we gotten an acknowledgement that they've received it yet?"

"No, sir. We haven't been able to establish comms on any of our normal nets," interjected Captain Carl Mullen. "What we wanted to do, Admiral, was to see if we need to revisit this whole port call issue with *Carl Vinson*, perhaps see if we should consider waving this entire thing off, at least until the threat level diminishes."

"I want those nets established ASAP, I don't care how many of those comm weenies we have to inconvenience."

"Yes sir," continued the ops officer, pressing Admiral Flowers as far as he dared press him. "But do you think that we need to put the brakes on this port call?"

"Put the brakes on this port call? Me? You gents seem to have an awfully short memory. I have been against this port call from day one. It interferes with the biggest exercise that's been conducted in this AOR in two years. I pushed this up the chain once and got told to sit down and shut up. This report of terrorist activity came down the chain of command, so if they know something more than these 'suspicions,' then they can wave this off. I've gone to the well once, that's enough. You all just work on getting the carrier notified, that's all."

The discussion among his small circle of close advisors continued as Admiral Flowers continued to emphasize that CARGRU SEVEN and *Carl Vinson* must be notified as soon as possible of the danger that they might encounter in Muscat. He forced them to work through every combination and permutation of methods to afford the carrier—and, more importantly, her sailors—the greatest possible degree of protection. Hardheaded as he might be, Vice Admiral Harry Flowers drew the line where the safety and security of Navy Bluejackets were concerned.

Their discussions were about finished when the duty yeoman pulled the sliding glass door to the conference room open. "Admiral," began the petty officer, "there's a Captain Perry on the line for you. I told him that you were in a meeting but he insisted that I tell you that it was very important that he speak with you."

"Tell him I'll be right there," the admiral replied. Then,

turning to his staff, he said, "I'm dissatisfied with the lack of progress in contacting the staff and the ship. Ops O, go over to the Watch Center and make something happen. This port visit's not going to get derailed, but I want Admiral Robinson and his people to know about the dangers they may face." Admiral Flowers moved quickly out of the conference room.

The staff was not certain why the admiral was unwilling to fight the *Carl Vinson*'s going into Muscat more vigorously than he was. Had they heard his conversation with Captain Perry, they would have been far less perplexed.

"Good morning, Admiral," Captain Perry began. "I am sorry to pull you out of a meeting sir, but things are moving quickly here."

"I'm sure that they are, Tom." Harry Flowers rarely displayed this degree of familiarity with officers junior to him, but Perry was an exception. Not only was he the admiral's protégé but Perry was his only reliable link with what was going on in the Pentagon, and he was the only one who could or would provide him with the minute-by-minute details of the deliberations of the National Security Council.

"Admiral," continued Perry, "as you know, intelligence is pouring in that strongly suggests some kind of terrorist attack against American forces in Muscat. We haven't gotten a formal CIA report yet, seems to be some hang-up at the agency, but all the circumstantial stuff points to it."

"I know that Tom, and we're working on warning the Carl Vinson Battle Group. We'll have them take all possible precautions."

"Admiral, these are strong signals. No one here is ready to go out on a limb and say that the attack is going to happen, but it looks extremely bad."

"I know Tom, I know." Flowers was vacillating between being understanding and being patronizing. Perry hadn't served in a ship at sea in a while, let alone in the Gulf. He didn't have the picture that the admiral had.

"But Admiral, can't we at least call off the port call? Maybe not let anyone go ashore?"

Now Flowers knew how detached Perry really was. He

should have known how hard he had fought the port visit. He didn't have time to give Perry a tutorial on it.

"Look Tom, it's too late for that. We have a huge liberty party ashore already. We're trying every means possible to alert the battle group's leadership to take all possible precautions. We're really doing everything humanly possible."

"I know Admiral, I just . . ."

Flowers cut him off. "You just keep me posted . . . hear?"

29

ANNE O'CONNOR AND CHRISSIE LINDER, AS WELL AS two other VS-35 Blue Wolf officers, alighted from the taxi in front of the Muscat Intercontinental Hotel. A doorman dressed in traditional garb with a heavily jeweled dagger opened the taxi door for them and made a deep bow. As they fished their bags out of the trunk of the cab, they were in a giddy mood. They had heard word that their advance crew had gotten one of the best junior suites in the hotel and that their admin was going to be the envy of the entire Airwing. They were ready to roll.

For Anne, this would be a welcome break. The flying had been great and she was at the top of her game professionally, but she felt a bit isolated on *Carl Vinson*. The Navy had looked like a great adventure—and it was—but there was no one to share it with, no one she could *really* talk to, no one she could confide in, except Chrissie. Oh sure, she was a member of the Blue Wolf Ready Room, and her fellow pilots had been friendly and cordial, but she was one of four *women* pilots in their ready room. And she couldn't just hang around with them that would make it look like they were a scared, clucking mess. Besides, Laura Meechan was recently married and all she could talk about was how hot her husband was, and Kate Von Dressel was so incredibly stuck up that *no one* wanted to talk with her. Even Chrissie was now engaged to a P-3 pilot on the East Coast and seemed to want to spend hours a day e-mailing him. Anne understood, and was happy for her, but she sure wasn't much fun to goof around with any more.

Anne was almost paranoid about having anything that even vaguely resembled a relationship with any of the other pilots in the Airwing. The horror stories about women officers who had gotten tangled up in "Airwing romances" made her feel that she had to be totally standoffish with her fellow pilots and flight officers. It was too bad, there were a ton of single guys in the Airwing. A lot of them seemed like really nice guys, and some of them were hunks, but Anne had decided that that was territory she didn't want to enter. There was just too big of a downside.

That's why she had agreed to play tennis with Rick. Rick had played on the tennis team at the University of Virginia, and she had played a lot of tennis before she had dedicated herself to varsity swimming at the Naval Academy. Swimming really wasn't much of a carryover sport, so since graduation she'd found herself getting back into tennis a lot. What they were doing was just tuning up their games—nothing else—and it wouldn't give anyone on the ship anything to talk about. As the OIC of the SEAL detachment, Rick was an outsider too, not part of the inner Airwing group, though the HS-4 bubbas were doing their best to adopt him. Anne felt that she could at least talk to him and not have every word make it back to the Airwing. It was going to be fun—she just hoped that her game hadn't fallen apart too badly on the ship.

In the heart of Muscat's downtown area, in a small garage, the men were finished packing a DHL van with 600 pounds of high explosives. The van had just been reported missing that morning, and Omani authorities had assured the company they would quickly find it. It was, after all, distinctively painted.

* * *

As Anne O'Connor, Chrissie Linder, and their friends entered the lobby of the Muscat Intercontinental, they paused to take it all in. The interior of the hotel was built around a huge atrium with lush plants, a cascading waterfall, and multi-level walks and well-appointed shops and restaurants. The entryway to each room on all of the floors opened up onto a walkway that, in turn, looked down on this impressive center area. In the middle of this spectacular scene stood a tall shaft with three large elevators, which whisked passengers to and from their rooms.

Anne and Chrissie were part of the Blue Wolf admin, but the summer rates at the Intercontinental were reasonable and Chrissie had talked Anne and Laura Meechan into springing for a room of their own. Laura had the duty today, but she'd be out tomorrow. It was a good plan, they thought; they'd hang with the guys in the squadron admin, but wouldn't have to stay there at night amidst the piles of beer cans and snoring male officers, to say nothing of having to fight two dozen guys for one of two bathrooms. Blend as they might, the women felt that they had to draw the line somewhere.

Anne and Chrissie finished checking in, grabbed their keys, and walked briskly to the glass-walled elevator for the quick ride up to the ninth floor. They walked out, found their room, 912, and pushed the door open. It was spectacular. Immediately below their room was the Intercontinental's spectacular swimming pool, half-covered to accommodate those who needed the shade, open at the near end for those who preferred to bake in the 100-plus degree heat. Beyond that was a large, lush, grassy area. To the right was the tennis complex—many courts, a small pro shop, and some indoor squash courts. Beyond that lay the Gulf of Oman. Anne drew in deeply, feeling the ambiance surround her. This was perfect.

One of the men returned to the garage and gave the all-clear. A small, nondescript car moved out of the garage first and proceeded down the narrow alley. The van followed a respectable distance beyond—it didn't need to follow too closely, that might arouse suspicion. They had driven the route before many times in another car, there would be no surprises, they had practiced this many times.

Rick, Jake, and some of the other HS-4 bubbas finally got to the Intercontinental and checked into their admin. Rick was enjoying his professional and personal association with these guys. They had brought him into the tight community of their ready room, and he was having the time of his life with them. Anne O'Connor had been a fun surprise, too. There was no one else on the ship who was much of a tennis player, but Anne was, well, pretty tough—and she took it kind of seriously. He knew that she had to be really careful about the semblance of any kind of "shipboard romance," but the idea of playing tennis together seemed like an innocent enough venue. Playing tennis also helped him remember his days at UVA, when life was a lot simpler. They'd go for it here in Muscat and see what happened.

That's why he felt dread every time he checked his e-mail from "his friends." He didn't want this to end. Going to sea, preparing for a tough job as a SEAL, flying as part of a Combat Search and Rescue team—Rick had decided that his new life might be better than the old one. He'd give it some time, but life was blissfully more straightforward doing what he was doing now. He thought that it wasn't likely to get much better than this. He wondered what the agency would think if he tried that one out on them. Maybe they weren't ready for that yet.

The car led the van through the streets purposefully, moving slowly, cautiously. Three men in the car, one man in the van. The others were already sanitizing the garage they had used so that no one would be able to trace their presence there. They knew that the Omani authorities would be under enormous pressure and would stop at nothing to track them down. It would be a futile attempt on their part.

30

THE HEAVY DOOR CLOSED BEHIND HIM AS THE FIFTH Fleet operations officer, Captain Carl Mullen, burst into the TFCC. He was in a full rage as he glowered over the watch-standers furiously working phones and radios. He shouted at the command duty officer, Commander Jose Gonzalas, demanding to know why he could not get through to CAR-GRU SEVEN aboard *Carl Vinson*. Admiral Flowers had ordered him to have the word of a probable attack against Navy personnel in Muscat passed to Admiral Robinson's staff, and now he was unable to make that happen.

"Commander, it is beyond belief, it is beyond fucking belief, that you cannot raise *Carl Vinson* on any net. What in the hell are you people doing in here?" shouted Mullen.

"Captain, I am trying," said Gonzalas. "I can't raise them on Task Group Command. No matter how many times I call, no one answers."

"Are you trying UHF satellite or HF?"

"HF. The satellite path doesn't give us reliable UHF coverage here. HF should work, but propagation paths have been unreliable of late."

"What else are you trying?" asked Mullen. With each invective from the ops officer, the petty officers manning the equipment in TFCC seemed to retreat into a deeper defensive crouch, as if his words could physically hurt them.

"The STEL line is not synching up, I think that either us or them have bad crypto. . . . I am trying to use the KY-68, and it sounds like I'm going out but they are not answering it at their end."

"What do you mean, not answering? I've been aboard

Carl Vinson. Their KY-68 is in their TFCC and it is manned twenty-four hours a day, in port and at sea. I can't believe this!"

Commander Gonzalas was a ninety-day reservist, sent to Fifth Fleet Headquarters in Bahrain to serve his active duty time. Such ninety-day hired help were not there long enough to be given "real jobs," so they were made permanent watchstanders. It was a source of consternation to the permanent Fifth Fleet staff members, but none of them were anxious to add standing watches to the brutal days that Admiral Flowers put them through, so they had resigned themselves to merely bitching about the lack of professionalism of the people manning their TFCC and did virtually nothing to help them do their jobs more effectively.

"Captain," offered the commander, "without actually being on *Carl Vinson*, I can't tell you what their problem is. All I can do is keep trying."

There was nothing else that Carl Mullen could do here. He directed Gonzalas to call the staff information operations officer—the N-6—Commander Beth McDaniel, who was responsible for C4I, the Navy acronym for Command, Control, Communications, Computers and Intelligence, and tell her to untangle this mess. He would report back to Admiral Flowers that he had "kicked butt" in TFCC and was going to have the N-6's ass for this. That should placate his boss for the moment.

With the departure of the raving operations officer, Commander Gonzalas was able to focus on trying to contact *Carl Vinson*. Ninety-day reservist or not, he was determined to do his best to warn his fellow Navy men and women. He assigned one petty officer to keep working the KY-68 continuously, while he had another draft a flash precedence message to CARGRU SEVEN, spelling out the danger in a few paragraphs. Even with all the sophisticated voice nets that were available, Gonzalas knew that a flash message, which was pushed through the system faster than any others, would reach the staff almost immediately. This done, he walked through the door on the right-hand side of TFCC and entered the Staff Intelligence Center. There he encountered Lieutenant Commander Ryan Shue, another ninety-day reservist, who was standing the intel watch.

"Ryan," he began. It seemed much easier for the reservists of different ranks to maintain a first-name familiarity than it did for the regular Navy types. "I've got to get some word to *Carl Vinson*, and I can't raise them on any of our nets. I'm drafting a flash message now, but do you have any way I can get to them faster?"

"Yeah, I think so," said Shue. "We've got classified e-mail via SIPRNET. I'll sit you down at our terminal, and you can bang something out to them."

"Great. Lead on," replied Gonzalas. This would have to be quick, as he wasn't supposed to leave his watch station in TFCC. Quick and to the point, basically a much shorter version of the flash message he had just dictated to the petty officer in TFCC. He considered running his proposed message by the operations officer, but every instinct told him to take his best shot and do this fast. After Shue set him up and entered the right code words into the terminal, Gonzalas sat down and typed furiously:

FROM: COMFIVEFLT
TO: CCG7
SUBJ: TERRORIST THREAT
PASSED FROM FIFTH FLEET COMMANDER TO ADMIRAL ROBINSON. DELIVER IMMEDIATELY.
THERE IS AN EXTREMELY HIGH PROBABILITY THAT HEZBOLLAH TERRORISTS IN-COUNTRY OMAN WILL ATTEMPT AN ATTACK ON U.S. NAVY PERSONNEL AT A LARGE PUBLIC PLACE IN MUSCAT. HOTELS HOUSING LARGE NUMBERS OF *CARL VINSON* SAILORS ARE CONSIDERED ESPECIALLY VULNERABLE. RECOMMEND THAT LARGE GATHERINGS OF *CARL VINSON* PERSONNEL BE AVOIDED AT ALL COSTS AND THAT EXTRA SECURITY PRECAUTIONS BE TAKEN ACROSS THE BOARD. COMFIFTHFLEET TFCC WATCH OFFICER SENDS.

Satisfied that he had done his best here, Gonzalas thanked Shue and returned to TFCC to see if his flash message was completed yet, and also to see if any progress had been made on getting through on the KY-68 or any other nets.

Aboard *Carl Vinson*, the normal swirl of activities incident to any first day in port was underway. The CARGRU SEVEN spaces were full of staff officers and enlisted men and women scurrying about, most departing on liberty, but a few preparing to stand their watches. The transition between the underway watch team, which populated TFCC, and the inport watch team, which had just one watchstander in TFCC, was not as seamless as it should have been. Operations Specialist Second Class Doug Lewis was assigned the TFCC radio watch, but he was also the security petty officer charged with ensuring that all safes were locked up during inport periods, as well as ensuring that no classified publications were left out and about. He had been royally chewed out by the chief of staff last inport period for not checking an obscure safe in the back of the ops office, and once was enough. He figured that they couldn't do anything for anybody while they were anchored, since all the warfare commander assignments had been dealt out already. He could leave TFCC for a few minutes.

Gonzalas hovered over the harried petty officer as she tried the KY-68 yet another time. "I'm sure that I'm getting through, Commander, but it just rings and rings."

"OK, just keep at it," responded Gonzalas.

An identical ringing punctuated the silence in TFCC aboard *Carl Vinson*. Petty Officer Lewis was checking safes in the operations office across the passageway from the War Room. The only person in the near vicinity was Lieutenant Hank Caine, one of *Carl Vinson*'s intel officers, who was standing the intel watch in SUPPLOT behind the heavy steel door adjacent to both TFCC and the War Room. Caine did not hear the insistent ringing of the KY-68 in TFCC next door. Having the watch sucked, but he was making the best of it and working on his Naval War College correspondence courses in the quiet of SUPPLOT. There was a mild *beep*, and Caine looked up to see an indication that a classified e-mail had popped up on his SIPRNET circuit. Probably some obscure intel factoid about something an ocean away. He almost decided to ignore it until he'd finished at least a chapter of his textbook on World War II, but he glanced up for just a second to ensure that the message was, in fact, unimportant nuisance info.

"Holy shit," Caine heard himself shout.

Caine stared at the e-mail on his screen. He could not believe what he was reading. He had been in Fifth Fleet's intel center and could picture one of the intel types there typing this out. This couldn't be a drill, could it? An exercise?

He pressed the bitch box that connected SUPPLOT with TFCC.

"TFCC, SUPPLOT!"

No answer.

"TFCC, SUPPLOT, over."

Still no answer.

Caine picked up his red phone and dialed SUPPLOT.

It just rang.

He dialed the War Room.

No answer.

Caine couldn't stand it anymore. He was a disciplined professional, but he had to find someone, anyone, to tell.

Caine dashed to the door of SUPPLOT and flung it open. It slammed hard behind him. He took the few steps into TFCC. No one. The phone was ringing, but he dared not pick it up—probably some meaningless call—all it would do was slow him down if he had to write down a message. He turned around and walked into the War Room. He looked to his left at the large slate-gray metallic door with one large star that led into Admiral Robinson's office and cabin. He had never been in the admiral's cabin. Should he call first? Should he knock?

Caine mustered up all the courage he could and rushed the door. He turned the handle. Locked. He turned it again, jiggling it. Nothing.

Suddenly, the door opened, and Admiral Robinson stood there in his white uniform, his large frame filling the doorway.

"Yes, Lieutenant?"

"Admiral, I, well, we . . . ," Caine stammered. Somehow he had not expected to see the admiral himself. An aide, perhaps, but the admiral! Caine tried to form the words, but his mouth just moved.

"Well, what is it, Lieutenant?"

Hank Caine watched the admiral's eyes grow wide and his jaw drop as he poured out the details of the message he had just received.

31

PATRICK COX HAD SUCCEEDED BEYOND HIS WILDEST expectations. A combination of having one of the finest facilities in Muscat, his reasonable rates, his willingness to work with the Navy to provide them with special deals, and his convincing the husbandry agent to push his hotel to the *Carl Vinson* and her embarked staffs had ensured a sellout for the entire inport period. Officers, chief petty officers, and common sailors had been lined up in his lobby to reserve rooms, making this a banner day for Cox, arguably the best he had ever had in the hotel business.

They drove the DHL van at just under the speed limit, determined to do nothing to attract any additional attention to themselves. They had chosen the right stolen vehicle carefully. With over a dozen of these vans in the city of Muscat, it was easy to blend in. They only had a few miles to travel from their garage to the Intercontinental, and they wanted to get there unchallenged. They also sent an advance car out ahead of the van to ensure that the van did not encounter any surprises during its travel.

*   *   *

Anne and Rick were halfway through their second set. The heat was beginning to slow them down a bit, causing them to work up quite a sweat and take more time on the court changeovers every two games. This gave them the opportunity to talk casually about life on an aircraft carrier, and Anne took advantage of the age-old right of a sailor to complain by letting Rick in on how hard it was to buy women's uniforms aboard ship and how she often felt like she was under a microscope, being one of only four female aviators and an unattached one at that. Slowly, Rick came to realize how unique he was as someone Anne could just unburden herself to.

Their advance car circled slowly through the Intercontinental's driveway. Only two cabs stood by for fares, and they were well off to the right of the main entry. It was late enough in the afternoon that few people were being dropped off. It looked like the van would have a clear path.

Anne and Rick were not the only ones enjoying themselves. Scores of *Carl Vinson* crewmembers, primarily officers, were lounging at the pool or at various spots around the hotel's expansive lawn. Others were using the small health club, unwilling to be away from a gym for even a day. Many others were simply enjoying the plush chairs and sofas in the large lobby, where even the extra waitresses brought in to handle the large influx had difficulty keeping up. Here, in air conditioned comfort, they could do what it was impossible to do aboard *Carl Vinson*—totally relax. Others could be found in the restaurants and cafes on the ground floor of the hotel. The Navy's invasion of the hotel had infused it with life and gave it a special ambiance that it had not seen in some time.

The driver of the DHL van now had the Intercontinental Hotel in sight. He continued to glance in his rearview mirror, ensuring that he was not being followed. Soon it would no longer matter. The van was shorter—by inches—than the entry doors of the hotel. He couldn't aim at them directly—the island displaced from the front entrance prevented that.

He would have to come up the circular driveway in the same fashion as the other cars, then, as he pulled up to the front entrance, he would have to turn sharply right, crash through the first set of doors, pass through the approximately twenty-foot entry, crash through the second set of doors, then hit the truck brakes and detonate his explosives. His comrades had determined that major structural members for the front facade of the hotel flanked the entry doors, and he hoped that the explosion would both collapse at least that portion of the building and also kill everyone anywhere on the several levels of the hotel in and around the lobby area. He pictured his mutilated body propelled by deadly explosives through the lobby area, flying by infidels as they breathed their last breath on earth. The thought pleased him.

Anne and Rick never did finish their second set. Their casual banter had extended so long that the next set of players had claimed the court. They headed over to the tennis clubhouse next to the two squash courts and grabbed some more Gatorade. Rick was pulling Anne's chain, telling her that her heavy Naval Academy ring was probably interfering with her tennis swing, when a deafening explosion literally knocked them both to the ground.

32

WORD OF THE EXPLOSION AT THE MUSCAT INTER-continental flashed worldwide instantly. Nowhere did this word travel faster than through U.S. military channels. Whatever faults the U.S. military might have, getting the word passed expeditiously regarding major events was not one of them. Smart commanders ensured that their command's communications system was airtight.

Captain Bill Durham, the CARGRU SEVEN operations officer, had been lounging at the Intercontinental pool when he heard the blast and saw portions of the hotel crumbling before his eyes. He resisted the urge to charge into the morass in response to the shrieks and screams of the injured. He immediately called the CARGRU SEVEN duty officer, Lieutenant Commander Jason Sloan, on his cellular phone. Initially Sloan did not believe what he was hearing, but Durham persisted, finally telling the junior officer to go into the "listen mode" and do precisely as he was instructed to do.

Armed with as detailed a description of the events as the operations officer could provide him, Sloan broke out his Duty Officer Notebook and turned to the OPREP III—NAVY PINNACLE/FRONT BURNER section, which described the type of report that must be sent in the event of an attack on United States forces. The first phone call was to Fifth Fleet Headquarters in Bahrain. The second was to CENTCOM. The next was to the National Military Command Center in the Pentagon.

In the field, at commands like Fifth Fleet and CENTCOM, each headquarters went through some very basic procedures regarding actions they took and people they informed. At Fifth Fleet, Admiral Flowers's staff concentrated on assessing exactly what had happened and on alerting other Navy forces in the AOR, notifying the various U.S. embassies and consulates in the area, as well as making recommendations to CENTCOM regarding increasing the THREATCON—threat condition—throughout the littoral.

The level of activity in the field was intense, but this level of intensity paled by comparison to the level of activity inside the Washington beltway. The National Military Command Center received the early word of the disaster, and quickly passed this word to the Joint Staff, and then to the watch officer at the National Security Council. Michael Curtis was informed immediately and requested an urgent audience with the president.

The president rose from his chair as Curtis entered the Oval Office. "Michael, you said a hotel in Muscat has been blown up? The Intercontinental?"

"Yes, Mr. President. We had a large number of *Carl Vinson* personnel staying there. No numbers yet on dead or wounded, but the initial reports suggest that the losses will be staggering."

"Terrorists?"

"Yes, Mr. President. The intelligence agencies were picking up information that terrorists who had recently departed camps in Iran were somewhere in Muscat. These had to be them."

"We don't want to jump to conclusions, Michael, but surely we'd have to think of Iran as the primary suspect behind this."

"Yes we do, Mr. President, and pending nailing this down with certainty, I recommend we begin to prepare to take action, if necessary."

"Michael, we don't want to jump the gun. We need to consult with our allies. We need to get more intelligence."

Curtis almost interrupted the president, but he waited for him to finish his sentence. This was a time for action, not diplomatic considerations. More intelligence? The intelligence agencies had botched this already by not providing timely enough information about the possibility of an attack. The hostile act that Curtis had secretly hoped for had happened. He had not anticipated that it would be an act of this magnitude, though, and he was shaken by it. However, it seemed almost certain that they would be able to link it to Iran. He had to keep the president focused.

"Mr. President, regardless of who did this, we can't just sit on our hands. We have to get forces moving, then increase readiness postures, then follow through with OPLANS. With all due respect, we can't just wait."

Curtis stopped his impassioned monologue long enough to stop flipping through his briefing book and to look up momentarily. The president sat at his desk with his head buried in his hands.

At CNN Headquarters in Atlanta, directives were going out to field teams throughout the Arabian Gulf as fast as the United States military was giving instructions to its forces. This story would receive top priority, and a team from Atlanta was already assembling to board the first available aircraft and fly to Muscat to supplement in-theater teams. It was going to be a full-fledged, long-term news effort that would stretch the resources of CNN as well as those of the United States military. The network would be first on scene with the greatest breadth and depth of news possible.

An aide in Michael Curtis's office was already watching, taking notes.

33

ONLY THE MOST EXTRAORDINARY DEGREE OF MILITARY discipline kept *Carl Vinson* from being plunged into total chaos. They knew that several hundred of their own were dead or wounded in the carnage at the Intercontinental, they knew that they had to take the lead in trying to save those that they still could, they knew that they had to begin the notification process for the families whose loved ones had perished in the blast. Beyond all that, though, they knew that this had been a terrorist act aimed at the government of the United States, and that as the primary striking force of that government in the Gulf, they would somehow have to gather up their remaining forces and carry out attacks against whoever had perpetrated this horrendous crime—Iran, most assumed.

Although this was a tall order, it galvanized the crew in a way that only such events can. As word of the bombing spread through Muscat, all of *Carl Vinson*'s sailors returned to the fleet landing to catch one of the liberty boats back to their ship. As these men and women streamed into the landing, *Carl Vinson*'s administrative officer, Lieutenant Commander Pete Otterey, directed traffic. Standing on a platform hastily assembled from wooden pallets, he gave instructions using a small bullhorn.

"Listen up folks. I know that you all had buddies in that hotel. Right now I can't tell you anything for certain regarding who's hurt and who's not. What I need now is medical people, and I need all of them I can get. I want corpsmen, I want dental techs, and I want all the strikers who have worked with them even for a short time."

"I'm the Medical Department chief," said Chief Petty Officer Don Long, raising his hand and pressing closer to Otterey. "I'll take charge of these people. What about medical supplies?"

"I've got Dr. Berg on his way in on a boat as we speak with as much equipment and supplies as he could grab in a hurry. There will be more to follow as soon as we get some additional people back on board to gather them up."

"Commander, we ought to get HS-4 primed to start flying the wounded that we can treat back out to the carrier as soon as we can," said Chief Weiss, now next to Otterey and assuming the role of his principal assistant.

"Already got that turned on, Chief. Senior Medical Officer was already at the hotel and we haven't heard from him, so we fear the worst. Dr. Berg wants us to triage everyone on site, then bring those we can to *Carl Vinson*. The more seriously wounded we're taking to Muscat hospitals. We think that they may get overwhelmed, and the ambassador is already working with the Omani government to have CENTCOM bring in Army and Air Force medics to supplement them."

"Aye, aye, sir, it looks like we've already got about a half-dozen corpsmen and dental techs gathered up. If it's OK I'll grab any vehicle that I can and we'll wait for Dr. Berg's boat to land, then head directly up to the hotel."

"Thanks, Chief," said Otterey, happy that the senior medic was taking charge.

Back aboard *Carl Vinson*, Admiral Robinson and a portion of his staff were trying to assess where they were and where they needed to go. The admiral knew that this was a major catastrophe, but he also knew that, at one level, he was fortunate. All of his senior staff and senior commanders had survived the blast and were already back aboard *Carl Vin-*

son. It was really a quirk of fate that they had been spared, because, like him, most of them were staying at the Intercontinental and could have just as easily been there during the blast. However, it had not happened that way. Wizard Foster and some of his CVW-14 staff had been at Omani Aviation Administration, trying to clarify the rules that they would have to follow while flying in the Omani Flight Information Region. Craig Vandegrift and Jim Hughes had grabbed the Captain's Gig and had gone directly to the souk, determined to do their shopping before the hordes of *Carl Vinson*'s sailors came ashore and flooded the outdoor marketplace. His chief of staff and his operations officer had gotten off the ship a bit later, and had been headed for the souk when word of the blast hit. Small compensation in the sea of death and destruction, but Robinson knew that he needed these men—and needed them now—to turn *Carl Vinson* into a fighting machine once again.

At the Intercontinental, the devastation was unbelievable. The blast had collapsed the entire front facade of the hotel, leaving a pile of rubble, itself over two stories high—broken concrete, shattered glass, twisted steel, shreds of furniture, and bodies, contorted bodies, broken bodies, and even more gruesome, parts of bodies amid the rubble. Beyond the front facade, the two adjacent sides of the hotel had suffered somewhat less damage, but doors were blown off rooms, balconies collapsed, and much of the hotel looked as though it could also fall apart at any moment. In the huge lobby, the human carnage was worse—and most obvious. All of those sitting there had been in the direct path of the blast and, mercifully, had probably died instantly, a better fate than that which befell those who were buried alive in the wreckage at the front of the hotel.

The first order of business for rescuers on scene, including Omani police and firefighters, Navy personnel who were on the grounds surrounding the hotel, and ordinary Omani citizens who came from the small shopping center across the street from the hotel was to try to find survivors in the pile of rubble that was once the Intercontinental. It was inefficient business, as there was no one in charge. The Omani authorities made a stab at taking control, but the Navy people who had survived the blast were hell bent on rescuing their comrades. Still, they tried not to interfere with each other as they worked to reduce the size of the pile of rubble and look for bodies—hopefully alive—under it.

The rescuers could do nothing for the dead, save identify them. The wounded they pulled from the rubble were brought to the broad lawn between the hotel and the ocean, where a makeshift triage station had been set up. *Carl Vinson*'s senior medical officer, Lieutenant Commander Hank Gillerin, had been lounging at the pool and had taken charge of the medical treatment, directing two *Carl Vinson* corpsmen, one dental tech, and several other sailors who knew something about medicine—or at least basic first aid—in triaging and treating those he could.

Although neither Rick Holden nor Anne O'Connor had any specialized medical training—just the basic first aid that most folks in the military are exposed to—their instincts took over as they pitched in to help Doc Gillerin in any way that they could. As they found themselves working side by side tending to the wounded, Rick quickly realized Anne was no shrinking violet when it came to dealing with emergencies. He was enough of a chauvinist to think that Anne would be overcome by the carnage and would not be much help, but his attitude changed as he watched her help the injured. Soon, he found himself deferring to her.

"Anne, over here," he said. "This guy's unconscious and his breathing sounds really labored. He's bleeding pretty badly from both his legs and I'm not sure I can stop it."

"Let me have a look," Anne replied, kneeling next to him and inspecting the sailor's wounds. "We've got to stop this blood loss or he'll go into shock. The medics are pretty tied up. We'll have to deal with him as best we can for now."

"I know, but—" Rick began to protest.

Anne did not let him finish. "Just give me something that I can make a tourniquet from, anything . . . there," she said, pointing to his tennis shoes, "give me both of your laces, and that towel, there. We can improvise something. Come on, we've got to hurry."

Rick and Anne finished helping the sailor and then moved to the next injured man they found. It was grim business.

The principals were gathered around Admiral Robinson's small table—*Carl Vinson*'s CO, CAG, the DESRON commander, chief of staff, intelligence officer, air ops, surface ops, and a few others. They were a grim-looking lot. The admiral wasted no time with pleasantries.

"Gents, we took devastating losses in the explosion at the Intercontinental. It will probably be many hours before we are able to fully understand the number of our shipmates who were killed or wounded. Intel, what do we know so far?"

"Admiral," began Captain Rocky Jacobson, "as we piece together the reports after the fact, it looks like the chain of command tried to let us know that the Intercontinental was being targeted but we couldn't get the word to the hotel fast enough."

"I know that," replied the admiral impatiently. "As soon as Lieutenant Caine showed me that report, I knew we were in trouble. We can piece together all of that later. What I want to know now is who did this. What do we know?"

Jacobson could see the strain the admiral was under. "Admiral, from what we've been able to piece together at the scene, particularly what the ops o reported to us—he's still there and is taking charge of the rescue efforts. From what he can determine, it appears that someone drove a van packed with explosives right through the front entrance of the hotel. There must have been a lot of punch in those explosives, because ops o says that the entire front facade of the hotel collapsed. He said it looks worse than Oklahoma City and way worse than Khobar Towers." Jacobson paused to let the admiral absorb that.

The admiral just stared straight ahead for a moment. Finally, his chief of staff, Captain George Sampson, broke the ice.

"Admiral, as Rocky said, ops o is going to stay on scene for a while directing the rescue effort as best he can. We've mustered most of our medical folks and they're treating the wounded there and we've got every able-bodied battle group officer, chief, and sailor who was not injured sifting through the rubble looking for survivors. That's the primary focus of our efforts right now."

"What are the local authorities doing?" asked the admiral.

"They're on scene and trying to help, Admiral, but this is a small country and ops o reports that they don't have a great deal to offer. They're cooperating, though, and following the directions our people are giving them. The good news is that they are really helping a lot with transporting the seriously wounded to their hospitals."

"Fine, I just placed a call to the ambassador. She pledged her cooperation and should be arriving on-scene soon. I'm counting on her to get the local authorities totally mobilized to help. Now, Rocky, tell me what else we know about who may have done this."

"We don't know a great deal, Admiral. The van that eyewitnesses saw drive into the entrance was one of those courier vans, a DHL one in this case. As you might imagine, the van is nothing but little pieces, but we've already checked with the local authorities and a DHL van was reported stolen a few days ago."

"This is a helluva way to find it," said the admiral, his rage simmering just below the surface.

"Yes sir," continued Jacobson. "While we're not jumping to conclusions, all of this would seem to be connected to the Hezbollah agents that were reported to have entered Muscat a short while ago. It seems to track based on what little we know now."

"Chief of Staff," said the admiral, turning now toward George Sampson, "are we about completed with our preps to get underway?"

"We are, Admiral, duty section has gotten things started, and as soon as the ship has a few more boatloads of its sailors aboard, we should be getting underway."

"Good," replied the admiral. "Are we leaving enough people on the beach to help our wounded and tend to those we don't bring back aboard?"

"Yes sir," replied the chief of staff. "Fifth Fleet also has a contingent of folks moving towards Muscat to help the people we're leaving on scene. Ops o will helo out to us when he's convinced that the people they send can take charge. CENTCOM is also sending a contingent of docs and medics from JTF-SWA. The Omanis have opened up all of their hospitals, but they're small and we will probably overload them quickly."

His staff could see that Admiral Robinson was torn—torn between mustering the full resources of his battle group to help his wounded sailors and getting *Carl Vinson* underway for what were likely to be retaliatory strikes against Iran. His staff convinced him that they were doing all they could for those left behind. It was time to get underway.

"All right," said the admiral. "Captain. Get as many of your folks back aboard as you can, but I want us underway in the next four hours. CAG, let's get aircraft preflighted, and pilots briefed. We need to be ready to put airplanes in the air ASAP."

The admiral rose as the others got up and began to file out of his cabin.

Heater Robinson felt the weight of the world on his shoulders.

34

AS *CARL VINSON* PASSED THROUGH THE NARROWEST portions of the Strait of Hormuz, the perpetual haze that hung over this body of water made it impossible to see the shore on either side of the ship. *Carl Vinson*'s navigation team plotted their fixes as best they could using radar navigation, a methodology with more certainty than "cutting" visual fixes. Still, the ship plowed on at a steady eighteen knots, accompanied by her Aegis cruiser, USS *Shiloh*, which had sprinted south through the Strait of Hormuz to meet the carrier.

Captain Craig Vandegrift sat in his bridge chair on the port side of *Carl Vinson*'s wide bridge and surveyed the flight deck below him. Brown-shirted linemen, green-shirted mechanics, red-shirted ordnancemen, and white-shirted supervisors from the various squadrons within Airwing Fourteen swarmed over their aircraft fixing "gripes," installing many of the spare parts that they had picked up in Muscat. Sailors worked feverishly to put every aircraft in prime operating condition.

As commanding officer of this warship, Craig Vandegrift felt the loss of all the officers, chiefs, and sailors—whether they were ship's company, Airwing, or staff—perhaps more deeply than anyone else on the ship. He mourned for each of the men and women, and he knew that he would mourn for a long time to come. Beyond that mourning, though, was concern, concern that *Carl Vinson* could complete its mission. The losses among the officer corps were particularly significant, and his executive officer, Commander Pete Chanick, had just arrived on the bridge to go over the awful toll with him.

"XO, thanks for coming up," Vandegrift began. "I'm pretty much stuck up here until we pass through the Strait. Tell me how bad our losses were."

"Captain, you may know some or all of this already. We had at least one hundred twenty-five people killed in that blast. The number still isn't firm because not everyone is accounted for yet. At this point, they're still searching through the rubble and don't expect to have that completed by tomorrow night. Lots more wounded though, and some really badly hurt. We'll get constant updates on the most critically injured. Some of those will remain in the hospital in Muscat, others are being MEDEVACED to military hospitals in Europe. All told, Captain, we sailed without a total of three hundred eighty people. Counting another forty or so in our sick bay who won't be in condition to go back to work for a while, and a few score others who aren't in sick bay but who are banged up pretty bad, we've got well over five hundred people out of action."

"That's ten percent of the crew, XO. Based on who makes up those five hundred, can you estimate the impact on our upcoming operations?"

"Biggest problem is pilots and NFOs in Airwing Fourteen, Captain. I've put it all down here," he said, showing the captain a neatly columnized sheet with a squadron-by-squadron breakdown of pilots and naval flight officers who were either killed, injured, or missing. Even in this largely depersonalized accounting, it was impossible to miss the full spectrum of this disaster. Ironically, because they were young, and thus more likely to frequent the Intercontinental, the pilots and NFOs in Airwing Fourteen led the casualty list. The numbers were staggering. *Carl Vinson* had sailed without four pilots and two NFOs from the Red Rippers of VF-11, five pilots and one NFO from the Tomcatters of VF-31, three pilots from the Fisties of VFA-25, a total of six pilots from the Stingers of VFA-113 . . . the list went on and on.

"This is bad, really bad, XO. Is that the list of ship's company officers?"

"Yes sir," said Chanick as he showed him the ship's company list. The captain read down the list, and Chanick could see that he was having trouble controlling his emotions. One hundred and twenty-three names. Sixty-seven of those were dead, while twelve others were in critical condition. The ship's navigator, Captain Bart Collins, Mini-Boss Commander Bob Stuyvesant, six other officers, five lieutenants, and a lieutenant junior grade were all dead. Vandegrift knew he would soon be writing condolence letters to their wives and families. It would not be easy. Still other key officers were wounded and would be out of action for a while. Significant numbers of *Carl Vinson*'s chief petty officers and enlisted men and women were killed or injured. The captain continued to stare at the list, and the XO spoke just to break his trance.

"Captain, these are tragic losses and these were all fine, fine people. We are pressing on, sir, and in every case the assistants to these principals have stepped up and are throwing their full energy into these jobs."

"I know that we will, XO. I know that we will . . ." said

Vandegrift as he continued to stare at the paper, glancing only occasionally out the window.

Six decks below, Wizard Foster had gathered each of his squadron commanding officers in his cabin—all save two. Fisties skipper Commander Alex Sheehan had been in his squadron's admin at the time of the blast and was in critical condition and not expected to live, and Blue Wolf's skipper, Commander Walt Burns, had been killed instantly as he sat in the Intercontinental's broad lobby. Both of their XOs were at the meeting, stepping in—one permanently, the other hoped only temporarily—but both ready to lead their squadrons and both wishing that they had come to command under different circumstances.

"You all know why I've called you together," CAG began. "The loss to our Airwing and to the Navy is staggering. We are all having difficulty coping with it. We have dead to bury, families to console, wounded to care for, and teams to build back up. Those things will all have to happen and will happen in due course. Right now, though, the immediate need is for us to be ready for combat. I know that our leaders in Washington are wrestling with exactly what we are going to do and who we are going to do it to, but there's no doubt in my mind, and there shouldn't be any doubt in yours, that we'll be dropping ordnance in the very near future. Our job is to be ready. The good news is that we have been practicing what we will actually do with Exercise Swift Sword for the past several weeks. Let's just use this time to review our target folders and get as much updated intel as we can on the location of Iranian forces. I want your most senior guys flying strike lead. This isn't training anymore."

He paused as he surveyed the sea of faces around him. They were all warriors, all about fortyish, with almost two decades of flying experience each. They were somber, their jaws set, ready to lead their strike teams against whatever enemy challenged them. CAG knew that they would get the job done.

"Tell me about how our loss of aviators will affect each of the strike teams you led in the latter stages of Exercise

Swift Sword, the portions where we conducted our biggest strikes."

Hound Dog McLain, CO of the Stingers of VFA-113 and the Airwing's most experienced strike leader outside of CAG and DCAG themselves, spoke first. "We lost some experienced aviators, CAG, no doubt about it. They were our friends and our shipmates, but everybody is ready to suck it up and fly more missions to rain steel down on the bastards who did this."

"I'm sure they are, Hound Dog," replied CAG. "There's no doubt in my mind that we'll all do our duty—and more. What I want to know is if we have the experience to do what we're gonna be asked to do."

"We can, CAG," replied Hound Dog. "Exercise Swift Sword has been going on long enough that we've had the chance to roll a lot of folks through as strike leaders. In addition to the COs and XOs, we've had all of our senior department heads—and even some of the more junior ones—flying strike lead throughout the exercise. That's not going to be the problem, CAG. It's gonna be just total number of pilots and NFOs."

"I suspected that, Hound Dog. Just how bad is it?"

"It all depends on how we strike and how long we sustain it. When we did our SURGEX during workups to see how many sorties we could generate over ninety-six hours, the forcing function was aircrews; mainly pilots and, to some extent, NFOs. You remember that Airwing Eleven supplemented us with a number of crews, but by the end of the SURGEX, even with the extra crews, we were all pretty ragged. Now, if we're going into this with the aircrew losses you've been briefed on already, it's gonna be awfully tight. We can do it for a few days, maybe, CAG, but not for a very long campaign."

Across the Blue Tile passageway, Heater Robinson was still waiting for Admiral Flowers to come on the line. This wasn't uncommon; the Fifth Fleet commander had a habit of having his aides and assistants get those junior to him on the phone and then have them wait—just to show them who was in charge.

"Admiral Flowers is on the line now, Admiral Robinson. I'll connect you now sir," said the Fifth Fleet aide.

"Robinson, you got your carrier back in the Gulf yet?" the admiral snarled. Heater Robinson could already tell that the Fifth Fleet commander's mood was even more foul than usual.

"Yes sir, Admiral, we are passing through the Strait now. It's been a normal transit thus far."

"Good. There will be missions for you shortly, I am sure. Just when do you plan on beginning flying again exactly?"

Heater Robinson was having trouble maintaining his composure. Granted, Flowers wasn't exactly the "hug 'em and love 'em" type, but this was the first time that he had spoken to him since the explosion at the Intercontinental. He could have at least expressed some sympathy for the losses that his men and women had sustained.

"We are going to continue to do maintenance today, Admiral, but expect to fly again starting late tomorrow afternoon."

"Late tomorrow afternoon? I thought that our ops officers had talked," said Flowers, sounding incredulous that the battle group commander was waiting this long to begin flying again.

"I think that they have, Admiral, and we have talked about it out here."

Admiral Flowers now felt that his orders were being ignored. "You don't need to second-guess me. If it comes from my ops officer, it comes from me. I fail to see why you feel you have to wait so long before you fly again," said Flowers, his tone nasty and his manner condescending.

Heater Robinson was now on the defensive, and he lashed back. "Admiral, as you know, we've had some staggering losses. We are still assessing where we stand. We have dead to bury, decedent affairs to take care of. Every pilot in my Airwing lost a close buddy, and the ship has lost key people. I have to be sure that we are ready to fly before I just start shooting people back into the air. I don't think that you understand just how bad things are."

That was it. The gloves were off. Admiral Flowers was not going to be challenged like this. He had kept it just below the surface, and now he blurted it out.

"Well, Admiral Robinson, you wouldn't have this problem if you'd done what the hell I told you to do. I told you not to have any of your people—*any of your people*—step ashore until your force protection people had things airtight. Far as I can tell, you failed in that mission. Your people clearly let you down—"

"But Admiral," interrupted Heater Robinson, "we had a good force protection plan that we implemented to the letter of the law after chopping it through your staff. My people did their job to the best of their ability."

"Well, Admiral, then if your people did their jobs, we have found the source of the problem. Clearly, you let your people down. Their blood is on your hands."

Heater Robinson stood up and pulled the phone away from his ear. He looked at the handpiece, looked at the phone cradle on his desk, then slammed the phone down.

35

IT WAS AT TIMES LIKE THIS THAT MICHAEL CURTIS felt the enormous power of the national security adviser's job. The circle of the president's closest advisors—a former captain of industry, an enormously successful career diplomat, the nation's most senior military men—had just left with the president's thanks, assured that they would be notified as soon as the president made his final decision. But they all knew that the president would not make this decision alone. They knew that Michael Curtis would have a major input into whatever the final decision would be.

"Michael, we certainly heard arguments across a wide spectrum. Although I know that there's not a consensus here, we have to come up with a plan of action. I take it that you're pretty firm on the fact that we need to take action against Iran?"

Curtis paused a moment before answering. Although he had rehearsed what he was going to say innumerable times, he realized that the president was seeking his counsel above all others, and he understood the incredible implications of what he was about to recommend. Such a "solution" would not pass muster here. What was needed was a swift and sure strike that would bring the Iranian regime to its knees.

"Mr. President, I recognize the enormity of the decision that you must make," Curtis began. "The decision to launch Desert Storm in 1991 did not involve such momentous consequences. I think that it is very safe to say that the overwhelming number of your advisors, and certainly the mood of the nation, favor swift action to punish the Iranian regime—"

The president interrupted, asking almost rhetorically, "But we don't really have a convincing smoking gun."

"No, we don't, Mr. President, not in the classic sense of the term, but the circumstantial evidence is almost overwhelming. Philip Quinn told us how strongly the court of world opinion is behind us already—and the full death count has not yet been made public!" Curtis felt himself getting more and more worked up. "There really isn't any doubt in any rational person's mind that this attack was conceived, planned, supported, and encouraged by the Islamic Republic."

"I suppose you're right," responded the president, finding himself being swayed by the national security advisor's calm but convincing arguments. "Do you think that we would be criticized anywhere outside the Arab world for taking action against Iran in this case? I know that you're advocating pretty decisive action beyond just hitting the terrorist training camps. Do you really believe that such a step is absolutely necessary?"

"Mr. President, we *must* take decisive action well beyond hitting the camps. First of all, the safety of our forces demands it. You have witnessed the devastation just one martyr can do. Imagine an army of martyrs. We must put their Air Force, their air defense system, and especially their

Navy out of action before they can attack the Carl Vinson Task Group or any of our other units in the Gulf."

"But do we even have the capability to do that?" asked the president.

"We have the forces in place and moving toward the Gulf, Mr. President. *Carl Vinson* has been rehearsing just such strikes over the past several weeks in Exercise Swift Sword. We need to issue an execute order to make it all happen, and we probably need to do that very soon."

"When you all were discussing the types of weapons you were to use, I got the distinct impression that you were interested in doing more than temporary damage to their forces and installations."

"You are correct, Mr. President. That is our goal. Iran is still far and away the most powerful nation in the Gulf. Temporary damage to her military machine—a machine which is growing faster than any third world country—would leave her free to threaten us again in the very near future. Mr. President, the clerical regime in Iran is not going to change. Unlike Iraq, there isn't any organized internal unrest that is strong enough to threaten the regime. President Habibi is no more than the puppet of the head mullah. He knows that his actions are severely proscribed and that the radical elements within the government really control the political agenda, and that agenda is to rid the Gulf of the United States. We can fix it now, Mr. President, or we can deal with it year after year."

"You're talking about having a lot of our people take a lot of extra risk to do this, aren't you?"

"Not if we do it right, Mr. President. Throughout Exercise Swift Sword I consulted with Admiral Monroe and he is convinced that, while it will take longer to hit Iran in this fashion, it involves no greater threat to our troops. We will just have to use the full spectrum of our weapons, both Navy and Air Force tactical aviation, as well as an awful lot of cruise missiles, to inflict the damage that we need to inflict." He'd almost said "intend to inflict."

"After these attacks are complete, how much will their ability to threaten us erode?"

"Terrorism is very easy to run on the cheap, Mr. President. But the important thing is that they lose the ability to defend themselves. Once they lose that, and once they have seen us respond to terrorist actions, we are certain that they will think twice about supporting terrorism to the same extent that they have in the past. They'd be totally naked to any attacks we would make against them."

"If we denuded them that much, what would it do to the balance of power in the region? Wouldn't they be especially vulnerable to an attack by Iraq?"

"Not really, sir. You recall that Iraq invaded almost two decades ago, and that war lasted almost ten years. But it was, virtually exclusively, a ground war. We're not going after their Army. It doesn't threaten us or any of her neighbors that we particularly care about. Her Navy and Air Force can reach out and touch us. We need to destroy them now and forever."

Patrick Browne thought for a long while as he let things sink in. Most of what the national security adviser told him he had heard before in one way or another, but Curtis had the ability to package it all together in a coherent fashion that made sense to the president. It all now appeared much clearer than it had just a few minutes earlier.

"Our military commanders are confident that they can execute this?"

"Yes they are, Mr. President. This is something that they have trained for, something that they know they can—and must—do."

The national security adviser kept his eyes on the president as he was obviously deep in thought. All of the planning, all of the briefings, all of the work winning the president to his way of thinking—it was finally paying off.

"Mr. President?" said Curtis after what seemed like an agonizing interlude.

"Yes?"

"Sir, we need your concurrence to proceed with this plan." *Say the words*, thought Curtis, *just say the words*.

"Michael, the case you have laid out is compelling. Compelling from a military standpoint and no doubt achievable by our brave warriors. But, from a political standpoint, it just won't wash. The rule of law has got to prevail if we are to have any international credibility. Clearly terrorists struck our brave sailors. Compellingly, but with no sure smoking gun, Iran seems to be behind this attack. We can lash out at the terrorist camps, but we cannot, and I will not authorize, taking down an entire nation as we lash out."

Michael Curtis was dumbfounded. He couldn't believe what he had just heard. The president had seem so convinced. He had convinced him. He knew he had. He had to turn this around.

"Mr. President, if I may . . ."

The president would not let him continue. "Michael, I have no doubts about how strongly you believe in the position you—and our key military advisors—have advocated. You've presented your views most cogently. But as commander in chief, the final decision is mine and mine alone. I must live with the consequences of the actions we take. This isn't nation against nation. It is the United States against international terrorism. That is what has struck us, and that is where we must strike. We must strike there and there alone."

The national security adviser sat gaping, as if he had been hit in the solar plexus. He tried to speak but could not.

Mercifully, the president continued. "Michael, I have benefited from your brilliance for a long time. Now I need to be served by your loyalty. I want to be briefed on strikes against the terrorist camps as soon as possible. We need to move out smartly while the court of world opinion is still on our side."

"Yes, Mr. President," was all Curtis could say as he beat a hasty retreat from the president's office. He had calls to make, and he needed to make them now.

Seven thousand miles away, in another presidential office, President Habibi sat rigid at his desk as his foreign minister and his military chief were brought into his office. Habibi did not rise, but let the two men be seated by his secretary. When she had closed the door behind her, he began.

"So, Minister Velayati, your attack on the Intercontinental has been completed. The explosion at that hotel has completely dominated the international news media since it happened over thirty-six hours ago."

Velayati stared back at Habibi, sullen.

"Mr. Minister, I have yet to see anything on these news broadcasts about our cause, or about American attempts to dominate the Gulf. No, what I see instead is pictures of broken bodies, of tearful parents and spouses back in America. I see news reports of the American secretary of state and secretary of defense making bold statements about catching and prosecuting the people who did this, and they are making thinly veiled references to us as the culprits. Call them what you will, the Americans are not idiots. They know that we did this."

Najafi fidgeted in his chair.

"Our radar stations report that, far from running away, the American aircraft carrier is coming back into the Gulf! What can that portend, Mr. Minister? General? Have we just signed the death warrant for our Republic?" Habibi was pounding his fist on his desk now, startling both of his visitors.

Both Velayati and Najafi knew that Habibi was enraged. Though he had bought into this plan some time ago, they recognized that now that the aftermath of this attack was playing itself out, Habibi might not be up to the task of dealing with the repercussions. More importantly, they feared that he might not be willing to take the next steps that he must take.

General Najafi spoke first. "Mr. President. We should exercise caution and not jump to conclusions. We have been watching the American statements carefully—just as you have. Though they saber-rattle, they have not definitely traced this attack to us. They may in time, but it is not certain that they have yet."

"What about the carrier moving back into the Gulf? Have you been watching that carefully too, General?" Habibi replied.

"Yes, Mr. President. The movement of the American carrier is routine. They are barely through one-half of their standard three-month assignment in the Gulf. They were supposed to come back into the Gulf as a matter of course."

"Except that now they will rain down destruction on us, General!"

"They may in fact want to do that, Mr. President. But much has to happen before they can do that. They must get the carrier into position. We will have ample warning, Mr. President, and we will be prepared to deal with it. As I told you in our last meeting, we have a plan to neutralize the carrier itself, and with it, any ability of the Americans to threaten us."

"You have told me of your plan to have this transport plane embark on this mission. Are you certain that this will succeed?" Habibi had softened his tone, now recognizing that he needed the general to protect the Republic.

"Mr. President, nothing in war is certain, but this plan is blissfully simple and straightforward. The fact that we are using a transport plane on a commercial route makes it virtually fail-safe. Ever since USS *Vincennes* shot down our Airbus, the Americans—and the American Navy in particular—have been paranoid over shooting down another airliner. They take extraordinary pains to check and double check before shooting at anything."

Habibi just nodded, seemingly convinced that the general's plan was a good one. Emboldened by this positive reaction, Velayati decided to speak.

"Mr. President, if, and it still is 'if,' the Americans take action against us I am certain that the plan that the general has will succeed. But as further insurance, I have told Shiekholeslam to set the plans in motion to have our brave operatives prepare to take these attacks to the American homeland."

"You spoke of these 'operatives' when we last met, Minister Velayati, but you were unwilling to tell me anything at all about them," replied Habibi. "Under the circumstances, do you think that you might reveal more of this to me now?"

"Mr. President, I assure you that I am not holding back anything from you at all. The reason that I do not even know many details is to protect our regime. The less all of us know of the details of the matter, the better our regime is protected—"

"Enough!" Habibi interrupted, springing out of his chair.

"Everything. I want to know everything you know right now!" he shouted.

The shocked Velayati stammered, then replied. "Mr. President, Shiekholeslam is running this on our behalf. I do know that he has several, as many as half a dozen, perhaps, operatives in major cities in the United States. New York and Washington, I am almost sure, perhaps Chicago and maybe a city in California. They each have been supplied a cache of nerve gas which has been smuggled into the United States from Vancouver, Canada. These men await his instructions to release it in these cities. . . ." Velayati was talking quickly and excitedly, wanting to get the entire story on the table now that he had begun.

"What will these attacks accomplish, Mr. Minister. Why would we do them?"

"Mr. President, these attacks would only be done to stay the hand of the Americans. Terror attacks paralyze them. If their carrier should strike us, we will strike them in their cities. There is enough pressure throughout America to limit their worldwide commitments. The average American sees no reason to protect corrupt regimes like the Saudis. Attack them in their homeland. Kill their women and children in their cities. They will demand that all of their forces pull out of the Gulf—forever!"

36

"ATTENTION ON DECK," SAID THE VFA-113 SDO AS Admiral Robinson, CAG, and CARGRU SEVEN COS, as well as a small number of other staff and Airwing officers, entered the Stingers' ready room.

"Seats, gents," said Heater Robinson. The assembled officers couldn't help but notice that the normally buoyant admiral seemed drained by the events of the last few days, yet his jaw was set with a sense of purposefulness, and he appeared to be all business. The admiral saw that six ready room chairs were empty, and that a border of black felt framed each of the name tags that identified the pilot who had formerly sat in that chair. The Stingers had been decimated more than any other squadron in the Airwing. It gave Heater Robinson pause, but he shifted his attention to Hound Dog McLain, who would lead the first strike against Iran.

The task group had not received an execute order yet to conduct strikes—they had just received a general warning order—but the forces were coalescing and they all pointed to strikes against the main elements of the Islamic Republic of Iran's Navy, Air Force, and integrated air defense system, followed by strikes against the terrorist camps once the Iranian forces that could threaten the task force were neutralized. Admiral Flowers had told Admiral Robinson to go into detailed planning and to "anticipate" getting authorization to execute the plan in the very near future.

The Stingers' skipper was standing in front of the ready room next to the pull-down screen, ready to present his "power point" strike briefing to the admiral and the others. VF-11's skipper, Benny Tallent, stood off to the side. He would lead the second strike, and his brief would follow Hound Dog's. The admiral wanted to get a sense of what these initial strikes would look like, and he wanted to be satisfied that the strikes would be successful.

"Good morning, Admiral, CAG, Chief of Staff," began Hound Dog. "I'm going to present the strike brief for Strike Alpha. This will be a coordinated TACAIR and TLAM strike. Then I'll be followed by Commander Tallent, who will brief Strike Bravo—"

Admiral Robinson interrupted. "Hound Dog, I know that you've got a well-wired brief put together—and that Benny does too. But before we begin, I need to know how long we can sustain these strikes with the officer losses the Airwing has suffered. Your squadron got hurt worse than any others, although it's bad across the board. I know that you all can suck it up and press for a while, but we can't do this forever without replacements. Tell me how it impacts your strike, for example."

CAG wanted to jump in, but he could tell by the admiral's body language that he wanted Hound Dog to answer the question. He was glad that he had anticipated the admiral's question and had gone over it earlier with his skippers and execs. Hound Dog thought for a moment and then answered the admiral as forthrightly as he could.

"Admiral, this is an eighteen-plane strike—plus twelve Tomahawks—against the Bandar Abbas naval base. Intel shows that they've got their ships still pretty bunched up, though we need to send up a TARPS mission to confirm that. As long as they're there, we can get some pretty good Pks [kill probabilities] with a reasonable number of missiles, planes, and bomb loads. Even with our losses with the Stingers, I can meet a really ambitious flight schedule the next day, too. After that it starts getting harder."

"OK," said the admiral, "but we need to look at this closely—across the board . . ."

The slight hesitation gave Wizard Foster the opportunity to weigh in. "Admiral, I think that Hound Dog hit the nail on the head. Even with our losses, we can strike and restrike Iran for a number of days, perhaps as long as a week, that's all the bombs we probably have anyway, as long as we are just striking. We've built all of these plans around having the Air Force fighters in the Qatar AEF fly the majority of our DCA and ASR missions. We all recognize the political sensibilities that would prevent them from doing strikes, but as long as they cover the other stuff, we should be OK."

"And if they don't?" said the admiral.

"Admiral, if they don't, depending on the level of the threat to the task group, we could be stretched really, really thin. We've already talked with AIRPAC, and as you know, they're making contingency plans to send us aviators from Airwing Eleven."

"I think that we'd better put those plans in motion, just in case," said the admiral.

"I'll make that happen," responded Wizard.

While the strike brief was going on, other missions were being flown. Commander Nasty McCabe sat in his F-14D Tomcat, Ripper 100, on cat 2, ready to launch on his mission. A naval flight officer and the squadron commander, Nasty was flying with one of his junior pilots, Lieutenant Andy Bacon. Nasty thought about what a small world naval aviation—especially fighter aviation—was. When he was a brand-new "nugget" NFO, then-Commander Heater Robinson had been his pilot. He'd learned a lot from Heater, and he was determined to pass it on to his own junior officers. Today, he and Andy were on a TARPS—tactical airborne reconnaissance pod—mission close to Iran to take pictures of Iranian military emplacements. His wingman, Ripper 102, was running up on cat 3.

Nasty loved the Super Tomcat. With its AWG-9 fire control system, the aircraft could detect and track up to twenty-four targets and simultaneously engage up to six targets with its hundred-mile-plus range AIM-54 Phoenix missiles. For closer in fighting, the Super Tomcat also carried AIM-7 Sparrow and AIM-9 Sidewinder missiles, in addition to its 20-millimeter cannon. The aircraft was a pilot's dream, and Nasty knew how to maximize its capabilities.

Nasty and Andy completed their control checks as they sat on cat 2, waiting for the catapult officer—the shooter—to signal that they were next. The shooter gave them the appropriate signals, and Andy pushed the throttles forward. The two GE F110-400 turbofan engines roared with over 50,000 pounds of thrust. After exchanging salutes with Andy, the topside petty officer knelt and pointed forward, and the shooter in the bubble punched the firing button. The shuttle ran forward along the track, moving the 70,000-pound Super Tomcat from 0 to 110 knots in less than two seconds. Andy and Nasty were thrust back into their seats by the force of the cat shot, and within seconds their aircraft was climbing away from the ship, heading for the mission tanker at 7,000 feet. Ripper 102 climbed up right behind them.

Hound Dog and Benny had given comprehensive briefings on their strikes, and they now waited for the admiral to comment. There was a long silence throughout the ready room as Heater Robinson let the briefing sink in. The strikes were well planned out and brought the potent combined firepower of the Carl Vinson Task Group to bear effectively on their enemy. The first two strikes would be on the naval bases of Bushehr and Bandar Abbas, and then subsequent strikes would be made on these two major naval facilities, all of her major air bases, and a huge portion of her IADS. Once this four-day-long campaign was complete, the terrorist camps could be struck and restruck with virtual impunity.

"That's a good plan, fellas," said the admiral. "Let's send these two by secure fax to the Fifth Fleet ops o with a little outline of what we have planned for the other strikes. I think that we should give Vice Admiral Flowers and his staff as much time as possible to look over these plans."

"Can do, Admiral," said Rocky Jacobson.

Turning to his aide, the admiral continued, "Let's see if we can get Fifth Fleet on the line on the KY-68. I want to let Admiral Flowers know that the task group is ready."

Nasty vectored Andy to his position off the coast of Iran. They were going on a straightforward mission—get updated photos of the Bushehr naval base, specifically to see which Iranian ships and boats were in their berths. Bushehr would be a primary target in any strike, and knowing where the Iranian Navy was berthed was crucial to the targeting process. As Ripper 100 leveled off at 12,000 feet heading south-south-east, Ripper 102 joined on Nasty's wing. They were in radio silence for this mission, with Black Eagle 601 another ten miles to the west, watching them as they cruised just outside the twelve-mile limit of Iranian territorial waters.

Nasty was just settling into his seat when the electronic warning system went off with a sickening, high-pitched tone. He yelled at Rick Bacon in the Tomcat's front seat at the top of his lungs.

"JINK LEFT, JINK LEFT, ACTIVATING COUNTERMEASURES!!"

His pilot needed no further urging as he snapped the stick to the left, chopped the throttles, and dove for the deck in a desperate maneuver to avoid the incoming missile.

Nasty hung on as he smashed out flares.

37

As he sat at his desk and looked out on the neat garden beyond the far end of his office, Vice Admiral Flowers grew angrier and angrier. A week ago he undoubtedly would have been furious at Admiral Robinson for being too conservative with his precious battle group. But Robinson was seeing things more his way. The strike briefings that he had sent him had been almost exactly what he was looking for. Aggressive, comprehensive strikes that would cripple the entire Iranian military machine, at least the part that he cared about—strikes that would set that nation back at least a decade as an effective military force. Maybe the fact that his people had been killed and maimed in Muscat had brought the junior admiral around and stiffened his spine. Flowers had gotten the chain of command under him fixed; now he needed to work on that portion above him.

He was angry because he had exploded at General Lawrence and now regretted it, not because he had any angst about arguing with a senior officer but because he recognized that this would just make it tougher to conduct business in the future. How could they have let this happen? How could they? Echoes of the conversation still rang in his ears.

". . . Admiral, I'm only going to say this one more time. You are to have the Carl Vinson Task Group strike a total of nine terrorist camps in Iran. The target list is still being scrubbed inside the beltway, but I've been authorized to provide you with a tentative list so you can begin your strike planning. The NCA wants this to be a proportionate response to the terrorist attack against the Muscat Intercontinental," said the CENTCOM commander.

"But General," began Admiral Flowers. "The entire campaign plan that we've practiced during Exercise Swift Sword revolves around first taking out the forces that can threaten our task group, then going after the terrorist training camps once that is accomplished. I can't guarantee that our forces will be safe if they go after the camps first."

"Nothing about combat is 'safe,' Admiral," replied the general. He wanted to say "except in the comfort of a nuclear submarine, where warfare is little more than a glorified Nintendo game," but he didn't. "We have our orders from the NCA. Now we're supposed to carry them out."

"With all due respect, General. I don't think that we've had this entire plan get a full hearing at the NCA level. If it would be helpful to you, I can certainly be on a plane today and brief the Joint Chiefs or anyone else on the efficacy of this plan."

General Lawrence was dumbfounded. Not only was Admiral Flowers accusing him of not understanding the big picture and worse—of not representing his subordinate commander to higher authority effectively, a charge that suggested dereliction of duty and bordered on insubordination—but he was also broadly hinting that he was prepared to go over his head in presenting this plan directly to the Joint Chiefs of Staff. This maverick needed to be put in his place, and put there quickly.

"Admiral, I'm going to say this one time and one time only, so start listening. . . ."

As Admiral Flowers pondered this disastrous conversation, he tried to think of a way to get his superiors to see things his way—not just because it was his plan but because it was the right thing to do. He knew that he had to get Captain Tom Perry to bend the ear of the national security adviser. He knew that he could do it.

"Yeoman," the admiral shouted to no one in particular, just whoever happened to be within earshot, "get me Captain Perry at the NSC on the line and get him on the line right now."

"Aye, aye, sir," responded the harried yeoman.

Harry Flowers knew that once he got the word from the top from Tom Perry, whatever cautions General Lawrence had would be inconsequential. He had to admit to himself that the fact that he could go over the head of this "dumb jock" pleased him greatly.

"Morning, Tom," the admiral began. "There seems to be a bit of 'confusion' up my chain as to what is going to happen with these strikes out here in the wake of the hotel bombing. I've got my battle group commander preparing to lay waste to the Islamic Republic. I assume that you all have those plans that we sent you—"

"Admiral," Tom Perry interrupted. He did not like doing that, but he correctly surmised that the more Admiral Flowers told him, the more disappointed the Fifth Fleet commander was going to be once he told him what he now had to tell him. Damn, Perry thought, why did he have to be the one to break the bad news? Even though he was Flowers's protégé, shooting the messenger was something that Harry Flowers was not adverse to doing. "I need to tell you about the strikes, sir.

"Admiral, the national security adviser met with the president less than six hours ago. Sir, he pressed his case hard for the types of strikes that we know we must do. However, the president was not willing to proceed on this course. He is only willing to hit the terrorist camps—nine in all, Admiral—and we are not to hit them until we get a detailed execute order—"

"WHAT?" shouted the admiral as he shot out of his chair. His aide came running into his office, but Flowers angrily waved him away. Calming only slightly, he continued, "What are they thinking of? Are you certain of this, Tom? Are you sure that you have interpreted Mr. Curtis's statements correctly?"

"I am absolutely certain, Admiral," replied Perry. "The national security adviser laid all of this out in detail, recounting even the most minute details of his conversation with the president. He left nothing out, Admiral. I am personally convinced that he went to the wall on this one and that he was rebuffed."

There was silence again on the line as Admiral Flowers let this all sink in. This tracked completely with what General Lawrence had told him. Now that he knew he could no longer influence the outcome of events, he needed to be "on board" and carry out the wishes of his masters.

"Admiral," said the puzzled Tom Perry.

"I got it loud and clear, Tom. Please convey to the national security adviser that I am here to carry out the orders of the president to the letter. We will execute smartly and plan to take out these camps— and these camps alone."

"Thank you, Admiral," replied Perry.

"Don't thank me, Tom, I'm just doing my job."

The next stage of which was telling Admiral Robinson to reorient his plans, which Robinson was sure to interpret as him relenting.

38

HEATER ROBINSON SAT IN HIS LARGE, HIGH-BACKED chair in *Carl Vinson*'s TFCC, right next to his Flag TAO. The NTCS-A readout on the right-hand, large-screen display showed the admiral how his forces had fanned out and were now distributed throughout the Gulf. *Carl Vinson* was in the Central Gulf, the perfect position for delivering air strikes simultaneously against both the Bushehr and Bandar Abbas naval bases. *Shiloh* and several other ships were in their "launch baskets" in the Northern Gulf, ready to launch Tomahawk cruise missiles against the Bushehr naval base, while other units were in the Southern Gulf, ready to hit the Bandar Abbas naval base in southern Iran.

Airwing Fourteen was in a state of constant rehearsal,

launching four simulated strike packages that day that were mirror image strikes into Bushehr and Bandar Abbas. Additionally, other aircraft were conducting ACM—air combat maneuvering training—getting ready for any Iranian aircraft that might try to challenge the battle group; AIC—air intercept training—practicing vectoring fighters to attack various enemy targets; and other missions, such as the TARPS mission that Nasty was flying near Iran.

Suddenly, an excited voice broke into the Battle Group Command circuit.

"This is Black Eagle 601 on guard! Report from Ripper 102. Ripper 100 has been hit. Ripper 100 has been hit! Mayday, Mayday, Mayday!"

The admiral stared at his TAO as the E-2C positioned twenty miles east of *Carl Vinson* continued his report on the guard frequency. "This is Black Eagle 601. Ripper 100 has gone down. Reported a missile lock on, then no transmissions. Ripper 102 saw the missile hit and scrammed to the west. Ripper 102 reports no chutes, repeat, no chutes from Ripper 100."

The entire watch team in TFCC stood in stony silence as Heater Robinson stared at his TAO. "Who's in Ripper 100?" asked the admiral.

"Pilot is Lieutenant Bacon, Admiral," replied the TAO seconds after looking at the recovery status board to his left, which listed the pilots of every airborne aircraft that was going to be involved in the aircraft recovery a half hour hence.

"And the NFO?" asked the admiral.

"I'll find out, sir," said the TAO as he picked up the Bogen phone.

"When you call him, tell him to tell the captain to send the ship to General Quarters. This could be the prelude to something bigger. We need to have the ship ready."

"Yes sir, Admiral."

The E-2C continued transmitting on guard. "This is 601. Appears to be a missile fired out of Bushehr. Don't know what type. Maybe I-Hawk. Went straight for Ripper 100. Black Eagle 601 is scramming to the west too." This was a precaution, as it was only twenty-five miles west of Bushehr, well within range of several of the enemy's missile systems there.

Seconds later, the TAO said, "Admiral, the NFO was Commander McCabe."

"Are you sure?" responded the admiral.

"Sir, I can ask again," replied the TAO, uncertain as to why the admiral would question his information.

"Yes, ask again. Ask Air Ops this time!"

As he completed his sentence, the ship's 1 MC blared, "General Quarters, General Quarters, all hands man your battle stations . . . Now launch the Alert 7 package, now launch the Alert 7 package!"

The TAO was confused by the admiral's instructions, but he complied. After less than a minute on the phone, he turned toward the admiral.

"Sir, Air Ops confirms that the crew was Bacon and McCabe."

Heater Robinson stared at the TAO but did not say anything.

"Admiral?"

By that time, TFCC had filled with senior CARGRU SEVEN staff members who had heard the word of the shootdown of Ripper 100 and by others who were responding to the General Quarters calls. Petty officers broke out sound-powered phone sets, and all watchstanders donned their flash hoods and gloves and had their gas masks at the ready. The chief of staff, the ops officer, the air and surface ops officers, and others all crowded in. Orders were shouted by anyone who had something to say.

"Get back to Black Eagle, ask him again about chutes."

"Let's get the war council formed. Meet in the War Room in ten minutes."

"We need to get a SAR helo up toward Black Eagle's position."

"TAO, have you called Fifth Fleet yet?"

"Admiral?" the TAO said again.

Admiral Robinson knew his staff was doing everything possible to make sense of the situation and do the right thing. He knew what "no chutes" meant, though.

"GQ time, one minute," continued the voice on the 1 MC.

"I'm going back to my cabin to call Admiral Flowers," said the admiral.

Heater Robinson walked the few steps back to his cabin as he had walked them a thousand times before, but this time he had trouble putting one foot in front of the other. How tragic to lose two good men. And to lose Nasty. It seemed like yesterday that he had taken him up on his first Tomcat hop in a fleet squadron. They had flown together in Desert Storm. Why did he have to die like this?

He sat down heavily in his chair and dialed the Fifth Fleet commander himself. After a brief word to his yeoman, Heater Robinson was put through to his boss.

"Robinson, sorry to hear about the loss of your aircraft," Admiral Flowers began. The junior admiral was surprised that Flowers already knew of the shootdown, which had happened less than ten minutes ago. "We heard the transmission from the E-2C on guard. We will get to the bottom of it in time, but it appears that your Tomcat strayed into Iranian airspace—"

"Admiral—" Heater Robinson began, but Flowers quickly interrupted him.

"Look, there, Admiral Robinson, I know that you are going to defend your crew. Quite frankly, I don't have time to get into a pissing contest with you right now over whether they did or whether they didn't. There are more important things that we need to talk about. Had you not called me I was about to call you."

Flowers was beyond cavalier about the loss of the Tomcat and the probable deaths of two brave men. Robinson was about to snap at him, but the senior admiral continued.

"Now I'm going to tell you something that you won't like, you won't like it a bit. Off the record, I am as angry as you are going to be about it. . . ."

Heater Robinson had no idea what the Fifth Fleet commander was talking about. With his deepening shock over the loss of his crew and his increasing rage at Flowers for writing it off as a crew screwup, all Robinson could do was listen.

"I have just been told that all of the preparations that you are making to strike the wide spectrum of targets in Iran must immediately cease. You will be provided an execute order in the next day or two to conduct strikes against terrorist camps and only against terrorist camps. No other targets and no convenient collateral damage. Do you have that loud and clear?"

"Admiral, you know the danger our pilots—"

"Robinson, now hear me and hear me good. I put my professional ass on the line to lobby for a stronger posture and for more robust strikes against Iran. Hell, I had to convince you when you first got to the AOR, as I recall. Your first order of business was just to protect your battle group and do nothing else. I pushed hard for these comprehensive strikes and got it shoved back in my face by CENTCOM—"

"I know, Admiral, but—" replied Heater Robinson, just trying to get a word in edgewise, but the senior admiral would not let him.

"Don't 'but' me, Robinson, just listen," Flowers shouted. "I thought strongly enough that this was the right thing to do that I went over Lawrence's head. Now if you ever tell anyone this I'll deny it a thousand times. But I went straight to the National Security Council. Straight to the top. Don't you ever repeat this, Robinson, but these orders came from the president himself over the protests of his national security adviser. So there's not a damn thing that you or I are going to change down here in the trenches!"

"GQ time, two minutes. Now set Zebra, main deck and below," continued the voice on the 1 MC.

Heater Robinson was letting it all sink in. Flowers could have no idea how much this news would anger him—even if it hadn't come now.

"This is unfortunate that your Tomcat crew was lost," Flowers continued, "but it doesn't change the final equation. We aren't going to change the nature of the kind of attacks we do just because of that. I'm going to be straight with you, Admiral. I think your boys screwed up and got shot down because they were somewhere they shouldn't have been."

Heater Robinson was too shocked to even speak. All he could manage was a weak "Yes Admiral," in response to the raving Flowers.

"All right, Robinson, I know you have things to do. If we're only going to strike these camps, then we had better be prepared to do it right. You and your people get your strike planning done, then get back to me."

"Yes, Admiral," replied Heater Robinson as he hung up the phone.

"Admiral."

The CARGRU SEVEN chief of staff, Captain George Sampson, then repeated his name, respectfully, but insistently. "Admiral."

Heater Robinson turned in his chair to face his chief of staff. He had been staring at the bulkhead for seconds, minutes, hours it seemed after finishing his call with Admiral Flowers. His staff was accustomed to the fact that calls with the Fifth Fleet commander usually were not pleasant ones for their boss, but after this call, the admiral had not emerged from his cabin for over twenty minutes.

"Yes COS?"

"Admiral, we've had two of our SAR helos scour the area where Ripper 100 went down. They heard nothing from survival radios. They see nothing in the water. We even vectored USS *Jarrett* over there to search with her two LAMPS helos, but they found nothing. Sir, we need to call off the search and get our helos back to support the CAP we're putting up. We've got no indications that the Iranians are doing anything else that is threatening, but we wanted to be in a defensive posture, just in case."

"All right, Chief of Staff, make it so," replied Heater Robinson absently.

"Admiral, was there any news from Admiral Flowers?"

"Yes, yes, he had news for us. He definitely had news." George Sampson was baffled by Heater Robinson's cryptic replies.

"Admiral, is there anything that you would like me to do, sir?"

"No, COS, you can go."

George Sampson knew enough not to pry.

As soon as his chief of staff left, Heater Robinson buried his face in his hands and wept. When he could finally move again, he pulled open his bottom desk drawer, the one where he kept all manner of things that he didn't use on a real-time basis. He dug around in the back of the drawer until he found his aviator's log books, where every flight he had flown was recorded. He picked up volume three of his four-volume set and found the time period when he had had his command tour.

There it was, flight after flight, wonderful memories of his CO tour, and scores of flights with Nasty McCabe. He found his first flight with him, a training hop at NAS Miramar. He closed his eyes and pictured their Tomcat crossing the California coastline west of Miramar and climbing out over the blue Pacific. Thumbing ahead a dozen pages, he found their last flight flying off USS *Ranger* at the completion of their deployment. He recalled thinking then that Nasty would make a great Fighter CO one day, and, sure enough, it had happened. Robinson had been the guest speaker when Nasty had taken over the Red Rippers just eight months ago. Now Nasty was gone—and now they were going to do nothing about it—nothing at all. He buried his head in his hands again.

He'd been completely loyal to his Navy and his nation for over three decades, but this was too egregious, too unbelievable. It could not stand. Heater Robinson was too much of a man, too much of a warrior to turn his back on this. The people who did this would pay—they would pay dearly.

39

MICHAEL CURTIS SAT AT HIS DESK AND ATTEMPTED TO shake the cobwebs from his brain. He had been up since 4:30 A.M. and it was approaching midnight. He no longer tried to hide his fatigue as Admiral Monroe entered his office to update him on the Joint Staff's work in selecting a viable COA—Course of Action—to hit the Iranian terrorist camps and issue an execute order to CENTCOM to carry out these strikes.

"Come in, Admiral," he began. "Seems like we've been at this a while today. I know that your staff has been working mightily to refine the COAs that General Lawrence has provided us. Do we finally have one that will pass muster with the president?"

"I think we do sir," replied the chairman of the Joint Chiefs of Staff.

"Let's run through it tonight then, and your folks can work it up through the rest of the night and morning. We can present it to the president before noon tomorrow."

Admiral Monroe motioned to his aide, who was standing a respectful distance away in the doorway of the national security adviser's office. Two other assistants instantly appeared with a laptop computer and a large-scale chart of the Arabian Gulf. He clicked to the first slide of his power point brief and began to walk through his briefing.

"Mr. Curtis, as you can see, the preferred option is a combined TACAIR and TLAM strike against the terrorist camps in Iran. Since our primary targets are concentrations of people, we'll want to strike at night while the terrorists are in their barracks, and we'll want to hit all the camps simultaneously or nearly so. If we hit some of them and don't strike the others until, say, the next day, it is too easy for them to simply break camp and move away, totally thwarting our efforts."

"That all makes sense, Admiral."

"As you know, Carl Vinson Task Group represents our only striking force in the region. They only have fifty fighter and attack aircraft, and only a discrete number of Tomahawk missiles. Spreading them around a dozen camps leaves us pretty thin across the board."

"We've taken a hard look at the situation with respect to our Air Force assets?" asked Curtis, though he knew the answer to the question already.

"Yes sir. Our JTF-SWA assets in Saudi Arabia will have to pull down all of the OSW missions over Iraq. This would be the worst possible time to let up the pressure on Saddam—especially in the wake of our shooting down his fighter."

"Are we still trying to work the AEF in Qatar?"

"Yes sir, we are. State has started an intense dialogue with the Qataris, but there's little likelihood that they'll let us fly out of there, especially if it involves attacking Iran. The Islamic Republic just has too much clout in the Gulf for the Qataris to want to risk antagonizing them."

"So *Carl Vinson*'s got this lock, stock, and barrel, is that what you're telling me?"

"Essentially that's it sir."

"Can they execute the mission without putting themselves at undue risk?"

"Mr. Curtis," he began, "there is always risk in any military operation. You know that all too well. The COAs we've been given, and the one we're inclined to go with, represent the best military options given the constraints we're working with. We've discussed the option of waiting until we move more forces into the area—you've already been briefed that the Theodore Roosevelt Battle Group enters the Mediterranean in two days, and it could be sent through the Suez Canal and on to the Gulf in about a week, but you've expressed the president's desire to move quickly in response to the attack against our people in Muscat. . . ."

The national security adviser was losing patience with Admiral Monroe. "Admiral, you know that waiting is not an option, so let's not waste time bringing it up again. Are you comfortable enough with the COA we've picked so that we can brief it to the president in the morning and have you issue an execute order by the end of the day to put this all in motion?"

The JCS chairman was torn. Nothing in his thirty-five years of military experience had prepared him for this crucible. There was only one answer that the national security adviser wanted to hear and only one answer that Admiral Monroe—chairman of the Joint Chiefs for just over two years but a Navy man for three and one half decades—could give. To give any other answer would be to suggest that carrier battle groups—the sine qua non of Navy striking power—were somehow not up to the task. Any task.

"Mr. Curtis, I'm comfortable that we can do this mission."

"Good. So am I, Admiral. Then let's get to it. We all have a lot of work to do."

Admiral Monroe took his cue. He had his assistants quickly gather their materials, and they departed the national security adviser's office. He was deep in thought as he headed back to the Pentagon. He was gambling with the Carl Vinson Battle Group. He hoped he was right.

Michael Curtis did not share the admiral's angst. He was focused on his long-term goal. The JCS chairman was barely out of his office when he buzzed his secretary.

"Ask Captain Perry to step in."

"Yes sir."

Within moments, Captain Tom Perry materialized. Even at this late hour, the national security adviser expected his principal assistants to be ready to respond instantaneously.

"Yes sir, Mr. Curtis."

"Tom, sit down," he began. "As you know, I've just had a session with Admiral Monroe. He's prepared to support the COA we discussed early this evening. You know what this means, don't you?"

"Yes sir. I know that we got set back when the president decided not to proceed in the manner we recommended—destroying Iran's naval and air forces before striking the camps. But if we hit the camps as hard as this COA plans for, it's a virtual certainty that the Islamic Republic will lash back against the Carl Vinson Battle Group with their naval and air forces. Carl Vinson can attrite them and then press the attack to units that have not sortied. We'll accomplish essentially the same thing this way."

"We may—but attacking ships at sea or shooting down aircraft in the air is a lot tougher problem than attacking them before they steam out of port or take off from their airfields."

"Yes sir, you're right. But we've got to think that Carl Vinson Battle Group is up to the task."

"Yes, we do have to assume that, don't we? But do we really think that, Tom?"

"With some degree of risk, yes sir. But if that risk is too great, and the battle group gets overwhelmed by the Iranian backlash, then I'm not sure that we're prepared to deal with the consequences."

"The consequences?"

"Yes sir, the consequences of a U.S. aircraft carrier being attacked and damaged or even sunk."

"That would be unfortunate, Tom, most unfortunate. But then think of what the reaction of this nation would be, and think how the president's attitude would change regarding how much damage he was willing to inflict on the Islamic Republic."

"I hadn't thought of it in just those terms, sir."

"No, but I have, Tom. That's my job and that's what I'm paid to do. No matter what happens in the next several days, Carl Vinson Battle Group will be the vehicle that brings an end to the Islamic Republic as a regional power."

Captain Tom Perry was thus dismissed as quickly as he had been summoned. He left with mixed emotions. His loyalty to his nation, to his Navy, and to his boss was absolute. Was the national security adviser gambling with the lives of the eight thousand sailors of the Carl Vinson Battle Group?

40

"YOU WANTED TO SEE ME, ADMIRAL?" HE SAID AS Robinson motioned him into the cabin. It had now been six hours since the shootdown of Ripper 100. The appropriate messages had been sent, the type wing commander back in NAS Oceana—VF-11's home base—had personally notified Nasty's wife, while his chief staff officer had notified Lieutenant Bacon's wife.

Diplomatic protests were flying regarding the shootdown,

but it appeared that at the highest levels of government, the Islamic Republic was claiming, and the United States was buying, the story that the aircraft had strayed into Iranian airspace and was inadvertently shot down.

Maybe U.S. policy makers had gotten themselves in a bind. Maybe this was too much like the shootdown of the Iraqi Foxbat, and the United States did not want to be accused of playing by a different set of rules when it found itself on the other side of an aircraft shootdown. Maybe the United States didn't want to tip its hand before the strike on the terrorist camps; if it made a lot of noise about the Tomcat shootdown, perhaps the Iranians would be more alert and looking for the attacks on those camps. Oh, U.S. policy makers might make all manner of excuses, but this wasn't just a singular event—this was a long and sordid history of vacillation and failure to do the right thing. Heater Robinson was determined that it had gone far enough.

He had not had that long to think about this, and he had not fully worked out in his own mind precisely how he intended to carry out his plan, but he was determined to act and act now. He needed to set the wheels in motion and start events spinning in the direction he wanted them to go or else it would be too late.

"Admiral?"

"Yes, COS," he began. George Sampson had been a loyal and trusted number two man for Heater Robinson, and lying to him pained him greatly. But it was a means to an end, he told himself. "I wanted to tell you where we stand, George, please sit down."

George Sampson did so and opened up the memo pad.

"George, I have just gotten off the secure phone with the Fifth Fleet commander. This is all verbal now—we will see message tasking soon—but we must act quickly, so I want you to assemble the war council immediately."

"Yes, Admiral," replied his chief of staff.

"I have spoken with Admiral Flowers and we will be getting orders soon to conduct strikes against the Islamic Republic. We did not discuss specific details, since those communications will, of course, have to be carried over top secret channels, but suffice it to say that these strikes will be large strikes and will be strikes that will devastate Iran."

George Sampson was writing furiously in his pad.

"George, I got the distinct impression that they would be massive strikes using all of our assets. I can't answer the 'when' part, we will just have to wait and see what our tasking message says. But what I want to do now is get a jump start on the planning, get our strike teams solidified, have them start doing detailed planning on target folders, that sort of thing."

"WILCO, Admiral, we can set all that in motion. It sure will be good to get that tasking message to get into more specifics of exactly what our missions will be."

"We can't sit around waiting for that, Chief of Staff!" replied the admiral, his voice rising several octaves. "Trust me. I was here during Desert Storm. We had a months-long buildup then, and even at that we were getting target folders to work at the last minute. We never did get it exactly right—too much time compression. We won't have nearly that much time now. We need to start planning today. Right now. I need you to drive this, Chief of Staff, not sit back and wait for things to happen!"

"Yes sir, I'll get right on it," George Sampson replied. He was stung by the admiral's suggestion that he would drag his feet on this. But more than worrying about his personal and professional feelings, George Sampson was perplexed. He had watched his boss do battle with the Fifth Fleet commander as Admiral Flowers had tried to make the battle group take a more aggressive stance in the Gulf, only to see Admiral Robinson shot down time and time again whenever he suggested using his battle group in a more conservative manner. Now, Admiral Robinson was really leaning forward, getting out ahead of the problem and ordering the battle group to begin detailed planning for strikes in advance of any formal tasking from the chain of command.

"Good, COS, I need a bit of time alone now. Let me know when you can have everyone assembled, and I'll kick off the meeting."

"Yes sir," replied the chief of staff. George Sampson was as loyal as the day was long. However, the admiral's actions were giving him pause.

41

"GENTLEMEN, THE PRESIDENT," ANNOUNCED THE NA-tional security adviser as he preceded President Patrick Browne into the Cabinet Room. All of his advisors rose as he entered the room. They quickly took their seats as the president took his at the head of the table.

"All right, what do we have, Michael?" the president said, turning to his national security adviser.

"Mr. President, this will be a presentation on Operation Resilient Response, our attack on nine terrorist camps in the Islamic Republic of Iran. The DCI will provide background on what we have done to discover a smoking gun—a gun held by the Islamic Republic—on this one. Then Admiral Monroe will go through the detailed operation plan for our attack on the camps. We have a few more briefs standing by."

"Fine, let's just get on with it," responded the president wearily. The bombing of the Intercontinental was the low point of his presidency. The Marine barracks in Beirut, the Khobar Towers, the embassies in Kenya and Tanzania, none of those had been as spectacular. Collectively, they had not resulted in as large a loss of life as this terrorist attack, which had occurred during his presidency, on his watch. Maybe if he'd acted more decisively earlier in his tenure. No, he wouldn't second-guess himself. That was past. He had to look forward.

"Certainly, Mr. President," replied the national security adviser, "Mr. Hernandez will begin the briefing."

Peter Hernandez stood and began a detailed briefing on the activities that took place in the Iranian terrorist camps. Even though his briefing got down into what some would call real minutiae, Patrick Browne marveled at how the United States could gather such comprehensive knowledge of something that happened in a foreign country, especially one that was as closed a society as the Islamic Republic was.

Hernandez put up slide after slide, speaking in a dull monotone. As he finished, he asked the president if he had any questions.

"No Peter, good brief, thank you."

"Admiral Monroe," said the national security adviser.

"Good morning, Mr. President," said the chairman of the Joint Chiefs.

Like Peter Hernandez before him, Admiral Monroe put up slide after slide, describing how the Carl Vinson Battle Group would attack the terrorist camps. This briefing did not hold the president's attention any more than the presentation by Peter Hernandez had.

"Do you have any questions about our plan, Mr. President?" he inquired.

"No, no, Admiral. Not at all. As usual, outstanding brief. Thank you."

They got up in succession after this. The secretary of state. The head of FEMA. The president's own press secretary. Finally, they were finished. There was silence. The president sat with his chin propped on his extended fingers.

"Mr. President?" said Michael Curtis as gently as possible.

"Yes, I know. You all are waiting for a decision."

"We are, Mr. President."

"Admiral Monroe, is this the plan that General Lawrence favors?"

"Yes sir," replied Admiral Monroe. "The CENTCOM commander is very solidly behind this plan."

"Good, then I think that we should approve it, don't you, Admiral?"

"Yes sir, I do," he replied.

"Fine, well, thank you, gentlemen," said the president as he rose. The others rose too, and then just stared as Patrick Browne strode out of the room. They had given their briefings. The president had listened. He had asked no questions, and he had approved of their plan completely. It was over just like that. Quick. Antiseptic.

Michael Curtis followed the president out of the room as the remainder of his advisors talked in hushed whispers, trying to absorb what had just happened.

Several minutes later, the national security adviser followed the president into the Oval Office. Instinctively, Patrick Browne knew what Michael Curtis was going to say, and he spoke first.

"Michael, I know that you were looking for a little more dialogue in there, but there wasn't much else to say. You all had the plan pretty well laid out. I saw no need to meddle with it. You know how to arrange the timing of this thing. Within the operational constraints that we're working with, time it for the maximum impact on the evening network news shows. Pete knows all that."

"Mr. President, thank you for endorsing this plan. I know, sir, that this is not something that you relish doing. It is the right thing, though, and we can carry it out effectively—though with some risk—"

"There's always risk, Michael," the president snapped.

"There would be less if we rolled back the Iranian military capability first!" There, he had said it, the national security adviser thought. He had been brooding ever since he had met with the president initially on this issue. He had hoped—no, he had done more than that; he had planted just the right words with the chairman of the Joint Chiefs and others—that as questions were asked about striking just the terrorist camps, the president would again consider striking Iranian military targets. That had not happened. This was his last chance.

"Sit down, Michael!" It was not a request from the president, it was an order.

Curtis sat down in the high-backed chair in front of the president's desk.

"When we last had this discussion, Michael, I told you that I had been well-served by your brilliance, and that now I needed your loyalty. That loyalty extends into the private as well as the public realm. You didn't second-guess me publicly, and I commend you for that. Now don't do it privately.

I've made my decision. Now, I'm sure that you have more important things that you must do rather than just sit here."

With that the president rose, giving Curtis the unmistakable signal that he should leave. The president was through with him. He couldn't ever remember being kicked out of the Oval Office before.

Had they been on firmer ground, Minister Velayati and General Najafi would have been angry that they were being summoned to President Habibi's office so frequently. But they were not on firm ground. They did not have full control of the forces of the Islamic Republic. They each had their own agenda, but they could not carry it out if their underlings kept letting things get out of hand.

The bombing of the Intercontinental had been too much, too soon. Velayati had supported Shiekholeslam in his desire to unleash his operatives to strike at American interests in the Gulf, but the man had gone too far. Over three hundred Americans killed, and in such a spectacular fashion. World opinion had turned strongly against the Islamic Republic.

Velayati and General Najafi now faced a fuming Habibi again.

"So, General, you say that you do not understand yet why your I-Hawk battery shot down the American Tomcat."

"I do not, Mr. President. I have ordered a full investigation and have summoned all those in charge of the missile batteries to Tehran to explain why this happened."

"You may not have had that intention, General, but the result is that the Americans have lost their plane and two pilots with it. We can forget any thought that they might stay their hand against us!"

"They would not stay their hand with or without this shootdown or, for that matter, with or without the bombing at the Intercontinental," said Velayati. "Mr. President, surely you recall that we sat in this very office not that many days ago and warned you that the Americans were conducting this aggressive exercise dubbed 'Swift Sword' that directly threatened us. They need precious little excuse to attack us whenever they want to."

"Mr. President, we have told the international press that the Tomcat strayed over our territorial sea and was heading right for our territory. It is well known that the Americans operate their jets aggressively. It is not too much to believe that they would violate our territory," said General Najafi.

"It matters not what the international press thinks, General. We should care what the Americans think!" shouted Habibi.

"Mr. President," Velayati continued, "again, we do not know if the *Carl Vinson* will strike the Islamic Republic. But if it strikes once, it will have to strike many, many times to really harm our Republic. Shiekholeslam has his men in place, and they are ready to release their nerve gas when ordered to do so. One strike by an American plane or a missile, and American citizens will start to die instantly. The strikes by the American pigs will stop immediately after that!" he continued, finishing with a flourish.

"And if they don't? If the Americans just strike again with more weapons?"

"Then my aircraft will destroy the American aircraft carrier. That I promise you, Mr. President."

The dialogue continued for a long time, with each man trying to convince President Habibi that the mission could be accomplished. When they left his office, they were not certain that he believed they would succeed. But there was no doubt in their minds that they would.

42

THE UNITED STATES MILITARY DID SOME THINGS WELL
and some things not so well. One of the things that it does
best is develop and update war plans—"on the shelf" plans
that provide detailed instructions for either quick strikes or
sustained campaigns against various countries around the
globe. The planning that goes into figuring what targets need
to be hit, with what types of weapons, in what sequence, and
over what time period is a Byzantine science practiced by a
cadre of analysts and military planners working in the bow-
els of the Pentagon on the Joint Staff and at the Headquarters of the Unified Commanders responsible for specific
geographic regions of the world.

For a few select countries—rogue nations that threaten
American interests most directly—the war plans on the shelf
are detailed and have numerous iterations. Such is the case
with Iran. The long-term threat to U.S. interests presented
by the clerical regime necessitated the evolution of a series
of war plans that included large target sets to be hit during
an ongoing military campaign. This long-term campaign in
turn had numerous subsets that would destroy targets over
a more discrete geographic area. One subset of the overall
Mountain Crucible campaign designed to bring the entire
Islamic Republic to its knees was called Mountain Divide.
Mountain Divide did not attack regime stability—it attacked
only military targets. That name was circulating through his
warfare commanders—just a few key players on Admiral
Robinson's staff. That's what the men around the table were
about to discuss.

"Gentlemen," said Admiral Robinson as they took their
seats around the table in his cabin, a group of laminated

maps of Iran serving as a multi-layered, multi-colored table-cloth for the admiral's conference table.

His closest advisors, his own chief of staff, ops officer, and intel officer were joined by CAG, *Carl Vinson*'s skipper, and the DESRON commander. That was all. Mountain Divide had to be so closely held that these were the only men who needed to know about the operation at this juncture. As they got closer to execution, more would be "read in" to the operation, but for now, this small group had the weight on their shoulders alone.

"Admiral, over the past several hours we've taken a good look at what you've given us and we have a few questions, sir," began Wizard Foster. As CAG he was the air combat commander, responsible for offensive strike warfare. He would have to take the detailed "off the shelf" contingency plan, add whatever additional, specific tasking the NCA provided, and vet these targets against the targets the battle group had practiced against during Exercise Swift Sword. Time was the enemy here. There was an enormous amount of planning that would have to be done in a very short time.

"I'm sure that you do, CAG. When we get this sort of short-fused tasking, especially when it's verbal as it is from the Fifth Fleet commander, our planning process goes into overdrive. That's why I felt it was crucial to get this moving immediately—even in the absence of all the message traffic that will flow in time."

"We all appreciate that, Admiral," continued CAG—and he really did. At his level and that of his people he was far less concerned about the niceties of formal tasking from above—hell, it was too hard to get at those messages. They were all top secret and higher and never left the intelligence officer's tiny office in CVIC. No, CAG was under enormous pressure to get on with planning strikes that would both get the mission done and bring his pilots home safely.

"Admiral, from the squadron's perspective, I can move our ships around to allow the shooters to be in their launch baskets when CAG wants them there," said Jim Hughes. "CAG, are you going to have every Tomahawk platform shoot during this operation?"

"I sure am, Commodore," CAG replied. "These are going

to be massive strikes. I'm gonna need every weapon that I can use—and then some."

"You got it, CAG. I'll move them into position as soon as you give me the word."

"OK," chimed in the ops officer. "I think that we shouldn't move anything yet until we complete our planning and until the execute order is issued. That way we won't tip our hand, and—"

"Well, hold on now," Admiral Robinson interrupted. "I don't think that our leadership is going to wait long at all before they order us to strike. I don't think we'd be tipping our hand if we at least moved our ships to the right areas."

Bill Durham quickly recovered. "Of course not, Admiral. The Commodore will move them as you indicated. He can start doing that immediately."

"Good. Rocky, what do your intel boys say about the overall threat and whether this plan is executable or not?"

"Admiral," began Rocky Jacobson. "There are major elements of what we have been tasked to do that closely resemble portions of Exercise Swift Sword. So from the standpoint of having current target folders and, I think—CAG, correct me if I'm wrong—from the standpoint of aircrews being familiar with the targets and Tomahawk missions being already planned, we are way ahead of the power curve."

"We are, Admiral," said CAG. "With the exception of the actual terrorist camps there are very few targets, no more than a handful, that are not fully planned out. The camps themselves should be easy to plan, they are all soft targets and, with the exception of the camps near Tehran, none of them present any particular ingress or egress challenges. I can't give you an exact time, Admiral, but I think that very conservatively, we can have this entire mission ready to go, all planned out, in less than thirty-six hours."

The dialogue between and among the key players continued, with Heater Robinson presiding but saying very little and giving no specific direction or orders. He wanted this to be their plan, one they would execute without question or hesitation.

At a very basic level, Heater Robinson hated deluding

these men, his closest advisors and his senior warriors. But he had reconciled his decision. If his nation refused to take appropriate action for the death of over three hundred of his officers, chief petty officers, men and women, then he would. The shootdown of Nasty's Tomcat was merely the last straw—the cowardly murder of two fine patriots.

Heater Robinson was no fool. Though the enormous pressure that he was under might have clouded his judgment and brought him to the brink where these last two events could have pushed him over, he had thought through how he would put his plan in motion. He would allow his staff to plan out a full-blown Mountain Divide campaign—that would be kept secret, of course, from the entire chain of command. Just before the order came to take out the terrorist camps, he would instigate a provocation by the Iranians—he thought that an attack on one of his ships would be sufficient—so that he would be authorized to simultaneously retaliate against the base or bases that the attacking unit came from.

No further "planning" would be needed, as he would just let the campaign, which encompassed those targets, flow. After these events were complete, they would finally recognize his plotting, but that did not matter to him. He was a man on a mission operating with no authority but his own. There was only one more person that he needed to bring on board. He called his front office to put through the call.

"Yes sir, Admiral," replied Becky Philips to the buzz of the intercom.

"Oh, Flag Sec, wasn't trying to reach you, I was looking for flag lieutenant or flag writer, just trying to place a call to Fifth Fleet."

"They aren't here, Admiral. I'm the only one in the office. I'd be happy to place it for you."

"Well, don't want to bother you, know that you're busy," Heater Robinson replied. Philips was the junior department head on the staff and was incredibly overworked. He didn't want to use her for such mundane tasks.

"Can do easy, Admiral. I'll buzz you when I get their front office on the line."

*   *   *

"Admiral, telephone call on the STU-III sir, Admiral Robinson is on the line," said his aide as he walked into Admiral Flowers's well-appointed office.

"Oh, well, all right, send it in," he replied. He was so accustomed to calling Robinson to chew him out for one thing or another that when his subordinate called him it was actually quite surprising.

Back on *Carl Vinson*, Becky Philips was stuck. She usually didn't get involved in placing calls for her boss. She had worked in the Pentagon and had watched executive assistants for flag and general officers stay on the line to take notes for their bosses. She didn't know whether the admiral expected her to do that or not, didn't have the flag lieutenant or flag writer around to query, and she was too embarrassed to ask herself. She decided that it was easier to beg forgiveness than to ask permission and decided to discreetly listen to the phone call between Admiral Flowers and Admiral Robinson just in case she was expected to capture the conversation for the admiral the way EAs do.

"Good afternoon, Admiral Robinson," Admiral Flowers said as the call was put through.

"Good afternoon, Admiral. I know you are terribly busy sir, but I wanted to update you on our preparations for striking the terrorist camps in Iran, Admiral, just to keep you absolutely up to speed."

Admiral Flowers recalled how he had chewed Robinson out during their last phone conversation, but Flowers still needed Robinson on board for the strikes on these terrorist camps. He decided to soften his approach ever so slightly.

"Admiral, why, yes, thank you for calling. I appreciate you keeping me in the loop. At this end, we haven't gotten the execute order yet, but I sense that you are going to need a bit more time with your planning anyway, aren't you?"

"We are, Admiral," Heater Robinson said. "We want to strike these terrorist camps and strike them hard, but the extra planning time that we are getting is being put to good use by our strike planners."

"That's good," replied Harry Flowers.

There was a long, pregnant pause before Heater Robinson spoke next. He was about to utter the most important sentences of his three-decade career. He had thought about them hard. He had recalled his numerous earlier conversations with Admiral Flowers, recalled how the admiral was clearly interested in enhancing the Navy's prestige in the Gulf, how Flowers wanted him to use his battle group more aggressively, how the admiral wanted to lean way forward but how he, in turn, was being hamstrung by the CENTCOM commander.

And most importantly, he knew what Admiral Flowers *really* wanted—to strike and strike hard.

"Admiral, I roger for everything that you told me in our last conversation about hitting the terrorist camps and only the terrorist camps. That is precisely what my strike planners are working on right now. They will have a comprehensive plan that will work and work well."

"That's good, Admiral." Flowers was pleased that Robinson was carrying out his instructions and even acting cheerful about it. Maybe he would bend this man to his will sooner than he thought.

"Thank you, Admiral. What we are also working on, sir, is a series of pre-planned responses. Playing out all of the 'what-ifs' that could happen after we strike. These include many things that you pointed out to me, sir, when we first checked into the AOR. We are coming up with plans to retaliate against their ships if they strike us and strike against their naval bases if more ships appear ready to sortie."

"Well, yes, it appears that would be prudent, wouldn't it?"

"Yes sir, it is, Admiral, but I think that we need this to be more than reactionary. I think that we couldn't respond quickly enough. Now, if we knew, or suspected, in advance, that one of their ships was about to do something, we could plan a counterstrike against that ship."

"Yes, I suppose you could, if you were clairvoyant," Flowers responded. Admiral Robinson thought that he detected his voice softening and his interest being piqued.

"Yes, sir, Admiral. We would find it only prudent to go after the base or bases that these ships came from, just to ensure that another unit wasn't coming out to attack us."

"Yes, I suppose you would."

"But Admiral, you know how well coordinated and planned our strikes have to be. If we are in the midst of hitting the terrorist camps, and then we have to hit an Iranian ship—let's say—that attacks us, and then if we have to subsequently go after a naval base—and of course we'd have to take out the IADS protecting that base—then, Admiral, those attacks would be terribly uncoordinated."

"Nothing you say is incorrect, Admiral Robinson. What is the punchline, though?"

The bet had finally reached him. It was time to up the stakes.

"Admiral, if we were to get such a provocation by an Iranian ship—one that necessitated this level of response—right before the attack on the terrorist camps, we would be better served by a coordinated attack on the camps, the Iranian Navy, their IADS, their entire network."

"Robinson, this sounds a lot like something we have been told we would not do," replied Flowers, his voice inquisitive but not harsh.

"It does, Admiral, but of course, it would only be for self-defense, if we were, in fact, attacked."

"You wouldn't initiate this without authorization, then?"

"Not without your authorization, sir. I do think that we ought to be prepared for such an eventuality, don't you, sir?"

Admiral Flowers understood completely where Robinson was going with this. It was the best of all worlds. He would be prepared to strike the Islamic Republic with everything he had, and need only respond to the provocation. Fifth Fleet would just be a bystander. There would be no personal risk to him. Admiral Robinson would be the lightning rod for this action.

"What do you want me to do then, Admiral Robinson?"

"Well, sir, I think that I would just want your OK to respond to a provocation against the battle group. I would handle the rest. The Iranians are becoming very aggressive at sea. When I receive an execute order for this operation I will be watching the Iranian Navy very carefully."

"All right, Admiral Robinson, but you keep me informed, is that clear?"

"Perfectly clear, sir," responded Heater Robinson. Then he hung up the phone.

Becky Philips held the phone receiver up to her ear for what seemed like an eternity after the conversation between the two admirals ended. What had she just heard?

43

HARRY FLOWERS WAS NOT AN OVERLY CAUTIOUS MAN, but even he could only reel from Heater Robinson's phone call.

Initially, he was primarily interested only in covering himself, ensuring that the plan concocted by Robinson did not implicate him somehow in any plotting against the chain of command. Once he was convinced that that was accomplished, he had time to reflect on the overall feasibility of the plan.

Robinson had clearly thought this through. The plan was simple and straightforward and was actually, though he hated to admit it, brilliant in its conception and easy in its execution. What puzzled him was the why; why was Heater Robinson now hell-bent on wreaking havoc on the Islamic Republic, when only a short while ago he'd seemed intent on keeping his precious battle group out of any action?

"Admiral, you wanted to talk to me about these fitness reports?" asked Bolter Dennis as he absently walked in through the private passageway between their offices. The damn chief of staff must have been raised by wolves, thought Flowers, who chafed at his constant interruptions. But now he thought that he might turn this into an opportunity.

"Chief of Staff, yes, we can do that a little later. I just got off the phone with Admiral Robinson. It appears that all of the plans to execute these strikes against the terrorist camps are coming together nicely."

"I think that they are, Admiral," replied Dennis.

"I must admit, though, that he did seem a little, well, a little different. I guess that he is very upset about the loss of all his people at the Intercontinental. He has every right to be. But there seems to be something more, something deeper."

"Admiral, I am sure that you know that he is especially affected by the loss of his Tomcat over the Gulf."

"Yes, but the aircraft was where it wasn't supposed to be. Tragic as that incident was, you have to understand that in the wake of the Foxbat shootdown, we don't have much of a leg to stand on if our aircraft get shot at or shot down where they aren't supposed to be."

Typical non-aviator response, thought Dennis. The normal hazards associated with naval aviation were exacerbated by the tough mission in the Gulf: the battle group was surrounded by hostile nations and the rules of engagement were especially strict. Non-flyers expected a single pilot or a crew of two to make perfect decisions the first time, every time; to avoid shooting down planes they weren't supposed to as they avoided getting shot down themselves, all while hurtling along in a cramped cockpit going close to the speed of sound. He needed to tell the admiral the full story.

"Admiral," said Dennis, getting worked up and raising his voice. "The squadron CO, Nasty McCabe, was in the back of that aircraft. He had been the admiral's nugget NFO when the admiral had squadron command. They made a combat cruise here to the Gulf during Desert Storm. He probably spent more time with Nasty than with anyone in the world except his wife—and that's probably a coin toss. I think that he has a right to be a little upset by that. I think that might be affecting him just a little bit, especially since, after this happened, the National Command Authorities didn't do a damn thing about it and basically told him that it was Nasty's fault. We all know that's a crock!"

Dennis stopped suddenly, realizing that he was all but attacking Admiral Flowers. He prepared himself for the blast.

So that's it, thought Flowers. Now he thought he understood what was driving this man.

"Well, Chief of Staff. Thanks for enlightening me. Yes, I agree with you. Admiral Robinson has every reason to be upset. Perhaps I don't understand everything there is to know about this Tomcat shootdown, but understand that the decision not to retaliate against the Iranians for this single act was not mine to make."

Bolter Dennis was shocked by this softer approach from his boss. He hurriedly replied, "Yes sir," as he turned to leave.

Robinson's thinking now was clear, and so was Flowers's next action. He was not sanguine that Admiral Robinson could pull this entire operation off as he intended to—even with his tacit approval. There was one more person who had to be brought onboard.

"Tom, are you there?" Flowers said.

"I'm listening, Admiral. Your yeoman said that it was extremely urgent, Admiral. How can I help you sir?" Perry sounded a bit perplexed—and groggy, it being 4:30 A.M. in Washington.

"Now just listen, Tom. We are about great things out here. Here is what I want you to do, and here is what I want you to tell Mr. Curtis. . . ."

44

BECKY PHILIPS LOOKED OUT ON THE ARABIAN GULF as she pounded away on the stair stepper on the Flag Bridge. She usually listened to her Walkman, or brought a book or magazine to read when she worked out, but today she just pumped away and stared—and thought.

The conversation she had overheard had been too strange to make any sense of. She'd tried to busy herself with paperwork when the flag writer returned to the office, but she'd found it impossible to concentrate. She had to escape to think, and working out always cleared her brain.

Admiral Robinson had always been so conservative. Now, was he really doing this? Was he talking about disobeying the orders of the president? And was he deceiving the Fifth Fleet commander and the entire chain of command? She reflected that the admiral had not seemed to be himself lately. As one of his close personal assistants, she would know that better than anyone else—but could he have gone off the deep end? She couldn't believe any of this, but she was worried enough that she was unwilling to write this off to something that she just didn't understand. She decided then and there, with perspiration flowing as she passed the half-hour mark on the stair stepper, that she needed to do something about this. She knew just what to do.

Seven thousand feet above *Carl Vinson*, Anne O'Connor and her crew were in the tanker track again, refueling Airwing Fourteen's strike aircraft as they practiced mirror-image strikes in the Central Arabian Gulf.

The Airwing had ratcheted up the level of flying dramatically, now generating over one hundred thirty sorties a day, practicing strikes against the terrorist camps. CAG Foster wanted to give all his strikers practice with just the kind of ordnance they would use against the camps and practice flying the kind of profiles they would fly in getting to and from their targets. They used most of the length and width of the Northern Arabian Gulf to practice flying the substantial distance overland to reach their targets in Iran.

That was one of the reasons that Anne was flying this much. If the jets were going to go on a long overland mission, they needed topping off just prior to crossing the coastline and going inland. CAG was determined that the Airwing would fight like it trained, and he wanted his pilots to go through the drill of tanking on the mission tanker prior to flying over Iran. That way, when the order to execute this operation came down the chain of command, the Airwing would be absolutely ready to do it.

"What's this, number four this flight, Anne?" said Mike Hart. Mike's sense of humor kept Anne going most of the time. She was still down, as were all on the *Carl Vinson*, about the attack on the Intercontinental. But Anne was feeling it a bit more directly—she had been one of the first on the scene, she had pulled broken bodies out of the wreckage, she had heard the cries of the wounded and dying, she had held the hand of men and women who knew that they were going to die and who just wanted someone to hold them for the last few minutes they had on earth.

"I think it is, Mike, and there's more where these guys came from. Think we can gas up about three more. Then they're sending 702 our way while we recover on the 15:45 cycle, gas up, and come back up here for some more."

"I'm up for it. How are you doing, Anne?"

"Fine, Mike. Just fine."

Becky Philips knocked on the open door of the chief of staff's tiny office, adjacent to the Flag Staff wardroom lounge. A far cry from the admiral's cabin, which Heater Robinson found almost embarrassingly big, George Sampson's area could be charitably described as a cubbyhole: it was five feet wide by about seven feet long, crammed with a desk, a chair for himself, and a small chair for a visitor. Over his desk he had a 13-inch TV constantly tuned to CNN and a smaller screen, which always displayed the PLAT camera focused on the flight deck. A desktop computer, laptop, and two phones took up the majority of the space on his desk. He was hunched over his laptop answering e-mail from the Navy's personnel bureau when Becky knocked.

"Got a minute, Chief of Staff?" she said. George Sampson discouraged "drop in" visits by the majority of the CARGRU SEVEN staff, but he worked so closely with Becky and with the admiral's aide, Mike Lumme, that they had open access anytime.

"Yeah, Flag Sec, not doing anything that can't wait. What's on your mind?"

"Sir, do you mind if I close the door?" she said. When

Sampson didn't object, she shut the door, making the cramped office seem even smaller.

"Chief of Staff, I don't know where to begin. I . . . I am still trying to put it all together myself, but well, I overheard something that I need to tell someone."

George Sampson listened impassively. Becky was a surface warfare officer like himself, the one "union" in the Navy that considered themselves the most solid, the most professional—not "flaky," like some Airedales. He didn't think that this was just going to be something inconsequential.

"Sir," Becky continued, "you know that Admiral Robinson has told us all verbally that we are going to strike Iran as part of Operation Mountain Divide?"

"Yes, I know that," replied the chief of staff. "How much of this are you read into, Flag Sec?"

"Not all the details, COS, just enough to do my job as Staff TAO. But I have the basics down, strikes against the Iranian military, especially their Navy and their IADS, followed by attacks on their terrorist camps. Do I have that about right?"

"Yes you do," he replied, more than a little bit puzzled.

"Sir, I was in the admin office when Admiral Robinson called us to place a call to Admiral Flowers. The aide or the writer usually handle that, but both were gone so I placed the call. Then, well sir, I got a little confused as to whether I was supposed to be an EA and take notes on the call for Admiral Robinson. So I decided it would be best to listen in and then recap the conversation for the admiral."

"Well, COS, I listened, and it seems that Admiral Robinson and Admiral Flowers discussed the fact that only strikes against the terrorist camps were authorized. But then Admiral Robinson said that he was planning to find a way to strike at more sites, you know sir, naval facilities, that sort of thing—"

"Wait a minute, Becky," he interrupted. "Do you know what you're saying? Now first of all, only a few people are read into the entire operation, and unfortunately you aren't one of them. But, yes, the strikes against Iran have nothing to do with hitting just terrorist camps. Think about it logically, will you? Doing just that would put our pilots in terrible jeopardy. Are you sure you didn't misinterpret what you heard?"

"No sir, I don't think so. I recall Admiral Flowers saying that the plan was just to hit the terrorist camps, then Admiral Robinson telling him that he was going to continue to plan to hit everything at once and even find a provocation to do that."

Becky was not backing down. As much respect as he had for her, he could not cross the bar. He could not even begin to make himself believe that she had heard what she thought she had heard.

"OK, Becky, look. Let's suppose—and I mean just suppose—for a minute that you actually heard what you think you heard. Do you know what that would mean? Do you have any *idea* what that would mean to our Navy? To our *country*?" George Sampson was raising his voice now in a way that Becky had never heard before.

"Well sir, yes, I think I do," she stammered. Becky Philips didn't often lose her cool, but she was losing it now. The chief of staff wasn't listening any more, he was lecturing.

"I don't think you do. If you *really* believe that you heard what you think you heard you are talking about sedition, do you realize that? You are talking about high treason! Is there anything that Admiral Robinson has done or said in the entire time that you've known him to make you think he would do something like this?"

"No, sir, there isn't, but—"

"Of course there isn't *Lieutenant Commander Philips*," he interrupted again. "And another thing. I think I do a pretty good job of sheltering those of you further down the chain of command from it, but you *might* have noticed that Admiral Robinson is under enormous pressure courtesy of his boss, Admiral Flowers. Now this is never to leave this room, but our boss has taken major, major hits from the Fifth Fleet commander and he has never complained. Does that sound like the kind of relationship that would lead to two people *conspiring* to sedition?"

"Sir, Chief of Staff, I don't know what to say." Becky's confidence was now almost totally shaken.

"Well, Becky, look," Sampson continued. "We're all under a lot of pressure out here. You were listening in on a conversation that was probably a continuation of several conversations you didn't hear. It's easy to get things out of context if you don't have the big picture. I can, I really can, understand how you might have gotten confused about this—"

"Yes, Chief of Staff, yes, I could have," Becky interrupted this time, now so embarrassed that she just wanted to get out of the chief of staff's office, an office that now seemed positively claustrophobic.

"Yes, it's nothing you need to feel badly about. It could happen to anyone. The point, though, is that you must put all this completely out of your mind. There can't be any loose talk, any speculation on your part about any of this. Admiral Robinson is Navy Blue from his head to his toes. Think how he would feel if he thought that one of his closest advisors could possibly consider this."

"Yes, sir, I see, sir," Becky stammered, now looking down at the carpet in the chief of staff's office.

"Good, then we won't hear any more of this," said the chief of staff as he stood up. He reached over and opened the door, latching it back. Becky knew that this was her cue to leave.

George Sampson gave her a friendly wave as she departed, and he sat back down to his work. The incident was now in his rearview mirror.

Just forty feet forward, Brian McDonald stood hunched over a large table in the center of CVIC. The bulkheads around him were covered with charts and other planning tools, and the other members of his strike team swirled around him in almost perpetual motion.

Brian was torn. On the one hand, he was one of the most junior strike leads in the Airwing. It was a great honor and a significant career plum and indicated that he was on the "fast track" in the TACAIR community. There were about six to eight strike leads in the Airwing senior to him, and under normal circumstances he would have been assigned a smaller strike or even would have been used as a secondary strike lead. But so many Airwing pilots had been killed or severely wounded in the attack at the Intercontinental that he had moved up rapidly in seniority and was now leading the planning of one of the biggest strikes in the campaign—a strike against the naval base at Bushehr.

While he was honored to be doing this, Brian chafed over the amount of time he was spending planning and how little time he was actually flying. He had last been airborne three days ago, and that only for a short 1+15 ASR hop. He could feel himself getting rusty. He thought how ironic it was; he had just seen Anne O'Connor in the dirty-shirts wardroom earlier in the day—she was going up for her second hop of the day, her fifth of the week thus far. He reflected on the fact that he was her mentor and reminded himself to give her a bad time about flying so much while he slaved away in CVIC.

Becky Philips couldn't go work out again to clear her mind. That would seem too strange, so she decided to take a walk around *Carl Vinson*'s cavernous hangar bay instead. She dropped down the three decks from the O-3 level and began to walk, weaving her way carefully around the twenty-four aircraft parked there undergoing various kinds of maintenance. As she watched the young mechanics working in the 110+ degree heat, doing hard, honest work, she reminded herself that above all else, she needed to do the right thing. The chief of staff had been no help. What could she do now?

Was he right and was she wrong? Becky ducked under a Tomcat that was undergoing an engine change as she tossed that question around in her brain. She had heard what she had heard. Had the chief of staff really listened to what she'd had to say?

As Becky walked past elevator four and looked out at the horizon at USS *Shiloh*, the AEGIS cruiser serving as shotgun for the *Carl Vinson*, she thought back to her previous sea duty tour aboard the AEGIS cruiser *Chancellorsville*. What a great ship and what a great CO—Captain Terry O'Donnell had gotten her a super set of orders coming off that ship and had written a strong letter of recommendation when she had applied for the Flag Secretary job on the

CARGRU SEVEN staff. As she walked forward to the farthest forward part of the hangar bay, where the vast complex of AIMD shops were located, she wondered where he was now. Then she realized: he was the one.

Back in her tiny stateroom, Becky clicked on her desktop computer. Through a series of satellite data links she was connected on the SIPRNET network with literally hundreds of commands Navy and DOD wide. She had one address that she needed to find.

Becky was adept at manipulating the system to work for her. Part of it was a by-product of her job—as flag secretary she needed to be connected to numerous other commands about a host of issues—and part of it was her natural curiosity and her familiarity with computers. She thought that she remembered that he was serving on the Joint Staff. A pulldown of DOD addresses in the greater Capitol area confirmed that he was there, and a short time surfing the Joint Chiefs of Staff web page confirmed his precise billet, phone number, and e-mail address. Becky was not sure that she could compose herself properly for a phone call, so she began to put her concerns in an e-mail. She typed and then erased and then typed and erased some more. Finally, she had something that she thought made sense.

Captain O'Donnell. Hello. This is Becky Philips. It has been a while since we served in *Chancellorsville* together. I am enjoying my job as Flag Secretary on CARGRU SEVEN staff, and I really appreciate your helping me to get it.

Captain, I have a bit of a dilemma here. I almost don't know how to begin. It all involves the recent terrorist attack on the Intercontinental Hotel. I am sure that you are very involved in this in your job on the Joint Staff. I know that we are going to strike Iran, I just don't know what the extent of these strikes will be.

I guess that even though this SIPRNET is classified, there is a limit to how specific I can get, but Captain, here is where I am really, really confused. Our Admiral briefed the staff that we are going after a full range of targets in Iran. But I overheard (I was trying to be an EA for the Admiral, just in case he needed me to do that) the Admiral talking with the Fifth Fleet Commander and alluding to the fact that only strikes against the terrorist camps were authorized, but that he was going to cause some kind of provocation and use it as an excuse to attack other targets. I tried to tell my Chief of Staff about it—he is really a good guy—but he just blew me off and there is no one else I can ask. I don't know how I got in the middle of this, but can you tell me, Captain, what the real story is?

If it's true that we are supposed to strike only the terrorist camps, then something is really wrong out here. If we are supposed to hit all these other targets, then I have totally misunderstood what is going on and I apologize for bothering you with this. I'm just trying to do the right thing, Captain, and I appreciate your looking at this. I look forward to hearing back from you, sir. Very respectfully, Becky.

P.S. Sir, please respond as soon as you can.

Satisfied with what she had composed, she took a deep breath and hit the Send button.

45

THE HOT SUN CAME UP IN THE EASTERN SKY AND IT was not yet 6:00 A.M., but the action onboard *Carl Vinson* was already frenetic.

Wizard Foster stood next to the captain's chair on *Carl Vinson*'s expansive bridge and waited for Craig Vandegrift to complete his conversation with *Carl Vinson*'s air boss.

The captain was even more engaged in events on the flight deck than he usually was, feeling he needed to provide even more extensive oversight as *Carl Vinson*'s flight tempo picked up.

"Sorry, CAG, Boss is working hard and I don't want him to miss anything," said the captain.

"No worries, Captain," replied CAG. "I reckon he could use some help. First time our sortie count's going to climb past 140 this cruise. We doing OK?"

"Yeah, CAG, we can handle it. Kids on the flight deck are working awfully hard, though," he replied as they both looked down on the flight deck, five decks below their high perch on the bridge. The last aircraft on this large, twenty-two plane launch was on cat 3.

"You know, we can talk with the admiral again about this," said the captain, "but he was pretty adamant about getting ready for these strikes against Iran. Until we get an execute order I think he's gonna keep putting a ton of planes in the air every day so we're all tuned up."

"I'm all for getting tuned up, too, but my pilots are getting burned out," replied CAG. "They're trying to make up for the pilots we lost by just working harder and flying more sorties. I know that some of the squadrons are shading crew rest rules already—and that's just based on what some of the pilots admit. I keep seeing that thousand-yard stare when I walk through the ready rooms."

"I know what you're saying," the captain continued. "I see it just passing some guys walking down the passageway."

"I haven't been really worried until the last two days, Craig. I don't know how much longer we can keep up this pace."

After the morning Flag Brief and the subsequent warfare commanders' meeting had finally ended—both had been exceptionally long as the admiral had insisted on wringing out all of the details of the battle group's preparations for the strikes against Iran—Wizard Foster and Craig Vandegrift stayed behind to talk with Heater Robinson.

"OK fellas, what's on your minds?" replied Robinson in a monotone. Both men could see that the admiral was distracted, almost distant. Something had changed, but neither man could tell what it was.

"Admiral," CAG began. "We're watching the sortie ramp up very carefully. Think that we may be pushing the outer limits of what we can sustain, sir, and we think that we may want to turn down the gain just a little bit."

"You think that we're flying too much, CAG?" the admiral replied, looking at Foster. It sounded more like an accusation than a question. "You think so, too?" he continued, looking at Craig Vandegrift.

"I do, Admiral," the captain replied. "People on the flight deck are getting a little ragged, Admiral. I'm not sure how long we can sustain this before we have an accident."

Heater Robinson paused for a long while before he spoke.

"Look, gents. The concerns you raise are legitimate. I know our people are getting tired. But it is only a matter of time—a very short time, I think—before we get the order to strike the Islamic Republic. That is going to be a tough mission. I have got to be sure that we are absolutely ready. Everybody needs a final tune-up before the real thing. I may have to buy some element of risk if we're going to be combat ready."

"I know that, Admiral," replied CAG. "But with our losses at the Intercontinental, I can barely make the flight schedule, and that's with double and triple cycling a lot of folks."

"Same thing on the flight deck, Admiral. I'm seeing the same type of fatigue, maybe worse, than I saw when we lost Petty Officer Parker. It's getting shaky out there," added Craig Vandegrift.

"All right, fellas, all right. Look, we all flew during Storm in the Gulf. We all got tired. But we all made it. Now we need to be just as ready."

His officers knew that there was no use in arguing.

"Easy with it."
"Power."
"Left for lineup."
"Easy with the power."
SLAM! The Viking caught the three wire. *Perfect*, thought

Anne O'Connor as the wire ran out and jerked her aircraft to a halt just sixty feet from the end of the angle deck.

"You still got it, Annie," said Mike Hart. "Double cycle mission and you still hit the three wire. You're my hero."

"Team effort, Mike. Let's get this beast parked and get the hop debriefed. I think that the intel boys will be interested in the contacts we picked up. Then it's rack time for me so we can rest up for our late afternoon flight."

"I'm with you, boss—well, I mean, not like that, you know. I'm spoken for and all that."

"Hart, you've got to be the most sex-starved NFO in the squadron. What have you been thinking about all the time?"

"That, mostly. Hey, I'm getting a little bit punchy. I need some rack time too."

Anne knew exactly where Mike Hart was coming from. The fatigue was really beginning to show in the Blue Wolf Ready Room. Their hop had been a double-cycle armed surface recee hop—just two-and-one-half hours. They'd launched just after 0900, and they were back on deck shortly before noon. A debrief in CVIC, some quick chow in the dirty-shirts wardroom, finish the rest of the paperwork at maintenance control, a fast shower . . . Anne figured that she could be in the rack by 1330—and get a few hours of sleep before her late afternoon hop. She'd need it, that would be a tanker hop, the same routine that Chrissie was going through now.

Anne was worried about Chrissie. She had looked more and more worn down over the past several days—even more so than most of the other Blue Wolf officers. Chrissie was a pro and didn't cut corners, which worked to her disadvantage now as she dotted every i and crossed every t of her duties. She was living on little more than a few hours' sleep a night. She even fell asleep during the brief. Worse, Chrissie had drawn tanker duty today, and just as Anne was landing, the replacement tanker went down on the cat. They decided to "yo-yo" Chrissie, refuel her and send her up to tank again, while Blue Wolf maintenance sorted out the aircraft situation.

Anne finished up her paperwork in maintenance control. As she was about to leave, she asked the maintenance control chief, Senior Chief McCarthy, if Chrissie had landed yet.

"No, ma'am," replied the chief. "Board says she's coming back with this recovery that started a few minutes ago. She'll probably be last down."

"Rog, thanks Chief," replied Anne. It had been a while since Anne had had "tower flower" duty serving as the squadron pilot assigned to stand by in *Carl Vinson*'s primary control tower to assist with any situation that came up with a squadron aircraft. Some sixth sense told her to head on up the seven decks to *Carl Vinson*'s tower to see Chrissie come in.

Anne arrived in the tower as the air boss was catching the last half-dozen aircraft in the recovery. Brian McDonald was up there already, taking his turn as tower flower for the Stingers.

"Set 'em up, Hornet," intoned the air boss, letting everyone in the tower know that an F/A-18 would be landing next. That would cause a certain tension to be set in the arresting cable rooms and would determine a particular setting for the meatball.

"Hornet ball, 4.4."

"Roger, ball," replied the LSO, his voice calls to the Hornet being piped into the tower. Anne watched Brian crane his neck to see his squadronmate catch a two wire. "Not bad," Brian murmured.

The last few aircraft all trapped successfully. As Chief McCarthy predicted, Chrissie Linder was the last plane in the groove. It was after 1300. She'd been flying for four-and-a-half hours. Anne knew that she'd be exhausted.

"Viking ball, 5.8."

"Roger, ball," replied Viking paddles. "Work it in, Chrissie."

It wasn't the smoothest approach that Anne or the others in the tower had ever seen. Chrissie was wobbly, she was overcorrecting as she came down the glide slope. Paddles was giving rapid instructions.

"Left for lineup, 704."

"Easy with the power."

"You're drifting right."

"Bring it back."

"Easy, *easy*, with the power."

"Power!"

Just get it down on deck Chrissie. This doesn't have to be the greatest pass you've ever made. Just get the jet on the deck, thought Anne.

"Easy . . . hold it."

SLAM! Chrissie's aircraft hit the deck, but she bunted the nose forward as she dove for it. As the Viking's nose pitched forward, the tail hook lifted away from the deck just a few inches—just enough to miss the arresting wire.

"Bolter, bolter, bolter," shouted the air boss. "Power and go!"

The Viking skidded down the flight deck and lumbered back into the air. Fred Beasal, her COTAC, chattered at Chrissie constantly.

"You got it Chrissie . . . hook-skip bolter was just bad luck . . . you made a great pass . . . just bring it around again . . . piece of cake . . . you've done this a thousand times. . . ." Fred Beasal didn't believe what he was telling Chrissie. He knew that she was struggling, but he needed to help her now—no time for bad news.

In the tower, Anne shot Brian a furtive, worried glance. She knew that he had hundreds more traps than she did, and her body language told him that she wanted his opinion on how Chrissie was doing. The look that he shot back was not encouraging. Even if she had not boltered, her pass had looked pretty awful.

As the tension mounted in the tower, Chrissie turned downwind for another try. Boomer Davison tried mightily to keep his voice calm. He reminded Paddles to do the same.

"OK, 704, just had a little hook skip there, bring it around and we'll trap you. Piece of cake. The deck's all yours," said Davison, hoping to calm Chrissie down as much as he could.

Chrissie rolled final.

"Viking ball, 5.2."

"Roger, ball," replied Paddles. Her LSO had talked with the air boss, and they shared the concern that this would be a tough catch. Linder was usually a good ball flyer, one of the better pilots among the Blue Wolves. Her last pass was marginal at best. They needed to give her all the help that they could to get her on deck.

"Deck's looking real good, 704, keep it coming," continued Paddles. His voice was calm, almost a whisper. He wanted Chrissie to feel like he was in the cockpit with her, helping to work the Viking down.

"Right for lineup, 704, easy with it."

"Little power."

"Don't overcorrect, just easy with it."

Paddles was on the horns of a dilemma. Chrissie was controlling the Viking erratically, her scan was clearly breaking down. Paddles had to correct her position on the glide path, but he knew that every correction he gave her would make her more and more nervous and induce even more corrections. He had to walk a fine line. He hoped he was right.

In the aircraft, Fred Beasal backed up Chrissie on the instruments. He could see that she was struggling. He knew that fatigue was overtaking her and that the bolter had stripped away what little confidence she had left. For the first time in all of the missions he had flown with her, he was worried. Furtively, he tightened all of his straps and harnesses.

In the tower, Anne, Brian, the air boss, and the other dozen-plus professionals there stood frozen in anticipation. It was a helpless feeling as they watched the Viking gyrate down the glide slope. It was all up to Chrissie and Paddles now to bring the Viking back on deck.

"Looking good, 704," said Paddles, although he knew he was really stretching it. Chrissie was all over the sky. He continued to work her.

"Little left for lineup now."

"Easy with the power."

"Easy."

"Don't settle."

Paddle's calls were coming more rapidly now as the Viking passed inside a half mile. At 120 knots, Chrissie would be over the deck in less than ten seconds.

"You're on centerline, just hold it."

"Little power."

"Little more power."

"Easy with it 704, *easy with it*."

"You're settling."

The Viking was inside a quarter mile. Chrissie's reactions were sluggish. She was now clearly behind the aircraft. Fred Beasal tried to coax her to respond to Paddles.

"Chrissie, he wants power, give it some power," he said, trying not to let his voice reveal the desperation he felt.

Chrissie was no longer flying the aircraft, it was flying her. The fine, fingertip touch on the stick had degenerated to a hand wrapped around the stick so hard that it seemed to want to squeeze the paint right out of it. Her hand on the throttle had the same tight grip. Her eyes no longer danced around the instrument panel, scanning her gauges and scanning the deck and the meatball.

"Power, 704, give me some power," said Paddles, his voice raising octaves rapidly as he spoke.

The Viking was settling, Chrissie was much too slow with the power. With her left hand wrapped tightly around the throttle, she barely knew where the throttle control was.

"POWER, 704, POWER!" Paddles was now insistent, demanding. Calm no longer worked, he just had to make her do what he said.

Fred Beasal was desperate now. "Power Chrissie, damn it, do it, DO IT NOW."

"POWER, POWER, POWER," shouted Paddles as the Viking approached the ramp. In that instant he knew that Chrissie had no chance of making a landing. He did the only thing that he could.

"WAVE OFF, 704, WAVE OFF, WAVE OFF!" As he said it, Paddles activated the switch that turned on the flashing red lights surrounding the meatball.

"POWER CHRISSIE, POWER DAMN IT, DO IT, DO IT," shouted Fred Beasal, desperately trying to get her to respond.

It was too late. The Viking was settling below the ramp. Even as Chrissie added power she could not overcome the laws of physics. The Viking had settled too far below the glide path. No amount of power, no movement of the controls could keep the Viking from striking the ramp.

Paddles saw it first and issued his next, fateful order.

"704, EJECT, EJECT!"

Fred Beasal heard the order and reached for his ejection handle. But it all happened too fast for Chrissie. Only a handful of the five thousand men and women on *Carl Vinson* had ever seen a ramp strike, but they all knew, instinctively, what was about to happen. Everyone on the LSO platform dove into the net just outboard and below the platform. On the flight deck people started running away from the ramp, trying to put as much distance between them and the aircraft about to impale itself on the ship. . . .

SLAM! The Viking hit the ramp with a sickening thud, breaking the aircraft's back and causing an instant fireball as the fuel tanks ruptured and the 5,000 pounds of jet fuel ignited. Pieces of aircraft shot a hundred feet in the air, and aircraft parts, large and small, hurtled down the deck like missiles. A single chute shot upward like a missile.

Anne's eyes grew wide with horror as everyone in the tower instinctively ducked for cover, even though it was highly unlikely that any of the flying debris would reach that high and forward, let alone penetrate primary's thick, shatterproof, glass windows. Seconds after the initial impact, everyone in the tower peeked over the console to see, they hoped, a second chute carrying Chrissie Linder to safety. There was none.

Anne began to shake, almost uncontrollably. She turned her back and ran out of primary. Brian stood stunned for a moment, then ran after her as she bolted down the ladders and away from the scene.

46

GENERAL NAJAFI WALKED UP TO ONE OF THE LOW concrete block buildings on the outskirts of what had once been an active base for the Army of the Islamic Republic. Rocky, barren, surrounded by distant mountains, the base had once been a bustling training facility, but now it was officially closed—another victim of the desperate economic times facing his country. He had flown from Tehran to Qom via military transport, then driven the forty miles from Qom to this facility.

Security was tight at this building, and the general was pleased with what he saw—double chain-link fences topped by deadly concertina wire, guard towers with machine guns loaded, soldiers with dogs patrolling on foot, armored vehicles with soldiers in full battle fatigues making constant patrols on both the inside and the outside of the perimeter fences.

He was met at the outer door by the chief scientist at the facility, Doctor Hashemi, who greeted him and his party.

"Welcome, General," he began. "We are honored to have you visit us, I think you will be pleased with what we have to show you."

"I am sure I will be," Najafi replied. For the head of the Islamic Armed Forces to visit this remote a site was a rare occurrence. The chief scientist knew that it was for one reason only.

"Here we have the receiving areas," Dr. Bani Hashemi said as he shepherded the general through the facility. "Here is one of the three main storage areas, the other two are in the building just to our west. Here on the right is our calibration laboratory. Right this way, General, and we will enter the main assembly area."

The nature of the general's visit had been unspecified—and short-fused—and Dr. Hashemi was doing his best to anticipate what he might want to see.

"General, here we are," said the chief scientist as he ushered the general past a guarded blastproof door and into the main assembly area.

It was half as big as a soccer field, stark, extremely well lit, with white-washed concrete floors, gleaming machinery, humming air-conditioning, racks and racks of computer bays, and dozens of white-coated workers moving purposefully throughout the facility. The general paused to take it all in as Dr. Hashemi continued to babble away.

"So, Dr. Hashemi, you have done well with this project. How soon will you be ready to put the weapon on one of our aircraft?"

The chief scientist was shocked by the general's remark. There had been no warning about this. This was not scheduled. They had been given a timeline, and they were actually slightly ahead of schedule. Preposterous. He just did not understand.

"General, as you see, our assembly is nearly complete. Working at this pace we will have it put together in a week to a week and a half."

"At this pace?" said the general.

"Yes, General. We are not funded for even two shifts, let alone around the clock operations. We put in a very efficient eight- to ten-hour day," the chief scientist began, now giving General Najafi a tutorial of their problems. "Once we complete the assembly, we must complete the testing. There are extensive fidelity checks to run, other more complicated tests—"

"How long will those tests take?" asked the general, interrupting the chief scientist and sounding a bit annoyed.

"It is almost impossible to say, General—"

Again, General Najafi interrupted. "Dr. Hashemi, is this absolutely the best you can do?"

The chief scientist had dealt with the bureaucrats in the Ministry of Defense for years. He had been assigned to this project two years ago and had dedicated almost every waking moment to ensuring its success. He had prevailed in spite of every obstacle. The drawings the Koreans had given them had been flawed. They had not gotten the material in time. Their technicians had too little training. Now he was close to completion. The Islamic Republic's first nuclear device. It was his proudest achievement. He would not allow some military fool, even if he was the head of the armed forces, to hurry his work.

"General, it is, and may I say we are working extraordinarily hard just to make that schedule." Several of the other white coats around him nodded agreement.

"That is good that you are working hard, Doctor," said General Najafi sarcastically, "but I need you to work harder. I want this weapon ready to load on my transport plane in ninety-six hours."

There was a collective gasp in the room. Then a murmur. Then Dr. Hashemi spoke.

"General, that is impossible."

"Impossible, Doctor?"

"Yes, General, quite impossible." The chief scientist and General Najafi stared at each other.

"Doctor Hashemi, who is your deputy?"

"My deputy, General?"

"Yes, your deputy, your second in command."

"I am," said one of the white coats as he stepped forward. "I am Dr. Mohammad Samimi, I am the chief scientist's principal assistant."

"Good," replied General Najafi. "Good," he said again as he went over to shake the man's hand. He stepped back from the man and turned back toward the chief scientist, giving the man a hard stare.

"This is the best you can do, Doctor," he said, challenging him again.

"Absolutely, General," he replied firmly, now giving the general a defiant stare.

General Najafi said nothing as his right hand reached down and undid the one clip holding down the flap of his service revolver. With a smooth motion he took the gun out of the holster, brought it up parallel to the floor, pointed it directly at the chief scientist.

The bullet hit the chief scientist square on the forehead, and the back of his head came off, sending bone, skin, and blood everywhere, splattering those close to him. Hashemi dropped like a rock, his lifeless eyes wide with shock. No one else in the room moved for what seemed like an eternity.

"Doctor Samimi, you have ninety-six hours," Najafi said as he strode out of the room.

At the Iranian naval bases of Bushehr and Bandar Abbas the level of activity was intense. Sailors sweated and strained to load stores and supplies and prepare their craft to get underway. Though the Iranian Navy had numerous ships and craft conducting comprehensive "Victory" series naval exercises in the Arabian Gulf at least yearly, it was not accustomed to leaving port on short notice.

At the highest levels of government, it was clear that this was the prudent thing to do. If the Americans attacked in retaliation for the bombing at the Intercontinental, they did not want to have their ships in their poorly defended ports to be sunk at their piers by American airplanes. That made sense to the senior Navy captains and commanders. What made less sense was the high-priority mission assigned to two ships' captains, Commander Mohammad Mohtaj on the Saam Class frigate *Sabalan*, putting out to sea from Bushehr, and Commander Farhad Kani on another Saam Class frigate, *Alborz*, putting out to sea from Bandar Abbas.

Commander Mohammad Mohtaj called his executive officer into his cabin.

"Abbas Sohrabi, you are my right-hand man. Although my orders are not to share this information with anyone, as my second in command, I must tell you.

"While many of our Navy vessels are putting out to sea simply so they are not sitting ducks for an American attack, we—along with *Alborz*—are to find the American aircraft carrier *Carl Vinson*."

Abbas Sohrabi gasped. He was as brave as any man, but

this was tantamount to suicide. Their small frigate, taking on an American battle group.

"I can see the concern in your eyes, Abbas Sohrabi. But do not fear. Our orders are not to attack the *Carl Vinson*, only to observe the American ship. Our leaders fear that the Americans may order a preemptive attack on the Islamic Republic. Our role, and that of *Alborz*, is merely to observe the actions of the carrier and listen to its transmissions. It is unlikely that it will be able to hide the fact that it is launching a huge number of aircraft to strike our beloved country."

"But Captain," Abbas Sohrabi replied, "we have learned that the Americans value their carriers above all else. Given the level of tension between our two countries, is it likely that they will let us operate anywhere near them? They fear our C-802 missiles and would not let us get anywhere within range of their prized carriers."

"That may be the desire of the carrier commander, but there has been no declaration by the Americans that our nation is behind these attacks, even though in their press, some of their right-wing journalists scream for retaliation. No, Abbas Sohrabi, we are merely patrolling in international waters. We can come close to their ships with impunity. There is nothing that they can do."

"Yes, Captain, we will follow our orders. We will be ready to put to sea in less than twelve hours," replied Abbas Sohrabi. Although he was unconvinced that his ship—or any other—could operate freely around an American aircraft carrier, he had his orders.

At the presidential offices in Tehran, four hundred and fifty miles away from Bushehr as the crow flies, much longer via Iran's antiquated road system, General Najafi was escorted into the office of President Habibi.

"General," Habibi said as he motioned Najafi to a chair in front of his desk. "I understand that you have visited the site where the nuclear weapon is being built."

"Yes, Mr. President. I have impressed upon the staff there the importance of completing this weapon immediately. I have the aircraft ready and the crew trained and briefed. I told them I wanted the weapon completed in ninety-six hours. I am certain that they will not disobey my orders. We will be ready and we will deliver the weapon against the American aircraft carrier."

Habibi paused a moment. The general was leaning forward—that he could abide—but he was now taking national policy into his own hands.

"When did you intend to deploy this weapon, General?"

"Why, immediately after it is completed, Mr. President. We will eliminate the danger to our Islamic Republic in one blow."

Habibi had trouble believing what he was hearing. Najafi was getting way, way, out in front. He was going to single-handedly start a war with the United States.

"General, we are not sure if the Americans intend to attack us. Even if they did attack us first, we still have ample ways to respond and we would also have world opinion on our side. Is this something you have carefully considered?"

Najafi was confused. He thought he had carte blanche to defend the Islamic Republic in any way he saw fit. Now President Habibi was temporizing.

"Mr. President, my sole purpose in life is the defense of the Islamic Republic. I have devised the most effective plan that I can to defend our country. I will be ready in just a few days. We need to defang the Americans before they can attack us."

"General," Habibi began. "You are our republic's military leader. You have established a record of excellence in your stewardship of our military. You deserve to have a legacy that generations can honor. That is why it is *crucial* that you not move with undue haste. You have told me where this facility is where your weapon is being prepared and you have told me how you intend to have your aircraft carry it. You are secure from attack by the Americans. They have far more inviting targets at our naval bases and our military airfields."

Najafi continued to listen.

"You have told me also, General, how you will have your ships shadow the *Carl Vinson*. You will know if they intend to attack, and you can then unleash your weapon, but not until then. Promise me, General, that you won't move until the Americans attack. We will depend on many nations to back us in our struggle. If we attack preemptively, especially with a nuclear weapon, we will be the scourge of the international community. Wait for the Americans to move—if they move—and we will see even nations who are against us rally to our cause."

General Najafi sat silently, weighing Habibi's words. He was beginning to see Habibi's point of view. He was not willing to admit it fully, but it was something he would consider.

"Mr. President, your words carry wisdom, I will consider them strongly," he said as he rose. Habibi had intended to continue the conversation, but Najafi was finished.

Habibi stood silently as Najafi strode off, wondering if he had convinced the general.

A short distance away from where Habibi was using all of his powers of persuasion, Foreign Minister Velayati had no such concerns. He and Shiekholeslam were of like minds. He had told Shiekholeslam to put his agents where they could have the greatest impact and do the most damage, and he, in turn, had instructed three men—the first to be activated—three of his best, to deploy in New York City, in Washington, D.C., and in San Diego.

Each man was a trusted underling who Shiekholeslam felt would gladly give his life for the cause if necessary. Each had been provided a quantity of deadly VX nerve gas and instructions on how to release it. Each was instructed to pick a crowded public place to release this nerve gas. Once they had reported where this place was, they were each to take a small hotel room very close to the location where their gas would ultimately be released and wait for Shiekholeslam to contact them on their pagers. They were to be ready day or night to carry out their tasks. Now all they had to do was wait.

47

CAPTAIN TERRY O'DONNELL STARED AT HIS COMPUTER screen and read Becky Philips's e-mail message for the third time. Each time he read it he became more and more perplexed. Could this really be true? Could this really be happening on *Carl Vinson*? He scrolled up and hit the printer icon on his display, tapping his fingers nervously as his printer hummed to life. As soon as the single page appeared, he grabbed it and rushed out into the broad corridor.

Colonel Dave Laird was in a meeting, and O'Donnell paced nervously outside his office waiting to be shown in. The Army sergeant manning the reception desk glanced at the captain every few minutes, wondering what was distressing him. For O'Donnell, the wait gave him time to sort through his thoughts. What would he tell Laird, his immediate boss? He had to tell someone, and Laird was the only one he could think to tell. If Becky's story was true, it was a matter of the utmost urgency. But what if it weren't true? What if she had somehow misunderstood the conversation between Robinson and Flowers? He wanted to do the right thing, but he didn't want to take the bullet for some mistake made seven thousand miles away.

The meeting broke up and the people who had been in the meeting with Colonel Laird filed out. The sergeant didn't need to announce O'Donnell to Laird, as the anxious captain just walked right into his office.

"What is it, Captain? I didn't expect to see you up here today. Thought that you were working that budget proposal and the answers to those congressional inquiries." Beyond being his immediate boss, Colonel Dave Laird was three years senior to Captain Terry O'Donnell and seemed to go out of his way to remind him of that.

"Colonel, I needed to see you right away. There may be a 'development' aboard one of our aircraft carriers, something that may affect national security. I thought that I needed to bring this to your attention."

"A 'development' aboard an aircraft carrier," Laird said a bit sarcastically. "Hell, Captain, you forget, we're the J-5 Directorate . . . we're not much into current operations. Why did this 'development' hit your desk?"

"This is why, Colonel," replied O'Donnell as he laid Becky's e-mail in front of Laird.

Laird read it quickly, then O'Donnell saw him reading it again slowly. He heard a long, slow hiss as the colonel sucked wind through his teeth.

"Have you shown this to anyone else?" asked Laird.

"No, you are the first one. I got this less than a half hour ago. It would have been in front of you sooner, but you were tied up in a meeting. Do you know what she is talking about in here?"

"Only scuttlebutt, the guys in the Ops Directorate are running this situation. I've heard—and it seems logical—that we might make some kind of a strike, but who, where, and when is being run by the J-3 folks. Even at that, it's very close hold, no one is talking much. I don't know the real answer."

"What should we do?" asked O'Donnell.

"This may be nothing, but we can't sit on it. My boss, Brigadier General Williams, is on leave, and the 'acting' is Colonel Baker. After General Williams, our chain goes to the J-5 as you know, but Vice Admiral Putnam is visiting STRATCOM, won't be back until late tomorrow. We need to get this to the Ops Directorate right now!"

"Are you going to jump the whole chain?"

"I'm going to give Randy Ziemba a call and tell him I'm running with this. I know General Allen's executive assistant pretty well. I think that the EA can get us on the calendar in a hurry."

This was all happening faster than Terry O'Donnell could absorb it. He could be minutes away from seeing one of the most powerful three-stars in the military—the director of operations for the Joint Chiefs of Staff—and explaining what this all meant. And some complain about bureaucratic inertia.

"Dave," O'Donnell said, hoping that the personal touch might work with him, "don't you think we ought to talk about what we're going to say, I mean, how we're going to present this? We may want to run it through some lower levels first—"

"We're the lower levels, Terry," interrupted Laird. "We know about this. I don't know how you Navy guys work, but if we had two Air Force generals conspiring to attack somebody we didn't authorize them to attack, we'd sure as hell try to get to the bottom of it as a matter of priority and not stand on ceremony or worry about being wrong." Laird's voice was almost condescending, making it sound as if the junior officer was trying to cover up a Navy problem. He didn't give O'Donnell a chance to reply as he dialed the phone.

Fifteen minutes later both men had passed through a maze of offices and stood outside of the office of Lieutenant General Robert Allen, director of operations for the Joint Staff and the officer responsible for directing any action dictated by the National Command Authorities through the chairman of the Joint Chiefs of Staff. He was the primary link to the Unified Commanders worldwide. In time of crisis, he became the focal point for much of the nation's military efforts.

They were ushered in without ceremony and without General Allen's having been given any background of why these two officers from a totally different part of the Joint Staff were in his office.

"Good morning, fellas. My EA, Captain Ziemba, said that you both needed to see me right away." He could see that both men were extremely nervous.

"General, we appreciate your seeing us," said Colonel Laird. "We wouldn't have bothered you unless we felt that this was crucial, real time information that you needed to have."

"I'm sure that you wouldn't have, Colonel. Well, let's have it."

Colonel Dave Laird began to pour out his story, everything that he and Captain O'Donnell had discussed over the last hour. Finally, he produced Becky Philips's e-mail.

General Allen read it slowly and then looked up at Terry O'Donnell.

"You know this person, Captain?"

"Yes, sir, I do."

"Is she some kind of wild-eyed, impressionable flake?"

"No sir, she's a solid officer. Served in my command for almost two years. If she's gone outside the chain of command like this, I think that there's a problem."

"You all stand by, we are going to see the chairman about this."

Both Terry O'Donnell and Dave Laird felt their eyes go wide.

Within an hour they had all seen the chairman. He had been as shocked as General Allen had been. Admiral Monroe had been incredulous about the story. A short while ago he had defended Admiral Robinson's shootdown of the Iraqi Foxbat to the president. Now this. He knew that he had to get to the bottom of this immediately, and he decided that the best course was to have General Allen call Admiral Robinson directly. General Allen had shooed away Laird and O'Donnell. After getting Admiral Robinson's direct dial STU III number from one of his assistants, he left strict instructions not to be disturbed.

It was 1100 Washington time, 1800 in the Arabian Gulf. Heater Robinson was sitting at the head of the table in the Flag Mess beginning the evening meal with his wardroom. The Stu III rang three times at Admiral Robinson's desk before tripping over to his admin office. His flag writer, Chief Petty Officer Carol Weaver, answered the phone. After a polite skirmish with General Allen's secretary, she ran into the Flag Mess to get the admiral.

"Admiral," she began, standing just a few feet away in the

Wardroom Mess lounge area, "General Allen of the Joint Staff is on the phone for you."

"Bob Allen? Sure. We were at National War College together. What's he want? 'Scuse me," he said as he got up from the table. "I'll take it in my cabin, Chief."

Heater Robinson strode purposefully the few steps to his cabin. The operations director on the Joint Staff was calling him directly. Maybe the operation to strike Iran was a "go" already. Once he was seated at his desk, Heater Robinson picked up the phone.

"Robinson?" said General Allen once his secretary put him on the line.

"Yes, sir, good to hear from you, General. It's been a long time since the National War College sir," said Heater Robinson, trying for a friendly and familiar connection with the general.

"Admiral Robinson, I just wanted to ask you about the upcoming operation against Iran and your preparations for it."

So this wasn't a call to give him an execute order, thought Robinson. What was the general driving at? Why was he skipping two echelons in the chain of command to call him directly?

"Yes, sir, General, we are preparing vigorously. We are doing mirror-image strikes preparing for an execute order from the Joint Staff. I thought you might be calling about that, sir."

"No, that will come in due course, Admiral. What I am calling about is the nature of those strikes and about any, well, potential 'misunderstandings' about what those strikes will entail. You've gotten the warning order, you're clear that these strikes will be against the terrorist targets and only against the terrorist targets."

So that was it, thought Robinson. His mind raced. How did Allen know this? Had Flowers ratted him out? He and Flowers were the only ones who had discussed this. Heater Robinson at once went from open conversation with General Allen to a very guarded one. He had to defuse this at once.

"Very clear, General. Only the terrorist camps. Nothing

else. That has been the focus of our planning."

"Yes, Admiral, but there's a concern that there might have been conversations that suggested hitting other targets, too. A major ratcheting up against the Islamic Republic. We want to absolutely ensure that this is not the case."

Now he knew that someone had let General Allen in on the exact contents of his conversation with Admiral Flowers. Flowers? No, he was implicated now. There must be a leak somewhere . . . somewhere internal. *Think, Mike, think*, he told himself. You've got to extricate yourself from this somehow. Finally it hit him.

"General, you know that we go to extraordinary lengths with operational deception to keep the Iranians off balance. The last thing we want to do is telegraph our exact plans to the Islamic Republic. We think that their monitoring of our radio communications—even our secure communications— is quite sophisticated. I have my command and control people planting all kinds of false communications to confuse the Iranians. Every other day I launch a big package of aircraft that heads down toward their base at Bandar Abbas just to keep them guessing. My communications experts even suggested that I have a conversation with the Fifth Fleet commander talking about strikes that weren't going to happen. That was a stretch, you know. Admiral Flowers isn't an aviator like you and me, and I had to coach him through a lot of the dialogue—but we made it work. I'd like to think that we were pretty convincing. Anyway, General, we're just trying to be as thorough as we possibly can, and we think that we've got the Iranians off balance."

General Allen had listened intently. At first skeptical, he was brought around to Admiral Robinson's seemingly sound logic. He tried to think of another question to ask, but he couldn't.

"Admiral, I see. Well, I understand what you are doing. We just got an offhand report, that's all. Maybe if you had let someone on the Joint Staff know that you were doing this, we could have turned off the alarm bells before they got too loud."

"That would have been a much better idea, General. Thanks for suggesting it. And we definitely will do that next time. On the subject sir, do you have any insights into when we will get an execute order?"

"Not yet, Admiral. We will keep you informed. Thanks for your feedback. You keep us informed, hear?"

"Good-bye, General."

Satisfied with Heater Robinson's explanation, General Allen hung up the phone. He dutifully reported this to the chairman, and then, still chagrined that he had not checked this out more thoroughly before raising it to Admiral Monroe's level, he called in Laird and O'Donnell and had a large piece of their butts.

Certain that he had totally derailed this crisis, Admiral Robinson rejoined his staff at the dinner table. They had slowed down their supper and made it transparent that the admiral was ever gone. Buoyed that he had extricated himself from this trap, he seemed to his staff to be in a chipper mood. But was thinking. Who had done this? How was he going to catch them?

"Welcome back, Admiral. Glad you didn't have too long a conversation, this steak is too good to miss. Anything up, sir?" said George Sampson.

"No, COS, nothing important." Looking around the table and seeing the empty chair, he asked, "Where's Commander Philips?"

"Oh, she just excused herself right after you got up, sir."

"I see," said the admiral. "Ops o, pass that steak sauce," said Robinson, changing the conversation. *Very interesting*, thought the admiral. Was this just a coincidence?

Forty feet away, Becky Philips sat alone in the admin office. As soon as she arrived, she dismissed the flag writer. Then she very furtively picked up the phone and listened to the entire conversation between the admiral and General Allen. Now she had no doubts.

48

BECKY PHILIPS SAT ALONE IN HER STATEROOM SHORTLY after reveille and read her e-mail. What stared back at her from her screen was so frustrating that she had a hard time believing it. But given the events of the last twelve hours, it actually was the logical result of what had transpired.

Dear Becky. Thank you for your e-mail. It was great to hear from you. I can tell that you are doing the same professional job there on CARGRU SEVEN staff as you did for me in *Chancellorsville*. I appreciate your contacting me with your concerns and for letting me have an opportunity to run this to ground.

While I am not at liberty to discuss too many details, I can tell you that I ran this up the chain right to the top. We have looked at it very, very carefully out here and some very senior officers were involved in finding a solution. I can tell you that we did not take this lightly, we did not take this lightly at all. However, in the final analysis, we are convinced that Admiral Robinson fully understands, and is completely onboard with, JCS policy on this matter. He understands that he is to attack the terrorist camps and only the terrorist camps. Any conversations that he may have had with Admiral Flowers discussing anything else were for operational deception purposes. I am personally confident that he will carry out his exact orders.

Becky, please don't take this the wrong way, but perhaps you should take such matters up with Admiral Robinson himself, before going outside the lifelines. That way any confusion generated can be resolved at the source before it bubbles up and gets out of control. Hang in there and keep up the great work.

How could they be so naive? Becky thought. *Operational deception* indeed! Admiral Robinson had deceived the Joint Staff lock, stock, and broomstick. General Allen had bought Robinson's lies and hadn't had the smarts to check them out some other way to see if they were the truth or not. Becky had heard the entire conversation, and she knew the entire truth. She pondered what to do next as she put on her uniform and headed down to the admin office.

Admiral Robinson sat at his desk as the radioman explained the procedures one more time. Radioman First Class Mike Lopresti—the admiral's "private" radioman—a senior first class petty officer in the staff comm shack, was the one the admiral had designated to read and deliver SPECAT messages. No one else, not even the comm officer, was allowed to see them. He let what he had told the admiral sink in and then listened patiently as the admiral asked one or two last questions.

"So to use this older phone I key on the lighted buttons. When one of these lights up, it indicates that there is a conversation going on on that line. I just need to press the button and pick up the handset. Neither caller will know that I'm on the line because my handset speaker has been disabled. Do I have this about right?"

"Precisely, Admiral," replied Lopresti. He had wondered why the admiral was having another phone system put in his cabin, but he did not know how to ask. Finally, the admiral broached the subject for him.

"Probably looks like a strange lashup to you, RM1. Wish I could tell you precisely why you're doing this, but all I can tell you is that we are trying to plug a huge security breach. I have got to get involved personally. You've done your usual exceptional job in handling the technical aspects of this. Once again, I am proud of you and I remind you that you may not discuss this with anyone."

"Oh, no, sir, certainly not, sir. You have my assurance of that," replied Lopresti.

"Very well, you're dismissed."

Heater Robinson stared at the Plexiglas buttons that RM1 Lopresti had numbered for him. One for the flag lieutenant's number, two for the flag writer's number, three for the flag secretary's number, four for the operations officer's number, and so on down the line. He had his strong suspicions, and he would be watching line number three just a little closer than all of the others.

As flag secretary, Becky Philips was the senior person who worked in the admin office. When she wanted to, it was her prerogative to order the other people there to carry out duties in other parts of the ship, including clearing the office when she had some particularly urgent message to write or other duty to perform that was time critical and required her full concentration.

This day she waited until evening chow on the messdecks when all of her yeoman would be gone anyway. The flag lieutenant was working out. Only the flag writer remained. She asked Chief Weaver to give her some time alone, and the chief complied. It was time for chow in the chief's mess anyway. Almost 1700 aboard *Carl Vinson*, 1000 in the Pentagon. She had found his phone number in the Department of Defense phone book. Captain O'Donnell would most likely be at his desk. She took a deep breath and dialed the number. It rang only once.

"J-5 Directorate, Captain O'Donnell, speaking."

"Captain, this is Becky Philips, sir."

"Becky. Well, I'm surprised to hear from you. This connection sounds really good. Did you get my e-mail?"

"Yes I did, Captain."

"Well, I hope that it explained everything. I appreciate your trying to do a good professional job, but I think that this may be a case where you just didn't have the big picture and maybe misunderstood what was said."

"I didn't misunderstand anything, Captain."

"Becky, look, I probably shouldn't even be discussing this with you, but we have assurances that there is nothing untoward happening here." O'Donnell sounded just a bit annoyed that Becky was persisting.

"Captain, I listened to the entire conversation between General Allen and Admiral Robinson. What Robinson told him was pure, unadulterated bull. It was a lie, and your general bought it hook, line, and sinker. Look, Captain, I know what is going on down here. This entire ship, this entire battle group, is planning major strikes against the entire military infrastructure within Iran. I know, Captain. I have friends in the Airwing who are on strike teams. They know what they are supposed to hit. People on our staff are carrying around target folders. They are for much more than terrorist camps."

"Becky, this entire process is very convoluted. There is a lot to it. Perhaps these people are part of the operational deception plan. Perhaps not everyone has the entire story. Becky, don't you see, you are challenging a battle group commander, a man who has given his life to the Navy for thirty years. Why in God's name would he do something like this?"

"Why do you have to ask, Captain?" shouted Becky as loud as she dared. This was not turning out at all the way she wanted it to. Captain O'Donnell was supposed to be on her side. Why did he doubt her?

"Becky, look, I'm sorry, OK. I will take your story up the chain one more time. You can imagine what kind of a reception I'm going to get. If we hadn't served together for as long as we did, and if I didn't have the deepest professional respect for you, I wouldn't do this. You understand that, don't you?"

"I understand that, Captain. I appreciate your running with this. I think that we had better hurry. I have a feeling that these strikes will be happening soon."

"We will hurry it up at this end, Becky. You just be careful out there, will you?"

"Don't worry about me, Captain," she replied as she hung up the phone.

Across the passageway, less than thirty feet from where Becky sat, Heater Robinson placed the phone back in its cradle. He had not missed a word. He would need to take action and soon.

On the flight deck, the first plane shot down the cat with Brian McDonald in Stinger 204. It was the first of four night launches for practice strikes. Every pilot was flying every day and night, except Anne O'Connor.

49

CAPTAIN TERRY O'DONNELL SAT AT HIS DESK IN HIS small cubicle in his Pentagon office with his head buried in his hands. Two days ago, life in his job in the J-5 Directorate was fairly routine. Now, after an exchange of e-mails with Becky Philips, a lightning series of meetings with senior officers on the Joint Staff, including the chairman himself, and the phone call from Becky, he was adrift as to how to proceed.

It had not been this way during his command of a Spruance Class Destroyer during Desert Storm, when he had peppered Iraq with Tomahawk cruise missiles, or during his command of *Chancellorsville,* when he had been AW—air defense coordinator—for the Kitty Hawk Battle Group, on the line in the Arabian Gulf during various crises. No, during those tours he had made major decisions every day. He had seen combat. He had put his ship in harm's way and fought his ship well. He had been responsible for the lives of the three-hundred-plus sailors aboard his ship. He had been a warrior.

Now, he couldn't remember really making a decision for the last eighteen months—his time on the Joint Staff. He had written countless position papers, floated up numerous ideas, given his opinion when asked, "chopped" the point papers and studies of others, gone to literally hundreds of meetings where he did nothing more than listen and report back to his immediate boss, and stood by "in case he was needed." He simply had abrogated the tough-minded decision-making talent that had gotten him to and through two command tours in the Navy and had taken on the anonymous role of a staff officer who didn't make decisions.

But he had to make one now. He thought the issue was put to bed, but what Becky had told him over the phone was shocking . . . alarming. He tried and tried to convince himself that maybe she was unbalanced, maybe she was overreacting, maybe she just didn't know what she was talking about—but he could not. He knew her too well, and what she'd told him was too compelling.

He could go see Colonel Laird again, and they could repeat the tortuous route up the chain of command once more. But at any step along the way, one officer in the chain could say enough—table the discussion and put it to bed—and he would be done. He would have to stop there or be subject to extreme censure for disobeying a direct order. No, he felt that he had only one recourse, if he chose to take it.

The chairman's office was on the E-ring, the premier ring in the vast Pentagon. It was quite a way from Captain Terry O'Donnell's office in the J-5 Directorate, and he was winded by the time he arrived there— another hazard of commanding a desk. While the chairman's office was on the outside of the E-ring, with an impressive view, his waiting room was across the corridor, on the inboard side of the ring. Terry O'Donnell stood in the middle of the corridor between them. Scylla and Charybdis.

O'Donnell turned left, entered room 2E872, and walked right up to the chairman's executive assistant, who looked up, startled.

"May I help you, Captain?" said the admiral's EA, looking a bit annoyed that O'Donnell had shown up totally unannounced. For a senior national security official like the chairman of the Joint Chiefs of Staff, there was a small army of aides and assistants who micro-managed his schedule literally down to the minute. Having anyone, even a three- or four-star officer, drop in unexpectedly was anathema. Having a mere captain standing in front of the desk of the chairman's EA was tantamount to an extreme emergency.

"Captain O'Donnell of the J-5 Directorate. I was up here yesterday with General Allen to see the chairman. We had some unfinished business with the chairman. I'd like a moment of his time, if you can arrange it." O'Donnell's brain was in overdrive and he was talking as fast as he was thinking. Had he had time to reflect on just how bizarre his behavior was, he would have taken flight back to his office. He didn't have time to reflect, he was just reacting and following his instincts.

"Yes, Captain, I remember you, but I don't see you on the admiral's calendar today," replied the EA matter-of-factly.

"No, no, you don't. This is a follow-up, though, and I just need a moment of the chairman's time."

"Well, the Chairman *is* very busy, *Captain*."

"I wouldn't be here unless it was important. Please, just work me in. Anytime today would be great," said O'Donnell, now trying to cajole the EA.

It was not working. "Look, *Captain*," the EA said. "I work my ass off to try to squeeze in three-stars who want to get in with the chairman a week from now—and he knows every one of them personally. What makes you think that I could possibly work you in— even if I wanted to?"

"Look, this is a matter of national security. I need you to work me in and I need you to do it now!" O'Donnell instantly abandoned the friendly tone and challenged the EA directly. The tension in the room was getting intense.

"Captain, let me make it easy for you," the EA shouted. "Hell could freeze over before I even attempt to get you on the chairman's calendar, today, or any day. Now if you'll excuse me, I have work to do."

This guy will make a great maître d' if he ever leaves the service, O'Donnell thought. "I'll wait until the chairman comes out if I have to, but I am going to see him today."

"The hell you are!" replied the EA, standing for the first time and now pointing his finger at O'Donnell.

"Watch me," shouted O'Donnell.

"Beat it, Captain, before I call security!" the EA shouted back.

"Not gonna happen, man, not gonna happen," O'Donnell

said as he moved around the desk toward the EA.

Suddenly, apparently noticing the level of noise in his outer office, Admiral Monroe appeared.

"Gentlemen!" he said loudly. "Just what in the hell is going on here?"

"Sir, this captain is trying to force his way onto your calendar," began the EA. "I was just trying to explain to him that it was quite impossible just to squeeze him in."

"Captain, I see from your badge that you work here on the Joint Staff. You must know, then, that we have procedures here."

"Yes sir, I do," began Terry O'Donnell, but the admiral interrupted him.

"Wait a minute, Captain. Weren't you up here yesterday with General Allen?"

"Yes sir, I was."

"Yes, 'that matter,' yes. We had closure on that, didn't we? We had a misunderstanding by one officer that I think we cleared up."

"It wasn't cleared up, Admiral, it's worse than we thought, sir."

"Maybe you'd better come in my office, Captain." Turning to his EA, he said, "Carl, hold all my calls and then come in too."

Seated in the low cushioned chair in the admiral's spacious office, Terry O'Donnell told the chairman of his latest conversation with Becky Philips as the EA took copious notes. Finally, he finished. The chairman took a long, deep breath.

"This is disturbing, Captain. Perhaps most disturbing because I just got an e-mail this morning from Admiral Beard at AIRPAC. He is asking the CNO to move assets from AIRLANT so that he can fill urgent requisitions for Airwing Fourteen. He says that CAG is asking for an incredible amount of weapons, far in excess of anything that he could possibly need to strike a few terrorist camps in the middle of nowhere. CAG is telling him that he needs a ton of spares, too, and we see from his AMRR that he's flying almost one hundred fifty sorties a day. It doesn't look like he's ramping up just to hit some camps."

"That's because he's not, Admiral. Sir, I quizzed Lieutenant Commander Philips when she called me. She *knows* what's going on aboard *Carl Vinson*. Admiral, it would seem that we can check out her story if we want to, but I know that what she is telling me is absolutely true. I'd stake my career on it," replied O'Donnell with a flourish.

"If what you say is true, Captain, then there's a hell of a lot more than your career at stake here, a hell of a lot more."

With that, the chairman rose. "All right. Captain, thanks for coming forward again and thanks for pressing to see me. Afraid that I may need you again soon, so please stay put in your office. Carl," he said, turning to his EA, "I need to see the national security adviser right now. No phone call, this has to be in person. Use whatever means you have to and make that happen."

"Will do," he replied and left. O'Donnell tried not to smirk.

50

ADMIRAL ROBINSON SAT IN HIS CABIN AND WAITED. He knew the staff's routine, and he had planned this accordingly. He had told his chief of staff that he was skipping dinner that night, something that he did when red meat was offered in the Flag Mess.

Shortly after 1800, when the majority of his staff who were not on watch was seated for the meal, he walked up to the Flag Bridge. As he expected, it was deserted and dark. The sun had set forty-five minutes ago, and nightfall had already made the Arabian Gulf a dark shroud. He sat in his bridge chair and looked out on the smooth water. If he was going to cast the die, he would have to do it now.

* * *

Five decks below the Flag Bridge and far forward, Anne O'Connor sat in the dirty shirts wardroom finishing dinner. She sat with Mike Hart, Fred Barber, and Fred's COTAC, Laura Meechan. They were all in a somber mood, still mourning Chrissie Linder's death. Though they all were down Anne was feeling it most, having been so close to Chrissie, such that, in spite of the Blue Wolves' intense flying and Anne's professionalism, skipper Lynch had elected to keep her grounded for one more day until the flight surgeon could give her clearance to fly. Anne wanted desperately to be back in the air, but she knew herself well enough and knew she wasn't one hundred percent yet. She would see the flight surgeon first thing in the morning and hopefully get her "up-chit" right away.

Anne finished eating a bit before her squadronmates and got up to leave.

"Anne, hang in there with us, we'll be finished soon," said Fred. "We'll walk back aft to the ready room with ya."

"No, thanks guys, I gotta stop by my stateroom for a minute. I'll see you all back there in a little bit. What time did the ops o say the AOM was?"

"All officer's meeting is at 1900, Anne," said Mike. "Don't be late or XO will put you on his list." Mike Hart knew Anne better than most of the other officers in VS-35 and was working mightily to cheer her up.

"I'll be there, Mike, thanks," Anne replied. As she got up, they could see that the usual bounce was gone. Anne moved as if she were in a daze. She was barely plodding along.

Rick Holden was finishing up his meal with a group of the HS-4 bubbas and saw Anne leaving out of the corner of his eye. As she moved toward the door, he excused himself and got up and started to leave, too. As Anne reached the large, silver door on the port side in the after end of the wardroom, Rick reached behind her and held the door open.

"I got it shipmate, good to see you."

"Oh, hi," Anne said absently. "Good to see you. How ya been?" she continued as she walked aft in the passageway and Rick followed.

"I've been OK. The question is, how have you been?"

"Been better, to tell you the truth, but I'm hanging in there."

They stopped in an alcove near an AFFF fire-fighting station to let a few maintenance folks pass by on their way out to the catwalk. Rick had an idea.

"You got five minutes you can spare?"

"Sure, I guess so," said Anne, not knowing what Rick wanted but pretty much not having the energy right now to think of why she might say no.

"Great, let's follow these guys out onto the catwalk. Won't be as much traffic out there as there is here in the passageway."

"OK," was all that Anne said as she followed along behind him.

As Rick opened the huge blast door and walked out onto the catwalk, the hot, sticky night air hit him. Anne felt it too as she closed the hatch behind them and headed for the starboard side catwalk.

They both leaned on the rail on the catwalk and stared out at the sea. Finally Rick spoke.

"Look, Anne, we hardly know each other and if I'm being too forward just tell me to shut up and I'll bug out," Rick began. Anne looked sideways and made what passed for eye contact in the dark night.

"It's just that I think that I have gotten to know you a little bit on this cruise and I know how close you and Chrissie were. I know that this is tearing you up inside. Anne, no one else on this ship knows this, but I've lost buddies in tough situations like this. I've had to bury people I was incredibly close to, and then I've had to move on. I know that Chrissie's death is probably the worst thing that's ever happened in your life—"

"It is, Rick, you just don't know, but it is," she said, interrupting him. "I just have to deal with it, that's all."

"I know you do, and I don't rate telling you what you should or shouldn't do. But I saw you in action at the Intercontinental. I saw what you did to help people you knew and people you didn't know. You are solid and you're a pro. I know you know that we need you at a hundred percent out here. I just wanted you to know that I'm in your corner and rooting for you, that's all."

Rick started to question himself. He had gotten up spontaneously in the dirty-shirts wardroom. Was all of his babbling making any sense to her—or to him?

Anne pondered what Rick was telling her. She knew that he was right, and she knew that she had to get on with it. Her squadronmates were depending on her. But she also knew that she couldn't keep this inside forever. She'd kept it light with Rick up until now. But she had to get it out. If not him, who?

"Rick, you don't know how much I appreciate that," said Anne, letting a deep breath go. "Chrissie was more than a roommate, she was my soul mate. I shared everything with her. Maybe you understand in a general sense, but you couldn't have known how really close we were. I still don't believe that this really happened. Our flight surgeon says that I'm in denial. I might be. I just hope that I wake up and find out that none of this ever happened."

"You won't, Anne, that's the point," Rick continued, moving closer to her and speaking only in a whisper. "But we need you, Anne. Your squadron needs you back in the air. We *all* need you back, Anne."

"Rick, you are the best. I know that you have other things on your mind. I know that this CSAR business is high-stress stuff too. You know that I can't really 'blink' in front of any of my Airwing bubbas. I really appreciate you just listening. I really, really do."

"Anytime, Anne. Listen, let's get you back to your ready room before your XO freaks out." She patted him on the arm as they went back inside.

Back on the Flag Bridge, Heater Robinson picked up the Bogen phone and hit 24, connecting him instantly to Flag Admin. He knew who would answer.

"Flag Admin, Lieutenant Commander Philips speaking," was the response. Becky had eaten early chow tonight, and the admiral was confident that she would be in Admin. He wasn't disappointed.

"Flag Sec, Admiral here. I'm up on the Flag Bridge, trying

to get some paperwork finished. Thought I'd finish looking at the end-of-tour award for *Shiloh*'s CO. Do you have it ready yet?"

Becky had been wordsmithing that award all afternoon. It had made it through the chief of staff and was finally ready for the admiral's signature. She wondered why he wanted it now—it was dark up there, and all the admiral had was a small, red light above his chair.

"It's ready, Admiral, and I'm on the way up with it."

Two minutes later, Becky was on the Flag Bridge. She looked toward the admiral's chair and saw the one white star on a blue background decorating it, but he wasn't there. No one was there on the port side of the Flag Bridge. She looked left and right. Nothing. It was dark up here, with only the lights on the flight deck making a reflected glow inside their bridge.

Becky walked forward and looked across to the starboard side of the bridge. It was very dark over there, but she thought she saw something. She headed that way.

"Admiral?"

"Over here, Flag Sec," came the voice that Becky recognized as Heater Robinson's. Becky had just come from the bright neon lights inside the ship, and she had no night adaptation at all. She could hardly see a thing and was a bit disoriented.

Becky continued to the far side of the Flag Bridge and saw the form of Heater Robinson sitting in the chief of staff's chair next to the window on the starboard side.

"Hello, Admiral," said Becky, trying to see him as best she could. The admiral sat in total darkness, a form more than a person. It was eerily quiet.

"Yes, Flag Sec, thanks for coming all the way up here. Hope that I'm not taking you away from anything important."

"No sir, nothing is more important than these awards," she said, handing the award write-up to the admiral.

Heater Robinson reached up and turned on the small red spotlight over the chief of staff's chair. The glow of the dim red bulb framed the admiral in just a hint of light.

"Well, you may be right at that. Here, let's have a look," he said as he took the folder from Becky.

While Heater Robinson studied the document, Becky looked at the aerobic equipment that clogged the entire starboard side of the Flag Bridge. How little time—but what big events—had passed since she first came up here to think after hearing the admiral's conversation with Admiral Flowers. Now, the admiral was just reading paperwork like it was business as usual.

"Well, this is a typically outstanding Philips product. You do terrific work, Becky, and you have a bright future in the Navy."

"Thank you, Admiral," she replied. Heater Robinson was always complimentary of her work, and his words seemed like more of the same.

"There are some issues that we need to clear up, though," he said as he got out of his chair. Becky backed up a step. The admiral seemed very close to her.

"Issues, Admiral?" said Becky. She didn't know where this was going, but she suddenly wished that there were someone else besides the two of them on the Flag Bridge.

"Yes, Becky, issues. It really goes to our staff being a team. You know, having issues—big issues—that we need to deal with, and especially not taking those issues outside the lifelines of this ship."

"Admiral, I'm not sure what you mean," replied Becky, suddenly feeling her skin crawl.

"Well, I think you do. It goes to the issue of when friends, *friends* on the same staff know things that they should keep among their fellow friends. It goes to keeping absolutely everything to ourselves here on the staff. Keeping everything, well, very private."

Becky thought she finally knew exactly what the admiral was talking about, while hoping against hope that she wasn't correct.

"Admiral, I think that I take great pains to keep everything we do here 'private.' I'm not sure what you are referring to," she replied, though as soon as the words left her mouth she realized that he wouldn't believe that. He must know too much already.

Heater Robinson was under too much stress to be coy with Becky Philips any longer. Taking a step toward her, he laid his cards on the table.

"Commander, were you or were you not listening to my phone conversation with Admiral Flowers?" he said. No longer the fatherly mentor, he was the accuser. "And didn't you subsequently call someone on the Joint Staff and relate your version of events to him?"

Becky was trapped. She couldn't lie about it now. The admiral probably knew everything. How? Had he been listening to her conversation with Terry O'Donnell? She summoned up all the courage she had and took the offensive.

"Admiral, look. It's clear to me what you're doing. Don't you realize that you have to stop? You can't take national policy into your own hands. I only did what I did because I had to do it. I heard your conversation with Admiral Flowers by mistake—I really did, Admiral. But once I knew, I couldn't not do anything. Don't you see, sir? Please stop doing this. We can get everything back to normal and just do what we are supposed to do," said Becky as firmly as she dared.

"Now, look, Becky," said the admiral, softening his tone. He had to convince her that there was no other way out of this. He was near panic. This wasn't going the way he wanted it to go. "I think that you might have misunderstood what Admiral Flowers and I were discussing. We were really just talking OPDEC, we thought someone might have been listening and we wanted to throw them off . . ." but as soon as he said those words he realized how utterly ridiculous they were. He moved even closer toward Becky.

"Admiral, God, please sir, don't lie to me," said Becky, backing away. "Admiral, you just need to stop all of this. You need to tell the chain of command above Admiral Flowers about this and you need to stop thinking about hitting these other targets and just hit the terrorist camps. You haven't done anything wrong—yet—sir."

Ah, the blissful ignorance of youth, thought Heater Robinson. What was she thinking? If he admitted one scintilla of this, he would be off the ship within twenty-four hours, relieved in disgrace—but more importantly, no longer able to exact revenge on the Islamic Republic.

"Becky, look, you have to understand. This is all part of a much grander scheme that has support right up to the top of the chain of command. If you will just give me time and let events play out, you will see. It will become clear to you—"

Becky couldn't stand being next to the man for a moment longer. "Admiral, look, we've said enough here. I'm leaving."

Heater Robinson moved a step closer to Becky and grasped her arm, turning as he did to place himself between her and the passage back toward the port side of the Flag Bridge. As Becky tried to shake her arm free, the admiral just squeezed it tighter.

"Admiral, you're hurting me. Please let go of my arm."

He just held her arm tightly and said, "Come on, do the right thing, Becky. Think about what you're doing."

He was inches from her now. She could feel the heat of his breath on her forehead. She shook her arm violently and momentarily broke free. She broke for the back of the Flag Bridge and for the freedom that the door at the aft end of the narrow passage would bring her. She took two steps, trying to work her way around the aerobic gear, but it impeded her progress.

The admiral had her left arm again. There was no time to think—only to react.

"Becky, stop!" said the admiral angrily.

She wheeled, and, with her free hand, hit him with all her might on the right side of the face with her right fist. She heard an audible *pop* and watched the admiral flinch as he again released his grasp on her arm. She jumped up on the treadmill and tried to work her way toward the door—and freedom.

"Argghhh," came the cry from behind her as the admiral lunged at her. His 240 pounds fell on top of Becky as he tried to tackle her to keep her from leaving. With a resounding crash they both fell half on the treadmill and half on the deck. Heater Robinson lay still for a moment, then pushed himself up and got ready to grab Becky, but she didn't move.

The admiral stood there heaving, trying to catch his breath. Becky still didn't move. He knelt down beside her and started to balance himself on one hand, but as his hand hit the ground it was immediately covered by something wet and sticky. Becky remained motionless. Heater Robinson turned her over and immediately recognized what the wet, sticky substance was. It was blood. Becky's face was covered with it, and even in the dim light of the bridge he could see that her skull was cracked open. It had evidently hit the side of the treadmill.

Heater Robinson completely panicked. What had he done? What would they think? Then, primal instincts took over. Someone knew that Becky was calling the Joint Staff to report about him. They would draw the only possible conclusion if she was discovered dead. If she was discovered. Heater Robinson looked up toward the door at the back of the Flag Bridge—the door that led to an outside platform—the same door that Becky had looked to for freedom.

His mind racing, adrenaline coursing through his body, he picked up the lifeless body of Becky Philips and headed for the door. He stepped over and around the remaining aerobic equipment. Holding her body on his hip, he opened first the joiner door, then the blast door, and got out onto the platform. He felt the hot night air and heard the sound of the water being pushed aside by the ship.

Heater Robinson was now working only on instinct. He stripped her uniform off her and dropped her shirt and pants on the metal grating. Then, using all his strength, he picked her up and thrust her lifeless body over the guard rail and into the gentle waters of the Arabian Gulf. Though in a state of panic, he grabbed her uniform and went back inside to clean up the blood on the deck. It was difficult to see, but he held his penlight flashlight between his teeth and worked mightily to get it all up. He thought that he got it all. That mission complete, he returned back out to the platform and cast the uniform into the sea.

51

THEY SPOKE IN HUSHED TONES, SPECULATING IN groups of two or three what the turn of events would bring. They were waiting patiently in the Cabinet Room—at least as patiently as individuals as high-powered as these could wait. They knew that Michael Curtis was with the president at that very moment and that he would join them just as soon as he could. It made the waiting just bearable.

Among such high-powered people there were no real secrets. None of them had gotten to such positions of responsibility without having well-developed networks of associates who moved heaven and earth to keep them informed. The price of not having real-time information on what was going to happen was just too high—they would be marginalized and their effectiveness and upward mobility would be seriously degraded.

Most of them knew that there was a crisis in the Arabian Gulf and that crisis involved the aircraft carrier *Carl Vinson*—the same ship that was preparing to conduct strikes against terrorist camps in Iran. They knew that there had been a number of emergency meetings within the Joint Staff and that Admiral Monroe had personally briefed the national security adviser earlier that day. It had taken most of the day to extract them from their other duties and convene this meeting this evening.

Michael Curtis entered, and everyone else quickly took their seats. All eyes were on him as he quickly strode to the head of the table and tossed his briefing books down. He was clearly in an extremely foul mood.

"All right," he growled. "We might as well get started. Bad news doesn't get any better with age. I had a meeting with Admiral Monroe early this morning," he continued, looking toward the JCS chairman, who nodded his assent, "and my immediate staff filled in some essential details throughout the day."

Everyone was riveted on him. Although most of them thought that they knew most of the story, they wanted to hear it straight from him.

"I have just spent almost an hour with the president. I am sure that all of you understand what that comports. The president insists on immediate and decisive action. We are here at this hour to determine precisely how to do that. Admiral Monroe is closest to the issue, and I'll let him bring all of you up to speed with respect to details."

"Thank you, Mr. Curtis," said Admiral Monroe as he stood at his chair. "As you know, military planning has been ongoing to attack nine terrorist camps in Iran. The decision to proceed with these strikes was made three days ago and our planning to do this has continued at a brisk pace." He had no slides and no notes, making what he said all the more compelling.

"It has come to our attention that the battle group commander embarked in the aircraft carrier has, for reasons known only to him, decided to attack not only these terrorist camps but also a number of military targets in Iran."

There was a gasp by those in the room who did not know even this much of the story.

"After consulting with the national security adviser, my recommendation is that we immediately relieve Admiral Robinson of his duties. This relief needs to be done on scene in order that planning and preparation for the strikes on the terrorist camps continue unimpeded. My recommendation is that Admiral Harry Flowers, the Fifth Fleet commander, relieve Admiral Robinson immediately," said Admiral Monroe. He felt his mouth go bitter at the idea of relieving a warrior like Heater Robinson—regardless of what he had done or intended to do—with a . . . a dilettante like Harry Flowers.

"The president concurs with Admiral Monroe's assessment and with his recommendation," added Michael Curtis. "We just need to get on with it."

For Michael Curtis this was a bitter moment. He had pressed hard for more robust strikes against Iran. Secretly, he had hoped that some event like a provocation from Iran would result in his nation's upping the ante and ultimately raining down major attacks on the Islamic Republic. Now this renegade admiral, for reasons not clear to the national security adviser, was threatening to up the ante on his own, and the president was ordering them to take draconian steps to prevent this from happening. Any hopes that Michael Curtis had of ratcheting up the crisis were dashed.

"Admiral, we need to continue planning for the strikes against the terrorist camps, but we will take no action to initiate strikes until Admiral Robinson is off USS *Carl Vinson*. You need to have Admiral Flowers relieve him on the spot and have Flowers take control of the battle group. The president wants a report immediately. Day or night, he wants to be notified when Admiral Flowers is in command of the battle group."

"We'll make that happen, Mr. Curtis," Admiral Monroe replied. The JCS chairman could feel the chill from the national security adviser, his tone of voice·and his body language conveying that the military—and specifically the Navy—had screwed this up and that they had better fix it and fix it fast.

Events had happened so quickly that the chairman of the Joint Chiefs of Staff was still trying to piece together the disparate pieces. He had hated sending Heater Robinson that stern message less than a week ago. He still liked him very much. Years of flying together in the fighter community had made the men not only professional associates but also fast friends with a similar view of the world.

But now there seemed to be proof positive that Admiral Robinson was operating as a maverick. In addition to Becky's call and anecdotal evidence, there was the odd report by Admiral Flowers. Monroe couldn't abide him, much less trust him, but what Flowers had reported hearing from Admiral Robinson was absolutely consistent with what had been reported from other sources. Admiral Monroe couldn't understand why Flowers had not unilaterally relieved Robinson on the spot for even suggesting what he had, but that was water over the dam now. It was time to get on with it.

52

In three major cities in the United States, three men with the same mission were doing the same thing They were waiting. Waiting for a call that they were certain would come. Waiting for a call from their leader for whom each would gladly give his life. Waiting, as instructed, for their pagers to go off.

None of the three men knew each other. That was by design. Though there was little chance of any of them being caught, no link to any other was provided. Each was to be contacted individually by Hossein Shiekholeslam and directed to commence his mission. Each man was to embark on his mission in response to his pager and not communicate with anyone until after his mission was complete. It was a straightforward, but by no means simple, mission.

In New York, Mejid Homani had picked out the spot on the United Nations concourse where he would release his deadly nerve gas. He had spent the better part of the previous day observing the patterns of movement, evaluating his ability to hide the gas, and balancing that against having it released in an area where the largest number of people would be passing through. He had evaluated several locations. The good news was that there were so many that were adequate that it was just a question of picking from among the best choices.

His choice of location complete, he holed up in a small room on the fourth floor of a nearby hotel. A small color television set sat on the bureau that dominated one wall of the room. Constantly tuned to CNN, the television revealed nothing significant about world events, certainly nothing even vaguely resembling an attack against the Islamic Republic by the United States. Could the United States have kept an attack secret from the world? He doubted it, but wondered nonetheless. He had to trust that Shiekholeslam would contact him as he said he would.

In the nation's capital, Hala Karomi walked out of Union Station for what he thought would be the next to last time. When he returned, it would be to release his nerve gas and then immediately jump on the Metro to a location several stops away from his hotel. Shiekholeslam had instructed him to take a hotel room close to the station, but Karomi was both put off by the high cost of some of the upscale hotels immediately adjacent to Union Station, and concerned by the huge number of police that patrolled in and around the station. He thought that by disappearing into the anonymity of the Metro, he could be certain that he had shaken any pursuers before returning to his hotel to await further instructions.

That was the one part of the mission that Karomi hated the most—staying in Washington after the attack he was about to unleash. He had learned enough during his time here to know that Americans treated their capital city with near reverence. He would never feel totally safe until he was on an airplane back to the Middle East. But he also knew enough about Shiekholeslam's desire to control this entire operation from start to finish. So he, too, stayed in his hotel room and waited while CNN droned on.

In San Diego, California, home to the overwhelming majority of the ships in the United States Pacific Fleet, Achmed Boleshari stood on the ground floor of Horton Plaza, a busy shopping mall less than two miles from the United States Navy base. It was the perfect location. Teeming crowds streamed by throughout the day, and the traffic got extremely heavy in the late afternoon. Above him, multiple levels of the shopping plaza stood exposed to any gas that would waft upward.

He wanted desperately to be somewhere else, to be at the

nearby Navy base. There, the ships that threatened his nation stood idly at their piers—their crews not alerted, their guard down, their billion-dollar ships inviting targets for the havoc that he knew he could wreak directly on them. That would deliver the message most clearly and conclusively, he thought. Alas, it was only a dream. Above all, Shiekholeslam taught obedience, and Boleshari put those thoughts out of his mind as he returned to his tiny hotel room, just a block from where he would act. How long would he have to wait?

Hossein Shiekholeslam sat in his hidden location, a location known only to a handful of his underlings and to no one else—not to Foreign Minister Velayati and certainly not to President Habibi. If the United States attacked the Islamic Republic, he would release these men on their holy mission. He would not hesitate, and he certainly wouldn't ask permission of those politicians, of those sycophants that lived permanently in Tehran. He had decided above all else that this mission must not fail.

53

"ADMIRAL, WE HAVE ALL THE PRINCIPALS ASSEMBLED in the War Room," said George Sampson as he cracked open the door to the admiral's cabin. It was 0900, and no one had seen Heater Robinson since Bill Durham had brought in the night orders at 1930 the night before. The ops officer had mentioned to the chief of staff that the admiral had looked very shaken for some reason. He had attributed it to stress. Shortly after that, the admiral had called the Staff TAO to tell him he was retiring for the evening and had locked his doors.

"On the way in, COS," replied Heater Robinson. The admiral was indeed shaken. Rationalizing that he was performing a higher duty by ratcheting up what were intended to be surgical strikes against terrorist camps to a wholesale attack on another nation, that was one thing. Killing another person, let alone someone who had been one of his closest personal advisors—and a woman at that—was something else again. He had taken twice the normal dose of the sedatives he had browbeat out of the flight surgeon, and he had finally gotten to sleep. He had only been awake for a half hour this morning and was still groggy.

His key warfare commanders were standing behind their chairs when the admiral entered the War Room. He quickly sat down, and all the others followed suit. CAG stood up to begin the briefing.

"Admiral, this is an overview brief for the strikes against the Islamic Republic. We are going to conduct a three-day rolling campaign against the main naval facilities, air defense units, major airfields, and, eventually, the terrorist camps. This briefing is classified Top Secret, and everyone is reminded that some extremely sensitive targeting information is being displayed."

The admiral was silent, so Wizard continued. But he paused before going on, knowing that he was now going to tread on uncomfortable ground.

"Our planning has exactly mimicked the campaign plan for Operation Mountain Divide. In the absence of detailed instructions or an execute order, and especially going on only the verbal guidance that you have obtained from Fifth Fleet, Admiral, this is our best professional recommendation as to how to conduct these strikes for maximum effectiveness. We made a few adjustments to the Mountain Divide campaign plan, but those were specifically designed to take maximum advantage of our particular aircraft weapons systems and Tomahawk loadout."

Even in his state, Heater Robinson could tell that CAG was fishing, expressing his frustration that all of this was being done based on verbal guidance—in direct contravention to the way they had trained. The admiral knew that once he blessed this plan, detailed discussions might tip their hand to others outside the staff. He had a plan for that, too.

"Right, CAG. We have no indication from Fifth Fleet when we might get that definitive guidance by message," replied the admiral, his tone somewhere between weary and annoyed. "For now, I just have to take the word of the three-star naval officer in charge of Fifth Fleet," he said as he glared at Foster. CAG picked up the message quickly.

"Yes, sir. I will present the overall plan and briefly discuss the eight aircraft strike packages, as well as the overall presentation of the hundred-and fifty-plus Tomahawk missiles we intend to shoot. Then Commander Tallent and Lieutenant Commander McDonald will brief the two initial strikes on day one. I have the other strike leads standing by, but don't intend to have them brief their plans in detail at this time."

"Fine, CAG, just proceed," said Heater Robinson. All assembled could see that the admiral was subdued, even morose. They just didn't know why.

As Wizard Foster was beginning his brief, sixty nautical miles east-south-east of *Carl Vinson*'s position Commander Farhud Kani stood on the bridge of the Saam Class frigate *Alborz* and looked over the shoulder of his radar operator. The young sailor was nervous but did his best to relate the information that his captain wanted.

"Ali, is that the *Sabalan* that is standing out of Bushehr naval base?"

"Captain, according to the coordinates we have been given, and the track that was predicted for her, that should be *Sabalan*."

"Captain Mohtaj told me that he would make a speed of fifteen knots and proceed on a course of due west. Is that the speed you have him going?"

"Yes, Captain, the average speed of the ship is just that, perhaps a little faster, but yes, fifteen knots."

"Officer of the deck, increase your speed to twenty-two knots, set a rendezvous course to intercept *Sabalan* due north of here." Turning to his executive officer, Mohammad Sali, he said, "Captain Mohtaj is the senior among us and I will follow his directions. We will meet with him and follow his lead. Then we will approach *Carl Vinson* from both the east and the west and observe her movements and listen to her transmission."

"Yes, Captain," replied Sali, who was visibly nervous. "What if the American carrier wishes to silence us? We will be no match for her attack planes."

"No we won't, Sali. But we will have done our duty. The admiral informs me that upon our warning, a most terrible vengeance will be launched against the Americans. We will have done our duty."

Mohammad Sali took little solace in this and merely nodded as the captain turned to other matters.

Now sixty miles to the northwest of where Captain Kani steered *Alborz* toward her rendezvous with *Sabalan*, Petty Officer Andrew Tyson operated his radar display in *Carl Vinson*'s Combat Direction Center. What he saw was interesting enough to call over his supervisor, Chief House, to take a look.

"What do you have, Tyson?" said the chief.

"Look at this, will you. We usually have guys going about six, maybe eight knots up and down the Iranian coast, usually dhows or small tankers. See this guy over here, Chief," he said, moving his cursor to stop on top of *Sabalan*. "He's going about fifteen knots, heading due west, on his present course, he'll pass within about ten miles of us."

"I see him," replied the chief, though he didn't act especially interested.

"But down here, Chief," Tyson continued, putting his cursor on *Alborz*, "this guy is making twenty knots, and he's making a beeline for our first guy."

"OK," replied the chief. He was getting off watch in fifteen minutes and didn't want to generate any additional excitement. Not now.

"Should I report this to the TAO, Chief?"

"Nah, not unless you have something more significant to tell him than that. Continue to track them both. Point them out to Chief Butterworth when he relieves me."

"All right, Chief," replied Tyson. He was troubled by the contacts, but the chief had the last word.

Just thirty feet from where Petty Officer Tyson held these two troublesome contacts on his radar, the strike briefs were finally wrapping up after almost two and a half hours.

"Admiral, that about wraps it up," said CAG. "We'll take on board your comments and those of your staff and make the adjustments you indicated. Bottom line, sir, I think that we have an executable plan."

"I do too," replied Heater Robinson. "But now that we have articulated this we must deny the enemy any opportunity to derail any aspect of this plan. Commo?" he said, looking around the room for his staff communicator, Lieutenant Commander Wilson.

"Yes sir," she replied.

"I think that it's time we executed total emission control for radio transmissions, don't you think?"

"WILCO, Admiral," she replied as the admiral rose to leave, going directly back into his cabin.

The rest of his people let this order sink in. They were going to go into total radio silence in preparation for the strike against Iran. This would keep them from giving away their position via very traceable radio transmissions. Tactically, the move appeared sound. Heater Robinson had another agenda none of them could suspect.

Admiral Robinson shuffled back into his cabin, still in a daze both from the events that had taken place and the enormity of what he was planning. He was just gathering his thoughts as to how he would execute his attacks on the Islamic Republic when the door to his cabin opened and his flag writer entered.

"Sir, we've got things backing up in the office, waiting for Commander Philips chop," Chief Carol Weaver said. "I was told that she had an urgent mission at Fifth Fleet, sir, but it's not like her to just leave without instructions for the rest of us to carry on while she is gone."

The admiral sensed danger. Did they know anything?

"Well, Chief, she probably didn't have time to tell you all because I told her to get her bags packed and get on the first COD with about fifteen minutes' notice. We have got some major awards snafus at Fifth Fleet and I have gotten tired of dealing with Admiral Flowers about things like this that are supposed to be handled three to four paygrades below mine. She'll get it straightened out now that she's there."

"Do you know when she'll be back, Admiral?"

"She'll get back when she gets these damned awards straightened out, Chief!" said Heater Robinson, his voice rising several octaves.

"Yes sir," responded Chief Weaver as she hustled out of the admiral's cabin.

Admiral Robinson continued to think of how he would precipitate a full-blown attack on the Islamic Republic. He needed a provocation of some kind, something that would threaten the *Carl Vinson* and the entire battle group. If he got that provocation, he could unleash devastating attacks against the Islamic Republic. He had been watching his JMCIS display, and the appearance of two unknown surface contacts validated an idea that had been bubbling.

———————— 54 ————————

ADMIRAL FLOWERS LOOKED OVER THE SMALL GARDEN outside his office window. The last several days had been a blur. He had almost become too closely embroiled in the maneuverings of Admiral Robinson, but he had been extraordinarily careful about what he had said. He had taken every precaution to distance himself from what Heater Robinson was plotting. He had left neither trail nor finger pointing his way. He had achieved plausible deniability. He reflected that it was only a matter of time until events played themselves out fully.

He had just finished berating his flag lieutenant for some protocol miscue when the yeoman burst into his office.

"Admiral," he began. "I have Lieutenant General Allen's office on the line, sir."

"The Joint Staff?" said the admiral, recognizing instantly who was calling. The yeoman responded that it was the Joint Staff operations director.

"Yes, well, wait, I just need a moment. Don't put him through yet. Not yet. You can wait outside, I'll buzz you when I'm ready to take the call," he said. The yeoman thought that Admiral Flowers suddenly looked extremely nervous. He left as instructed.

Flowers felt his heart start beating faster. Had someone found something out? Did they now suspect that he had something to do with what was being planned aboard *Carl Vinson*? He noticed his palms were sticky.

He sagged deeper into his chair. What would he say? What would he do? He needed time to think. Should he have the yeoman tell him that he wasn't in his office? No, the man had already blurted out that he was there. It was too late for that. After collecting his thoughts for as long as he dared to hold off the inevitable, he buzzed the yeoman and within a minute, General Allen came on the phone.

"Admiral Flowers, is that you?"

"Yes sir, General, it is. How are things in Washington?"

"Busy, Admiral, busy. But they are about to become busier in your AOR . . ."

General Allen began to pour out everything that they had learned about Admiral Robinson's actions, information they had gained from Becky Philips's e-mails, as well as the fall-out from Flowers's secretive communications with Tom Perry. Flowers listened to the general's entire fifteen-minute monologue, exhaling, it seemed, only when he stopped. He had made no accusation against Flowers.

"General, that is an astounding story. I thought that I knew Admiral Robinson a lot better than I evidently did," he said. The suspense was driving him mad, so he pressed. "General has . . . has my performance been . . . been satisfactory?"

Allen was perplexed by the question, but he answered.

"Of course, Admiral. That is one of the reasons that I am calling and that was about what I was getting to. The chairman, Admiral Monroe, has directed that you immediately fly out to *Carl Vinson* and relieve Admiral Robinson on the spot."

General Allen paused to let this sink in, but he did not wait long enough to allow Admiral Flowers to respond.

"You are to take control of the battle group, cancel any strikes against any of the Iranian military infrastructure— *any* of it, and then, once that is accomplished, conduct attacks that the NCA has ordered against the terrorist camps."

Admiral Flowers just sat there gaping straight ahead. He was relieved—relieved beyond words—that he had not been found out. But now, beyond that, he was going to *take over* the battle group.

"Admiral, did you hear me?"

"Yes, General, yes, of course sir. I will do so immediately, General. Please convey to the chairman my thanks for this vote of confidence in my abilities. . . ."

Allen didn't need to hear any more of this gratuitous dribble. "Look, Admiral, we've got a few things on our plate here. Just get out there in a hurry and report back when you have taken charge."

"Will there be any written follow-up guidance once I effect this?" he asked.

"Flowers, damnit, just do it and do it fast, man!" said General Allen as Harry Flowers heard the phone slam down.

Harry Flowers sat for a long time, trying to think through the sheer magnitude of what he was about to do. He finally sorted it out enough in his own mind to give his staff the direction they needed. He called his chief of staff over the intercom.

As soon as Bolter Dennis walked in, Flowers said, "I think that I need to pay Admiral Robinson a visit. Let's see if we can get me out there, OK?"

"Certainly, Admiral," replied Dennis, while writing in his notebook. He was shocked. Admiral Flowers hated flying and didn't enjoy visiting any ships. But he pressed ahead. "When would you like to plan to visit, Admiral?"

"Today, Chief of Staff."

"Today, sir?" said Dennis, now openly shocked. A visit by a flag officer was usually a well-planned and fully orchestrated event. A week was usually the minimum lead time needed—and that was pushing it.

"TODAY!" Flowers shouted, jumping up from his chair. "Don't patronize me, Chief of Staff. Call the damn ship, tell them to send in one of their helos or that claptrap C-2, I don't give a damn which, and get me out there this afternoon, is that clear!"

"Yes sir," said Dennis as he rushed out of the Executive spaces and headed for TFCC, grabbing the ops officer as he went by his office.

"Get *Carl Vinson* on the Command Circuit right now," Dennis said to the watch officer there.

Dennis and Carl Mullen watched as the harried watch officer called *Carl Vinson* several times on Battle Group Command. There was no response to his multiple call-ups. Thwarted in his attempts, he turned toward the chief of staff.

"COS, it's no use. It looks like they may have gone into radio silence on *Carl Vinson*. We haven't heard any calls from them in the last four to five hours."

"Great, how do we get to them? We've got to get them to send an aircraft to pick up the admiral and bring him out to the boat!" said Dennis. He did not want to have to go back and tell Admiral Flowers that he could not carry out his orders.

"Sir," one of the other watchstanders chimed in, "there's one COD at the Aviation Support Unit. Their flight plan says that they are planning to take a load of cargo out to *Carl Vinson* late this afternoon. Maybe we could tell them to hurry their preps along and take the admiral out as soon as he wants to go."

"He wants to go now!" shouted Dennis, now frantic to get transportation for the admiral. "Get a hold of the COD crew and tell them to get ready for VIP transport to the carrier, and tell them to hurry it up!"

55

THE FLOOR OF THE NATIONAL MILITARY COMMAND Center, typically a busy place, was now the center of frenetic activity. Generals and admirals buzzed about, issuing and carrying out orders, talking on telephones, and looking at displays or TV monitors. In the command area of the NMCC, fewer people were present, and the level of activity, while intense, was somewhat more orderly, due to nothing but the smaller number of people who worked here. Brigadier General Roger Kissel commanded a small watch team that comprised the action arm of NMCC.

General Allen had become a permanent fixture in the command center. Brigadier General Kissel chafed a bit at the constant presence of the operations director for the Joint Staff, who was directing virtually every effort—something General Kissel thought he should be doing. Then again, he thought, with as many times as the chairman and several other of the Joint Chiefs had been in the NMCC insisting on being updated on the situation in the Arabian Gulf, he wasn't completely upset that it was General Allen who fielded their questions and fended off their unintended—but constant—attempts to micro-manage the situation.

It was relatively calm—no high-powered visitors for the moment—when the Army Major manning one of the phones announced, "General, I have Admiral Flowers's office on the line, sir."

General Kissel moved toward the phone, but General Allen quickly preempted him. "I'll take it over here, Major," he said, pointing to a seat right next to the man.

"Allen here," he said into the receiver.

"Yes, General," Flowers began. "I wanted to update you

on what I am doing to carry out your orders to relieve Admiral Robinson. It seems, sir, that the battle group commander has put the carrier into total emission control. We have not gotten any radio call from them in several hours, and every attempt that we make to contact them via any circuit is met with absolutely no response."

Allen was stunned. He had given Harry Flowers direct and explicit orders to do something, something that the chairman himself, articulating a decision of the National Security Council, had directed. Was this admiral now telling him that he had not even begun to carry out these orders?

"Admiral Flowers, we spoke hours—*hours*—ago, did we not? I am, frankly, staggered that you are calling me from your headquarters and not from *Carl Vinson*. I expected you to be on the ship already carrying out your orders. This is a national emergency, Admiral, a national emergency!"

"Yes sir, General," said Admiral Flowers, trying to recover. "I am proceeding out to *Carl Vinson* very shortly sir. Since I was not able to contact *Carl Vinson* they could not provide me an aircraft to fly out. Unfortunately, both CH-53E helos are down for maintenance and my Desert Duck H-3s just don't have the legs to fly out there . . ."

"Admiral, I don't give a tinker's damn about your helos or your problems. This is coming from the president! Relieve Admiral Robinson. Do it right now! Don't give me a bunch of babbling minutiae about how you are going to do it, man!"

"Yes, sir, General," replied Admiral Flowers, desperately trying to recover. "I will be lifting off—"

"DAMNIT FLOWERS. Just friggin' get there!" shouted Allen as he slammed down the phone in its cradle.

Throughout the NMCC, on dozens of television sets, news stories continued about the crisis in the Arabian Gulf. The shootdown of the Iraqi Foxbat had been a footnote, the ongoing standoff with Iran a bothersome fact of life, the continuous Operation Southern Watch flights a nuisance at best. But the explosion at the Intercontinental had galvanized America and riveted its attention. Citizens from every walk of life had demanded that the perpetrators be found and justice done.

Elsewhere in the NMCC, at a board mimicking the display that General Kissel and General Allen saw, a Navy commander and an Air Force major watched their display. It showed the Carl Vinson Battle Group proceeding along a predictable northwest to southeast track. It showed dozens of other tracks moving all about the screen. It also showed two high-speed tracks converging directly on *Carl Vinson*. The commander picked up the phone that connected him with the general.

56

ABOARD *CARL VINSON*, IN A COOL, DIMLY LIT CORNER of CDC, Petty Officer Tyson continued to track the two fast-moving contacts that he had picked up a little over an hour and a half ago. He remembered his guidance from Chief House, but now he could wait no longer. He called Chief Butterworth over to his screen.

"Chief, I pointed these guys out to Chief House just before you relieved him and he told me to continue to track them. I've been doing just that, and nothing has changed in the time that you've been here. They just continue to converge and will come together just twenty miles southeast of us. We don't have any ESM on them. Think that we need to let the TAO know, Chief?"

Butterworth looked over Tyson's shoulder and assessed the situation. He called another OS chief over to validate what he saw. After several minutes of conferring, they made their decision.

*   *   *

The watch team in CDC took a while to assess the information that Petty Officer Tyson had developed on his scope. There were so many ways to get spurious information into the system, so many ways to be "wrong," that TAOs learned, and faithfully practiced, caution in fully assessing information before passing it up the chain of command.

Lieutenant Cutler Hedley evaluated what his team was presenting him. He factored in their EMCON condition, where all radio transmissions were prohibited and where radars were being operated in low power. He reminded himself that radar propagation paths in the Arabian Gulf were unlike those anywhere else in the world. He remembered that Petty Officer Tyson was new to this watch team and watch station and that he had not had the seasoning that some of his other petty officers had experienced. He decided to wait.

At the Aviation Support Unit several miles away from Fifth Fleet Headquarters, Captain Dennis had just finished an angry confrontation with the COD pilots. Only by issuing them a direct order and threatening them with all manner of censure was he able to convince them to fly their aircraft out to *Carl Vinson*. The unpleasant conversation still rang in his ears.

"Captain, we can't take off for the carrier until we file a flight plan with them and we can't do that until we can talk with them. We are trying sir," said the first pilot.

"You can file in the air, damnit," responded Dennis, reaching deep into his kit bag to come up with a quick solution to something that they were making so hard.

"We can, Captain," countered the second pilot, "but we're not sure where *Carl Vinson* is and we can't fake the hand-off from Bahraini air controllers. They always want to know exactly where we're going, Captain," he said. Then, feeling a little bit emboldened, he added, "You're an aviator too, you know where we're coming from, sir."

That comment set Dennis off. He knew Admiral Flowers would be there soon. He needed the COD to be ready to go.

"You're damn right I'm an aviator, son, and the reason I've gotten where I have in my career is that I haven't offered some pussy excuse every time a mission I was assigned to wasn't exactly to my liking. So I'm going to make it easy for you. This is a direct order. *You are to fly Admiral Flowers to the* Carl Vinson *immediately.* Is that clear enough for you? If anyone yells at you, Lieutenant, you just tell them to come see me, is that clear?" he shouted, staring at the aircraft commander. "This is a matter of the highest importance, an issue of national security!" he said, finishing with a flourish. He hadn't wanted to get this fired up—or this specific—but he dared not risk Flowers's wrath.

"We will do what you are telling us, *sir*, but I am filing a report when I return. This is not a safe evolution and it's not even a legal evolution. You're doing the wrong thing, Captain. I'm doing this because you've made it a direct order—but that's the only reason."

"That's all the reason you need!" Dennis replied, then wheeled and walked away.

Now he stood near the maintenance hangar—the same one where the CH-53E had been destroyed—waiting for Admiral Flowers to arrive as the COD sat on the field with both engines turning and the ramp down. Flowers couldn't possibly be disappointed.

Aboard *Carl Vinson*, Captain Craig Vandegrift sat in his bridge chair and listened impassively as his TAO reported the approach of the two suspicious craft. The timing could not have been worse: he was pointing into the wind, about to launch a major package—eighteen aircraft—and then had to recover twenty-one others. The wind in the Gulf was almost dead calm, and he was making almost thirty-two knots to generate enough wind over the deck to safely launch and recover his bomb-laden aircraft.

"If I keep doing this, TAO, where will these guys be right after the launch?"

"They'll be less than ten miles from us, Captain, maybe less if the launch and recovery get stretched out at all."

"OK, I've got it. I'll tell the handler not to totally juggle the launch sequence plan, but if he can get any of those armed surface recce S-3s off the deck early, I need him to do it. I'm turning them over to the commodore—he needs them badly."

"Yes sir," was all that the harried TAO said in reply. After hearing from the aircraft handler, he called the commodore's Zulu Module and told him that the fifth aircraft coming off the cat would be an armed S-3 up for his control.

A few frames forward of where the CDC team was now keeping a very wary eye on these worrisome contacts, the CARGRU SEVEN TAO received a call from *Carl Vinson's* TAO. Concurrently, Craig Vandegrift called the admiral in his cabin to report the developing situation. Within moments the admiral had made his decision. The staff TAO contacted the carrier's shotgun ship via flashing light.

"*Shiloh*, this is Xray Bravo, over."

"Xray Bravo, this is *Shiloh*, roger, over."

"*Shiloh*, do you hold the two fast-moving contacts coming up from the south-south-east?"

"Roger, hold them on the SPY."

"*Shiloh*, Xray Bravo, you are directed to keep those contacts away from *Carl Vinson* while the ship completes this launch and recovery cycle. Use whatever means necessary."

"This is *Shiloh*, roger, out."

Admiral Flowers listened with a pained expression as the COD crew chief delivered the standard safety brief to him, while his aide fumbled with the gear the admiral was bringing along. It included a large envelope containing a formal letter relieving Admiral Robinson. A stickler for details, Admiral Flowers had insisted that such a letter be typed so he could formally relieve the admiral.

He sat in the front seat, but that meant looking backwards in the COD—the "tube of shame," as some wags dubbed it. Essentially the same airframe as the E-2C, the C-2A Greyhound was anything but a greyhound. It was slow, ponderous, and had the aerodynamics of a truck.

Admiral Flowers adjusted his straps as the pilots turned the aircraft up and got ready to taxi. The admiral knew that the flight to *Carl Vinson* would take almost forty-five minutes, so he tried to do what he could to get comfortable.

Aboard *Sabalan*, Commander Mohammad Mohtaj had seen the aircraft heading to the northwest—they were aircraft heading toward the carrier's marshall stack—confirming in his mind that the large contact in that direction was the *Carl Vinson*. He signaled that fact to Commander Farhad Kani on *Alborz*. Together, they decided that *Alborz* would go west of *Carl Vinson* and *Sabalan* would go east, each ship giving the American carrier a respectable five-mile standoff. From those vantage points they would watch its every move. They had long chafed over the American naval presence in the Arabian Gulf. Now they were in a position to do something about it. Both proceeded at flank speed.

The level of intensity aboard *Carl Vinson* was picking up. The launch was complete. Now the jets overhead had to be recovered, because they were reaching critical fuel states. The ship plowed on into the wind toward the contacts when Petty Officer Tyson shouted, "Chief Butterworth!"

The chief appeared quickly and looked over his shoulder. "What ya got, son?"

"Chief, I've been tracking these guys for a long time. It definitely looks like they've picked up speed."

"Tell the TAO now," he said.

Aboard *Shiloh*, Captain Jake Busch had both Iranian ships on his powerful SPY radar. His CDC team did some quick calculations. The ship to the west would come closest to the carrier. Convinced that it was the most immediate threat, he proceeded toward it. He was also working furiously to get his LAMPS helicopter out of the hangar, spread, and launched so he could visually ID that ship. At ten miles away in the Arabian Gulf haze, all he could tell was that it was a warship. That was enough to make him decide to close in at full speed.

His orders were to keep these ships away from *Carl Vinson*. But what did that mean? He hoped that his mere presence—he intended to place *Shiloh* between the *Alborz* and the carrier—would suffice. But what if it didn't? What if the Iranian continued to close? These people had bombed a hotel and shot a Tomcat out of the sky. They were capable of anything, he thought to himself. The rules of engagement were still murky. Shoulder the ship? Fire a shot across its bow? Jake Busch had never spoken to the admiral directly about this. He was basing all of his actions on the flashing light message received from the Flag TAO. He ran through his options as *Shiloh* and *Alborz* converged at a combined speed of over fifty knots.

As the junior captain among the two ships, Kani was very inexperienced. In command for only four months, he had taken his ship to sea a grand total of eight days before today. He had not had much experience at sea in any capacity in the past several years, coming off a staff assignment at naval headquarters just prior to this tour. He knew that Commander Mohtaj, many years his senior and already selected for captain, was watching, and that he was expected to close the carrier as he had been ordered. Kani stood in the center of his bridge and gripped the gyrocompass tightly. He gave the order.

"Helmsman, turn right forty degrees. Point your bow at the starboard bow of the aircraft carrier and keep it there."

Shiloh's bridge team saw the sharp maneuver. They were now less than four miles from the Iranian ship. The Iranian was making a beeline for the carrier. It defied belief. Jake Busch ordered flank speed as *Shiloh* took a course to place it between the Iranian warship and *Carl Vinson*. That would be only three miles from the carrier.

Commander Kani steeled himself for the confrontation. He knew that he was now committed. This American cruiser was attempting to keep him from complying with his orders. He could not fail Commander Mohtaj. Too much was at stake. He held his course.

Jake Busch saw that *Carl Vinson* was still recovering aircraft—aircraft that were low on gas and that had no alternative but to land on the carrier. He knew that Craig Vandegrift had to hold the carrier on a steady heading that would put him dangerously close to *Alborz*. As he got closer to *Alborz*, Jake Busch called the ship on bridge to bridge, warning him off the carrier, but he received no reply.

When Jake Busch saw the Iranian unmask his batteries, he made his move. He set *Shiloh* on a course up inside of the *Alborz*'s port bow, which would cause it to collide with *Alborz* if the Iranian did not change course. Then he made a critical move. He pointed his gun at Kani's ship and activated his fire control radar. He personally grabbed the bridge-to-bridge radio from his officer of the deck and yelled at the Iranian ship to back off.

Commander Kani heard the diatribe over bridge-to-bridge at the very moment he heard the alarmed voice of his combat information center officer. "Captain, the American has us lit off with his fire control radar." Kani panicked. The American captain yelling at him, his ship on a collision course, and now a definite hostile act, locking him up with his fire control radar. Captain Mohtaj was watching. He made his decision in an instant. "Fire a warning shot ahead of the American's bow."

His men were keyed up and primed for action. His gunner did not stop to ask the captain how far in front of *Shiloh* he should shoot or how many rounds he should fire. He pumped out three rounds in quick succession, two passing just ahead of *Shiloh*. The third, though, struck the cruiser's bow.

Jake Busch was not the type who needed to be told something twice before he got the message. He had to think of more than just his ship, though. If this Iranian was bold enough to shoot at him, he might shoot at *Carl Vinson* also—and *Carl Vinson* was in no position to maneuver to defend itself. Busch's SPY radar showed at least a half-dozen aircraft still preparing to land. He gave the order to his gunners.

Flames leapt out of the barrel of *Shiloh*'s five-inch, fifty-four caliber gun as round after round found *Alborz* with deadly accuracy. The gunner's mates, well-practiced from the almost daily drilling that Busch gave them, poured round after round into *Alborz*. The lightly armored Iranian frigate was no match for this concentrated, highly accurate fire. Holes were ripped into the superstructure across the entire length of the ship. Fires broke out everywhere. *Shiloh* kept firing as *Alborz* slowly decelerated and the crew of the Iranian vessel ran about madly breaking out hoses to contain the rapidly growing fires.

Aboard *Sabalan*, Captain Mohtaj watched in horror as his sister ship took this merciless pounding. He was eight miles from *Shiloh* and did the only thing that he thought he could do: he pointed his ship directly at the American cruiser and told his gunners to prepare to fire. Win or lose, he would not let the American pound one of his ships with impunity.

Aloft in Blue Wolf 703, Lieutenant Mike Doyle was watching the action between the ships. He broke radio silence and called the Zulu Module, talking directly with Commodore Jim Hughes.

"Commodore, Blue Wolf 703, I've got a bead on the Iranian ship moving toward *Shiloh*, request weapons release."

"Granted, 703," was all that the commodore needed to say.

Doyle brought his aircraft screaming out of the sky and directly toward *Sabalan*. He had the frigate squarely in his sights as he hit the pickle switch and pulled up. Mk 82 500-pound bombs rained down on the Iranian frigate.

Captain Mohtaj never saw the Viking screaming down at him. He was totally focused on *Shiloh*. As he was coming up dead astern of her, he figured that he would get a clear shot off before the American ever saw him. He was not sure that his ship would win the contest with *Shiloh*, but he had confidence in the C-802 missiles that he carried. Most importantly, his radio operator was already calling Bushehr on a secure radio, telling of the American attack on *Alborz*, and warning that the U.S. aircraft carrier could launch strikes at any moment.

Captain Mohtaj probably felt the explosion before he heard it. Every man on *Sabalan* was instantly knocked off his feet. Ominously, the engines wound down, and *Sabalan* slowed precipitously, mortally wounded. Captain Mohtaj knew immediately that he had lost his ship. His only goal now was to save as many of his men as he could before the ship went to the bottom of the Arabian Gulf.

In TFCC on *Carl Vinson*, Heater Robinson stood behind his TAO, watching the surface action. No direction was needed by the flag staff, as *Shiloh* handled one contact and the commodore handled the other with a single Viking. They merely watched the action on the JMCIS display and listened to the reports over the Battle Group Command circuit. It was crisp, almost antiseptic, as the Iranian ships were taken out effortlessly.

For Heater Robinson it was an ominous sign. Were the Iranians conducting a wholesale assault on his battle group? If so, it meant that the entire Iranian fleet was sortieing from its ports. That would defeat his attack plan to catch all of those ships there. He decided that Operation Mountain Divide could not wait.

The C-2A Greyhound sat on the tarmac at Bahrain International Airport. Harry Flowers was incensed as he sat in the back of the rumbling aircraft, sweat pouring off him in the stifling COD. His aide tried unsuccessfully to explain that the pilots were trying to get clearance from the often-uncooperative Bahraini air controllers, who seemed to periodically take great delight in delaying the launch of American military aircraft. Nothing the enraged Flowers or the hapless pilots could do sped the process along.

57

"CAPTAIN, LOOK AT THIS, WILL YOU?" SAID LIEUTEN-
ant Colonel Bill Mansalo.

"I see it, but I'm not sure I'm believing it Bill," replied
Captain Mike Ruggles.

The two officers were closely monitoring their worldwide
JMCIS display on the floor of the NMCC. Though the display gave them the position of all U.S. military units worldwide, as well as tracks put in by these units, their team had
focused in on the Northern Arabian Gulf and specifically on
the area immediately surrounding USS *Carl Vinson*. They
had tracked *Carl Vinson* south-south-east and had watched
as *Shiloh* moved close to the carrier as two unknown surface
contacts continued to close both U.S. ships. They had
watched with great concern as the symbology for the two
tracks had changed from "unknown" to "hostile."

Now one of the tracks had disappeared.

Bill Mansalo noticed it first, and asked the senior Navy
officer to confirm his suspicions.

"Do tracks just drop out of the system like that, Captain?"

"Not likely, Bill, let's see what corroborating evidence we
can find," Ruggles replied.

The two officers instructed the enlisted watchstanders to
check the data bases, running various checks, trying to determine exactly why one of these two hostile tracks had disappeared. None of the normal checks revealed any more
specificity about the status of the tracks. Soon, though, loud
voices penetrated their area.

"OPREP Three Pinnacle/Front Burner from USS *Shiloh*,
voice report two minutes ago, message will be in soon. *Shiloh* reports shooting up an Iranian frigate that was threat-

ening *Carl Vinson. Shiloh* also reports *Carl Vinson* aircraft is attacking another Iranian frigate in the immediate area!"

The news was electrifying, for it represented a major escalation to a standoff that had been brewing for a while. What had precipitated the American attacks? The speculation was intense all throughout the NMCC as everyone from junior watchstanders to General Allen and other senior officers waited for details to flesh out. Watching the displays just prior to the contacts' disappearing as they converged on *Carl Vinson* fueled all kinds of speculation—from preemptive attacks against the Iranian vessels by *Shiloh* to some kind of defensive engagement in response to an Iranian attack. The last several decades had seen U.S. naval engagements cover a wide spectrum, from the Tonkin Gulf engagement off Vietnam, to action against Libyan surface craft, to action against units of this Navy a decade ago, where the first reports of what took place did not always accurately reflect reality. They hoped that the soon-to-be-received OPREPS would provide more detailed—and accurate—information.

Soon, the OPREPS from *Shiloh* and from *Carl Vinson* appeared and fleshed out some areas where there had been an information void. They painted a comprehensive picture of the way that the battle group had defended itself from the attacks by the Iranian frigates. While no one would venture a guess as to why these Iranian ships had attacked, the consensus was that the battle group had done the proper thing in defending itself.

While the very brief voice reports and the more comprehensive OPREPS had been a good start, they had not been enough. What they wanted to hear, but what was conspicuous by its absence, was a voice report by Admiral Robinson, a recap by the battle group commander of what had gone on—a formal OPREP THREE PINNACLE FRONT BURNER from the admiral himself, filling in the Flag-level details and providing his personal assessment of the situation. They knew that the admiral had put the group in emission control to make it more difficult for the Iranians to locate his ships, but they hoped that he might have chosen to communicate directly with them. He hadn't. Beyond that strange silence, the watch team noticed something else.

"Couch, what do you make of these ship posits?" said Captain Mike Ruggles to another one of his watch team, Lieutenant Commander Hank Couch.

"Let me put up some overlays and I'll try to tell you?" he replied. Couch was a surface warfare officer who was an expert in Tomahawk employment. He was searching for overlays that would depict the geographic area where each of the Tomahawk ships would have to launch their missiles in an attack against Iran. Couch manipulated the JMCIS display for another minute.

"There they are, Captain," he replied as he drew some wind through his teeth.

"Yeah, I see it, it's every one, isn't it?"

"Sure is, Captain. They've got every TLAM shooter positioned right where they need to be to launch strikes against targets in Iran."

"Are you sure it's not just a coincidence that they happen to be where they are?"

"No way, Captain, look at this," Couch said as he moved his laser pointer around the screen. "These two guys down here are tucked in close to the Iranian land mass, someplace that they'd never be unless or until they were going to shoot Tomahawks at Iran."

"I see. Are they the only ones in odd positions?" replied Ruggles.

"No, Captain," continued Couch, "what's really strange is the way all of the ships doing maritime intercept operations have moved away from their positions in the northern Gulf and taken up other positions. It's strange for two reasons. One is that we never totally back off on enforcing sanctions against Iraq, no matter what else is going on. The other is that he's got tremendous overkill for shooting Tomahawks."

"How so?" asked Captain Ruggles.

"Sir," replied Couch, "I've sat in on some of the overall targeting sessions for the strikes against the Iranian terrorist camps. TACAIR is providing most of the firepower, we're only shooting twenty-six Tomahawks, total, against all of the camps. Captain, he could get that from one or two ships. He's got every Tomahawk shooter—with a total of over three hundred twenty-five missiles—in position ready to fire against Iran."

"Maybe he just wants backups in case some missiles fail," replied Ruggles. He was not an expert in Tomahawk matters and was just trying to play devil's advocate.

"That would be a stretch, Captain. What this really looks like, sir, is the force laydown for Mountain Divide."

"You're right. It's just like we've wargamed it."

"We need to tell the boss," said Couch.

"I agree," replied Captain Ruggles as he reached for the phone at his watchstation.

As the word from these watchstanders worked its way up through the Joint Staff, it confirmed what those near the top of the chain knew already—that Heater Robinson was planning to attack the Islamic Republic with massive TACAIR and Tomahawk strikes. That was already known. What made the situation more ominous was the fact that the renegade admiral had already placed his TLAM ships in precise position to fire their deadly missiles. What was more, based on the large sortie counts he had been putting in the air, the attack appeared to be imminent.

General Allen entered the chairman's office with the latest news.

"Admiral," Allen began, "we've been pulling together a lot of information. The long and the short of it is that it appears that Admiral Robinson may be prepared to launch his full-blown attacks against Iran sooner than we anticipated."

"It looks like he may," responded the chairman. As a naval officer and former battle group commander who had led George Washington Battle Group in the Arabian Gulf years ago, it was even more clear to Jake Monroe what was about to happen.

"Any further action on our part right now, Admiral?" asked General Allen.

"No, we've got it from here," replied the chairman, who seemed suddenly distant.

As General Allen departed the chairman's office, Admiral

Jake Monroe told his EA to get Michael Curtis on the line, then pondered the situation. They knew what Heater Robinson was planning. Now it appeared that he had moved up his timeline significantly. He had Admiral Harry Flowers in an aircraft headed out to *Carl Vinson* at this very moment. But what would happen when Flowers got there? If Heater Robinson was this close to carrying out his attacks, would he even listen to Flowers or just ignore him? Would he even let him land? Would he hold him as a hostage onboard if he had really gone over the deep end? Jake's EA broke his reverie to let him know the national security adviser's office was waiting.

"Admiral, it's good to hear from you," Curtis said. "My secretary said that it was urgent."

"It is, sir. The timetable for events in the Arabian Gulf has picked up. I believe that we need an emergency meeting of the NSC immediately."

"Is this about the Iranian ships that just threatened *Carl Vinson*, the ones that just got taken out?"

"That and more, Mr. Curtis. Please sir, we need to move on this one."

Within an hour, the principals were reconvened at their now-familiar places in the Cabinet Room, waiting for Michael Curtis. Although they dared not voice it, they were getting weary of these constant meetings. There wasn't time to implement all of the things that they had agreed upon—or, more accurately, that Michael Curtis had directed them to do—before they were meeting again to take on new actions.

The principals rose as Curtis and Monroe entered. Immediately, they sensed that they were all now about to become third parties to actions and decisions already underway.

"Thank you all for coming on such short notice," Curtis said. "I assure you that the urgency of the situation made this a necessary meeting.

"Based on some heads-up play and on good analysis by watchstanders in the NMCC, Admiral Monroe has confirmed that the evidence that *Carl Vinson* is going to launch attacks against a full range of targets in Iran is now overwhelming. Further, he suggests that the timetable for these attacks could be much more imminent than we initially thought.

"Admiral Flowers is airborne as we speak, en route to *Carl Vinson* to relieve Admiral Robinson on the spot. We hope that this goes smoothly. However, if it doesn't, we need to hedge against that possibility and be ready to take other action. I've assembled all of you here to discuss options."

There was silence in the room. They were not prepared for this meeting. None of their underlings had prepared the requisite position papers or briefing packages. They were left to their own instincts and their own wits.

Michael Curtis surveyed the sea of faces. No one made eye contact. They all shifted uneasily in their chairs.

"Ideas?" said Curtis, his voice betraying his annoyance.

Still silence.

"All right," said the national security adviser. "Maybe it was unfair of me to gather you all so soon. Shortly, we'll know if Admiral Flowers was successful in his mission. Admiral Monroe will keep us posted. Meanwhile, I want you to come up with contingency plans."

As they filed out, they heard Curtis call after them, "Four hours. I want to reconvene in four hours to look at your options!"

58

THE C-2A LURCHED DOWN RUNWAY 30 AT BAHRAIN International Airport and lumbered into the air, a terrified Harry Flowers facing aft, sitting next to one of only two small, round windows in the entire cabin. The damned Bahraini air controllers had delayed them on the tarmac for over forty-five minutes, then had had them taxi the entire length of the twelve-thousand-foot runway to take off northwest on runway 30. His khakis were already soaked through and they still had thirty to forty minutes left in the air before they reached *Carl Vinson*.

Flowers hated to fly—hated the Greyhound worst of all—and had the disposition of a doomed man. Only by reminding himself that he was about to command a battle group, a position that had eluded him throughout his career, and wreak havoc on the Iranian terrorist camps at the very least, was he able to keep his spirits up.

Sitting in the Greyhound's cockpit, Lieutenant Frank Barrett and Lieutenant Steve Green discussed their options.

"I am really pissed that we got browbeat into this mission, Frank," said Green, the junior pilot of the two.

"I am too, Steve, and I know it was my call as aircraft commander, but Captain Dennis gave us a direct order and the admiral sure rubbed it in when he got to the plane. Let's just get him onboard the boat and get the heck back to base. I'm filing a report with the skipper back at North Island and I hope he runs it right to the admiral at AIRPAC. This shit has got to stop."

"First we got to find the boat," said Steve Green. "The chief of staff said he thought they'd be down here just south of Bushehr. We'll look there first. Why don't you pick up a heading of 050 magnetic and we'll check it out."

"WILCO, but we'll have to get right on top of them. This order by the admiral and the chief of staff to turn our transponder off so our arrival is a surprise is total bullshit, but I don't give a damn anymore. They can order me to fly upside down if they want to. I just want to get this over with."

"Me too, buddy, me too," said Green as the COD droned ahead.

Carl Vinson and *Shiloh* continued northwest toward the furthermost corner of the northern operating area, trying to put as much distance between themselves and the Iranian naval bases and airfields—and buy as much reaction time—as possible should the Iranians try a major attack. Both ships remained at General Quarters in the wake of the sinking of the one Iranian frigate and the disabling of the other.

Heater Robinson kept the group in radio EMCON, the only exceptions being his direction to each of the group's TLAM shooters to move to their launch baskets, spin up their missiles, and await further orders, and the very brief OPREP report of the *Shiloh* disabling *Alborz* and of the Viking sinking of *Sabalan*. Once that was complete, he reimposed radio silence and charged his entire staff to actively monitor the electronic spectrum to ensure that there were no transmissions.

The tension aboard *Carl Vinson* and aboard *Shiloh* was incredibly high. Although they had "won" the engagement with the frigates, they were not convinced they could so handily defeat multiple attacks by similar determined units. More ominously, at all levels of the battle group, there was great concern that these attacks had been mere probes—sacrificial attacks designed to test the battle group's defensive systems, precursors to massive coordinated Iranian attacks against the battle group. Shipboard radars swept the skies in all directions, looking for airborne contacts as the flight deck was alive with activity to load ordnance on aircraft getting ready to launch for strikes.

Flowers's aide crawled up into the cockpit of the COD to talk to the pilots. "The admiral wants to know when we are going to arrive onboard *Carl Vinson*."

"We've got to find the damn boat first," replied Steve Green as the COD did a lazy circle in the central Gulf, scanning the horizon for a ship that was not there.

As the admiral's aide returned to the COD cabin to deliver this report to Admiral Flowers—the pilots hoped he got his ass kicked—Green turned to Barrett: "OK Frank, you're aircraft commander, what next?"

"I was afraid of this, Steve," he replied. "Don't know what these yokels were telling us about the carrier being here. Bum gouge to be sure. I'm gonna take us northwest up to where *Carl Vinson* usually operates. We'll find her there."

"Think you're right, Frank. It's about our only option, isn't it?"

"Yep, that's the way I see it," he replied.

"Just make sure that you give Bushehr a wide berth, Frank, no sense getting shot at by them."

Carl Vinson and *Shiloh* had now been at General Quarters for several hours. In the VS-35 Ready Room, pilots, naval flight officers, and naval aircrewmen bustled in and out of the ready room, coming and going from their missions, still pushing the edge of the envelope, flying to the limits of their endurance, making up for the loss of Chrissie, as well as making up for Anne's temporary absence.

Anne sat in her ready room chair watching the pace of activity and thinking. Early that morning she had gone running with Rick—he had suggested it the night before—and he had followed up on his earlier advice and counsel to her. Nothing heavy-handed, no advice that she hadn't asked for, no pushing her to make a decision, just wise, sage counsel as they pounded out four miles on the unyielding steel deck. What he had told her had made a lot of sense, and the way he had listened had been wonderful. She knew that now she needed to make a decision.

As the COD continued to fly northwest, the pilots had no knowledge of the recent surface action in the northern Gulf, but they felt incredibly vulnerable nonetheless. It was one thing to fly out to an aircraft carrier—even one that had been their home for almost two years—without filing a flight plan with them. It was another to be searching the Gulf for the ship because they didn't know the carrier's exact position. And they were doing this without benefit of radios. But the most unsatisfactory part of this mission was flying without their IFF—identification friend or foe—transponder on, the one sure way that they could identify themselves as a friendly aircraft.

Sure, a three-star admiral was aboard, and his aviator chief of staff had ordered them to launch on this mission. He had even pulled them aside after he had blasted them and all but apologized, telling them in the strictest confidence that this was not a routine visit by any means and that Admiral Flowers would not be returning from *Carl Vinson* for quite some time. Based on the number of bags that the aide had lugged onboard it did appear that Admiral Flowers was embarking for a while. Maybe some huge operation that required the presence of a three-star admiral was in the offing.

That thought at least gave them some comfort as they pressed on at 9,000 feet and 240 knots, not so much flying through the air as beating it into submission with two huge propellers. Admiral Flowers sat in the back fuming, trying to relax as much as he could but frustrated that the constant noise and the ceaseless shaking were fraying his nerves even more than they already were.

Carl Vinson and *Shiloh* remained on alert, scanning the seas and skies around them. Visibility was less than five miles, and the anxiety level was incredibly high. Petty Officer Sandy Martinez, manning his scope in *Shiloh*'s CDC, was the first to spot it.

"I've got an airborne contact at bearing 130 for eighty-five miles. Course 325, speed two hundred fifty knots, altitude twenty-three thousand feet. No modes, no codes." The last portion of his report told his superiors that they were interrogating the aircraft with IFF but that it was not responding at all.

"Roger," replied the watch supervisor.

After tracking the contact for a while to ensure that it was what they thought it was and to further refine course and speed, the watch supervisor passed this information up the chain, where ultimately the TAO evaluated it. When he finally made his report to the captain, the contact was at less than seventy miles.

"What do you think, Alan?" said *Shiloh*'s commanding officer to his TAO.

"We need to watch this one closely, Captain," replied Lieutenant Commander Alan Mellon. "It emanated from the vicinity of Bushehr. Slow speed tells me it probably isn't a high-performance fighter or attack plane, but they could be going this slowly deliberately to throw off anyone tracking them."

"I agree, Alan, we need to break radio silence and let the Flag TAO aboard *Carl Vinson* know."

"WILCO, boss," Mellon replied as he now tracked the contact inside of sixty miles.

Aboard *Carl Vinson*, the Flag TAO called Heater Robinson. An unknown aircraft inbound to them with "no squawk" was a serious concern. Although he had all but sequestered himself in his cabin, Heater Robinson appeared in TFCC and watched the contact on both the ACDS and JMCIS displays. As the contact closed to within fifty miles, he broke radio silence again and directed *Shiloh*'s CO to issue level one warnings to the aircraft and directed *Carl Vinson*'s CO to launch Alert 7 fighters. It was time to give this contact a closer look.

Aboard *Shiloh*, the captain had seen enough. He ordered his TAO to issue level one warnings, but the plane kept on coming.

The action on the flight deck was frantic as *Carl Vinson* turned back into the wind to launch the Alert 7 fighters. Lieutenant Rudy Garcia in Fist 206 got his Hornet started first and, following the yellow shirt director, headed for cat 3. A minute later, Lieutenant Pat Whaley in Fist 209 started his aircraft and was ready to taxi to cat 4. The two Fistie pilots had been a little surprised by the call for the alert launch and were just a bit behind. It had been five minutes since the alert was called away, and Whaley, in particular, was worried about busting the seven-minute limit.

The flight deck yellow shirts usually moved aircraft with well-choreographed precision, but these men were feeling the effects of the tremendous rampup in flight tempo over the last several days. They didn't cross-check and double-check as they usually did. The yellow shirts directing Pat Whaley got him moving just a bit too fast and overshot the corner to bring him on to cat 4. The air boss caught it first and grabbed the 5 MC.

"On the flight deck, yellow shirt directing Fist 209, emergency stop. I say again, emergency stop!" shouted the air boss.

But it was too late. With a sickening crunch, the radome of Fist 209 smashed into the right wing of Fist 206 as it turned up on cat 4. The flight deck crew scrambled for cover as Pat Whaley desperately slammed on the brakes in response to the yellow shirt's frantic signal. Pieces of aircraft flew everywhere as both Whaley and Garcia quickly shut down their aircraft. Mercifully, no one on the flight deck was seriously injured by the flying debris, but emergency crews swarmed about the two Hornets prepared for the worst. Someone thought they saw smoke coming out of Fist 206, and the crash cart sprayed a layer of foam to fight the non-existent fire.

One deck below, both *Carl Vinson*'s TAO and the Flag TAO watched in horror. Beyond their concerns for the safety of the men on deck, they realized that there would be a delay in launching any interceptors from *Carl Vinson*. The unknown air contact was now at forty miles, headed directly for them.

Aboard *Shiloh* the tension was palpable. Level one warnings had not deterred the aircraft. The TAO issued level two warnings to the aircraft:

"Unidentified aircraft bearing 125 at fifty miles from my position and flying at twenty-three thousand feet, on course 305, speed approximately two hundred fifty knots; you are approaching a United States Navy warship operating in international waters. Your identity is not known and your intentions are unclear. You are standing into danger and may be subject to United States defensive measures. Request you establish communications now or alter your course immediately to remain clear of me. Request you alter course to 090 to remain clear!"

No response.

"Again," said the captain. He could feel his palms sweating.

"Unknown aircraft . . . to remain clear!" said the TAO, repeating the warning precisely.

Again there was no response.

Green and Barrett were still searching in vain.

"Frank, the haze is getting pretty bad up here, do you want to try to break out below? Won't be able to see as far, but maybe the visibility will be a little bit better."

"Let's try it, Steve, let's take it down to three thousand feet, we may be able to see a bit better down there. What have we got to lose?"

"WILCO," said Frank Barrett as he pushed the yoke forward.

Heater Robinson himself grabbed the UHF radio and called *Shiloh*.

"Xray Whiskey, this is Xray Bravo. Emergency on *Carl Vinson*'s flight deck. I repeat, emergency on *Carl Vinson*'s flight deck. Unable to launch DLIs. Unable to launch DLIs. Show air contact still closing the force. Request intentions!" Heater Robinson was leading *Shiloh*'s CO—a lot. The captain was getting it loud and clear from the admiral. He had an absolute obligation to defend the force, and he was going to get no airborne help. It was *Shiloh* and her missiles.

Aboard *Shiloh*, the captain was about to respond to the admiral, when, from across the cruiser's CDC, the petty officer manning the scope made his call.

"Airborne contact at twenty-eight miles, two hundred seventy knots descending rapidly, passing through seven thousand feet. It looks like an attack profile sir!"

"Take it with birds!" shouted the captain.

His order was repeated back, and within seconds, two SM-2 ER—standard missiles extended range—leapt out of *Shiloh*'s forward vertical launch magazine.

Almost thirty feet long, and weighing almost 3,000 pounds, the SM-2 was accurate out to over twenty-five nautical miles, and they proceeded with deadly precision toward the COD. At two-and-a-half times the speed of sound, the missiles would be airborne in less than a minute-and-a-half.

The AWACS airborne over Saudi Arabia had been tracking the COD for its entire flight, from the time it departed Bahrain. Long accustomed to the transit of these aircraft between Bahrain International and the carrier, the operators on board did not focus intently on the aircraft. They thought that its flight path was a bit circuitous and ascribed that to those Navy boys just not telling each other where they were—something that never happened in the Air Force. They noticed that the aircraft did not seem to have an operating transponder, again, something they could easily write off to a lack of pride in their gear and a baffling willingness to fly their aircraft in a degraded mode. They almost missed them, but finally picked up missiles streaking up from USS *Shiloh* and impacting the aircraft. After a moment of stunned silence, they rapidly began to communicate with higher echelons about this extraordinary event.

59

"GENERAL, IT'S AN OPREP PINNACLE/FRONT BURNER voice report from *Carl Vinson*," said Colonel Jay Williams as he put the receiver down in its cradle.

"What does it say?" said General Allen. He had just watched the JMCIS display and thought that he knew precisely what the report would say, but he had to let his watchstander report it in accordance with their procedures.

"Sir, *Shiloh* reports shooting down an unknown aircraft with negative squawk that was closing *Carl Vinson* and descending on an attack profile."

"Shot down with *Shiloh* birds?"

"Yes sir," replied Williams.

"Any visual ID?"

"No, General. Accident on *Carl Vinson*'s flight deck prevented them from launching any DLIs. *Shiloh* shot BVR."

"I see," replied General Allen. "I'll take care of calling the chairman, make sure that this is passed to the White House Situation Room."

"Yes sir, General," he replied.

General Allen had just departed the NMCC to head back

toward the J-3 Directorate when Colonel Williams received another OPREP Pinnacle report.

"Admiral," he said, turning to Rear Admiral Walt Morrin, "OPREP just received from the AWACS over Saudi."

"Go ahead," he responded.

"Sir, they report that the *Shiloh* just shot down the COD aircraft that was flying out to *Carl Vinson* from Bahrain."

"No, there's obviously some confusion by the AWACS crew. *Shiloh* just shot down an Iranian aircraft approaching from Bushehr."

"Sir, they said that they tracked this aircraft from the time it departed Bahrain International. They double-checked with Bahrain Approach, and they confirmed that the COD took off at exactly the time that the AWACS began tracking it. They said that there's no doubt, sir."

"SHIT," shouted Admiral Morrin. "Colonel, get General Allen back in here now!"

"Yes sir," he replied.

"And have someone get back on the net and get *Carl Vinson* and *Shiloh* patched back in. We need to sort this out."

"Admiral," responded the shaken Colonel Williams, "the battle group has gone back into radio silence."

"DAMNIT!" shouted Morrin as he rushed from the room.

Within minutes the full power of the Joint Staff was mobilized to try to deconflict the two radically different stories about the aircraft shootdown. Phone calls were made, tapes reviewed, aircraft specifications double-checked, and other resources were brought into play. In twenty minutes they had made their assessment. It confirmed their worst fears.

General Allen sat in the chairman's office as Admiral Monroe called the national security adviser. The news was as unbelievable as anything they had ever heard. He could see that the chairman had trouble even expressing the words over the phone. Somehow he expected that the imminent meeting of the NSC would be even worse. He felt more confident that the plan they were going to propose, draconian as it was, would be accepted.

*　　*　　*

The principals took their seats in the Situation Room. The mood was beyond somber; it approached despair. Each one admitted to themselves that they wished they were anywhere else, doing almost anything else. This time, Michael Curtis was at his seat, staring straight ahead as the others filed in.

"You all know why you're here," he began. "I assume that the word of the shootdown of Admiral Flowers's aircraft has reached all of you already. Admiral Monroe will briefly recap these events so that you all understand fully what happened, but there is no doubt that his aircraft was shot out of the sky as it approached *Carl Vinson*. Admiral."

"Thank you, Mr. Curtis," replied Jake Monroe as he stood up. One of his aides placed a map of the Arabian Gulf on an easel, and the admiral went through the chain of events. Afterward, there was the obligatory question or two as to whether he was certain that this had occurred. He assured them that it had. When he finished, all eyes turned toward Michael Curtis.

"When I sent you away earlier today to come up with a backup solution to removing Admiral Robinson from *Carl Vinson*, the worst scenario I envisioned was his refusing to yield to Admiral Flowers's authority and not letting the Fifth Fleet commander take over. We . . . I . . . had no concept that the battle group commander had raised the stakes and the level of violence to the point that he would shoot his plane out of the sky and kill seven innocent people in the process. You are going to hear two options briefed this evening that will sound radical. I hope that you will agree with me that the nature of this crisis demands that we carefully consider both options. Admiral Monroe will begin, followed by Mr. Hernandez."

Admiral Monroe stood up once again as aides put up different charts on a set of easels. They showed a now-familiar chart of the Arabian Gulf, a picture of USS *Carl Vinson*, and a picture of a submarine. The admiral let his aides finish setting up and had them leave the room before he spoke.

"Ladies and gentlemen," he began, "Admiral Robinson has *Carl Vinson* in position ready to conduct massive strikes against Iran. He could conduct these strikes at any moment, though we suspect that he will most likely do so sometime in the next twenty-four to thirty-six hours, depending on how fast he can upload his ordnance. The key is to prevent the aircraft carrier from doing that, to disable it and negate its ability to conduct these strikes."

Admiral Monroe paused to look around the room. Every eye was on him.

"USS *Jefferson City*, one of our Los Angeles Class attack boats, is in the Southern Arabian Gulf. We propose to have her make best speed north to the vicinity of *Carl Vinson* and disable the carrier by shooting torpedoes into her screws. If the carrier can't make way through the water, it can't launch and recover aircraft. While not an ideal solution, given the urgency of the situation, it is our best option."

The admiral went on to explain some of the technical details of *Jefferson City*'s capabilities, the specifications of the torpedo, how the sub would conduct the attack, and other details. He then asked for questions.

"How can you be sure that the torpedo won't sink *Carl Vinson*?"

"These are highly accurate fish, we can place them precisely where we want them."

"Can the sub actually find the ship?"

"We'll give *Jefferson City* locating data on the carrier's precise position."

"After the screws are hit, how long will the carrier be disabled?"

"As drastic as this sounds, replacing the screw on an aircraft carrier—or any other ship, for that matter—is a relatively straightforward matter. Much less complex than repairing hull damage from a torpedo."

"What about the strikes on the terrorist camps?"

"We have not completed our analysis yet, but once Admiral Robinson is removed from *Carl Vinson*, we intend to order his replacement to attack the terrorist camps with Tomahawk cruise missiles."

The admiral continued to field questions until Michael Curtis weighed in.

"Before we get into too much more detail regarding Admiral Monroe's option, I want you to hear from Mr. Hernandez," said the national security adviser, working mightily to keep the meeting on track.

Pete Hernandez stood up slowly. He had neither charts nor assistants like Admiral Monroe did. His body language conveyed the fact that he did not like doing what he was about to do. There was silence in the room as he prepared to speak.

"Ladies and gentlemen, the option I propose is quite simple, perhaps even simplistic, compared to that offered by Admiral Monroe. We have had an agency operative embarked in *Carl Vinson* since the beginning of her deployment. He is assigned there as a Navy SEAL and has, in fact, been with the SEALs for several years. He recently completed a mission for us in another area, and our intent was to keep him on hold for a while, just conducting his normal Navy duties until such time that we needed him again."

Pete Hernandez could tell by the look on their faces that they had no idea where he was going with this. He got right to the point.

"We are in daily contact with this man. We propose to contact him and have him disable Admiral Robinson—by whatever means necessary—to prevent him from conducting these attacks. Based on a communication Admiral Monroe received from the ship, we assess that the entire crew is not behind Admiral Robinson, that it is highly likely that he has duped them all into believing that a full-blown attack against Iran has been ordered by competent authority. We believe that once he is disabled, order can be restored."

The questions came hot and heavy.

"What if he refuses to do it?"

"This individual has put his life on the line for his country before, we have no doubts that he will carry out his orders."

"Can one person accomplish this, no matter how capable he is?"

"Again, this is a uniquely qualified individual. He can do this mission."

"Who will be in command if Admiral Robinson is disabled?"

"Temporarily, his chief of staff, Captain George Sampson, will be in charge as the next senior man. However, we are preparing to send another flag officer to take his place very soon after that."

"Will this individual just disable, or will he kill Admiral Robinson?"

"His orders will be to disable him by whatever means necessary."

There were a few more questions for the DCI, and Michael Curtis let his colleagues ask them. Finally there were no more, and Curtis stood up.

"Ladies and gentlemen," he began, "these are very draconian proposals, but they are necessary because wo must stop Admiral Robinson at all costs. I am not going to ask you to choose between the two of them—I think that the urgency of the situation demands that we put both plans in motion right away. We can afford to have redundancy in this mission, we just can't afford to fail."

The nodding of heads around the table told Michael Curtis all he needed to know.

60

THE CHIEF OF NAVAL OPERATIONS CONVENED AN emergency meeting of his close advisors immediately after meeting with the National Security Council. He had made his suggestion to the chairman of the Joint Chiefs of Staff not expecting that it would be accepted. Now that this option was on the table and had been accepted by the National Security Council, it was up to him and his key advisors to make it happen. It was not going to be easy.

The CNO gathered a small group of his close advisors in his spacious E-ring office. Once they reconciled the fact that a Navy submarine was going to fire torpedoes at a multi-billion-dollar Navy aircraft carrier, there was nothing terribly complex or involved with making this happen. They decided that the order should come directly from COMSUBPAC, *Jefferson City*'s operational commander, with a concurrent message from the chief of Naval Operations, letting the boat's CO know a bit more of the overarching mission. The decision finalized, the real business of putting the plan into action got underway. Getting the word to USS *Jefferson City* instantly became job number one for the United States Navy.

Seven time zones away from the Pentagon, Commander Willard stood in the control room of USS *Jefferson City*, directing the actions of his crew of one hundred thirty-five. Willard loved this boat, loved command, and loved what *Jefferson City* could do as a war machine. Armed with a mix of huge Mk 48 wire-guided, active/passive torpedoes, as well as deadly Tomahawk cruise missiles, possessing the most sophisticated combat data, weapons control, and sonar systems, *Jefferson City* was more than a match for anything else in or on the oceans. Displacing 6,000 tons, *Jefferson City* could stay submerged indefinitely, and her two turbines driving her single shaft could propel the boat at over 30 knots.

The tremendous capability of his boat, however, was just what was causing Willard angst at this very moment. He was in his eighth straight day of watching to see if any Iranian Kilo Class submarines got underway. It was a boring, routine duty and a mission that prevented him from training to hone the skills of his crew. Joe Willard could feel the barnacles growing on their readiness every day that they sat there. He was roused from his musing by his executive officer, Lieutenant Commander Alex Hines.

"Captain, SPECAT message has just come in for you. RM2 Jeeter is standing by outside of your cabin."

"SPECAT message?"

"Yes sir," responded the exec.

The captain hurried back to his cabin and grabbed the message from the one radioman on board who was authorized to handle them. He signed for it and dismissed Jeeter.

He closed the door to his cabin and took a deep breath before opening up the message and laying it out on his desk.

FROM: COMSUBPAC
TO: USS JEFFERSON CITY
TOP SECRET SPECAT PERSONAL FOR COMMANDING OF-
FICER FROM COMSUBPAC
SUBJ/JEFFERSON CITY MISSION//
1.(TS) COMMANDER, THIS IS NOT A DRILL. REPEAT, THIS
IS NOT A DRILL. UPON RECEIPT YOU ARE TO PROCEED
NORTH AT BEST SPEED TO THE NORTHERN ARABIAN
GULF. UPON ARRIVAL YOU WILL LOCATE USS CARL VIN-
SON. ONCE LOCATED, YOU WILL SET UP FOR A DELIB-
ERATE ATTACK TO DISABLE, REPEAT, DISABLE, CARL
VINSON. IT IS PREFERRED THAT YOU DO SO BY FIRING
TORPEDOES INTO THE CARRIER'S SCREWS, BUT THE AC-
TUAL TACTICS ARE TO BE OF YOUR CHOOSING. THE
REASON FOR YOUR TASKING IS EXTREMELY DELICATE
AND SHALL NOT BE DIVULGED TO ANYONE; THE BAT-
TLE GROUP COMMANDER HAS ELECTED, FOR REASONS
KNOWN ONLY TO HIM, TO ATTACK THE ISLAMIC REPUB-
LIC OF IRAN. YOU MUST DISABLE CARL VINSON BEFORE
HE CONDUCTS THESE ATTACKS. BEST ESTIMATE OF THE
TIME OF THESE ATTACKS IS 24 TO 36 HOURS FROM NOW.
THE IMPORTANCE OF YOUR MISSION CANNOT BE OVER-
STATED. GOOD LUCK AND GOOD HUNTING. THIS IS NOT
A DRILL, REPEAT, THIS IS NOT A DRILL. COMSUBPAC,
REAR ADMIRAL DEUTERMANN.
DECL/X4//

Joe Willard read the message three times, then grabbed a sheath of yellow legal paper and started to fashion a response to COMSUBPAC. This could not be happening. Twenty years of submarine service, including some dangerous and harrowing missions—one so dangerous that it had won his boat's captain the Silver Star—had not prepared him for this. He wrote and scratched and wrote and scratched as time stood still. He did not realize that almost an hour had passed when there was a knock on his door.

"Yes," he replied.

"Captain, Petty Officer Jetter. Sir, another SPECAT for you."

Thank God, Willard thought, surely this was another message from SUBPAC canceling the original message. He was beyond relief. He grabbed the message from Jeeter, hastily signed for it, then closed and locked the door to his tiny cabin once again. He opened the message and laid it before him, his anticipated relief already welling up.

FROM: CHIEF OF NAVAL OPERATIONS
TO: USS JEFFERSON CITY
TOP SECRET SPECAT PERSONAL FOR COMMANDING OFFICER FROM CLOWARD
SUBJ/MISSION VALIDATION//
1. (TS) CAPTAIN. YOU HAVE JUST RECEIVED A SPECAT PERSONAL FROM COMSUBPAC. UNDOUBTEDLY, IT HAS GIVEN YOU PAUSE AND PERHAPS EVEN MADE YOU WONDER IF THIS IS SOME CRUEL JOKE VESTED ON YOU AND YOUR FINE CREW. LET ME ASSURE YOU THAT IT IS NOT. THE THREAT NOT JUST TO NATIONAL SECURITY BUT TO WORLDWIDE PEACE AND STABILITY IS VERY, VERY, REAL. I HAVE SAT WITH THE CHAIRMAN OF THE JOINT CHIEFS OF STAFF AND THE NATIONAL SECURITY ADVISER AND GIVEN THEM MY PERSONAL AND PROFESSIONAL ASSURANCE THAT YOU ARE THE RIGHT MAN, IN COMMAND OF THE RIGHT BOAT, AT THE RIGHT TIME, FOR THIS EXTRAORDINARILY DIFFICULT ASSIGNMENT. YOU HAVE MY PERSONAL GUARANTEE THAT THE ENTIRE NAVY AND THE ENTIRE DEPARTMENT OF DEFENSE ARE BEHIND YOU ONE HUNDRED PERCENT. YOU AND YOUR CREW ARE ALL THAT STANDS BETWEEN EVENTS SO CATACLYSMIC THAT THEY ALMOST DEFY EXPLANATION. NO RESPONSE, EXCEPT A RECEIPT ACKNOWLEDGMENT, IS REQUIRED OR DESIRED, CAPTAIN. GO FORWARD AND DO YOUR WORK AND GODSPEED. CLOWARD.
DECL/X4//

As he did with the message from COMSUBPAC, Willard read this message over and over, then scribbled on the yellow legal pad. Finally, he put both messages securely in his safe and emerged from his cabin. He strode into the Control Room and looked directly at his officer of the Deck.

"Wilson, we have been ordered to break off this mission. Disengage from this position, turn to the northwest, and when clear the shallows, make your speed twenty knots. Have the exec gather the department heads in the Wardroom and then call me when this is done."

The two men had never been in the director's office before. Intuitively, they knew that if they were being called there, it had to have something to do with their "friend." Their jobs at the agency as field agents would never lead them to a meeting like this, at least without first briefing what they had found to about six levels of the bureaucracy first.

Like the chairman of the Joint Chiefs and the chief of Naval Operations, Pete Hernandez had presented his option under extreme time duress. He had presented it as just that, an option, not thinking that it would be given serious consideration. But it had been accepted. Now that it was too late to consider the wisdom of this decision, he just needed to act and act quickly.

They stood as he entered the office, then quickly sat down again as he motioned to them. Hernandez was under too much stress and was thinking too far ahead to think to try to put the two men at ease.

"I know that you wonder why I have called you in. It regards the other mission you two have been assigned. First, it goes without saying that what I am about to tell you must never be broached—even hinted at—outside of the channels that I am authorizing you to work in.

"You are to contact your 'friend' aboard the *Carl Vinson*. He is to conduct a mission that is so crucial that we have spent the last four hours writing and rewriting explicit and detailed instructions for him. You are to e-mail this information to him, then destroy this paper, then purge your e-mail files. Once your friend acknowledges receipt of this message, you are to contact me or the deputy director immediately, day or night, with this acknowledgment. Is that clear?"

The two men could only nod. They couldn't even begin to speculate what the DCI wanted them to do. He pushed a single piece of paper across his desk, and each man held it in one hand. They both nodded as they read it. They looked at the director, and he looked back at them. They sat rigid in their chairs and waited for further explanation, for some granularity regarding what they were to do. There was none, and they did not know how to ask for any.

"I can only guess what you are thinking," said the DCI. "These are astounding instructions, I know, and I truly wish that I could explain more to you. But I cannot. Transmit the message."

With that, he rose, and the two men did also. They departed quickly to carry out their instructions.

Rick Holden returned to his tiny stateroom tired but satisfied. The level of intensity onboard *Carl Vinson* had reached fever pitch, and he was happy to be part of something important, something meaningful. His training with HS-4 had been absolutely superb, and they were more than ready for any CSAR mission that might come their way. They could not, would not, fail.

He was also satisfied that he had been getting through to Anne. There was no good reason why he was caught up in this, he just had an intuitive sense that he was doing the right thing. He, perhaps uniquely among anyone else on the ship, had gone where she was going and knew what she was dealing with. Getting her through the loss of the best friend that she had ever had and getting her back to flying was a huge challenge, but one that he took an enormous deal of satisfaction and pride in.

The confluence of these two "missions"—preparing to save his fellow warriors and returning Anne to her full professional duties—had another leavening effect on Rick. It helped him to push the agency even further into the background. His occasional thoughts about changing professions had become more and more frequent, and now it was a very serious, daily consideration.

As he sat down at his desk, he could feel the tension easing out of his body. Just two minutes for his obligatory daily e-mail check and he'd hit the rack for hours of blissful sleep. He had it coming, he mused. Rick logged on, clicked on the familiar address, and prepared to read the typical two lines. He read something else.

Holden, you have been assigned a mission that you must complete in the next 36 hours. These orders come directly from the National Security Council and from the DCI who has personally authorized us to transit this message to you—code word—"Houseboat."

The Admiral commanding the battle group has disobeyed military orders and intends to attack Iran in a way that he is not authorized to do. Indications here are that he has deceived his entire staff and duped them into believing that he has orders from higher authority to conduct these attacks. Only attacks on the terrorist camps were authorized and now these must be held in abeyance.

The Admiral is considered dangerous and possibly deranged. The NCA had sent the Fifth Fleet Commander to relieve him in person, but Admiral Flowers' COD was shot out of the sky hours ago, a fact that has probably been hidden from all on board. The admiral concocted a story that it was an Iranian aircraft bent on destroying the group. It was not. Therefore, you are to consider the admiral extremely unbalanced. Do not try to reason with him. Do not try to convince him to change what he is doing. Find him, disable him, and, if necessary, kill him, to prevent him from launching these attacks. Then, explain the contents of this message to the second in command, Captain Sampson.

Code word "Houseboat" applies. Acknowledge receipt of this message only with "message A received." Good luck, Holden.

Rick felt himself shaking. He stood up, paced around his tiny stateroom, sat down and read the message again. He could not control the shaking. He had to get a grip long enough to respond to his handlers. Then he had to complete his mission. Was he prepared to do this? Had he been living a normal existence too long?

61

CAPTAIN BOLTER DENNIS STOOD IN TFCC AT FIFTH Fleet Headquarters and held the phone receiver a few inches from his ear, certain that he would be able to hear the loud voice of the four-star general with the phone at that distance. He was fielding his third call from General Lawrence in the last hour. Although these calls were ostensibly to ascertain more information about the tragic shootdown of the Fifth Fleet commander and the overall situation with respect to the *Carl Vinson* Battle Group, the "questions" from the CENTCOM commander always seemed to turn into accusations. The fact that he himself had all but browbeat the pilots into launching on this mission made his guilt and grief for those lost even stronger.

"Dennis, are you there?" said General Lawrence.

It wasn't a shout, it was a normal voice.

"Yes sir, General, Chief of Staff here, sir."

"Captain Dennis, we all mourn the loss of your commander and the other professionals in the C-2 that was shot down. There is some more information that I need to share with you. Do you have the capability to take this call in private?"

"Yes sir, General. I'm in TFCC now, but I can have this transferred back to my office. If I may put you on hold for about two minutes, I'll sprint back there sir."

"Thank you, Captain. I'll wait," replied General Lawrence. Dennis was perplexed by this request—and doubly perplexed that it was a request and not an order—but he was even more astounded by the change in the general's tone. He hurried back to his office, eager to hear more.

"I'm at my desk now, General," said Dennis into his STU-III phone.

"Captain Dennis, what I am going to tell you now is to go no further than you as acting commander. This is to be held extremely close. Is that understood?"

"Yes, General, of course."

"Good Captain, the OPREP sent by *Carl Vinson* when the COD was shot down indicated that it was an Iranian fighter out of Bushehr that was threatening the battle group. That story made sense to us and to everyone up the chain up through the NMCC and the White House Situation Room. However, a short time later a report from the AWACS working over Saudi and reporting to JTF-SWA indicated that it had tracked the COD from the time it took off from Bahrain International until the time it was shot down twenty-five miles from *Carl Vinson*."

"The AWACS is sure of that?" asked Dennis, surprising himself that he was now playing the inquisitor with Lawrence.

"Absolutely positive, Captain. What's more, the preliminary analysis here and in Washington is that given the systems onboard *Carl Vinson* and *Shiloh*, particularly Link 16 and the SPY radar, it is all but inconceivable that this fact was not known on both of those ships."

"General, I'm not certain what you are suggesting."

"Captain, given the strange behavior that Admiral Robinson has demonstrated thus far, and given the fact that Admiral Flowers was flying out to relieve him of his duties, the possibility—and I would make it a significant possibility—exists that Admiral Robinson intentionally had Admiral Flowers's aircraft shot down. We can't know that with certainty, and won't until we get someone aboard *Carl Vinson*, but for now we have to assume the worst and act accordingly."

"General, I roger everything you say. What actions would you like us to take here, sir?"

"Nothing right now, Captain. Again, you have my condolences over this tragic loss. But it's important now that you engage your casualty control people and get them moving to make the proper notifications of the people we lost in the COD. I know that Mrs. Flowers is still in Washington, D.C. and that the CNO has personally visited her. I'll leave it to you to take care of the rest of the folks."

"We'll do that, General. Is there anything else, sir?"

"Yes, Chief of Staff, there is. Due to the nature of these extraordinary events, I need to be in theater and I don't need to be in the middle of the Saudi desert. My people will give yours details, but I will be boarding one of our aircraft within the hour. Expect me at your headquarters in about eighteen hours."

62

ABOARD *CARL VINSON* ALL BRACED FOR A FULL ASSAULT by the Islamic Republic. Rocky Jacobson and his people were peppered by the entire staff for more information—information about what the Iranians would do next, information they could not provide. Jacobson and his people lived in a world of capabilities—orders of battle, military strengths and weakness, what the enemy could do if he intended to. But they could not divine intentions, and that was exactly what the entire battle group, and especially her senior leadership, desperately needed to know.

Admiral Robinson was shaken by the shootdown—shaken that an Iranian aircraft had come within weapons release range of his flagship before it was shot down, and shaken by the fact that the Iranians might mount a full-scale attack on his battle group. He decided on his own what he would do. Normally, this was a decision that he would make in the collegial milieu of his warfare commanders. No longer. He could no longer look these men in the eye. He sat at his desk and picked up the Bogen phone that connected him to his chief of staff in his tiny cabin just twenty feet away across the Flag Mess.

"Chief of Staff," responded George Sampson as he picked up the Bogen on the first ring.

"COS, Admiral here. This attack by the Iranian aircraft is worrisome, and Rocky and his boys can't tell us a damn thing about what to expect next. I think that we need to accelerate our timeline for attacks against the Islamic Republic before they lash out at us again."

"We can do that, Admiral, I think. I'll have to get with CAG and with our Surface Strike people. Bomb buildup is proceeding on schedule—certainly not ahead of it, and missiles are being worked as we speak." George Sampson had learned to be positive and upbeat when talking with the admiral, but he knew intuitively that making these attacks earlier would be extraordinarily difficult. "Would you like me to gather the warfare commanders in your cabin?" he asked cautiously.

"No, COS, no I don't. I think that this is something that you all ought to be able to figure out without having another group-grope. Just get with CAG and figure out how much earlier we can push H-hour and get back to me ASAP."

"Yes, Admiral," replied the chief of staff as he wheeled out of his office and headed across the passageway to talk with CAG. George Sampson knew that this wasn't going to work, and he dreaded having to hear CAG vent when presented with yet another demand, but he was going to carry out the admiral's orders.

Anne would be on the flight schedule tomorrow. She had decided that her period of mourning for Chrissie was over. It needed to be over. She had loved Chrissie as a best friend and she had loved her like a sister, but it was time to move into a different stage of mourning and continue with her professional duties. She needed to get back in the cockpit. No, it wasn't just her love of flying, although that certainly played a part. She recognized that she needed to carry her end of the log. Her fellow pilots were carrying the load for their shipmates lost at the Intercontinental, and now they were carrying it for Chrissie. They couldn't carry it indefinitely for her too. She needed to be up there doing her part on a daily basis.

As Anne headed for her destination, she reflected on the fact that she hadn't made this decision on her own. She didn't know if she could have—at least she didn't think that she would have made it this soon, or with this level of assurance. Rick Holden, singularly, had been the one person aboard *Carl Vinson* who had helped her work through this terrible tragedy. Rick had been through this before, and she was taken by how well and with what level of understanding he had helped her through it. Not only had he enabled her to make this decision with a high level of confidence but this confidence had also spilled over during her interview with the Airwing flight surgeon, with her XO, and finally with her skipper. They all agreed, without question, that Anne O'Connor needed to be back in the cockpit.

Now she was looking for Rick. She needed to share the good news with him and thank him. He was the reason she was now holding her head up and looking at the world positively again. She remembered from the day's Air Plan— Anne always scrutinized the Air Plan whether she was flying or not—that HS-4 had several CSAR events that day. Rick was certainly involved, and she headed down to the Black Knight Ready Room to look for him. She didn't want to talk to him for long, not yet, and not in a venue that might cause him embarrassment. But every instinct she had told her that she wanted to tell him now.

Anne walked aft down the starboard passageway and arrived at the back door of the HS-4 Ready Room. The briefing for the CSAR event was over, and the crew was going in different directions to do a myriad of tasks. Rick was out the back door and headed aft toward the Black Knight paraloft to draw his gear, needing to fly on this mission just to keep things as normal as possible. He was, however, almost totally distracted by the e-mail he had just received. He breezed by Anne without looking up, missing her completely.

"Rick," she called out softly, not wanting to attract undue attention.

"Anne, I sure didn't expect to see you here. Miss the turn

for the Blue Wolf Ready Room?" he joked. The VS-35 Ready Room was right next door to HS-4's, barely a few steps away. Occasionally a yeoman delivering a flight schedule or others not fully aware of their surroundings would venture into the wrong one—but never a pilot.

"No, Rick, I really wanted to see you. I wanted to talk with you for just a minute."

"Anne, we just briefed for this mission and I'm gonna be late if I don't hustle up to the flight deck and man up. I'd love to talk with you later on, OK?"

It was not really a request, it was a statement, and Rick walked away from her and toward the paraloft. Just a minute, that's all she wanted. Was he that busy? Was he that distracted?

"Rick?" she said as she ran the few steps to catch up with him right outside the door to the paraloft.

"Anne, not now!" he hissed and disappeared inside the door.

Anne's instincts were on overdrive. This was not just someone who was busy. There was something else on his mind, and Anne wanted to know what it was. She wheeled to go back to her ready room and determined that she would find out. That was the least she could do for him.

63

Patrick Browne sat in the Oval Office waiting for his meeting with the national security adviser. Michael Curtis had asked for a private session and had further asked that a full two hours be scheduled—an unprecedented amount of time on the president's schedule, especially for a one-on-one session.

The president was in a foul mood. The crisis in the Arabian Gulf was spinning out of control and was distracting him from all of his other duties. He had tried to stay disengaged, tried to stay out of the Situation Room as much as possible, but he dared not distance himself too much for fear of being labeled a weak commander in chief. No, he had appeared there from time to time, but he had attempted to keep a full calendar, too.

"Michael?" said Patrick Browne. "Come in please." The national security adviser could tell that the crisis was wearing on the president. That usual hail-fellow-well-met demeanor was totally absent. The president all but sagged in his chair.

After he sat down, Michael Curtis opened his thick briefing book and held it on his lap. "Mr. President, a great deal has happened in the last forty-eight hours regarding this crisis in the Arabian Gulf. I know that you have been kept up to speed somewhat, but with your permission, sir, I would like to go over the events for you and then lead into the recommendations that we have just evolved in our NSC meeting two hours ago."

"Proceed, Michael," said the president. This was one of the reasons the president liked his national security adviser; his ability to recap events in a way that brought them into sharper focus and enabled the president to either make a decision or validate one the NSC had made. The president recalled that he had specifically charged the NSC to come up with a solution, and he recognized that he should be receptive to what they proposed.

After almost an hour of constant talking, with very few interruptions by the president for questions or clarification, Curtis concluded, "So these are our two plans, Mr. President, and pending your final approval, I have put both plans in motion concurrently."

"These plans are moving forward now?"

"Yes, Mr. President."

"Are you certain that these are the only solutions that you have to this problem?"

"Yes, Mr. President, and having these solutions available was a very near thing. We were lucky that *Jefferson City* was in the Gulf and not far away on some other mission, and we were lucky that this CIA agent was onboard *Carl Vinson* and not some other ship."

"Yes, that sounds fortunate," said the president, his head beginning that slow sway from side to side which signaled he did not fully agree with him. "I know that you have brought the full resources of the National Security apparatus together on this, Michael. I shudder at the thought of one of our own subs attacking our aircraft carrier, but I think that I see that this is an effective way to negate any aircraft strikes. And I see that Admiral Robinson must be stopped, but I cannot, I will not, condone murder in this case or in any other. My God, Michael, we have *laws* about assassinating other heads of state. To condone murdering one of our own flag officers, no, I won't have it."

The national security adviser had anticipated this. The president was aboveboard and didn't like any of the cloak-and-dagger operations that were an unfortunate fact of life in the world in which they worked.

"Mr. President, the orders to this agent were to disable the admiral if at all possible. He will take him down, figuratively, then report the full details of the situation to the second-in-command, the battle group chief of staff. Once Captain Sampson takes control of the battle group, the chairman has a Navy group in place to take over for their staff, a group headed by Rear Admiral Bart Katz, one of the best battle group commanders we've ever had."

"All right, Michael. I see your point. But make sure that this agent understands this explicitly."

"Yes, Mr. President. Sir, there is one other matter. In the event that Admiral Robinson is not stopped in time, we might want to consider the option of informing the Islamic Republic of what might transpire, just so they don't think that this attack is being ordered at the highest levels of our government."

"Is this your recommendation?"

"No, it isn't, Mr. President. It would be a good hedge, but it is impractical."

"Then let's not do that, Michael," the president said.

Less than two miles from where the president and the national security adviser were discussing these matters, a nervous Hala Karomi made his fourth trip to Union Station. He had already made his decision as to where to place his agents, it was now time to wait. Still, he could not sit in his hotel room, and returned, now to see where he would carry out his work.

He watched the hundreds of commuters stream by and tried to imagine what would happen to people like these as soon as he released his agents. He felt neither compassion nor true hatred, just indifference. They were merely pawns, pawns in a giant chess game, who had to be sacrificed to achieve the greater good.

64

ABOARD THE *JEFFERSON CITY*, JOE WILLARD SAT IN HIS cabin considering how he was going to accomplish his mission. He was concerned about another issue too—how to brief this mission to his crew. The SPECAT messages had been quite specific regarding what he could and could not tell his people. He knew the level of detail that his people needed to know far better than anyone else. The chairman and the CNO could be excused for not knowing what he had to tell his men: they were not submariners. But COMSUBPAC should know better. Then again, it had been too many years since he had commanded his own boat. He had forgotten too much.

Joe Willard opened the door to his cabin and walked the few steps into the control room. He asked his quartermaster to lay out chart 62032, which depicted the entire Arabian Gulf. He looked at the position of their boat, just thirty-five miles west of Bandar Abbas now. He let his eyes wander up the chart toward the extreme northern Arabian Gulf, where the *Carl Vinson* was operating. What he saw was not what he wanted to see—vast stretches of clear, deep ocean depths, a submariner's joy. Instead he saw shallow water and a sea full of obstructions—seamounts, wrecks, and primarily oil platforms, massive rigs that were sturdy enough to break his boat if he was not extremely careful. Maneuvering in these waters at high speed was going to be a challenge.

His exec broke him out of his musing. "Captain, had to get the M3s to finish cleaning up after lunch, it's all clear in the wardroom now and I have the department heads assembled and ready to meet with you sir."

"Good. Lead on, XO," he replied as they headed for the wardroom. He needed to tell these men first.

Just over three hundred miles north, Rick Holden sat in his tiny stateroom and opened his e-mail, hoping to find a message from his "friends." To his chagrin, there was none.

This was the second time that he had e-mailed back his handlers. The first time he expressed his astonishment at receiving their direction, asked them for an incredible amount of detail, and was told to just complete his mission as ordered. This time he was more specific, asking questions about follow-on actions that he would need to do, getting into a level of granularity that he felt he needed to know. Their failure to respond thus far disturbed him deeply. They owed him more than this, at least an explanation at some level of detail.

He did not appreciate the fact that his handlers had told him not to get "hung up" on the semantics of whether he was going to kill or just disable Admiral Robinson. Semantics? It cut to the very core of what he believed in and what he stood for. How could they be so cavalier about what happened to another human being—even one *suspected* of doing what Admiral Robinson was being accused of? At least they had given him permission to disable the admiral rather than the permanent alternative, which was some measure of relief for him.

65

"WELCOME, GENERAL," SAID PRESIDENT HABIBI AS the secretary ushered the general into his office. He could tell that Najafi was under enormous stress, and he knew instinctively that this would be a difficult meeting.

It almost surprised him that Najafi had waited this long for an audience, and didn't blame the general for pressing him. After all, ultimately, it was he who was charged with the defense of the Islamic Republic. In that regard, he was glad that General Najafi had a single focus. It was his job as president to balance all the factors and rein in the general when necessary.

"Mr. President," General Najafi began, "the Americans are becoming more aggressive and I fear that they may attack soon."

"What makes you so certain of this, General?"

"Mr. President, the American bandits have sunk one of our ships and crippled another—ships that were exercising their rights in international waters. They were not threatening the Americans in any way. Oh, I am certain that they will make up some sort of cover story about us shooting first, but I assure you, Mr. President, that they did not. We have reviewed the tapes of the radio transmissions from both *Sabalan* and *Alborz* and they were attacked without provocation by the Americans."

"I understand that, General. How many sailors did we lose?"

"We are not certain yet, Mr. President. *Alborz* was shot up very badly but is still functional, while *Sabalan* was sunk with American bombs. *Alborz* is seaworthy under her own power and is picking up survivors from *Sabalan*. Commander Kani tells us that they have lost many men from *Sabalan* and that it is too early to tell how many have been lost from *Alborz*."

"What did the Americans do after the engagement?"

"Nothing, Mr. President. They just withdrew from the area and kept launching airplanes. They did nothing to help search for survivors as required by international law."

"Nothing?"

"No sir, Mr. President, nothing. Once the American carrier was well clear of the area we sent our Orion aircraft there to drop life rafts and medical supplies. We have also gotten another ship underway from Bushehr to assist *Alborz*. We hope to have both ships and all survivors back in port by tomorrow night."

"This was a tragedy to be sure, General," Habibi demurred. "The Americans, of course, are playing it up in the international press that we attacked their precious carrier. I wonder what credibility they have now that they have proven so trigger happy that they have shot down one of their own aircraft."

"This is most troubling, Mr. President. The Americans are portraying this shootdown of their C-2A transport as a mistake, and it surely was, but the only conclusion that we can draw is that they shot down this plane because they thought it was one of ours. They are desperately afraid that we will interrupt their attack planning and will see that they are about to launch strikes against us. That is why we must act now!"

"General, I have no doubt that you have looked at this very, very carefully. I am completely confident that you have analyzed it thoroughly. And I have no doubt that the Americans harbor ill will toward our Islamic Republic. But isn't it possible that the Americans are merely in a defensive mode, trying to protect their carrier at all costs? As tragic as these losses are to us, they evidently have the ear of the world press and have convinced them that they were merely defending themselves. Do you really think that an attack against us is imminent?"

"I do, Mr. President."

"I tend to agree with you, General, more than I did just

a day ago. But, still, we cannot attack the American carrier without their first striking us—striking our homeland."

"Mr. President!" Najafi said. "You must reconsider—"

But Habibi would not let him finish. He needed to hammer home his point.

"General, you told me earlier that your weapon was 'almost' ready. Is it fully prepared yet?"

"No, Mr. President, but I am confident that it will be—and very soon—perhaps today and certainly tomorrow. As soon as it is ready, I can put it on our aircraft and execute our plan."

"I think that we should do a portion of what you say. Finish assembling the weapon and load it on your aircraft. Tell your crew to be ready on short notice to do what we have discussed, but do not do this preemptively, General. Do not, or you will force me to take measures that will be extraordinarily severe."

"Mr. President—"

Habibi raised his hand and cut the general off again. "Even as we speak our diplomats are attempting to shape world opinion in our favor. Losing *Sabalan* and having *Alborz* damaged, as well as losing all those sailors, was a tragedy, but this reckless act by the Americans is slowly tilting the scales in our favor. We need to continue this. Drop a nuclear weapon on their carrier and we will not only incur the wrath of the world for starting a full-scale war but we will be censured by the community of nations for letting the nuclear genie out of the bottle. We will, and I assure you I will, use this weapon if we are attacked—but it will be used to stay the hand of the Americans once they start attacking. It can be no other way!"

General Najafi admitted to himself that he had not considered all of the factors that Habibi had just articulated. He had renewed respect for the president. He would just as soon have released this weapon against the Americans the moment it was ready, but, upon reflection, he decided that Habibi's plan was a good one. He would support the president every way that he could.

As General Najafi departed, it occurred to President Habibi that the efforts that he and the general were making covered the gamut from strategy, to policy, to military action, to diplomacy. If only they had a diplomatic opening to the United States, they could defuse this crisis. That was in the hands of the foreign minister. At this point in these escalating hostilities, Minister Velayati should be talking with the American secretary of state and eventually, as president of the Islamic Republic, he should be talking with the American president, Patrick Browne.

But Habibi quickly brought himself back to reality. There was no channel between him and the American president because during his three years as foreign minister, Velayati had done absolutely nothing to open up a rapprochement with the United States. Hostage to the ayatollahs, Velayati had used all manner of excuses to spurn the tentative feelers from the United States to end their "dual containment" policy. He, Habibi, had no more possibility of talking with the American president than that madman Saddam Hussein did. Velayati had seen to that.

It was one thing to be ideologically pure and not associate with the United States. It was another to not have the means to defuse a crisis like this. He knew that Velayati had an agenda and that agenda was one he had tacitly agreed to let go on. He wondered how long he would be able to let that happen. He could not even call the foreign minister now. He was "unavailable." Habibi had a vision of what Velayati was doing. He and this madman Shiekholeslam were no doubt plotting further terrorist attacks against American interests. Habibi knew instinctively that they had already taken this too far. He was at a loss as to how to stop them. He had to regain control of the situation, and he eventually had to find a way to speak with the American president.

66

"ADMIRAL, WE'RE READY," SAID MIKE LUMME AS HE opened the door to the admiral's cabin. Over the last several days, the staff had learned to exercise extreme caution around the admiral. He had all but sequestered himself in his cabin and acted annoyed and even hostile whenever anyone entered for any reason. This was a meeting that he had asked for, though.

"OK, Mike, let's go," replied the admiral as he rose and headed for his place at the end of the small table in his cabin.

His warfare commanders quickly filed in and took their seats. He looked around at the sea of faces. They were drawn and haggard, and he could see that the strain of the last few days was taking its toll on them. It still grieved him that he had to delude them—he actually thought of bringing them in on his plan but rejected that notion for two reasons. Clearly, one or more of them might protest, and that would greatly complicate things. But more than that, if they did join him in this plan, out of loyalty to him or because he was able to convince them that it was a righteous plan, they would suffer the same fate he knew would befall him in the aftermath of these momentous events.

"Gentleman, thanks for coming together again. I have just spoken with Fifth Fleet Headquarters and they have received the execute order for Operation Mountain Divide. The attacks are on, gentlemen. Fifth Fleet will bound the problem for us in the sense that they will give us a no-earlier-than and no-later-than time to conduct these strikes. I expect the no-earlier-than time to happen rather quickly, so we should prepare to do them within no more than the next six to twelve hours at the outside. We need to assess our ability to do that."

"Admiral, we've completed our practice strikes, and the Airwing is more than ready to conduct these attacks," CAG began. "We have given all of our strike leads plenty of practice and we are ready in all respects, sir."

"Good, CAG," responded the admiral. "Captain?"

"Admiral, we have most of the ordnance built up and staged. I still have some in the magazines, but once I load a lot of what I have on the flight deck I can bring that up right away. I anticipate being able to support the launch plan for a good two to two-and-a-half days of sustained operations."

"Good, Captain," Admiral Robinson replied. "Will you have enough sea room for the big launches we'll need?"

"Yes sir, no problem, wind has been out of the northwest still and I've got more than enough room."

"Good. Jim?"

"Admiral, all our shooters are in their launch baskets," replied Commodore Jim Hughes. "They're all ready to go with their launches. I've worked closely with CAG and the captain to ensure that no aircraft come too close to the route of flight for our Tomahawks."

"Good," the admiral replied. "Ops O?"

"Admiral, our overall assessment is that we are ready. We have prepared and prepared well. It's almost a little disconcerting that Iran is not at a higher state of readiness and anticipating strikes by us, but we've never been able to psyche them out about anything else. No sir, we're ready to go. We just need the word."

"OK, Ops, thanks," the admiral replied. "George, you're the cleanup hitter."

"Admiral, I agree with Ops O," replied George Sampson. "The battle group is completely ready. Our folks are mighty tired, so I think that the sooner we get this going the better off we'll be."

"I agree with you, COS," said Heater Robinson. "All right, gents, let's get to work."

* * *

George Sampson walked back to his small office thinking that he would just return to his usual mound of paperwork. He found CAG, the commodore, and Craig Vandegrift waiting for him.

"What's up?" said Sampson. He knew precisely what they wanted but thought that he would at least attempt to disarm them.

"COS, we've been good soldiers about all of this and have gone along with the admiral's plans to prep for this attack," began CAG, serving as the spokesman for the group. "But you have got to talk with him. We can't go into this without an execute order. You know that. We can't understand why he's got this hotline between him and Fifth Fleet. If this is that sensitive that CENTCOM can't transmit it to us via the normal message channels—even back channel means—then, hell, put your flag sec on an aircraft and have her bring it out. She's been in there for two days."

George Sampson knew that he owed them a better answer than he was about to give them. He also knew that the idea of Becky Philips bringing the execute order out was a good one. He was still puzzled by the special mission that the admiral had sent her to Fifth Fleet Headquarters on and had looked for an opportunity to ask the admiral about it, but the admiral had been so noncommunicative about it that he had let it ride.

"Look fellas," George Sampson began, "we can't get wrapped around the axle about the niceties of what the textbooks say about how the JOPES system works. If the admiral says that he's talked with the Fifth Fleet commander about this, that's good enough for me. I hope that it's good enough for you!"

"It is," replied Jim Hughes. "We hear you, COS. We just want to be sure that we get it right."

"I know, fellas, and I appreciate your cautions. Let's just press ahead."

Satisfied that they had raised the issue to the proper level, the three men left to complete their work.

A hundred frames forward, Anne O'Connor stood outside the door of Rick Holden's stateroom. There was no way to sugarcoat it, he had blown her off in the passageway outside of their ready rooms. She was completely baffled. Was this the same man who had patiently but firmly guided her back into flight status?

If Rick hadn't done all this for her, his actions would be easier to understand. She figured that maybe he had just had a bad moment there. She checked with Jake McLaughlin and found out that although they had briefed really early, Rick wouldn't be going on his CSAR training mission for another several hours. She figured that he might be back in his stateroom. Maybe he would want to talk with her now.

Anne knocked.

"Who is it?" came the voice from within.

"Rick, it's Anne. I just wanted to talk for a minute."

There was a long delay, then Rick opened his door a crack —but only a crack.

"Hi Anne. Look, I really can't talk now. I've got something that I've got to do. You understand, don't you?"

Anne looked at Rick and couldn't help but notice that he looked stressed, even drained. This wasn't the confident, even cocky, SEAL that she knew. This was a man who was wrestling with a huge dilemma.

"Rick, sure, OK, I understand. I may come back later, all right?"

"Sure, Anne, later would be good, thanks," he said as he shut the door slowly on an even more perplexed Anne.

—————— **67** ——————

ONE OF THE THINGS THAT HAD ATTRACTED PATRICK Browne to politics was power—the power to make decisions, the power to control events, the power to do great things. This was the currency of his trade, the rewards that made all the campaigning, all the fund-raisers, all the compromises, all the distasteful deals worthwhile.

The president felt none of that power now. He felt like a hostage to his national security apparatus. Oh, they were all well-meaning enough, and he was sure that in their heart of hearts they had the interests of the nation in the forefront and, by extrapolation, his interests there too. But it wasn't working, those interests weren't being well represented, he felt that they were being overtaken by events and were powerless to be masters of their own destiny.

Michael Curtis was surprised by the short-notice summons to the Oval Office—the president usually didn't work this way—and found himself a bit out of breath as he reached the Oval Office. The president's secretary told him that he was expected and that he should go right in. Inside, he was surprised to see the president already talking with Secretary of State Philip Quinn. Curtis hesitated, but the president waved him in.

"Hello, Mr. President. Mr. Secretary." The national security adviser's mind was in overdrive. What did the president want? Why was the secretary of state here?

"Michael," said Philip Quinn. The secretary looked so self-assured that Curtis began to worry that he and the president had already evolved some sort of decision which might muck up his own plans.

"Michael, please sit down," began the president. "I asked Secretary Quinn to come over and brief me on our diplomatic options vis-à-vis the Islamic Republic and what we could possibly do to make some sort of rapprochement with President Habibi."

So that was it. At the eleventh hour, the fuzzy-headed diplomats at Foggy Bottom thought that they had a better idea and could defuse a crisis that the rest of them couldn't. Damnit, he didn't like getting blindsided like this. Philip Quinn had never mentioned these thoughts to him in any of their numerous meetings over the last several days.

"Options, Mr. President?" the national security adviser responded, his tone just a bit incredulous to note he was being hit cold on this one. "I thought that we had addressed that in our previous meeting, sir. If we tip our hand to the Islamic Republic we could put our military forces in jeopardy. No sir, I stand by my previous recommendation—what is going on must remain sub-rosa to Iran. Job one for us is to stop Admiral Robinson from launching these comprehensive attacks on Iran. Next, when we reassert control of the battle group and put Admiral Katz in control of it, we need to follow through with our original plan to strike the terrorist camps. Iran can't be allowed to think that terrorism can stand without serious consequences. Beyond that, I think that Secretary Quinn is right to seek a long-term dialogue with the Islamic Republic—although there are factors, as you know, which would mitigate against it being a very fruitful exchange."

He thought for a moment and suddenly wished that he hadn't uttered that last sentence—at least not in that context.

"Michael, I agree with you up to a point," the president began, "and you should know that Secretary Quinn did not initiate this meeting, I did. I know how strongly you feel from a long-term geopolitical standpoint about the prospects for more normalized relations with the Islamic Republic, but my concern is more immediate. Whatever we do to Iran must have a purpose and I must be able to communicate with their head of state—with President Habibi—and end this crisis at some point."

"Yes, Mr. President, your point is well-taken." Curtis didn't want to cross swords with the president unnecessarily.

"Michael," said Philip Quinn, "as you know, our communications with Iran right now—even before this crisis started—are, at best, awkward. We have made virtually no progress since our embassy was sacked and our diplomats taken prisoner coincident with the overthrow of the shah over two decades ago. When we have wanted to talk with them, we have used the good offices of other embassies, but it is not an effective means to communicate."

"I understand that, Mr. Secretary," Michael Curtis replied.

"Then you also understand," Philip Quinn continued, genuinely trying not to sound like he was giving the national security adviser a tutorial, "that President Habibi is a voice of moderation in Iran. He may, in fact, be very approachable and may want to open up a dialogue with the president. I am sure that you have had the same briefs that I have had about the way his foreign minister, Velayati, and the head of the Iranian armed forces, General Najafi, operate almost autonomously, but Habibi was elected with a huge popular mandate, and we think that if the president communicates with him and gives him all the facts at hand, he might be able to force a more moderate approach by these people and others. We just need to get to first base—to communicate with him at all."

Michael Curtis was no neophyte. He knew that this is what the president wanted. He would stand aside and let Philip Quinn try to open up this path.

"Mr. Secretary, I agree that opening up this path is important—once we follow through with our plans to retaliate for these terrorist attacks. At some point, yes, the president will have to enable President Habibi to back down gracefully from his country's aggression against us and against our interests."

"Good, Michael, I'm glad that you agree," said the president. "Now, please tell us about the progress we are making in stopping Admiral Robinson before he carries out these strikes."

"Certainly, Mr. President," Curtis replied as he once again recapped what he knew, as well as what he didn't know: the progress of USS *Jefferson City* and the progress of Rick Holden.

68

IMMEDIATELY AFTER BRIEFING HIS DEPARTMENT HEADS, Commander Joe Willard took extraordinary pains to lay out their current track, one that would take *Jefferson City* swiftly—but safely—north through the unforgiving waters of the Arabian Gulf to its destiny with USS *Carl Vinson*. After leaving their gateguard position, they had gone due south to remain well clear of Qeshm Island. Clearing that, they took up a west-south-westerly course remaining just north of the Salah Oil Field. Turning more westerly now, Captain Willard maneuvered *Jefferson City* south of the Western Traffic Separation Scheme, slipping through the deep water south of the Greater and Lesser Tunbs and north of Abu Musa Island. He kept his boat at a slow five knots as he crept between Forur and Bani Forur Islands. West of these islands the water depth became a comfortable 85 meters, and he increased *Jefferson City*'s speed to fifteen knots. He maneuvered the boat in a northwesterly direction in order to pick up and use Kish Island north of his course as a navigation landmark.

Then Willard again met his exec, operations, and weapons officers, this time to review their options.

"Captain," began his exec, "I think that Ops and Weps have looked at this really hard. They know what our goal is, temporarily cripple *Carl Vinson* so she can't launch airplanes, but don't permanently damage her."

"OK," Willard responded. "What's the plan as you all see it?"

"Captain, the Mk 48 is a really capable torpedo, as you know," his weapons officer began. "We recommend a close-in shot, aiming right for her screws. That will definitely stop her or at least slow her down to a really slow speed—"

"What about permanent damage? Screws are a pretty difficult part to repair," interrupted the captain. They could tell that he was not sanguine about their ability to successfully complete their mission.

"Screws are pretty major, Captain, but they are replaceable in a dry dock and it should be the kind of job that could easily be done in a week or so. It would be major but, under the circumstances, it's the best possibility."

"Ops O, tactically, can we get in that close and take that kind of shot?"

"It will be a gamble, Captain. All depends, of course, on whether we are spotted or not and what kind of I&W and defenses they have."

"I've got to think that their I&W will be real good. A carrier battle group draws on a wide array of sensors and systems. They should pretty much have a good command of what's going on around them."

"And we are counting on that, Captain," replied his OPS officer. "Biggest thing that we're counting on is them knowing that Iran's three Kilo Class submarines are inport Bandar Abbas. If they know that, they should be totally unsuspecting of an attack. If a Kilo does get underway, then that changes the entire equation and they will be alert and searching for a sub for all they're worth."

"But even if they don't get underway, we need to count on *Carl Vinson* having near-continuous intelligence to assure themselves that the Kilos are inport. If they lose the bubble, they will assume the worst," offered his exec.

"Fine. We can refine our tactics as we go north. And let's hope that those Kilos don't make a move," Willard said.

Captain Willard steered *Jefferson City* southwest from the area near Kish Island and skirted the rich oil fields east of Qatar. A collision with one of the numerous oil platforms in this area would spell catastrophe, but Willard knew the position of every one. He moved through the waters of the Great Pearl Bank, past Abu Al Bukhush and Salih Oil Fields, through the Maydan Maham Oil Field and south of the Rostam Oil Field. During most of this journey the water was at least 30 meters deep, but on occasion it shallowed to just over 20 meters. He knew that his orders were to engage *Carl Vinson* as soon as possible, but he needed to ensure that his boat got there safely, so he proceeded at a cautious ten knots, coming up frequently to communications depth to listen for any amplifying instructions from COMSUB-PAC. There were none—and he pressed ahead with his mission.

69

RICK HAD SPENT A LONG TIME IN HIS STATEROOM REC-onciling his mission. Reluctant as he was to admit it at first, he now recognized that Admiral Robinson had to be stopped.

How to do it was the conundrum he now faced. He was glad that they had seemingly acceded to his input regarding disabling instead of killing the admiral. The next great unknown was whether the admiral was acting alone or whether he had co-opted his entire staff. That was something that he was not totally comfortable with, but he ultimately felt the former was the case.

There wasn't any compelling evidence that pointed to this, just little snippets of information, scuttlebutt that passed through the staff/ship/Airwing junior officer circuit. Word that the admiral had been taking medication for stress; knowledge that he had lost his former RIO; statements by many CARGRU SEVEN staff members, even senior ones, that they couldn't figure out where the admiral was coming from; word that he had been sequestered in his stateroom for days; and other hints led him to the strong suspicion that Heater Robinson was acting alone.

Rick didn't know exactly where to begin on his mission.

He didn't even know the area where the admiral worked. He had no familiarity with the Blue Tile Area—junior officers knew both intuitively and from the experience of their fellow JOs that they should avoid it. He knew that he could avoid it no longer. He left his stateroom and went aft for some initial scouting.

As much as Anne had confidence in her ability as a naval aviator to "compartmentalize" things and not bring personal problems into the cockpit, her concern for Rick was too big an issue for her to leave unresolved and then go flying. Which led to her returning to stateroom 03-45-4-L. She knocked, but got no answer. Another knock received the same. This was odd. She thought that she had timed it better. Rick wasn't briefing or flying, she had checked the Black Knight flight schedule. It wasn't chow time, so he couldn't be eating. Flight ops were going on, so he couldn't be jogging on the flight deck. Maybe he was working out in *Carl Vinson*'s gym. Even Rick couldn't do that forever, she thought, and it would look dumb walking back and forth between her stateroom and his. She tried the doorknob. It turned and she opened the door cautiously. The room was empty.

Anne shut herself in and flicked on the light. The room wasn't in the state of disarray that Anne thought most guys' rooms were. Rick had had the room to himself for about ten days while his roommate, Lieutenant Pete Carroll, was officer-in-charge of the EOD det and was in Kuwait doing an exercise. It made the room less cramped and made it easier for Anne to make her decision to wait for him there. She knew this would look odd if someone else came along, but she needed to talk to Rick right away.

Anne paced for a few minutes but finally sat down in the chair in front of Rick's tiny pull-out desk and laptop computer. As she stared at the gung-ho screen-saver with the Navy SEAL logo and some action shots of SEALs doing macho things, she thought, *Typical.* As she turned to examine her surroundings most carefully, she bumped the desk, and the slight movement disabled the screen-saver. What she saw on the screen was Rick's e-mail account with a list of e-mails in his inbox and an e-mail opened up off to the side.

Anne was sensitive to invading Rick's privacy. Maybe what was upsetting him had come by e-mail. Her curiosity overcame her and she started to read the one e-mail that was open. She just thought she'd give it a quick scan—maybe it was that dreaded "dear John" letter from a girl-friend, or a message from a family member describing some illness to someone in his family, which would help explain his recent actions. She just had to know. Anne read the short message.

> We are sensitive to your concerns as to whether you should kill the admiral outright or whether it is possible to just disable him. We have run this up through the highest levels. You may disable him, but you must not fail in your mission. He must be stopped. This must now be accomplished within the next 24 hours. Acknowledge receipt of this now and tell us within the next eight hours how you intend to accomplish this and when it will take place. There is no other alternative. YFATA.

Anne pushed her chair away from the desk. What had she just read? This had to be some kind of a joke, some SEAL thing, some cryptic exercise or something. She looked at the closed door, looked at the round doorknob. It didn't move.

She had to find out more. She looked at the return address on the e-mail she had just read: walkerk@corg.com. She scanned the list of e-mails that he had saved in his queue, looking for ones with the same address. She found one from the day before and opened it.

> We have received your reply. This is not a mistake or any problem on our end. You are to carry out your mis-sion. There is no other alternative. YFATA.

YFATA? thought Anne. A name? An organization? Someone or some entity—or some *country* was telling Rick to do this. Her heart was now pounding and her stomach churning. It felt like her first cat shot all over again. She closed that e-mail and looked at the list of incoming e-mails for another one. There was one right above this, and, cross-checking the times, she saw that it was only about six hours older than the one she had just read.

Our friend. It is time that you perform a mission for us. You must take down Admiral Robinson and neutralize him at all costs. This is a most important mission. We cannot give you any more details or any more guidance at this time. You must move swiftly, before the admiral attacks the Islamic Republic. Time is of the essence. YFATA.

Not let the admiral attack Iran? Was Rick an agent for a foreign government? Impossible? She needed to see what his responses to these e-mails were. She closed the e-mail she was reading and closed the incoming e-mail screen. She looked at the door again. No Rick. What would she do if he walked in now? What would she say? She felt herself breaking out into a full sweat. She opened the outgoing e-mail screen and looked for a list of outgoing e-mails. There was none. Rick probably had gotten into the habit of not saving his outgoing e-mails once he sent them. And if he was a sleeper, he must have been so for so long he's let down his guard enough to trust another wouldn't see the incoming messages.

Rick walked cautiously, but as casually as he could across the athwartship passageway outside of Strike Ops and Plans, which marked the forward boundary of the Blue Tile Area. As he crossed over from the port side of the ship to the starboard side, Rick reminded himself to be as observant as he possibly could. Remember where doors are, he told himself, where the admiral's cabin is, where the closest ladders are up and down. Which doors have regular locks, which ones have cipher locks, how much traffic there is in the passageway, and any other details—small or large—that would help him put together his plan to take down Heater Robinson.

He realized that he didn't have unlimited time to scout all

of this out. The timeline YFATA—"your friends at the agency"—had given him was short. He would look at this now, then return in the middle of the night for a final check. Then he would make his move. Exactly what that would be, he didn't know. He first had to get the basic lay of the land. He had left his fatigues in his stateroom and had put on a regular khaki uniform, figuring that he would blend with the CARGRU SEVEN staff better that way and not attract as much notice.

Rick turned right at the end of the athwartships passageway and entered the Blue Tile passageway. The door to the Flag Mess was on his right, and the CAG's stateroom was forward a few feet on his left. His head was on a swivel as he tried to absorb every nuance. He knew that he couldn't just stop, but he decided that if he gave way to everyone else who came through the passageway, it would slow down his movement considerably and let him absorb as much as possible. Doing this at night would be easier from many standpoints, but if the red lighting that pervaded the rest of the ship was used here at night, he would be able to see very little. Going through here later with a flashlight was a nonstarter—that would surely attract just the kind of attention he didn't want.

A commander and a lieutenant commander from the staff were coming the other way, and he ducked into the small alcove outside of the Flag Mess and let them pass through on their way forward. He nodded respectfully, but they just blew by him. He paused for a few seconds, as long as he dared, and was about to continue aft. A sailor emerged from CAG's stateroom carrying several bags of laundry. He was moving slowly, so Rick fell in behind this slow-moving sailor and continued aft. This wasn't as difficult as he thought it would be. He could see the flag admin office up ahead on his left as he kept taking it all in, his mind in overdrive as he made a mental map of everything that he saw.

Twenty feet up ahead a crowd of officers emerged from the War Room—a meeting had evidently just broken up— and the sailor in front of him moved aside to let them pass. Rick stopped in his tracks as the passageway momentarily went into gridlock. He happened to stop right in front of the admiral's cabin. As he looked right he saw the burly master-at-arms in his fatigue uniform assigned to stand in the tiny alcove outside the admiral's door.

"May I help you, sir?" the man said to Rick.

"Just passing through, mister, thanks," he said, his tone dismissive. The crowd was breaking up outside the War Room and people were starting to move again, slowly, perfect for what Rick needed to do.

"Sir, this passageway is for Flag Staff only, do you have business here, sir?"

Rick hadn't anticipated being challenged by some over-eager master-at-arms. Sure, the man was here to be a sentry for the admiral, and this was certainly something valuable for Rick to know, but he didn't need this kind of challenge—not now.

"Right, just moving out, sailor."

Maybe it was Rick's tone that made this sailor—a second-class petty officer who normally wouldn't challenge a lieutenant in this way—take the offensive.

"Who do you have business with, *sir*?" the MAA asked.

Rick saw that there were still a number of CARGRU SEVEN staff officers up ahead who were within earshot. He couldn't bluff this well.

"Don't have business here, sailor, just passing through like I said," Rick said, his anger starting to burn through.

"Sir, then I'll have to *respectfully* request that you go back forward and go around another way. This passageway is only for the admiral's *immediate* staff."

Rick glared at the man.

"*Sir?*" said the MAA, his tone and body language conveying unmistakably to Rick that he didn't intend to give way on this one.

"Sure, sailor, no problem," replied Rick as he turned around and walked forward, a bit shaken by the encounter. A full look at the Blue Tile passageway would have to wait, he thought as he headed back down to his stateroom.

Anne had tried several functions and just couldn't find a way to retrieve any outgoing e-mails. She was getting extremely nervous now. Rick was sure to return any minute. She couldn't have a normal conversation with him now. She quickly reread the three e-mails that she had seen and then returned Rick's computer to its original configuration. She stood up and put the chair back where she remembered it had been. She slowly twisted the doorknob and opened the door. The passageway was deserted. She pulled the door closed behind her and hurried away.

70

MICHAEL CURTIS SAT AT HIS DESK IN THE OLD EXecutive Office Building and assessed the crisis in the Arabian Gulf. So much had happened in such a short time that he was having difficulty just keeping track of events, let alone controlling them. He needed time to think, time to analyze, time to put all of this in context and bound the problem. All he was doing now was lurching from event to event. That fact alone made him angry.

He tried to think of a way to regain control of the situation but it was slowly slipping away from him. He knew that he couldn't do it all alone—he knew that all too well—but he was not sanguine that those who were responsible for stemming various aspects of this crisis saw the picture in the same way as he did or had the same focus that he had. He had decided to use his most-trusted assistant as a sounding board and was almost relieved when he knocked.

"Come in, Tom," he said as Captain Tom Perry entered his office.

"I came right over when you called, sir. Your secretary said that it was urgent."

"Not really urgent from an action standpoint, Tom, but there are issues that we need to sort out here and now, issues that can't wait."

"It's been an eventful few days, sir, that's for certain," Tom Perry replied. He could tell intuitively that the national security adviser wanted to use him as a sounding board—it was a role he was becoming increasingly accustomed to.

"Tom, what do you hear from your contacts at State? Secretary Quinn is on a mission to establish a link between the president and President Habibi. Is that moving forward and are we going to get some last minute peace offering that will cause us to stop our strikes against the terrorist camps once Admiral Katz has control of the battle group?"

"No sir. Reestablishing some sort of dialogue with Iran has not been as easy as Secretary Quinn first assumed. They've made it their number one priority over at Foggy Bottom, and I think that they'll eventually get there, but there is a lot of inertia on both sides against doing this."

"I see, so nothing in the offing for right now on that score as you see it," replied Michael Curtis.

"No, sir, nothing soon at all."

"I see. The other thing on my mind is how this whole process of stopping Admiral Robinson is going. We bought into two concurrent plans—hell—I *sold* the president on these plans. But now that we've let the Pentagon run with their plan and the DCI run with his, it's like getting blood out of a stone to get them to keep us informed on the progress of both of these efforts. Hell, do I have to convene a meeting multiple times a day just to find out what is going on?"

"No sir, you shouldn't have to do that. You shouldn't have to do that at all," responded Tom Perry. He was not just agreeing with the national security adviser to be agreeable; he believed what he was saying. Perry saw the same things that Michael Curtis saw, though not at as high a level.

"When does the Pentagon say that their sub will get to *Carl Vinson*, and what do they think down in the Situation Room?"

"Both estimates line up pretty closely, sir," he responded. The *Jefferson City* is making steady progress on her journey north. Assuming that she has no trouble actually finding the carrier, she should be there in about twelve to fifteen hours. The best guess is that the captain will set up carefully for an attack—"

"Set up carefully!" interrupted the national security adviser, his frustration showing, "doesn't he understand that if Robinson launches the attacks he has planned, it will be too damn late and he might as well turn around and abort his mission?"

Tom Perry knew that he needed to mollify his boss. "Sir, I'm certain that *Jeff City* understands the urgency of the situation. I know the skipper, Joe Willard. He was two years behind me at the Academy. He's no shrinking violet. He has his orders, he'll carry them out as swiftly as he can."

"OK, fine," replied Michael Curtis. "I just wish we'd get more frequent updates from the Pentagon. How about this agent that Pete Hernandez thinks can stop the admiral. What's the latest on him?"

"We have been kept pretty well-informed by the DCI on that, sir. Evidently, his handlers have had several e-mail exchanges with him."

"Several exchanges?"

"Yes sir, the working level people at CIA tell me that at first, the guy on *Carl Vinson* didn't believe that they were assigning him this mission. He finally got on board and acknowledges that he has to stop the admiral. Trouble is, we have absolutely no way of knowing what he is doing or what progress he is making. The agency just told him to get it done, period, and he finally acknowledged that he would."

"Not a lot to go on, is it, Tom?"

"No sir, it isn't."

"So when it really comes right down to it, we have no idea which one of these actions will transpire first—if either one of them happen at all. Damn, Tom, this is a hell of a way to deal with what is probably the most critical foreign policy crisis we have had in a decade."

"It is, sir," replied Tom Perry, trying to keep Michael Curtis from getting any angrier.

"OK. Tom, let's do this. I need to have Admiral Monroe and Mr. Hernandez come over here and talk to me about this. Things are moving too fast to have me getting this third or fourth hand."

"We'll make that happen sir," said Tom Perry as he hurried from the room. He heard a weariness in the national security adviser's voice. He was determined to carry out his boss's orders. He would do his best. But intuitively he knew that his chances of making the chairman of the Joint Chiefs of Staff and the DCI appear before the national security adviser were diminishing every hour.

71

ANNE DIDN'T REMEMBER HOW FAR OR HOW LONG SHE had walked after leaving Rick's stateroom. She thought that she had actually seen him out of her peripheral vision coming around a corner just after she left, and that had caused her to move quickly away from the stateroom area of the O-3 level. She remembered walking all the way forward and down a deck to the fo'c'sle, then going down to the hangar bay, and finally coming back to her stateroom and throwing herself on her bed. The pressure of all the flying, Chrissie's death, and now . . . now, the one person that she thought she could talk to who had any time to talk to her might be an . . . an *assassin*. It was almost too much to bear, and Anne had felt her head spinning as she lay facedown on her small rack.

She didn't know how long she had slept, but it was probably a good thing that she had. Her head felt a bit clearer. Rick had always changed the subject on the few occasions when she had asked about his past. She recalled the conversations that they had had on the tennis court in Muscat. He always seemed to want to talk about something else when she asked those kinds of questions about him. He had never been really clear about how he had been commissioned or how he had come to be assigned as OIC of the SEAL platoon on *Carl Vinson*. She had a number of academy buddies who had gone through SEAL training in Coronado, and had been to a few of their parties, but she had never seen Rick there or heard any stories about him, stories that were usually bandied about in small warfare communities like the SEALs. Rick was older too, over thirty at least, while other SEALs who had his type of job were just a year or two out of college. It was all looking extremely odd to Anne.

She knew that she couldn't deal with this all by herself; she needed to talk with someone else, someone with a little more experience and perspective of the big picture of what was going on. She knew that Brian had her best interests at heart and that he would listen, and she was almost certain that she knew where to find him right now.

Anne walked aft from her stateroom down the starboard side passageway. She reached CVIC and paused by the info board right outside of the intel complex. Anne tried to be as unobtrusive as possible while standing in this busy passageway but that was a challenge in itself, as it was one of the two main thoroughfares on the 0-3 level. So she busied herself reading the bits of information displayed and looking at the photo of the day—a picture of a ship taken by one of the Airwing's aircraft that the intel bubbas had dubbed the "best shot." It was just one more tiny competition in the intensely competitive world of naval aviation. Then she spent some time walking a few dozen frames forward—she couldn't go aft, since the Blue Tile Area was just a few dozen feet away—and then returning to the board. She was counting on Brian showing up soon—he had virtually lived down here for the last several days.

Fortunately, she wasn't just standing there but was returning from one of her strolls when she spotted him coming around the corner from Strike Ops. He was in the lead with about six other pilots and NFOs.

"Hi Brian, you got a minute?" asked Anne as casually as possible.

"Oh hi, Anne," replied Brian as they both moved closer to the inboard bulkhead of the passageway to let the other aircrew continue into CVIC. One of his fellow pilots shot

Brian a glance that said he needed to be in CVIC with the rest of them.

"Brian, I have a problem and I need to talk with you."

Brian could see that Anne was worried . . . her face was flushed, her eyes looked red, and she seemed really, really stressed. He could see that and he wanted to stop and talk with her, but this was such incredibly bad timing.

"Anne, I . . . I want to talk with you too, but, Anne, I'm just heading into CVIC to give the strike brief for our attack on Bushehr. CAG moved these briefs up so that everyone will have more time at their unit briefs after this overall brief. Anne, I can't not give this brief and I've got to give it right now."

"Sure, Brian, sure," she replied. Anne desperately needed to talk with Brian, but realized that he needed to do this. "I'll catch you after the brief, OK?"

"That would be great, Anne, and I really do want to talk with you."

With that, Brian turned and walked into CVIC. She had wanted to remind Brian that it was important, but she'd hesitated. With a moment's reflection, she was glad she'd kept quiet. What was she trying to do to him? He was about to brief to fly into combat—not just fly himself, but take responsibility for a large number of other aviators too. The last thing she wanted to do was give him one more thing to worry about. Anne realized that she wasn't thinking clearly. The time pressure was now on her big time. She was supposed to brief for her flight in less than two hours, but she was determined to get this resolved one way or the other before then.

In his tiny stateroom Rick Holden brought up his e-mail account. That bothered him—the mission was still a go—as did the feeling that something was odd about his room. Something was different. Was it a scent? Hadn't he encountered it before?

He couldn't tell. So he simply erased the messages from his friends and left. He would try the Blue Tile Area again in a little while, perhaps hit it from the other end, away from the sentry.

72

JEFFERSON CITY CONTINUED TO WORK HER WAY north. Joe Willard was in and out of the control room constantly. He was proud to see that his crew was performing magnificently. He had briefed them all not long ago on their mission and its incredible importance, and despite any misgivings anyone might have, they had together risen to the task. A captain could ask for nothing more, nothing less.

Eventually, the boat reached a predetermined point where he felt that he needed to take another visual fix.

"Up periscope," he commanded.

Joe Willard was on the scope handles of number one scope as soon as they rose to the level of his shoulders. Slowly, he moved in a circle.

"There it is," he shouted.

"Aye, Captain," said his officer of the deck.

"Mark. Shah Allum Shoal Light, bearing 082."

"Shah Allum Shoal Light, bearing 082," the OOD replied, repeating the bearing back exactly.

"Range, approximately eight to ten miles."

"Aye Captain."

"Down periscope."

"Fathometer?"

"Sixty meters, Captain."

As Joe Willard stepped away from the scope he looked over to the small chart table, where his quartermaster dutifully plotted the position of his boat. The position coincided well with where he thought *Jefferson City* was located. Silently, he congratulated himself on his navigational prowess thus far.

"Make your heading 330 degrees true," he said to his

OOD. He would head slightly more to the north-north-west in order to avoid the large collection of oil wells approximately fifty miles north of the tip of Qatar. He knew he had a long way to go to reach *Carl Vinson*. He only hoped they reached their objective in time.

Joe Willard had been back in his cabin for about fifteen minutes, trying to relax, when a knock came at the door. "Enter," he said.

"Hello, Captain," said his chief of the boat, Sonarman Senior Chief Nikola.

"Hello COB, what's on your mind?" he said. The chief of the boat, or COB, was the senior enlisted man on a U.S. submarine and was the one man the captain depended upon to have the true pulse of the boat—to know what the crew was thinking and what they were worried about.

"Captain, I've been talking to the men, sir. Ever since your announcement, they have been seeking me out in droves."

"I imagine that they have been, COB. This is an extraordinarily important mission. I hope that they appreciate the fact that I gave it to them straight."

"They do, Captain. But . . . sir, the long and short of it is that the men want you to warn *Carl Vinson* before we fire any torpedoes at them."

Joe Willard just stared at the COB. He did not believe what he was hearing.

73

ANNE LOOKED AT HER WATCH. IT WAS FINALLY lunchtime. She needed to eat and she needed to get out of her stateroom. Normally a place of refuge from the hectic pace of life on an aircraft carrier, Anne's stateroom had become a prison, evoking too many memories of Chrissie. Her ready room and the easy camaraderie of her fellow officers, all of whom really cared about her and were going out of their way to try to help her work through this, was a better place to be, but for now she just wanted a little time to herself. She headed up to Wardroom 1 at the forward end of the O-3 level, figuring if she got there right at the beginning of the meal, she could find an out-of-the-way table and just eat and think for fifteen to twenty minutes.

Anne pushed her tray through the serving line and grabbed a burger and fries and found one of the small round tables at the after end of the wardroom. The table was a bit hidden by a partition, and she looked forward to just a few minutes of alone time. She was two bites into her burger when she sensed a figure standing above her and heard a familiar voice.

"Mind if I join you?"

"Uh, hi Rick," she replied, trying not to look as startled as she was. "Sure."

Anne's mind was racing. Did he know that she had been in his stateroom reading his e-mail? Had he come to see if she would admit that she'd been there? Why here, someplace that was so visible? She didn't know what to expect from Rick, and secretly wished that the wardroom would instantly fill up with other officers, but there were only two other pilots at the far end of this section.

"Good burgers?" Rick said as he sat next to her.

Anne knew that she had to act like everything was normal. She didn't want to look at Rick, didn't think that she could make eye contact with him, but she knew that she needed to do just that. She pulled that resolve from deep down inside and responded.

"Rick, for you SEALs I'm sure that this is haute cuisine. But I must admit, this is better than it is out in the field, isn't it?" She wanted to keep the banter light, keep things seeming like they were as normal as possible.

Light banter was exactly what Rick was looking for. The encounter with the MAA outside of the admiral's cabin had disturbed him, as if he had tipped his hand. "That's an understatement. Those box lunches we get on our CSAR training missions leave much to be desired."

"I bet that they do, Rick. Say, do you have a training mission today?"

"No, have the day off from that perspective. Have some other stuff that I have to take care of, though."

"Oh, what's that?" Anne asked. She was treading lightly. This was dangerous ground.

"There's just, well, just some things that I have to take care of. I've really been wrestling with a lot of things, you know . . ."

"There is a lot going on out here, Rick," responded Anne, taking her cue from his pause. Anne hadn't seen Rick like this before. Was he trying to trap her? She started to overcome her desire to just get away from him and now decided that she wanted to hear more. Maybe she would learn whether he really intended to do something to the admiral.

"Yeah, there is," he replied. "It's just that there are such major things going on that none of us have much visibility into down here at our level."

"That's the truth, isn't it?"

"Well, we are all brought up and brought along believing that our senior leaders are doing what's right for the Navy and for the nation. I don't know, sometimes that may be too much of a leap of faith."

"You're probably right," she replied. "I think that at least out here at the battle group level we're pretty focused on doing the right thing."

"Do you think that the right thing is to lay waste to the entire military infrastructure of Iran? That's going to put a lot of pilots at risk and it won't be something that we can take back once we start it."

"Rick, I think that it may, but that's our mission. That's what has been handed down from higher authority. We all have to take those risks if that's what we're ordered to do."

"I know. But I wonder if we ever stop to think if the people at the top, at the very top, are doing the right thing. Sometimes I don't think that they consider what the impact of their actions is going to be down here at our level. Sometimes I think that they just press forward without thinking.

374

There are situations where those people have to be stopped."

Rick was really reaching. He seemed to be almost in a trance, talking not so much to Anne but to himself. Now Anne was confused. She was a little less concerned that he suspected her of being in his stateroom, although she realized that she might not be totally out of the woods. Rick seemed to be trying to reconcile his mission. Maybe he was being forced to do this and now he was having second thoughts. In any event, Anne was even more sure than when she was in his stateroom that Rick intended to do something to Admiral Robinson, and she believed that he was going to do something soon.

"Rick, there are all sorts of issues out there. I guess at my level I just try to do what I did at the academy and put my head down and swim. I really have trouble dealing with some of this big picture, political stuff."

"Well, the politics of the situation is probably driving all of us to do the things that we do. I can't get away from it."

"Maybe not," she replied.

There was a long, pregnant pause as they both munched away. Anne thought that she had validated what Rick was going to do. Now she was sure that she needed to do something about it. She needed to extricate herself from this and move. Rick could try to carry out his mission at any time. Somehow she suspected that he would try to do this at night, but she might not have that long.

"Rick, it was good seeing you, but I'm flying in a little while, so I'd better get down to my ready room. I'll see you around, OK?"

"Sure Anne, sure," he replied. "Fly 'em safe, OK?"

"You bet," she said as she got up. "Thanks again for everything, Rick."

"You got it."

Anne grabbed her tray and took it back to the window, where the food service attendant stood ready to take it, and kept moving aft and out of Wardroom 1. She had learned a lot from this chance encounter, and there was only one place that she could go with this information. And she didn't have much time to do it.

74

THE NEON SIGN OUTSIDE HIS WINDOW FLASHED WHAT seemed like every second and sent a surreal glow into his hotel room. Mejid Homani lay on his bed with his remote in his right hand, idly clicking through the channels, but always returning to CNN. He slid his left hand to his side, feeling for his pager. It was still there. It was still silent.

Mejid was only twenty-three, but he had been a soldier for Shiekholeslam for almost seven years. He had been orphaned after the Iran-Iraq war and had been passed from relative to relative, but he'd mainly grown up on the streets. He had finally found Shiekholeslam—or, more correctly, Shiekholeslam had found him—and been brought to the camps. Mejid had trained diligently and had proven himself against men a decade older.

But that is all that it had been for all of those years—training. He had done the same repetitive things month after month, year after year, always being promised that he would be given a mission "someday." Now, "someday" had come, and he had been selected, he was sure, for his devotion and his willingness to die for his cause if necessary. He had found his contact and received his supply of the agent, which he scrupulously guarded. He had picked out the location and returned to that site once just to recheck absolutely everything. He had followed his instructions to the letter. Now he just had to wait. All the years of training. All the dedication to the cause. And all he had to do was wait a little longer before putting them into practice.

Mejid returned to CNN and was about to continue scanning the channels when he saw a map of the Arabian Gulf appear behind a reporter providing the latest news on the crisis there:

> *"And in the Arabian Gulf, the simmering crisis between the United States and the Islamic Republic of Iran continues and threatens to intensify. Yesterday, two Iranian frigates, the* Alborz *and the* Sabalan, *attempted to attack the American carrier USS* Carl Vinson *in the northern portion of the Gulf. The Navy cruiser USS* Shiloh, *shown here, severely damaged one frigate while attack planes from* Carl Vinson *sank the other. There were no U.S. casualties and there is no reliable data as to Iranian casualties.*
>
> *"Later that same day, USS* Shiloh *shot down an Iranian aircraft that was closing the battle group in a threatening manner. The aircraft did not respond to warnings by* Shiloh *and was in an 'attack profile' and coming within weapons release range. Iranian officials deny that one of their aircraft was approaching the battle group.*
>
> *"Meanwhile, at the United Nations, the Iranian ambassador to the United Nations decried the attack on the Iranian frigates, stipulating that they were operating in international waters and calling the Americans 'pirates and bandits' for attacking these ships. He called for a United Nations resolution condemning the United States for these barbaric acts.*
>
> *"Pentagon officials declined to comment on the action in the northern Arabian Gulf, indicating only that the matter was under investigation. These officials also refused to comment on the overall level of U.S. activity in the Gulf and would not speculate regarding possible American attacks on Iran in the wake of the bombing of the Muscat Intercontinental Hotel and the shootdown of the Navy Tomcat aircraft off the coast of Iran.*
>
> *"Meanwhile, at the U.S. Capitol. . . ."*

Mejid Homani hit the mute button. He did not want to hear any more. The American pigs were sinking Iranian ships and killing Iranian sailors. They were shooting down his homeland's airplanes whether or not his government wanted to admit it or not. And still, he was not unleashed. They had not ordered him to act. He fingered his pager once again, as if he were trying to coax it into going off. How long would he have to wait?

He did not know how long he had been asleep. It was dark. The neon light outside of his hotel room, dim in the daylight, was now a bright, pulsating strobe that flooded his room in waves. He shot out of bed. Had he missed a call from Shiekholeslam? His pager's tiny red light indicated that it was on. No, he would have heard it.

Mejid could not stay in the tiny hotel room any longer. He needed to do something. He felt that his moment might pass him by. What were they waiting for? He was not "political," and he feared that those who were might be interfering with what the holy man had promised them they would do. He tied his shoes and checked on his agent. It was safely under the hotel bed, hidden in a box labeled Jewelry Samples. He hurried out of the room and locked the door behind him.

Mejid walked the three blocks to the United Nations Plaza. It was 9 P.M., and the plaza was virtually deserted. He walked up to the glass doors that led to the concourse and put his nose against the glass. There, he could see where he would place the agent. It was ideal. He had studied the traffic patterns and understood what the effect of the gas would be on those busy workers and visitors who would be the victims of his attack. He could not have planned it any better.

75

ANNE NEEDED TIME, SO ALTHOUGH IT WENT ENTIRELY against her professional instincts, she decided that she needed to come off the Blue Wolf flight schedule. She and she alone had to get to the bottom of what Rick was doing, and, as much as she hated to admit it, she couldn't do that in the air.

She also needed help. And if Brian was unavailable—for good reason—then she would tell her squadron skipper and then depend on his good judgment to help her stop Admiral Robinson. She wasn't exactly sure exactly how she was going to do that, but if she couldn't trust him, who could she trust?

The ready room was not packed, just the usual assemblage of pilots and naval flight officers. Anne walked toward the skipper's chair at the front.

"Hey, Anne," said Lieutenant Luke Meyer, the Blue Wolf duty officer, he had a duty desk near the back of the ready room. "Brief goes down in fifteen minutes. You're early. Good to have you back flying."

"Yeah, thanks," she replied without enthusiasm.

Anne continued forward, scanning the front row of ready room seats. She didn't see a head rising over the top of her skipper's chair. As she reached the front of the ready room, a voice piped up:

"Hello O'Connor. Welcome back."

It was her XO, Bingo Reynolds. He was slouched in his chair reading the message board.

"Thanks, XO. Good to be back," she replied. "XO, is the skipper around, sir?"

"No, he's still flying, O'Connor. Something I can help you with?"

She really wanted to talk with her skipper. He was so easy to talk to, and she needed to have this be easy. The XO—well, he was just the XO and didn't ever seem to have her best interests at heart. But this couldn't wait.

"Actually, XO, there is." Anne looked around. There were about a dozen other officers in the ready room. Although none of them made eye contact with her, she knew just by the fact that she was standing in front of the ready room talking with the exec that almost everyone was listening to her conversation. "XO, sir. This is kind of a, well, a delicate matter sir," she continued in a whisper. "Could we discuss this in private, sir?"

As thick-headed and difficult to get along with as Bingo Reynolds was, he recognized that this was something that he needed to accommodate. Anne had been through a lot in the last few days. He rose. "Sure. We can do that. Let's talk in the passageway."

Anne followed the XO out the front door of the ready room. They passed Blue Wolf Maintenance Control, with its usual high level of activity—pilots reviewing aircraft discrepancy books, maintenance chiefs contacting troubleshooters to work on aircraft, and the like. It was not the place to try to talk.

"Looks a little jammed here, O'Connor. Let's go down to my stateroom."

She followed him aft for a few dozen frames. At his stateroom, Reynolds slipped his magnetic card into the door slot and pushed the door open, letting Anne enter first. He flicked on the neon overhead light as he entered and shut the door behind him. He motioned for Anne to sit on his desk chair as he sat on the edge of his pull-out bed, which doubled as a sofa.

"OK, O'Connor, what's on your mind?"

"XO, I don't really know where to begin. For right now, I think that I need to come off today's flight schedule."

Reynolds knew now that something was seriously wrong. He knew how much Anne loved to fly and he knew that she had worked hard to get back up and flying as soon as possible after Chrissie's death.

"Sure, Anne, sure, we can do that. Is there something else that you want to tell me?"

Anne was never comfortable with the exec, but she decided that she couldn't wait for the skipper; she had to tell the XO.

"XO, I think that I've walked into something that I'm having trouble dealing with. It's really, really complicated, but I think that we have a big problem on this ship."

"Problem? What kind of problem?"

"XO, this may take a while," she replied.

As the XO sat with rapt attention, Anne poured out the details of the e-mails that she had read in Rick's stateroom. She related the account of the lunch conversation she had just had with Rick. She reinforced all this by telling the XO that it was Rick who had helped her through her crisis after Chrissie's death as a way of assuring the XO that she knew Rick well enough to know that something had changed and she was certain that he was going to do what the e-mails told him to do. The XO never took his eyes off her for her entire outpouring.

"O'Connor," he said slowly, "I don't know where to begin. This is the most amazing and troubling story that I have ever heard. But first things first, we do need to get you off the flight schedule for right now. Walters was whining that he wasn't getting his fair share of flight time. I'll have the ops o pop him in there in your place. Then we'll dig into this matter."

76

MICHAEL CURTIS DID NOT REMEMBER HOW MANY times he had been in the Oval Office during the years that he had worked as the president's national security adviser. He had never thought to try to keep track of such a statistic. Surely it was hundreds of times. In all of those previous times he never could remember feeling that he had been summoned. It had always seemed collegial before—mutual respect between two professionals. It felt anything but that now.

Curtis breezed by the president's secretary as he entered the Oval Office. His aides had called ahead and related the president's exact words: "I think you better come over here right now—right now." Meanwhile, the White House staff made sure that calls were held, other staff members were shooed away, and any outside visitors were either canceled or relegated to that perpetual purgatory of being promised to be "worked in" at another time.

The president had his back to the door as he sat in his high-backed chair and looked out the window. His desk was clear, and it appeared to Curtis that he was not doing anything particular at all. The national security adviser had seen him do this before—whenever the president faced something that he thought was a serious crisis he cleared his calendar and cleared his desk. It seemed to clear his mind so that he could focus on the immediate problem at hand.

"You wanted to see me, Mr. President?"

"Yes, Michael. I don't feel like I am getting brought up to speed on events in the Gulf fast enough. I know that we often joke about CNN being ahead of our intelligence people in reporting world events, but in this case I think that it might be true."

Michael Curtis was caught between a rock and a hard place. He couldn't get the Pentagon or the agency to keep him updated frequently enough, and the president came to him and him alone to vent his frustrations regarding his not being kept up to speed. It was frustrating beyond words.

"Mr. President, events are moving rapidly. Admiral Monroe and Mr. Jacobs are executing their plan to send the submarine to stop *Carl Vinson*, and the DCI has given his agent explicit instructions about stopping Admiral Robinson. Those plans are being executed as we speak, Mr. President."

"Yes, I understand all of that, Michael, but with all of the communications networks and the like that we have you would think that we could do better than being totally in the dark about what is happening and when it is happening."

"You would think that we would, Mr. President," he replied, agreeing with the president. "Sir, I have taken every measure that I can to get updates from Admiral Monroe and Mr. Hernandez. You would think that the few miles between here and the Pentagon and the ten between here and Langley were a thousand miles. I get all manner of reasons why they can't keep us informed."

Michael Curtis's frustration was boiling over. He didn't want to look or act like he was putting his colleagues "on report" with the president, but he was under too much pressure as it was to take the heat for two senior national security officials who ought to know better than to keep him and the commander in chief in the dark.

"I know that it's frustrating, Michael, and I don't want to get fortress mentality over here in the White House, but there are larger issues to deal with than just the minor piece-parts that the Pentagon and the agency are working on."

"I know that sir."

"I'm not certain that you do fully, Michael. I had discussed with you all the idea of letting the president of the Islamic Republic know what was happening with the *Carl Vinson* Battle Group. You all convinced me at that time not to, and, as I recall, you all were vocal in your insistence that I wait!"

The president was getting worked up in a way that Michael Curtis had seen only on rare occasions.

"Yes sir, and, Mr. President, I think that was sound advice at the time."

"But now? Is it still sound advice?"

"Mr. President, I—"

"No, Michael," the president interrupted, "it is absolutely terrible advice!" Michael Curtis could see that the president was going to get this out and that he should just listen.

"Michael, I never pretended to be a grand strategist or to be especially knowledgeable about military matters. That's why I brought professionals such as yourself to work here—people who had that broad strategic background and vision. And yes, I wanted the focus of my administration to be economic. But there are some basic things that I think you all are missing."

Michael Curtis wanted to respond, but he held his tongue.

"I know that this terrorist attack on our people was a dreadful, barbaric act. And I know that the subsequent shootdown of our Tomcat aircraft was a hostile act, as well as the Iranian ships attacking *Carl Vinson*. Put in the context of Iran's long-term intransigence toward us, it looks even worse. I understand all that and you know I do."

"Yes, Mr. President," was all that Michael Curtis said.

"But you are seeing right now how much trouble we have just getting subordinates to merely inform us of their actions—and we live in what is probably the most open society on earth!"

"So here we have Iran, which as near as I can figure doesn't have one power center, it must have a dozen, and we assume that their president has full control of his military, his police, his foreign policy apparatus, everything. Do you really believe that he does?"

"He may not, Mr. President," Michael Curtis replied. The president's questions were all over the map, and he didn't feel well prepared to respond to any of them.

"Exactly. I am not convinced that President Habibi condoned or countenanced any of these things. And yet, we have a mad admiral who may rain destruction down on military bases and airfields and God knows what else and you all *insist* that I not contact Habibi and warn him that there is a part of our arsenal that we may not have full control of!"

The national security adviser saw where the president was coming from. There was nothing the president said he could really disagree with. He wanted to support the president and he wanted to do the right thing for his country—not just now, but for the long term. He was caught on the horns of a dilemma.

For Michael Curtis this was the toughest personal and professional conundrum he had ever faced. His loyalty to his president was absolute, as was his loyalty to his nation. Michael Curtis believed fervently that the Islamic Republic posed a real and compelling long-term danger to the United States. And if . . . and only if . . . they failed to stop Admiral Robinson and he delivered the attacks they now knew he was planning, Iran's ability to threaten the United States would be dismantled for a least a decade—perhaps more. Importantly, the United States could then be absolved of any real responsibility for this—they could blame it all on a renegade military officer. It was the opportunity of a lifetime to accomplish great things at virtually no cost.

But if the president made overtures to President Habibi, the Islamic Republic might have a better chance of blunting the American attacks and, more importantly, of dispersing their naval and air forces to avoid them. Robinson undoubtedly would attack with full force over a short time period, so if the initial flurry of attacks hit empty naval facilities and deserted air bases, it was doubtful that he would have enough weapons to conduct an ongoing campaign to attack any of these dispersed units. Moreover, by that time, one plan to stop the mad admiral would surely have reached fruition. He knew, however, that he could not ignore the president's request.

"Mr. President, you have a valid point, sir. We should, at a minimum, establish a way for you to contact President Habibi. I know that Secretary Quinn has been working on upgrading our diplomatic networks to reach out to the Islamic Republic. I recommend that we let him run with this as an urgent priority and get this line established right away!" replied the national security adviser.

"Good, then we are agreed, Michael. Shall I call the secretary?"

"No sir, I will be talking to him in a very short while on another matter. I will ensure that he gets on this right away."

"Thank you, Michael," responded the president as the national security adviser departed. Michael Curtis would speak with Secretary Quinn—in due course.

77

WIZARD FOSTER SAT BEHIND HIS DESK TRYING TO make sense of the strange story that Bingo Reynolds then, for confirmation, Anne herself had just told him. He was sure the others—Deputy CAG, her CO, and the ship's XO were doing the same.

"You've told us an amazing and shocking story, Lieutenant," CAG said, "and we're going to take this step by step. I want to thank you for coming forward. Now, would you mind giving us a few moments? I'd appreciate it if you would stand by in your ready room."

"Sure, CAG." Anne got up as CAG came out from behind his large desk and extended his hand. Anne shook it but she couldn't help notice that he didn't make eye contact.

No sooner had Anne left the room than CAG looked to those assembled. "Impressions?"

"Her story is the same as the one she told me earlier. I think that she really believes that Holden is out to assassinate the admiral," replied Bingo Reynolds.

"OK, well, that's good, her story is consistent," replied CAG.

"I think that we need to get to the bottom of these

e-mails," replied *Carl Vinson*'s XO. "We need to see exactly what they say."

"Good idea, XO," replied CAG. "Can you find a window when Holden isn't there to do that?"

"Should be soon, CAG, I was scanning the Air Plan while we were waiting for Lieutenant O'Connor to come down here. HS-4 is flying a ton of practice CSAR missions in preparation for our strikes, and Holden will likely be in the air for those. I'll check for sure and then check his e-mails right away."

"Good, XO, thanks," replied CAG, as the XO left his cabin.

"Skipper?" said CAG, looking directly at the Blue Wolves' CO.

"CAG, Lieutenant O'Connor is one of my best nugget pilots. She has had an outstanding workup period and a great cruise thus far. She may be my high-time pilot this month—"

"So she's flying a lot?" interrupted CAG. He wanted to draw as much as he could out of the skipper. He was, ultimately, the one person who should have the pulse of what was happening to one of his junior officers.

"Really banging out the hops, CAG. Of course, you know that I took her off the flight schedule after the death of Lieutenant Linder. But she got cleared by medical after a few days and was ready to go flying again . . . at least until she came down and talked with the XO just now."

"Lot of pressure doing that much flying, particularly here in the Gulf. How close was she to Linder? Wasn't she her roommate?"

"She was, CAG, and they had been roomies for a while. I'd say that they were really close, wouldn't you, XO?"

"They were incredibly close, CAG. She took Chrissie's death hard. I don't know if you know it, CAG, but she was in the tower when Chrissie hit the ramp."

"No, I didn't know that," CAG replied. "How has she been dealing with being one of our few women aviators, skipper?"

"I think that she's been doing, OK, CAG. There's no question that she's put a lot of self-imposed stress on herself, you know, trying to prove she's as good as the men, if not better—but I'm not going to fault her for that. I'd like to have a dozen more like her."

"Yeah, CAG, I think that O'Connor is a little unique in our squadron. She's the only woman in the squadron who isn't either married or attached to a significant other. The other women just don't seem as hell-bent-for-leather to excel every minute. I think that the skipper and I probably have O'Connor pegged as one of the few really planning on making the Navy a career," said the XO.

"CAG, I agree with everything that the XO says. As far as off-ship attachments we're pretty sure that O'Connor doesn't have any. But the scuttlebutt around the ready room is that she's been seeing this Holden a lot. She told you that they jog together, but, well, you know, CAG, just talk among the JOs, that's all."

"Talk that there's some sort of romantic involvement?"

"Yeah, you know, the usual stuff."

"I see," replied CAG.

He hadn't spoken yet, but CAG's deputy, Captain Walt "Stretch" Purcell, had listened impassively to the entire conversation. The dialogue about a possible romantic link between Anne and Rick struck a responsive chord with him.

"CAG," Purcell began, "I've been listening to all of this and trying to reconstruct the time line in my brain. I was down getting a burger in Wardroom 1 just a little while ago and I swear that I saw O'Connor and Holden having lunch together in an out-of-the-way corner of the wardroom. It was right before she said she talked to you, XO, so it must have been after she read the e-mail. Would she have been having lunch with the guy in a quiet corner, if she thought he was an assassin or something?"

"I don't know, Deputy, I'm getting a little confused."

As they continued to "what if" the situation, there was a knock on the door.

"Enter," said CAG. *Carl Vinson*'s XO stepped in. "Big XO, have you found out anything?"

"I have, CAG," he said as he took a seat in front of CAG's desk. "As soon as I left here, I confirmed that Holden was flying with HS-4. I went down to his stateroom and let myself in. His laptop was open and on, just like O'Connor had told us. I went right to his e-mail account and found about two dozen incoming e-mails, of varying age, sitting in his queue. CAG, I read every one of them. There wasn't one that was even vaguely like the ones O'Connor described. There wasn't one telling him to do anything."

"Are you sure, XO?"

"CAG, I'm really sure. Look, I'm not a computer genius, sir, but I gave it a good solid look. I went beyond just his incoming queue and looked at all his files, even files that were labeled as something innocuous. I opened them. It didn't take long because he just doesn't have much on his machine. There is nothing in there that could lead any reasonable person to believe that Holden is involved in anything untoward."

"Nothing?" replied CAG.

"Nothing sir. I suppose we could turn this over to our legal department and formally charge him with a crime, confiscate his laptop and have some real experts go through this, but I think that I may have a little insight on where O'Connor is coming from."

"Yes, go ahead."

"CAG, there were three e-mails in there from someone named 'Laura.' Well, sir, they're not mushy, but it sounds like it's a serious relationship. She's evidently a semi-steady girlfriend."

"Did they look like they've been on his machine for a while?"

"Yes, sir. The most recent one is from two days ago and the others are a little older."

Deputy CAG chimed in. "So, XO, are you thinking that maybe O'Connor read those e-mails?"

"I don't want to jump to conclusions, Deputy," said the XO, "but that's my general train of thought. Skipper and XO here tell us that she's kind of 'seeing' Holden. She goes down to his stateroom and reads these e-mails from some other woman. I guess I could see where she'd be a little peeved. I don't know, maybe it's a stretch, but I could see where she'd be pissed enough to try to get him in some kind of trouble. Making up a story that he's trying to take out

Admiral Robinson might seem like a big leap, but who knows. I have to defer to her skipper and XO again. If they say she's been under a lot of stress, maybe she stopped thinking and snapped."

"I know, I had a girlfriend once who would rat me out to God if she thought I ever looked at anyone else," said Bingo Reynolds.

"Whoa, we're really taking a leap here," said CAG. "I'm not sure we should be ready to cashier O'Connor quite yet."

"I'm not saying that we should, CAG," chimed in Anne's skipper, "but she's our officer, and now I'm genuinely concerned about her. I think that as a minimum, we should have her evaluated. I think that our CAG flight surgeon and our senior medical officer need to give her a thorough . . . well, CAG, a thorough psychological evaluation. I think that we should take this very, very seriously. I don't want her tripping over the edge."

"I'll leave that to your good judgment," responded CAG. "Now, what do you all think that we should do regarding Holden? If these accusations are true, we obviously need to do something about it. Do we think that there is any chance that they are true?"

His deputy spoke first. "CAG, based on what we know right now, there doesn't appear to be a shred of evidence against him. The only 'evidence' that O'Connor related just doesn't exist, and now we think we have reason to believe she just might have reason to manufacture these charges—"

"Deputy, I don't think we ought to hang that on O'Connor yet," interrupted Bingo Reynolds. As much of a hard-nose as Bingo was, when it came to accusing one of their JOs, he drew the line.

"All right, XO, we're not *accusing* her of anything. We're trying to decide if there is enough to go on to accuse Holden of anything—at least accuse him formally—and where she is coming from plays into that."

"I think that we would be on very, very shaky legal ground doing anything to Holden based on the info that we have thus far," added *Carl Vinson*'s XO.

"OK, OK," shouted CAG, not wanting to lose control of the meeting. "We're getting a little far afield here. Here's what we are going to do. Skipper, XO, I want you to take O'Connor and get her checked out. Big XO, Deputy, I want you to work with whatever investigators you have onboard and see if we can at least keep track of what Holden is doing until we get a handle on this. I need to take everything we know to the chief of staff. Let's get this resolved soon, gents, we do have a war about to start!"

VS-35's CO and XO found Anne in the Blue Wolf Ready Room. Her eyes grew wide as her skipper began to tell her what they were going to do.

78

JOE WILLARD SAT WITH HIS COB FOR OVER AN HOUR, listening to his concern, explaining the mission to him over and over again, trying to come up with options that were less draconian than what he was about to do. There was no easy answer, though.

The captain reflected that when COB had first broached the subject of warning *Carl Vinson*, he had been taken aback. He had—for a moment—been bitterly disappointed that his crew, despite appearances, was not a hundred percent behind the mission that their Captain had laid out to them. Upon reflection, he began to recognize that these men, who, like him, also had sworn to support and defend the Constitution, were right to have doubts about an order to torpedo a United States Navy nuclear aircraft carrier. Nothing like this had ever been asked of them before.

He realized that he and the COB needed to get closure and decide what they were going to do next.

"Captain," the COB began, "I think that the men would be satisfied if you went back up the chain of command and at least asked the question again, asked if warning *Carl Vinson* was an option for us as we try to complete our mission."

"COB, I can ask the question if you want me to. I will do that. But I've got two messages here—from COMSUBPAC and from CNO—that tell me that I must attack *Carl Vinson*. They don't authorize me to warn the carrier—something that could put the success of the mission in jeopardy if our warning them lets them evade us."

"But it doesn't tell us we can't do that, Captain," replied the COB. "That's all the men are looking for, Captain, just the fact that you've asked the question again."

Joe Willard sat silent for several moments as he considered what the COB was telling him. Finally, COB broke the ice.

"Sir, this crew would follow you anywhere. I think that all they need to know is that you asked higher authority for clarification so they would know that you are being responsive to their concerns. Captain, you and I both know what we are going to be told when we ask the question—they're going to tell us to complete our mission as assigned and tell us explicitly not to warn the carrier. We know that. But they don't, sir."

"COB, you really believe the crew thinks that we would ever be authorized to warn the carrier?"

"Captain, most of the men came into the Navy when the cold war was just a memory. They don't know anything about some of the clandestine ops we used to be involved in. They are pretty idealistic. They think that we can make combat a casualty free Nintendo game. It's hard to overcome all the years of socialization that has led them here. We just need to keep faith with them, Captain, that's all."

"All right, COB, I think that I understand. Let me turn this over in my brain for just a minute, will you?"

"Sure, Captain. I'll be standing by when you need me."

"I know that you will, COB, thanks."

As the COB left, Joe Willard saw his dilemma was simple. He needed to complete his mission. He needed to keep faith with his men. It was the reconciliation that was hard. He reflected for a long time, then he pulled out his yellow legal paper and began to write.

*   *   *

Joe Willard stood in *Jefferson City*'s Control Room and continued to monitor his boat's progress north. He was navigating in more and more constrained waters and felt that he needed to be in the Control Room even more than he had been. As good as his cadre of young officers and men was, safe passage was ultimately his responsibility. Joe Willard had never felt the weight of command more than he did at this moment.

As the periscope reached the full up position, Joe Willard rested on its outstretched arms. Slowly, he pivoted around 360 degrees. He saw nothing except for the one light that he had hoped to see.

"Navigator!"

"Yes, Captain."

"Ra's Tanura Racon, bearing 012, mark."

"Ra's Tanura Racon, bearing 012, Captain. Estimated distance?"

"Distance three, no, four miles."

"Yes, Captain."

"Fathometer?"

"Fifty-two meters, Captain."

"Down scope."

Satisfied that he had once more fixed his navigation precisely, the captain gave the order.

"Make your course 316, speed ten knots."

"Make my course 316, speed ten knots, aye sir," responded his officer of the deck.

Jefferson City continued to move north-north-west, roughly paralleling the coast of Saudi Arabia. There was reasonable water here as the captain kept the boat just east of the shallow water of the kingdom's offshore oil fields—Al Qatif, Al Barri, and Manifah. He walked the few feet to his tiny cabin and saw the radioman waiting for him.

"I have the message typed out, Captain."

"Good, Mercer. Let me see it."

He pushed open the door to his cabin, sat down in his chair, and laid the message on his desk.

FLASH
FM USS JEFFERSON CITY
TO COMSUBPAC
BT
TOP SECRET SPECAT PERSONAL FOR COMSUBPAC FROM
WILLARD.
MSGID/GENADMIN/JEFFERSON CITY/
SUBJ/JEFFERSON CITY MISSION//
RMKS/1. (TS) ADMIRAL DEUTERMANN. JEFFERSON CITY
HAS BEEN PROCEEDING NORTH AS ORDERED IN ORDER
TO INTERCEPT AND ATTACK CARL VINSON. OUR CUR-
RENT POSITION IS 27 10 N 50 15 E, JUST WEST OF THE
JU'AYMAH RACON. JEFFERSON CITY IS READY TO
CARRY OUT THE TASKING THAT YOU PROVIDED IN
YOUR MESSAGE. ALL WEAPONS SYSTEMS HAVE BEEN
CHECKED AND TESTED AND CONTINUITY CHECKS RE-
VEAL NO PROBLEMS WHATSOEVER.
2. (TS) ADMIRAL, LENGTHY DISCUSSIONS WITH MY COB
AND OTHERS HAVE REVEALED CONSIDERABLE CON-
CERN ON THE PART OF MY CREW REGARDING TORPE-
DOING A US NAVY SHIP. A POSSIBLE ALTERNATIVE TO
OUR CURRENT TASKING WOULD BE TO FIRST WARN
CARL VINSON PRIOR TO FIRING TORPEDOES AT HER.
THIS WOULD ENABLE HER CREW TO, FIRST, VOLUNTAR-
ILY ELECT TO CEASE THIS MISSION, BUT, FAILING THAT,
WOULD AT LEAST ENSURE THAT THEY ARE PREPARED
TO TAKE PROPER DAMAGE CONTROL PROCEDURES TO
KEEP FROM LOSING THEIR SHIP. DUE TO THE EXTRAOR-
DINARY NATURE OF THIS MISSION, I RESPECTFULLY RE-
QUEST THAT YOU CONSIDER AUTHORIZING US TO MAKE
THIS WARNING TO CARL VINSON.
3. (U) VERY RESPECTFULLY, JOE WILLARD.//
DECL/X4//

The captain read the message carefully, once, then again.
Then he affixed his initial to the top right-hand corner of
the paper and handed it back to the radioman.

"Send it."

A flash precedence message had priority over all others.
Joe Willard waited at communication depth for COMSUB-

PAC to send his answer. Less than twenty minutes later, it came.

```
FLASH
FM COMSUBPAC
TO USS JEFFERSON CITY
BT
TOP SECRET SPECAT PERSONAL FOR COMMANDING OF-
FICER FROM COMSUBPAC
MSGID/GENADMIN/JEFFERSON CITY/
SUBJ/JEFFERSON CITY MISSION//
1. RMKS (TS) CARRY OUT YOUR MISSION AS ORDERED.
2. (U) WARM REGARDS, DEUTERMANN.
DECL/X4//
```

79

"HELLO LIEUTENANT," SAID HIS WEAPONS PETTY OF-
ficer as Rick Holden found Petty Officer First Class Ed
Vickers on the starboard side of hangar bay one.

"Hello, Vickers. How's business?"

"Booming, sir, booming," said Vickers, smiling. Bos'n
Mate First Class Edward Vickers had been a SEAL for sixteen years. He had seen action in Desert Storm and in the
Balkans and was combat tested through and through. He
had been in enough scuffles on liberty, however, that he was
never going to be selected for chief petty officer, so he was
just serving out his last four years trying to get his job done.
And although he thought the request was a bit strange, he
figured he could bend the rules a bit when it came to issuing
weapons to his fellow SEAL team members—especially his
officer-in-charge.

Hell, thought Vickers, these ship drones could set all the

damn rules that they wanted to, but he and his fellow SEALs were probably going to be on the ground in "Indian country" soon. They needed to be ready to shoot and shoot straight on the first mission—there was no batting practice or warm-up game. Anything that he could do to get weapons into the hands of his comrades so they could be more ready—hell, he'd bend any idiotic rule that the ship had about issue control, weapons checks, or the like. They weren't paying him to be a glorified equipment manager!

"That's good, that's really good. I hope that we're not making your job any harder than it has to be with weapons issue and all."

"Not at all, Lieutenant. I think that if we get 'em out there, we'll be more than ready for our mission. Any intel on when the strikes are gonna happen, sir?"

"No, nothing exact, but I'd be really surprised if it was any later than tomorrow or the next day at the very latest. All the signs are there. Airwing is full up and ready to go."

"We'll be ready for CSAR sir—or for anything else. The men are really pumped."

"I know that they are, Vickers. Now I need to be ready to do my part. Not gonna be much of an example if the lieutenant can't shoot straight."

"That's for sure, sir. What's your pleasure today?"

"I think that I'll work with the nine millimeter and forty-five caliber. Both have pros and cons, so I might as well get up to speed with each. Better give me enough ammo to really get warmed up. That way, once I start using these I don't have to come looking for you again."

"That's not a problem, sir. I'm here whenever you need me. But I'll give ya a few extra boxes of ammo, just for practice."

"Thanks, I'll try to hit something with 'em."

Rick took the nine millimeter from the man and inserted the clip into it. Then he did the same thing with the forty-five caliber. Rick wanted to be sure that he had plenty of ammo in reserve if it came down to the point of having to shoot it out with any of Admiral Robinson's men to finally get to the admiral. He put both weapons and all of the ammo in the aviator's helmet bag that the HS-4 bubbas had given him, and started aft.

"See you, Vickers."

"See ya, sir. And remember, if there's gonna be any action, don't forget who your best killer is."

"I will, Vickers, I will."

Passing through *Carl Vinson*'s hangar bay, Rick thought about just how he could complete his mission to stop Admiral Robinson without being one of those killers. It was going to be tough.

He needed to be alone so he could think. He worked his way past a Tomcat parked in Hangar Bay II and started up the port side ladder. As he closed the hatch behind him, he had the strangest feeling that someone was following him. He looked around and didn't see anyone, but he couldn't lose that nagging feeling that someone was there.

Rick slipped into his stateroom with his weapons and ran through his options. He could just shoot the Admiral outright and be done with it. He would be taken into custody, of course, handled roughly by the staff, maybe even beaten by investigators trying to determine if he was part of a conspiracy. He was prepared for that. Then he would tell his story to the chief of staff—the next senior man aboard—invite him to check the veracity of his story with the agency, and then wait for justice to lurch ahead. The planned strikes would be called off, and the nation would be saved a long and bloody conflict with an enraged Islamic Republic. It was a plan simple in its conception and straightforward in its execution.

This was not a scenario, however, he could bring himself to implement. That was why he had lobbied his handlers so hard to let him disable Admiral Robinson instead of killing him. That would be far tougher, though.

His thoughts flashed back to the hangar bay; had someone been following him? Who, one of the admiral's staff? Based on just the slightest chance that it could be someone who would try to stop him, he recognized that he couldn't stay in his stateroom any longer. It would be too easy to trap him here. He had to move.

Rick put the nine millimeter inside the front of his waistband, while he put the forty-five caliber between his waistband and the small of his back. Fortunately, the camouflage uniform was sufficiently baggy that it hid both. He then distributed the extra ammo as discreetly as he could in the various pockets of his jacket. He was armed and ready. He just needed one more thing.

Rick dropped back down to the hangar bay. Now, as he moved, he always looked furtively around, looking for anyone who might be following him. He went forward and found Petty Officer Vickers again.

"Hi sir, come back for another weapon?" he asked, clearly ready and willing to arm up his officer-in-charge as well as he could.

"No, just want to get a walkie-talkie from you. We're gonna need to do some coordination with the ship. I need to be able to talk to the usual cast."

"No problem, sir, I have one right here, all charged up."

"Thanks, I won't lose it."

"No problem, sir, if you do, it'll come out of your pay, not mine."

Rick gave him a friendly wave and sought out somewhere to complete his planning. As far as he was concerned, he had to assume that he was a hunted man. The walkie-talkie would let him eavesdrop on the actions that the ship might be taking to find him. More importantly, he knew from experience that the master-at-arms force used these to alert MAAs of the admiral's movements so they could make sure that the route he picked to travel was clear of obstructions, excess personnel, and the like.

Rick walked aft through Hangar Bay II. As he did, he continued to look over his shoulder. *Damn*, he thought, *there is someone watching me. I just know there is.*

80

ACHMED BOLESHARI SAT BOLT UPRIGHT IN HIS BED IN his tiny hotel room just two blocks away from Horton Plaza. The "Special Report" on CNN had just appeared with a lead-in featuring a picture of both the American and Iranian flags. He flicked the volume up and listened:

"Iranian Foreign Minister Ali Akbar Velayati again condemned the United States for its attacks on two Iranian frigates in the Northern Arabian Gulf. In a prepared statement, Velayati condemned 'continued American aggression in the Arabian Gulf and America's Rambo actions in attacking these ships in international waters, as well as America's total disregard for common decency in refusing to pick up survivors of these Alborz *and* Sabalan *in violation of customary international law.' Minister Velayati went on to note that 'a total of one hundred thirty-four brave sailors died in this action,' many of whom undoubtedly would have not perished had the U.S. Navy ships in the area attempted to provide any lifesaving assistance.*

"Meanwhile, at the United Nations, the Iranian ambassador renewed his call for a resolution condemning the United States for these attacks. He called on all peace-loving nations to join Iran in supporting this resolution. Further, he petitioned United Nations Secretary General Kofi Annan to demand monetary compensation of six hundred and seventy million dollars—five million dollars for each victim—for the families of those lost on both ships. He indicated that unless or until this compensation was paid 'the Islamic Republic

*will wage a worldwide fatwah against the interests of
the United States all over the world.'*

*"At the Pentagon, U.S. military officials insisted that
the attacks on the Iranian frigates were strictly in self-
defense and that the United States would take 'appropriate measures' to beef up the defenses of all U.S.
forces in the Gulf. One high-ranking official, speaking
on condition of anonymity, noted that he could not
think of a plausible scenario that would not result in
retaliation by the United States for the attack on the
Muscat Intercontinental Hotel.*

*"In the United States House of Representatives, Con-
gressman Parker Jay of California called for 'immediate and unrelenting attacks on the Islamic Republic of
Iran,' citing 'over two decades of extreme hostility toward the United States and a pattern of supporting terrorism that is malignant and pervasive.' In a
remarkable bipartisan response, over a hundred and
eighty Republicans and eighty-four Democrats joined
Parker in this resolution."*

The talking head continued, and Boleshari could feel himself becoming more and more enraged. One hundred and
thirty-four of his brothers slaughtered. Achmed knew that
he could kill twice that number of American sailors if he
was unleashed on the American Navy Base just a ten-minute
taxi ride from his hotel. What if he attacked on his own? He
certainly had enough gas to attack a ship and also conduct
the planned attack in Horton Plaza.

What would they do? Condemn him? He thought not. No,
he would forever be a hero of the Islamic Republic, honored
and revered for his determination and his bravery in taking
the fight to the United States in a way that retaliated most
directly for the heinous attack on the brave men on *Sabalan*
and *Alborz*. He closed his eyes and envisioned these American sailors dying as they tried to find their way off their
ship, trapped in a steel casket.

As part of his training, he had been on many United
States military bases. It was easy to gain access—very easy.
The Americans were prideful above all else, conducting

tours of their ships, which they opened to the general public. One needed neither a pass nor special permission. Over and above that, their security, such that it was, was a sieve. Vendors, pizza delivery men, contractors selling everything from soap to bombs, Federal Express, United Parcel Service, the list went on and on. Achmed felt himself getting more and more worked up over the possibility.

He flicked off the television, knowing that whatever he missed on CNN would be played again and again, and packed those things that were important in his knapsack. Pausing only a moment to pray, he dashed out of his room and down the two flights of steps, emptying him out on Market Street on the fringes of San Diego's Gaslamp District. He hailed the first taxi that he saw.

"Where to, buddy?" said the driver as Achmed scrambled into the backseat, carefully cradling his knapsack.

"San Diego Naval Station."

81

ANNE SAT ALONE IN EXAM ROOM TWO IN *CARL VINSON*'s sick bay, reflecting on the last several hours.

The interview with and examination by the ship's Senior Medical Officer, Captain Roger Joyce, came first. Anne asked him several times why she was being examined, but the SMO was evasive, saying only that "her chain of command was concerned about her." That was code for the fact that they thought she was going off the deep end. She kept her responses professional, but curt. Finally, after a very thorough examination—more comprehensive than Anne had ever received on an aviation flight physical—Anne asked if he had found anything wrong. He said no.

* * *

Then Lieutenant Commander Cummings grilled her.

". . . so Lieutenant, as you were saying, you don't know why you are down here in sick bay."

"No, I really don't, Commander. Maybe you could enlighten me," Anne responded. Once she saw her welcoming committee in sick bay, instincts that had been honed at the Naval Academy took over, and she decided to play hard ball. She wouldn't volunteer any information.

"Well, it seems that your chain of command is very concerned about you, Lieutenant O'Connor, or may I call you Anne?"

"You can call me anything that you want, Doc. Why is my chain of command 'concerned' about me?"

Cummings was not anticipating this hostile response and was thrown a bit off balance. Still, he knew that he could maintain the upper hand with any patient.

"Well, *Anne*, it seems that they note, first of all, that you have been under incredible stress—"

"All of us have, Doc. In case you haven't noticed, we're about to thump up on a pretty big local bully. If you think I'm the only one stressed, you must not get out much!" she replied, then instantly regretted that she had come on that strong.

"Well, yes, Anne, I know that many people onboard, especially you pilots, are under a lot of stress. Of course, not everyone has witnessed their roommate and best friend die in a fiery crash right before their eyes."

"No they haven't, Doc, but you know what, I was checked out by your buddies down here right after that and given an up chit. They didn't think that I had a problem getting over it."

"No, they didn't at that time. But subsequently, you asked to be pulled off the flight schedule before beginning your first hop back. Could it have been because you had second thoughts about getting back into the cockpit?"

"No, *Doc*, it couldn't have been for that reason, but it *could* be because we have an assassin loose on the ship getting ready to take out Admiral Robinson!"

"Oh, that story," he replied.

"What do you mean, 'oh that story'?"

"I mean this idea that Lieutenant Holden is some sort of assassin is just a fantasy."

"A fantasy? Try this, Doc, why don't you go to his stateroom and read the e-mails that he's received—the ones telling him to kill Admiral Robinson."

"We have read all his e-mails."

"And?"

"And, *Anne*, there are absolutely no e-mails saying anything incriminating. None. The XO himself checked, and then had one of the ship's computer experts check. There is nothing of the sort on there."

"What do you mean? I saw them. They were there on his machine."

"They are not there now—if they ever were."

"If they ever were! I'm tired of this bullshit Doc, I'm outta here!"

"You will stay right here, *Lieutenant*. That's an order!"

Anne wasn't prepared for that. She seethed, her eyes burning through him.

"What we did find were some letters from someone named Laura. Does that ring a bell?"

"Laura? No. That doesn't mean anything. What is that supposed to mean?" Anne knew that she was sounding defensive. It was hard not to, though.

"Well, Anne, it seems that Laura may be Lieutenant Holden's steady girlfriend—his *very* steady girlfriend. There were some intimate things in her e-mails that might upset someone else who was *seeing* him."

"Seeing him? You think that I'm *seeing* Holden?"

"Anne, it's nothing to be ashamed of. You are both young, independent people. There's no crime in seeing someone. You two have been seen in many places about the ship. It isn't something that needs to be a secret. It's only a problem if you let relationships get in the way of your good judgment," he said soothingly.

"There is no f-ing relationship Doc. What planet are you on? This is just some BS that you're making up."

"No, Anne, it's not. All right. You say that you did not read any of this woman's e-mails and you are not trying to retaliate against Holden out of jealousy. Good. Now convince me that this is true and convince me that there is evidence enough to believe your story."

"There *were* e-mails there!" said Anne in semi-desperation. "Why else would I tell all of this to my exec?"

"Well, Anne, you see, that's the part that we're having a little trouble with too. Now, I believe you, I really do," he lied, "but DCAG says that he saw you having lunch with Holden after you were in his stateroom but before you went down to your ready room. He says you were in a corner of Wardroom 1 having a very private conversation. . . ." Cummings let his voice trail off, inviting Anne to jump in.

Damnit, she thought. That was the part she hadn't told CAG. Now what was she going to do?

"OK, Doc, look, I don't have control of who goes where or who does what on this boat, OK? I was trying to collect my thoughts and Holden just showed up. I thought that it would look suspicious if I told him he couldn't join me."

"Well it might," replied Cummings.

The interview went on for at least another hour, Cummings always seeming to agree with her, seeming to be on her side. Anne was wary but found herself revealing more than she wanted to to him. Finally he said:

"Well, Lieutenant O'Connor. That about wraps it up unless there is anything else you want to share with me."

"This guy Holden is an assassin and you guys need to stop him. Now let me out of here and let's get on with it."

"Oh, I don't think that you will be going just yet. The CAG flight surgeon needs to see you first—and I need to file my report."

"Your report? Well, what is *your report* going to say, Doc?"

"I'm afraid that is privileged information, Lieutenant," he said as he quickly left the room, leaving Anne stunned and speechless.

Anne was left alone in the exam room for another ten minutes as her mind went into overdrive. Finally, Commander Alex Fitzgerald entered.

"Hello, Anne," he said, his tone friendly, his expression understanding.

"Hello, Doc," she replied. "You all have me outnumbered today. Am I pretty close to getting out of here?" The ten minutes alone had given her time to plan her strategy; be friendly and upbeat and act as normal as possible.

"Well, yes, we have conferred and I am about to release you. I am going to ask you if you would go ahead and sit on the bench for a few days—no flying—and just to make it official I need to give you a grounding chit."

"Fine Doc, fine," she replied, gathering herself up to leave.

"Anne, this means no flying, of course, but it also means that you need to return down here in two to three days for a reexamination. We want you to be back in the air as much as you do, but, well, I must tell you that Doctor Cummings's report is, well, troubling. I am giving you the benefit of the doubt and giving you a few days to work things out in your own mind."

Anne had known Commander Fitzgerald for over a year and genuinely liked him. But now he was telling her, albeit in the kindest and most gentle way, that she was not right mentally! That damn worm Cummings had worked his psycho-babble on the CAG flight surgeon, and he had bought it.

Anne made her decision. These men not only didn't believe anything that she said but, worse, they were now treating her as if she needed to be handled. This was beyond belief. Years of being a team player had socialized her to go along to get along, to believe in the system. Now the system was cashiering her! Anne decided to quit the team and take matters into her own hands.

"OK, Doc. I get it and I agree with you. I just need a few more days to get over things. I will come back in a couple of days so you can let me get flying again," she said cheerfully as she hopped off the table.

"Good, Anne, I think that will be best for all concerned," replied Fitzgerald, apparently happy she would do as they wanted.

But as Anne hurried out of sick bay and bounded up the four ladders to the O-3 level, she was already planning her mission and how to enlist the help of one other person.

82

GEORGE SAMPSON WAS BECOMING ACCUSTOMED TO people closing his door after entering his tiny office. Now it was CAG.

"George, there is something that we need to talk about: one of our JOs just told me the wildest tale that I've ever heard in my career." He went on to report Anne's accusation and his assessment that she had made the whole thing up.

"Damn, Wizard, that is quite a tale. You don't think that this O'Connor is going to do something crazy, do you?"

"No. After meeting with the other docs, she had a good session with my CAG flight surgeon."

"And no evidence supports her?"

"None. As a precaution, I even talked to the ship's skipper. We are going to have some of his master-at-arms people watch Holden. Very discreetly, of course, on the one-in-a-thousand chance that, in fact, there is something to what O'Connor is saying. But COS, believe me, there is nothing there. The only reason that I'm even telling you this is just to keep you filled in."

George Sampson reflected a moment. "But what if she is right?" he replied. "What if Holden really is after the admiral?"

"COS—"

"Even if it is a 'one-in-a-thousand' chance," he interrupted, "we have an obligation to protect the admiral."

The COS was a pretty good guy, CAG told himself, but he was a typical Blackshoe, overreacting to any stimulus. Now he was sorry that he had told him anything.

"I said that Craig has his guys watching Holden. If he is

some kind of agent—and I think that is really a stretch—we'll see what he's up to—"

George Sampson interrupted him again. "But you may not be able to stop him in time. My primary responsibility is to the admiral. Look, we'll do it discreetly, but I'm going to have the staff protect the admiral at all costs."

"All right, George, you do what you need to do. We'll do our best to do our mission."

"Are you certain that there's no way that we can lock up this Holden? At least until we check things out?"

"We can do anything that we want to, George. But without any evidence—I think watching him will be a good compromise."

"All right, Wizard, but you'd better watch him closely."

"You can count on it."

Forty frames aft, Anne O'Connor sat in the Blue Wolf Ready Room watching the strike brief on SITE TV. She had not spoken to any of her squadronmates since returning from sick bay. She was too embarrassed. She knew that it had to be common knowledge that she was marched down to medical by her skipper and exec—such things were impossible to keep secret in a close-knit community like this. How could she face any of her fellow warriors?

Anne was specifically watching Brian McDonald. She knew he would have time to talk with her now. There was time built in between the overall strike brief, which Brian had just delivered to all ready rooms via SITE TV, and the element briefs for the various types of aircraft. Anne arrived outside of CVIC confident that Brian would be out soon. In just a few minutes, he appeared.

"Brian, I have got to talk with you. This is a matter of life or death!"

"Anne, what do you mean?"

"Brian, please listen to me. We need to talk and talk now!"

Brian saw the look of desperation on her face and the sound of panic in her voice. "Fine, fine. Look, let's go to your stateroom, OK?"

"Yeah, come on."

Brian followed her down the starboard side passageway, totally perplexed.

In her stateroom, he tried to be patient. "I can tell you're upset. What's the problem?"

"Brian, I'm going to give you the short version. Rick Holden is an assassin. My best guess is that he's an Iranian agent. He is going to kill Admiral Robinson. We have to stop him and we have to stop him now!"

Brian couldn't find any words to respond.

"I know what you're thinking, Brian, but here's where I am coming from on this. . . ." With that, she related the entire story of what she knew and how she came to know it, sparing neither time nor detail. Brian took it all in and, to his credit, let her go through the entire story. When she was finished, he spoke.

"Anne, I don't know what to say. This is serious. Deadly serious. We have to get the ship to do something to stop him. They need to arrest him!"

"Brian, have you heard anything that I've said? I've tried to go there but I got shot down. They are not going to do a thing. Nothing. I'm on my own and I need your help."

"Anne, you're talking about taking the law into your own hands. What are you going to do when you confront him? Do you think that he's going to just stop? Anne, I . . . I don't know what you want me to do."

"You can help me stop him!"

"Anne . . . the strike . . . I mean, I launch in just a few hours . . . Anne, you know what this strike means to our overall campaign. . . ."

"Brian, I hate to get you involved, but you are the only one I can trust. I almost wound up in a straightjacket when I tried this on my chain of command. I'm not going to go there again. Look, if you can't help me, I am going to go after him alone."

"Anne, I can't let you do that."

"Then help me, Brian. Please."

Brian looked deep into her eyes. He couldn't say no to her.

"Anne, I've got to tell DCAG that he needs to drop me

off the schedule. You know that this is going to raise a ton of questions. I'll cover as best I can, but what we're doing may come out."

"And if we don't stop Rick, our admiral may be dead. What do you think will happen to the strikes then?"

"I know, I know. Look, just let me get out of this as gracefully as I can for now. Once I do that, we can come up with a plan to stop Rick. Anne, are you—"

She cut him off as gently as she could. "Brian, I am really, really sure. I read the e-mails. You have got to believe me on this."

"I do, Anne. I really do."

George Sampson found Admiral Robinson in TFCC and asked him if he and CAG could have a private moment with him in his cabin. The admiral was reluctant to leave TFCC, but finally followed them into his cabin.

"OK, COS, what's so damned important that it can't wait?"

George Sampson poured out the entire story to Heater Robinson and watched the admiral's eyes grow wide with disbelief.

83

JOE WILLARD WAS NOW SPENDING VIRTUALLY EVERY minute in *Jefferson City*'s control room as his boat continued to work its way north. He was in the most dangerous waters of the Gulf now. Using extraordinary care and double- and triple-checking his navigation, he picked his way through the shallows southwest and west of Farsi Island, then past the numerous oil wells northwest of that island.

He put his best conning officer and his full sea and anchor detail team on watch as they entered the Lawhah Oil Field, an area containing a large number of oil wells, and was at a heightened state of alert as they entered the Fereydun Oil Field, containing even more oil wells. Willard knew that even incidental contact between his boat and one of these massive oil drilling structures could be catastrophic.

The captain had ordered the boat to slow to eight knots— a safer speed for picking his way through the maze of oil wells and also a better speed to give his passive sonar a chance to hear *Carl Vinson*'s powerful screws. This was tough water to operate in, shallow, a mixed gradient, nothing good about it at all. This was further complicated by the constant man-made noise put in the water—shipping of all kinds—but especially the constant mechanical noise put into the water by all of the machinery that operated on each oil well. Still, *Jefferson City*'s sonarmen were trained and ready to pick out the unique sound of a 100,000-ton aircraft carrier pushed through the water by four powerful screws.

"Officer of the Deck, Sonar, I have screw noises, bearing 335."

"Sonar, roger," replied the OOD. The OOD moved to the small nav table and consulted his chart just as the captain did. Bearing 335 pointed toward the massive offshore Sirus Oil Terminal, where the largest supertankers took on oil and began their journey to destinations in Europe, Asia, and North America. Joe Willard did not want to overreact to this contact; it might be the carrier or it might be one of these supertankers.

"Sonar, Captain. Give me a course recommendation as soon as you can."

"Aye, aye, Captain," replied Petty Officer First Class David Green, manning the sonar stack. *Jefferson City* was heading on a course that did not optimize the ability of her towed array to hear contacts ahead of the boat. As sonar continued to refine the bearing they had, they would pick a course for the boat to turn to unmask the towed array—the long line of hydrophones that were towed behind the boat—and allow it to have a clear listening path to the contact, without interference from *Jefferson City*'s hull.

Joe Willard consulted with his OOD and ops officer, Lieutenant Commander Walt Capen. They were in the tactical thick of things and needed to bring their combined three decades of experience and expertise to bear at this precise moment.

"Walt, what's your assessment?"

"I looked at sonar's display, Captain, it looks like it could be the carrier. I think that once sonar gives us a new course to steer, we'll be able to resolve any ambiguity."

"I agree. Do you concur that we need to go to battle stations?"

"I do, Captain."

"So do I. Pass the word. No announcements. Quiet ship."

"Aye, aye, Captain," Capen replied. The captain was taking every possible precaution. Announcing battle stations over the sub's general announcing system would have just put more noise in the water.

"Officer of the Deck, Sonar. Sonar recommends coming to course 070 to clear the towed array and give us a clear bearing angle."

"Officer of the Deck, aye," replied Capen as he moved to the chart table again. Huddled with the captain, they decided that this would be a safe course that would keep them clear of oil wells and give them sufficient maneuvering room.

"Make it so," Joe Willard said.

Jefferson City came around slowly, gliding through the water at eight knots, her sonar techs straining to hear the contact more clearly. The boat had been settled on her new course for about ten minutes when the call came from sonar.

"Officer of the Deck, Sonar. Sir, this definitely sounds like an aircraft carrier. I'm picking up her screws really well now."

"What do you estimate the range to be?" said Joe Willard, suddenly appearing behind Petty Officer Green in the tight confines of his stacks.

"Captain, our environmental programs estimate that the maximum range allowing us to hear a carrier in these waters is about eighteen thousand to twenty thousand yards—that's absolute max, Captain, and that's if she's making twenty knots or so. Based on how faint this signal is, and the fact that we've just been hearing it for a short while, I'd estimate that it is around the fifteen thousand yard range right now."

"Roger, fifteen thousand yards. Continue to refine the bearing," replied Willard.

"Aye, Captain, contact now bears 328 degrees."

In their attempts to unmask the towed array and resolve the contact, the captain and his team were actually moving the sub away from *Carl Vinson* on a tangent. Willard knew that he would soon have to alter course to the north and close the contact. He would continue this tactical dance for a short time longer to refine the tactical picture.

Throughout *Jefferson City*, every man tensed at his station. They were as honed and ready as they could possibly be. The captain had listened to the COB and had asked the chain of command to reconfirm that they were to attack *Carl Vinson*. Their skipper had paid for that—receiving a curt reply from Admiral Deutermann instructing him to not only carry out his mission but also to stop questioning his orders. Still, they knew that he had tried. That was good enough for them.

"Captain, screw noise is getting fainter, it sounds like the carrier is moving away from us sir."

"Roger, bearing now?"

"Bearing 325 degrees, Captain. Noise is getting fainter."

It was crunch time. Joe Willard needed to decide now. Close the contact rapidly or continue to maneuver carefully and set up for a time when he was certain that the carrier would run south again. He knew that the prevailing wind was typically from the northwest, and he guessed that *Carl Vinson* was probably launching and recovering aircraft at this moment.

"Officer of the Deck, come left, steer course 325. Make your depth sixty feet. Prepare to raise the scope."

That order electrified the control room. At fifteen thousand yards and opening, they were too far for a torpedo shot, so his crew knew instantly that the captain wanted to ensure that this contact was indeed the carrier before making an attack.

Slowly, *Jefferson City* turned to her ordered course and

came to periscope depth. Once the boat was stabilized, the captain gave the order.

The number one periscope came up rapidly, but the captain was already on it as it locked up into place. He scanned the horizon in all directions. Satisfied that there were no contacts close by and no threats to his boat, he looked in the direction that sonar had reported the noise—325 degrees.

The damn visibility in the Gulf was as poor as it typically was. He strained his eyes, looking toward the horizon, trying to make out the carrier. He saw haze and thought he might be seeing a contact, but he couldn't be sure.

"Officer of the Deck, have a look."

Walt Capen stepped up to the periscope and looked. Nothing. He too stepped back. Then he stepped forward again. Still nothing . . . no . . . there might be.

"Officer of the Deck, Sonar, sounds are getting fainter, sir, I'm starting to lose contact."

"Officer of the Deck, aye," Capen responded. "Captain, there might be something out there. I can't be sure. Look out here at 330, sir."

As Joe Willard stepped up to the scope again, Lieutenant Tiny Baker and Lieutenant Dave Wallstadt piloted their Hornets back toward *Carl Vinson*, high above *Jefferson City*. They had just been part of a simulated strike mission against the Iranian naval base at Bandar Abbas.

"Tiny! Dave," he said over their squadron common frequency.

"Go Dave."

"Tiny, it's the damnedest thing, but I think I just saw a sub periscope down there."

"Where?"

"Just passed below us."

"Another look?"

"Roger, we'd better."

Tiny, flying lead, broke left, and Dave followed on his wing. Their nav systems were tight, and soon they reversed the course they had taken to the carrier.

"I'm looking, Dave."

Wallstadt clicked his mike twice in acknowledgement.

Both pilots scanned the water three thousand feet below them. Nothing. Then Tiny saw it.

"Dave, you're right. Down there. One o'clock low. It looks like a periscope feather," the small wake of white water that a periscope made as the sub drove through the water with the scope raised. "Let's drop down to angels one to have a closer look."

Both pilots chopped their power and put their Hornets into a gradual descent as they began a shallow turn to arc around the periscope at 1,000 feet and keep it in their field of view. They began to circle around it, keeping far enough away to make a gentle arc.

"Dave, you got any doubts?"

"None, Tiny. I've seen one or two before in exercises. That's the real deal."

"I got it. I'm calling strike and reporting it."

"Roger, let's head back now, my fuel's getting near red line."

With that, they banked back toward the northwest toward *Carl Vinson*.

"Strike, Stinger 304 and flight."

"Go ahead 304."

"Strike, we've just passed over a periscope. We confirmed it by reversing course and flying over it a second time. Stinger 307 confirms it also. We are on *Carl Vinson*'s 150 for eight point two miles. Returning to ship."

"Stinger 304, confirm a periscope!"

"Affirmative, Strike. A periscope. We are certain of that."

"Roger, 304, we'll pass it."

Aboard *Jefferson City*, neither Joe Willard nor his officer of the deck could make out anything definite on the horizon. They were so intent on looking down the bearing line that they did not notice the Hornets overhead. The captain knew that they needed to close the contact if they were to have any assurance that it was, in fact, *Carl Vinson*.

"Down scope."

The number one scope dropped rapidly and locked in its down position.

"Make your depth one hundred seventy feet. Increase speed to twenty knots."

Jefferson City would put more noise in the water at this speed. But Joe Willard had made his decision. He was going after his target.

In *Carl Vinson's* CDC, OS1 Sanders turned to his chief.

"I just got a report from one of the Hornets returning to the ship. He says he saw a periscope."

"Yeah, and I'm captain of this ship," replied Chief Brewer, his voice dripping with sarcasm. How many times before had these flyboys sent them a bogus report?

"Chief, he said that both he and his wingman saw it and that they flew back over it a second time to be sure."

"Where is it?"

"About eight miles away, Chief."

"All right, tell the TAO, but don't get all excited. We're gonna find out it's a bogus report."

84

CARL VINSON'S TAO, LIEUTENANT ANDY BOGLE, MADE Petty Officer Sanders repeat his story twice. Only when his chief confirmed that Sanders was a crackerjack petty officer did the TAO finally believe that he had actually gotten his story straight, that the Hornet had sighted a sub periscope. After it sank in, Bogle began to issue orders in rapid-fire fashion.

"Fred, call Flag TAO on the Bogen. Tell 'em the whole story—slowly—make sure that they get it right."

"Wilco."

"Art, walk over to the SCC Module and tell them exactly what happened. I'm gonna call 'em over the Battle Group

Command net, but I want them to hear it from you, first."

"Chief Walton."

"Yes sir."

"That's got to be an Iranian Kilo out there. Go down to CVIC and find Commander Armstrong. They can get the latest imagery on Bandar Abbas. We've got to know what they have on the three Kilos."

"Wilco, Lieutenant," he replied.

Then Lieutenant Andy Bogle picked up the red phone—the Battle Group Command circuit that connected him to all the major players in the battle group.

"Xray Bravo, this is USS *Carl Vinson*. Aircraft from *Carl Vinson* have sighted a submarine periscope bearing 150, distance eight miles from the ship. Break. Xray Zulu, acknowledge."

Bogle had used the most abbreviated shorthand possible over the net, ensuring that the battle group commander—Xray Bravo—knew what was going on and that the officer who needed to take action—Xray Zulu, Commodore Hughes—heard the report and was going to report to the admiral that they did.

"This is Xray Zulu. Roger. Out."

Seconds later, his phone rang. It was the captain. After a brief exchange, he hung up.

"GENERAL QUARTERS, GENERAL QUARTERS, all hands man your battle stations. Go up and forward on the starboard side, down and aft on the port side. Expedite setting Zebra. Repeat, expedite setting Zebra. Hostile submarine in the area!"

Carl Vinson's crew needed no further motivation, and men and women moved with alacrity to set Zebra. Finally, the real thing!

As Andy Bogle had anticipated, Commodore Jim Hughes was soon standing next to him.

"TAO, I need aircraft at the datum."

"I've already alerted CAG, Commodore. We'll have to respot the deck to get you some ASW aircraft. First guy off the deck for you might be one of the HS-4 helos, 'cause we need to run downwind for a while so we have plenty of sea room for the next launch."

"OK, I need to brief the admiral in person," he added as he turned to leave CDC.

Commodore Jim Hughes entered TFCC and immediately felt the level of intensity in that space envelop him. The admiral turned toward him.

"Submarine, Commodore?"

"Yes sir, Admiral, it appears so. I need to get some ASW aircraft over datum immediately and check this out. In the meantime, Admiral, I heard that we intend to turn downwind as soon as we catch these last few aircraft. I'd like to request that we don't do that. I want to put as much distance between us and the sub as I can."

"Commodore, look at the JMCIS display. Ship is going to run out of sea room in just a few miles. There's nowhere to go up here and you know all too well how quickly the water shallows."

"Yes sir, I know Admiral, but—"

"Look, Jim, just get with those pilots when they land and get the rest of their story. Then get some ASW aircraft prepped, keep 'em light, 'cause I'm gonna launch 'em downwind. I need to get some sea room to get ready to launch my strikes. I don't have a choice."

Jim Hughes could understand the admiral's skepticism. False sub sightings were an unfortunate fact of life in any naval operation. Add the fact that everyone was springloaded to attack the Islamic Republic and that the Iranians had used their Kilos aggressively in their naval exercises, and it was understandable that people could "see" a submarine that wasn't there.

"Aye, aye, sir," he replied. "We'll find it and pin it down."

"I'm counting on you, Commodore."

After Jim Hughes left, the chief of staff spoke to the admiral in a hushed whisper.

"Admiral, would you please reconsider moving from TFCC? We really think that if this assassin is going to move against you, it's going to be here. We can protect you far better if we keep moving, sir."

"We've had this discussion before, COS. I've got confidence that you all can 'protect' me right here—that is, if I need 'protecting'—and I'm not certain that I really do. No, we're about to conduct the strikes that we trained for and that our National Command Authorities have directed us to conduct. My place is right here."

Sampson tried to trust that the admiral knew what he was doing.

85

SEVERAL HOURS LATER, AS OPERATION MOUNTAIN DIvide moved forward, the admiral said to his battle watch captain, Commander Pete Turville, "Let's recap where we are, Pete."

"Admiral, we've launched the SH-60F and he's proceeding to the datum under Xray Zulu's control. We've got an S-3 on cat 4 and another one arming and manning up and getting ready to move to the cats. That should give the commodore enough assets to see if this is really a sub or not."

"OK, so the commodore's covered on that score. How's the timeline for our strikes?"

"H-hour is two hours and twenty-five minutes from now, Admiral. We'll turn back into the wind and set up to launch well before that, just to get in the proper position."

"How about our TLAM shooters?"

"All units are in their launch baskets. Missiles are spun up. They'll execute on command at H-hour."

"Fine, any loose ends?"

"Nothing major, Admiral. COPS watch tells us that they're doing a little reshuffle on the flight deck. Seems that the strike leader for the first attack on Bushehr, Lieutenant Commander McDonald, dropped out of the flight at the last minute. CAG has put the alternate strike leader in charge of the mission. No real impact on the strike, just strange that a strike lead would drop out at the last moment."

"Sure is. But we can't focus on that right now. We need to get as much info as we can about what's going on at the sub datum."

"Wilco, Admiral," he replied.

Heater Robinson continued to monitor the action and was content with what was happening. He was broken out of his musing as the chief of staff and the captain suddenly appeared in TFCC. Having the captain leave the bridge at such a critical juncture was highly unusual, and the admiral's antennae went up.

George Sampson began, "Captain and I wondered if we could drag you out of TFCC for a few moments. There's something urgent we need to tell you."

"Do we have to do this now, COS? We're just getting spooled up for the strikes."

"It can't wait, Admiral," interjected Craig Vandegrift. The admiral's antennae went up even higher as he walked with them toward his cabin.

"All right, what's so damned important that it can't wait?" he said to them both, not trying to hide the annoyance in his voice.

"Admiral, it's about this alleged assassin," Craig Vandegrift began.

"Not that again? Captain, I've just been through this with the chief of staff and CAG. What is this, the tag team approach?"

"No Admiral, it's not. We have just come up with some new information. Sir, as you know, we had all but discounted this story by Lieutenant O'Connor—she just has too many reasons to be confused, or worse, have an ax to grind—"

"Fine, I know all that," he interrupted.

"Yes sir, Admiral, but just as a precaution, we have been following this Lieutenant Holden as best we can to try to determine if he is doing anything suspicious. We haven't put a close tail on him—definitely didn't want to alert him to our efforts—but we've maintained a sense of where he's been and what he's done."

"All right, so far you haven't told me anything that makes it worth me leaving TFCC when we're about to conduct the biggest military operation this country has conducted in over a decade!"

"Yes sir," responded the captain. "Admiral, we know that he visited the work area the SEALs use on the hangar bay. We talked to the petty officer who handles their weapons— Vickers is his name—and he told us that Holden drew two service weapons earlier today, a nine millimeter and a 45-caliber. Said that he was going to practice firing them so he could get ready for his CSAR mission."

"So far I don't see anything all that alarming," said the admiral, his impatience burning through.

"Admiral. We don't let folks just shoot weapons any time they want. We schedule FAM fires for our folks who use weapons—the MAAs, the SEALs and others several times a week. There are definite times that we do this. There hasn't been a FAM fire time scheduled since Holden drew these weapons. The rules are really clear; you draw your weapon right before a FAM fire, use it, then return it right away. When you go on a mission, you do the same thing. You don't just check out two weapons and keep them indefinitely."

"No, well, has anyone asked this Holden what he thinks he's doing? These SEALs are all kind of independent operators anyway."

"No, we didn't want to alert him," replied the captain. "The other disturbing thing, Admiral, is that he checked out an awful lot of ammo—several boxes, and he checked out a walkie-talkie."

"That much ammo? Why would he want a walkie-talkie?"

"We're not certain, Admiral. But it stands to reason that he might be interested in knowing your exact movements. Admiral, we have got to at least complicate his efforts to reach you, sir."

"All right, but we are going to have to keep me in constant contact with TFCC. We must stay on our timeline to launch strikes. And if we are this sure that Holden is an assassin, Captain, don't you want your men to try to pick him up?"

"I do, Admiral. I talked it over with my JAG and with my master-at-arms. I think that I can find a reasonable pretense to bring him in—just the fact that he's violated ship's policy on weapons should be enough to at least bring him down to the master-at-arms office for questioning. He might just reveal what he's doing with that minor nudge. But while we do that, Admiral, we have to keep you moving."

"All right. You two have made your point. I'll agree to move, but you have to come up with a way to keep me in contact with TFCC."

"Admiral, we can use the walkie-talkies on a discreet channel. Unless Holden keeps changing freqs, he'll never land on yours. We won't do or say anything over them that would reveal your location. All we'll do is provide a constant flow, keeping you informed of the strike preparations. You can give us permission to proceed whenever you're ready."

"Let's do it that way then," Heater Robinson replied. "COS, I want you here in TFCC the entire time. You're second in command. Captain, I know that you need to be on the bridge. I'll travel with just flag lieutenant, master chief, and one or two other people on the staff who can handle a weapon. Who do you recommend, COS?"

"Admiral, air ops is pretty good with weapons, I think that he shot pistol at the academy."

"Then grab him—one guy with a gun should be enough—and get him down to the armory ASAP so the captain can have his people issue him a weapon. Then I also want ops o with me while I'm on the move. I think that the four of us can keep a low enough profile and not attract any undue attention."

"Yes sir, we'll make that happen," responded the chief of staff, relieved.

Four decks below, Rick Holden had planned his mission as best he knew how. He was confident that he could use his walkie-talkie to keep up to speed on where the admiral was. He knew that the admiral rarely went anywhere outside of the Blue Tile Area and that if he stayed on the fringes of that area he would eventually be able to close in on him.

Rick had not worked this out precisely—there were just too many possibilities—but his initial thought was that if he could either catch the admiral in transit to or from the Flag Bridge, or catch him alone in his stateroom, he would have a good chance of disabling him. Once he subdued him, it got a bit murkier for Rick. He did not want to kill the man. His hope was that once he subdued him he could tell him that the entire chain of command had found him out. After he had done that, the admiral might just admit what he was doing. At a minimum, though, keeping him from launching the strikes was the key.

This business with the submarine was puzzling to him. With the ship at General Quarters, his movements would be restricted somewhat—more hatches to open and close—but that wouldn't be a major factor. He didn't put any credence in the report, mainly because false alarms were almost legendary. What he needed to focus on was stopping the admiral from launching strikes. He knew that he didn't have any more than an hour or two to accomplish his mission. He left the safety of the corner of the hangar bay and looked for a ladder to begin to climb.

On the O-3 level, Anne and Brian knew that they needed to find Rick and find him fast. On a ship as large as an aircraft carrier, this effort initially seemed all but impossible, but as it sunk in that their mission was to keep Rick from attacking the admiral, they began to realize that if they simply kept themselves close enough to Heater Robinson to intercept Rick, they should have a good chance of protecting the admiral. But they had to be careful not to let Admiral Robinson or anyone on his staff know they were doing this: Anne had come close enough to being locked up herself as it was.

The sub alert puzzled Anne, too. It seemed inconceivable to her that an Iranian Kilo sub could have slipped out of

Bandar Abbas. The United States just had too many assets looking for these subs. She knew that her squadronmates were airborne now, looking for that Kilo sub, and they would find it.

"Anne, are we agreed on our plan?" asked Brian.

"I think so. We'll cycle through the Blue Tile Area every fifteen minutes or so, close to each other but not precisely together. Between the two of us, if Rick is there, we'll see him."

"Do you still want to make first contact?"

"I do, Brian. We have had an ongoing dialogue, and I think that it would be a lot more natural if I went up to him and started talking. Once I get him engaged, you can close in and help me stop him."

"We haven't really decided how we're going to do that, though," said Brian.

"I think that we might be a lot closer than we think. The thing that Rick thinks he has going for him is surprise. If he's confronted, and if we tell him that we all are on to him, he might just give it up right there."

"I suppose that's what we've got to count on, but if it starts to turn into an ugly confrontation, we—you—need to back away before things start to get out of control."

"I'll watch out for myself—you just take care of yourself, OK?"

"OK. Ready to move?"

"Yeah, let's go," said Anne. She led Brian aft.

86

SHIEKHOLESLAM WAS RECEIVING CALLS FROM VELAYATI several times a day as the crisis with the Americans continued to unfold. The latest report from the foreign minister convinced him it was time to act. There could be no doubt now that the Americans were preparing for an imminent attack. He wanted to ensure that Mejid and the others were absolutely ready to carry out their plans immediately after the pigs struck so that there would be no doubt in the Americans' minds that they were paying for their military striking the Islamic Republic.

He toyed with the idea of not contacting them—they were all young, and he did not want to confuse them with excessive communications. But he was so sure that they would have to act soon—perhaps within a few hours—that he wanted to be absolutely certain that they were ready. He decided to send them a short communication. He dialed the first number.

It was not yet dawn. Hala Karomi was sitting on the Metro a few minutes out of Union Station when his pager went off. Karomi took the pager off his belt and scrolled through the message once, then twice to be sure:

> HALA, YOU ARE TO BE ABSOLUTELY READY TO CARRY OUT YOUR MISSION IN THE NEXT FEW HOURS. WE WILL STRIKE AND WE WILL STRIKE HARD. READY YOUR AGENT AND BE PREPARED TO SET IT OFF. MY NEXT COMMUNICATION WILL BE ORDERS TO DO JUST THIS.

Hala Karomi looked at the pager with relief and satisfaction; relief that he was not ordered to carry out his attack right now—this foolish riding back and forth on the Metro had put him in the worst possible position to do that—but satisfaction that he was actually going to conduct his attack. As the train arrived at Union Station, he got off quickly to return to his hotel.

In New York and in San Diego, Mejid Homani and Achmed Boleshari received identical messages and felt a thrill similar to Karomi's.

87

CARL VINSON HAD BEEN AT GENERAL QUARTERS SINCE the original sub sighting, and the ship was "locked down" with very little movement about her decks. Passageways and ladders that were typically full of people coming and going were now virtually deserted as all of the carrier's officers, chiefs, and sailors were at their battle stations.

Dressed in his desert camouflage uniform, Rick Holden stood out on the hangar bay, but he counted on the fact that the crew was accustomed to SEALs being just about anywhere, and doing almost anything, to make his movements transparent to them. He knew that once he began his assent to the ship's upper decks, dogged-down hatches or large, tight groups of sailors in damage control parties would impede his progress; therefore he looked for a way to get as close to the Blue Tile Area as possible. He walked aft in the hangar bay until he spotted it; the Captain's Ladder. Normally reserved just for the captain and the flag staff, he knew that it would be unused during GQ. He could make his way up the three decks via that ladder and be very close to where he thought he would find the admiral.

On the O-3 level, Brian and Anne were starting to exhaust

ways to patrol the Blue Tile Area without themselves looking suspicious. They both were in their flight suits, and both
had gone to the paraloft to grab their helmet bags, survival
vests, and other gear so that they both could look like pilots
en route to and from their ready rooms.

Now they were conferring in the passageway at the far-
aft end of the Blue Tile Area. It led outboard to the Captain's Ladder, going up to the flight deck. It was a good
vantage point, since they had a clear view of the starboard
side fore and aft passageway, as well as of the door to the
downward Captain's Ladder.

"Anne, I think that this MAA is getting awfully suspicious
of our movements back and forth. We'd better go around
the port side for a while."

"I agree," she replied. "Maybe we don't need to cycle
back and forth so often. One way we can do this is to split
up and one of us can watch each end of the passageway.
There's no way he could get by us then."

Brian reflected. That might put Anne in jeopardy if she
ended up having to confront Rick alone. He opted for a
safer course. "No, I think that we should stick together."

Rick undogged the hatch and began to work his way up the
three ladders. For a ship housing almost five thousand people, the ladderwell was eerily quiet. Rick put his hand on
the weapon in his belt—it was there and he was ready. He
whipped his arm behind his back and quickly felt for the
other one. It was there too.

Brian and Anne were ready to cycle back to the other side
of the Blue Tile Area when the door leading to the downward Captain's Ladder opened. Only a half-dozen feet away,
Anne was closest to it—right outside the Flag Material Office—while Brian was on the other side of a half-bulkhead
further inboard. She riveted her attention on the door. Suddenly, Rick emerged.

"Anne!" he almost shouted. He was more startled than
she was. "What are you doing here?"

She quickly regained her composure. "Oh, just going

down to my ready room," she lied. "I didn't think that I'd see you coming up from the hangar bay, thought that you'd be down in the HS-4 Ready Room getting ready for a CSAR event."

Anne was fencing now, trying to act as calm as possible, hoping that Rick didn't hear fear or alarm in her voice, hoping that he didn't hear her heart pounding. She needed to buy time until she could think what to do next.

"No, well, I mean, I am, just had to check with my guys down on the hangar bay. Headin' to the ready room now, actually."

Rick didn't like lying to Anne, that's why he had fended her off when she had tried to see him, figuring that avoiding her completely was the best idea. He had let his guard down when he'd sat with her over lunch in Wardroom 1, but the encounter with the MAA had shaken his confidence badly, and he had just lit on a familiar face. Now he needed her not to be a part of this. Someday, maybe, he would be able to explain it all to her.

"Well, yeah, I'm heading back to mine too. Want to walk there together?"

Anne knew that Brian was on the other side of the bulkhead. She didn't think that Rick saw him yet. Now, confronting him, the panic set in. They had not really thought this through beyond catching up with Rick. They really didn't have a plan. They just hoped he would stop doing what he was going to do. Now that plan seemed as weak as it actually was.

"No, I don't want to hold you up. I may go up toward CVIC for a minute, then head on back, actually," he said. He needed to extricate himself from her, and that was the only way he knew how to do it.

Anne knew that if he headed forward he would be that much closer to the admiral. Putting her hand gently on his arm, she tried to delay him.

"Gee Rick, I really thought you could give me a minute or two. Can't you just walk me back to my ready room and talk for just a minute? Honestly, it will be just a minute." Anne wasn't sure where she was going with this or what good it would do. She was just buying time. She kept her hand on his arm, even though he subtly pulled back a bit.

Rick was insistent. "Look, Anne, I'd like to talk, but I have something very important to do and I need to do it alone. You're just going to have to trust me on this." He gently pushed her hand away.

"Rick, I need just a minute."

"Sorry."

Anne wasn't getting anywhere with this tactic. Rick was almost at the bulkhead and would see Brian imminently. She swallowed hard and said, "I know what's up, Rick."

That stopped him.

She stepped carefully. "I know that sometimes people may ask you to do something. I know that it may not always be something that you want to do. I want you to know that if you don't want to do it, you don't have to."

Rick's mind was racing. What did she mean by all this? Was this just a general admonition, or was she focusing on something specific? Could she know anything about his mission?

"Anne, I'm not sure what you mean. Do you think that I have some sort of . . . of agenda?" he asked, choosing his words carefully.

"Rick, I just think that, well, people sometimes get put into positions that they don't want to get put into, and they make, well, poor decisions. But until you do something wrong there is no harm really done—not if you don't do something illegal—or worse." Anne was now sweating profusely, and she knew that she sounded rattled. At least he wasn't moving any longer, at least not for now.

"Anne, I'm not really exactly sure what you're talking about. Do you think that I'm doing something that I shouldn't be doing?"

"Rick, there's nothing you've done that can't be undone. You can turn back now. Just don't do this."

How could she know? He was close to Anne now, as she had subtly put her body between him and the hatch leading to where Brian still lay in wait. Anne's sweating made her scent stronger. That scent! Rick had smelled that before. In his stateroom!

"Do what, Anne?" Now he grabbed her arm.

"Rick, just don't do . . . do anything. You just need to think it through before you do anything." Anne twisted her arm, but Rick did not relax his grip.

"But what do you think that I'd do, Anne?"

"Ow, Rick, you're hurting me, stop!"

Suddenly, Brian rushed from behind the bulkhead.

"Let her go!" he commanded.

"You too?" Rick said, stepping back from Anne and looking right at Brian.

"It's over," Brian said.

"I don't think so. You're meddling in something too big for you to even know about. Back away!" Rick said as he moved toward the hatch that led toward TFCC.

Brian put his body in front of him. "I said that we're taking this up the chain. You're not going anywhere."

"Watch me." Rick pushed past Brian and made for the opening, but Brian threw himself in Rick's way. Rick grabbed him, and that was all it took. Both men were on each other in a full-scale assault. Fists doubled, they traded punches. At first, Brian held his own, but Rick started landing more and more blows as Brian staggered back. He was no longer trying to slip away now. Rick was trying to beat Brian into submission.

Brian found the wall behind him with his foot, however, and used it to launch himself at Rick, slamming his body against him, pinning him to the bulkhead. He heard the *crack* as Rick's head hit the steel.

Momentarily dazed, as Brian leaned his heavier weight on him, Rick slackened some, so Brian loosened his hold slightly, and that was all Rick needed. He spun around and pinned Brian against the same bulkhead and began hammering his fists into him, delivering body blow after body blow.

"You couldn't leave it alone, could you?" Rick gasped.

Anne's instincts took over. She hadn't been able to do much as Rick and Brian went toe-to-toe, but now she leaped on Rick's back, locking her left arm around his neck while hammering the right side of his immobilized head with her fist.

Having her on his back shocked Rick, but his adrenaline

was so high that as Brian started to slump down against the bulkhead, he wheeled and literally flung Anne against the opposite bulkhead. As he did, the pistol he held in the small of his back fell out and clattered to the deck. The blow almost knocked her out, and she lay slumped on the deck.

The combination of a few moments of relief from Rick's blows and seeing him fling Anne off of him like a rag doll let Brian reach deep down inside with renewed energy as he came at Rick. Now both of their blows were heavy as both men slammed each other, their primal instincts taking over.

Anne broke out of her daze and saw the gun on the deck, grabbing it. Rick saw her out of his peripheral vision and lunged at her, but Brian, with his last ounce of energy, grabbed Rick's leg, keeping him from reaching her.

"Run, Anne, run!" he shouted, and Anne, horror in her eyes, complied and scrambled away, heading back down the Captain's Ladder.

Brian bore the brunt of Rick losing one of his weapons and having one of his accusers get away. Rick slammed him repeatedly against the bulkhead.

Brian knew that he couldn't fight back much longer and finally wrapped his left arm around Rick's neck, holding on for all he was worth.

But Rick simply ripped Brian's arm away from him and threw him on the ground. Then he landed on him with both knees on both arms.

Snap.

Brian went suddenly cold as Rick's right knee snapped his arm right above the elbow. The excruciating pain caused him to lose all the fight he had in him, and he collapsed on the deck, panting.

Rick was focused on his mission, and the sight of another man in intense pain was not enough to deter him or even give him pause; it never had before. He just needed to ensure that Brian was no longer a threat. Rick looked around for a place to hide Brian. He didn't have to look far before he spotted the Captain's galley a few feet away. Rarely used when the ship was underway, the galley and the entire inport cabin area were sure to be deserted during GQ.

Rick opened the door, and, grabbing Brian by his good

arm, dragged him inside, down a narrow hallway and into the galley. He let Brian go, and he slumped helplessly to the deck. Ripping through the shelves in the galley pantry, Rick found a large roll of duct tape and began to bind Brian. Brian recovered enough of his composure to try to talk to him one last time as directly as he possibly could. There was no time to be coy.

"Rick, look, it's not too late to stop. You can't do what you plan to do to Admiral Robinson. Rick, don't you see, it's murder, pure and simple. The officers around the admiral will shoot you if you try to get close to him, and the Navy will execute you if you succeed."

"How did you know I was going to do this?" asked Rick as he continued to wrap the duct tape around Brian's feet. "Did Anne read my e-mails?"

"Yes, she did, but it's not her fault. She never intended to, but once she read them, what did you expect her to do?"

Rick saw no point in being coy with Brian either. The bond between two men who had just engaged in near-mortal combat wouldn't permit that.

"Listen, I'm not necessarily trying to kill Robinson, but I will if I have to. These strikes against Iranian bases that you all have been practicing—they are illegal."

Brian grimaced in pain as Rick moved his arms and bound them with duct tape. Rick didn't have any choice. Brian couldn't be allowed to get loose.

"The only strikes authorized are the strikes against the terrorist camps. The admiral is intent on starting his own war, and he's lied to everyone on the staff, everyone on the ship."

"I don't believe you. Why do you want to assassinate him?"

"Come on Brian, think! How hard would it be to get a 'foreign agent' into a Navy uniform? And don't you think that it's a little strange that no one has seen an execute order for these strikes—it's all verbal between Admiral Flowers and Admiral Robinson? Do you think that there is any other reason for the admiral to put the entire battle group into radio silence for this long? Add it up, Brian. One man has five thousand of you duped."

"Rick, no, you—" but Brian was cut off as Rick roughly wrapped the duct tape around his mouth. Brian struggled to continue to talk, but the duct tape was completely effective in cutting off any words.

That complete, Rick dragged Brian into the far reaches of the Captain's galley, laying him out in front of the reefer in the most out-of-the-way corner he could find. Brian struggled against the duct tape, if for no other reason than to show Rick that his spirit had not completely been broken. Rick turned off the galley lights and closed the door behind him.

Rick stood in the narrow passageway inside the captain's inport cabin, collecting his thoughts. Where had Anne run away to? Should he go after her or go after the admiral?

88

JEFFERSON CITY HAD LOST CONTACT WITH CARL VINSON as soon as Willard had turned his boat's bow toward it and increased speed to twenty knots.

At the navigation table, his exec, weapons officer, and navigator now all huddled over the chart table trying to come up with their best estimate of where the carrier might be as they waited for his sonar to pick it up again. But as they continued ahead, every instinct told Willard he was closing on the carrier.

Several miles south, Lieutenant Commander Bob Labuda was the pilot of Blue Wolf 706 and was scene of action commander at the datum that had been reported by the two Hornets. It had taken a while to get his Viking off the deck armed with a full sonobuoy load, but he had arrived at the datum ten minutes after the SH-60F. The helo had been dipping at the datum without success. With an active sonar range of only 4,000 yards it was doubtful that the helo would gain contact, but the Seahawk stayed at datum, dipping, then moving, then doing so again.

"Black Knight 612, Blue Wolf 706. Clear the area to the east, I say again, clear the area to the east. I will be sowing a buoy field right around datum."

"Wilco, 706," said Lieutenant Scott Fielder as he banked the helo hard to clear as expeditiously as possible.

Labuda then began the highly scripted process of seeding the ocean with DIFAR sonobuoys. As he captured each fly-to-point on his multipurpose display, another DIFAR spit out of the belly of the Viking. Designed with geometric precision based on water conditions, type of target, and type of tactics used, the pattern was constructed to afford the maximum possibility of catching a submarine.

Labuda's buoy field was two-thirds complete when he received a call from his playmate.

"Blue Wolf 706, this is Blue Wolf 701."

"Roger, 701. At datum, angels four. Request you remain at angels six until I complete my buoy field."

"Wilco, 706. Blue Wolf 701 has full sonobuoy loadout and two torps, repeat, two torps."

"Roger 701, no contact yet, will keep you filled in."

"Roger, 706."

The three aircraft continued working the datum. When the buoy field was complete, Blue Wolf 706 had a total of thirty-six highly accurate DIFAR sonobuoys in the water. That completed, Labuda called Black Knight 612 back in to continue dipping, and divided the area into eastern and western halves. Labuda took the western portion and 701 took the eastern portion. In the back of each Viking, the sensor operators listened carefully to each DIFAR buoy in sequence, waiting to hear submarine noises. There were none.

Unbeknownst to the surface world, *Jefferson City* had cleared the datum—by miles. Thus Willard had no knowledge that he was being hunted himself.

His exec came up from the chart table and stood at the captain's side. "Captain, by our calculations we have been closing the carrier for some time. Our best estimates, if the ship hasn't turned or changed speed, is that we are now just under ten thousand yards away."

"Good estimate?" Willard asked, knowing the answer, but wanting to be doubly sure.

"Really solid, Captain. We even could be a little closer, Captain. We all agree that we should take a look."

"Roger, let's just keep driving for a little bit longer. I only want to have to take one look."

And although he didn't like his orders, once he sighted *Carl Vinson*, he would move in for the kill.

High above the water, Bob Labuda continued to direct the actions of the aircraft at the datum. They had been joined by Saberhawk 48, the SH-60B LAMPS helo off of *Shiloh*, as Commodore Hughes tried to put as many aircraft at the datum as possible. The buoy field, however, remained completely cold.

"Ninety-nine, this is 706. We're cold here, gonna move toward the carrier with our buoy fields. Blue Wolf 701, walk a pattern on a northerly heading from the datum. Put the first one in four thousand yards north of DIFAR 22, that's our most northerly buoy. Saberhawk 48, you put a sixteen-buoy field in just to the east of where 701 is sowing his. Black Knight 612, I want you to move north and west— make it six thousand yards and start to dip on a line toward the carrier."

After 701 and 612 rang in, the LAMPS helo crew said, "Saberhawk's got it. 706, we clear to do radar flooding?" They wanted to know if they could use their powerful APS-124 radar to search for a submarine periscope.

"Affirmative Saberhawk, 701 and 706 are using radar, periscope detection mode. You look with us."

"Roger."

Convinced that he had built the best tactical plan that he could, Labuda called back to Commodore Hughes.

"Xray Zulu, this is Blue Wolf 706. Datum is cold, repeat,

datum is cold. Moving buoy fields north toward carrier and having Black Knight dip in that direction also."

"Roger, 706, keep the press on."

"Officer of the Deck, make your speed five knots, make your depth sixty feet."

The OOD repeated the order back to the captain and then gave his orders to the diving officer and the helmsman. *Jefferson City* slowed and began her gradual ascent. Finally she was at depth and on speed.

"Up scope."

All eyes in the control room were on the captain, who popped the handles of the scope down and spun 360 degrees, ensuring that there were no contacts close by. Finally, he looked in a northerly direction.

"There it is! It's the carrier!" he shouted, not trying to hide his excitement. "Bearing 342 . . . range . . . eight thousand yards and opening. Mr. Capen, have a look!"

The captain stepped away, and the OOD stepped up to the eyepiece. After a few seconds he nodded to the captain, signaling that he agreed with his sighting.

"Downscope," ordered Joe Willard. "Make your depth one hundred feet, increase speed to fifteen knots."

"Blue Wolf 706, Saberhawk 48, radar sinker, radar sinker, bearing 350, range sixty-five hundred yards from my posit! Vectoring to the datum!"

The news electrified every aircraft. The LAMPS helo was working north and west as it had been ordered to do. If Saberhawk had actually seen a periscope, then the Kilo submarine was only a few miles from *Carl Vinson*. If the helo reported radar sinker, then the sub must have had its periscope up for only the briefest time—a classic attack profile for a submarine. Labuda knew that he needed to get to the sub fast.

"Saberhawk, roger, when you get to datum, I want you to put in a four buoy field right around datum, then put in the rest of your DIFAR on a line just north of that. Then I want you to clear the datum and move three miles to the east. You're carrying two torps, right?"

"Affirmative on the torps, we'll call as soon as we're clear."

"Roger, I'm at angels four now, maneuvering to come on top—break—Blue Wolf 701. As soon as Saberhawk reports clear, I want you to put a containment pattern around the new datum, then walk that pattern north."

"Roger, 706, I've got Saberhawk's datum entered in my system."

"Black Knight, I want you standing by to dip as soon as we get a buoy hot."

"Wilco."

"Roger. OK folks, we're not gonna lose this guy."

The aircraft went through their procedures, spitting a new round of sonobuoys, knowing that now that they had a fresh datum they would have a much higher probability of localizing and attacking the Kilo submarine that was after their carrier.

"All right. Suggestions?" said Joe Willard to his OOD and to the other officers standing in the Control Room.

"Captain, I recommend that we continue on this course for six to eight more minutes. At that point we'll be set up for a close shot on her screws, just like you wanted. Take one quick look through the scope when we get there and we'll have a perfect firing solution," responded Walt Capen.

"I agree," said his exec. "We've got it set up just right, Captain. Thus far I think that they're totally unaware that we're here. Looks like they're just worrying about flight ops."

"Blue Wolf 706, this is Saberhawk 48, hot contact, I say again, hot contact on DIFAR 13 and DIFAR 28. I say again, HOT CONTACT!"

89

ANNE DID NOT KNOW HOW LONG SHE HAD BEEN SIT-
ting in the Joint Air Operations Center, Rick's gun beside
her. It was dark inside the JAOC, save for the few computer
screens that had been left on as the people working on air
plans had scrambled out of the space when GQ was
sounded. A good place to collect her thoughts and herself.

What had Rick done to Brian? Had he killed him? She
couldn't live with the thought. Could she have done more?
She wanted to go back up to the O-3 level and see what had
become of him, but she couldn't. Not yet.

Thoughts of Brian and of how much he had done for her
came rushing back. From his first intervention at the Naval
Academy, to his continuing encouragement throughout her
career as a midshipman, as a flight student, and as a naval
aviator, to his agreeing to help her stop Rick and giving up
the most important mission he was ever going to fly; Anne
thought of how much she had depended on him and how
she had needed him. Now she had let him down and had
caused him to be beaten to a pulp—or worse.

But thoughts on what Brian had done for her and what
he would want her to do now filled her with sudden resolve.
Summoning up all the courage she could muster, she knew
she had to stop the Navy SEAL—and who knew what else—
herself.

Admiral Robinson stalked out of TFCC again and entered
his cabin, followed by CAG, the CO and XO of VS-35, and
his own chief of staff. He waited until the door closed behind
the chief of staff, then exploded.

"Chief of Staff, what is so goddamned important that you all have to drag me out of TFCC again!"

"Admiral, we have come up with some more information that bears directly on this Lieutenant Holden." He took Robinson's silence, not his glare, as a signal to continue. "While we have doubted Lieutenant O'Connor from the beginning, perhaps wrongly, we don't believe she's doubted herself at all. Because now she's missing."

"You don't think Holden killed her, do you?"

"No sir. We think that she might have gone after Holden herself."

"That changes things, Chief of Staff. That changes things a great deal," replied the admiral, then he left them behind and headed back into TFCC.

Anne figured that the admiral was probably in TFCC, especially since the ship was at GQ in response to the threat of attack by an Iranian Kilo submarine. The MAA stood outside the door to the admiral's cabin, but he wouldn't be in a position to stop Rick if he tried to get to the admiral while he was in TFCC. All Rick had to do was get into the War Room—he might even have the combination to the cipher lock—and once he was in there he had a clear path into TFCC. Once in TFCC, he would surprise the admiral and kill him. It was all too easy.

So how could she stop it? Anne figured that if she confronted Rick when he just came up to the Blue Tile Area, it might take him some time to get his bearings, observe what was going on around the O-3 level, come up with a definitive plan, and then go after the admiral. She counted on that time to allow her to catch up with him and stop him before he struck.

Or was he coming after her? She had his gun! Was it the only one he had? If it was, he could do nothing to the admiral until he got it back. Would he be looking for her to try to wrest it away from her? She finally decided that she couldn't count on his not having another gun and just wait for him to look for her. She had to go after him before he got to Admiral Robinson.

It occurred to Anne to check the gun that she had picked

up. She hadn't fired a weapon since plebe year at the Naval Academy, but she felt confident that she could handle it. She checked the clip. There was ammo enough for what she needed to do. This was the easy part. The other half of the equation was the hardest.

Could she actually do it? Could she pull the trigger and shoot another human being—even one with such evil intentions—in cold blood? When she got to this point, her blacks and whites turned to grays. She honestly didn't know what she would do. She hoped that when it came down to it her instincts would take over.

With that, she crept out of the JAOC.

90

MEJID HOMANI COULD ALMOST WALK FROM HIS HOTEL room to the United Nations in his sleep. It was good that he could. Keyed up, he slept fitfully when he did sleep at all. It was a half hour before dawn when the message to be ready appeared on his pager. The only way that he knew to be ready was to go to the United Nations and sit and wait for the final notification. Mejid rolled out of bed and went to the closet in his tiny hotel room. He unzipped the backpack. His agent was secure and ready for deployment.

First light was just breaking on Manhattan's Upper East Side as Mejid walked along on the nearly deserted streets, the only other signs of life an occasional jogger or the ubiquitous city garbage trucks. Mejid walked quickly, not just because he was focused on his mission but because he feared the New York streets. He had been sent here many months ago on a student visa and had been uncomfortable during his entire time here. He was happy that his mission would soon be over and that he would be able to return to his beloved Islamic Republic.

Mejid had never been to the United Nations this early and was surprised to find that the building was not yet open. He felt conspicuous standing outside of the building until the grand concourse finally opened. Resolved to be as close as he could be and as ready as he could be, Mejid Homani walked across the street and entered a small coffee shop, selecting a spot where he could watch the entry of the concourse. He wanted to be one of the first to enter.

In Washington, Hala Karomi did not have the same leisurely time that Mejid had in New York. Near panic when his pager went off, he fidgeted nervously as the Metro approached Union Station. Why had he gotten into this idiotic habit of riding the train? Sure, it calmed his nerves, but now he was separated from his agent, and Shiekholeslam might instruct him to carry out his attacks at any time. The instructions on his page—"TO BE ABSOLUTELY READY TO CARRY OUT YOUR MISSION"—resonated in his brain until his head ached. Now, at the moment of truth, this stupid diversion might cause him to fail to carry out his mission. Shiekholeslam would never forgive him. In that instant, Hala Karomi decided that if he failed he would take his own life.

He bolted off the train as soon as it entered Union Station, pushing past the commuters who already crowded the train. As it was in New York, it was before dawn in Washington and the train was full of earnest government employees who had to be at their desks before their lower-level bosses arrived, so that they could be prepared for the middle-level bosses and bureaucrats, so they in turn could be prepared for the upper-level political appointees and career civil servants who came in early as it was to start their stress-filled, twelve-hour days. Hala wondered why the Americans inflicted such stress on themselves—like Mejid, he could not wait to leave this cursed country.

Hala crossed the overpass and headed down the stairs to wait for the train that would take him the three stops back to his hotel room. He would then have to rush up to his room, grab his agent, return to the Metro, jump on an even more crowded train, and return to the spot he had selected to release his agent. Hala Karomi prayed as fervently as he ever had that he could make it back to Union Station in time.

In San Diego, Achmed Boleshari bolted from a deep sleep as his pager went off. It was only three-thirty in the morning there. Like Mejid, he was not in a huge rush; he knew that there would be no shoppers in Horton Plaza at this early hour of the morning. He would just have to check his agent, dress, and then prepare himself to wait.

He hoped that Shiekholeslam understood the time difference between San Diego and Iran. If Shiekholeslam gave his next order in just an hour, Achmed would be releasing his agent in a deserted plaza. Surely Shiekholeslam did not intend this. But then how long should he wait? For the first group of morning workers? Until the midmorning shoppers began to fill up the mall? Until late in the afternoon, when the plaza would be busiest? Until the evening, when he would be most inconspicuous placing the agent in the spot that he had selected? Prior to coming here Shiekholeslam had emphasized how critical timing was to every operation and how important it was to carry out his instructions to the letter of the law. Now those two considerations collided.

Achmed was really questioning his courage, and that thought pained him. He had reconciled what he intended to do—at least explored the possibility of deploying his agent on a U.S. Navy ship at the San Diego Naval Station. He had thought it all through during the short taxi ride down to the station's front gate. But when he'd gotten to the gate, he'd been surprised. Instead of the lone sentry that usually manned the gate—typically a very junior petty officer who could be talked into admitting almost anyone—a full security force, armed gate sentries, military working dogs, and Marines in full battle dress had confronted Achmed. A large sign announced that the base was in "THREATCON ALPHA."

Achmed had instructed the taxi driver to make a U-turn

and deposit him on Harbor Drive near the front gate. He had watched the action from across the street for some time—long enough to convince himself that entry would be extremely difficult. After over an hour of agonizing, he walked north along Harbor Drive, back toward his hotel. Few taxis had come by, and none would have stopped for a young man with a dark complexion walking alone in this part of town in the middle of the night.

Now he cursed that decision. If he had been bolder, he would be in position, hiding somewhere on that sprawling base, and would deploy his agent on one of the large American ships at the piers there. No, that would not happen. Instead, he might be ordered to deploy his agent in an empty or nearly empty shopping mall. Achmed was becoming increasingly frustrated as he trudged along the dark downtown streets, the only other humans there the street people who slept in the doorways of the stores along Market Street and the area near Horton Plaza.

91

"ADMIRAL, WE'RE READY TO MOVE."

"All right. Let's go," replied Heater Robinson. His staff could tell by the tone of his voice and his body language that he did not want to do this, that he felt that his place was in TFCC directing the strikes. They had finally convinced him to move—that Anne might be hunting Rick seemed good evidence for the actual existence of Rick's e-mails—but he still didn't like the fact that he had to.

"Chief of Staff, I want to know absolutely everything that happens. Work with the captain and CAG to try to move the strikes earlier, the sooner we get them moving the better."

"Will do, Admiral," replied George Sampson.

"I want to know about this damned submarine, too. So far I see a lot of excitement, but all anybody has is passive contact. That's not good enough to make me certain that there is one. Has anyone debriefed those Hornet pilots who said they saw a periscope?"

"Yes sir, Admiral," replied Carl Mullen. "Intel officer says that they got debriefed thoroughly down in CVIC. Rocky says that they are sure of what they saw."

"Has Rocky got any imagery of the base at Bandar Abbas to confirm that there's a Kilo missing?"

"No, not yet, he's hoping to get something really soon, Admiral."

"Yeah, and I'm hoping to find a Mercedes in my driveway when I get back home," he replied.

"Yes sir," was all that his operations officer could reply.

Less than twenty feet away, Rick Holden moved furtively through the O-3 level port side passageway. Normally a busy thoroughfare, it was deserted now that GQ was set. No battle stations here. There wasn't a hint of another person as far as he looked, either fore or aft.

Rick thought about using the back entrance to TFCC. The hatch was closed during GQ. Was it locked from the inside? He was fairly certain that the admiral was in TFCC. But if he weren't, he would have tipped his hand. It was one thing for a SEAL to come into the War Room, wander into TFCC, be told that he really wasn't supposed to be there, and leave. It was another to come in the back door of TFCC—an entrance normally used by watchstanders—during GQ.

Rick rejected that idea. He might confront and surprise the admiral, or he might just run into a group of his staff and then be stuck in TFCC vainly trying to explain what he was doing there. He decided that he would continue forward, cross over on the athwartships passageway just aft of Strike Operations, and then approach the Blue Tile Area from the other direction.

Rick stole carefully across the passageway, his heart pounding. One person walking through the passageway could foil his plan. What would he say if he was asked what he was doing there? He couldn't begin to think of a believable story. Would he have to take that person out the same way he intended to take Admiral Robinson out? How far was this going to go?

Admiral Robinson breezed out of TFCC and through the War Room, followed by a few of his staff. He now believed that there was someone out to cause him harm, his guilt over disobeying orders a convincing bit of evidence itself. He hadn't had a spare moment to reflect and therefore did not have a clear idea in his own mind just how this assassin happened to be on his ship, or how he intended to do it. For now, he was willing to follow the wishes of his staff and stay mobile until the strikes were completed.

"We ready to move?" he asked his ops officer.

"Yes sir, Admiral. Master-at-Arms outside the door will proceed us. We'll head up to the Flag Bridge, it's absolutely secure. The MAA has a side arm and air ops has one too. He'll follow behind us."

"I've got your walkie-talkie to keep us in contact with TFCC, Admiral," said Mike Lumme.

"All right, make sure you do," replied the admiral. "Let's get on with it, then."

Carl Mullen opened the door of the admiral's cabin and signaled the MAA to start moving aft. He followed, letting Mike Lumme go behind him, followed by the admiral. Carl came next, followed by air ops. Commander Bob Fischer, who packed his nine millimeter, brought up the rear.

92

THE WORDS "HOT CONTACT" ELECTRIFIED EVERY CREW member in the four aircraft at datum, as well as everyone in the Sea Combat Commander Module. Jim Hughes knew that Bob Labuda had good control of the aircraft at datum and was utilizing each of them to the maximum extent of their capabilities, but he wanted to ensure that he was doing everything that he could back aboard *Carl Vinson* to optimize the chances of catching the Kilo submarine.

The commodore reflected on the fact that "optimizing his chances" sounded too antiseptic for what they were really about. Their battle group had bloodied, and had been bloodied by, Iran. Well over a hundred Iranian sailors had met their deaths in these very waters less than twenty-four hours ago in the duel between *Shiloh* and the two Iranian frigates. Now he had every reason to believe that this Kilo submarine intended to send *Carl Vinson* to the bottom of the ocean. They could not let the sub get a decent shot off   not at this range.

He energized his watch team to extract more information from the aircraft at the datum. Soon, they learned that the new datum was seven thousand yards astern of the carrier and that the submarine was on a course directly for the carrier at a speed somewhere near fifteen knots. It was up to the four aircraft now.

They were flying close enough together for each to see all the others. Although Bob Labuda had directed altitude separation between each aircraft, every pilot had to take on the additional responsibility of not colliding with one of his playmates. In the intense action surrounding a submarine prosecution, such accidents were far too common as aircrews often got overfocused on the tactical problem and ignored basic flying rules.

Bob Labuda had flown over—"on-topped"—DIFAR 28, one of the hot buoys and made that the anchor of his tactical picture. From his perch at four thousand feet, he directed the actions of the other aircraft.

"Blue Wolf 701, take angels three, mark on top DIFAR 28 and lay a barrier north of it, three thousand yard spacing."

"Roger, 706."

"Saberhawk, keep to the west while 701 spits his buoys. Fly MAD trapping circles after that and let's see if we can get him nailed."

"Wilco, 706. Will run 'em at four hundred feet, OK."

Labuda wanted the LAMPS helo to use his MAD for precise localization of the sub. The MAD, or magnetic anomaly detector device, was a towed body streamed behind the helo on a two-hundred-foot-long cable. When the towed body, which was approximately the size of a small missile, detected an anomaly in the earth's magnetic field for that location— an anomaly caused by a metal object such as a submarine— the crew in the helicopter received an alert. Subsequent passes over the same location would reconfirm a submarine's exact location in preparation for a torpedo attack.

While Saberhawk 48 deployed its towed body, Labuda continued to issue instructions.

"Black Knight 612, stay about two miles to the east of datum. As soon as we get clearance from Xray Zulu we'll bring you in to dip. When you do, I want you to dip right on the contact. I mean, right on him."

"Roger, 706," replied the crew of the HS-4 helo. Thus far, Labuda was conducting passive tracking of the sub, trying not to alert the Kilo to the fact that there were aircraft prosecuting him. Once his location was fairly well refined, and a precise location was determined for a torpedo attack, Labuda would ask the commodore for "hammer"—authorization to use active, pinging sonobuoys as well as the highly accurate dipping sonar carried by the HS-4 SH-60F. Events would move quickly then. Once the active sensors were deployed, he knew that the Kilo would become evasive.

As Blue Wolf 701 spit out more and more passive sonobuoys, the other aircraft at datum continued to update the submarine's location based on the continuously refined passive track. All the aircraft continued to zero in on the Kilo's location, and Bob Labuda passed this information back to the Zulu module. They were coming closer and closer to gaining an attack solution on the submarine.

Joe Willard continued to press toward *Carl Vinson*. At fifteen knots, his passive sensors had to contend with so much own-ship's noise that they did not pick up the sounds of the passive sonobuoys hitting the water and deploying their long hydrophone array cable below them.

Jefferson City was as ready as he could make the boat for this attack. He had trained these men for the last year and a half and knew that once they got him in position to fire his torpedoes, they would find their mark in the carrier's huge screws.

Blue Wolf 701 completed spitting her passive sonobuoys. Labuda ordered Saberhawk 48 toward the datum and into the action.

"Saberhawk 48, Blue Wolf 706, looks like we've got a pretty good track, how are you holding him?"

"Got a well-defined track, 706, should be no problem getting a MAD."

"Roger, proceed to datum, 48."

Lieutenant Pete Howe banked his SH-60B helo and headed toward the datum as his copilot and ATO in the left seat, Lieutenant Frank Meyers, continued to refine the sub's track. The workload was intense inside the helo as they prepared to pinpoint the location of the sub in preparation for a torpedo attack.

"How's the track looking, Frank?" Howe asked.

"We've got this guy nailed, Pete, fly-to-point is coming up!"

"Roger, I'll home in on that. Senso," he said to his anti-submarine sensor operator, Petty Officer Carl White, in the back of the aircraft, "as soon as you get a MAD sing it out. We don't want to lose this guy."

"Wilco, sir," replied McCray.

This was the most intense flying that any of them had ever experienced. Nowhere in their training had they ever encountered anything like this. Although Howe was a "second-cruise" pilot, he had only been an aircraft commander for four months. He could feel the adrenaline rushing through his body.

"One mile to fly-to-point, Pete."

"Roger, gonna nail this sucker," Howe replied as he pointed the nose of the helo at the datum. High above him, the two Vikings continued to circle and, to the east, the SH-60F remained ready to pounce on the sub once Howe and his crew got the first MAD contact.

As they approached the datum, the Seahawk crew let their situational awareness break down for a moment. Totally focused on getting to datum and getting a MADMAN, Howe neglected to engage his radar altimeter hold on his automatic flight control system—a system that would have held the helo at a steady four hundred feet. The SH-60B started to descend, slowly, almost imperceptibly, as Howe and Meyers remained task-overloaded and did not notice the gradual descent.

"Half-mile to fly-to-point."

"Got it, Frank. How far is the HS-4 bird?"

"He's about a mile off, ready to come in when we get a few MADs. Once he dips and gets solid active contact, they'll call us in for an attack."

"I'm ready, buddy."

Howe and Meyers were thinking ahead of the problem, which was good. What was not good was that they were still descending slowly.

"Captain!"

"What, sonar?"

"Sir, just heard a loud noise on the conformal array. Very close, sounds like something dropping into the water."

"Confirm."

"I'm certain sir. A loud splash. It's a little hard to make out, going as fast as we are, sir, but it definitely was something dropped right into the water, close aboard."

Joe Willard instantly knew aircraft were out there hunting him—and he had been detected. He didn't have time to wonder why or agonize over what to do. He just needed to press his attack—an attack that had suddenly become more urgent.

"What was that?" shouted Pete Howe as a tug seemed to jerk his aircraft backwards. As it did, Howe quickly scanned his instruments, looking for signs of engine failure or a gearbox problem.

"Oh shit!" said Frank Meyers, looking at his altimeter, but immediately knowing what it was. "We just lost the MAD towed body. Shit, Pete, we just dragged it through the water and it snapped off!"

"Blue Wolf 706, Saberhawk 48. We just lost our towed body. Repeat, we just lost our towed body!"

Bob Labuda cursed to himself. They would have to go active sooner than he wanted to.

"Roger 48, clear to the north, no further than a half-mile. Break. Ninety-nine, Saberhawk has lost his MAD, we're gonna try to go active. Break. Black Knight 612, proceed to datum, I say again, proceed to datum."

"Wiloo, 706."

"Xray Zulu, Blue Wolf 706, request hammer, I say again, request hammer."

Commodore Jim Hughes took the radio himself. He had heard the first call about the LAMPS helo losing the MAD and anticipated that Labuda's next alternative had to be active sensors. The Kilo was just fifty-five hundred yards behind the carrier now; there was no advantage in trying to remain passive. They had to go active, localize, and attack him now.

"Blue Wolf 706, you are cleared to release active buoys. Repeat, you are cleared to release active buoys."

"Roger, Xray Zulu. Request authorization to drop torpedoes when we have him localized."

"You've got it, 706."

Permission to conduct a torpedo attack was normally issued only after a contact had been localized with active buoys and sonars and after some deliberation. The problem was moving too fast for that. Jim Hughes needed to get this sub before it got the carrier.

"Blue Wolf 706, you have torpedo release, repeat, you have torpedo release," Hughes shouted. He knew that once they went active, the sub might go evasive, or knowing that it was located, might decide to attack right away. The next few minutes would be crucial.

Once they heard the torpedo release call, the crew of Black Knight 612 did not wait for further instructions for Blue Wolf 706. Performing a maneuver they had practiced scores of times, they descended rapidly from five hundred feet and arrived in a hover at sixty feet right on the best datum that they had, based on the passive sonobuoy track.

Joe Willard considered his options.

"Navigator, what's your estimated distance to the carrier?"

"Unless she's picked up speed, Captain, inside of six thousand yards, maybe less than five thousand."

"Weps, how do you feel about a torp shot from here?"

"Would like to get a little closer, Captain, but we can take it from here."

"We'll hit the screws?"

"Yes sir, based on the stern aspect of the carrier that we've seen. I think that—"

"CAPTAIN, SONAR, I HAVE ACTIVE SONAR CLOSE ABOARD. SOUNDS LIKE A DIPPER SIR. SOUNDS LIKE A DIPPER!"

Now there was no doubt. The hunters knew that they were there, and worse, had them precisely located. There was not more time to discuss options or weigh alternatives. They had two choices: run or shoot.

It took several *pings* before the sensor operator in the back of Black Knight 612 had solid contact on the submarine.

"Pilot, Senso, I've got him. I've got him! Bearing 035, twelve hundred yards, down doppler!"

"Blue Wolf 706, Black Knight 612, solid contact on my

ball. Bearing 035, twelve hundred yards from my posit, down doppler."

Bob Labuda instantly assessed the tactical situation. The contact that 612 had was close, close enough to convince him that they really had the sub nailed. Down doppler meant that the sub was moving away from the place where the helo was dipping—toward the carrier. Before long, the HS helo would lose contact as the sub slipped out of range of its dipping sonar. The helo could break dip, get closer, and dip again in an attempt to get and maintain an even more refined solution, or he could hope that the dipping helo would hold contact long enough to vector another aircraft with torpedoes on top of the contact to place its fish in the water. Labuda made his decision. He keyed the mike.

Aboard *Carl Vinson*, Jim Hughes knew that, in addition to the aircraft prosecuting the datum, the carrier had one other weapon to escape from the submarine—speed. He did not feel that he needed to consult with the admiral's staff to give the aircraft prosecuting the datum permission to use both active sensors and torpedoes; that was his job as the sea combat commander, but he did need to motivate them to use that speed. He picked up the Bogen phone and called TFCC.

"Flag TAO, sir," said Lieutenant Commander Harry Vance.

"This is the commodore, I need to speak with the admiral right now."

Clack, clack, clack. The first aircraft shot down the catapult.

"Sir, he's not here," replied Vance.

"Well, where is he?"

"Commodore, he is on the move. Chief of staff is here. Do you want to speak with him?" offered Vance.

"Absolutely!"

The harried TAO handed the Bogen phone to George Sampson.

"COS here, Commodore."

"George. This damned sub is just five or six thousand

yards astern. Aircraft are pounding him with active sonar and active buoys and are trying to get a torpedo shot off, but he may shoot soon. We have got to get the ship moving out to the north as fast as we can."

"Commodore, Admiral's not here now and he left explicit instructions to hold this course and speed. We're launching our strikes and you see how far north we are already. If we speed up we may run out of sea room before we get them all launched."

"George, if we don't outrun the sub, the aircraft that launch may not have a carrier to come home to!" shouted Jim Hughes.

"I know that, Jim. You've got four aircraft at datum pounding the hell out of him. I can't move the ship any faster, not unless I talk with the admiral."

"Well talk with him, damnit!" shouted the commodore, loudly enough that George Sampson pulled the Bogen phone away from his ear.

"All right, Jim, all right! I'll call you back!"

Clack, clack, clack. The second aircraft roared down the cat.

Jim Hughes slammed the Bogen phone down. He was powerless to do anything at his end. It was all up to the aircraft at datum.

"Get the admiral on the walkie-talkie," George Sampson said to the staff TAO, "and hurry up."

Joe Willard balanced his two options and found one wanting. He made his decision. "Slow to five knots."

The CO was not going to run. He was going to shoot.

"Sonar, we're slowing. I want you listening for all you're worth. As we slow, you get me a solid passive bearing on the carrier. We shoot on that bearing."

"Roger, skipper."

"OOD, I want two straight runners. Tubes one and three. Fire down the bearing line as soon as you have it. Carrier is going to be moving away from us rapidly, so I don't want any delay."

"Yes, Captain."

They all stood transfixed in the Control Room, waiting for *Jefferson City*'s speed to bleed off. Twelve knots, ten knots . . . the pinging of the dipping sonar echoed in their ears, as did the pinging of the active sonobuoys that Blue Wolf 701 was seeding ahead of them. Eight knots. Seven. The torpedo room reported that the number one and three tubes had been flooded.

"Sir, sonar has good contact on the carrier. Bearing 025. Very strong."

"OOD, fire down the bearing line!" shouted Joe Willard.

First one *whoosh*. The boat shuddered. Then another, as it shuddered again. The water slugs ejected the two huge Mk 48 torpedoes from their tubes. *Jefferson City*'s crew held on as the fish swam away.

"Officer of the Deck, let's get out of here," said the captain. "Let's turn smartly, speed up and go deep."

"Helmsman, come right to course 060. Increase speed to twenty-five knots. Make your depth one hundred fifty feet," said the OOD. Walt Capen had worked with Joe Willard long enough to know exactly what the captain wanted.

"TORPEDOES IN THE WATER, TORPEDOES IN THE WATER!" Flying at one thousand feet above the water, and dropping sonobuoys ahead of the contact, the crew of Blue Wolf 701 saw the torpedoes first and alerted the other aircraft at the datum. Already urgent, their need to get the sub multiplied exponentially.

Bob Labuda had already ordered Saberhawk 48 to close the contact held by Black Knight 612. In their SH-60B, Pete Howe and Frank Meyers bore down on the contact, ready to drop their deadly Mk 46 torpedoes.

"Drop 48, drop!" shouted Labuda, reinforcing the instructions he had already given them, but injecting a new sense of urgency.

"Fifteen seconds to fly-to-point," Frank Meyers shouted over the radio. Pete Howe just continued to bear down, following the number one needle on his compass, while Meyers held his finger over the torpedo release button on the center console.

"Torpedo away," said Meyers as Howe wrapped the Sea-hawk into a hard right turn and began to time the first fish. They would drop a second one as soon as the first had run out for the appropriate number of minutes.

93

THE DARK BLUE CURTAIN HANGING AT THE END OF the Blue Tile Area, which broke it from the athwartship passageway that Rick was standing in, gave him perfect cover to observe what was going on. He saw the MAA standing motionless in front of the door to the admiral's cabin, and he could see all the way up and down the fore and aft passageway. There had been no movement for ten minutes. Rick pondered his next move. He knew that strike aircraft were being launched and he did not have much time. The sound of the catapult shuttle was now incessant, with aircraft being launched less than a minute apart.

He had decided that if he circled around on the port side again he could approach the Blue Tile Area from the other direction and maybe, just maybe, bolt into the War Room before the MAA, who sometimes let himself step back into the tiny alcove closer to the door to the admiral's cabin, taking the entry door to the War Room out of his direct view. Rick had learned the combination to the War Room door from listening to staff members tell others who were new how to get in. Once in, he figured that he had a clear path to Admiral Robinson.

Rick was about to begin circling around when the MAA moved. Had he spotted him? He was about to beat a hasty retreat when he observed the MAA heading aft, away from him. Soon, other figures emerged from the admiral's cabin—the admiral, the aide, the ops officer, and another officer

Rick did not recognize. The entire group headed aft, and he saw them take a left turn at the end of the Blue Tile Area and head outboard toward the Captain's Ladder. As soon as the last person in the group turned the corner, Rick quickly set out after them. Now or never.

Anne O'Connor had reached the top of the Captain's Ladder, and she grabbed the handle of the blue door leading to the passageway that she had been in a short time earlier. She hesitated for a moment before opening it, then made herself turn the handle and push. She looked left and right. No one. She looked right again and then walked a few steps that way, into the passageway outside of the captain's galley. No Brian! Anne was elated. If Brian was not lying dead or wounded in this passageway, she hoped that it meant that he had escaped from Rick! For a moment, nothing else in the world mattered to Anne. She felt relief beyond words or comprehension. Now she could get on with her mission with her mind even more focused.

But where had Rick gone? She wasn't sure, but she thought that he might be moving toward TFCC. Anne walked the few steps to the fore and aft passageway. As she looked forward, she saw a group of people emerging from the admiral's cabin, with the MAA leading the way. What should she do? She didn't think that she wanted them to see her stalking around the Blue Tile Area with a weapon! Anne took a quick left and hid behind the dark blue curtain marking the aft limit of the Blue Tile Area, peeking through the narrow crack between the curtain and the bulkhead at the group of men moving toward her.

She recognized Admiral Robinson walking behind the MAA, followed by three other men—she thought that one of them was the admiral's aide. Anne pressed herself against the steel bulkhead, ensuring that they didn't see her. The men were moving quickly and purposefully. If they continued straight ahead beyond the curtain, they would be literally on top of her. She prayed as hard as she had ever prayed that they would turn left and not see her.

She heard the footsteps continue to come nearer. Her heart beat hard, the pounding drowning out her shallow breathing. Anne felt her hands turn clammy and her knees grow weak. Please, oh please, let them turn left. Anne had never wanted anything more in her life.

Ask and ye shall receive. She sensed the entourage turning left, probably going to the Flag Bridge to see the last of the strikers launch. Anne peered carefully through the crack to try to identify the last few people following the admiral as they passed to her right. As her eyes left the last man following the admiral, she let them drift back up the passageway. She soon saw another figure. It was Rick! He had found the admiral and was sneaking up behind him. He was going to follow him up to the Flag Bridge!

Anne flattened herself against the bulkhead in momentary panic. Thank God he hadn't seen her. She had only one recourse. She had to follow Rick. If the admiral wound up on the Flag Bridge and Rick caught up with him there, there was only one other way out—the back exit on the port side—and it was a tough door to get to. The admiral would be a sitting duck. Anne was sure now that Rick had a weapon; otherwise, he wouldn't be following the admiral.

Anne waited until she no longer heard his footsteps, then peered right around the curtain. He was gone. Now it was up to her to catch up with him and stop him before he shot the admiral. There was no more stalking, no more finesse, not even any more thinking. It just had to be a headlong rush to stop him and stop him now.

Anne gripped the forty-five caliber Hechler & Koch pistol tightly as she swung out from behind the curtain. No Rick. She wound her way cautiously around the narrow passageway, past Flag Material, past the Captain's galley, past the Signal's Exploitation Space, and finally up to the Captain's Ladder. She bounded up the ladder, then hesitated before she opened the door to the O-4 level. Rick might be there. She cracked the door open with her left hand and then pushed it open slightly further with her foot while she kept both hands on her weapon. Finally, opening it a quarter of the way, she peered out carefully. No Rick. She stepped out into this small passageway and walked by the dogged hatch leading to the flight deck and started up the next ladder. When she reached the top of that, she cracked open the door in the same fashion she had the previous one. Still no sign of life as she stepped out onto the O-5 level passageway.

Had she missed them? Why was she so sure that they were headed for the Flag Bridge? Anne was beset with self-doubt, but she determined to continue to head up the three remaining decks to the Flag Bridge. Maybe they were just outdistancing her. She decided to pick up the pace.

Anne turned the corner on the O-5 level and moved quickly up the next ladder. Halfway up she looked up and saw feet on the exposed ladder above her, the hint of a desert uniform stuffed into tan desert boots. It had to be Rick! That was exactly what he had been wearing when he'd confronted her in the passageway below! Now was the moment of truth; he was almost on the O-7 level, just one away from the Flag Bridge.

Still holding her weapon with two hands, Anne spun around in front of the Meteorology Office. She turned and quickly covered the few steps to the next ladder, starting up after Rick. When she was three steps up the ladder to the O-7 level, she brought her gun up into firing position and pointed it at Rick.

Her steps up the ladder must have been heavier than she thought, because as she got to the middle of the ladder, Rick turned around and looked at her. There was shock in his eyes as he looked at her, then at her gun. His eyes met hers, uncomprehending. Was she trying to stop him alone? This was madness. His weapon was still tucked in his belt. There was no way that he could draw it in time to shoot her before she could shoot him. Could he shoot her? Was his mission that crucial? Rick did not have time to think, just to react. He bolted away from Anne and spun around the passageway to head up the last ladder to the O-8 level.

Anne could do nothing but chase him. He was out of her sights before she even realized it. She bounded up the ladder and got ready to turn the corner—

WHAM. The sound was deafening as a shot rang out in the narrow, enclosed passageway. Anne heard a shout, then a loud clattering as Rick tumbled down the ladder toward her. Momentarily panicked, Anne ran down ladder after ladder and back toward the O-3 level. Her heart was beating faster again, but she was almost relieved—the admiral's men had stopped Rick—but her relief was short-lived as she heard the 1 MC blare, "Torpedo in the water, I say again, torpedo in the water astern, ship is maneuvering, stand by for heavy rolls!"

94

JOE WILLARD STOOD IN THE CONTROL ROOM WITH A stopwatch, listening to his two Mk 48 torpedoes run out, estimating the time of impact on the carrier. Willard knew that he could not stay around for follow-on shots—at least not until he shook his pursuers, and he was not sure that he would. Even though the Los Angeles Class submarine was one of the most advanced in the world, shaking a determined group of pursuers would not be easy.

He was maneuvering away from the datum using the best tactics he could come up with. Speed and depth were his allies now. The pinging by the helo sonar was getting less intense, they may have escaped the net—

"Captain, torpedo in the water, torpedo in the water," shouted the sonar watch supervisor. The call was the most dreaded that a submariner could hear. Now they were no longer the hunters—they were the hunted—and the aircraft above them had every intention of sending their boat to the bottom of the Arabian Gulf. Those thoughts would only confuse him. He had to get away from this torpedo.

"Activate countermeasures," he shouted to the OOD.

"Launch the Mk 2 torpedo decoy," the OOD ordered.

"Flank speed! Make your depth one hundred forty feet."

The other men in the control room stood transfixed. The water depth in this portion of the Arabian Gulf was only one hundred sixty feet. The captain was coming perilously close to bottoming the boat. And, at flank speed, it only took a momentary sticking of the diving planes to literally drive the boat into the mud—a watery grave they would never escape.

The crew knew what the captain was trying to do. He was trying to lure the torpedo to the bottom. If the torpedo homed in on them, it might not be able to pull out of its dive and might head straight into the bottom of the Gulf. That was his tactic—and it was a good one—but it put them all at tremendous risk. *Jefferson City* slowly pushed her speed above thirty knots and dove.

The stern lookout and a small group of sailors watched in horror as the two torpedoes, one leading the other by about a thousand yards, bore down on their ship. *Carl Vinson* was turning rapidly but was not gaining much speed, the skidding turn bleeding off much of the energy gained by the increase in torque of her four huge screws. The aft lookout talked rapidly into his sound-powered phones, trying in his shock and excitement to give as accurate a position as possible of both torpedoes.

"First one is at five o'clock, estimate less than one thousand yards, think that it's gonna be close."

On the bridge, the bos'n mate took the reports and relayed them as quickly as he could to the bridge watch team.

"First torp now moving through six o'clock," the lookout continued. "Think it's gonna pass just astern, not by much though."

There was a momentary pause.

"Second one is at six o'clock. It's running really close to the starboard side. This is gonna be really close!"

His reports now came in rapid-fire fashion. The bos'n mate on the bridge tried to report what he heard to the watch team just as he was hearing it.

"First torp missed. It missed. It's outbound!"

A five-second pause.

"Second torp is close aboard starboard side. Six o'clock. Six o'clock. It's gonna hit!"

*   *   *

Four miles away from *Carl Vinson*, *Jefferson City* had a torpedo on her tail as the OOD punched out countermeasures. The LAMPS helo had dropped a second torp two minutes after the first, and the sub's sonarmen heard the distinctive sound of a second set of screws.

WHAM. The Mk 46 torpedo struck *Jefferson City* in the after part of her sail. The shock wave literally knocked most of the sub's crewmen off their feet and caused the boat to suddenly become dark. Gear went flying, and alarms went off. There was confusion and terror throughout the boat. *Jefferson City*'s crew was stunned and dazed as they tried to get their bearings.

"Damage estimates," shouted the captain.

Reports started to stream in. As the shock of the torpedo strike started to wear off, the initial reports were encouraging. The boat still had propulsion, there was only relatively minor flooding, and most systems seemed to still be functioning. The captain leveled the boat at one hundred twenty-five feet but continued ahead at close to thirty knots.

"Torpedo in the water! Torpedo in the water!"

The shout by the sonar watch supervisor sent the crew of *Jefferson City* into overload. They had to evade this fish too.

"Activate countermeasures," shouted the OOD, not waiting to be prompted by the captain.

"Sir, countermeasures are completely expended."

"Sir, it's headed right for us. It's heading right for us!" shouted the after lookout as the torpedo continued to bear down on *Carl Vinson*. "It's inside of five hundred yards. It's gonna hit!"

The captain himself grabbed the 1 MC mike from the bos'n mate.

"Torpedo inbound. Torpedo inbound. All hands brace for shock. I say again, all hands brace—"

KABOOM! The huge Mk 48 torpedo hit *Carl Vinson*'s number one screw, throwing a huge plume of water skyward. The sound was transmitted throughout the ship as sailors were knocked off their feet, gear shattered, and lights blinked off and then on again.

*   *   *

"Hard right rudder," shouted the OOD as he tried one last tactic, putting a knuckle of water created by the boat's churning screw into the water to try to lure the torpedo away from the sub.

Jefferson City continued to turn as the high-pitched whir of the torpedo homed in on the boat.

WHAM! The second torpedo struck, but this time the jolt was much more severe, knocking men down so hard that some cried out in pain. Not far from the Control Room, Joe Willard heard water rushing into his boat. They had been hit and hit hard. He had only one choice to try to save his boat.

Emergency blow!

Slowly, *Jefferson City* rose, her role as a hunter finished, her crew desperately hoping that their boat could get to the surface of a gulf most had never seen before coming apart and sending them to depths all had often imagined.

Above the wave tops, the ASW aircraft knew that they had scored when they heard the underwater explosions. They didn't know how well they had done until they heard the transmission from Blue Wolf 701.

"Ninety-nine, Blue Wolf 701, sub is breaking the surface. I say again, sub is breaking the surface!"

There was a pause as all of the airmen watched, transfixed, as *Jefferson City* broke the surface. There was complete silence on the net until Bob Labuda all but shouted over it.

"It's not a Kilo. It's not a Kilo! It's a U.S. Los Angeles Class!"

95

ANNE HAD REACHED THE O-5 LEVEL WHEN SHE FELT the jolt of the torpedo hitting *Carl Vinson*. The huge ship shuddered, and Anne grabbed on to the ladder railing to keep from being toppled.

"Torpedo hit aft! Torpedo hit aft!" blared the 1 MC.

Anne continued to scamper down the ladder, not certain if Rick was really dead or just wounded by the admiral's men. Was he following her down? Were they following her down? If they saw her with that weapon, would they think that she was an assassin also working with Rick? She did not have time to debate the possibilities; she just needed to get away, and she continued down the ladder toward the O-3 level.

In the Captain's galley, Brain was still bound with duct tape. He had passed out from pain and exhaustion after the beating Rick had given him, and his broken arm was throbbing now. He lay there groggy—he had lost track of time. Then the torpedo explosion and the 1 MC announcements energized him, and he managed to pull himself up and stand against the counter in the Captain's galley.

He was confident that Rick was no longer nearby. Now his thoughts turned to getting out of this space and out of this predicament. Brian struggled with all his might against the duct tape, but Rick had bound him so well and so tightly—his feet were tight against each other and his wrists were bound together—that he had trouble moving at all.

He looked at the door. The push-in lock held it tightly shut. Sweating and straining, Brian retrieved a fork from a counter and picked at the lock with it. Finally he got the button to pop out. Halfway there. He slapped at the door handle with the back of his hand, trying to get it to turn. It wouldn't budge. He moved next to it and tried to roll the side of his body against it, getting it to turn. It was all to no avail. There was nothing that he could do to turn the handle to open the door. Out of frustration, he slammed his left shoulder against it. The metal door resonated with a heavy clang.

This might be his chance! The door made a loud enough sound when he hit it that it might attract someone's attention, as deserted as the passageways were during GQ. He continued to bang against the door, biting back the quickly mounting pain.

Anne made it down to the O-3 level unsure of what to do next. She did not hear Rick or any of the admiral's men following her, but she wanted to be sure. She parked herself at the bottom of the Captain's Ladder on the O-3 level, confident she would see who was coming through the door on the O-4 level in enough time to slip away, perhaps to the Module, before they saw her.

She had been waiting at the bottom of the ladder for just a few minutes and was becoming confident that no one was coming down after her when she heard a clanging. Something against metal. At first she discounted it. A carrier at sea had a cacophony of noises of all kinds that sometimes defied objective definition. She listened more carefully. It was a dull clanging of something against metal. It had a rhythm to it. A clang, a few seconds' wait, another clang, the same number of seconds, a clang again. Anne moved a few feet closer to the entrance to the Captain's Cabin. The noise got louder. Was it coming from inside?

Anne looked back at the Captain's Ladder. No one. She decided to crack open the door to the Captain's Cabin. The noise got louder. What was it? The type of sound and where it was coming from did not track for Anne at all. She opened the door wide and now heard the noise very clearly. It sounded like it was coming from the captain's galley. Anne called out.

"Who's there?"

The pounding increased in magnitude, and the noises

came much closer together. Was there someone trapped in the galley? Someone who had responded to her voice?

Anne moved quickly to open the door to the galley. She issued a warning first. "Whoever's in there, I'm coming in!" She heard scuffling inside. Rapid movement. She turned the handle and swung the door open. "BRIAN!" she heard herself cry out.

Near tears, she undid the duct tape, causing Brian to wince as she pulled hair from around his face and head.

"Brian, I'm so glad that you're OK. I thought . . . thought that he had killed you! I'm so glad that you're alive. I can't tell you—"

"Anne, I thought you were in trouble. Did he come after you? Where did you hide?"

Their mutual joy in finding each other alive and relatively intact overwhelmed both of them for a moment before Brian got down to the heart of the matter.

"Rick told me an incredible story as he was tying me up."

"I'm not sure I'd believe anything that he said," Anne said as she continued to unbind him.

"I wouldn't either, not earlier. I told him why we were after him; he looked shocked when I accused him of doing something wrong. He told me that the strikes against the Iranian bases are illegal. He said that the only strikes authorized were those against the terrorist camps. He told me that the higher echelons in the Pentagon and all around Washington think that Admiral Robinson wants to start his own war for some unknown reason. They don't know exactly why, he said, but that he had been ordered to stop him—to disable him if he could but to kill him if he had to."

"And you believed all this?" said Anne, trying to hide her skepticism.

"At first, no, but then I started to think. Why would he lie to me? I was going to be tied up and helpless. But I'll tell you Anne, these strikes have come together in a very strange way. There has been no execute order. It's all being done on the fly based on phone calls between Admiral Robinson and Admiral Flowers. No one on CAG's staff can contact their counterparts at Fifth Fleet to get any more information. Rick's story is starting to make sense to me."

"Look, Brian, Rick was after the admiral. I was after Rick and was about to catch him, but the admiral's men shot him. I don't know if he's dead or alive, I just got out of there as fast as I could."

"But what about the admiral? What about the strikes?" asked Brian.

Anne knew that Brian had been through a harrowing ordeal, and she didn't want to rub in just how wrong he was. Rick was an assassin—plain and simple.

"OK Brian, look. Let's take it a step at a time. Before I heard you, I was heading to the SCC Module to see what's going on with this Kilo that nailed us with the torpedo. Come over to the Module with me. Then we can figure what to do next."

Brian had no choice but to go along with her.

High above *Carl Vinson*, three-quarters of the strike aircraft were overhead the ship and already refueling from their mission tankers. The strike leads were dialoguing furiously with Strike, trying to decide whether to push with the aircraft they had in the air, or wait for *Carl Vinson* to pick up speed and launch her remaining aircraft. Miles away from *Carl Vinson*, each Tomahawk shooter began the countdown for their deadly missiles

---

96

TWENTY MILES WEST OF BUSHEHR NAVAL BASE, THE Iranian P-3 Orion flew its daily maritime patrol. Purchased from the United States during the shah's regime, and maintained for decades with parts obtained on the black market, the P-3 was the eyes and ears of the Islamic Republic over the Arabian Gulf. U.S. forces had become so accustomed to the daily "marpats" that they paid little attention to them.

Khalil Sadr had been a plane commander for only a few months. This was only his sixth marpat as plane commander. He was elated to be in command of the huge four-engine plane, but he felt incredibly vulnerable as he flew above the Gulf.

The Islamic Republic and the United States were at war. Nothing had been declared but, to Sadr, that meant nothing. Word of the sinking of one of their frigates and the disabling of the other by United States Navy ships had spread like wildfire. Now, the U.S. carrier was operating aggressively in the northern Gulf, flying what could only be mirror-image strikes in preparation for massive strikes against the Islamic Republic. Sadr's mission was to fly a profile that looked exactly like a "typical" marpat mission and alert his military headquarters if the carrier launched strikes.

Sadr was no fool. He knew that the Americans knew about these marpats—they probably knew their schedules as well as he did. He knew that if the Americans wanted to shoot him down they could do so in an instant, either with a missile from one of their AEGIS cruisers or with one of the fighters from *Carl Vinson*. Sadr continuously thought about possible escape routes and ways that he could flee over land before he was targeted and shot down.

He had been airborne for about a half hour when he noticed them. They had been gathering slowly but continuously, and now there were almost thirty that he could pick out—aircraft that seemed to be holding just over and slightly east of the American carrier. The Americans had never done this before, and not with this many aircraft! There could be no other reason for it—they were preparing a massive strike to attack the Islamic Republic! Khalil Sadr keyed his mike and made his report.

Headquarters following procedures, would then pass it as rapidly as possible to Tehran. It would reach the Office of the president, the foreign ministry, and the military headquarters nearly simultaneously, causing three different men to react in three completely different ways.

*   *   *

President Habibi listened impassively as his chief of staff reported the news. This is what Habibi had feared more than anything else—a massive air attack by American carrier jets. He knew that his nation's defenses were weak and that the American jets could pound his country day after day. In spite of the plans that others said they could put into effect, he was not sanguine that he had any way to really defend his nation.

Habibi railed against his own indecisiveness. He had told them he wanted to have a way to communicate with the American president. They had dragged their feet and offered all manner of excuses. Now he could wait no longer. He was going to make this happen.

Foreign Minister Ali Akbar Velayati smiled as he put the receiver back in its cradle. He knew that his country was about to suffer devastating attacks. That was unavoidable. He was confident about his country's ability to absorb the blows. After all, Saddam had been absorbing strikes by the United States for over a decade, and each time he'd come back stronger. His nation was at least as resilient as the Iraqi dictator's.

What the attacks did was give him license to carry out the final step of his plan. Oh, he would step away from it and deny responsibility, saying that it was that madman Shiekholeslam run amok, but it would achieve the goal that he had set out—punish the United States and make them leave the Arabian Gulf for good.

Velayati picked up the phone to call Shiekholeslam. Few words would need to be exchanged.

General Najafi had had a great deal of time to reflect on what he was about to do. It had been well over a half-century since the United States had let the nuclear genie out of the bottle. The so-called cold war between the American and Soviet empires had been about keeping that genie quiet. Now, he was going to be the one to unleash it.

The general reconciled what he was about to do with the urgent need to defend his country, a relatively small, peace-loving nation of only sixty million people about to be pummeled by the world's only superpower. How could anyone fault him for using whatever means he had to make these aggressors back off? Though there would undoubtedly be some minor nuclear fallout around the Gulf littoral, the fact that all the nations around the Gulf saw a United States Navy aircraft carrier mortally wounded and perhaps even sent to the bottom would more than make up for whatever negative factors accompanied this attack.

General Najafi phoned the base. The officer picked it up on the first ring. He assured the general that the plane would launch immediately.

97

COMMODORE JIM HUGHES AND HIS TEAM WERE WIND-ing down from the intense action of the ASW prosecution—from having their number-one crew hit and probably destroyed, although they retained manueverability and lost only a few knots speed and from the call by Bob Labuda that the submarine that they had successfully attacked was a U.S. Los Angeles Class boat. While the Commodore and his team were discussing all this, Anne and Brian staggered into the SCC Module.

They were an incredible sight. Anne was still cradling her weapon, and Brian was beaten bloody and clearly in pain. Though he tried not to, the commodore gaped at the pair. Anne finally broke the ice.

"Did I hear you correctly, sir? Did you say we were fired upon by one of our boats? How much damage is there? Aren't we going evasive any more?"

As taken aback by Anne's irrepressible presumption as by her and Brian's appearance, the commodore answered, "Yes, USS *Jefferson City*. Its skipper is Joe Willard, a solid,

solid, guy—I spent some time with him at the National War College—which makes this is all the more unbelievable."

"Perhaps he mistook us for an Iranian ship," Anne offered.

"Perhaps. It's the best I can figure. Otherwise, it's the biggest error in U.S. naval history. We'll know for sure in a few moments when he arrives."

Anne's mind started to put a number of disparate pieces together. They'd been attacked by a U.S. submarine—and by a sub skipper whom the commodore personally vouched for—but attacked in such a way as to only cripple *Carl Vinson*, not sink her. And Brian had been convinced by the story Rick had told him, a story that Anne had rejected out of hand—then.

"Commodore, I need to talk to that sub skipper now!"

Jim Hughes was further thrown off balance. He liked Anne, but his patience had its limits, he wasn't accustomed to taking orders from junior lieutenants. What's more, Anne hadn't begun to explain why she was carrying a weapon or why Brian looked the way he did.

"Well, Anne, he'll be here in ten minutes or so. We'll get him down here for a debrief and we can all begin to try to piece this together."

"Commodore, I need to talk with him now. There may not be time to wait to bring him back here. I really, really need to talk with him right now. I'll explain it all in a minute."

Commodore Jim Hughes had worked closely with Anne over the past year and considered himself a mentor. He trusted her instincts and was willing to accede to her wishes. But she had best be right.

"All right, let me talk to Black Knight first," he said.

Commodore Hughes slipped on the mike-headset that his watchstander handed him and called the HS-4 bird.

"Black Knight 612, this is Xray Zulu, over."

"Xray Zulu, Black Knight 612, roger, over."

"Black Knight, I need you to put on the sub's captain on the net for a moment."

"Roger Xray Zulu."

Within moments, Joe Willard was put on the line.

"Joe, this is Commodore Jim Hughes. We're vectoring *Shiloh* to assist you. She should be to your boat before long. Are any of your men hurt?"

Willard was surprised to hear the voice of someone he knew. "No sir, they're all basically OK. Some fellas got banged up a bit when we took your . . . ah . . . the torps, but nothing really serious. I saw *Shiloh* on the horizon when they lifted me off the boat. She should be there soon."

"All right, Joe. Look, you'll be onboard in a few minutes and you can tell me more then, but I've got one of our pilots here who wants to talk to you in the worst way. There's something going on here and I'm just going to let her talk to you. I'm putting Lieutenant O'Connor on."

"Skipper, can you hear me?" said Anne into the mike.

"Yes, I can."

"Sir, I know that there is a lot to sort out but I need to know why you were attacking *Carl Vinson*."

Joe Willard was concerned about what he should or shouldn't say over the radio. "Lieutenant, I think that maybe I'd better wait until I can see all of you and Commodore Hughes face to face, then I can—"

"Skipper, we can't wait for that. We are forming up strikes to devastate Iran. We have only minutes to stop the person who is orchestrating them—if you confirm for me what I think you are going to confirm."

He was too overwhelmed to argue. "The strikes are going now?"

"Yes, skipper, they are overhead getting ready to push."

Joe Willard lost any reluctance to talk to Anne. He poured out his whole story.

"Lieutenant, I don't know where you fit into this overall scheme of things, but I'm just going to lay it out for you and trust that you will pass it along to the right people."

"Fair enough, sir."

"I received tasking from COMSUBPAC several days ago ordering me to attack *Carl Vinson*. The orders were to disable the ship, not sink it, that's why I shot at the screws. The message said the battle group commander had decided to attack the Islamic Republic of Iran and that I needed to disable the carrier before this happened. The message was very unambiguous. I got another message shortly after that from the chief of naval operations, Admiral Cloward, himself confirming that this was my mission. . . ."

All eyes in the SCC Module were on Anne as she listened to Willard. She was the only one who could hear him, and they waited for her to tell them what the sub skipper was saying, but Anne just listened.

"Even with these two messages in hand, I still sent a message back to COMSUBPAC and asked for confirmation that this was my mission. I was told in no uncertain terms that it was. I still find it unbelievable, Lieutenant, that a flag officer would do something crazy like this. I really don't believe it."

"We'll ensure that you get a full brief when you get onboard, Skipper," said Anne. She ripped the mike off her head. That was all the confirmation she needed. Admiral Robinson *was* conducting completely unauthorized strikes against Iran. Rick had been on a righteous mission all along. And she and Brian had tried to stop him, perhaps even caused him to get shot.

Now Anne knew there was only one way to redeem herself.

"Come on, Brian," Anne said, pulling toward the door.

"O'Connor, what did you find out from Captain Willard?" asked the commodore, figuring that the least Anne could do would be to tell him that much.

"No time, Commodore," she replied as she turned the handle to the door. "Skipper will be aboard in a little bit and tell you the whole story—"

"But, wait—" Jim Hughes shouted as Anne and Brian departed. He now had more questions than he could deal with.

Anne steered Brian to the right as they moved aft in the passageway. They exited the Blue Tile Area and went by the same blue curtain that Anne had hidden behind earlier.

"Brian, you were right about Rick. That conversation with the sub skipper confirmed everything he told you. It seems incredible that the admiral would do this, but now we don't have time to wonder about it."

"We've got to stop him, Anne."

"Brian, you can barely move. Your arm has got to be killing you. I've got to stop him," she said, nodding toward her gun.

The MAA worked his way carefully down the ladder to the O-7 level, his weapon ready, prepared to put rounds into the supine figure. When he was a few feet away, he said, just to be sure, "Freeze."

No answer. He moved a step closer. Still no movement.

"Get up, Holden."

No sign of life. He approached the body and pushed it with his foot.

"Ooohhhh."

The MAA couldn't resist jumping back a few feet. He signaled the air ops officer at the top of the ladder to come down toward him, as he spoke into the walkie-talkie to the admiral's aide.

"I'm over Holden now, sir. He's alive but barely moving. I think that it's safe to move out."

"Roger," came the reply.

The MAA and the air ops officer bent over Rick Holden. He had taken a slug in the shoulder and was banged up and bloody from tumbling down the ladder. He was barely conscious.

"Admiral, Holden isn't a threat anymore. They say he's knocked out and they are going to get some rope from the signal bridge and tie him up. MAA will stay with him. I think that we can move out sir."

"Let's go," replied the admiral. "Ops O, where are we with TFCC?"

"COS says that the strike aircraft are overhead tanking and getting ready to push for their missions. Captain and CAG were trying to decide whether to launch the remaining strikers, think there are about seven or eight more to go, or send these guys ahead with each strike group a little light."

"That's not a decision that they can make on their own.

We need to get down to TFCC," the admiral replied. Turning to his aide, he said, "Lead on, Mike."

Mike Lumme led the admiral and ops officer off the Flag Bridge. They walked down the first ladder and saw the MAA tying up Rick Holden. He nodded that he had the situation under control. Air ops fell in with them, and the four men headed down the ladders.

98

NATIONAL INTELLIGENCE SYSTEMS PICK UP AN INCREDible amount of data every day—more data than the intelligence agencies can possibly process, let alone turn into any useful information. During a major crisis, the efforts of analysts are shifted to allow them to focus on specific, critical information. Such was the case with the Gulf today.

The action in the Arabian Gulf was so frenetic that it outpaced the ability of the National Military Command Center and the White House Situation Room to even keep track of events, let alone analyze and interpret them. Senior military officers were being roundly chewed out by their superiors for not having complete answers to a myriad of questions. That only added to the frenzy as these officers, in turn, sought out less senior officers and sent them scurrying about in search of answers. There were none.

The duty watch at NSA had received the scattered reports between 3 A.M. and 5 A.M. Eastern Daylight time. Reports were coming in about the proximity to the aircraft carrier. Additional reports dealt with large numbers of aircraft milling about close to *Carl Vinson*.

The early alertment at NSA provided just enough data to confuse and confound, but did not provide enough granularity to allow analysts to really come to grips with what was happening. NSA alerted the NMCC via the NMJIC—the National Military Joint Intelligence Center—as well as the Situation Room, but neither location fully understood what was going on in the Gulf until the OPREP THREE PINNACLE messages began to arrive at the NMCC from both *Carl Vinson* and from *Jefferson City*, indicating that both units were under attack. Key watchstanders at the NMCC knew that *Jefferson City* was on a highly secret special operation classified under the Top Secret program.

It was clear—but it wasn't clear. *Carl Vinson* had been hit by *Jefferson City*. *Jefferson City* had been hit by torpedoes dropped by ASW aircraft under control of *Carl Vinson*. Aircraft were still launching from *Carl Vinson*, and a large gaggle of aircraft was forming up near the carrier, apparently headed for Iran. And to make matters worse, there was no report from the CIA agent aboard *Carl Vinson* as to what was happening with regard to his efforts to stop Admiral Robinson. That was a critical piece of information that the entire operation hinged on.

Admiral Monroe was a fixture in the NMCC, hoping by his very presence to somehow bring order out of chaos. The president had all but ordered him to come to the White House and be a fixture in the Situation Room, but Monroe assessed that his presence in the NMCC was more important—and he was right. He was one of the few who were read into *Jefferson City*'s mission, and he was able to steer watchstanders in trying to evaluate the information that they did have without speculating on what they didn't know.

At the CIA, Pete Hernandez pressed the control officers to try to find out what Rick Holden was doing on *Carl Vinson*. They had no way of knowing that he had been shot and was now in custody aboard the ship—labeled a traitor, an assassin, and worse. Hernandez was enough of a bureaucrat to know that there was no gain in standing in front of the president and admitting that he did not really know what was going on. In spite of the president's personal urging, Hernandez had begged "special needs" and had remained at his headquarters in Langley.

So there was no one at the White House of sufficient rank

or stature for President Patrick Browne to vent at except Michael Curtis.

"Michael, every time I walk down to the Situation Room I come away more confused about this operation. And I am the man who makes the decisions. What else have you heard since our briefing an hour-and-a-half ago."

"Nothing, Mr. President," he replied. "I have pressed the chairman for more information, and he tells me that reports are still coming in regarding action between *Carl Vinson* and *Jefferson City*, but there is nothing definitive. I'm afraid that it is still completely unsettled, Mr. President."

"Is Secretary Quinn making any progress getting a communication network set up with President Habibi?"

"He's working on it, Mr. President," he lied. Curtis had reached a low-level functionary and had made this request. The man probably would take days just writing his memo to send up the chain to have this done. By then it would be too late. He had carried the message forward—he had just left it, purposely, in inept hands.

"Well tell him to get it done, damnit! Get it done now!"

"I'll see to it, Mr. President."

One hundred and twenty miles as the crow flies from the warm waters of the Arabian Gulf an aircraft was launching.

"Four thousand feet remaining . . . three thousand feet . . . you need to rotate now, Mohammad—"

"Airspeed isn't high enough yet, Bani—"

"Almost two thousand feet now, you must rotate, rotate, now!"

"No, we will stall—"

"Less than a thousand feet remaining. ROTATE, RO-TATE, or we will run off the runway!"

His hands frozen on the yoke, Mohammad Sallihab pulled back gently and lifted the C-130 off the deck at Shiraz Airport. The weapon was primitive and was enormously heavy. His calculations told him he should make it, it wasn't supposed to be this close, but there had been absolutely no wind, and this had complicated things.

Sallihab climbed slowly and began a slow clearing turn to

join the airway. He would climb to just the right altitude and go at just the right speed as he headed his aircraft toward Kuwait, knowing that he and his crew would never reach there.

99

In the skies above *Carl Vinson*, the thirsty Tomcats, Hornets, and Prowlers in the strike group sucked gas from the Vikings sent aloft as mission tankers. The Blue Wolves had scrambled to put enough aircraft aloft—they had sent two aircraft to prosecute the submarine and had launched every up aircraft they had on the flight deck in order to get enough gas to give the strike aircraft full bags of fuel so they could fly deep into Iran and deliver their weapons.

DCAG was the senior aviator in the air and was on the radio with *Carl Vinson*'s CO, dealing with the issue of whether to wait to launch the remaining strike aircraft before pushing toward Iran. The strike groups had been carefully constructed with very little redundancy, so they wanted to get as many aircraft as possible airborne to join the strike package. There was a limit to how long they could wait— and they were reaching that limit.

Once DCAG and the captain had made their decision, the captain passed it to TFCC to get Admiral Robinson's concurrence. They reached the chief of staff, who gave them a "wait out" while he tried to reach the admiral. The chief of staff had to leave the captain and DCAG hanging.

In the absence of guidance from the admiral or his staff, Craig Vandegrift decided to launch a total of six more strike aircraft and send them aloft to join DCAG's group. By the time they got there and refueled, it would be pushing the outside of the envelope for the window to launch the strikes at all.

Black Knight 612 touched down on spot 4 on *Carl Vinson*, and the ATO moved quickly to the helo's cabin door and assisted Joe Willard in getting out of the helo while the powerful rotors continued to spin. He was whisked down to the SCC Module to meet immediately with Commodore Jim Hughes.

"Joe, it was important that I talk with you face-to-face. I wasn't privy to your side of the call with Lieutenant O'Connor. From listening to her side, I expect you told her just what in the hell you are doing out here shooting at *Carl Vinson*."

Joe Willard was a little off balance already, and the commodore's comments only made him more so. He had laid everything out for this lieutenant; hadn't she told the commodore anything? Or maybe she had.

"Commodore, as I told the lieutenant, I received a naval message from my boss at SUBPAC and another from the CNO himself directing me to fire a torpedo at *Carl Vinson* and disable her. The message from SUBPAC told me that the admiral on board the carrier was going to conduct an unauthorized attack against Iran and that this was the only way to stop this from happening. I questioned that order, sir, by sending a message back to COMSUBPAC, but was told that I was to carry out my orders to the letter."

"What did you do after they confirmed your mission for you?" asked the commodore.

"I have been working my way north through the Gulf to get in position to take this shot. I don't know what damage, if any, I've done to *Carl Vinson*, but I can tell you that my boat is in very, very bad shape. The first torp hit my sail with fairly minimal damage. The next one hit my hull and I had to surface or risk losing the boat. I need rescue and assistance parties to help me save it, sir."

"*Shiloh* is on her way," continued the commodore. Could Willard's tale be true?

"Commodore, I know that this may not be the time or place, but you said my torpedo hit *Carl Vinson*?"

"Yeah, got us in the number one screw. That will take a while to get repaired—but we will. Now, Captain, tell me more about this . . . this . . . accusation in the message you received from COMSUBPAC alleging that the admiral was going to conduct strikes that were unauthorized."

"As I told the lieutenant, the message from COMSUB-PAC was clear. It said, 'the battle group commander had elected, for reasons known only to him, to attack the Islamic Republic of Iran.' I know what the message said, Commodore, I must have read it a hundred times."

"I'm sure that you did, Joe. But did you know that our orders were to conduct those very attacks that SUBPAC told you were not authorized?"

"No, then there must be some incredible mix-up some-where—that dwarfs any other kind of military snafu I've ever seen or heard about."

"Commodore," his chief staff officer chimed in, "these or-ders for us to do these strikes have all been verbal. No naval message has come down from the chain of command—"

Now it was Joe Willard's turn to interrupt. "You are con-ducting these strikes on verbal orders?"

"They are verbal orders that the admiral has received di-rectly from the Fifth Fleet commander."

"Commodore, even so, this really casts doubt on the en-tire mission," continued his CSO. "Don't you see, sir. If we are going on *verbal* orders to attack, and the skipper here has *a naval message* telling him that this isn't what is sup-posed to be happening, then something is wrong, sir. At a minimum, we need to ask the chain of command what they really want us to do."

"We're in radio silence for a reason, CSO. We have to disguise our position and our intentions from our enemy."

"I think that we might be disguising more than that, sir," chimed in Joe Willard. "Sir, can't we break radio silence long enough just to check with Fifth Fleet Headquarters as your CSO suggests? We sure aren't giving away our position any more than the frigates we dueled with have already."

"All right, I'll talk with the chief of staff. The admiral is on the Flag Bridge now near as I can figure. Yes, I think we can make a case for contacting Fifth Fleet."

"I just hope that we do whatever we are going to do soon," said the CSO. "And we need to find out what was wrong with O'Connor and that other pilot she was in here with," he continued.

100

He dared not use his name.

"My friend. As I speak, the American jets are forming up over their aircraft carrier, prepared to fly over our nation and drop their deadly bombs on our homes and on our women and our children. Our brave seamen have died dueling with them, we have shot down one of their fighter jets before it crossed our coast, and their AEGIS cruiser has shot down another aircraft that they only could have thought was ours. All of this, and still their government is silent—allowing their bandit carrier battle group to rain down destruction on our Islamic Republic. . . . ," barked Foreign Minister Ali Akbar Velayati into the phone. He did not intend to give Shiekholeslam a tutorial; he hadn't planned on saying more than a few sentences, but he grew more enraged by the minute over the recent chain of events.

"Yes, Mr. Minister," was his only response.

"They do all of this and their government does not even attempt to contact ours. Not at the presidential level, not at the ministerial level, not even informally via third parties. And do you know why they don't do this? Do you know why they treat us with such disdain?"

"I do not, Mr. Minister," Shiekholeslam replied.

"They treat us with this disdain because we do not threaten them. We experimented with ballistic missiles that could reach the United States, but these missiles never lived up to their promise. The Americans laughed at us—a country such as ours was not advanced enough, not worthy enough, to have such missiles. Now they spit at us. We cannot hurt them, so they can continue to act with impunity. That is the problem. You understand that, don't you?"

"Yes, Mr. Minister."

"The time has come, my friend. You are to instruct those brave men in the United States to release the agents in the places they selected. We will take this fight to the enemy. As bombs are raining down on our country, Americans will be dying in the streets. We will be the ones who will be laughing."

"It will be done, Mr. Minister."

"I know that it will, my friend. But it must be timed precisely. That will have the maximum impact. They all must release their agents at precisely the same time. Can you ensure that, my friend?"

"I can, Mr. Minister."

"Good. It is now 1030 Greenwich Mean Time. They are to carry out their attacks at precisely 1145 Greenwich Mean Time. Can you ensure that they do just that?"

"Yes, Mr. Minister. I have only to pick up the phone and it is complete. I have warned them to be absolutely ready, and these men are already at the locations that they are assigned. We are ready to carry out your orders."

"Excellent," he replied. Shiekholeslam's thorough preparations and his calm responses put Velayati at ease somewhat—but not completely.

"Is there anything else, Mr. Minister?"

"Yes, my friend, allahu akbar. God is great."

"Allahu akbar."

Shiekholeslam put the phone down and pulled a sheet of paper out of his desk. He scratched at it quickly until he had the words precisely correct. He put the pen down—

THE MOMENT HAS COME. THE AMERICAN PIGS ARE ATTACKING OUR ISLAMIC REPUBLIC. YOU ARE AUTHORIZED TO CARRY OUT THE ATTACKS THAT YOU HAVE BEEN INSTRUCTED TO CONDUCT. YOU ARE TO RELEASE YOUR AGENTS IN THE APPOINTED PLACES AT PRECISELY 1145 GREENWICH MEAN TIME. NOT BEFORE. NOT

AFTER. THE SUCCESS OF OUR NATION'S DEFENSE DE-
PENDS ON YOU. AT 1145 GMT, PRECISELY. ALLAHU AK-
BAR.

—and dialed the first number.

In New York, Mejid Homani hoped the United Nations concourse would be open then. If not, what would he do? Worried, he hurriedly left the coffee shop and crossed the street
as the sun rose over the East River. He would try the doors
to the United Nations. Maybe it would be open.

Hala Karomi received the message next, just as he was
boarding the Metro to head back to Union Station, his agent
tucked firmly under his arm. He was relieved. He would
arrive in time.

Achmed Boleshari read his pager carefully and quickly
calculated what this time translated to in San Diego. It
would be barely dawn. Horton Plaza would be nearly deserted. What was Shiekholeslam thinking? He could not believe that was what he wanted him to do. Achmed Boleshari
sat in the coffee shop across the street from Horton Plaza
and weighed his options.

101

ANNE AND BRIAN LEANED AGAINST THE STEEL BULK-
head, debating what to do next.

"Once I get the drop on the admiral," Anne said, "I can
tell the other senior officers around what is going on and we
can end this."

"But what if they are in on it too, Anne? What if they are
part of the plot?" he replied.

"Brian, that's just too big a stretch, that a whole group of people could have decided to plot this. You know guys like CAG. There is no way!"

"We thought we knew the admiral too, Anne, and he's really gone off the deep end. If he could, then so could everyone else."

"Yes, but the messages that you tell me Rick got, and what *Jeff City*'s CO told me, make it sound like the admiral was working alone. If he isn't, if they're all involved, there's no way that we can stop what is going to happen. We've got to hope that the admiral is a solo actor here—and Brian— I believe that he is. I'll find out as soon as I find him."

"Where do you think he is now?"

"I gotta think that he's still on the Flag Bridge. That's where he was headed when I saw Rick following him. Then I heard shots and saw Rick fall down the ladder. They're probably waiting to see if the coast is really clear. Wait, there's one thing that I have to check."

Anne stepped out from behind the curtain, took a few steps forward, and peered down the passageway toward the admiral's cabin, then she returned.

"What were you doing?" said Brian.

"I needed to see if the MAA was there. He wasn't, so I've got to figure that the admiral is still on the Flag Bridge. I think that it's best if we just wait here. He'll have to pass by us to get back to TFCC. If we're this close to pushing the strikers, he's bound to go back there soon."

"So what's your plan? You—"

Anne raised her hand suddenly, signaling him to stop speaking. She had heard voices—faint, but close by. Without further comment or signal, both Anne and Brian pressed themselves against the bulkhead again.

The voices got closer, and now words could be picked out.

"Keep moving, Flag Lieutenant, I don't want to get to TFCC after all the strikes are finished."

"Yes, sir."

The footsteps and the voices were now closer still and were coming toward the fore and aft passageway where they hid. In a few feet, the group would have to turn. If they turned right, they would stay in the Blue Tile passageway and head for TFCC. If they turned left they would literally be on top of Anne and Brian.

The voices grew louder.

"Ops, as soon as we get to TFCC, find out the status of the strikers. I want to know exactly where they are and exactly when they think they're going to push."

"Yes sir, Admiral."

"And I want to know where the TLAM shooters are on their countdown."

"Got it, Admiral."

The voices were almost on top of them. Anne held her breath.

"I don't know why the hell we went up to the Flag Bridge anyway. Chief of staff convinced me against my best instincts—"

The voices were right there. They dared not breathe or move.

"Admiral, we'll be back there in just a moment," his ops officer said. The voices were growing softer. They were moving forward. They were moving away!

The footsteps and the voices grew fainter still as the four men moved away down the passageway. Anne hazarded a peek from behind the curtain. They were past the SCC Module and were now more than twenty feet away, almost to the War Room.

There was no waiting now. Neither Anne nor Brian dared utter a word. She started to move forward.

Brian grabbed her arm with his good one. Their eyes met. He mouthed the words "Be careful," then he released his grip.

Anne gave him a hard stare, then wrapped both hands tightly around her .45 caliber pistol and pressed on.

102

MOHAMMAD SALLIHAB HAD FOLLOWED THE AIRWAY precisely for over one hundred miles. Even at twelve thousand feet he could see the coastline of Iran in the distance. He knew that once he arrived there he would have to act quickly. He would have to leave the airway, descend rapidly, and then find *Carl Vinson* in the perpetual haze that hung over the Arabian Gulf. Then he would have to penetrate the carrier's defense and crash his aircraft on its flight deck, exploding his weapon with deadly force.

He did not fear dying, nor did the rest of their crew. For them, martyrdom was the highest calling. It had taken many days of intense instruction to teach them how to fly the C-130 transport—they did not even know how to operate all of its systems—but they knew enough to get it off the deck and to its destination. And the Americans would be powerless to stop them.

Miles from where Sallihab's aircraft was about to cross the coastline, Jake Busch stalked back and forth in *Shiloh*'s Combat Direction Center. *Shiloh* had been at General Quarters for longer than Busch could ever remember being at GQ. *Shiloh*'s powerful SPY radar scanned the crowded skies around the carrier. They were shotgun for the carrier and needed to continuously scan the skies around the battle group to be prepared to deal with any hostile aircraft attempting to reach *Carl Vinson*. Satisfied that things were running properly in CDC, Busch turned toward his TAO, Lieutenant Bob Long.

"I'm going up to the bridge to oversee this rescue and assistance effort. If you get anything—and I mean anything—hot down here, you let me know ASAP!"

"Yes sir," Long replied as the captain bounded out of CDC.

Petty Officer Alex Davillo sat at his console and did his best to sort out the airborne traffic while his ship pounded through the seas toward *Jefferson City*, ready to lend assistance to the wounded submarine. In addition to the over thirty aircraft milling around getting ready to push off on their strike mission, there were the aircraft that had prosecuted *Jefferson City*, still at the datum, as well as the commercial traffic on nearby commercial airways. *Shiloh* had the airways depicted on her large-screen displays in CDC for ready reference, and Davillo and his fellow OSs were confident that they could sort friend from foe out of the maze of aircraft.

Mohammad Sallihab was over the water now. His copilot held the nautical chart in his lap while he held the aerial chart in his right hand and continuously cross-checked the two. Their superiors had marked the spot on the nautical chart where the carrier was supposed to be. His eyes shot back and forth between the map and the chart as he kept up a running dialogue with Sallihab, telling him where he was and where he thought the carrier was.

For his part, Sallihab concentrated mightily on keeping his aircraft precisely on the airway and traveling at the prescribed speed.

His copilot lifted his eyes from his charts and looked at Sallihab.

"We are at the closest point of approach to where the carrier is supposed to be. Here is the spot where you must turn," Bani said.

"Turn to what course?" said Sallihab.

"Turn to course 205."

"Course 205. I am starting my descent," Sallihab replied. "I am leaving twelve thousand feet. I will level out at one thousand feet."

"Yes, Mohammad."

With that, Mohammad Sallihab pushed the yoke forward

and turned sharply as the huge aircraft shuddered at this change.

Aboard *Shiloh*, Petty Officer Davillo stared at his radar scope and eased forward to the edge of his chair. He blinked. Then he changed scales on his radar. Then he changed back to the original scale. It was still there.

"Chief."

"What is it, Davillo?"

"Chief, I've got this airborne contact at 035. I think that he was on the airway, but he dropped off of it. He's headed right at us and descending rapidly. Chief, I'd better tell the TAO."

"Do it!" shouted the chief as his eyes fixed on the same contact. It took him only seconds to make the same analysis that Davillo had. The aircraft that had been innocently plodding along the commercial airway was now making a beeline for the *Shiloh* and *Carl Vinson*, only eight miles away from the cruiser.

"Mr. Long!"

The TAO, Lieutenant Bob Long, walked up behind him. "What is it, Davillo?"

"Right here on my screen, sir. Chief confirms it. This contact is headed straight for us at two hundred thirty-five knots."

"Did he come off the airway?"

"Yes sir, he did."

"Is he squawking emergency?"

"No, sir, he's not squawking anything."

Long pressed the bitch box to the bridge.

"Captain, TAO. Your presence is requested in CDC!"

They were descending through eight thousand feet as the aircraft continued to shudder.

"There, Bali!"

"Where?"

"There, there, at one o'clock low. Look at them. There must be twenty of them. All over the sky. All over the sky!"

"Yes, I see them, I see the specks!" Bali replied.

Mohammad Sallihab praised Allah and praised the intelligence men who had plotted the likely position of *Carl Vinson* on their chart. If those aircraft were all milling around above it, the carrier must be close by. While the Gulf haze often limited visibility near the deck to a half-dozen miles, above the haze, where he flew, Mohammad had virtually unlimited visibility, and the glint of the sun off the aircraft circling high above and east of *Carl Vinson* was difficult to miss.

"I am turning ten degrees to head directly toward them, Bali, but now that we know where the carrier is, we must accelerate our descent to get under the clouds before these aircraft see us."

Jake Busch was standing next to Bob Long within twenty seconds. "What?"

"This contact, Captain. No squawk. Coming right at the carrier—"

"Give him level two warnings. Don't waste your time with level one."

"Captain?"

"DO IT!" shouted Busch. There was a chance that it might be a friendly aircraft. He needed to find out right away.

"Unidentified aircraft bearing 035, six thousand feet, on course 205, two hundred thirty-five knots, you are approaching a United States Navy warship operating in international waters. Your identity is not known and your intentions are unclear. You are standing into danger and may be subject to United States defensive measures. Request you establish communications now or alter your course immediately to remain clear of me. Request you alter course to 010 to remain clear."

No answer.

"Again."

"Unidentified aircraft. . . ." The TAO repeated these instructions verbatim.

Still no answer.

"Take him with birds!" shouted Busch.

"Captain, we need to ask Xray Bravo!"

"No we don't, damnit, DO IT NOW!" Busch had almost

waited too long the day before when the other Iranian aircraft had approached them. That one had not made the devious move this one had, in trying to look like a commercial airliner. This one had even more evil intentions, he was sure.

Within seconds they felt first one jolt, then another as the deadly SM-2 missiles leapt from the vertical launch magazine.

Mohammed Sallihab held the yoke forward with all his might as the C-130 shuddered violently, protesting the rapid descent. Sallihab looked at his attitude gyro for as long as he could, trying to keep his wings level and keep the aircraft in balanced flight . . .

103

ANNE STARTED DOWN THE PASSAGEWAY, GUN IN HER right hand. Ahead, the ops officer and air ops officer entered the War Room; the admiral's aide and the admiral were still a few steps away. The admiral was bringing up the rear, his men undoubtedly going ahead of him just to ensure that the coast was still clear. Even though they had just shot the assassin, they were still wary.

Anne closed to within ten feet of the admiral and held her .45 at arm's length. She knew that she couldn't miss from this distance.

She had a clear shot at the back of his head. All she had to do was take the shot and the admiral would be dead and this ordeal would be over. One shot and it was over. One shot and Anne would stop the battle group from launching these devastating strikes against Iran. Her finger slowly started to put pressure on the trigger. . . .

Anne couldn't do it, not in the back of the head. She shouted out, "Admiral!"

Heater Robinson turned and looked at Anne. He froze, his eyes wide with disbelief. Was there another assassin on this ship? His eyes met hers, searching for something, anything, to tell him why she was doing this. There was none. Just a cold, hard stare from Anne as she slowly stepped even closer to him.

Mike Lumme had turned when the admiral had. As he did, he inadvertently let go of the handle to the War Room door, and it slammed shut as the ops officer and the air ops officer continued ahead to TFCC. Lumme stood frozen for a moment, just like the admiral. He then moved out in front of the admiral, putting himself between him and Anne.

"Lieutenant, don't do this," he said. "I don't know what you are doing, but you have to stop. You can't do this. You have to understand. You can't do this." He was slowly moving closer as he spoke.

"That's far enough. Stop right there!" Anne shouted at Lumme, bringing her gun up just a little higher and holding it out just a little straighter in front of her.

"Look, Lieutenant, you don't want to shoot anyone. This is just a big misunderstanding. We can clear this up." He continued, one step at a time.

She took a step back to buy time, but Lumme just moved a step closer to her. Now he had his hand up and was shaking his head as if to say "no, you can't do this."

"Stop, stop right there!" she shouted at him, momentarily pointing her gun at Admiral Robinson, indicating to him that he shouldn't move either. The admiral took the hint.

"You're not going to do this," said Lumme as he stepped toward Anne, his face now contorted with anger. He would be on top of her in seconds, and Anne had not pulled the trigger. It didn't look like she could.

Suddenly, from behind Anne, heavy footsteps! Brian had been watching the action as he too had crept up the passageway, unnoticed by the other three in the intensity of the moment. Cradling his broken arm close in to his body, Brian ran like a running back, brushed by Anne, and crashed into Lumme just before he reached Anne, knocking him to the deck. As they hit the deck, Brian called up every ounce of strength to keep from crying out in agony. He rolled on top of the shocked Lumme and began to pummel him with his good arm.

Anne was as shocked as Lumme was by Brian's instantaneous presence; so shocked that as he brushed by her, he knocked the gun out of her hand. It slid along the deck toward where he and Lumme fought.

Heater Robinson got his wits about him first and tried to escape. He was at the War Room door and only feet from safety. Once inside, he would be safe from these new assassins. He grabbed the handle of the door to the War Room and turned it. It would not open. He had to try the cipher lock. He tried to think of the combination. He rarely came into the War Room this way.

It didn't take Mike Lumme long to get the upper hand on Brian. Lumme saw the gun on the deck and started to belly-crawl toward it, but Brian saw what he was doing and grabbed his leg and held on to it with all he had.

Admiral Robinson finally remembered the combination and was about to punch it in when he was knocked off his feet. Anne had hurdled the two struggling men on the deck and had thrown herself headlong into the admiral. The two came crashing down on the deck just forward of the War Room.

The shock of Anne crashing into him and the adrenaline rushing through Anne's body momentarily let her get the upper hand on the admiral. She used the advantage to lay into him with all she could, delivering blow after blow, trying to at least knock him out.

While Anne struggled with the admiral, Mike Lumme continued inching toward the gun as Brian hung on to his leg, twisting it, fighting him for every inch that he crawled. Brian had found that place beyond pain, so focused was he on his grip, and Lumme was getting there driving to the gun, when the door to the War Room suddenly opened, and the chief of staff and the air ops officer looked out on the commotion. The air ops officer cut to the quick by drawing his own gun, leveling it on all of them. He shouted, "STOP IT,

STOP IT RIGHT THERE. EVERYONE FREEZE. NOW EVERYONE JUST FREEZE."

They all turned on the new threat.

"Admiral, are you all right?" said the chief of staff as he rushed to help the admiral to his feet. Heater Robinson didn't say anything.

The air ops officer saw the gun on the deck. Keeping his weapon leveled at Anne and Brian, he said to Mike Lumme, "Flag Lieutenant, go pick up that gun."

"Yes sir," said Mike Lumme as he pulled free of the writhing Brian.

"Admiral, did they try to shoot you?" asked the chief of staff.

"She did," he said, pointing at Anne. "How many damn assassins are there on this ship, Lieutenant, besides you and this Holden and this other officer down here?" he said, looking at the figure on the deck but not recognizing Brian.

It was a rhetorical question cold and harsh, the admiral's pride ruptured at being taken down by a woman.

The air ops officer kept his weapon trained on Anne and Brian as Anne slowly got to her feet. She was totally exhausted from her struggle with Admiral Robinson and stood hunched over with her hands on her knees, trying to catch her breath. Brian struggled to get up, his badly broken arm now hanging grotesquely at his side.

The chief of staff took charge as best he could. "Flag Lieutenant, I want you to assist the admiral and get into TFCC, the strikes are on their way and I know that he wants to monitor them. The minute you get in there, I want you to call the ship's Master-at-Arms office and get several MAAs up here. Tell them to break through whatever Zebra fittings they have to, they just need to get here and get here now."

"Yes sir," he replied.

"You two are under arrest," the chief of staff continued. "You are traitors, both of you, and you will pay for your crimes—"

"NO WE'RE NOT," Anne shouted.

At her shout, Brian forced himself up and stood facing the admiral.

"McDonald, is that you? You were supposed to be leading

one of these strikes, what the hell are you doing with this
. . . this . . . woman stalking me?"

Before Brian could answer, there was noise coming toward them from the back end of the Blue Tile Area. The commotion of the fighting there had, even through the thick metal door, gotten the attention of the people in the SCC Module, the only other space in the Blue Tile Area that was manned during GQ. The commodore and Joe Willard appeared.

"Commodore," said the chief of staff, "these two assassins tried to kill the admiral. They almost succeeded. We shot one of their coconspirators up on the O-7 level just a few minutes ago. We have these two, but we don't know how many more there are."

"I have something to tell you and you'd better listen," replied Jim Hughes, now fully sizing up the situation.

"This is Joe Willard, George, the skipper of *Jefferson City*. He has told me why he was ordered to shoot at this ship— and shoot to wound us, too, not to sink us. I'll let him explain."

Ordered? Sampson thought.

"Chief of Staff. I've received messages from both COM-SUBPAC and CNO telling me to disable *Carl Vinson* before the carrier launched strikes against Iran. I was told that the admiral had taken matters into his own hands and was directing completely unauthorized strikes. As I told the commodore, I questioned those orders but was told by Admiral Deutermann himself that I was to proceed with my mission as a matter of urgency. I followed my orders, sir, that's all."

"George, don't you see what's happening?" said the commodore.

"I see that this is very, very strange," replied the chief of staff. "We are authorized to conduct strikes. We have orders directly from Fifth Fleet."

By now, Brian had recovered enough to speak. "Sir, the Airwing has been planning these strikes based on verbal authority only. All of our doctrine, all of our training, everything that I have done for my whole career, all that we have been told by our senior officers, is that these kind of strikes are never, never tasked verbally. There is just too much that can go wrong. We must have hard-copy naval messages to do these kind of strikes."

"I'm the one who read Holden's e-mails," Anne said, jumping into the dialogue. "He had just the same kind of instructions the skipper of the sub had."

"It's all bullshit," shouted Heater Robinson, interrupting the discussion. "Lock them up, lock them all up!"

"Admiral, how do you expect to prove that all these people are wrong and you are right?" said the commodore.

"I DON'T HAVE TO PROVE A GODDAMNED THING," he shouted. "Now, Chief of Staff, are you going to order them locked up or do I have to do it myself?"

George Sampson's eyes darted from one horn of his dilemma to the other.

"Wait," said Brian, "there's one way to find out what's true."

"What's that?" said the chief of staff.

"We've been in radio silence for no apparent reason. There's no reason to be there anymore, we won't give our position away any more than it is known already. Break radio silence, Chief of Staff. Call Fifth Fleet. They know what the score is. They know what has or hasn't been authorized. Call them and they'll confirm it!"

George Sampson thought for a moment, then looked at the commodore for validation.

"Do it, George," Jim Hughes said.

"No, Chief of Staff, you are not authorized to break radio silence, you are not authorized!" shouted Heater Robinson.

"Admiral . . . I—"

"Do it, George, do it!" said Jim Hughes. "Do it or I will!"

George Sampson stood frozen in his spot, unable to go against the admiral's orders. Jim Hughes pushed by him and headed into the War Room.

Bill Durham was directing the group in the War Room as the strikers moved toward the coast of Iran. The aircraft striking Bandar Abbas had pushed first due to the long distance involved in getting to the southern part of Iran. CAG was in TFCC with him, and they were giving directions to the other strike aircraft. They were startled when Jim Hughes burst in.

"Commodore, great job nailing the sub, what's up now?" said Bill Durham.

"We've got a crisis, Bill. We need to call Fifth Fleet right now about these strikes!"

"Commodore, we're in radio silence. We can't break that now, not without a change that the admiral directs."

"We have to and we will!" he shouted, startling everyone in TFCC. "Either you do it in here or I'll do it from my module!" Both Durham and CAG could tell that the commodore was serious, but orders were orders. Hughes could see their dilemma, and continued, "It's these strikes, CAG, and what we're supposed to hit. At this point this has all been based on verbal orders—conversations between the admiral and Admiral Flowers. Now there is some doubt about what was actually ordered. We need to get to the bottom of—"

"But Commodore, the admiral—" Bill Durham interrupted.

"YOU DO IT OR I DO IT!" shouted the commodore, interrupting Durham again. Bill Durham stared at him hard, but he decided that he needed to make the call from TFCC. He picked up the Battle Group Command Net.

"Alpha, Alpha, this is Xray Bravo."

"I'll remember this," the Commodore noted to himself.

"Xray Bravo, this is Alpha Alpha," replied the startled Fifth Fleet watchstander. *Carl Vinson* had been off the net for a while, and they were surprised that they were initiating a communication.

"This is CARGRU SEVEN Ops Officer, Captain Durham. I need to talk with your ops officer, Captain Mullen, ASAP."

"Yes, sir, stand by, sir," he replied.

The wait was only minutes, but it seemed like hours. Someone's career, perhaps several careers, were about to be ruined.

"Carl Mullen here," said the voice on the other end of the line.

"Carl, this is Bill Durham. We have multiple crises working here and I don't have a lot of time to explain. I need clarification and I need it now. Tell me about these strikes against Iran that we're launching. There is a ton of confusion. What is authorized and why didn't we get hard copy for them yet? All this was supposedly worked out between Admiral Robinson and Admiral Flowers, but now there are unanswered questions. Carl, these strikes are on their way now, what is going on?"

Members of the military have a sixth sense for snafus, and Carl Mullen's was tingling madly. He gathered himself the best he could and answered, "Bill, we have a crisis here and it all involves *Carl Vinson*. Admiral Flowers is dead. Your guys shot down his COD! You are supposed to be flying strikes against the terrorist camps, that's all. We have the execute order here, but you all are in radio silence and we can't get it to you. Those are the only strikes that are authorized, nothing else. What are you all doing out there?"

Bill Durham's whole spine went cold at once. Only the strikes against the terrorist camps were authorized?

"Carl, I—"

"Bill, General Lawrence is on his way to our HQ to take over. He arrives in a few hours. Admiral Flowers was flying out to *Carl Vinson* to relieve your boss because there was proof that he was a renegade doing completely unauthorized things. Bill, please, you've got to be the one to stop it all. Don't let those strikes keep going. Talk to your chief of staff. Isn't he the next most senior one out there?"

"He is, but—" Bill Durham couldn't believe what he was hearing. Could his admiral have been lying to all of them this entire time? The weight of evidence was compelling.

"Carl, I'll do everything that I can to call them off. I'll leave CAG on the line with you for now, I've got to do something right now."

"All right, just stop those strikes."

"I will," Durham replied. Then, as an afterthought, he said, "I know that we've been in radio silence, but we've been waiting for you to send info back with our flag sec, Lieutenant Commander Philips."

"Philips? Your admin officer? She isn't here."

"Sure she is. She went in on the COD three days ago."

"Bill, she's not here. Never has been. I'd know about those things. Why did you think she was?"

"Carl, the admiral—" But he caught himself. What else was the admiral hiding from them? He turned to Jim Hughes. "Let's go, Commodore," he said, and the two of them left TFCC.

Bill Durham and the commodore appeared again in the Blue Tile passageway as the chief of staff and the air ops officer continued to hold their weapons on Anne and Brian. Admiral Robinson stood there too, telling the air ops officer what to do with the two "prisoners." He wasn't making a lot of sense to anyone else standing there, and the entire scene had a surrealistic feeling about it.

"What did they say, Bill?" said the chief of staff.

The ops officer did not answer immediately, so George Sampson turned toward him. Durham was white.

"Bill?"

"We shot down Admiral Flowers's plane and killed everyone on board."

"We what?"

"Remember that contact that *Shiloh* shot down yesterday? The one that wouldn't respond to warnings? That was the COD. Admiral Flowers was on it."

"My God!"

"And another surprise, COS. Becky Philips isn't at Fifth Fleet Headquarters. Never was, according to them."

"But Admiral," began George Sampson, "you told us . . . ."

It came together for George Sampson in a flash. Becky had come to see him, making some wild accusations against the admiral. And it was the admiral who had made up this obviously contrived story about her being at Fifth Fleet on a "special mission." And now Fifth Fleet had told Bill Durham that the verbal orders that Admiral Robinson had supposedly gotten from the Fifth Fleet commander hadn't happened—and couldn't have happened because Admiral Flowers was dead when Admiral Robinson was ostensibly talking with him. George Sampson asked the hardest question he had ever asked.

"Admiral, these are pretty serious charges. Sir, tell me that none of it is true. Please tell me that, sir."

Heater Robinson could play it one of two ways. He decided to put all his cards on the table.

"Don't you all see? Iran is the real enemy. They have murdered our shipmates—on the ground and in the air. They must be destroyed. We hold the hammer. If we don't act now, our country will never have the will again. How many more people will have to die at the hands of terrorists? Our leaders didn't have the guts to move forward, so I moved forward without them. Each of you would have done the same thing in my position." He looked from person to person, trying to make them understand his point of view.

"Work with me on this," the admiral continued. "There shouldn't be any reason that we turn back now. We have come this far together, let's stick together on this. These people have our long-term destruction uppermost in their minds. We have to hit them first. We have to hit them hard. You all need to be with me on this. We have to hit them hard. I've tried to do it alone—that was a mistake—now I need you to join with me."

No one said anything. Heater Robinson thought that he had them on his team.

"Air Ops," said George Sampson, "take the admiral into custody. Put him in his cabin under guard for right now."

104

"GET ME THE NATIONAL SECURITY ADVISER!" SAID ADmiral Monroe to the watch officer. The admiral's towering presence and booming voice made the man nervous, but he dialed the number quickly and handed the phone to the admiral. After a quick skirmish with the watch officer at the White House Situation Room, he was on the line with Michael Curtis.

"Yes, Admiral, what is it?"

"Mr. Curtis," he began, "I just got off the line with the acting commander at Fifth Fleet Headquarters. They finally received a communication from CARGRU SEVEN aboard *Carl Vinson*."

"You mean the carrier is finally out of radio silence?" Curtis said, his pent-up frustration already starting to ease now that the damned carrier was talking with the outside world again.

"Yes sir, and Captain Dennis had a great deal to report. I will head over to the Situation Room and brief you more fully there, but for now, here is what we know. Admiral Robinson has been taken into custody—"

"He has?" exclaimed Curtis.

"Yes sir, but a lot has happened in the interim. USS *Jefferson City* attacked *Carl Vinson* and put one torpedo in her screw, but did only minor damage—the carrier is essentially operating as before. *Carl Vinson*, in turn, put two torpedoes into *Jefferson City* and almost sank her. She was forced to the surface, but is still intact."

"Was anyone killed or hurt?"

"No sir, not there. Onboard *Carl Vinson*, the Navy SEAL that was sent to take out Admiral Robinson was shot by Robinson's immediate staff before he could complete his mission, but two other officers, for reasons that we cannot yet figure out, actually attacked the admiral and stopped him. Between what these officers told him and what the CO of the submarine told him, the chief of staff and commodore decided to break radio silence and have the staff ops officer call Fifth Fleet."

"They were told that the strikes that Admiral Robinson claimed had been authorized by Admiral Flowers were not authorized at all. It was only then that the staff on *Carl Vinson* found out that they had shot down the COD carrying Admiral Flowers."

"Go on."

"There has been other action, sir. In addition to the running gun battle *Shiloh* has had with the Iranian frigates, she also shot down an Iranian aircraft making an attack on *Carl Vinson*. We are not certain what one plane—and one traveling at a relatively slow speed—was hoping to accomplish, but one theory is that it was a suicide aircraft. If the Iranians were resorting to that, it might have been the last card they played. They may not have anything else to throw against us."

"So Admiral Robinson is in custody and the CARGRU SEVEN staff is talking to Fifth Fleet and Iran is no longer threatening the battle group. Is everything settled then, with the strikes and everything? Are we sure that they are not going to strike anything until they are authorized—in writing—to do so?" asked the national security adviser.

"No sir, that part isn't completely settled yet. The battle group has told the Tomahawk shooters to hold fire. But the aircraft strikes had all pushed off toward their targets. *Carl Vinson* is attempting to call them all back, Mr. Curtis."

"Attempting to call them back?"

"They are trying, sir, via every means available. But these strikes were timed to all happen simultaneously to ensure military surprise throughout Iran. The strikers that had the furthest to go—the ones that were assigned to attack Bandar Abbas—were pushed off first. They are the ones that they may have trouble getting to hold off. You're getting this thirdhand and slightly time-late, Mr. Curtis. I'm trying to get more information to clear this up as best I can."

"You damn well better," snapped Curtis. "I'm not going to go to the president with some half-cocked story."

"You won't have to do that sir, I'll see to it personally. I will get you the information."

"You need to and you need to fast, Admiral."

"Yes sir." He needed to get on the net directly to the battle group and to whoever was in charge at the moment. He did not want to think about what might be happening to his friend Heater Robinson right now.

In the Situation Room, Michael Curtis announced, "I'll be with the president," and quickly headed upstairs.

105

ADMIRAL ROBINSON SAT ON HIS SOFA WITH HIS ARMS folded. One MAA sat at the other end of the sofa, while two other MAAs stood by the door to the War Room and the door to the Flag Mess. The admiral did not speak to them, and they were ordered not to initiate conversation. They were further instructed to keep him in their sight at all times.

Just twenty feet away, George Sampson tried to take control in TFCC and use his watchstanders and others to do the multitude of things they needed to do almost instantaneously. The chief of staff did so with considerable angst, trying to put out of his mind the role he may have played in Becky Philips's disappearance. She had trusted him, had confided in him, had tried to get him to help her get to the bottom of her suspicions, but he had blown her off, treated her like some rattled schoolgirl. And what had happened to her? Given the other things that the admiral had done and his state of mind, Sampson feared the worst. Robinson had done something to her—and he, Sampson, had effectively set her up.

"Steve," he said to the Flag TAO, "you and your team contact each of our five TLAM shooters. Tell them to cancel their missions and power down their missiles. I want you talking to each CO individually. Get positive affirmation—and I mean positive affirmation—that they understand this. Then confirm each with me. Got it?"

"Yes sir."

"Good. That's the long pole in the tent. Aircraft we can call back. Tomahawks we can't."

"Paul," he said to Lieutenant Paul Barton, who was manning the air display console, "I want you to get me the E-2C. Tell them to reach me on the J-1 circuit. I'm going to use them to reach the strikers and have 'em call back each strike group individually. Once we have them moving this way we can worry about how to tank 'em, marshal 'em, and get 'em all back aboard safely."

"Will do, sir," Barton replied.

"Steve, I want reports from *Shiloh* right away with a reconstruction of the track of the aircraft they shot down. I want to know where it came from and exactly why they felt threatened."

"Wilco, COS."

"CAG," he said, turning to Wizard Foster, "you've got to work with Craig to find a way to get this many aircraft back aboard safely. I've got to tell him what's happened here and tell him that he can start moving southeast again—I know that he doesn't want to get trapped in the shallow water up here."

"I'll work with him on that, COS."

"Chief of Staff, I've got the E-2C on the J-1 circuit, sir."

George Sampson picked up the handset. "This is Captain Sampson, chief of staff for CARGRU SEVEN. Who's on this net?"

"Captain, Commander McCarthy, sir. I've got primary air control up here. What is it sir?"

"This is directive K.T. so I'm going to say it slowly. The strikes that just pushed are being recalled. I say again, the strikes are being recalled. You are to contact each of the strike leads ASAP and direct them to return to *Carl Vinson*, is that clear?"

Sampson knew the CO of the E-2 squadron very well, and they recognized each other's voices on the net. That helped convince McCarthy that this was the real deal—that the strikes were to be called off.

"I got it, Chief of Staff."

"Get back to me as soon as you get confirmation that you have turned them all around."

"Will do, sir," he replied.

Satisfied that he had initiated the crucial operational issues, George Sampson turned to other matters. "Mike," he said to the flag lieutenant who had now come into TFCC to follow the action, "what have we done with Lieutenant O'Connor and Lieutenant Commander McDonald?"

"Sir, Lieutenant Commander McDonald's arm is in really bad shape. They've got him down in medical right now, and the surgeon is working on him. Lieutenant O'Connor was a little shaken up, but she's basically OK. She's in admin now telling her story to our legal folks."

"What about Lieutenant Holden?"

"I know that he was alive when we went by him. The MAA was guarding him. I'll have to check on that, Chief of Staff."

"All right, we can find out more about that later. We shot the guy and now it turns out that he's a hero for trying to do his duty."

George Sampson picked up the Bogen phone and hit 28, which connected him instantly to the captain on the bridge.

"Captain," said Craig Vandegrift as he picked up the phone.

"Craig, COS here. We've just had some astounding things go on down here. We're recalling the strikes and CAG is going to talk to you in just a minute to try to figure out how to recover all the strikers. But for now, we're not threatened any more, so I think that it's OK to stand the ship down from GQ."

"Will do, COS."

"Craig, but would you do something for me?"

"Sure."

"There's a Lieutenant Holden that one of your MAAs is guarding up on the O-7 level. He's been shot, but he's one of the good guys. Can you get someone down there to assess his condition and then get him medical help ASAP?"

"Can do, COS."

"Thanks, Craig, I'll get back to you," he said. He hung up the Bogen.

"Chief of Staff, I have the E-2C mission commander on the J-1."

"Great, give me the handset."

"COS, K.T. here."

"Go ahead, K.T. Have we got all the strikers turned around yet?"

"No sir, not yet. Chief of Staff, there's a problem. I'm telling the guys this on our fleet air defense net, but they don't believe me. They think that it's either some sort of Iranian ruse or that I am confused and don't know what I'm talking about or something. But the best I've been able to do is to get some guys to hold at their present position for a short while. If I don't convince them, they're gonna push."

"You've got to convince them!"

"Sir, I'm trying, but we're losing time, and that's not the worst news, sir."

"Not the worst news! What is?"

"Chief of Staff, I've called the strike group heading toward Bandar Abbas a half-dozen times. They don't respond. Sir, they may be too low and too far away already. We may not be able to reach them at all!"

"Damnit, K.T., we need to be able to control what the hell we're doing," barked the chief of staff.

"Yes sir, Chief of Staff, DCAG's not too far from the southern strike group. I'll talk to him and see if he can reach them. In the meantime, we need to come up with a way to convince everyone airborne that they're supposed to turn back."

"I'm going to give you a 'wait out' for a minute, K.T., until we sort things out down here. In the meantime, keep trying to convince your boys to turn around."

"Wilco, sir."

George Sampson looked around TFCC. He had all the players he needed—ops, air ops, intel, CAG. He would get them to help him solve this problem. "All right, it looks like we've got the brain trust all assembled. Our E-2C skipper is airborne and is telling me that not all the strikers want to turn back, afraid that this latest order is an Iranian ruse. Worse, he says that the Bandar Abbas strike group pushed early and they are so far south and probably so low on the deck already that they aren't responding to his calls. He mentioned something about DCAG maybe being able to reach them. Jesus Christ, CAG, what does it take?"

"Chief of Staff, we have to move fast if we are going to

get results. Here's what I propose. I'll raise DCAG. He's in a Hornet and he can speed south and try to catch the southern strike group. While he's en route, he can tell everyone else that they should be turning back. Hearing it from him in the air and on a covered net will help."

"Will help?" said George Sampson.

"Right, Chief of Staff, but you need to put this out to everyone and put it out on Guard. Lay it all out from soup to nuts. The guys in the air will understand if it comes at them that way. I would go into as much detail as necessary and I'd do it right away."

"OK, OK, I'll do that," he replied. CAG rushed out of TFCC toward his module.

George Sampson huddled with his ops officer and air ops officer. Within a few minutes, they settled on what they were going to say.

First, George Sampson picked up the J-1 net.

"Black Eagle 601, Xray Bravo."

"Go ahead, sir."

"K.T., here's the plan. CAG is going out to DCAG to get him to tell everyone to call off the strikes, catch up with the southern strike group, and tell them to return also. I want you to go out on the net one more time and tell them to return to *Carl Vinson*."

"Wilco, sir."

George Sampson instructed his watch team to bring up a radio on Guard, the channel used almost exclusively for military distress. Every pilot always monitored Guard every time he flew. What he said would be heard by every aircraft airborne and by everyone with a UHF radio turned on. He keyed the mike.

"All airborne units, all airborne units, this is Xray Bravo on Guard, this is Xray Bravo on Guard. All units have been contacted by the Hawkeye, this message confirms that order. Do not, repeat, do not fly over Iran and do not conduct any attacks against Iran. All strike aircraft must return to *Carl Vinson* immediately. No attacks against Iran of any kind are authorized. Return to homeplate. A complete explanation will be provided when you are debriefed in CVIC."

George Sampson unkeyed the mike for a moment and then continued.

"All strike leaders report to the Hawkeye that you have received this instruction along with what has already been passed to you and that you will comply. Gentlemen, it is crucial, repeat crucial, that we call back all your strikes. Report to the Hawkeye immediately."

Satisfied that he had done everything that he possibly could, George Sampson put down the mike and picked up the J-1 net.

"K.T., chief of staff here."

"Yes sir?"

"I want to know immediately, and I mean immediately, K.T., when all of the strike groups have checked in with you and are returning."

"Wilco, sir. CAG has put out his radio message, too, and I think that the combination of his and yours will do the trick. He's speeding south now trying to catch up with the Bandar Abbas strike group."

"We'd better pray that he makes it."

106

THE MAJOR BRAKED THE STAFF CAR TO AN ABRUPT halt outside the military headquarters where General Najafi was conducting his inspection. After a brief conversation with the general's aide, the colonel approached him.

"General, Colonel Hiliah at Communications Headquarters has an urgent message for you."

"Yes, what is it?" said General Najafi. His instincts told him it was extremely urgent.

"We have intercepted transmissions from the American aircraft carrier. They did not try to be covert but transmitted this on their Guard frequency for all to hear—"

"The American carrier transmitted on Guard?" Najafi interrupted. He knew enough about U.S. military procedures that he understood how unusual this was.

"Yes sir, it is highly unusual as you know. But the nature of the transmission was even more alarming. General, the American carrier said that strikes had been launched against our Republic and that now those strikes were to be called back—canceled. General, our radar sites and air defense sites have been alerted. We see no planes yet, but we are ready."

The general paused to absorb this extraordinary information. That the Americans were striking the Islamic Republic was not that astounding. Their entire nation had been preparing to absorb these blows. That they were calling back their strikes was. He didn't know precisely what to make of it, but knew that he would soon be summoned to the presidential Palace.

Foreign Minister Velayati was at his desk in the Foreign Ministry when he received the news. What could this mean? Did the Americans suddenly have a change of heart? He also recognized that soon President Habibi would summon him. He did not want to give him that satisfaction. Velayati called for his staff car and prepared to leave the Foreign Ministry.

For Ali Akbar Velayati, the situation was suddenly very complex. The Americans were attacking and he had directed Shiekholeslam to unleash his agents in the United States. Now the attacks were being called off. What was he to do? Should he call Shiekholeslam now or wait until Habibi told him to? He decided that he would force his hand. He would make him tell him to do this. He, Velayati, would not be accused of getting cold feet. No, it would be on the president's head.

President Habibi was pacing behind his desk as the two men entered. They had arrived in his outer office almost simultaneously and were quickly ushered in by his assistant. Habibi had received word of the extraordinary transmission from the *Carl Vinson* earlier and had been trying to make sense of it with his personal staff. Habibi now wanted to validate that theory with his two key national security officials. He got down to business immediately.

"General, the American carrier now is recalling all of its aircraft. What do you make of this? Do you consider it the extraordinary event that we all do?"

"Yes I do, Mr. President. The carrier has been vigorous in defending itself. They had their bandit cruiser attack our ships. Our Orion aircraft reports that they attacked a submarine that they thought was ours but which turned out to be their own. They shot down our C-130 transport plane with the nuclear weapon. We fully expected them to lash out against us with their cursed aircraft, and we were fully ready to defend our beloved Republic to the last man—"

"Oh, I'm certain that you were, General," interrupted Habibi. He would warm to General Najafi a lot more if he lost most of his condescending hyperbole.

"Yes we were, Mr. President. This could, of course, be an American ruse to throw off our defenders."

"General, I want to make this clear. 'Just in case' the Americans really do intend to call off these strikes, I want you to take no provocative action. None at all. You can maintain your forces on whatever alert you choose to, but you are to do nothing, repeat, nothing, to make the Americans believe that you have hostile intentions. Is that clear?"

General Najafi was taken aback by how strongly President Habibi worded what he was saying to him.

"Yes, Mr. President. It will be done as you direct it."

Habibi turned to Velayati. "Mr. Foreign Minister, I look at this as the beginning of an American effort to defuse this situation. I assume that you have already canceled these attacks against American cities."

"I have not yet, Mr. President."

"You what?!"

"I have not canceled them, but will do so if those are your wishes."

"Yes! Those are my wishes! Could there be any doubt? Are you deliberately dragging your feet, Mr. Minister?"

Velayati knew that this was all a charade. He was indeed dragging his feet and knew Habibi knew that he was. He would just have to play this out as best he could.

"Mr. President, I will immediately call off these men if you order it, but it is a decision of enormous consequences. Would it not be better if the Americans felt the full force of our wrath on their home soil? We certainly have more than enough justification to do this. Just ask the families of the sailors whose bodies now lie entombed in our ship at the bottom of the Gulf. What are their lives worth, Mr. President?"

Habibi was beyond rage that Velayati would challenge him on this, but he was prepared. He pushed the intercom button.

"Send him in," he ordered his secretary.

The door opened and Colonel Mohammed Navez, assistant chief of the Tehran police force, entered with four of his men.

"Ah, Colonel Navez. You are to perform that mission that we discussed early this morning. You are to escort Minister Velayati to his office. There he will contact an individual and direct him to call off his agents in the United States. After he does this, you will bring your men into the Foreign Ministry and 'assist' him in establishing the communications path directly with the United States that I instructed him to establish some days ago. . . ."

He paused to ensure that the colonel understood all this.

"Yes, Mr. President."

"You are to stay with him as he establishes communications with the United States Department of State, whom he will inform of our peaceful intentions. There he will be connected with the office of the American president, President Browne. You are to stay in constant communications with my office. If Minister Velayati fails to do any of these things, you are to place him immediately under arrest. Do you understand these instructions completely, Colonel?"

"Completely, Mr. President."

Velayati was furious and off-balance. Furious because of what was happening and off-balance because of the carefully scripted dialogue between Habibi and the police colonel.

This was no spur-of-the-moment outburst from the president. He had contrived this carefully. Suddenly Foreign Minister Velayati felt completely trapped.

Six hundred and fifty miles from Tehran, Lieutenant Commander Bill Weaver led his eight-plane strike group of Tomcats, Hornets, and Prowlers on a course of 130 degrees, roughly paralleling the coast of Iran. They had just refueled south of *Carl Vinson* and were on the deck at two hundred feet above the surface of the Arabian Gulf. Weaver's strike group was the first to push and was to be the first to hit the naval facility at Dandar Abbas.

There was an urgency to their mission, for once the Iranian vessels sortied from their port they would be extremely difficult to find and kill—particularly the submarines. Catch them at their piers and they would be easy targets.

Weaver turned his strike group east as they passed Qeshm Island, which pointed like a dagger directly at the port of Bandar Abbas. Once they reached the eastern end of the island, they would turn due north and run straight in at the port. It was a straightforward mission that they had practiced for well over a year, starting with the Airwing desert deployment at the Naval Air and Strike Warfare Center at Fallon, Nevada.

Back in Tehran, Foreign Minister Velayati suffered the indignity of being escorted into his own Foreign Ministry. He could not hide his rage at President Habibi and rambled at the police officers escorting him, as well as at anyone else around him in or near his offices. After fuming for some time, he called Shiekholeslam.

"Yes, Mr. Foreign Minister."

"I have a simple message for you. President Habibi has ordered that you tell your agents in the United States to stop—to call off their attacks. They are not to release their agents. Is that clear?"

"Perfectly clear, Mr. Foreign Minister. But, you see, this may be quite impossible. These men have already been given the go-ahead. The designated time is approaching. It may be impossible to tell them to stop."

Velayati looked up at the police officers surrounding him, eyeing the one officer who was discreetly listening on one of the other telephones in his office. He raged at Shiekholeslam.

"It is not impossible. You know that it is not. The hour that we have designated for them to conduct their attacks is still twenty minutes away. You alerted them by pager to conduct these attacks, you use the same method to tell them to stop them. This is an order, Shiekholeslam, you will obey it!"

Shiekholeslam thought Velayati was losing both his control and his nerve—he had never used his name over a phone line like this before.

"As you wish, Mr. Minister. I will do as you instruct. These brave men have put themselves at great personal risk, but they will do as you say."

"See that they do!" said Velayati as he slammed down the phone, more for effect than for any other reason. He wanted to ensure that those standing over him would report back to Habibi that he had done his bidding.

Shiekholeslam placed the phone back in its cradle. He would not let his anger get the best of him as it had Velayati. He would make the calls. There would be other opportunities.

Bill Weaver turned his strike group due north and pointed it straight at Bandar Abbas. The visibility in the Southern Arabian Gulf was unusually clear, and he could see more than ten miles. The port facility was easy to pick out, with its large, concentric breakwater, its submarine and other piers in the wide outer harbor and yet more piers in the restricted inner harbor.

The submarines would be the primary targets. Weaver and his wingman would attack first, followed by a section of Hornets that would reattack them. The other aircraft would fan out across the broad harbor and strike as many ships as possible at their piers. Working with data that was less than six hours old, they were confident that they knew precisely where every vessel in the harbor was located.

Weaver felt especially good about leading the first attack

against Iranian soil. Nasty had been his mentor and Andy Bacon had been a good friend. He wanted to be the first to deliver cold steel against the Iranians who had murdered his shipmates. Four miles from the breakwater, without signal from him, each jet flipped its Master Arm Switch to Arm.

107

SHIEKHOLESLAM SAT ALONE IN HIS TINY ROOM. HIS head ached and his stomach churned after his conversation with Velayati. The man had no spine. They were so close, so incredibly close, to taking the fight to the infidels. Shiekholeslam again considered ignoring Velayati's instructions but rejected the idea. The foreign minister could make his life very difficult if he went against him. The significant funds that he needed to support his camps were run through Velayati's Foreign Ministry. No, he reminded himself, there was a long-term war to be won; he would concede this skirmish.

He scribbled out a message on a piece of paper:

YOUR MISSION HAS BEEN CANCELED. YOUR MISSION HAS BEEN CANCELED. YOU ARE NOT TO RELEASE YOUR AGENTS. RETURN TO YOUR HOTEL ROOMS AND AWAIT FURTHER INSTRUCTIONS FROM ME.

Quick. To the point. Something that these young men could easily understand.

He then put the identical message out to each of their pagers.

Half a world away three men watched the clock and prayed for the success of their mission. They didn't pray for their own safety—just that they might be successful and that they might somehow kill as many of the American pigs as possible. They knew that there would be a manhunt looking for them once the authorities found out why these people were dying. They were prepared to take steps to become elusive.

In New York, Mejid Homani sat on a bench in an out-of-the-way area of the large concourse on the ground floor of the United Nations. It was still early and there weren't a huge number of people here, but there were enough—enough to die such that the infidels would recognize that the Islamic Republic could hit them where they lived.

He was surprised when his pager alerted him again. As discreetly as he could, he pulled it off his belt and looked at the message. Mejid scrolled through the words, then again. His heart began to beat faster and his hands grew damp. No, this could not be! Was this some American trick to throw him off his mission?

Mejid had come so far and was completely ready. All he needed to do was to release the agents. What if he just ignored the pager? That was it! He could say later that he just never received the message. He closed his eyes and prayed as fervently as he had ever prayed.

Mejid opened his eyes. He could not do it. His years of training would not let him do anything else. Mejid got up, and, with his agent securely under his arm, he hurried out of the United Nations. He couldn't get over the feeling that someone was watching him. He crossed the street and walked north on First Avenue. He could not go back to his hotel, not yet, so he walked north, his head still spinning.

Achmed Boleshari received the message in the coffee shop across the street from Horton Plaza. Like Mejid, he was surprised that his pager was ringing again and shocked at the message that he received. What was going on in the Islamic Republic? Didn't they know what they were doing? They issue an order and then change it an hour later.

Achmed was disappointed that the attack was being called off, but he was relieved in a way. The appointed hour to release his agents was in ten minutes and he was about to cross the street and enter Horton Plaza, but it was still virtually deserted. His agents would have no effect and his mission would have been a failure. If they were changing their minds like this, perhaps they would tell him to attack later when the plaza was full. Buoyed by this positive turn of events, Achmed discreetly put the pager back on his belt and signaled the waitress to bring him another cup of coffee.

In Washington, Hala Karomi got ready to get off the Metro, sweat pouring off his face. The next stop was his. It was going to be a close call whether he got to Union Station at the appointed time. The train had been much slower getting back than it should have been—did these Americans really ride these cursed trains every day?

As he predicted, the train was now jammed with commuters who jostled and bumped against one another. When the train lurched into the station, a score of people stood between him and the door, and most didn't appear to be getting off at this stop. Hala squirmed out of his seat and started to make his way to the door even before the train stopped, now frantic to get off the train.

Pushing and shoving, he squeezed his body between the unyielding commuters. These pigs did not move! In desperation, he clutched his agent and wedged between the passengers and out of the door seconds before it closed. As he ran for the steps up to the street level and into Union Station, he looked up at the clock overhead. Only ten minutes before the appointed hour.

On the floor of the crowded train, a fallen pager went off, and green letters appeared on the display. In the din made by the now rapidly moving Metro, no one heard it go off, just as they had not heard it hit the floor after it was stripped off Hala's belt as he pushed his way off the train.

Hala Karomi stood outside Union Station for just a moment, composing himself. He knew where he would release his agent, and he wanted to appear calm as he approached that place. This was not the time to draw attention to himself. He wanted to blend in with the other commuters who passed through this station during the morning rush hour.

Finally composed and with several minutes to spare, he walked to the newsstand in the center of the station and moved to the far corner of the small shop. He placed his backpack down on the floor and knelt next to it. No one was watching him, the single clerk was busy with a short line of customers. He broke the vial and pushed the backpack under a rack featuring sweatshirts with various logos of the Capitol region. He stood up and calmly walked out of the newsstand.

His training had told him that the gas would not release instantaneously and that he had time to exit the station without running. Hala forced himself to walk slowly, but found it even more difficult than sprinting up a steep hillside.

As he walked down the steps to the Metro, Hala Karomi began taking deep breaths. When he reached into his pocket to take out money for the train, he noticed that his pager was not on his belt. Frantically he checked his pockets, then realized it made no difference. He had delivered his agent. His masters would be proud.

108

THEY WERE ACCUSTOMED TO BEING SUMMONED TO the president's headquarters. They had been here so many times in the past several days that they knew the surroundings as well as they did their own offices. But this time they had not been summoned. They had insisted on meeting with President Habibi and had bullied their way past his secretaries and other horse holders until they were ushered into his large office. The president of the Islamic Republic clearly was not ready for this encounter, and it showed. So much the better, thought General Najafi and Foreign Minister Velayati.

The general spoke first. "Mr. President, we must prepare to take further action. The Americans continue to confound us with their perfidy. They attacked our ships without cause and they shot down our plane, although the attack on our plane I can understand, since it was sent out to attack their precious carrier."

"What is your point, General?"

"Mr. President, I am certain that *by now* you must have heard of the aerial attack on our naval base at Bandar Abbas." Najafi was reinforcing the fact that President Habibi did not always receive information about important military matters in real time—and often did not receive these reports at all.

"I have been briefed on the attack, General. I am told that our men acquitted themselves well in their efforts to defend the port."

"They did, Mr. President, and many brave men died attempting to put up this defense. But the point, Mr. President, is that this attack came a half hour *after* there were radio instructions to the American aircraft to cease and desist in these attacks. We can deduce now that these instructions represented an elaborate ruse to try to make our defenders let down their guard."

"Good, General?"

"Mr. President, the Americans are resorting to tactics which are repulsive to civilized nations. What they did was tantamount to walking up with a white flag and then shooting the enemy. Their actions cannot go unanswered, not while our nation still has the strength to fight at all."

Habibi could see that General Najafi was becoming extremely worked up. He wondered what he was going to come up with next.

"What do you propose, General?"

"The brave martyrs who flew our C-130 cargo plane are not the only martyrs in our country, Mr. President. We have many, many more. They are prepared to launch soon to take the attack to the carrier once again, and this time they will ride our jet airplanes, not the lumbering cargo plane."

"You are talking about launching massive strikes of jet aircraft against the American carrier?"

"Yes I am, Mr. President. Until we disable the carrier, the Americans can continue to launch strikes against us!" he shouted, getting out of his chair.

"Sit down, General. If I hear another outburst like that, you will leave, and by the time you return to your barracks you will have no soldiers to lead."

Najafi's eyes grew wide, and he slowly sat down.

"Minister Velayati?" said Habibi, now challenging the foreign minister to say something to him.

Velayati was unfazed by the dressing-down the general had just received. He immediately went on the attack.

"Mr. President, I have done as you have ordered. I have had the operatives in the United States contacted and directed to abandon their plans to strike at American cities. I did not agree with this, Mr. President, but obeyed your orders to the letter. Now, looking at what the Americans have done, I regret that decision."

"You regret it, Mr. Foreign Minister? Do you think that the Americans have done everything to us that they can do?"

"No, I don't, but—" He was interrupted in mid-sentence by one of the president's aides, who rushed in breathlessly.

"Turn on CNN," the man said. "Turn it on right now."

The man kept walking the entire time he talked and moved to the large TV in Habibi's office. Soon the television was on and the picture was of a reporter in front of a large building. The caption read, *"Mindy Cole, Washington, D.C."* Her voice sounded hard as she gave her report.

"Here at Union Station, the situation is chaotic. Early this morning, at the height of the morning commute, persons unknown released what appears to be a significant amount of nerve gas inside Union Station. Emergency officials on the scene refuse to speculate on how many people may have been killed or injured, but the D.C. coroner has been on scene, many of those being removed from the station who are still alive appear to be very sick.

"This attack comes only a short time after a reported attack by U.S. warplanes on the Iranian naval facility at Bandar Abbas in the southern Arabian Gulf. U.S. officials are refusing to say whether the Iranian regime is suspected of orchestrating this gas attack, but they

would not discount this possibility out of hand. The scene at the station is chaotic as emergency workers attempt to cordon off a large area around Union Station. District Police Chief Elmer Johnson has been on the scene and has requested the assistance of the FBI in determining who perpetrated this horrendous crime.

"We are going to follow the directions of the police and move further away from Union Station. This is Mindy Cole, reporting live near Union Station in Washington, District of Columbia."

Habibi turned to Velayati and hissed, "So you called off the attacks, Mr. Minister, did you?"

"I assure you that I did, Mr. President. I gave explicit, exact instructions that these attacks be called off—"

"Well," the president cut him off, "your underlings must not think much of the requirement to obey your commands. That is not what is important now. We have done this in their capital, within sight of the building that houses their Congress and only a few short miles from the White House. Do you know how they will respond?" Habibi's question was rhetorical, but he asked it out loud anyway.

"We will be prepared for anything they attempt to do, Mr. President," said General Najafi.

"I'm sure that you think that you will, General. Only the foreign minister will do absolutely everything in his power to ensure that you do not have to. Mr. Minister, have you obtained that direct link yet between me and the American president?"

"It is almost complete, Mr. President."

"Good. Until it is, you will remain at my headquarters and direct the efforts to finish it. Once that line is established, you let me know."

Velayati was beyond words. First he had been humiliated by being escorted to his Foreign Ministry. Now the president was making him a virtual prisoner in his offices until he completed this menial task.

"You are dismissed, General. See to your duties, Mr. Foreign Minister," said Habibi as he stalked out of the room.

109

THE EMERGENCY CREWS OUTSIDE UNION STATION were aggressive in cordoning off the area around the station so that ambulances and other official vehicles could pull up to the broad facade of the station. However, they were having trouble keeping the hordes of media away. Not only CNN but every major national news network and many local television, radio, and print media reporters descended on the station in droves. The initial calls to the media suggested that this disaster had the potential to be another Oklahoma City. Reporters were pulled off virtually every other story in the city and rushed to Union Station.

President Patrick Browne and his national security adviser sat in the Oval Office fixed to the TV. They had flipped through the channels and had settled on CNN. The cameras moved periodically from the talking head to scenes of stretchers being carried out of the station and put into ambulances. Many of the victims on the stretchers had blankets pulled over their heads, a very grim reminder that the death toll would be enormous.

The president and Michael Curtis continued to watch CNN as they waited for the secretary of defense, the secretary of state, and the chairman of the Joint Chiefs of Staff to converge on the Oval Office. Few words were exchanged between the president and the national security adviser as they sat transfixed by the scene being played out on CNN. Michael Curtis waited as long as he thought he dared before speaking.

"Mr. President, this certainly is an unbelievable tragedy; I'm afraid that the number of casualties will be very large."

"Yes," replied the president.

"Mr. President, we certainly don't want to jump to conclusions, but this attack has the Islamic Republic's fingerprints all over it."

"I know that it appears that way, Michael, but we need to get to the bottom of it before making that determination. I know that the FBI is completely mobilized and is working with the D.C. police to find the perpetrator."

"Mr. President, it could be weeks, maybe months, maybe years, before we catch the perpetrators—or we may never catch them. We can't wait, Mr. President!"

Patrick Browne looked to Curtis as if he was overwhelmed by the tragedy, but in fact he simply didn't want to discuss it with his national security adviser at that moment. "All right, Michael, you've made your point, thanks."

This hit Michael Curtis exactly the wrong way, and he lashed back at the president.

"Mr. President, may I remind you what has transpired recently. *Iran* has reinitiated training at terrorist camps that had long been closed, *Iran* viciously attacked the Intercontinental Hotel and killed more of our men and women than had been killed in any previous terrorist attack, *Iran* attacked the U33 *Carl Vinson* with two of her ships, *Iran* shot down our F-14 TARPS aircraft when it was innocently flying in international waters, *Iran* sent aircraft out to attack *Carl Vinson*. . . ."

The president stopped looking at the television screen long enough to look up at Michael Curtis, who was now standing and all but hovering over him. Browne had never seen the national security adviser so animated. He was about to speak, but Curtis continued his harangue.

"And what have *we* done, Mr. President, in response to these blatant attacks against our people and against our national interests? Nothing? No, Mr. President, we have done *less* than nothing. We have sent an American submarine to attack a U.S. Navy aircraft carrier! Mr. President, in over two centuries of our Republic's history we have never had one United States Navy ship attack another one—until now. Not only that, but we have unleashed an assassin to kill a Navy admiral who *might* be getting ready to attack the same Islamic Republic that has perpetrated these crimes. We have taken *extraordinary* pains to turn the other cheek and every time we have done that we have been slapped again and attacked again!"

The president now stood, facing Michael Curtis, but the national security adviser continued his diatribe.

"Don't you see, Mr. President, we could have predicted this gas attack by the Iranians. They hit us and we don't respond—hell, we even take extraordinary steps to thwart those forces in the field who try to do something, try to defend themselves! We cannot let this stand, Mr. President, we cannot let this stand! We need to respond swiftly and inflict the maximum amount of damage on the Islamic Republic while this incident is still fresh in the public's mind. The nation will stand behind you, Mr. President, I have no doubt of that."

Patrick Browne leveled his eyes and burned them deeply into Michael Curtis.

"Now Michael, I am only going to say this once, so I want you to listen," the president began. "I have followed the advice of you and the rest of my advisors throughout this crisis. I am not saying that you all gave me bad advice, but I am saying that I have never followed my instincts, in an effort to effect some sort of consensus among all of you."

"Mr. President, we all work for consensus," Curtis said when the president paused briefly.

"But I have worked for it more than anyone. I have to do what I think is right. Ultimately, I am responsible for the course this country takes."

"Of course you are, Mr. President," Curtis continued, breaking into just the briefest pause in the president's monologue.

"So that is why I need to do what I am going to do. Now, when the others get here, I want you to take them down to the Situation Room. Continue to get updates on this tragedy at Union Station. I am going to have a press conference to address the nation this evening, and I will need details on exactly what went on there. I will discuss this tragedy and will discuss other matters."

"Other matters, Mr. President?"

"Yes, Michael, other matters. Now go, go meet the others."

The president stood up and walked Michael Curtis to the door of the Oval Office, showed him out, and closed the door. The national security adviser left with the greatest fear of the unknown that he had ever felt.

110

HASAN EBRAHHIM HABIBI SAT IN HIS OFFICE, ALONE. The phone on his desk was still silent. His personal aide had told him that the president of the United States would be calling within the next two hours. Foreign Minister Velayati and General Najafi had been ushered from the presidential headquarters. Habibi had been manipulated by these two men for long enough.

That was past now. He would listen to them no longer. He was the properly elected president of the Islamic Republic. The only way that he would not have the power would be if he abdicated it. Now that was no longer going to happen. Hasan Ebrahhim Habibi was going to do what he thought was best for the country he loved.

He had brought in his military communications chief as soon as he had heard that the United States president would call. Working under enormous pressure from the president, he had established a reliable line that could connect him with anyone in the world. True, it was not a secure, scrambled net, but there was not much that needed to be hidden—that could be hidden—anymore. It was too late for that.

President Patrick Browne had instructed the White House Communications Office to establish a phone line that could reach the Islamic Republic. Once that office established the line, they tested it with the Iranian Presidential Headquarters. That done, the president asked for a short time to collect his thoughts before making the call.

No aides or secretaries interjected themselves in the process when Patrick Browne picked up the phone in the Oval Office and dialed the number that he had been given for the Office of President Habibi. The phone rang twice, then Habibi picked it up.

"President Habibi, speaking."

"Mr. President, this is Patrick Browne calling."

"Good day, Mr. President. Thank you for calling. I think that there is much that we should talk about."

"Indeed there is, Mr. President," Patrick Browne continued. "I think that this is a terrible state that our nations find themselves in, isn't it?"

"It is indeed, President Browne. First, I must say that I am very sorry for the deaths of your citizens in your capital city. I assure you that the attack by the terrorist who did this was not authorized by my government. It was not authorized at all. It was done by a man acting on his own volition, and for this we are extremely sorry."

"I believe that is as you say it is, Mr. President. But I must ask you this. Was the attack on the Intercontinental Hotel done by your nation?"

"I am afraid that I cannot deny that terrorists trained in my country probably perpetrated this horrible crime, Mr. President. We have not controlled this scourge of terrorism the way that we should. We have turned away while others have done these things and have not stepped in and stopped these attacks from happening. For that, we have no excuse. It is my government's strong desire to pay reparations to the families of those who were lost at the Intercontinental, as well as the families of those people tragically killed in the attack at Union Station."

"That is very gracious of you, President Habibi. I must now tell you, sir, that our aircraft that attacked your naval base at Bandar Abbas were not authorized to do so. True, they were launched on this mission, but they were launched by a rogue admiral who was absolutely not authorized to do this. He has been relieved of his duties and is no longer in a position to attack your nation. We wish to express the deepest regret for the damage done to your facility and to the ships there."

"This admiral you speak of, President Browne, why would he do such things without authorization?"

"We don't fully know that yet, Mr. President, but we are trying to get to the bottom of it. Sometimes men snap. In this case, it appears this admiral did. I can tell you truthfully, Mr. President, that we did everything in our power to stop this man before he launched any strikes against you. We sent one of our nuclear submarines on a high-speed chase with instructions to fire torpedoes at the carrier, and we instructed an operative aboard the carrier to seek out and disable the admiral. Still, these strikes were launched before we were able to stop him. Many strikes were launched; this is the only one that was not able to be called back."

"I see, Mr. President."

"May I make a suggestion, President Habibi?"

"Yes, by all means."

"I suggest that we have our forces disengage as quickly as possible. I will order *Carl Vinson* to exit the Strait of Hormuz as a signal to the world that we mean the Islamic Republic no harm. Once the carrier is clear of the Gulf, perhaps you can allow your forces to come off high alert. We both have fences to mend. I think that the sooner we do it, the better."

"I agree, Mr. President. Much harm has been done. It will take a while to undo it. I have let my country down by allowing others to make decisions for the Islamic Republic that are my responsibility and mine alone. That will no longer happen. Not as long as I am in office."

"I, too, have been captive to my advisors. Often their advice is so earnest that it is easy to go along with. Now I know that my instincts are often better than the advice I receive."

"Mr. President, your country is still the world leader. The Islamic Republic wishes to join the community of peace-loving nations. We will follow your lead in this. I give you my personal guarantee that I will do absolutely everything in my power to stamp out terrorism."

"That is all I can ask, Mr. President. That is all I can ask."

EPILOGUE

PATRICK BROWNE SAT SILENTLY AT HIS DESK IN THE wake of his phone call with President Habibi. He felt relieved beyond words that the crisis in the Arabian Gulf had been defused and that, most importantly, the killing had been stopped. Just as importantly, he felt that he had reasserted control of his presidency and that he was finally making the decisions. He was making them—not his secretary of defense, not his secretary of state, and certainly not his national security adviser.

The president called his secretary into the room and dictated a brief agenda. First there would be the phone calls to the principal members of his national security team. He did not need or want any more meetings. He had reconciled in his own mind what actions he wanted each of them to take. Next would be the phone calls he would make to important heads of state. Those would be brief and to the point. After that, he would meet with his press secretary and prepare for his press conference—but that would be straightforward. He knew exactly what he wanted to say.

Seven thousand miles away, in the presidential headquarters, President Hasan Ebrahhim Habibi was already taking action. Iranian military forces were stood down, the terrorist training camps were shut down, Iranian ships at sea were immediately recalled to their ports, and the president ordered the nation to immediately return to normal business throughout the Islamic Republic. It was an order that he intended to see carried out.

There was one action that Habibi decided he needed to do in person. Within an hour of his conversation with Patrick Browne, he had Foreign Minister Velayati brought to his office. When Velayati arrived, there was already an assemblage of persons in the president's office, including the senior judge of the Iranian High Court. There, in front of this large group, and using legal language provided by the judge, President Habibi formally cashiered Velayati for his complicity in terrorist operations and his failure to derail these operations once they were ordered to be stopped. Velayati was given an opportunity to tell him about the whereabouts of Hossein Shiekholeslam, but he refused.

Velayati's failure to help President Habibi ferret out Shiekholeslam and force him to stop supporting terrorist training prevented him from moving the Islamic Republic completely away from supporting terrorism. Although Habibi could see that the camps were closed down, along with the funding from Velayati's office, the fluid nature of the terrorist threat allowed Shiekholeslam to keep his network alive and moving from place to place—to be, in the end, an even more elusive target.

Michael Curtis was shocked by the president's phone call. A matter of such importance should have been discussed in person—the president should have at least afforded him that courtesy. Patrick Browne told him, in no uncertain terms, that a stated goal of his administration was now to mend fences with the Islamic Republic of Iran, to put an end to the simplistic "dual-containment" policy that had lingered for too many years. The national security adviser received this message silently. He still believed that Iran posed a deadly threat to the United States and to U.S. interests. How he would reconcile these beliefs with continued service under a Browne administration was something that he would need to ponder long and hard.

Secretary of Defense Bryce Jacobs called in the chairman of the Joint Chiefs of Staff and reviewed with him what they had been instructed to do. The military crisis in the Arabian

Gulf had to be defused and Admiral Robinson had to be dealt with.

The first task was not easy. Blood had been spilled, people had died, bombs had been dropped, and military hardware had been destroyed. Disengaging two military machines that were at each other's throats took deft handling and was not something that the secretary and the chairman entered upon lightly. Dealing with a highly volatile Central Command commander who was now on station in Bahrain at Fifth Fleet Headquarters made their job that much harder. But this challenge paled by comparison with the really tough issue—how to deal with the battle group commander.

Admiral "Heater" Robinson had been relieved of his duties and was under house arrest aboard his own flagship. That took care of the immediate problem but did not address the long-term one—what were the Navy and the nation going to do with Heater Robinson? They knew that they could not bring him to trial; neither the nation nor the world could ever know how perilously close one man had come to starting a war that could threaten to engulf an entire region of the globe, especially a region where even the hint of unrest could send world economies into recessions that would last for years.

No, the president had approved their recommendation to let Heater Robinson retire quietly. They covered his abrupt departure with a story that he had been relieved for "emergent medical reasons." Soon after his departure from *Carl Vinson* he was whisked by military jet directly from Bahrain to Andrews Air Force Base and then to the Washington Navy Yard and the Naval Criminal Investigative Service Headquarters, where he was thoroughly debriefed. Papers were signed, pledging his cooperation in return for receiving his pension, and he went quietly to a home he and his wife owned in Bonita, California. His name would never again be uttered in the context of these naval operations.

Far away from the weighty political and military matters that were being decided in the nation's capital, three young warriors began to deal with the aftermath of the crisis.

Anne O'Connor recovered from her minor injuries quickly and was back in the cockpit flying with the Blue Wolves within a week. Her love of flying was rekindled and would sustain her throughout her career. She even began to start to think seriously about applying for the United States Naval Test Pilot School.

Brian McDonald's injuries were more serious; his badly broken arm took him out of the cockpit and left him flying a desk, possibly for several months. His dedication and his heroism made those on *Carl Vinson* loath to lose him, and they were able to work a deal to transfer him from the Stingers to Wizard Foster's personal staff, a career plum for an officer as junior as he. There he was able to reaffirm his dedication to naval aviation and validating his career decision to keep flying.

Rick Holden was flown to Germany to recover from his gunshot wound. Though his wound was serious, he never was in mortal danger. However, the medical evacuation to Germany got him off *Carl Vinson* and was the first step in having him go underground again. Once again, he had performed heroically and, once again, the powers that be decided he was too valuable an asset to cast off.

In spite of the order for the military pullback and the damage done to various military units during the crisis, one constant stood out: USS *Carl Vinson* remained on station in the Arabian Gulf.

AFTERWORD

FOR DUTY AND HONOR IS A STORY WOVEN AROUND
the awesome power of a United States Navy carrier battle
group. For those unfamiliar with the operations of forward
deployed fleet units, the portrayal of the virtually autono-
mous power of a carrier battle group commander may appear to be a bit of a stretch. It's not. The Navy is long
accustomed to vesting paramount authority in the commanding officer of a Navy combatant ship. In a carrier battle
group this happens on a far larger scale. The Navy and the
nation entrust the lives of 8,000 people, national treasure in
the tens of billions of dollars, and devastating firepower in
the hands of one very carefully selected individual—the carrier battle group commander. No one person in any military
organization in any nation personally controls so much de-
structive power.

Having worked directly for six battle group commanders
over the course of almost seven years and through three
deployments—including two recent deployments to the Arabian Gulf—I would be the first to admit that the scenario
presented in this story is not one that I personally lost sleep
about. I never felt that any of my bosses—all of whom were
superb leaders—would ever be driven to the point that the
Admiral Robinson of this story was. But add the right mix
of political circumstances, an unhelpful blending of military
crises, a tense intersection of personalities, and a breakdown
of checks and balances, and the scenario painted here could
become all too real in short order. Put another way, the
question arises. Do we as a Navy and a nation try to produce

an Admiral Robinson in this story? No. Could we collectively fail to pay attention and push a military professional over the edge and create *Heart of Darkness* on an aircraft carrier? We might.

The overwhelming majority of military officers—especially senior military officers—focus exclusively on their duties and try not to be drawn into the political arena. However, this is a situation that is not always in their hands. They can be drawn into political and military intrigues not of their making, and when this happens, they are typically treading on unfamiliar turf with less than fully developed instincts as to how to extricate themselves.

Like most stories, this one has a beginning, a middle, and an end. It has good characters and evil characters. Most are well defined. But what about Admiral Robinson? What about Michael Curtis? Who bears the burden of the events put in motion in this story? As in many things in life, the person out in front, the person taking or personally direction the action, is the most exposed. In this case, Admiral Robinson was cashiered while Michael Curtis continued serving as National Security Adviser—albeit a somewhat chastened one.

And ships like the USS *Carl Vinson* are on the line—every day.

Captain George Galdorisi
Coronado, California
December 1999